MICK FARREN

was rock correspondent, ~~and~~ sometime editor of underground 1960s newspaper, *International Times* (*IT*); singer and founding father of the Deviants; and is unique in winning his *Nasty Tales* comic book obscenity trial. He brought the White Panther Party to the UK, and took a leading part in the semi-revolution that turned the Isle of Wight Festival of 1970 into a free-for-all festival. An early predictor and precursor of punk, Farren championed its cause whilst at legendary music paper, *New Musical Express*. Fleeing from Thatcher's Britain in 1979, he settled in New York and then LA, where he currently lives.

Mick Farren's autobiography, *Give The Anarchist A Cigarette,* was published in 2002 by Jonathan Cape; his novels include *Citizen Phaid, The Feelies* and *Jim Morrison's Adventures in the Afterlife.*

The
DNA
Cowboys
Trilogy

Mick Farren

THE DO-NOT PRESS

This collection first published in Great Britain in 2002 by
The Do-Not Press Limited
16 The Woodlands
London SE13 6TY
www.thedonotpress.co.uk
email: DNA@thedonotpress.co.uk

Casebound edition: ISBN 1 899 344 94 2
B-format paperback: ISBN 1 899344 93 4

British Library Cataloguing in Publication Data. A catalogue
record for this book is available from the British Library.

1 3 5 7 9 10 8 6 4 2

Printed and bound in Great Britain

Three of the people who were very close to the creation of this book have already vanished into the nothings. This is for...

Edward Barker
Ingrid von Essen
and Michael Dempsey

It's also for Phil Jones and Rich Deakin, who are very much alive, and have done so much to keep my tattered flag flying.

The DNA Cowboys Trilogy

Introduction by Mick Farren   9

The Quest of the DNA Cowboys   13

Synaptic Manhunt   185

The Neural Atrocity   385

A TAXI TO THE GATES OF EDEN

The creation you are about to read grew in a very specific petridish, at an equally specific time in recent history. *The DNA Cowboys* came to life in a top-floor apartment in Ladbroke Grove, London, in the middle of the highly confused 1970s. Odd tales would be told of my method of writing this back-to-back opus. Living-room legend claimed I worked with the curtains closed, the TV blasting and ripped out of my already fragile cortex on uncontrolled doses of windowpane acid supplied by ethical guerrillas of the Midnight Brotherhood. Nonsense. The curtains and the TV? Fair enough. That was standard. The role of acid in the process, except as deep background, was wholly fabricated. Although a perverse sense of self-aggrandizement caused me never to refute such fancy, and allow it to gently settle as myth, the plain truth was that these books were written on hashish, Coca-Cola, and chain-smoked Rothmans between robust bouts of nightlife in the taverns of the town, where I drank Jamieson's, and snorted anything that was put in front of me and didn't move of its own accord. I had not ingested any major league psyche-delics for a year or two, finding them too jaggedly strenuous for the prevailing mood.

In the street the rudies were restless, and snotty whiteboys banged Japanese Telecasters and howled Lou Reed songs in basements so they could be punks in a year. In the dark days before the computer, I scrawled on legal pads like a poet in a trench while Lemmy drifted through with small bags of speed and a brass tube with a dragon on it, wanting obsessively to borrow a couple of quid, and play *Teenage Head* by the Flaming Groovies on my stereo. Edward Barker would sketch cartoon animals in the corner, or talk logic to the cat. Nick Kent might waft a trail of scarves, used Kleenex, and empty milk cartons. The TV was flicking, dispensing *Kojak* and *Kung Fu*, and my girlfriend of some years maintained her Nordic equilibrium with amphetamine sulphate and yellow Valium, and wrote letters to Wayne Kramer in jail. The first full-color video games made Dalek noises in the boozers, and wideboys dressed like Rod Stewart could be caught in near Zen contemplation of *Breakout* or *Missile Command*. Sam Peckinpah movies were released in cinemas in the West End, and Ziggy played guitar.

Amid all this full-auto ground-clutter, I could only be gripped by a determination to put it all down on paper, but in a neo-surrealist fictional form that would give 'Naked Lunch' a run for its money. I further demanded space to include bouts of truly bizarre martial arts, a couple of really nasty religions, and the kind of depraved underage heroine that Julie Burchill would attempt to remake as flesh without even reading the book. I already had the structure. Didn't the environment in which I dwelled constantly prove itself a free-form montage of entropic chaos, punctuated by periods of unconsciousness, amnesia, and transcendental aimlessness? Why shouldn't a novel be crafted to such a template? Plot? What plot? Life has no plot. Why do the bloody DNA Cowboys need a plot? Why couldn't they stumble headlong through the internal movie of my creation just like the rest of us did through real life?

Not that Billy Oblivion, Reave Mekonta, and the Minstrel Boy by any means came fully formed out of a single environment. Unquestionably they were the product of much that had gone before. I, for instance, was still packing a mess of ideas generated in hundreds of variously intoxicated hours spent soaking up the oblique imagery of Bob Dylan. As late as the mid-1970s, Dylan still straddled popular culture like a colossus, and I wanted to lay claim to landscapes similar to those at which he hinted. I not only wanted to find out what lay beyond the Gates of Eden, but insisted on knowing what the entire population was wearing, what played on the radio there, and if I could find a cab. The character of the Minstrel Boy was supposed to lead me to such places, but, from the moment that he first walked the page, he peevishly refused to yield directions or show his passport. I saw the way the wind was blowin', and how I must ultimately rely on the stretch of my own half-tested imagination.

Thus I stretched, and, in stretching, I was treated to an array of enlightenments. One of the earliest was that when an artist starts to use his imagination he becomes endowed with the super-powers of Daffy Duck. The artist can walk off the cliff, and be perfectly safe as long as he or she never looks down. I also learned it was very wise to know as little as possible about the rules of the game. The fewer the rules, the less you become self-consciously aware of breaking them. It's only the rules that define the impossible. Without them, you just go right ahead and do it, like Joe Primitive did it a million years ago; the caveboy on the shore who cracked open an apparent rock and ate the slimy stuff inside. Joe Primitive discovered the first oyster by not knowing any better. As an additional benefit I found that psychedelic fiction could actually prove therapeutic, the perfect antidote to a day-labor in the weekly rock press. By pressure of deadline alone, the hack carries his own Lou Grant union rulebook, even when his subject matter is a narrow triangle defined by Evel Kneivel, Capt. Beefheart, and Squeaky Fromme. Returning home to the DNA Cowboys, I could kick up my hooves and roll on any last shreds of objectivity like a brewer's drayhorse out to pasture.

Perhaps the greatest secret I discovered was that the writing of a novel, aside from constituting a pitch for immortality, celebrity or both, can be a refuge from intrusive reality. I could steal away into my very own private world and have fabulous adventures as I made up the stories. The escape route of the disturbed infant, perhaps, but better than an invisible friend, is to have an invisible empire, peopled by hundreds of characters subservient to one's will. (Although when the fantasy heats up, one may become subservient to theirs.) Writers like to lay claim to the pain, talk woundedly about the birth pangs of literature, and boast how their business is like opening a vein, but take that with a grain, sweetheart. Forget Jack Nicholson in *The Shining*. He didn't do too much writing, anyway. More chasing of Shelly Duvall into the bathroom with a fire axe. The secret truth is that writers are quite happy when they're in the zone. It's the moving, the entering and exiting of the comfortable pod that's really responsible for all the angst, hard drinking, and 'Here's Johnny'.

And having let slip this crucial secret, friends and neighbours, come now and enter the theatre of imagination I inhabited a full quarter of a century ago, when so much was young and raw, and I thought I knew it all. The seats have been dusted and the bubblegum scraped from the floor. These books have been out of print for so long that they have developed a certain cachet of rarity. Some may say this is more than the work really deserves. (Although they do say it at risk of kneecapping and excommunication.) Me? I can no longer be subjective. You must enjoy the pages for yourselves. The lights are going down, you have your popcorn. The movie is starting...

Mick Farren, Los Angeles, 2002

THE
QUEST OF
THE DNA
COWBOYS

1

It was inevitable that they should up and leave Pleasant Gap. The most the people could say, and they said it often, was that Pleasant Gap was a good old town.

Good old town really summed it up. Pleasant Gap was built on one of the most stable points in the fabric, it nestled in a fold of the grey elevations that the people of Pleasant Gap liked to call the hills. There were maybe fifty houses, frame buildings with wooden shingles, front porches and neat front gardens with well-tended lawns and flowers. Then there was the church, Eli's Store, Jackson's Repair Shop, and down at the end of the main street, a couple of bars and, although nobody mentioned it in polite company, Miss Ettie's Sporting House, which must have been visited by every man in town at one time or another.

Beyond Miss Ettie's was the railroad track. Of course, the railroad didn't go anywhere, just ran around a fold in the hills and came back again. The main use of the railroad, apart from reminding people what time it was, was that the two boxcars concealed the faraday cages that hooked into the transporter beam from Stuff Central.

Pleasant Gap had a consumer contract with Stuff Central which gave them just about everything they needed, but the trouble was that a lot of people in town didn't like to see their cans of dog food, bolts of cloth, and new work shoes appear out of nothing in a flash of static. It reminded them too much of the wild things that happened in other places. And so, every morning the train chugged out of town empty, and every afternoon it chugged back in full of supplies.

These supplies were unloaded and delivered to Eli's Store where people then went and bought what they wanted with the money they picked up from the Welfare Bank.

This system worked fine, except that every year, when the Stuff contract had to be renegotiated, Stuff Central kept putting pressure on the town council to take more and more stuff. Eli would bitch and complain about how he would have to reduce prices and how that would be bad for business, and then the citizens would complain about the amount of stuff that they were expected to use up. Jed McArthur and his cousin Cal would sit on Eli's porch and complain to each other about just how many motor mowers a man was expected to keep in his tool shed.

That was about the extent of the troubles of Pleasant Gap, and the calm, placid life was due mostly to the huge stasis generator, as big as two city blocks, which stood, hidden by a grove of pines, down below the railroad track. It drew power straight from the fabric, and hummed away to itself all day and night keeping things in Pleasant Gap as they ought to be.

There hadn't been any trouble in Pleasant Gap for a long, long time. No disruptor had come near them in living memory, and the even pattern of life was rarely interrupted. Occasionally a small rupture would appear in a garden or the main street, but nothing worse than you could maybe catch your foot in. Once, a few years back, an anky-losaurus had wandered down Yew Street, but Ma Hoffman had chased it with a broom, and it had lolloped off into the hills. Apart from these little anomalies, the generator kept things pretty much as the people of Pleasant Gap wanted them.

Life in Pleasant Gap was safe, well regulated, but, to some, crushingly monotonous, and it was more than likely the monotony that started them having thoughts of moving out.

It was Billy who first brought it up. Billy liked people to call him Captain Oblivion, but most people called him Billy. It was a great disappointment. He felt his thin good looks and hard penetrating eyes merited a better title. Billy was secretly very vain.

He and his buddy Reave were lying in the back room of McTurk's Bar with the alphaset cranked up past euphoria. Reave was the stockier, more solid of the two. In another age he would have been a farmer. It was the middle of the day, nobody was about, and Billy was bored.

'I'm bored.'

His voice was slurred. It was very hard to talk against an alphaset running at full power. Reave rolled over slowly, and pushed his long greasy hair out of his eyes.

'What's the matter?'

'I'm bored.'

'Bored?'

'Bored.'

'So let's go down to the tracks, and watch the train come in.

'We must have watched the train come in maybe a thousand times.'

'So? Let's go watch it again.'

'Who needs it?'

Reave shrugged and said nothing. Billy was always having these fits of discontent, it didn't pay to take them too seriously. After a while another thought struck him.

'We could go down to Miss Ettie's.'

'Why?'

'I dunno, have a few drinks, get laid. It's something to do.'

'Maybe.'

There was another long silence, and then Billy stretched out and hit the off button on the alphaset, and their nervous systems came down with a bump.

'Shit, what did you do that for?'

Billy sat up. He had that kind of crazy look that people get when they've been soaking up alphas for too long.

'Let's split.'

Reave scratched his leg.

'That's what I said. Let's go down to Miss Ettie's.'

'I don't mean go to Miss Ettie's or the railroad track. Fuck Miss Ettie's and the railroad track. I mean split the town, leave Pleasant Gap and go somewhere else.'

Reave frowned and scratched his head.

'Yeah? Where? A man can get himself killed or lose his mind out there in the wild lands.'

Billy walked over to the window and stared out.

'A man could lose his brain hanging out in a town like this.'

Reave shrugged.

'It's easy enough, living in Pleasant Gap.'

Billy looked at Reave's placid, easygoing face and began to get annoyed.

'Sure it's easy. It's just that nothing happens. It just goes on, day after day.'

'So what do you want to do about it?'

'I want to get out of here.'

'Why?'

'There's got to be something out there that's better than this.'

Reave looked doubtful.

'What?'

Billy shrugged.

'How the fuck should I know until I find it?'

'So you want to set off looking for something, and you don't know what it is?'

'Right.'

'And you want me to come with you?'

'If you want to.'

'You've got to be crazy.'

'Maybe. Are you going to come?'

Reave hesitated for a moment, hitched up his dungarees and grinned.

'When do we leave?'

They spent the rest of the day going round town telling their friends and buddies that they were leaving. Their friends and buddies shook their heads and told them that they were crazy. After they'd left, the friends and buddies all shook their heads and told each other that Billy and Reave had always been no good.

Billy and Reave finally wound up at Miss Ettie's Sporting House, saying a special goodbye to some of the whores. The whores looked at them thoughtfully, but didn't shake their heads and say they were crazy.

The next morning saw them bright and early inside Eli's Store, clutching their final payments from the Welfare Bank. Eli shuffled out from behind the counter rubbing his hands together.

'Hear you boys are leaving town.'

'That's right, Mister Eli.'

'Nobody leaves this town, can't recall anybody leaving in years.'

'We're going to do it, Mister Eli.'

'Rather you than me, boys. It's supposed to be pretty dangerous out there. You wouldn't catch me going out into the wild lands. A couple of years ago a drifter came in on the train...'

Billy interrupted.

'The train doesn't go anywhere, Mister Eli. It just goes round in a circle.'

Eli appeared not to hear. Nobody in town was sure whether Eli was deaf, or just didn't want to listen to anything that conflicted with his own ideas.

'This old boy came in on the train, and the stories he told. You can't count on nothing out there. If you drop something you can't even count on it falling to the ground, you won't even know if the ground is going to be there from one minute to the next.'

Billy grinned.

'We'll take a chance on it, Mister Eli.'

Eli stroked his bald head.

'That's as maybe, but I can't stand here all day chatting with you boys. Did you want something?'

Billy nodded patiently.

'We want some stuff, Mister Eli. We want some stuff for our trip.'

Eli shuffled vaguely round the store.

'Plenty of stuff here, boys. That's what I'm here for. Stuff's my business.'

Billy and Reave wandered up and down the shelves and displays, picking things up and dumping them on the counter.

'One leather jacket, two pairs of jeans, two shoulder bags, a pair of cowboy boots.'

'You got any camping rations?'

The old man stacked a pile of packets on the counter.

'How about stasis machines? You got a couple of portapacs?'

Eli peered at a high shelf.

'Don't have much call for them.'

Billy began to get impatient.

'Have you got any?'

'Don't take that tone with me, lad. I think I've maybe two of them somewhere.'

He picked up two chrome boxes about the size of a half-pound box of chocolates, and blew the dust off them.

'I knew I had some somewhere. Is there anything else?'

'Yeah. You got any guns?'

'Guns? I haven't been asked for a gun in a long time. I've got some shotguns, and a couple of sporting rifles.'

Reave glanced at Billy.

'I don't much fancy toting a rifle all over the place.'

Billy looked at Eli.

'You got any hand guns?'

Eli scratched his head.

'I think I've got a couple of reproduction Navy Colts somewhere in the back.'

The old man shuffled out. Billy looked round the store. Its dark, dusty, cluttering interior seemed to stand for everything that was driving him to leave Pleasant Gap. Old Eli came back holding a pair of long-barrelled revolvers from another age. He placed them on the counter beside the other things. He reached under the counter.

'I've got two belts here. They have holsters that will take the guns, and some sort of do-hickey that will hold the portapacs. Reckon you'll need them.'

Billy picked up one of the belts, strapped it round his hips, and picked up one of the pistols. He spun it on his index finger, dropped it into the holster, and drew it in a single fluid motion. He grinned at Reave.

'Neat, huh?'

Reave nodded.

'Neat.'

Billy turned back to Eli.

'Okay old man, how much is all this stuff?'

Eli stood calculating under his breath.

'Three hundred and seventeen, boys.'

Billy pulled a roll of notes out of his shirt pocket.

'We'll give you three hundred. Call it a cash discount.'

Eli grunted.

'You'd make a poor man of me, but I'll do it, seeing as how you're leaving.'

Billy handed the old man three one-hundred bills. 'Nice to do business with you, old man.'

They stuffed the food, spare clothes and ammunition into the shoulder bags and strapped the gun belts round their hips. Billy pulled on his new cowboy boots, and shrugged into his leather jacket.

'How do I look, Reave old buddy?'

'Heavy.'

Billy pushed his fingers through his curly black hair. 'Just one more thing, old man. You got any sunglasses?'

Eli placed a pair of dark glasses on the counter. 'You can have those, son. Call them a going away present.'

Billy grinned.

'Thanks, Mister Eli.'

He put the glasses on. They seemed to make his pale face look even sharper under the mass of black hair.

'I guess we're about ready.'

Reave nodded.

'It looks like it.'

'So long, Mister Eli.'

Eli shook his head. 'You boys have got to be crazy.'

2

She/They floated free across the smooth chequered plane of Her/Their control zone. The light, ordered by Her/Their passing, shone brightly but without apparent source, casting no shadows except for a pale smudge below where Her/Their feet hung over the smooth surface.

Slowly She/They drifted forward, and although no other being heard, the motion was silent, and although no one watched, She/They adopted the regular triple form. The Trinity. The three identical women, who looked as one and moved as one. Their slim, erect figures were concealed by the white ankle-length cloaks that swayed gently with their motion, each in identical folds to the other two. Her/Their heads were encased in silver helmets with high crests and plates that curved round to cover the nose and cheek bones, leaving dark slits through which Her/Their eyes glittered steadily.

The control plain stretched, in regular dividing squares, uniformly to the horizon. Overhead the sky was bright, cloudless and a perfect white. Only a faint, tumbling, distant haze where sky and plain met gave evidence that Her/Their power to control was finite, limited by distance, and around the zone were the twisting chaos fringes.

She/They halted and appeared to gaze intently at a point on the dark, twisting fringe. At the point of Her/Their gaze the dark area appeared to expand, stretch out into the plain and rise a little into the sky.

'Disruption.'

The word seemed to hang in the air, displacing the silence.

'Possible rupture,' a phrase took its place.

'Freudpheno possible.'

The structure of the turbulence at the horizon changed; it began to revolve, forming an almost regular circle. The centre of the circle began to assume spatial depth. The silence that had resumed after the passing of the word was filled by a low hum that seemed to originate from the growing tube on the horizon.

More words cut across the hum.

'Freudpheno imminent.'

The hum grew louder, became a roar, and suddenly, straight from the mouth of the tunnel rushed a herd of rhinoceroses, close packed and charging straight for the triple form of Her/Them. The surface of the plain trembled under the rhinos' armoured weight. In their wake the fabric of the zone rose in boiling moiré patterns.

The centre unit of Her/Them raised the hand that held the energy wand. A yellow stinger of light flashed towards the rhinoceroses, who slowed to a halt and stood for a moment blinking, and then turned and trotted back the way they had come.

She/They lowered the energy wand, and watched as the animals disappeared back into the fringes. More words occupied the silence of the zone.

'Freudpheno returns.'

'Disruption at fringe still gains level.'

'Suspect proximate disturb module.'

The frenzied churning on the horizon continued to grow and even gradually advance into the zone. In the centre of the turbulence a solid cylindrical object appeared. Slowly it began to advance into the zone.

'Confirm disturb module.'

The module moved out into the zone, its blue metalflake body h/ buried in the surface of the plain. Its front end was an open intake + sucked in the fabric of the zone as it slid towards Her/Them. Beh it left a trail of swirling chaos that stretched back to merge with the fringes.

She/They again raised the energy wand. The module came steadily towards Her/Them, like an open-mawed reptile cutting through the surface of the plain, its smooth, shining sides reflecting the swirling colours of its wake. The stinging of yellow light flashed again, but had no appreciable effect on the machine. The thin path of light widened to a broad band. The metalflake skin of the module changed from blue to a pale green, but it still kept on coming. The yellow band of light hardened into a deep flaming red. The module became a shining grey/white, but still maintained its steady forward motion.

She/They experienced the novelty of horror as the band of light from the energy wand was forced, inexorably, up through the spectrum. Yellow, green, blue and finally violet, then fading and vanishing altogether.

The module was upon Her/Them.

As its gaping mouth engulfed Her/Them, the zone twisted and became unrecognizable. She/They was sucked into the interior of the module, losing form as Her/Their structure flowed and twisted, falling simultaneously in any number of directions, down through tunnels that squirmed in downward Möbius patterns, glowing with shifting pink, and faced with a soft cosmic tuck and roll.

She/They had never before been caught in the path of a module, and found Her/Their self fighting against patterns that threatened to destroy the integration of Her/Their fabric.

Desperately She/They pulled into a rough sphere to best withstand the pressures. As She/They managed to retain a grasp on Her/Their structure, the tunnels abruptly vanished, and, in total darkness, waves of hard energy washed over Her/Them. The environment seemed to contract and there was a sensation of falling, then suddenly everything snapped, and a phrase filled Her/Their consciousness.

'Folksymbol.'

She/They was standing in a hot, dusty street which was lined with wooden buildings. She/They was in a male structure and wearing a rough cotton shirt, denim trousers and heavy boots. Facing Her/Them was a man, similarly dressed, his eyes shaded by a wide-brimmed black hat. His arm hung loosely beside a heavy gun that was strapped to his right thigh.

'Reach, stranger!'

Her/Their hand, a man's hand, calloused and sunburned, clutched for the similar weapon that hung from Her/Their belt.

The male's gun was already in his hand, there was a roar as it fired.

*She/They tried desperately to rearrange Her/Their fabric as the metal
projectile tore through it. The experience of pain clouded Her/Their
consciousness, preventing the energy buildup needed to shift out of the
collective illusion of a Folksymbol. The shift was impossible, but the
wooden buildings did begin to fade, and the blue of the sky took on the
swirls of chaos. The male figure that She/They had been forced into
began to dissolve.*

*In its place, amid the pale ghost of the Western township, She/They
reverted to the triple form. Two standing erect, while one lay crumpled
in the dust.*

3

Billy and Reave stepped off the railroad track and started up the
bare grey hillside. It was easy to see where the field of the Pleasant
Gap generator stopped. All along a curved line the ground boiled
and fell away into a blue-grey smoke. The clear air inside the field also
became a swirling, multi-coloured mist. Billy and Reave walked up to
the line and hesitated.

'Do you just step into it?'

'It's like stepping off the edge of the world.'

'I don't like it.'

'We can't go back now. The portapacs should hold things together.'

They turned up the gain of the machines on their belts and, side by
side, stepped into the shimmering fog.

The portapac doesn't hold things together much beyond the area
immediately around the carrier, even when it's turned up. Billy and
Reave found that the fog in front of their faces turned into about a foot
of clear air, and a patch of solid ground formed each time they set a foot
down. They could breathe, walk and even talk to each other, although
their voices sounded muffled and distant. Reave looked at Billy in
alarm.

'How the hell do we know where we're going?'

Billy looked round at the shimmering fog and shrugged his shoulders.

'We don't know where we're going so we can only go on until we
find something else.'

'Suppose we don't find anything?'

'Then we'll just walk round for ever.'

Reave was about to call Billy crazy, but then he thought better of it
and shut his mouth.

They trudged through the bright flickering mist. There was no sense of time, and no indication that they were going anywhere. For all they knew, they might have been walking on a treadmill. The only changes in the total sameness were occasional shifts in the direction of gravity, which pitched them on their side like a sudden pile-driving wind. It was painful and annoying, but comforting in the way that the portapacs always seemed to be able to produce enough solid ground for them to fall on, even though it wasn't sometimes in exactly the right place.

Although they might have no sense of time, Billy and Reave realized they were progressively collecting an array of bruises and small cuts. Reave sucked his barked knuckles and spat into the haze.

'I sure wish I was leaning at the bar in Miss Ettie's. I'll tell you that for nothing.'

Billy plodded on.

'Miss Ettie's ain't even open yet.'

Reave looked at him in amazement.

'What do you mean, not open? We've got to have been walking all day. It must be about evening.'

'I don't figure we've been walking for more than an hour.'

Reave looked round bitterly at the changing colours.

'A day or an hour, what's the difference in this stuff? I don't figure there's anything else at all. Pleasant Gap's the only place left anywhere.'

Billy turned and scowled at him.

'What about Stuff Central, what about that, huh? That's got to exist somewhere.'

'Stuff Central? Is that what you're looking for?'

''Course it ain't, but it proves there's something else besides Pleasant Gap. Right?'

'It don't guarantee that we'll find it, though.'

Billy looked at Reave in disgust, and plodded on. Reave spat again, and hurried after him. They plodded on and on. The reality of their life began to look like a half-remembered dream. It was as though they'd been walking through the nothings for ever.

Just as despair was starting to edge its way into Billy's mind, he put his foot on something that was uneven. He looked down, and saw blades of green grass. He stopped and bent down. It was grass. He grinned up at Reave.

'It's grass, man! It's grass, growing on the bit of ground around my foot.'

'You've cracked up.'

'No, no, it's real.'

Billy picked one of the short blades and passed it to Reave, who turned it over slowly between his fingers.

'Sure looks like grass.'

'It is fucking grass. Listen, here's what we do, take two more steps forward, kind of carefully, and I've got a feeling we'll find something.'

Hand in hand, they took the first step. There was more grass at their feet, extending out for maybe four feet. They took a second step, and then a third, and they came out of the coloured nothings.

They were standing on a grassy slope that rose in front of them. Billy fell to his knees and rolled on the ground.

'We made it! We made it!'

Reave sat down and pulled at the straps of his bag.

'Want a beer?'

'You got some beers?'

'Sure, I nicked a six-pack while old Eli was out back.'

'That was sharp. Yeah, I'd really like a beer.'

Reave pulled out two cans of beer and passed one to Billy. Billy turned it over, looking at the label – Tree Frog Beer, the fat green frog squatting under the red lettering, grinning at you. For the first time Billy knew there was something called homesickness.

After a couple of moments, though, he snapped out of that particularly unique depression, pulled the ring on the can and gulped down the beer. When it was finished he wiped his mouth and flung the can at the wall of nothing. As it hit the mist the can melted, smoked and became nothing itself. Reave grunted.

'That's what'd happen to us if we didn't have no stasis generators.'

'Better not get caught without one.'

Billy stood up.

'Guess we better find out where we are.'

The sky above them was a uniform shining white without either sun or clouds. The air was warm, clear and still. The grass slope ran upwards for a matter of yards and then stopped at some kind of summit. Billy scrambled up it and, once at the top, turned and shouted down to Reave.

'It's a road, man. A goddamn road!'

'A road?'

Reave scrambled up to join him. The road ran flat and dead straight as far as they could see in either direction, a wide, six-lane highway. It was made out of a smooth composition material with a grassy central reservation. On either side were more banks of grass, like the one that Reave and Billy had stumbled upon. Beyond that there were the walls of shimmering nothing.

After prowling around for a few minutes, Billy and Reave came back to the central strip of grass.

'So what do we do? Start walking?'

Billy stared down the seemingly endless strip of highway.

'It looks a mite far to walk.'

'What do we do then?'

Billy sat down on the grass and tilted his dark glasses forward.

'Just sit here a while, take it easy and wait. I reckon somebody's got to use this road, and when they come by, we'll try and beg a ride.'

Reave looked doubtful.

'We could wait a good long time.'

Billy shook his head lazily.

'I don't think so. Nobody builds a big old road like this and then doesn't use it. That stands to reason.'

'Maybe.'

Reave sat down on the grass but still looked uncomfortable. Billy punched him on the arm.

'Come on, man. Relax, it's warm, we're out of that fucking fog, what more do you want? This is an adventure and we ain't in any hurry to get anywhere.'

He rummaged in his bag and pulled out a ration bar, snapped it in half and handed one of the halves to Reave.

'Have something to eat and take it easy. Something'll come by sooner or later.'

Reave munched on the food bar and stretched out on the grass beside Billy, feeling a bit more comfortable. Just as the two men were drifting off to sleep, they heard a humming way off in the distance. Billy sat up and shook Reave by the shoulder.

'Something's coming.'

Reave rubbed his eyes and looked around.

'Which way's it coming from?'

Billy listened intently.

'I don't know, it's hard to tell. It must be a good way off.'

Gradually, the humming grew louder, and a tiny speck appeared far off in the distance. The hum became a high whine which took on more body as it came closer. From a small speck, the object got bigger until Billy and Reave saw it was a huge truck bearing down on them. They jumped about and waved frantically, but the truck sped past them in a flash of chrome exhausts and black and white paint job. Then huge red warning lights flashed at the back and it screeched to a stop, about two hundred yards down the road. Billy and Reave started running and the truck started to back up. They met each other halfway, and a skinny little guy with a shaggy crewcut, long sideburns and a face like a shifty lizard, leaned down from a small door high up in the cab.

'Wanna lift?'

The truck was a huge semi, with an immaculate matt-black paint job on the cab and huge bonnet, it was trimmed in white. Huge chrome blowers reared from the top of the hood, and all the accessories, the wind horns, the military spots mounted high on the cab, the headlights on the fenders were also chrome. The sides of the trailer were of matt-finish aluminium, and JETSTREAM WILLIE was lettered on the cab door.

Reave and Billy climbed up the steel ladder on the side of the truck and ducked inside the cab. The driver sat in a high bucket seat behind a huge steering wheel. The dash panel was a mass of instruments. A pair of rabbit's feet on a thin silver chain dangled from the top of the windscreen. There was a long bench seat, upholstered in white leather with black piping, beside the driver's seat. Reave and Billy sat down on it. Billy grinned up at the driver.

'Some truck.'

The little lizard guy threw the truck into gear.

'Sure is. Seven speed, four pod 5-0-9, blown through. Hits three hundred when I floor her.'

He went through the gears like a master, and was soon at a speed that made Billy and Reave dizzy. Billy swallowed and grinned again.

'Is that your name painted on the side?'

'Sure is. Jetstream Willie, that's me.'

He swivelled round in his seat to show them the same lettering on the back of his black leather jump suit, and the truck swerved so alarmingly that Reave and Billy grabbed for the edge of their seats. Jetstream Willie laughed and accelerated even more.

'Where you boys from?'

'Pleasant Gap.'

'I never heard of a place of that name, not on the road.'

'It's not on the road.'

'Whadda you mean, it's not on the road? If it ain't on the road, then how the fuck did you get here?'

Billy pointed out to the side of the truck.

'We walked through the grey stuff.'

'Through the nothings? That ain't possible.'

Billy held up his portapac.

'Had these.'

'What's that?'

'Miniature generator.'

Jetstream Willie shook his head in disbelief. 'You two got to be crazy.'

Without waiting for an answer, he punched a button on the dash, and country and western music blared from concealed stereo speakers.

'"Ring of Fire" by Johnny Cash. Finest music the world ever known.'

Billy and Reave both nodded. They didn't know what the hell he was talking about. The truck seemed to be going at a suicidal speed, but Jetstream Willie held the wheel with one hand and went right on talking.

'So where are you crazy guys headed?'

'Anywhere. We're just drifting.'

'Drifting, hey? Long time since I picked up any drifters. I can take you as far as Graveyard.'

Reave looked puzzled.

'What's Graveyard?'

He found he had to shout to make himself heard above the roar of the engine, and the country music. Jetstream Willie looked amazed.

'You don't know what Graveyard is? You must have come out of the nothings. Graveyard's the end of the road. It's the truck stop. It's the wheelfreaks' paradise. That's where I got my camper, and that's where my little woman is, just a-waiting for me to come back. A-waiting in that there transparent neglig-ay that she got from the Stuff catalogue. A-waiting to give me something hot with my dinner, or at least she better be, or I'll kill the bitch.'

Reave waited until the tide of poetry had stopped.

'What's a wheelfreak?'

Jetstream Willie looked shocked.

'You asking what a wheelfreak is? You don't know nothing. You're looking at one. Us wheelfreaks are the lords of creation. We're the boys who ride these rigs, we're the only ones who got the balls. We haul them from Graveyard clear down to no-man's-land.'

'What do you carry in these trucks?'

'Carry? We don't carry nothing. Ain't nothing in the back of here 'cept one ol' big generator. How else do you think we keep this road together. Wouldn't stop turning into nothing for an hour if we weren't gunning these ol' boys up and down.'

He fumbled in the pocket of his leather jacket and produced a green plastic box, and popped a little white pill into his mouth.

'Yes sir, there wouldn't be no road or nothing if it wasn't for us, I can tell you.'

He offered the box to Reave and Billy.

'Have a benny.'

Each of them dutifully took a pill and settled back in his seat. They didn't want to ask any more fool questions, and risk upsetting a lord of creation.

Another truck flashed past in the opposite lane, going in the other direction. Briefly, as it passed, all its lights came on, and it shone like a Christmas tree. Jetstream Willie hit buttons on the dash and his own lights came on in reply.

'That's Long Sam. He's a good ol' boy.'

Jetstream Willie cut the lights, and pointed to a set of sockets on the dash panel.

'If you want to recharge them portables of yours, you could try plugging them in there, takes power from the engine.'

Reave and Billy unclipped the pacs from their belts and did as he indicated. Willie seemed to have lost interest in them because he now stared straight in front of him, and sang along with the music. It consisted of the same song, over and over again.

After an hour of this, by the dash panel clock, he swung the truck on to a slip road. Without apparently slackening speed, he jockeyed the truck up a steep ramp and out on to a huge expanse of flat, smooth concrete. He cut the engine and let it roll to a stop at the end of a line of about a dozen other huge baroque vehicles. They were of the same general shape and massive size, but each was unique in its elaborate design and paintwork.

Jetstream Willie caught them staring at a vast gold monster with black trim and enormous balloon tyres.

'That's Dirty Mary's. Sure is a fine-looking machine, but it's all show and no go. I can shut him down with a ten-minute head start before he's even hit the quarter line.'

They unplugged the portapacs, gathered up their bags and swung down from the cab. The truck still seemed to hum slightly, and Reave looked at it curiously. Jetstream Willie provided the answer.

'Always leave the generator on. All helps to keep things straight.'

At first sight Graveyard looked like one huge parking lot surrounded by buildings, and that, in fact, was what it was. Far over on one side was a row of trailers, with smoke curling up from chimneys and lines of washing hanging out to dry. They were dwarfed by the odd truck that was parked among them. On the other side of the lot, right by where Jetstream Willie had parked, was an immensely long single-storey building made of glass and chrome that stretched for a whole side of the roughly square lots. On its flat roof was mounted a huge replica of an ice-cream soda, which rose into the air for sixty or seventy feet.

The cherry on the top was illuminated from inside, and it flashed on and off like a beacon. Flashing in time with the cherry was a red and yellow neon sign that occupied most of the rest of the roof, and spelled out the words 'Vito's Cozy Drop-In' in twelve-foot letters. It was towards this structure that Jetstream Willie led. As they pushed through the revolving glass door, Willie looked at them warningly.

'You better keep yourselves to yourselves in here, some of the boys might not take too kindly to the way you look.'

The Cozy Drop-In was decorated in black and orange plastic. There were lines and lines of tables and seats. A bunch of men, all with similar suits and cropped haircuts to Willie's, queued at a long counter waiting to be served by a team of blonde girls with jutting breasts and short, yellow tunics. Willie pointed at a table away over in the corner.

'You best go and sit yourselves down there, and I'll bring you something over.'

Reave and Billy did as they were told, while Jetstream Willie joined the other men in a flurry of back-slapping and hee-haw laughter. Like their trucks, the wheelfreaks' suits were all basically similar, but each one had its own colour and design.

While they waited for Willie to come back, Billy and Reave looked cautiously round the room. One end of it was dominated by a vast juke box, as tall as a man and maybe eight feet across. Coloured lights kept changing the patterns of reflections on its elaborate chrome face and it seemed to be playing the same 'Ring of Fire' record that Willie had had in the truck. Another wall was filled by a row of pinball machines, but again they were much larger than anything that Billy and Reave had ever seen. Instead of standing in front of it, the player sat in a kind of pilot's chair that had complex flipper controls set in the arms.

Jetstream Willie came back with a tray of coffee and donuts. He banged them down on the orange plastic top of the table.

'Here you go, get some of that down you.'

He jerked his thumb towards the waitress who had served him.

'There's a hot little number. Sure like to crawl into her jeans.'

He winked and pushed a hand into the leg pocket of his suit.

'Might as well put a kick into this here coffee.'

He produced a bottle wrapped in brown paper. Reave looked at it curiously.

'What's that?'

Willie grinned and touched the side of his nose with his index finger.

'Good ol' crank-case gin. Put hairs on your chest.'

He topped up each coffee cup, and Reave and Billy both took a tentative sip. They coughed as the raw spirit hit their throats.

'Strong stuff, that.'

Jetstream Willie winked.

'Sure is.'

He gulped down his coffee in one, took a bite at a donut, and then a hit from the bottle.

'Listen, boys, can't hang round here all day. Got my little woman waiting there at home.'

He stood up.

'See you both later.'

'Yeah, thanks for the lift.'

'That's okay, see you all.'

They watched him walk away. It was strangely sad, somewhere beneath the wheelfreaks' frenetic confidence there seemed to be something doomed. Billy and Reave looked at each other, and there was a long silence. Then Reave let out his breath.

'So what do we do now?'

Billy shrugged.

'Hang round Graveyard and see what turns up. I don't have any ideas.'

As it happened, something turned up before they'd even finished their coffee.

A huge fat man in a scarlet leather suit with blue and white stars and the words 'Charlie Mountain' in white across the back, sauntered over and placed a heavy boot on the seat beside Reave.

'You the boys that came in with Jetstream Willie?'

They both nodded.

'Yeah, what of it?'

Charlie Mountain put two huge hands on the table and leaned forward threateningly.

'It's lucky that you came in with Willie, else we'd be doing something about you right now. As it is, I wouldn't stay too long if I was you. You don't fit in around here, we don't need your kind in Graveyard. You know what I mean?'

Billy and Reave said nothing, and Charlie Mountain straightened up and strolled away. They looked round and saw that every eye in the place was on them. Reave leaned close to Billy.

'Let's get the fuck out of here. I don't like this.'

'Yeah, you're right, but take it easy. We want to do it with class. If we run, they'll probably come after us.'

Billy leaned back in his seat, took a small thin cigar out of his pocket and lit it. He signalled to Reave.

'Okay, let's go.'

Slowly, they both stood up and walked carefully towards the revolving doors. Just as they reached them, one of the wheelfreaks sounded off behind them.

'Will you guys just look at those sweet things!'

Billy and Reave were left in no doubt as to who was being talked about. They hurried through the swing doors and out on to the lot. The white sky was still as bright and shining as it had been when they'd first come out on to the highway. They were both tired and Reave began to wonder if there was any day or night in this truckers' paradise. Billy put on his dark glasses, and they walked across the lot.

4

A Catto hadn't slept at all that night and now watched the sun come up through the clear bubble of the roof garden. It was only fitting that the Con-Lec tower generator could produce day and night. It was a pity that after a while even that became tedious. She turned her back on the view and trailed her silver nails in the water of the fountain.

It was very quiet in the roof garden. The only sound that could be heard was that of the dying party in the mirror room. Somewhere in that party was De Roulet Glick. He was aching to have her again, and as far as she was concerned he could ache. She had made the mistake of sleeping with him once, about a year earlier, and he disgusted her by talking too much and coming too quickly. She had no reason to suppose a second time would be any improvement.

The sounds from the party increased, it seemed as though they were coming out into the roof garden. AA Catto retreated towards the rose bushes that concealed the lift entrance, and pressed the call button. The voices grew louder. She thought she heard Glick. The lift doors opened with a hiss, and she stepped inside. Behind her Glick called out.

'AA, wait a moment.'

She laughed as the lift doors closed on his stupid, eager face.

Inside her apartment she unsnapped the metallic dress she had worn for the party and stepped into the shower. The needle jets seemed to wash the tiredness out of her body, and after the warm air vents had dried her, she stepped out and looked at herself in the full-length mirror.

There was no mistaking the fact that her body and face were almost perfect. It was little wonder that fools like Glick fell over themselves to try and get to her. The only trouble with her perfection was that no one man in the five families could in any way match her desirability. She was wanted, but for the most part she didn't want. Even the guests that arrived from the other citadels usually amounted to little more than a temporary exploration. A brief period of amusement that usually proved to be indistinguishable from all the others.

She pulled on a robe and debated with herself whether to remain awake for the rest of the day, or to sleep until evening. She picked up a small ornate case from a side table and looked at the two injectors; dormax, which would guarantee her eight hours' uninterrupted sleep, and altacaine, the alternative shot that would see she remained lively and talkative until late the following night.

The problem was that if she did decide to use the altacaine and stay up all day, what exactly was there to stay awake for? She walked over to the entertainment console and punched up the day's social programme. It was the usual round of talk, consumption of drink and drugs, and sexual assignations. Nobody was even putting on any kind of show or amusement, not even so much as bringing up a pair of sturdy L-4s to fight or copulate with each other. It looked like a blank day. Nobody seemed to have any imagination left.

Idly she wondered if anything was going on in the outside world, and reset the console to the newsfax channel. It was mainly concerned with the firestorm. That had been amusing a few days earlier when it had actually threatened Akio-Tech, but now that it was confined to L-4 dwellings it was no longer the least bit interesting.

She left the console chattering to itself and stepped out into the perspex blister that served her as a balcony.

Far beneath her was the ugly mess of shacks and ancient buildings that were the warrens of the L-4s. Maybe if they caught fire it would brighten up the day, but at the moment, the city looked safe and tranquil under its blanket of filth.

The outside had once filled her with fascination; there had been the abortive plan that she had hatched with Juno Meltzer to disguise themselves as L-4 prostitutes and slip out into the city, but the details became too complicated, and the plan had been abandoned. With the dropping of that scheme, most of her interest in life among the L-4s had faded.

She wandered back into her day-room. The console was now muttering about population figures and she cut it off. In the act of turning the switch she came to a decision. If nothing was going to happen that day, the best solution was to shut it out.

She picked up the dormax injector and walked into the bedroom. She adjusted the circular bed to a light vibration, slipped out of her robe, turned the temperature setting to sleep and lay down. She pressed the injector against her thigh, and squeezed the release. There was a cold tingling as the minute droplets penetrated the pores of her skin, and then consciousness began to fade.

5

We've all heard the legends that have grown up around the Minstrel Boy. Now the troubles are over, and the natural laws have been brought back, we tend to think of him as the romantic figure of the movies, off on his journey singing stories and telling poems through the length and breadth of the troubled lands.

Of course, the Minstrel Boy did exist, and he was even something like the artists depict him, the blue jeans and the black fur-trimmed jacket, the pale intense face with its sunken cheeks and large, penetrating eyes. When Billy and Reave first saw him in the parking lot at Graveyard, he looked more scuzzy than romantic. His clothes were dirty rather than funky, and his mouth, so sensitive in the paintings, was weak and petulant. He did have the dark glasses, though, much the same as Billy's, and the halo of light brown hair. He had the legendary silver guitar, too, slung over his shoulder, but even that caused confusion.

He was always telling people that it was an original National Steel, which would have made it incalculably old, whereas in fact it was only a Stuff Kustom Kopy, like Billy's and Reave's pistols. It was immediately clear from looking at the guitar that it couldn't be an original. It had a portapac built into the back.

The problem with the Minstrel Boy was that he was an inveterate liar, who generated legends about as quickly as he generated songs.

When Billy and Reave first saw him he was standing beside an electric blue metalflake monster trying to hustle the driver for a lift. The wheelfreak wasn't having any, and replied with an obscene gesture. The Minstrel Boy shrugged and wandered away. Reave and Billy caught up with him.

'You trying to get out of this place?'

The Minstrel Boy looked suspicious.

'Yeah, it ain't healthy, but what's that to you?'

The Minstrel Boy was also very paranoid. Billy and Reave fell into step beside him.

'We were just asking because we've got to split too. We just got run out of Vito's Cozy Drop-In.'

The Minstrel Boy twitched.

'You should have known better than to go in there in the first place.'

There was a short, awkward silence while they stood on the lot and wondered what to say next. Billy felt strangely drawn to the pale, desperate young man. He also felt challenged by the apparent lack of interest in either him or Reave. He didn't know it was one of the Minstrel Boy's most successful techniques for getting people under his influence. Finally Reave waved his hand in the direction of the line of parked trucks.

'What are the chances of getting a lift?'

'Slightly worse than the odds against getting your head broke for asking. I been trying for hours and I'm still here.'

'Is there any other way out of Graveyard except for riding a truck?'

The Minstrel Boy scratched his ribs, and pulled a face.

'I was coming round to thinking that maybe I was going to have to walk.'

Billy looked surprised.

'Walk? Walk where? I thought there was only the road, down to no-man's-land.'

'Well, I sure as hell don't want to go there, and even if I did, I sure wouldn't walk that far. No, you been talking to truckers. They always forget about the old road. They can't hold it together, and they can't run down it, so they don't think about it.'

Billy frowned.

'You mean the wheelfreaks didn't make the road?'

The Minstrel Boy looked at Billy as though he was looking at an idiot.

''Course the wheelfreaks didn't make the road. The road's been there for ever. They just hold it together. There's this other bit of road that goes on from here, it ruptures in places, but it goes right through to the plain.'

'The plain? What's the plain?'

The Minstrel Boy shuddered.

'Don't even talk about it. The only good thing about the plain is that the town of Dogbreath is in the middle of it, and you can get a stage from it. That's only a good thing, though, because everything else is bad.'

Reave looked anxious.

'Could we make it that way?'

The Minstrel Boy stared at the two of them speculatively.

'Maybe. I doubt if anyone could do it on their own, but three of us might, particularly when you've got those fancy guns. Can you use them?'

'Sure.'

Billy whipped out his gun, spun it and dropped it back into its holster. The trick made Billy feel that he was back on to a level with the Minstrel Boy. He might know more than Billy, but Billy was armed. It was Billy's turn to look speculative.

'Maybe the three of us should travel together?'

He turned to Reave and winked.

'You want to travel with this guy, brother?'

Reave shrugged.

'Maybe. I don't see no reason why we shouldn't.'

The Minstrel Boy's eyes flickered from Reave to Billy and back again.

'Who says that I want to travel with you guys?'

'You said one man couldn't do it on his own.'

'I never said whether I wanted to make it.'

'You don't want to get stuck inside of Graveyard.'

'Okay, okay. We'll travel together. There's no other way, we all know it. What are you two called, anyway? If I'm going to cross the plain with you, I might as well know your names.'

Billy grinned. 'I'm Billy, and he's Reave.'

'Glad to know you.'

'And what's your name?'

'People call me the Minstrel Boy.'

'So now we know each other, shall we get started?'

They walked across the parking lot and down the slip road. Billy walked slightly in front, while Reave walked with the Minstrel Boy, telling him about life in Pleasant Gap, and their walk through the nothings.

They started down the road, and after about a mile, Billy stopped and looked at the Minstrel Boy.

'How long before the Graveyard field stops?'

The Minstrel Boy tried to explain.

'It ain't like it actually stops. This ain't like the nothings. It kind of holds together in a way, only there are sort of holes in it. You know? You could maybe get right through without any kind of stasis machine, but it would be better to turn them on now, to be on the safe side. It'll save anyone who falls in a hole.'

They all halted, turned up the gain on their portapacs, and then walked on. After about another mile, they came across an elliptical hole in the surface of the highway. It was about four feet across, although the edges shimmered and fluctuated slightly. There didn't seem to be any bottom to the hole, and it was filled with a thin blue mist. Billy walked across and peered down into the hole. He glanced back at the Minstrel Boy.

'Is this how the road starts to come apart?'

The Minstrel Boy nodded.

'There's more and more of them as you go on.'

Billy carefully placed one foot above the hole, and a piece of highway surface obediently appeared to receive his foot.

'Lumps of the same nothing.'

They walked on, and the holes became more and more numerous. At times they had to thread their way along a flimsy network between a mass of openings. Despite their portapacs, they all tried their best to avoid stepping on the empty spaces.

After walking for a long time they came to a fairly clear section of road. The sky had changed from brilliant white to a dull metallic grey, and they found they were walking through a dim twilight. Reave stopped and dropped his bag.

'I'm exhausted, for Christ's sake let's stop here for the night. It's almost dark.'

Billy and the Minstrel Boy also stopped. The Minstrel Boy put down his guitar, and pushed his hair out of his eyes.

'We might as well stop here, but don't think it's nightfall, it ain't. That light the truckers use goes on twenty-four hours a day, we're just moving out of range of it. It's always dark along this stretch.'

Reave shook his head.

'I don't care anymore. Let's just stop here and sleep. I'm going to cave in any minute.'

Billy looked at the Minstrel Boy.

'What's the best way to sleep in this kind of country?'

The Minstrel Boy laughed.

'You boys'd be lost without me. It's simple. We hook up our three pacs in a series. That'll give us a field big enough to sleep inside of.'

They coupled up the power pacs, piled up their belongings, and unstrapped their belts. Billy tucked his gun inside his jacket and lay down on the grass of the central island. It was hard and cold, and he drew his knees up to his chest. Just as he was convincing himself that it was impossible to sleep in those conditions, his consciousness drifted away.

Billy wasn't sure what had woken him. He raised his head and looked around and saw to his surprise that the road was filled with people. He sat up in alarm, but none of them seemed to notice him.

It was a long column of people – men, women and children – hobbling and stumbling through the twilight. There were young and old, grandfathers limping on crutches, and young mothers holding clinging babies. Every one of them looked sick and exhausted. Their clothes were ragged and torn. They moved on and on, past where Billy crouched, coming from the same direction as he and the others had come.

They looked neither left nor right. They just trudged on, staring at the ground. They made no attempt to avoid the holes, but walked straight over them as though they didn't exist. Some pushed prams or carried suitcases, while others were bent under bundles on their backs. They came on and on in a never-ending, sluggish stream.

At intervals along the lines were armed guards on tall horses. They wore dark uniforms, and their faces were hidden by their steel helmets. Even the guards seemed bowed in their saddles, as if they too had travelled a terrible distance. Each time one of them passed him, Billy tried to make himself as small as possible, but although even in the twilight he must have been clearly visible, none of the guards seemed to notice him. The thing that really scared him was that both guards and prisoners seemed to have a strange, unnatural, ghostly translucence. Billy felt a cold sweat begin to trickle down his face and body. He stretched out a hand and shook the Minstrel Boy.

'What's happening?'

'Ssh!'

Billy put a finger to his lips and pointed at the awful procession.

'Look.'

'Dear God.'

'What is it?'

'I don't know. I don't think I want to know.'

'They don't seem to be able to see us.

'Thank Christ for that.'

For what seemed like hours, Billy and the Minstrel Boy crouched, shivering, as the inhuman column moved past them.

When it was finally past, they waited a little longer and then woke Reave. He was reassuringly human as he bitched and complained, and gathered up his things.

The three of them divided up the rations from Eli's Store, and washed them down with the last of Reave's beer. Billy and the Minstrel Boy didn't eat too much, but Reave appeared not to notice.

They disconnected the portapacs from each other, and hitched them back on their belts. The Minstrel Boy shouldered his guitar, Billy and Reave picked up their bags, and in single file they started down the gloomy highway.

6

*U*ttering a strange high sound like the keening of high-tension cables, She/They gathered up Her/Their fallen third in Her/Their arms, and slowly began to move forward.

'Grief.'

'Gather data, it is a unique situation.'

'We are wounded.'

'We are wounded.'

The wooden buildings of the township began to fade, and the multi-coloured mist flowed in its place. She/They noted that there was a greater density to the mist where there had been ground.

'Chaos below total.'

'Willeffort.'

The ground-mist became thicker, and the air-mist grew thinner. She/They continued to move slowly forward. The oppressive silence jangled with the presence of chaos. Even the words that filled it were blurred and indistinct. With a gesture of what might have been reluctance in a being of different form, the right-hand figure raised the energy wand. The mist around the figures was bathed in an orange glow. It twisted and swirled, and then began to fold in on itself, coiling into thick viscous strands that sluggishly settled to produce ground and air around the space where She/They hung suspended.

A bridge began to form in front of and behind Her/Them, a plain, stark structure without decoration or parapet. It was made of a dark blue material, and as it formed, the energy wand glowed brighter, its light shifting from orange to yellow. The bridge extended, not to the horizon, but a considerable way into the mist that still swirled in the distance. The bases of its piers were also obscured by the shimmering fog, but around Her/Them it was absolutely solid, and She/They floated above its surface, casting a slight shadow. Even the silence was most pure, and the words that formed in it were sharp and clear.

'All potential reduced proportionally.'

She/They drifted along the bridge, gathering momentum. As She/They approached it, the mist receded.

'Problem of continued existence.'

Despite the burden of the fallen third, She/They seemed less bowed by the weight.

'Problem necessitates an external stasis source. It is not possible to maintain control zone and heal. Insufficient power potential.'
The words flipped rapidly through the silence.
'Seek external source.'

7

The road abruptly stopped and the plain was in front of them. It was like a wide lake that had solidified and become a hard, smooth, but glowingly translucent material. The sky above it was pitch black, apart from an edging of the deepest blue where it met the horizon. All light came from beneath, from the plain itself. To look at everything in a soft, cold light that came from below was disconcerting. It was like being in some huge, ghostly ballroom. Billy and Reave hesitated before stepping off the last broken fragments of the road, and on to the surface of the plain. The Minstrel Boy, however, went straight ahead.

'You don't have to worry, it's quite safe to walk on. You can even shut your portapacs off. Stasis is the least of our worries.'

Doubtfully, Billy and Reave went ahead, and found that they could, in fact, walk on the plain's surface. Billy caught up with the Minstrel Boy.

'So what do we have to worry about?'

'Reaching Dogbreath. It's a fair distance.'

'Ah, come on now. You keep talking about this plain as though it was dangerous.'

'It can be.'

'So what do we have to look out for?'

'That's the trouble, you never know. You can't ever tell.'

'You must have some idea.'

'Maybe I have, and then again, maybe I haven't.'

Billy's temper snapped. He swung round and grabbed the Minstrel Boy by the lapels of his frayed velvet jacket.

'Listen smartass, tell me all you know and don't fuck around.'

'Let go of me or I ain't saying nothing. Okay?'

'Okay.'

Billy relaxed his grip. The Minstrel Boy stepped back and dusted himself off. Billy looked hard at him. 'I'm still waiting.'

'Okay, okay. You know what an anomal is?'

'Sure I know what an animal is.'

'No, no, an anomal.'

He spelled the word for Billy. Billy frowned.

'I think so. It's something that appears where it doesn't belong.'

The Minstrel Boy nodded like he was a teacher talking to a backward pupil.

'And it would seem that this plain is a high-density point for them.'

'So we've got to watch out for them?'

'That's the problem. Nobody knows where they come from. It's been suggested that people produce them themselves.'

Billy frowned.

'I don't understand.'

The Minstrel Boy pursed his lips impatiently.

'Look at it this way. Say you're walking down the road, thinking about elephants, and this herd of elephants shows up where no elephants ought to be, that's a self-produced anomal. Right?'

Billy nodded.

'Right. I get it. If we cross this plain with our guns drawn, looking over our shoulders all the time, the thing we fear is more than likely to jump out at us.'

'Something like that.'

Billy glanced round nervously.

'Surely if we blank out our minds, nothing's going to happen to us.'

The Minstrel Boy shook his head.

'It's not as easy as that. Try looking at it this way. Say you're walking down the road, and you ain't thinking about nothing 'cept where your next meal's coming from, and then a herd of elephants jump out on you where no elephants ought to be. How about that?'

Billy fiddled with his belt.

'I don't know. That just don't fit.'

'Well, according to the self-production theory, those elephants are left over from somebody else thinking about them. Somebody who might have passed by years before.'

Billy looked uncomfortable.

'So what you're trying to tell me is that we can expect anything, but it's dangerous to expect too hard.'

The Minstrel Boy nodded.

'That's about it.'

'You think we should tell Reave about it?'

The Minstrel Boy shrugged.

'You want to?'

Billy glanced at Reave plodding across the glowing plain.

'No. I guess what he don't know won't hurt him.'

They both hurried to catch up with Reave.

The next hour or so was completely uneventful, and Billy began to think that maybe the Minstrel Boy had just been trying to make him paranoid. They were approaching a rocky growth, a kind of jagged mesa that jutted up through the surface of the plain. Billy had just started to relax when a figure darted from around the rock and began running towards them. Billy jerked out his gun, but the Minstrel Boy signalled him to wait.

'I don't think he's anything to do with us.'

As the figure got closer Billy saw that it was a small fat man, naked, terrified, and obviously out of breath. As soon as he saw Billy, Reave and the Minstrel Boy, he shot off in a different direction.

'What I'd like to know is what he's running away from.'

They stood perfectly still, and waited. They didn't have to wait long; almost immediately a horde of naked, howling children came charging round the rock. They carried crude spears with fire-hardened tips, and their only garments were multi-coloured stocking caps or head bands.

Billy and Reave both had their guns out, but the wild children seemed to ignore them, and raced off in pursuit of the little fat man. They chased him for maybe a hundred yards, and then a well-flung rock brought him down. In an instant, the wild children were all over him. His screams were suddenly cut off short.

The Minstrel Boy swung round on Billy and Reave.

'Quick, let's get out of here.'

Reave continued to stare as the children milled round the man.

'What are they doing to him?'

The Minstrel Boy grimaced.

'Playing a game of tag. They play the terminal kind. Let's get out of here.'

The three of them broke into a run, their bags bumping against their hips. Their single purpose became to put as much distance between themselves and the children as possible while they still had the chance.

They ran as fast and as long as they could, but eventually had to stop for breath. The three of them stood together, their heads down and their hands on their knees, gasping for air. Finally, Reave straightened up and pushed his long, straight hair back from his forehead.

'Christ. Where in hell did those kids come from?'

The Minstrel Boy spread his hands.

'Who can tell? There's supposed to be hundreds of them roaming these plains.'

Reave shuddered, and hitched up his pack.

'Let's keep moving. The sooner we reach this here town, the better.'

The other two fell into step beside him. In the next hour of walking they saw a herd of huge misshapen apes plod across their path. They were well off in the distance, however, and didn't bother them. Later a monstrous flying thing swooped down ahead of them. Reave took a shot at it, but he missed. The thing croaked and flapped away. Finally, when they were just beginning to believe they were really lost, they saw the lights of Dogbreath. Honest yellow lights that shone out against the eerie glow of the plain.

As they came closer, they could make out the shapes of buildings, and finally they heard the sounds of people, laughter, shouting, a dog barking and a fiddle scraping.

Dogbreath was little more than a single main street. Down one side was a saloon, a bar, a slot arcade, another saloon, a whore house, another slot arcade, and a general store. Down the other side was a saloon, a slot arcade, another saloon, the Leon Trotsky Hotel, the town hall and the jail. Tucked away at the back of the main street were some dwelling houses and an abattoir. Dogbreath would have been a paradise of fun if it hadn't been so broken-down and ratty.

Whoever had erected the predominantly wooden buildings seemed to have been incapable of constructing a right angle. They staggered, and looked in imminent danger of collapse. The decorations on the outside had been done with an amazing lack of either skill or taste. The only redeeming feature was that the crude, garish paintwork had, at least, chipped, peeled and mellowed to a kind of uniformity.

Electric light bulbs had been strung along the fronts of the saloons and slot arcades to lend them some kind of glamour and excitement. The effect was rather spoiled by at least half of them being blown and dead.

Despite the air of decay and dilapidation, the place was alive with people, hustling and jostling, scuffling through the sand and garbage that covered the street and helped to block out the light from inside the plain.

Billy, Reave and the Minstrel Boy slowly made their way down the street, looking around at the passing crowds.

'Sure are some weird people in this town.'

The Minstrel Boy took Reave by the arm.

'You want to keep those kind of remarks to yourself, Reave, old buddy. People here don't like to be talked about as weird.'

Reave pointed back down the street.

'I just saw a guy with orange hair, and six fingers on each hand. There sure wasn't nothing like that back in Pleasant Gap.'

'That's as maybe, but there are a lot of weird folk in this town. They more than constitute a majority, and they're very touchy about strangers pointing fingers and calling names. If you go on the way you're going you're quite liable to get yourself lynched.'

Reave shrugged.

'Okay, okay. But some of these folks are sure strange looking.'

'Yeah, sure they are, but just keep it to yourself. Okay?'

'Okay.'

They stopped in front of one of the saloons. Billy wiped his mouth with the back of his hand.

'I sure could use a drink after all that walking.'

The Minstrel Boy glanced at him.

'You happen to have any money?'

Billy grinned.

'Sure, we got a bit left.'

'Let's go then.'

They pushed through the swing doors and a wave of noise, smoke and the smell of booze hit them like a slap in the face. They elbowed their way through the crowd and up to the bar. Reave's eyes were popping, but he kept his mouth shut. He had never seen such a diversity of skin colours, not only black, white, brown and yellow but green, blue, red and orange. There was an unimaginable variety of dress, style and even strange anatomical variations. Reave did his best to look straight ahead and show no surprise.

Billy hammered on the bar.

'Can we have some drinks over here?'

'Okay, okay, what do you want?'

'Three beers to start off with.'

'Three beers coming up.'

The bartender banged their mugs on the counter.

'Twenty-one.'

Billy fumbled in his pocket, and handed him three Pleasant Gap tens. The bartender looked at the bills blankly.

'What the fuck are these?'

Billy looked surprised.

'Money, of course. There's thirty there.'

The bartender began to look ugly.

'What kind of money do you call this?'

'Pleasant Gap money.'

'Then I suggest you fuck off back there and spend it. It ain't no good around here, we only take Dogbreath money.'

He signalled to two men on the other side of the room.

'Milt, Eddie. Throw these bums out of here.'

The three of them were grabbed by burly bouncers, hustled through the crowd and thrown out into the street. As the Minstrel Boy picked himself up, he looked at the other two and shook his head.

'You two really don't know nothing, do you?'

8

A Catto came out of the deep, total, dreamless sleep that came from dormax. She looked around the soft glow of the dimmed room, and stretched out a hand to the bedside console. The lights came slowly up, and she blinked again. The small clock on the console read 21.09. She became aware that she was hungry, and wondered if that was because she had become aware of the time. Did she feel hungry because she knew she ought to be hungry?

She slid off the bed and stood up. Through the perspex of the balcony, she saw that the sun was setting, turning an angry red through the shifting air, a romantic, Wagnerian sky looming like some terrible vengeance over the dark shadows of the ruined buildings and squalid shacks. AA Catto hoped her brother Valdo was watching. It would fit so well, particularly if he was still into his Nazi craze. She wasn't sure if he was, though. She hadn't seen him for a month or so.

She stared for a while at the screen of the entertainment console, tapping her silver nails on the plastic coating. She made a mental note that the silver would need redoing in a couple of days. Maybe she should have something different this time, maybe metalflake.

She punched a button, and a show sprang into life. It was the fight games. Four naked L-4 children, with the numbers one to four tattooed on their backs in different colours, were struggling on the sandy floor of a small walled area. A commentary drawled out of the speakers.

'...And don't forget, the combatants have all been starved for two days and then given massive injections of dinamene to make them fierce and aggressive. Right now they are struggling over the piece of meat, and so far, none of them have noticed that there is a heavy steel bar in one corner of the arena... And yes, number three has the meat, and one and two are both on him. You'll notice that the combatants have their heads shaved to stop...'

AA Catto flicked the channel selector round and came up with two fixed-smiling Hostess-1s attempting intercourse with a bored-looking donkey while gales of canned laughter roared from the speakers. She scowled at the screen and punched the off button.

She lay back down on the bed and rang for her personal Hostess. Moments later an almost too-pretty blonde in tight pink covers stood in the doorway.

'You rang, Miss?'

'I'm hungry.'

'You'd like to be served dinner here?'

'Screw dinner, I only just woke up. I want breakfast.'

'Shall I dial you a breakfast menu?'

AA Catto sat up and shook her head.

'No, no. I'll have orange juice, three poached eggs, wholemeal toast and coffee.'

The girl nodded.

'Yes, Miss.'

AA Catto liked to order her food directly through servants rather than dial it for herself. She knew that the only time the girl would taste any of the menu would be if she stole her leftovers. The girl turned to go, but AA Catto called her back.

'Tell me, girl, did you notice that I was naked?'

The girl coloured slightly and nodded. 'Yes, Miss.'

'You could hardly miss the fact?'

'No, Miss.'

'Do you like my body, girl?'

The girl blushed more. 'Yes, Miss.'

'Do you think it's a beautiful body?'

'Yes, Miss.'

'More beautiful than your body?'

'I think so, Miss.'

'Yes? Why?'

'Because you're one of the directorate, Miss. The directorate are the most beautiful people in the whole citadel.'

AA Catto smiled. This girl had been well trained.

'Tell me, girl, would you like to touch my body? Would you like to handle it, play with it?'

The girl began to look frightened.

'I think so, Miss. I think that would be a wonderful experience.'

Her training went deep. AA Catto laughed.

'Well, you won't get the chance. Go and get my breakfast.'

The girl hurried from the room. AA Catto stood up and reached for her robe. As she slipped into it, she smiled to herself. She really should try to resist baiting the servants, but it did relieve a few moments of boredom. She went back to the main console and punched for information. The screen flickered into life with the image of another pink-uniformed Hostess-1. This time she was a brunette.

'Information. May I help you?'

'What's happening?'

'Tonight, Miss Catto?'

'Not next year.'

'Tonight the Glick family are giving a formal dinner for Cynara Meltzer at 22.00.'

AA Catto scowled at the screen.

'Forget that. The Glicks are tiresome, Cynara Meltzer is tiresome, and the dinner will be tiresome. What else?'

'At 24.00 there is to be a party given by Juno Meltzer.'

AA Catto raised an eyebrow.

'Yes? Do you have any information as to what attractions she's providing?'

'No, Miss Catto, only that they are to be a surprise.'

AA Catto smiled. Juno Meltzer could be exceptionally wild at times. The surprises might even be surprising.

'Anything else?'

'I can get you the vu-screen schedules if you require them.'

AA Catto shook her head.

'If that's all, don't bother.'

'There is one thing, Miss Catto.'

'What?'

'I'm instructed to remind all callers that there is a full meeting of the directorate at 10.00 tomorrow.'

'Yeah sure, you reminded me.'

She snapped off the screen, and wandered idly to the entrance of the balcony. It was almost dark outside, and the perspex blister gave a distorted reflection of herself and the lighted room.

There was a hiss behind her as the door slid open, and her Hostess-1 came in with the breakfast tray. She hesitated inside the doorway.

'Would you like it here or in bed, Miss?'

'Oh, I'll go back to bed.'

The Hostess-1 nodded.

'Yes, Miss.'

She carried the tray through into AA Catto's bedroom, and AA Catto followed. She picked up the glass of orange juice and curled up on the bed.

'Run my bath.'

'Yes, Miss.'

'And then come back to attend me. You can help me bathe, it'll be another chance for you to look at my body. You might even get the chance to touch it.'

'Thank you, Miss.'

AA Catto laughed.

'You're very well trained.'

'Miss?'

'Never mind, attend to the bath.'

The girl disappeared into the bathroom, and AA Catto pushed a finger of toast into one of the eggs. The problem that remained was what to wear to Juno Meltzer's party.

She finished toying with breakfast, and lit a cigarette. It was one of her personal blend, a lovingly reproduced mixture of Turkish tobacco and ground Nepalese hashish. As she smoked it, she reflected on the time and trouble it must have taken to obtain the contents of the cigarette. She flicked the ash over the remains of the meal. AA Catto took a primitive delight in spoiling food.

The Hostess-l returned to tell her that the bath was ready, and AA Catto crossed the bedroom, slipped out of her robe and stepped into the sunken tub.

After she was dry again and the Hostess-l had massaged her and done her hair, she asked for the peacock cape outfit to be laid out. She had had it handmade from an archaic print that she had discovered one bored afternoon in the directorate library. She had added some modifications of her own, and it seemed suitably perverse for Juno Meltzer's party.

For a while she sat naked in front of the pink glass mirror, studying her face and body. It pleased her to think how many of the sub-class women in the citadel took their idea of beauty from her vid-lounge image.

She had herself made-up, and then stood up so the Hostess-1 could perfume and dress her. Once finally dressed, she turned.

'What time is it?'

'23.35, Miss.'

'Damn, that means I have an hour to kill, I can't possibly turn up on time. Switch the screen to an entertainment channel.'

The girl hurried to the console, punched buttons, and a bloody battle with tanks and infantry sprang into roaring life. Four men crouched behind a rock were incinerated by a burst of flame that lashed from the turret of a tank.

'Change the channel.'

A dozen or more couples writhed and squirmed in a tank of black oily liquid, to a background of electronic music.

'God no, try another.'

A comedian appeared, going through some sort of rapid-fire patter.

'Forget the channels.'

'What would you like, Miss?'

'A fast burst of 91 k.'

'After the quick, pleasant radiation bath, she dismissed the girl and, careful not to crush her dress and cape, she sat for half an hour watching an ancient movie. Then she shut down the console and picked up the box that held her injectors. She gently pulled up her long black skirt and pressed the one marked altacaine against her thigh, and gasped with pleasure as the first rush of the drug rocketed round her system. She pressed the button twice more. That would see her flying for at least twenty hours.

She was ready for the party.

9

They stood in the main street of Dogbreath and looked at each other.

'How the fuck was I supposed to know they didn't take Pleasant Gap money?'

The Minstrel Boy mimicked Billy.

'How the fuck was I supposed to know? How the fuck are you supposed to know anything? Oh yes, I've got some money, let's have a drink, and you pull out that funny money and we get the bum's rush.'

'I'm sorry. I didn't know.'

'No, you never fucking know.'

'Okay, okay. You made the point, what do we do now?'

'What do we do now? Nothing, man! We're fucking broke! We can't get a room, we can't get a meal and we can't get a drink. We can't even get the stage out of here.'

Billy and Reave fell silent. There didn't seem to be anything they could say. A drunk staggered out of the saloon, across the boardwalk and collapsed in the shadows. The Minstrel Boy grinned.

'I think we just fell on our feet.'

'Yeah?'

'Yeah. Follow me.'

The Minstrel Boy crossed to where the drunk was lying mumbling to himself, and crouched beside him. He started to go through his pockets. Reave looked at him in surprise.

'What are you doing?'

'Rolling a drunk, what do you think? Quick, come and help me.'

Billy and Reave knelt down beside the drunk. The Minstrel Boy gestured impatiently.

'Quick, go through his boots.'

They both pulled off a boot each, turned them upside down and shook them. The drunk protested feebly and then started giggling. A small package fell out. The Minstrel Boy leaned across and grabbed it.

'What's this?'

He unwrapped it.

'Fucking lucky day. Good quality heroin. We're doing all right, boys. Hundred and ten in coin, and about an ounce of smack in his boot. We can live with class for the next couple of days.'

They stood up and moved away from the drunk who was now snoring. Reave and Billy looked at the Minstrel Boy.

'What happens now?'

'Well, it'd be good to keep the scag and have ourselves a time, but we can't afford it. We'll take it down to the store and see what they'll give us for it.'

'Won't they want to know where we got it from?'

'Nah, they won't give two fucks. The only law and order in this town is dedicated to protect the mayor's interests and the police chief's interests. It doesn't extend to drunks on the street.'

They hurried down to the store. A small furtive man gave them a thousand in coin on the heroin, and they went off laughing. They avoided the saloon they'd been thrown out of, and in front of one of the others, the Minstrel Boy divided up the money.

'Remember to save at least a hundred for the stage, or we'll never get out of here.'

They pushed their way into the saloon. It was almost identical to the one they'd been thrown out of. This time they made their way through to the bar, ordered drinks with a flourish and paid in coin. The beers tasted good. The raw spirit that followed tasted even better.

A trio of girls walked past their table, pretending not to notice them. One of them, a tall black girl in shorts and halter of a metallic purple material, let her thigh brush against Reave's hand for a moment, before walking away with an exaggerated sway of her hips.

Reave began to get up to follow her, but the Minstrel Boy put a restraining hand on his arm.

'Hold on, man. Before you start having yourself a party, we ought to get ourselves a room at the hotel.'

Reave scowled.

'You sound like my mother.'

'You boys need a fucking mother, the way you handle things.

Reave sat down again.

'Yeah okay, you told us already.'

They finished their beers, left the saloon and made their way down the street to the Leon Trotsky Hotel. It looked dim and deserted in comparison with the bustle of the saloons. Billy pushed open the door. Reave and the Minstrel Boy followed him into a dim foyer. The hotel smelled of dirt and decay, and their boots echoed in the hollow silence.

The only light was a small yellow bulb above the dusty reception desk, and as their eyes got used to the darkness they saw that the only furniture was two beat-up sofas and an aspidistra that drooped sadly in its pot. Everything was covered in a thick layer of dust that looked like it hadn't been disturbed for centuries.

'Can I help you, gentlemen?'

The three of them started and turned to see that a figure had emerged from a bead-hung doorway behind the reception desk.

'We're looking for some rooms.'

He was a small man with narrow shoulders and a pot-belly. His large, pale, watery eyes watched from rimless glasses. His skin was a sallow olive colour, and he wore a dirty white suit, a rumpled black shirt and thin white tie. On top of his limp black hair he wore a dark red fez. He smiled ingratiatingly and rubbed his hands together.

'Three?'

Billy nodded.

'How long do you want them for?'

Billy looked at the other two.

'How long do we want to stay here?'

The Minstrel Boy glanced at the man.

'When does the next stage leave town?'

The little man consulted a yellowing timetable. 'Tomorrow, at midnight.'

'What time is it now?'

'Just after eleven.'

'Night or morning?'

'Night.'

'So we've got to wait twenty-five hours?'

'That's right.'

'That's how long we'll be staying.'

'That'll be twenty each. In advance.'

They all tossed coins on to the counter, and the little man scooped them up.

'My name's Mohammed. I'm your host.'

He picked three keys off a board behind him.

'If you follow me, I'll show you to your rooms.'

He came out from behind the desk and led them towards a flight of stairs that wound up towards pitch-dark upper floors. At the foot of them he stopped and turned on another dim yellow bulb on the first landing. A fat black cat that had been asleep on the third step raced past them and out of sight under one of the sofas.

They followed him up the first flight of stairs and along the landing. At the foot of the second flight he stopped, turned on another light, again dim and yellow, up on the second floor.

They went up four flights in this fashion. Stairs, landing, stop, click, and up again. On the fourth floor, Mohammed stopped and unlocked a door to a room. Billy let himself be ushered inside. He dropped his bag on the floor and Mohammed turned on the light.

'You like?'

'Uh... yeah.'

Mohammed slid out of the door and went to unlock the next two rooms for Reave and the Minstrel Boy.

Billy looked round the room. The kindest thing you could say about it was that it was minimal. Mohammed's slow-burning light bulb shed its sickly glow over a plain iron single bed with two grey blankets and a slightly less grey sheet. On the floor was a yard square strip of worn carpet. There was a chipped washstand and a wooden chair, and that was it, apart from a small sepia photograph of a camel that hung above the bed in a black frame.

Billy kicked his bag under the bed, and walked down to the next room. The Minstrel Boy was looking out of the window. Billy sat down on the bed.

'Some hotel.'

'I've been in better jails.'

'Are we going out?'

'Could stay here and tromp roaches.'

'I'll go and get Reave.'

They found that Mohammed had turned off all the lights on his way back down to the foyer, and the return trip on the stairs was a series of near disasters.

Mohammed reappeared as they walked back through the foyer, and beckoned furtively to them.

'Hey, boys. Come over here, I got something to show you.'

Reave, Billy and the Minstrel Boy looked at each other questioningly. Without saying a word they seemed to settle it and strolled over to the desk.

'Okay, Mohammed, what have you got to show us?'

The little man put a plastic cube on the counter.

'Filthy tri-di?'

Inside the clear cube was a miniaturized scene. Tiny doll-like figures performed within its substance. It was two blonde girls in short pink uniforms beating a third who was bound and naked. The naked one squirmed a little in mock pain, but all three showed distinct traces of boredom. After a matter of seconds it became clear that the cube had been produced on a loop system, and there was only a single, short action which went on repeating itself. Mohammed grinned and looked sideways at Reave, Billy and the Minstrel Boy.

'Pretty hot stuff, eh?'

Billy slowly shook his head.

'No.'

Mohammed looked disappointed.

'You no like?'

'No.'

'I got others, maybe you like them better.'

'No.'

Mohammed began to look as though he might burst into tears. He tried again.

'You boys going out to find some girls, maybe?'

'Maybe.'

'I can get you nice girls, they come right here, right to your room.'

'We'll find our own girls.'

They started to walk towards the door, but Mohammed came round the counter and stopped them.

'Listen, maybe you want to buy some hashish?'

The Minstrel Boy began to look annoyed. He took hold of one of Mohammed's lapels between two fingers.

'Why should we want to buy hashish off you? They sell as much as we could want right across the street at the store.'

'I sell much cheaper.'

Still holding him by the lapel, the Minstrel Boy walked Mohammed across to the reception desk.

'Your hustling is beginning to annoy me. Let's have a look at this wonderful hashish.'

The little man reached under the counter and produced a piece of black dope, about the size of a matchbox. The Minstrel Boy picked it up and sniffed it.

'How much?'

'Twenty.'

'Do the cops know that you're selling dope without a licence?'

'Fifteen.'

'I'll give you ten.'

'You'll break me.'

'Ten.'

'All right, all right. I was a fool to try and help ingrates like you.'

The Minstrel Boy pocketed the piece of hash and slapped a ten on the desk. He turned and made for the door. In the doorway, he turned and glanced back at Mohammed.

'If you've been through our bags when we get back, I'll kill you. Got it?'

Out in the street, things seemed to have slowed down a little. The crowds had thinned and a high proportion of drunks leaned against walls or lay in the gutter. The three strolled into the first saloon they came to. It was quieter and more peaceful on the inside as well. A poker game was in deep session in one corner. Beyond that the only signs of life were by the bar, where a number of men stood around, morosely drinking. About half the tables were taken up by drunks, their heads cradled in their arms, sleeping soundly. A string band was playing tired music on a small bandstand.

Reave went to the bar to get some drinks, while Billy and the Minstrel Boy sat down at a vacant table. The arrival of three new customers, apparently with money to spend, had an immediate effect on the bar girls. Within seconds three had closed in on the table, strutting and smiling.

'You gentlemen mind if we sit with you?'

Reave waved his arms in an expansive gesture.

'Go right ahead, be our guests.'

The ones who sat with Reave and the Minstrel Boy were attractive enough, but they could have easily come from Miss Ettie's. The one who sat beside Billy was the most amazing thing Reave had ever seen.

Her skin was a pale blue, and seemed to be made up of tiny reptilian scales. As far as he could see, she was completely without hair, but this enhanced, rather than detracted from her appearance.

The back of her head was covered by a kind of skull cap of multi-coloured sequins. Her long skirt was made of the same material, and slit up to her thigh. Apart from the cap, skirt and a pair of satin mules with ultra-high heels she was naked. A kind of necklace made of rows of much larger sequins hung in front of her small, firm breasts, but did little to obscure them.

Billy put a hand on her arm.

'Is your skin real? I mean, really real?'

The girl laughed.

'That could cost you money to find out.'

'Is that a promise?'

She patted his cheek.

'No, honey. It's a profession.'

'What's your name, babe?'

'Angelina.'

One of the other girls giggled.

'Angelina the whore. No limit.'

Angelina flashed round on her.

'You shut that come-inside mouth of yours, bitch, or I'll set Ruby to tear your face off.'

She turned back to Billy.

'Take no notice of her, honey, she don't have any idea of how to behave. She can't leave the grease gun alone.'

The Minstrel Boy, his silver guitar in one hand and his girl in the other, went over to sit in with the string band. A few minutes later Reave also stood up and, with a wink at Billy, followed his girl up the stairs at the back of the saloon. Billy sent over for a bottle of mescal, and he and Angelina began to get acquainted.

The operation was going very well when a commotion started on the other side of the room. One of the sleeping drunks had woken up, and was wildly staring round the place.

'Where's that goddamn pig with my money? Where's the blue-skinned bitch gone with my fucking money?'

He caught sight of Angelina, and staggered across the room towards where she and Billy were sitting.

'I paid you for time, bitch, and I ain't had nothing yet.'

Angelina looked at him coldly.

'You busted out, buddy. I can't help that you fell asleep.'

The drunk grabbed Angelina by the wrist.

'I aim to get what I paid for.'

Billy jackknifed to his feet.

'Take your hands off her.'

The drunk kept hold of Angelina, but swung round to look blearily at Billy.

'Butt out, sonny. I'm getting what's righteously mine.'

'I'm warning you. She's with me.'

'Fuck off, kid, or I'll rip your arms off.'

Billy swung at the drunk, and to his surprise he went down in a crash of overturning chairs. He came again, though, almost straight away, with a polished black tube in his hand. There was a shout from the bar.

'Laser!'

Everyone who was still awake hit the floor. A thin pencil of bright blue light flashed silently from the tube and swung down at Billy. Billy ducked and twisted, and it sliced through the table behind him. Billy found he had his own gun in his hand, and before the drunk could swing the laser back at him again, the gun exploded. There was a loud, frozen silence. A look of surprise came over the drunk's face. The laser slid from his fingers and, almost in slow motion, he crumpled to the floor. The saloon seemed to breathe out. The bartender came across to where Billy was standing over the drunk with his smoking gun still in his hand. He knelt beside the body and put an ear to its chest.

'You killed him.'

'He went for me with a laser.'

The bartender held up his hands.

'It's nothing to me, kid. I'm just saying that he's dead. You could leave a twenty for the cleanup crew, though.'

Billy dropped his gun into its hoister, and took a hit from the bottle of mescal. He tossed a twenty on to the table, and turned to Angelina.

'I've got to get out of here.'

She picked up her bag.

'Want me to come with you?'

'How much is that going to cost?'

She ran a pointed tongue round her blue lips.

'You just killed a man, honey. You can have me all for free.'

10

She/They moved forward, the two units carrying the fallen third cradled in Her/Their arms.

Forward, along the blue bridge that cut such a perfect line through the swirling kaleidoscope mists.

Forward, seeking a place of stasis where Her/Their power could be concentrated on healing Her/Their wounds.

Forward, creating the bridge in front of Her/Them.

Forward, with the bridge behind Her/Them smoking and boiling, finally becoming one with the swirling, shining, coloured chaos as Her/Their area of power moved on.

She/They had been alone from the beginning. It was Her/Their choice. The other beings who had, on occasion, used the order that She/They created for their own purposes had been so contaminated with the seeds of chaos that if they appeared too often, She/They had always moved on, removing the field of influence and leaving the area to disruptors and the shimmering mists. There could be no serenity and order where other beings came with their scattering influence. Since the beginning Her/Their being and purpose had been concentrated on creating an order sphere wherein She/They could find the real satisfaction.

She/They had devoted Her/Their infinite existence to that world of white sky, smooth surface resolved into perfect squares of alternate black and white, total density of the solid ground and total purity of clear air.

Her/Their being found its only satisfaction in the poetry of ultimate symmetry, in a purity of form that had been destroyed by the coming of the disruptors.

Her/Their memory of Her/Their life before the disruptors raged across the levels of the finite world was old and clouded. The most She/They could recall from that time was a longing for a cloistered, patterned existence. It came to Her/Them as indistinct fragments of pale contentment. She/They had long abandoned any hope that She/They might regain Her/Their place in that ordered work. The order that now maintained Her/Their being was the single purpose to reconstruct as much as She/They could of that which the disruptors had ruined and destroyed.

Her/Their wounds, the bridge across which She/They travelled, and most particularly the circling, twisting mists that insinuated, attacked and sought to engulf Her/Their sole symbol of order caused Her/Them pain and horror that were unique in Her/Their experience.

Although She/They used the entire residue of energy that was left from Her/Their creation of the bridge to break down, analyse and catalogue these impulses, She/They was intensely aware that the very existence of such phenomena as fear, pain and the awareness of danger had introduced disorder into the heart of Her/Their consciousness.

She/They loathed and hated the impulses that attacked Her/Them, but in that loathing She/They knew that She/They was Her/Their self producing disorder. The silence She/They prized so much was flawed with a high static sound, and the words that formed in it glowed a garish, ugly red.

'Irregular spiral.'
'Estimate product to be destructive.'
'Energy drain approaches critical.'
'Active destruct move at spiral results in tightening the circuits.'
'Emergency.'
'Willefort fails to negate trend.'
'Passive acceptance reduces trend but increases spiral motion.'
'Paradox.'
'Paradox is not.'
'Paradox exists therefore is.'
'Contradiction produced.'
'Warning warning.'
'Reduce trend or increase speed.'
'Solve paradox.'
'Energy drain.'

The words were burning with a hideous brightness, crackling against themselves. The silence began to break up under the strain of gusts of white noise.

'Attempt order production by mathematic route out.'
'Product of wave form.'
'Prime.'
'Root of wave form.'
'Prime.'
'Numerical escape blocked by prime number groups.'
'Out, out, out.'
'Negative.'

The bridge began to turn, it assumed an elliptical and downward form. Inexorably it started to corkscrew.

'Class A emergency.'
'Disorder in terminology.'
'Terminology by definition is a factor for order.'
'Disorder as term becomes factor of definition.'
'Reject.'
'Rejection tightens spiral.'
'Stop.'

She/They stopped.

'Paradox flow up four points.'

Cracks appeared in the bridge.

'Prepare passive state.'
'Wounds preclude total passivity.'

Her/Their form became spherical, but gradually one side began to flatten and streaks of colour began to creep across Her/Their reflective surface.

'Wounds render passivity partial.'

She/They resumed the triple form. A large section of the bridge fell away into the mist. Slowly She/They raised the energy wand. It glowed a dull red. She/They stood on the flat side of a blue hemisphere.

Slowly it began to rise, and the silence broke into a scream.

11

If Billy's mind hadn't been blown by the killing, it certainly was after Angelina had finished with him. She did everything that Miss Ettie's girls had ever done to him, and then took him into places that he had never been before.

Her blue skin was strangely cold. Afterwards, he told Reave that it was like fucking an energetic corpse. Fucking was, by no means, the end of it. It was little more than a beginning. After she'd sucked him and brought him on, she rushed him through to a series of numbers that took him higher and higher until he finally blew apart. That wasn't the end of it, either. She pulled a little induction coil from her bag. It didn't generate more than maybe ten volts, but it was sufficient to do alarming things to their nerves when each of them held a terminal and their bodies came in contact. Her arms slid round him like blue snakes, and they started again. This time with the added electric jolt.

Billy's head was spinning and his body was exhausted by the time they'd worked out all the possibilities of the shock machine. He lay on his back and stared at the ceiling while Angelina ran her fingernails over his chest.

He was drifting in a half sleep when there was a furious pounding on the door. Billy woke with a start and reached towards the gun in his belt.

'Who is it?'

'Never mind who it is, open up.'

Billy carefully got up, and draped a blanket over his shoulder.

'Hold on, I'm coming.'

Holding his gun in one hand, he opened the door a tiny crack with the other.

It was immediately kicked open and the barrel of a huge .70 calibre recoilless pistol was shoved under his chin.

'Police Department, freeze.'

Billy stood perfectly still as a huge beer gut of a man removed his gun, while his equally huge partner held the pistol at his throat.

The Dogbreath Police Department took pride in their appearance. They wore yellow metalflake helmets with a red star on the front and black visors. Their bodies were encased in black PVC one-piece suits with padding on the shoulders, ribs, elbows, crutch and knees, and decorated with a wealth of badges and insignia.

They were also well prepared. From a wide belt around their waists hung a riot stick, tear-gas canisters, a stock prod, handcuffs and a narrow-beam laser. All this was in addition to the .70 calibre recoilless that each of them held in their pudgy hands.

The pistol was taken away from Billy's throat.

'Okay, relax, but don't try nothing or I'll blow your head off.'

The cop holding Billy's gun looked at his partner. 'Is he the one that shot the guy?'

The one holding the gun on Billy grinned.

'Must be, Angelina's up here with her shock box.'

Angelina sat up in bed.

'Screw yourself, pig.'

'Shut your mouth, honey, or we'll book you for L and F.'

The one with the gun prodded Billy in the stomach.

'So you're the gun-happy kid?'

Billy tried to explain.

'Listen, he pulled a laser on me…'

The cop slapped Billy across the face. 'We'll tell you when to talk.'

He pointed with his gun to the upright chair.

'Sit.'

Billy sat. The two cops stood in front of him.

'So you're the killer who blasts down citizens of Dogbreath with his fancy reproduction pistol.'

The one with his gun spun it on his finger. Billy tried again.

'He was roughing up Angelina, I hit him and he pulled a laser.'

'So?'

'It was self-defence.'

'So?'

'I don't understand.'

'What makes you think Dogbreath has got any laws about self-defence?'

'It wasn't my fault.'

'No? You shot him, didn't you?'

'But…'

'It's lucky for you, kid, that Dogbreath don't have no laws about killing, or you'd be in trouble.'

Billy looked bewildered.

'So what are you here for?'

'We don't like gun-happy kids in town.'

'But you said there was no laws...'

'We kill who we don't like. The stage leaves at midnight. Don't miss it.'

Billy shook his head vigorously.

'I won't.'

The cop pulled a pad of printed forms from a pouch on his belt.

'Sign here.'

'What is it?'

'Statement exempting the People's Metropolis of Dogbreath from all claims by agents or relatives of the deceased.'

Billy signed.

'Okay, that'll be...'

The cop counted on his fingers.

'Conveyance Fee ten, Mortification Duty twenty, Disposal Fee twenty, and Law Enforcement Charge fifty. That's a round hundred altogether.'

'You mean I have to pay to go through this?'

'You better learn, kid. Nothing comes free.'

They gave him his gun back.

'Be on the stage.'

They left. Billy looked round at Angelina. 'What was that all about?'

'They shook you down for a hundred. You got taken, honey.'

'So what was I supposed to do?'

She licked her lips with a swift, lizard-like flick of the tongue.

'You could have killed them, and run.'

'Wouldn't that have been overdoing it?'

'You don't have any sense of class. No drama, no romance.'

Billy started to get into bed, but Angelina pushed him away.

'I've gone off you, honey. I don't think I want you any more.'

'What's the matter with you?'

'The way you handled those cops, you're just no good, babe.'

Billy began to get annoyed.

'I was good enough to handle your buddy with the laser.'

Angelina thought about it, and then slowly rubbed her thighs together.

'Yeah, I guess you were at that. Come on back to bed.'

After another strenuous hour with Angelina and the induction coil, Billy passed out.

He woke up with Reave shaking him. 'Wake up, old buddy. The stage leaves in an hour.'

Billy yawned.

'Have I been out for that long?'

'You have indeed.'

Billy sat up rubbing his eyes. 'Got a smoke?'

Reave handed him a cigar, and then struck a match. Billy inhaled and coughed.

'Did you have a good time last night?'

Reave grinned and winked.

'I'll say.'

Billy got out of bed and struggled into his clothes. Reave laughed.

'You look rough, did you have a heavy night?'

Billy pulled on one of his cowboy boots.

'Heavy.'

'Yeah? What happened? Did you come back here with that blue chick? She looked weird.'

'She was weird.'

Reave poked him in the ribs with his elbow.

'Come on Billy, it's me, Reave. What happened? Don't be so cagey.'

Billy took another cigar from Reave and sat down on the bed. He began reluctantly to tell him about the killing in the saloon and the scenes that followed.

'And then, to top it all, the fucking cops took a hundred off me.'

The atmosphere of all boys together telling tales dropped away. Reave stroked his chin and looked worried.

'How much money have you got left?'

'About eighty, why?'

Reave looked guilty.

'I don't have more than that left myself.'

'So? We've got a hundred and sixty between us, and the Minstrel Boy must have some more money.'

There was an awkward silence. Reave walked across to the window and looked down at the street.

'That's the trouble. I haven't seen him for hours.'

'You mean he hasn't been back?'

'There's not a sign of him, and the stage goes soon. I mean, if he don't show up in the next few minutes we're in trouble. We don't even know where the fucking stage goes to.'

Billy stuffed the last of his things into the bag and did up the straps.

'We don't need the Minstrel Boy to nursemaid us.'

He strapped on his gun belt.

'We'll go down to the stage, and if he doesn't get on it, we'll just ride it down to the next town and see what happens there.'

Reave slung his own bag over his shoulder. He still looked unhappy.
'I don't like it, Billy.'

Billy turned in the doorway.

'What's the matter with you? We've done okay so far. We don't need anyone to look after us.'

Reave shrugged, and followed Billy out of the door.

'Maybe you're right.'

In, the foyer Mohammed stood behind the counter and watched them walk to the door.

'Good luck on your journey, boys.'

Billy glanced back at him.

'Yeah, right.'

Whatever Billy and Reave had expected, the stage was a total surprise to them. It was like something out of a legend. Billy had seen pictures of things like it, back in Pleasant Gap. The battered wooden coach with its high spoked wheels, small square windows, three on each side, and the brass rail round the luggage rack on the roof. None of the pictures had shown anything like the four huge green lizards that were harnessed to it, and squatted on their haunches, waiting for the journey to start.

On the boardwalk, beside where the stage waited, there was a signboard. "Overland Hollow City and Dogbreath Stage Co. Passengers Wait Here." Only one man stood beside the sign. He wore a wide-brimmed bat hat with a band of silver and turquoise links, and an ankle-length, dirty yellow duster coat. His pinstripe trousers were tucked into high black boots. As Billy and Reave approached, he turned and they saw he had a weather-beaten brown face with a blond drooping moustache and short pointed beard. A strap across his chest, outside his denim work shirt, indicated that he was wearing a shoulder holster. He looked Billy and Reave up and down.

'Well now, two more for the stage. Where you boys headed?'

Billy shrugged.

'Anywhere, we're just drifting along.'

The man stroked his beard.

'You better stay on the stage right through to Hollow City. This here stage only stops at two other places. Sade and Galilee. Galilee is bad, and Sade you don't even want to talk about in broad daylight.'

Billy and Reave looked at each other.

'Looks like it's Hollow City for us.'

Two men came down the boardwalk. Both wore peaked caps and heavy fur coats. One carried a long whip, while the other cradled a wicked-looking riot gun in the crook of his arm. The one with the gun climbed up on to the driver's box of the stage, while the other stopped in front of Billy, Reave and the man in the hat and long coat.

'Stage is leaving, let's have your fares.'

The man dropped some coins in the driver's hands and climbed into the coach. Billy was the next in line.

'How much to Hollow City for the two of us?'

It didn't look as though the Minstrel Boy was going to show.

'Two hundred.'

Billy felt an empty feeling hit his stomach.

'How far can we get on seventy-five each?'

'Galilee.'

Billy thought about what the man in the hat had just said. Then he thought about what the police had said the night before.

'I guess it better be Galilee then.'

They paid the driver and climbed inside the coach. The man in the hat looked at them inquiringly.

'Thought you were going to Hollow City?'

Billy scowled.

'We were, but we found we only had enough money to make it as far as Galilee.'

The man shook his head.

'That's too bad, boys. Rather you than me.'

Reave looked at him.

'What's wrong with Galilee?'

'They don't like strangers.'

Billy was about to ask him to go into more detail when the coach gave a lurch and then slowly began to rattle down the main street of Dogbreath. Once out of the town, the driver whipped up the lizards and soon they were bouncing over the plain at a merry pace. Reave grinned at Billy.

'Sure beats walking.'

Billy sighed.

'I guess it does.'

The man took off his hat, and laid it on the seat beside him. He fished a flask out of his coat, took a hit from it and offered it to Billy. Billy accepted the flask and took a healthy swig. It felt as though his mouth and throat were on fire. His eyes watered, and he coughed.

'What in hell is this?'

The man winked.

'You know what they say. Don't ask no questions.'

Billy passed the flask to Reave, who, despite a little more caution, went through the same performance. He handed the flask back to the man, who took another swallow, put the cap back on the flask and pocketed it.

'If we're going to be travelling together, I'd best introduce myself. People call me the Rainman.'

He stuck out a hand. Billy and Reave both shook it.

'I'm Billy, and he's Reave.'

'Pleased to know you.'

The stage rattled on, and Billy wondered if he ought to ask the Rainman what exactly was wrong with Galilee. Before he could say anything, Reave started a conversation with him.

'If you don't mind me asking, why do people call you the Rainman?'

The Rainman laughed.

'Because I bring on the rain.'

'Huh?'

'These stasis towns, you know, they get bored and they hire me on. Ain't you never heard my slogan?'

Reave shook his head.

'Can't say I have.'

The Rainman recited.

'Change your weather, change your luck. Teach you how to... find yourself.'

'Neat slogan.'

'I think so.'

'What I can't figure is why these people want the weather changed. Nobody grows nothing since Stuff Central set up in business.'

The Rainman grinned knowingly.

'They don't. Not until I get to town.'

'So what happens?'

'Well, I just ramble into town, hang around for a couple of days, tell a few people about how the weather used to be in the ancient days. I tell them about rain, clouds, sunshine, showers, thunder and hurricanes, and pretty soon they get to thinking about how dull it gets with the old white sky and even temperature, and that's the time I make them an offer.'

'An offer for what?'

'An offer to lay on some weather.'

Reave looked impressed.

'You can really do that?'

'Sure can.'

He glanced up at his bag on the rack.

'Got me this little old limited-field disruptor, trapped it myself out in the nothings a few years back, and I ain't been short of a meal or a drink or a woman since.'

'So what exactly do you do?'

'It's simple, son. I just set up that disruptor in the middle of those bored old stasis towns and give him a couple of kicks to get him going, and bingo. They got weather. Rain, snow, heatwave, lightning, fog, as much weather as they could want. Of course, it ain't exactly like it was in the old days. They don't have the same weather for more than ten minutes at a time, and now and then things get a bit out of hand, and they maybe get a hurricane or an earthquake or something like that that they didn't exactly bargain for. When that happens, I find myself leaving town in a hurry, but it works out okay in the end.'

Reave scratched his head.

'What happens when these people get all this weather? We never had anything like that in Pleasant Gap.'

The Rainman laughed again.

'Son, you should see them go. They just about go crazy. Dancing about, singing and shouting. And the women, oh boy, you should see those women get it on. And me, well, I started it all and that puts the good old Rainman right at the front of the line.'

'Sure sounds like a good life.'

The Rainman nodded.

'It is. 'Cept most towns get tired of weather after a few days and begin to hanker after everything getting back to normal. That's when they pay me off and I shut off Wilbur, that's the pet name I call the disruptor, and it's time to move on. Like you say, though, it ain't a bad life.'

Billy started to take an interest in the conversation. He looked at the Rainman.

'You sound as though you don't have too much regard for these stasis towns.'

The Rainman shook his head.

'I don't, and I must have seen a hundred of them since I got hold of old Wilbur.'

'What's wrong with them?'

'Oh, nothing really. It's just that they're so goddamn self-satisfied, You know, they sit there, inside the field of their generator, everything they need coming in on a stuff beam. After a while they seem to fold in on themselves, refuse to believe there's anything different from their little world. They start to get so fucking narrow, some then really turn weird.'

'Weird?'

'Yeah, these little towns all get caught up on some stupid detail and build their whole lives round it.'

Billy looked interested.

'Is Galilee like that?'

'Yeah, they're all crazy.'

'Crazy?'

'Yeah, they have this thing about work. I mean, everything they need comes in on a stuff beam, but they have this kind of religion thing about work. They work all the time at these pointless jobs, hard physical work for maybe ten hours a day. They have this mad priesthood which keeps everybody hard at it. It's a terrible place to get busted for vagrancy. They'll have you breaking up rocks with a goddamn hammer. You wouldn't believe the way they carry on around Galilee.'

Reave looked alarmed.

'And this is the place we're heading for?'

The Rainman nodded sombrely.

'If I was you, I'd get the hell out of it as quick as possible. It's no place for freewheelers and ramblers.'

They rode on in silence for a while. All of them were lost in their own thoughts. Outside the coach, the glowing plain seemed to go on for ever. After about two hours, the driver leaned down and yelled.

'We're hitting the nothings, better switch on your generators.'

Billy punched the on button on his portapac and glanced at the Rainman.

'Doesn't this coach have its own generator?'

'Sure it does, it's under that canvas sheet at the back, but it's an old beat-up bunch of junk and it ain't too reliable.'

'Why are we going into the nothings at all?'

The Rainman looked at him as though he was an imbecile. 'If you don't go into the nothings, how the fuck do you get anywhere?'

'But how does the driver know where he's going?'

'He don't.'

Billy and Reave were beginning to get confused.

'Then how do we get anywhere?'

'The lizards.'

'The lizards?'

'Sure, them old lizards seem to know where to head when they get into the nothings. Leastways, they usually come out where they're supposed to.'

'Usually?'

Billy thought about his life being in the hands of the huge, lumbering, green monsters that had sat scratching themselves in the street at Dogbreath. The Rainman shrugged.

'A few stages don't turn up. That's why people don't move around much.'

Billy stared out of the window at the swirling colours that flashed and blended and faded back into the ever-present grey. Apart from the occasional lurch, there was no indication that the coach was moving in any direction at all. Looking out into the nothings Billy was filled with a deep depression that he could find no logical reason for. He began thinking about what the Rainman had told him about Galilee. It seemed as though they'd really made a mess of things by losing the Minstrel Boy. Billy didn't want to wind up on some religious nut's chain gang.

Then they were out of the nothings and running on a strip of barren, dusty desert. The only things that grew under the hot red sky were twisted thorns and stunted cacti. In the distance Billy could make out what looked like a walled city.

As they drew near, the city revealed itself to be a grim, forbidding place. It had high white walls, behind which Billy could make out the pointed tops of dark buildings. The coach seemed to be heading towards a pair of sinister gates made of some kind of embossed black metal. It was then that Billy saw something that made his stomach twist.

Outside the walls and a few yards from the gate was an enormous gibbet. It stood like a huge angular tree, or the mast of an ancient sailing ship that had sunk into the sand. There must have been a full fifty bodies hanging from it, men, women and children. Evil-looking crows circled the ghastly structure, picking choice titbits from the dead.

The driver didn't take the coach into the city, however. Before the trail reached the gate, it crossed another that ran parallel with the walls. At the intersection a figure was waiting. It had a broad black hat that flopped to hide its face, and a black cloak that concealed its body. The driver halted the coach beside it and hollered out.

'Sade.'

The figure opened the door of the coach and climbed inside. Billy had a brief flash of a deathly white hand with purple nails and heavy silver rings. Then it vanished beneath the cloak. The figure seated itself in the corner, as far as possible from Billy, Reave and the Rainman.

The Rainman held out his hand as he'd done to Billy and Reave.

'Howdy stranger. People call me the Rainman. Maybe we should get acquainted seeing as how it's a long ride to Hollow City.'

The stranger gave a sharp hiss, and moved even further into the corner. The Rainman shrugged.

'Suit yourself, just trying to be sociable.'

He settled back into his seat and stared out of the window. The coach was still rushing through the same parched landscape with its baleful red sky.

It was about then that the stage hit a rock or something and was jolted a foot into the air. The Rainman's bag crashed to the floor. As he reached down to pick it up, it began to smoke and dissolve. He looked at Billy and Reave in alarm.

'Wilbur's woken up, and he's mad. Grab hold of me, there's no knowing what can happen – and you, stranger.'

He reached out towards the figure in black, but it twisted violently away from him. The sudden movement tipped its hat, and for an instant showed the pale face of a beautiful but incredibly evil woman.

Then Wilbur started to move and everything shimmered and dissolved.

12

AA Catto walked at a suitably stately speed down the moving corridor that led to the Velvet Rooms. She looked at herself in a small pocket mirror. Her features were perfect, the straight aristocratic nose, the large pale blue eyes and the sensuous mouth with its trace of cruelty.

AA Catto was extremely satisfied with herself.

The Velvet Rooms were an ideal place for a party. Their floor, walls and ceiling were covered in purple velvet, and the main floor was hydroelastic and sections could be made soft or rigid by the touch of a control. Jutting out of the main floor was a broad terrace of pure white marble, with a baroque balustrade and a wide staircase that swept down to the floor.

It was on the terrace that AA Catto made her entrance. Directly she stepped inside the Velvet Rooms, the familiar atmosphere of opium smoke, incense and chatter swirled around her, and she looked across the party. Bruno Mudstrap and his yahoo friends already had the floor at soft and were rolling round, pawing each other. AA Catto decided to stay on the terrace. A Hostess-1 came up behind her with a tray of drinks and AA Catto took one. She took a careful sip. She was always careful with drinks at Juno Meltzer's parties. There was no knowing what pleasant concoctions Juno might serve to her guests.

AA Catto was attempting to guess the ingredients of the drink when she heard a languid voice from behind her.

'AA Catto, you came. How nice. I believe your brother's here somewhere.'

Juno Meltzer had spared no effort to be the most noticed person at her party. She was completely naked apart from her jewellery, and her body had been treated so the flesh had become transparent. It was as though she was made of clear plastic, inside which was the red and blue tracery of veins and arteries, the white moving muscles and pink candystick bones.

Her hair had been dressed so it looked like spun glass. AA Catto regarded her with frank admiration.

'You look very impressive, Juno.'

Juno Meltzer smiled.

'I thought I ought to make an effort for my own party.'

'Isn't it awfully dangerous?'

'I don't really care. What are a few cells, one way or another? And anyway, it's so exciting. Whoever I have tonight will be able to watch what happens inside me. That ought to do something for them.'

A frowned creased AA Catto's smooth forehead.

'It could be a little undignified.'

Juno Meltzer waved her hand in rejection of the idea.

'My lovers have seen me in every kind of position, darling, but I think I have enough breeding never to be undignified.'

Both women allowed themselves a brittle laugh, and then Juno Meltzer steered AA Catto to a long buffet table.

'Perhaps you'd like to eat something?'

The table was full of the rarest and most exotic delicacies, arranged in elaborate constructions. The centre piece of the whole buffet was a huge dish of chilled and crushed strawberries, upon which a beautiful young L-4 girl, she couldn't have been more than fourteen, lay perfectly still, her body providing a unique receptacle for all manner of sweetmeats. AA Catto picked up a silver spoon and took some chocolate ants that were heaped where the girl's pubic hair should have been. Then she put down the spoon and with her fingers took a morello cherry from one of the girl's nipples and popped it into her mouth. She turned to Juno Meltzer.

'Is the girl dead?'

It was hard to read Juno Meltzer's transparent face, but AA Catto thought she detected a trace of disappointment.

'Of course not. She's fully conscious. All we did was to have her prefrontals radiated out. She does exactly what she is told without a thought. Bruno and his gang will have a great time with her once all the food's been consumed.'

The two women parted and began to circulate, making the small talk with people they really didn't want to know that was the traditional preliminary to every party. A Hostess-1 presented AA Catto with a blue glass opium pipe, and when she finished it she felt ready to move into second gear. She sought out Juno Meltzer.

'When does the fun begin, darling? I hope the human plate wasn't the big surprise.'

Juno Meltzer shook her head most mysteriously.

'Any moment now the entertainment will start.'

The end section of the floor became rigid, and formed a low semi-circular stage. Some Hostess-1s politely persuaded Bruno Mudstrap and his cohorts that maybe they'd like to move back and watch the show.

AA Catto slowly descended the marble staircase and sank into a reclining position on the soft part of the velvet floor. De Roulet Glick spotted her, and hurried to her side.

'AA Catto, it's so wonderful to see you. I wonder…'

'Get lost, Glick. I find you loathsome.'

'But…'

'Loathsome, Glick.'

De Roulet Glick slunk away like a whipped puppy.

Hostesses moved among the guests with drinks and opium, and then the music faded and the lights dimmed. A troup of tiny people appeared from a concealed door and the lights focused on the impromptu stage.

They were L-4s who had been reduced to a height of not more than sixty centimetres by some kind of DNA adjustments. They played miniature instruments, sang and did acrobatics. AA Catto yawned. What kind of cornball idea was this? The transparency treatment must have damaged Juno Meltzer's brain.

The Hostess-1s moved among the guests again and, along with the others, AA Catto found herself handed an ornate, leaf-blade knife. The midgets continued with their absurd pantomime.

Gradually AA Catto found her mood was changing, she was becoming irritable. The irritability turned to anger, and the anger to a cold hate. She realized that there was a wide-band alphaset being used. Juno Meltzer's surprise was about to be sprung. It was the midgets that cracked first. One of them, a comparatively tall male, cried out in a high trilling voice.

'Now, brothers and sisters! Slay the oppressor!'

Squeaking, they rushed at their audience. Before AA Catto could get to her feet a tiny woman had struck at her with a small sword. As the blow fell it became clear that the sword was only painted balsa wood. It snapped and AA Catto swung her own inlaid steel blade at the L-4 and cut her practically in two. Leaping to her feet she hacked at the little people, cutting off heads and limbs in a savage fury. The rest of the guests were joining in with relish. In five minutes it was all over. The L-4s had all been slaughtered.

AA Catto felt her emotions change. Someone had adjusted the alphaset, and a feeling of wellbeing crept through the Velvet Rooms. A team of Hostess-2s cleared away the tiny corpses and removed the blood. AA Catto sank back to the floor.

She felt positively good. So good, in fact, that she was actively pleased when her brother Valdo pushed up her black skirt and began to caress her thighs.

13

Reave, Billy and the Rainman clung desperately together. There were no words to describe what they were going through. Disruption patterns filled the sky, and glowing things flashed past them.

Their sense of down kept shifting, and in their minds they seemed to be falling in constantly changing directions. In a similar way to when they had walked through the nothings, the idea of time became warped and twisted. One moment they floated through a curving, ribbed pink tube, and the next they were dropping past glowing perspective lines. The paradox was that although they seemed to slip rapidly from one plane to the next, while they were actually experiencing a phenomenon it was as though it had been going on for ever.

After what seemed like both an eternity and a few moments, they hit something. Billy fell heavily and twisted his shoulder. Painfully, he picked himself up and looked for the others. Reave and the Rainman were sprawled beside him, but there was no sign of the strange woman in black.

The three of them climbed to their feet and looked around. They were in a narrow stone-flagged alley, on each side of which were high, windowless granite walls. The place had a hard, forbidding atmosphere.

'So where are we?'

'Somewhere, and that's a comfort in itself.'

'Think we ought to take a look round? It's a gloomy kind of place.'

Grey seemed to be the keynote of everything they could see. The sky was the colour of slate, the granite buildings and flags echoed the same theme, and dark, dirty water trickled down a gutter in the middle of the alley. Reave shivered.

'It's none too warm.'

Billy nodded.

'This place gives me the creeps.'

The Rainman shrugged.

'We ain't going to improve matters by standing round complaining.'

He flipped a coin to see which way they should go. It came up tails, and they started down the alley. They'd only gone a few paces when men appeared at both ends of the alley. Calling them men was rather stretching the point. They had coarse, ape-like features and their arms hung nearly to their knees. They wore black tunics and leggings, and leather helmets with an iron strip that hung down to protect the nose. On the front of the tunics was a design that consisted of an eye surrounded by stylized flames. In their hands they held dull iron tubes that Billy assumed were guns of some kind.

'Halt!'

Billy started to run, but there was a deafening bang and a hail of nuts, bolts, nails and assorted lumps of metal whistled over his head. Billy stopped, and stood very still. A group of the men surrounded him. They were shorter than either Billy, Reave or the Rainman, but they had massive chests, shoulders and arms. A hand covered in warts and thick bristles was thrust under Billy's nose.

'Papers!'

'Papers?'

'Papers, snaga, papers!'

'I don't have any papers.'

'No papers? No papers? Everyone has papers, filth.'

'I don't have any papers. I just fell out of the nothings.'

One of the creatures punched Billy hard in the mouth, and Billy was knocked to the paving stones. The creature who had hit him roared down at him, showing sharp yellow teeth.

'The nothings are forbidden, worm. You are a prisoner of the Shirik.'

Billy was hauled roughly to his feet, his arms were dragged behind him, and a pair of manacles snapped round his wrists. Reave and the Rainman received similar treatment, and surrounded by the creatures who called themselves the Shirik, they were marched down the alley.

They turned into a wider street that was paved with the same granite as the alley and surrounded by the same high, menacing buildings. It was Billy's first chance really to look at the sinister new city. As far as he could see it was built from the same sombre grey stone, topped by steeply sloping roofs of darker grey slate. The total lack of colour touched Billy with an edge of fear. Another feature that seemed to be absent from the high dour buildings was windows. Billy could see no openings near the ground, and it was only high up under the roofs that he could make out some narrow slits. The most frightening thing about the city was that it was completely silent. Apart from the strange apemen that surrounded him, there was nobody in the streets, no birds fluttered round the roof tops, and the city looked totally deserted.

After walking for some three hundred yards, the party came to a doorway with writing over it in some strange script. Billy, Reave and the Rainman were bundled inside, pushed down a corridor and into a stone-floored room where another of the apemen sat behind a high wooden desk. He looked up as the room filled with people, and barked at Billy's captors.

'What's this? What's this?'

'Prisoners, Uruk sir. Wandering without papers.'

'No papers? No papers?'

He climbed down from his stool and came out from behind the desk. He jabbed at Billy with a thick stubby finger.

'Where's your papers, filth?'

'I don't have no papers. I only just arrived in the city.'

The finger jabbed again.

'Arrived? Arrived? How you arrive? You couldn't pass Black Gate without papers.'

'We came out of the nothings, a disruptor got us and we finished up here. We don't even know where we are.'

The Uruk's small red eyes narrowed and he peered intensely at Billy. He paced up and down. One of the group that had brought in Reave shuffled his feet and coughed.

'The Eight. P'raps we should report this to the Eight.'

The Uruk sprang across the room and punched the one who had spoken.

'Eight? Eight? I'm the Uruk for this section. I say what gets reported to the Eight.'

The Shirik wiped blood from his mouth and spat.

'You won't be Uruk for long if one of the Eight found out you'd not been telling things they wanted to know. You'd have the skin taken off you, and the flesh, too.'

The Uruk flashed round and kicked the Shirik hard in the groin. With a scream, the Shirik dropped to his knees. The Uruk swung his ironshod boot at the Shirik's head and the Shirik rolled over and lay still. The Uruk faced the other Shiriks.

'See that? See that? That's what'll happen to any others of you filth who talk fancy.'

He turned back to Billy, Reave and the Rainman.

'No papers, come from the nothings. What tale you scum trying to give me? The Eight going to hear about you. They'll deal with your tales.'

He swung round on the Shiriks.

'Six of you process them, and the rest back on patrol. Jump, I said!'

Billy, Reave and the Rainman were released from their manacles and hastily stripped. Their clothes and possessions were stacked on the Uruk's desk. He prodded the heap.

'We keep this for the Eight. Take them down.'

The three of them had their manacles replaced, this time with their arms in front of them instead of behind their backs, and were marched naked into another corridor. The guards in front of them stopped at an arched doorway, and one of them unlocked a huge door of dark wood studded with iron nails.

They descended a winding stone staircase with guards in front of them and behind. Narrow corridors radiated out from the foot of the stairs, and the three were pushed and kicked down one of them. The leading guard unlocked another door, this time a steel one with a small peephole in it, and they were all thrown into the same narrow cell.

The cell was about six feet wide and ten feet long. Its walls were made of the same granite, and in places it ran with slimy dampness. There were no windows in the cell, and the only light came from a yellow globe high up in the door. The floor was covered with damp straw, and an open drain ran along the far wall. Reave flopped to the ground.

'We really did it this time.'

Billy and the Rainman sat down as well. Billy tugged in frustration at his manacles, and winced as the metal bit into his wrists.

'If we only knew where the hell we were.'

He glanced at the Rainman.

'You got any idea what this place is?'

The Rainman shook his head.

'I never seen anything like this. It's not the usual stasis town. This looks like something different, something I ain't even heard about before. We're in trouble, boys.'

Reave slumped against the wall.

'You can say that again.'

A rat scuttled down the drain, and wriggled through the little opening where the drain continued into the next cell.

'We've really got to get out of here.'

'Yeah, but how?'

'Fuck knows.'

They lapsed into thought, and Billy's attention kept going to the hole through which the rat had gone. He stooped over, and knelt down beside the foul-smelling gutter.

'Hello, hello in there.'

There was a grunt from the other side of the hole, and then a blunt hairy hand was thrust through the space. It grabbed one of Billy's hands and tried to drag it into the next cell. Billy tugged it free, and looked round at the others.

'Don't look as though we're going to get any help from that direction.'

A glum silence fell over Billy, Reave and the Rainman. They slumped on the damp straw. The chill began to get to them. Reave watched his legs slowly turn blue, and very soon, all three's teeth had begun to chatter uncontrollably.

'Dear God, how long do we stay stuck in here?'

Billy jumped to his feet and hammered on the door with his fists.

'Hey out there. What the fuck's happening?'

His fist made little more than a dull thud on the thick wood of the door, and no sound came from the outside. Frustratedly he beat on the door and then sank to the floor.

'We've fucked up good.'

The other two shuddered and nodded.

The gloomy silence descended again. Only the occasional rustle of the straw punctuated their paranoia. Reave remembered Miss Ettie's. It was worlds away.

The lights of memory dimmed as the blackness of cold and despair closed around Reave. They wouldn't be wandering heroes. They'd blown it and wound up in a filthy cell. They'd lost the bet for fortune, adventure and experience.

Just as Reave had decided that he was a loser, a familiar voice echoed from outside the cell.

'...And you, shiteater. Under para 4, section 1, a registered minstrel gets himself into all and any public administration buildings. Here's my fucking card, so open the door. Got it?'

Billy's and Reave's heads both snapped up.

'The Minstrel Boy, here?'

They jumped up and stood by the door. More voices came from outside.

'Not possible. No one goes into cell till Ghâshnákh come to interrogate.'

'And it says in the Code that I go anywhere.'

'Not possible.'

'Shirik Precinct Houses come under the public administration order of the Ghâshnákh. Right?'

'Yes.'

'So Shirik Precinct Houses are public administration buildings? Right?'

'Yes?'

'So minstrels, and namely me, gets to go where I like in public administration buildings. That means Shirik buildings, so open up.'

'It's against regulations.'

'If you don't, it's against the Code, and I'll report it.'

'Code?'

'Code.'

'But regulations…'

'Look at it this way, scumbag. If you break the Code it's a hanging deal, and that's it. The regulations, the worst thing that can happen to you is a flogging. Know what I mean? Make it easy on yourself.'

'But…'

'Ever thought about it, piggio? Hanging, I mean, how it must feel and all, swinging away and choking, your hands tied behind your back, and just nothing you can do about it.'

There was a reluctant scraping of keys in the door, and it swung inwards. It was a very different Minstrel Boy who stepped into the cell.

The thin white face was hidden behind huge black multifaceted glasses that made him look like he had the eyes of some grotesque insect. The halo of hair was still there, but it had been dyed white. He wore a dark green lizard-skin frock coat over a black ruffled shirt, velvet trousers and high black boots with silver fastenings. The silver guitar hung from a heavy strap inlaid with coloured stones.

Billy and Reave bombarded him with questions.

'Where are we, man?'

'How the hell did you get here?'

'How do we get out of here?'

The Minstrel Boy held up his hands.

'Hold it! Hold it! Dumbo behind me might suddenly decide that there's nothing in the regulations says I get to talk to you. So listen. If you can just hold on a while longer I'll try and get you out of here. Okay?'

'How soon?'

'I don't know. It ain't easy. You won't be going anywhere.'

'Where are we?'

'Dur Shanzag.'

'Dur Shanzag?'

'I can't talk now. Don't worry, I'll swing it. I don't know how you could get into any more shit if you worked at it.'

'Okay, okay. We know, just try and get us out.'

'I told you, don't worry.'

He stepped back out of the cell and the door was slammed shut. Briefly it opened again.

'What's the other guy called?'

'The Rainman.'

'Okay, I'll see what I can do for him.'

The Minstrel Boy ducked out, and again the door was slammed. Billy and Reave looked at each other.

'What the hell. Did that happen?'

'Seemed to.'

'But his clothes and everything?'

'Who knows?'

The Rainman stood up.

'Who was your friend?'

'The Minstrel Boy, a guy we met on the road back in Graveyard.'

'Some useful friend to have in a strange city.'

'I sure hope so.'

'And me, boy, I can tell you. Say you met him in Graveyard?'

'Sure, we travelled with him from there to Dogbreath. You know Graveyard?'

'Graveyard, sure I know Graveyard. Jived up many a thunderstorm for them guys to slide their old rigs through.'

He looked at them intently.

'What did he look like, back in Graveyard?'

'Much the same, only with dirty blue jeans instead of those fancy clothes, and his hair was dark. Why?'

The Rainman shook his head.

'It's nothing. One of those things stuck in the back of your mind that you can't quite bring out. Maybe it'll come to me later.'

They waited, straining their ears for any possible footfall, but nothing happened. It had long ago become impossible to gauge the passage of time. Billy and Reave had lost that skill altogether when they first stepped into the nothings. The sudden appearance of the Minstrel Boy receded and became confused. They began to think it was an absurd way of snapping their minds. To add to their problems, they had begun to get ravenously hungry, and thirsty too. Nobody was ready to drink the foul trickle that ran along the guttering. At one point there was a commotion of voices a long way away, and they held their breath to see if it came nearer. Then the sounds died, and hope of immediate release faded.

It was just when any faith in the Minstrel Boy's return had all but disappeared that the door creaked open, and he walked in.

'I've done it, you're free.'

'Free?'

'Well, almost free. I've got a release order, and you don't have to be interrogated by the Ghâshnákh. You could say that you were substantively free.'

'We can get out of here?'

'Sure, right now.'

'That's great. Where do we go?'

The Minstrel Boy frowned.

'That's one of the problems, but I'll tell you about it when we're out of here.'

Billy shrugged.

'Just as long as we're out of this filthy cell.'

Again surrounded by guards, they walked out of the cell, along the corridor, and up the stairs. Groans and snarls came from the other cells as they walked past. The release of a prisoner seemed a great novelty.

They were again pushed into the stone-flagged room where the Uruk sat behind his high desk. Billy, Reave and the Rainman were lined up in front of him, and he scowled at them with distaste.

'Release orders? Release orders? You scum have friends in high places. They won't help you if I ever get my hands on your filthy bodies again.'

Two of their guards were dispatched to fetch their clothes, and the three of them hastily dressed. Their bags, portapacs, and even their guns were returned to them, and then the Minstrel Boy initialled a sheaf of forms. Finally they were released, and they followed the Minstrel Boy out into the street. Once outside, Billy caught up with him.

'Where are we going now?'

'To the barracks.'

'Barracks? What barracks?'

The Minstrel Boy avoided Billy's eyes.

'That was one of the things I had to do to get you out. In order to get the release papers, I had to enlist you in the Free Corps.'

'The Free Corps? What in hell is that?'

'It's... uh part of the army.'

Billy stopped dead in the street.

'The army? Are you trying to tell us that we've joined the goddamn army in this place?'

He swung round to Reave and the Rainman.

'This idiot's gone and got us into the army.'

The Minstrel Boy took Billy by the arm.

'Keep moving, you don't want to get arrested again. There was no other way, Billy. It was a case of jail or the Free Corps.'

They walked on, Billy shaking his head.

'I don't understand any of this. You better start from the beginning.'

'Okay, listen. This is Dur Shanzag, and it's a long way from Graveyard or Dogbreath.'

14

She/They rose slowly through the threatening mists. Her/Their mind was not required to continue the upward motion, and She/They allowed it to retreat into the memories of the almost infinite past. It drifted back to Her/Their hardly remembered birth, the fusion of shapes and colours that had condensed and blended and produced Her/Their triple form. She/They could go back no further than the triple form. Before that there had been something, an order that had enabled Her/Them to transcend and escape the chaos that had overtaken everything else.

The achievement of the triple form had been followed by centuries of contemplation while She/They had ordered and stabilized the space that She/They occupied. It was a long period of calm that had been savagely brought to an end by the arrival of the first disruptors.

The arrival of the disruptors had started the long battle that She/They had waged against the encroaching mists of the twisting chaos.

It was the start of a hateful, searching period in which She/They had moved across the fabric, attempting to stabilize the sectors She/They covered.

She/They had become the continual prey of the disruptors, and, for a very long time, She/They had directed Her/Their intelligence at the problem of what they were, and where they originated. It had never been possible to come in close proximity of the thing without Her/Their objectivity being damaged by the disruption process. All Her/Their observations led towards the assumption that the disruptors were some strange halfway point between animal and machine.

She/They had never solved the problem of their coming. Before the disruptors Her/Their triple form had not existed. There had been form and there had been consciousness, but beyond that, all memory was hazy and tattered. Her/Their creation was inexorably linked with their arrival. It was almost as though they had given Her/Them birth as they first tore into the fabric of reality.

She/They was produced out of the disruption. The logical opposite to disruptors and the wake of chaos. By the same logic it should follow that She/They was their equal. That would only be disproved either when they shattered Her/Them and diffused Her/Their form into the clouds of unstable fabric, or when She/They extended a state of unchanging order throughout Her/Their entire area of experience.

She/They, over the millennia of Her/Their struggle, had watched the behaviour of the disruptors, and the pattern that seemed to lie behind their attacks. She/They had, at times, entertained the proposition that an intelligence was directing the disruptors. For a few long periods, the movements of the disruptors had seemed regular as though they moved according to a directing logic. During other periods, their actions had become completely random, and the idea of an overall intelligence had been rejected by Her/Them as a product of chaos-induced paranoia.

She/They returned Her/Their mind to the present. The mist had taken on a more even quality, and was starting to glow a deep electric blue. Her/Their upward motion ceased. Her/Their two heads turned slowly. Deep in the blue mist something solid seemed to be moving.

15

'Dur Shanzag is the city of the Presence. Nobody seems to know any more exactly where the Presence came from. Seems as though he or it has been around for thousands of years.'

'He or it?'

Billy walked along with the Minstrel Boy, a confused look on his face.

'They say he was a man once, but, by all accounts, he's not any more. He's… well, he's the Presence. They say he's burned up with the idea of being the master. The lord of everything. They say he's had four or five empires, way back over hundreds of thousands of years.'

Billy shook his head.

'How does one man get to live a hundred thousand years? It just isn't possible.'

The Minstrel Boy shrugged.

'I'm just telling the story. I don't have to account for inconsistencies. The story goes that he ain't a man any more. It could be that he ain't the original one who built those empires, maybe he's just another crazy living out some fantasy that he got from some old book. I don't know, there's a whole lot of things that it doesn't pay to look too closely at. When it comes down to it, all I know is that there's a thing called the Presence, and this is his city.'

'What about those things that threw us in jail? This Presence was like one of those once?'

The Minstrel Boy shook his head.

'The Presence wasn't ever an apeman. Those things are his slaves. He created them. He bred them down through the centuries to serve him. The Shirik, they're the workers, soldiers and watchdogs of his citadel. The smarter ones are Uruks. They boss the Shirik, and pass on his orders.'

'What about the Ghâshnákh? What are they?'

'The Ghâshnákh? They're the next level of power after the Uruks. They're men, but slaves just the same. They're his officers, civil servants and secret police. They hate and fear him but are all loyal to him. I suppose each, in his own way, shares the same desire for power and conquest. His whole massive bureaucracy runs on a balance of greed and fear. It's not efficient, but I don't think he cares. It seems like he gets a kind of twisted pleasure out of watching it fuck up.'

'But surely that's not going to help him conquer the world?'

'I don't think he cares. The rumours say that all his concentration is fixed on the disruptors. He thinks that the way to power lies in the control of the disruptors. That was why I had so much trouble getting you out. You told the Uruk that you'd been hit by a disruptor, and disruptor cases are always interrogated by the Ghâshnákh. That's why I had to sign you into the Free Corps, in order to get your release papers. You'll still get questioned by the Ghâshnákh, but it'll only be a stage three. The Uruk would have handed you over for a stage one. There ain't too many who live through a stage one.'

'What's the Free Corps, then? What have you gotten us into?'

'Don't be like that about it. I did the best I could.'

Billy nodded.

'Yeah, yeah, I know. I'm sorry. Tell me about this Free Corps.'

'The Presence is at war. He's always at war. This time it's with the Regency of Harod. It's been going on for years. The Harodin will lose in the end, the neighbouring cities have all lost in the end.'

'I thought the Shirik did all the Presence's fighting. I don't see what he needs us for.'

'The Shirik make killer infantry, but they're too dumb to operate anything complicated. He needs mercenaries to man his fighting machines, and operate the big guns. That's the Free Corps. They're the crew of mercenaries who do the Presence's dirty work for him.'

'How does he treat them?'

'It ain't too bad. The Ghâshnákh make sure they have enough women and enough booze. They're the elite troops and they get treated that way. They're a rough mean bunch, though.'

'How long have you signed us on for?'

'Two years.'

'Jesus.'

'That's the minimum period, nothing else I could do.'

'What happens then?'

'You get paid off, and a free passage to the limits of the zone. Of course, they put the arm on you to re-enlist, but in the end, they let you go.'

'What about escaping?'

'Should be quite easy once you get to the front. It's up to you. I've done all I can.'

The Minstrel Boy halted, and pointed at a huge granite block, larger but otherwise identical to the Shirik House.

'That's the barracks. Go in and tell the guard that you're the new recruits. I'll see you later, okay?'

The Minstrel Boy started to walk away but Billy called him back.

'Just one question, Minstrel Boy. How did you get here? And the way you're dressed up?'

The Minstrel Boy shook his head sadly.

'Don't ask, Billy. Just don't ask.'

'But...'

'We all got to survive, Billy. Remember that.'

The Minstrel Boy turned on his heel and walked away. His boots echoed hollowly on the paving stones of the deserted street. Billy watched him go, and then followed the others inside the cold, forbidding building.

A huge man with a full, black, curly beard lounged behind a desk similar to the Uruk's. He wore an olive-green combat suit and a peaked fatigue cap. A cigar was clenched between his teeth, and a huge pair of combat boots were propped on the desk. The peak of his cap hung down over his eyes, and when Billy, Reave and the Rainman walked in, he raised it lazily with his forefinger. He stared at them for a while, and then lazily shifted the cigar to the side of his mouth.

'Whatcha want?'

'Recruits.'

'Recruits? Where the hell did you come from?'

'Our friend got us out of jail on the promise that we'd enlist.'

Billy thought it was best to keep quiet about the disruptor.

'Get lost in the nothings and wind up here?'

'Yeah, that's right.'

'That's how most of them get here. No one comes here from choice.'

'It's bad?'

'You'll see.'

He swung his legs off the desk, and his boots hit the floor with a crash. He stood up, and yelled towards a door behind him.

'Hey Skipper, there's three recruits out here. Wanna take a look at them?'

A man emerged from the doorway. He was a little wiry man with a clipped moustache. He wore a sheepskin jacket and dark blue trousers tucked into scuffed riding boots. On his head, he had a light blue cap with the same eye and flames badge that the Shirik wore. He looked the three of them up and down.

'Recruits?'

'That's right.'

'Just got out of jail?'

'That's right.'

'You better get signed in.'

He walked over to the desk and picked up a clipboard.

'Okay.'

He pointed at Reave.

'You, come over here.'

Reave sauntered over to him and stood in front of him with his hands in his pockets.

'I'm Sperry, kid. Master of Warriors. You train with me and I get to choose whether you train easy, or you train hard. You got that?'

Reave straightened his back and took his hands out of his pockets.

'I got it.'

'I got it, sir.'

'I got it, sir.'

'Okay, name?'

'Reave.'

'Place of origin?'

'Pleasant Gap.'

'Do-you-solemnly-swear-to-serve-in-the-Army-of-the-Sovereign-state-of-Dur-Shanzag-for-a-period-of-not-less-than-seven-hundred-days-in-accordance-with-the-Code-and-military-regulations-of-that-said-state? Say "I do".'

'I do.'

Sperry handed Reave the clipboard and pen.

'Make your mark here.'

Reave scrawled his name and handed them back. Sperry looked towards Billy.

'Next.'

Billy stepped up. 'Name?'

'Billy Oblivion.'

'Place of origin?'

'Pleasant Gap.'

'Do you solemnly swear what he just did?'

'I do.'

'Okay, make your mark and stand over there with him.'

Billy made his mark and stood by Reave.

'Next.'

The Rainman stood in front of Sperry. 'Name?'

'People call me the Rainman.'

'Ain't you got a proper name?'

'It's the only one people use.'

'Okay, Rainman. Place of origin?'

'Hell, how should I know? That's a helluva question to ask a travelling man.'

'Where was the last place you stopped? You remember that?'

'Why, sure I do, it was Dogbreath.'

'Okay, Dogbreath. I gotta put something. Do you swear too?'

'Sure, I ain't got no choice.'

'You should remember that. Make your mark and get over with the others.'

Once the Rainman was in line with Billy and Reave, Sperry came over and inspected them.

'You got any weapons?'

Billy nodded.

'We all got handguns.'

'Okay, fetch 'em out.'

He looked at Billy's and Reave's reproduction Colts and sniffed.

'They'll have to do.'

He seemed more impressed with the Rainman's spiral needler on .75 frame.

'Yeah, okay, put them away again. Your clothes are all right too.'

Reave looked surprised.

'You mean we don't get uniforms?'

'Only when the things that you got wear out.'

He jerked his thumb towards the door he'd come out from. 'Go through there, and tell the guy inside that you're reporting for training.'

Training consisted of an intense ten days of being run around and shouted at by veterans who had been wounded at the front. Billy and Reave flopped into their bunks exhausted each night, and, all too soon, were roused out by Simp the one-eyed trooper, who seemed to be primarily in charge of them.

The command structure of the Free Corps was loose and haphazard. The only thing that Billy and Reave knew for sure was that they were very definitely the lowest of the low. The only group beneath them in the pecking order were the Shirik, who seemed universally loathed by the Free Corps mercenaries.

Surprisingly, the Rainman appeared very little worried by the hard training regime. He went through everything at the same leisurely pace, and treated the yelling officers with smiling contempt.

The final night, after they had completed the course, the three of them were given a recreation pass. This entitled them to spend an evening in yet another granite building, drinking flat beer and raw spirits in the company of a small group of depressed whores.

The next day they were due to leave for the front. Billy was rudely awakened by Simp shaking him.

'Come on out of it.'

'It ain't time yet.'

'Sure it is. You want to die in bed?'

'Would suit me fine.'

Simp tugged at the blankets.

'Come on, start moving. Inspection in half an hour. Got it?'

Billy dragged himself out of his bunk and staggered across to the stone wash-trough. His head was splitting from the bad booze that he'd poured down himself the night before. He splashed cold water on his face and neck, and struggled into his shirt. He was pleased that the Free Corps barracks didn't run to mirrors. He felt that that particular morning he really couldn't face the sight of himself.

After a breakfast of grey porridge, Simp assembled the next recruits on the windswept expanse of stone that served as a parade ground. Sperry made a short preliminary speech, and then moved down the line giving the recruits their assignments to the front. He stopped in front of Billy, Reave and the Rainman. He stared at them for a moment with one eyebrow raised.

'For reasons unknown, the powers have decided to keep you sorry trio intact. As of now you're a machine crew. You'll pick one up from motorpool and join the Seventeenth Gorbûkh at Hill 471.'

He handed Billy an envelope.

'Here's your written orders, you're off my hands now.'

The Rainman grinned.

'Ain't you gonna wish us luck... sir?'

Sperry sneered.

'Why bother. You're past help.'

The three of them were dismissed, and they walked to pick up the fighting machine.

The Dur Shanzag fighting machine was a squat iron construction. Its square, box-shaped body, with riveted plates and tiny slit windows, housed the crew of three. Mounted on top was a small circular turret from which the gunner could direct fire from either the flamer or the repeating bolt gun. At each end were the huge spiked rollers which, driven by a low-gear flutter engine, carried the dull grey monster along the ground at something like the speed of a man running.

The Rainman signed out the machine from a motorpool orderly with a bald head and thick, horn-rimmed glasses. As they climbed inside it, the orderly waved.

'Don't scratch the paint now.'

Reave gave him the finger, and slammed the iron door. Crouched inside, the Rainman grinned round at the others.

'Either of you mind if I drive this here rig for a while?'

Billy and Reave shook their heads.

'Go right ahead. It's okay by us, we'll just take it easy.'

The Rainman brought the motor to life, and the cabin reverberated with a teeth-jarring hum. The fighting machine wasn't built for comfort. He guided it through the empty streets of Dur Shanzag to the Black Gate, and then they were out of the city and running along a road that stretched out into the bleak desert. The Rainman gave the machine full power, but it was incapable of going any faster than the stage that had carried them out of Dogbreath. It seemed that the fighting machines weren't built for speed either.

The journey across the desert very soon became monotonous as they clanked and rattled along the desert road. Occasionally they would pass columns of Shirik heading for the front at a fast, loping trot, and once they passed a train of wagons pulled by scrawny mules, returning to Dur Shanzag loaded with Shirik wounded.

Reave pointed out of the narrow slit window.

'They must lose millions of those dumb brutes, the rate they seem to be sending them out to the front.'

The Rainman grimaced.

'I hope they don't lose millions of us dumb brutes as well.'

The three of them fell silent, and Billy stared out at the endless dull brown dust. The only break in the desert was the odd clump of thorn trees. Apart from that, it was completely barren. Only the continuous jolting of the machine stopped Billy from falling asleep.

After riding for hours they began to hear the rumble of distant gunfire above the noise of the engine. Very soon, they could see a pall of smoke along the horizon and they knew that they were entering the battle zone.

At a fork in the road an Uruk appeared to be directing traffic. Billy pressed his face to the window and shouted.

'Hill 471?'

'Hill what? Hill what?'

'4–7–1.'

The Uruk stared at the ground frowning, and then jerked an arm towards the right.

'Straight down. Can't miss it.'

The Rainman swung the fighting machine down the right-hand fork.

After a series of false trails and a dozen wrong turnings, they finally pulled up at a low hill that was crisscrossed with trenches and coils of barbed wire. One side of the hill was honeycombed with foxholes and bunkers. The Shirik were swarming over it like a colony of burrowing ants. Billy spotted an Uruk who was standing over a squad of Shirik labouring on a trench. Every so often he encouraged them with a knotted rope.

'Hey! Hey you! Uruk. This Hill 471?'

'Who wants to know?'

Billy pushed his pistol through the slit.

'We want to know, shiteater.'

The Uruk responded happily to threat and abuse.

'Sure, sure. This 471.'

'Where do we find the Free Corps command post?'

The Uruk pointed.

'Down that way.'

The Rainman put the machine in motion and swung it down a deeply rutted track. They were now in the heart of the Dur Shanzag lines. The snouts of light cannon and mortars poked from foxholes. Shell craters dotted the landscape, and all round them squads of Shirik sappers sweated with picks and shovels enlarging the foxholes and dugouts.

They passed a Shirik stripped of his uniform, suspended by his hands from a wooden frame that had been erected beside the track. He was obviously undergoing some kind of punishment. Around his neck hung a placard on which was a single word in the strange script they had seen used throughout Dur Shanzag.

A ditch ran for some distance along the side of the track, and every so often Billy noticed huddled shapes, the bodies of men and mules that lay half in and half out of the muddy water, where they had been pushed off the road and left to rot. They rolled past crisscrossings of tangled barbed wire and Billy saw to his horror that in the middle of a particularly thick section, a skeleton was hanging with shreds of clothing still adhering to it. It seemed as though the war had crossed this area and moved on.

Eventually they found what they were looking for. A huge dugout where a collection of olive-green tents huddled under the protection of sandbagged ramparts. In front of the tents and tunnel entrances, a group of humans lounged round a huge black field piece. Three fighting machines, similar to their own, were parked beside it.

The Rainman pulled in beside the other machines, and the three of them climbed down and walked over to the men squatting round the cannon. They were all unshaven and filthy, and wore a motley assortment of combat suits and work clothes. At their belts they carried a vicious array of knives and side arms. None of them looked up as Reave, Billy and the Rainman approached. They seemed totally to lack interest in anything that went on around them. Billy stopped and cleared his throat.

'Where can we find whoever's in charge?'

A big man with blond hair and a black eye patch spat a stream of tobacco juice in the dust.

'I am, I'm Axmann, M of W for this section. You replacements?'

Billy nodded, and gave him the envelope.

'These are our orders.'

Axmann seemed to have no interest in opening them.

'You better get settled in.'

He glanced back at the men beside the gun.

'You, Duck. Show these replacements where to bunk, and explain the facts of life to them.'

A little bald man with a rodent's face and extremely short legs scrambled to his feet. Axmann turned back to Billy, Reave and the Rainman.

'Duck will show you round. Oh, just one thing. You boys don't plan to be heroes, do you?'

'It's not our greatest ambition.'

'Good. The last thing we need is heroes.'

Duck led them inside the bunker. It stretched way back inside the hill, and housed the command post, stores and sleeping quarters. The roof was low, scarcely four feet high in places, and they had to move in a half crouch. The walls of the excavation were shored up with an assortment of scrap timber, and here and there someone had stuck a pin-up. These served to highlight rather than disguise the appalling squalor. Duck pointed at three empty wooden bunks.

'You can take them three. The guys they belonged to took a direct hit. They won't be needing them any more.'

They dumped their gear on the beds, and Duck led them out of the bunker and up the hill a little way.

'If you keep your heads down you'll be okay. You can see the whole battle zone from here.'

The plain beneath them was gouged with craters and scarred by trenches. At irregular intervals a boom and an eruption of dust would mark a shell landing. Small figures would scamper out of a trench, and rush into the section of no-man's-land that ran between the lines of either side. Inevitably, before they'd gone very far, the figures would fall and lie still. Overhead, off in the distance, two clumsy flying machines, cigar-shaped objects with a collection of umbrella-like repulsors on their top sides, circled each other warily. One carried the eye and flames markings of Dur Shanzag, while the other bore the seven-pointed star of Harod. Billy watched in appalled fascination.

'How long has this been going on?'

Duck shrugged.

'Who knows? Maybe a generation. Maybe more.'

'But I thought the Presence was winning.'

'Sure he's winning. We've gained maybe a hundred yards this year. I guess another twenty years will see us at the gates of Harod.'

'Twenty years.'

Duck dug the heel of his boot into the dirt.

'Twenty, maybe twenty-five. Attrition's the name of the game. The only thing that could prevent it was if the Shirik stopped breeding. The Shirik do most of the fighting. They're sent up the line. They rush the enemy, most of them get slaughtered, but they keep coming, and we keep gaining little bits of ground. If they start losing too many of them, we have to take our tin cans in and sort it out. Beyond that we try and keep out of the fighting and stay healthy.'

'Doesn't anyone want to fight?'

Duck scowled.

'Who needs it? Except the Shirik, who can't get enough. Occasionally one of our boys goes kill-crazy, but when that happens they usually start on the Shirik, and we have to go down and fuse them before they do too much damage. Beyond that, it's like I said, we do our best to keep out of it. We all hate this goddamn war.'

Billy scratched his head.'

'I don't see why any of us go on with it.'

Duck looked at Billy in contempt.

'Did you ask to come here?'

'Nah, we were in jail. We didn't have no choice.'

'Neither did anyone else, sonny boy. Get stuck inside of Dur Shanzag and you wind up at the front before you know it.'

'What are the enemy like?'

'I ain't seen 'em close to 'cept maybe a few times. They looked like regular guys to me. Just like us, 'cept they're fighting for their lives. You'll get called out soon enough, and then you'll see for yourselves.'

16

AA Catto came home from the party in another artificial sunrise. Once again, she was bored, Juno Meltzer had done her best, but when AA Catto finally came down to it, nothing new really happened. It was yet another party where she had finished up with her brother. It was an indictment of the lack of stimuli that someone like Valdo was superior to most of the other available men.

She made a mental note that she really should stop doing it with him, particularly in public. People were beginning to label them, and there was nothing more tiresome than being labelled.

Inside her apartment AA Catto tore off her black Art Nouveau party dress and flopped on the bed in her underwear. She grinned at how her silk stockings and basque corset had come from the pornography of a slightly later period, but nobody had even noticed. With the exception of Valdo, she decided, the people she knew were exceedingly ignorant.

She kicked her legs and stared at the ceiling. It was the morning problem again. Sleep or stay awake. It was a choice between dormax or altacaine. AA Catto rolled over and watched the sunlight begin to filter through the perspex of the balcony. She glanced at the clock. It was 08.15. She reached out and punched up Information. The blonde in the pink uniform flickered into life and smiled.

'Information. May I help you?'

'What's going on this morning?'

'There is a full directorate meeting at 10.00. All family members are expected to attend, Miss Catto.'

'Don't tell me what to do.'

'I'm sorry, Miss Catto. I'm only relaying information.'

'All right, all right.'

She hit the off button. The directorate meeting would wipe out anything happening for most of the day. She might as well sleep right through it. She was reaching for the dormax when a thought struck her. Maybe it would be fun to go to a meeting once. If Valdo was there to back her up, between them they might throw some shocks into those old fools. She punched Valdo's combination, and another pink-clad Hostess-1 appeared.

'Mr Catto's residence.'

'Is Valdo conscious?'

'If you'll wait one moment, please, Miss Catto, I'll find out.'

The screen dissolved into a pattern of neutral colours. It stayed that way for almost a minute, and AA Catto tapped her silver nails impatiently on the console. Finally Valdo's image appeared on the screen.

AA Catto had often thought that the reason she liked her brother so much was that he resembled her so closely. He had the same straight nose and large blue eyes. He even had the same full mouth. It was something that didn't quite fit on a male. Valdo revelled in the fact that he was definitely borderline.

The image on the screen was far from Valdo at his best.

He still had on the pale blue wig that he had worn the night before, and his makeup was smudged and streaked.

'What do you want, sister? I thought you'd be dormaxed out by now.'

'You look awful, brother. What do you plan to do this morning?'

'Sleep. There's nothing happening except a directorate meeting.'

AA Catto pretended to be scandalized.

'You mean you're going to miss a directorate meeting?'

Valdo scowled.

'What are you talking about? We always miss directorate meetings.'

'I thought we ought to go to this one.'

'You're joking?'

'I thought it would be a good idea if we went to the meeting.'

'Have you gone mad, sister? Directorate meetings are boring, tedious, and, very positively, no place to be.'

'Think about it, brother. If we took on maybe three payloads of altacaine, and then went along and caused trouble for the parents, I thought it would be fun.'

'Aren't you rather scraping the barrel?'

'I thought if we worked on it, we might be able to force through some dictates that could make life more amusing.'

Valdo looked unconvinced. 'Like what, sister?'

'Maybe we could have a war.'

'There's no one worth having a war with.'

AA Catto waved his objections aside.

'I only just thought of it. We can work out details later. Say you'll come.'

'No.'

'Why not?'

'Listen, sister, I'd rather sleep than spend the day with those boring old farts.'

'But we could take it over, brother. We could really put them through.'

'It still seems like a waste of time. A whole day spent in pursuit of the tiresome. It almost seems an insult to good drugs to take on a load and then sit with awful, OLD people.'

'It's because we never go to meetings that these old awful people have it their own way. That's the reason that the entertainments are so wretched.'

'My dear sister. Is it that you've become a concerned citizen?'

AA Catto's eyes flashed with anger.

'Don't be disgusting.'

'It does rather sound like it. I never thought I'd see my dear sister wanting to go to a meeting. Perhaps you're getting old.'

'You can be very insulting when you try.'

'That kind of remark isn't going to persuade me to come with you.'

'Then will you come?'

'I'll consider it. You haven't tried to bribe me yet.'

'What do you want?'

'I don't know. There's very little that you have that I want.'

AA Catto's mouth twisted.

'You didn't say that four hours ago, brother.'

'I was simply accommodating you, sister dear.'

'Then accommodate me now.'

'Will you promise to come back here and allow me to use you in a cruel and original manner for a whole hour if this meeting's as boring and loathsome as I fear it will be?'

AA Catto nodded quickly.

'Yes, yes, anything you like. Say you'll come?'

'I'll come.'

'Wonderful. I'll see you at 10.00 outside the Boardroom.'

Valdo grimaced.

'Oh God, sister, don't say you want to be punctual.'

'Sorry, make it 10.45.'

'That's a little better.'

'Thank you, brother. You won't be disappointed.'

Valdo yawned.

'Anything to amuse my little sister.'

17

Like a wave of coarse flesh the Shirik poured out from trenches and dugouts and charged howling towards the Harodin lines. The enemy immediately opened a withering fire and dead Shirik fell one on top of another. Some dropped like stones while others fell twisting and snarling, clawing at their wounds. Although they died in their hundreds, still more came on, clambering over the bodies to get at the enemy.

One small group actually made it across no-man's-land and reached the opposite trenches. They discharged their single-shot scrap guns and then fell on the remaining defenders, clubbing, hacking and biting. They were shot down, but the Harodin line was breached and more Shirik poured into the gap. A horrible slaughter began in the narrow confines of the Harodin trenches.

Billy wiped the sweat from his face. It was their first time in action. They had hung round the dugout for five days, and then, along with two other machines, they had been ordered to back up and consolidate the Shirik assault.

As he watched, a handful of Harodin leaped from the forward trenches and tried to run away. They had only gone a few yards when they were cut down by blasts of scrap metal from Shirik guns. The men who had run seemed indistinguishable from the mercenaries. Duck had been right when he'd described them as being regular guys.

From the driver's seat, the Rainman grunted.

'Looks like we'll be moving up soon.'

Billy swivelled the turret a little to look at the other two fighting machines. Sure enough, a red flag appeared through the turret hatch of the lead machine. Billy glanced at the Rainman.

'Okay, here we go, roll it.'

The Rainman eased the machine into gear and it began to move forward in formation with the other two. Billy licked his dry lips and glanced down at Reave, who crouched in the stand-by position, ready to move if anything happened to either of the other two. Billy grinned tensely at him.

'This is it, kid.'

Reave shook his head.

'How the fuck did we get ourselves into this?'

'Don't ask, man. Just don't ask.'

The fighting machines crossed the Shirik trenches and started across no-man's-land, towards the huge gap the apemen had carved in the Harodin defences. The wheels crunched over the thickly littered Shirik bodies, crushing them into the dust. Billy fought to keep himself from being sick. He dropped a burst of bolts on a section of the forward trench, but saw that it was already in Shirik hands and stopped firing. There seemed to be nothing left for them to do.

At Harodin machine gun opened up on them from an isolated foxhole, and bullets clanged against the machine's armour. Billy swung the flamer round. As he fired he saw the gun was manned by two haggard, bearded men in dirty blue tunics. They looked surprised as the tongue of flame lanced towards them. It was the same look of surprise that had crossed the face of the man he'd shot in Dogbreath. The next instant the flame caught them, and they turned into blazing inhuman things. Billy lost sight of them as the machine dipped and lurched across the first enemy trench. His stomach twisted but he managed not to be sick.

The formation stopped just beyond the Harodin advance trench and took up a defensive position. The Shirik mopped up the last of the defenders. Once the trench was cleared it was their job to guard against a possible counter-attack, while Uruk engineers reconstructed the newly won fortifications.

No counter-attack came, and at nightfall the mercenaries dismounted from their machines and made a temporary camp. The killing was too strong in Billy's mind to allow him to sit and relax with the other crews. He wandered along the trench, until he came to a group of Shirik huddled round a small fire. Without going too close he watched the strange subhuman creatures and listened to their grunted conversation. The Shirik seemed to have been issued with fresh meat, possibly as a reward for their victory. They snuffled and grunted over large bones.

'Fight huh? Fight?'

'Some fight. Some fight.'

'Plenty kill, huh?'

'Listen…'

'Huh?'

'Listen… I fight.'

'I fight, I fight.'

'I fight, I hit 'em, I kick 'em an' bit 'em. I had to fight, huh?'

'They get on top of you?'

'Nah… I fight. I kill 'em.'

'Yeah.'

'Yeah.'

'All fight.'

'All attack.'

'Hey.'

'Wha'?'

'I… fight.'

'Sure, all fight.'

'No, no, I remember.'

'Wha'?'

'I remember.'

'Wha'?'

'I… I don't remember.'

'You forget.'

'It was before, before.'

'Didn't we surround 'em?'

'Kill 'em.'

'Plenty good killing, huh?'

One of the Shirik waved his bone in the air.

'Good killing, good eating.'

He wiped his mouth with a strip of blue uniform, and in a flash Billy realized. The fresh meat was human. The Shirik were eating the bodies of the Harodin. He backed away in silent panic, and as soon as he was well away from the Shirik, he bolted along the trench towards where the machine crews were camped. He stumbled across a figure lying in the darkness.

'Fuck off, I'm trying to sleep.'

It was Reave.

'It's me, it's Billy. Listen, I just saw…'

The words stuck in his throat.

'I… I…'

Reave looked at him in alarm.

'What's wrong, man? You look like you seen a ghost.'

'It's worse than that, man. Much worse.'

'What is it, Billy? You look terrible.'

'You remember how Duck told us about the guys who went kill crazy. How they always attacked the Shirik?'

Reave nodded.

'Sure, I remember.'

'Reave...'

Billy's hysteria was holding off by only a fraction.

'... I found out why. The Shirik, man. Those fucking animals eat the dead! They're out there, eating the men they killed today!'

Reave closed his eyes.

'Jesus! You saw this? You saw it happening?'

'I saw it, Reave. I saw it and heard them talking. It was horrible. We got to get out of here.'

He clutched at Reave and sobbed into his jacket. Reave put an arm out and stroked Billy's hair.

'It's all right, kid. We'll get away from this place. We did in Dogbreath, and we can do it here.'

Billy said nothing, and for a long time they clung together in silence. A figure emerged out of the darkness.

'What's the matter with you two? Never had you tagged as queers.'

Reave looked up, and saw Axmann standing over him. Axmann had been in command of the lead tank.

'My partner cracked up when he saw the Shirik eating the dead.'

'Didn't Duck warn you what it was like?'

'He didn't tell us they were cannibals.'

Axmann scratched the stubble on his chin.

'That's too bad. It must have been a shock to just stumble on to it. We all stay close to camp after a victory. Nobody wants to get close to the Shirik.'

Billy looked up at him.

'It's okay for you to talk. You've got used to it.'

Axmann put a hand on Billy's shoulder.

'Nobody gets used to that. I've been here for five years, and I never got used to it. The best you can hope for is to be able to close off your mind to it.'

He fumbled in the pocket of his combat coat, produced a small bottle and shook some of the contents into his hand. He handed Reave two flat, white pills.

'Give him these, they'll put him out for the rest of the night.'

Axmann turned and walked away. Reave gave Billy the pills and some water to wash them down with. A few minutes after Billy had swallowed them, he fell into a deep, dreamless sleep.

The next thing that Billy remembered was being shaken awake by Reave.

'Come on, man, move. We're under attack.'

There was an explosion close by, and Billy shook his head to make his brain work.

'What's going on?'

'The Harodin are counter-attacking. There's thousands of them. I guess they want to get their own back on the Shirik.'

There was another explosion, and Billy scrambled to his feet.

'Get inside the machine. It'll be safer than out here in the open.'

Billy and Reave climbed out of the trench and sprinted towards the parked machines. Bullets spattered around their feet. Bearing down on the Dun Shanzag lines was a wall of blue uniforms. The air was filled with snarls and howls as the Shirik prepared to meet the enemy.

They reached the fighting machine, and Reave tugged open the door.

'Quick, inside.'

They dived inside.

'Where's the Rainman?'

'Dunno, I ain't seen him.'

Reave pointed out through the observation slit.

'There. There he is. He's coming.'

The Rainman was ducking and weaving towards the machine, attempting to dodge the crossfire from the Shirik and the Harodin. He was only ten yards from the machine when he stumbled, spun round and hit the ground. Reave looked at Billy in alarm.

'He's been hit. He's gone down.'

The Rainman was on his hands and knees, slowly crawling towards the machine. Reave reached for the door.

'I'm going out to get him.'

There was the clang of bullets hitting the side of the machine. Billy grabbed Reave by the arm.

'Don't be a fool. You'll get killed out there.'

'I can't leave him lying out there wounded.'

As he spoke, more bullets hit the Rainman, he jerked convulsively and lay still. Reave pulled away from Billy and began opening the door.

'I can't leave him out there.'

Billy pushed Reave hard into his seat.

'There's nothing you can do. He's dead.'

'But we can't leave him out there. Those goddamn creatures will eat him.'

'You can't go out and get him. You'll be killed yourself.'

Reave slumped in his seat, and covered his face with his hands.

'Okay, okay, I know it. I know it. Why did we ever get involved in this? Curse this fucking, absurd war.'

Billy dropped into the driver's seat, and threw the machine into gear.

'Get into the turret, Reave. Get yourself together. The Rainman's dead, and we've got to get out of here.'

Reave climbed slowly into the turret, and Billy started the machine rolling. The other two machines were also on the move, cutting into the Harodin lines with their turrets spitting bolts and belching fire. Billy swung away from them, and turned sharp right. He pushed the machine as fast as it would go, running parallel to the trenches, between the attackers and the defenders. Bullets hammered against the armour and the fighting machine bucked and skidded as shells exploded nearby. Reave yelled at Billy in alarm.

'You gone crazy? You'll get us killed. Where the fuck do you think you're going?'

Billy clung grimly to the steering gear as a near miss rocked the machine.

'I'm getting us out of this. Away from this insanity.'

'But where are you heading?'

'I don't know. I'm just getting away.'

'If you keep running along in no-man's-land we're just going to get ourselves blown up.'

'All right, all right.'

Billy swung the machine to the left and plunged across the trenches, crushing Shirik under the spiked wheels. Soon they were running towards the rear. Confused Uruks gesticulated at them as they cut through supply columns and rolled across dugouts. The battle zone seemed to go on and on but after thirty minutes they left the last shell hole and excavation behind. They were in the bare, open desert. Billy brought the machine to a halt.

'We made it. We got out of their war.'

'It's too bad the Rainman didn't make it.'

'Yeah. It's too bad.'

'Where do we go from here?'

Billy slid down in his seat.

'Who knows? Just keep on going until we hit something. We've never known where we've been going before. Something'll turn up.'

There was a long silence. Each of them was absorbed in his own thoughts. The quiet of the desert was strangely deafening after the roar of battle. The occasional rumble of distant gunfire was the only reminder that it still existed. After a while, Reave took a deep breath.

'Billy?'

'Yeah.'

'You got any idea what you're looking for?'

'Not really. No more than I had back in Pleasant Gap. I just know there's something, and I'm going to keep looking for it. One thing's for sure, we can't go back.'

Reave nodded.

'That's true enough.'

Billy glanced up at him.

'You regretting this whole thing? You wishing you were back in Pleasant Gap?'

Reave shook his head.

'No. I don't regret nothing. I'll go along with anything. It's just…'

'It's just what?'

'It's just that I don't have your faith that there's something out there waiting for us.'

Billy laughed.

'Shit man, I don't have no faith. I didn't leave Pleasant Gap to find no divine destiny. The only thing to look forward to in Pleasant Gap was growing old and ending up like old Eli.'

Reave grinned despite himself.

'That's true enough. There doesn't seem to be anything to do except go on.'

Billy started the engine again and dropped the machine into gear, and they moved forward across the desert. Billy halted the machine again and looked up at Reave.

'Want to drive for a spell?'

Reave climbed down from the turret.

'Sure.'

He took Billy's place behind the controls. Billy slid into the standby seat and the machine moved forward again. They rolled across the desert for another few hours. Billy had dropped into a half sleep when the engine coughed and died. Reave fiddled with the controls. Billy sat up and leaned over his shoulder.

'What's the trouble?'

Reave banged the speed control backwards and forwards.

'It just died on me. One minute it was going, and the next it wasn't.'

'Move over. Let's take a look at it.'

Billy squeezed past Reave and studied the controls. He flicked at a couple of switches and moved some of the levers.

'Sure looks like it's dead.'

Reave nodded.

'Just faded out on me. What do we do now?'

'Foot it, I guess.'

'You mean just trek off into the desert?'

'I don't like this any more than you do, but we can't stay here.'

Reave took a last kick at the controls, and then opened the door.

'I don't need walking across this fucking desert.'

'I don't see any way round it.'

Reave jumped down into the dust, and looked back up at Billy.

'What are we going to take with us?'

'I'll see what we've got and pass it down to you.'

Billy stripped everything he could out of the fighting machine and passed it out to Reave. When there was nothing left he joined Reave and looked at the stuff laid out on the ground. Reave squatted down on his heels.

'We ain't going to be able to hump this lot on our backs. We'll have to leave most of it behind.'

Billy looked at the mass of stuff, and scratched his head.

'We'll just have to take essentials.'

Reave picked up the steel water container and shook it.

'Ain't too much water left.'

'Pour it out into the small bottles and dump the can.'

Reave transferred the water to two canteens and he and Billy slung one each over their shoulders.

'We'll need the portapacs.'

They clipped them on their belts. 'And food.'

'It's a pity we left our bags back in the bunker.'

'We'll just have to stash as much as we can in our pockets, and eat what's left.'

They sat in the shade of the machine and chewed their way through the surplus of flat, tasteless ration bars. When they'd finished Billy took a mouthful of water and stood up.

'Might as well get moving. There's no use hanging round here.'

He hitched up his gun belt, and started walking slowly away from the machine in the direction it had been going when it stopped. Reave clambered to his feet and reluctantly followed him.

It got hotter and hotter. Billy took off his dark glasses and wiped the sweat out of his eyes. There was nothing in sight but sand and thorn bushes under a steel-coloured sky, no sign of a track or habitation. He waited for Reave to catch up, and then started walking again. The heat got worse and then, at last, the sky began to dim, and it grew dark. Billy and Reave slept huddled together on the hard ground. The nights were as cold as the days were hot. They walked on through the second day. They didn't speak to each other. They didn't even think. Life shut down until it consisted of nothing more than putting one foot in front of the other. Billy kept his eyes carefully fixed on the ground. He found if he stared at the horizon he began to hallucinate.

He stopped and wearily pulled the top from his canteen. He put it to his lips, and nothing happened. He tilted it further. Still nothing. The canteen was empty. He turned and waited for Reave.

'I'm out of water.'

Reave held his canteen to his ear and shook it.

'I don't have more than a mouthful left.'

'We're in trouble.'

Reave looked around.

'There ain't nothing we can do about it except keep on walking, and hope we find something.'

They kept on walking. Their lips dried and cracked. Their tongues became rough and parched. They began to feel sick and dizzy. Billy's feet seemed a long way away. Then his legs gave way and he crumpled to the ground. Reave stumbled to where he lay.

'Come on, man. Try to keep going. Only a bit further. We got to find water soon.'

'I can't. I've got to have water. I'm burning up.'

'Come on, Billy. Try and make it.'

'It's no good, man. You'll have to go on without me.'

Reave hauled Billy to his feet, and supported him while they staggered on for another hundred yards. Then they both collapsed and fell to the sand. Billy rolled over on to his back.

'We've had it, Reave. This goddamn desert goes on for ever. We've had it.'

Reave looked up, and for a long while he stared at the horizon.

'I don't believe it!'

Billy looked blankly at the sky.

'It's true, man. We've had it.'

'No, no. Look!'

'It's no good, man. If you stare at anything too long, you start to hallucinate.'

'This isn't a hallucination. I can see it! I can really see it!'

Billy rolled on to his side.

'It's a mirage.'

'It's not, Billy. There's trees and water. I can see them.'

Billy painfully raised his head.

'Holy shit! You're right. I can see it too.'

Stumbling and crawling, they made their way towards the oasis. Billy expected it to disappear at any moment, but, as they fought their way forward, it remained and came closer. They were in the shade of tall spreading palms. On their knees they reached the edge of the pool of clear water. They stooped to drink. Then a voice came from behind them.

'Hold it right there!'

18

'*Cease upward motion.*'
    '*Turn fifty-seven degrees.*'
    '*Object.*'
'*Object responds as solid body.*'
'*Probe.*'
'*Probe non-responding. Nature of body concealed.*'
'*Assume protective formation.*'

She/They shimmered and slowly closed in on Her/Their self. She/They took on the protective spherical form, but once again the sphere was discoloured and dented on one side. In every form Her/Their injuries had their effect.

'*Move forward and observe.*'
'*Caution.*'
'*Caution is maintained.*'

She/They moved towards the object that was concealed in the blue mist. She/They halted some distance from the object.

'*Probe again. High density.*'

A round spot on the side of the sphere glowed yellow, and a thin pencil of light cut through the blue mist.

'*Partial response on probe.*'
'*Organically arranged mineral construction.*'
'*Structure familiar.*'

She/They moved a little closer and probed again. This time, the result of the probe struck a trigger response in Her/Their consciousness.

'*Alarm. Object conforms to data on disruption modules.*'
'*Object does not conform to normal mass or dimension information stored from previous encounters.*'
'*Object has ceased to move.*'
'*Assumption that object is small dormant disruptor.*'

'No record of such phenomenon.'

'Lack of information does not preclude its existence.'

'Hypothesis. Small dormant disruption module will reawaken if probing continues.'

'Assumption that object is dead disruption module.'

'Insufficient data.'

'Data may be gathered by probing.'

'Probing could activate.'

'Close and probe. Increase caution level.'

She/They, still in Her/Their spherical form, closed with the object. It was now visible through the blue mist. She/They probed again.

'Object remains dormant.'

It was definitely a disruptor, although it was much smaller than any that She/They had previously encountered. Its body, instead of the usual smooth, gleaming, metalflake skin, was a dull black, and its surface was cracked and pitted.

'Assumption is that the disruption module has been subjected to damage, energy drain or burnout.'

'Assumption would warrant further probe.'

She/They probed again. The disruptor showed no signs of awakening.

'Indication of external tampering.'

'Indication of non-functional human interference.'

Along the side of the disruptor, in crude white letters, was the word WILBUR.

19

'Hold it!'

Billy looked up in dull surprise.

'Huh?'

A huge albino stood behind them. He had large incongruous breasts, small pink eyes, and straight white hair that fell to his shoulders.

'What are you two doing, making free with my water?'

'Your water?'

'Sure it's my water. Who told you that you could go drinking it?'

Billy looked at him in disbelief. His voice was a dry croak. 'We're dying of thirst. We just came across the goddamn desert.'

'I can't help that. There ain't too many people come this way, I'll admit, but all the ones that do want water. If more folks started coming here I'd have no water left at all.'

Billy pushed himself up on to his knees, and pulled out his gun.

'Listen. I don't know who you are, or what you do here, but we've got to have water and nobody's going to stop us.'

The albino held up his hands.

'There's no call to take it like that. I wasn't saying you couldn't have no water. I just like to be asked first. Good manners don't cost nothing.'

Billy sighed and dropped the gun back into its holster. 'Could we please have some water?'

The albino beamed.

'Sure, fellas. Help yourselves, take all you want.'

Billy and Reave drank deeply and splashed water over their heads and necks. When they had finally finished they turned and faced their host.

'We're much obliged to you, mister. We were just about dying.'

'Think nothing of it, boys. I'm always glad to oblige. By the way, what do people call you?'

'I'm Billy, and he's Reave.'

'Billy and Reave, hey. Pleased to make your acquaintance. I'm called Burt the Medicine.'

'Hi.'

'Maybe you'd like to come over to the shack and take the weight off your feet.'

'Sure.'

Billy and Reave followed Burt the Medicine towards a log shack under the palms. There were a table and some canvas chairs in front of the ramshackle building. They were shaded by a multi-coloured beach umbrella. Burt the Medicine waved a limp hand.

'Sit yourselves down, boys. Make yourselves at home.'

Billy and Reave flopped into two of the chairs, and Burt the Medicine took another.

'What brings you way out here?'

'We were getting away from the war.'

'The war, hey. It's still going on?'

'It's still going on.'

'You wouldn't believe the way they could drag it out.'

'When we ran, it looked like it would go on for ever.'

'It's amazing what some folks will do for amusement.'

Reave scowled.

'We didn't find it too amusing.'

Burt the Medicine smiled.

'You done well to get out then.'

Billy and Reave both nodded, and the conversation flagged in the way it does between people who have only just met. The albino pulled a deck of tattered cards from somewhere inside his robe.

'Fancy a game of Loser Take Nothing?'

Billy shook his head.

''Fraid we don't play, and besides, we don't have any money.'

Burt the Medicine put the cards away.

'That's too bad. I don't get too much company out here. In fact, I ain't had a good game since the last time Quinn was here.'

'Quinn?'

Burt the Medicine looked surprised.

'You don't know Quinn? I thought everyone knew Quinn.'

'I don't recall ever meeting anyone called Quinn.'

'If you'd met him, you'd remember. When Quinn gets here, everybody jumps for joy.'

'Maybe we should meet him.'

'You ought to. Where are you fellas planning to go from here?'

Billy shrugged.

'No idea. We'll just travel on until we come to something.'

Burt the Medicine looked surprised.

'You're weird.'

'Maybe.'

'Still, it takes all kinds.'

He struck himself on the forehead.

'Here I am, chattering on, and you're probably starving.'

Billy and Reave both nodded.

'We are kind of hungry.'

The albino stood up.

'I'll see what I can do. There should be something in on the stuff beam.'

'You've got stuff beams out here?'

Burt the Medicine put a hand on his hip and pouted.

'Well of course. This isn't the outback.'

'We didn't mean that. It was just that they didn't have any stuff receivers in Dur Shanzag.'

'Well, they wouldn't, would they?'

Billy looked confused.

'No, I suppose not.'

The albino disappeared inside the shack, and returned with a laden tray.

'Here you go, boys. It's all cold, I'm afraid. I got a bit wary of hot stuff down the beam. The war zone, you know, it sets up some kind of interference. A roast chicken went wrong one time, and that's how I grew these tits.'

Billy and Reave looked suspiciously at the food, but Burt the Medicine waved aside their fears.

'Eat up, fellas. I guarantee nothing won't happen to you.'

Billy took a speculative mouthful.

'Tastes all right.'

''Course it does.'

They began to eat. Reave looked questioningly at Burt the Medicine.

'Must have been quite a shock, growing those tits and all.'

The albino finished chewing.

'It came as a kind of a surprise at first, I can tell you, but I soon got used to it. After a while I quite got to like it.'

He jiggled one of his breasts.

'I mean, I never was the sort of guy who had much truck with women, so it didn't make that much difference, if you know what I mean.'

They went on with the meal. They had just started on a dish of ice-cream and stuff beam strawberries when a high-pitched buzz started away in the distance. It grew louder and nearer. Burt the Medicine leaped to his feet.

'Fuck the bastards. It's another one. You two better get down on the ground.'

After their experiences in battle, Billy and Reave didn't ask any questions. They dived from their chairs and hit the dust.

A small, red, propeller-driven airplane with multiple wings was coming straight at the oasis, almost at ground level. It sprayed a burst of machine-gun fire at the shack, and pealed off, circling for another run.

Burt the Medicine leaped to his feet and ran to the edge of the trees. He whipped the cover off a pair of tripod-mounted, twin-field lasers and swung them towards the plane as it came in for a second low-level attack.

Twin pencils of white light sprang from the lasers as the albino pressed the triggers. They sliced neatly through one of the sets of wings, and the plane rolled over. It dropped like a stone, hit the ground and exploded, scattering pieces of wreckage across the sand. Burt the Medicine replaced the cover on the laser and came back dusting off his robe.

'Well, that takes care of another one.'

Billy and Reave got up off the ground.

'What in hell was that?'

'Quin-plane auto-pirate.'

'What?'

'It's some little gizmo they dreamed up over in Dur Shanzag a while back. Automatic killers. They let 'em loose and ever since, they've been buzzing round looking for live targets. I've taken out maybe a dozen so far. The control system ain't too smart, so they're quite easy to deal with.'

He sat back down at the table.

'Guess we might as well finish our meal. I really hate being interrupted while I'm eating.'

They finished their dessert, and then the albino produced Turkish coffee and a bottle of Stuff Central's best cognac. The sky was already starting to dim, and by the time the bottle was drunk it was quite dark. The albino stood up and yawned.

'I could sit here talking with you boys all night, but it's past my bedtime. You two look like you could use some sleep.'

Billy and Reave both nodded. The brandy had wiped out what little was left of their energy. The albino cleared away the remains of the meal, and started to rig up a hammock between two of the palm trees.

'There's room for one of you to sleep in the shack, and the other can sleep in this here hammock. It's plenty warm enough on account of how it zips up like a sleeping bag.'

He demonstrated. Billy and Reave looked at each other. 'Who's going to take the hammock?'

'We could flip a coin for it if we had a coin to flip.'

Billy shrugged.

'I'll take the hammock, I could sleep anywhere.'

'If you're sure you don't mind.'

Billy tested his weight on it. 'No, I don't mind.'

Billy took off his jacket, boots and gun belt.

'You can take these into the house with you. I'd hate to lose them in the night.'

'Sure. Goodnight.'

Reave took Billy's things and followed Burt the Medicine into the shack. Billy zipped himself into the hammock, and within minutes was asleep.

It was light again when Billy woke up. He felt better than he had at any time since leaving Pleasant Gap. Even the memory of the Shirik had diminished to a dull nightmare. He pulled down the zip on the hammock and swung his feet to the ground. Neither Reave nor Burt the Medicine seemed to be up and about yet. He walked over to the pool and had a leisurely wash.

Feeling clean and refreshed, Billy looked round for some sign of life, but nobody had yet emerged from the shack, so he walked to the partly open doorway in his bare feet.

The interior of Burt the Medicine's shack had none of the makeshift appearance of the outside. Although it was only one room, the floor was carpeted and the walls were hung with tapestries and finely wrought brasswork. Light filtered in through venetian blinds over the windows. It revealed that the room was crowded with ornate furniture and *objets d'art*.

At one end of the room was a huge bed made of dark, carved wood. Billy moved quietly towards the bed. To his surprise he found, naked under the covers, Reave and Burt the Medicine curled up together in each other's arms. They were sound asleep.

Billy backed quietly away from the bed, grinning to himself. He'd never thought that Reave was that sexually adventurous. His boots, belt and jacket were lying on a chair, so he picked them up and tiptoed out of the shack.

He sat by the pool for nearly an hour before anybody emerged. The albino was the first to appear. He wore a white brocade robe and oddly dainty silver sandals. He came over to where Billy was sitting.

'Breakfast?'

'Yes, please.'

'Be ready in a few minutes.'

'Great.'

Burt the Medicine strolled back to the shack. A while later Reave appeared. He walked over and joined Billy. He looked a little sheepish.

'You got your stuff out of the shack, then?'

'Uh-huh.'

'I guess I must have been asleep at the time.'

Billy tried hard to keep a straight face.

'That's right.'

'In bed with Burt?'

'Yeah, as far as I could see.'

'I... uh... was pretty drunk last night.'

'Yeah?'

'I... er...'

Billy laughed.

'Don't worry about it, man. I don't care who you ball.'

'But...'

'It doesn't matter, Reave. We ain't in Pleasant Gap now. There aren't any rules any more.'

'I guess not.'

'So stop looking so fucking guilty. Did you have a good time?'

'He was pretty weird.'

'Yeah. He's coming back, so leave it for now.'

The albino set a tray down on the table. There was chilled melon, sliced ham, croissants and a pitcher of cold milk. He grinned at them.

'Breakfast, boys.'

For the next half hour they ate and made small talk, and then, while Burt the Medicine was clearing away the meal, Reave looked at Billy.

'What do we do now?'

'I guess we should move on sooner or later.'

'On foot? Back into the desert?'

'Maybe we should talk to Burt the Medicine about it.'

'Talk to Burt the Medicine about it.'

He had returned from the shack. Billy glanced up at him.

'We were talking about moving on.'

'Moving on? You only just got here. What's the matter, don't you like it here?'

He looked sideways at Reave. 'Bored already?'

Reave coloured. 'No, no. It's just that...'

He quickly borrowed a phrase from the Rainman. 'We're travelling men.'

Burt the Medicine stared out into the distance.

'Travelling men.'

His voice was wistful.

'A lot of travelling men used to come through here before the war started.'

He switched his attention back to the present.

'What do you want to do then?'

'Billy spread his hands.

'That's the trouble, we don't really know. I suppose this desert doesn't go on for ever.'

'No, but it goes on for quite a way. I suppose you want to go on to the river?'

'The river?'

'That's the only place to go, except back to the war.'

'What happens on the river?'

Burt the Medicine grinned.

'Just about everything you could think of. You'd best head for Port Judas. From there you can take a river boat all the way down past Dropville, Arthurburg and right through to the nothings.'

'How far is it? How long will it take us to get there?'

The albino shrugged.

'Depends how you go.'

'I guess we'll be going the same way we came.'

'You came on foot.'

'That's what I mean.'

'It takes a week to reach Port Judas on foot. You'd probably die before you got there.'

Billy frowned.

'Then we're in trouble.'

The albino smiled.

'Not really. I'm sure I can fix something. I'll see what I can jive up on the stuff beam after we've eaten lunch.'

Billy grinned.

'Sure do a lot of eating round here.'

Burt the Medicine shot Reave another sidelong glance.

'That's true.'

He stood up, and bustled back to the shack. Billy and Reave continued to sit at the table. Burt the Medicine came back with a bottle of Campari, a soda syphon and a dish of ice. He put them down on the table.

'This'll keep you two amused until lunch. I've got a few chores to do.'

He disappeared inside the shack again. Billy and Reave drank Campari and soda until the albino appeared with yet another meal. When they'd finished, Burt the Medicine took a deep breath, as though he was about to make an announcement.

'I've been looking through the Stuff catalogue. There's a nifty little two-seat buggy. I think I could get it for you without them wanting to push up my quota. That's if you've really got to go.'

'We've got to move on, I'm afraid.'

Burt the Medicine stood up.

'I'll go and dial up the buggy for you. It'll take me a while to set up the large cage. If you just wait here, I'll bring it round to you.'

He went round to the back of the shack, and after a few minutes there was an intense flash of static and then the low hum of a flux motor. Burt the Medicine swung round the outside of the shack in a small two-seat pink buggy with huge, white balloon tyres. He halted it just outside the line of trees. Billy and Reave hurried over to join him. He climbed out and patted the fibreglass body.

'There you go, boys. That should get you to Port Judas inside of two days.'

Reave scratched his head.

'I don't know how we can ever pay you back for this.'

The albino laughed.

'Don't bother about it. Stuff Central are always getting on to me about how I ought to consume more. It's like you're helping me out.'

Billy and Reave came over adolescent tongue-tied.

'Well, thanks.'

They threw their few belongings into the buggy, and Burt the Medicine once again disappeared inside the shack. He returned moments later carrying a wicker basket.

'I just packed up some food for your trip.'

Billy was about to make a crack about grandmother's house, but decided it would be unkind.

'Thanks.'

'Be sure and stop by here again.'

'We will.'

Reave set the buggy in motion, and they pulled away from the oasis. Their last glimpse of Burt the Medicine was as he stood waving, a solitary white figure between the palm trees.

20

At ten forty-five sharp, exactly three quarters of an hour after the meeting had started, A.A.and Valdo Catto entered the Boardroom. It was a grand entrance. AA Catto had made sure of that. Both she and her brother were dressed in white. He wore a uniform modelled on ancient film of the legendary hero Hermann Goering, while she had on what she liked to refer to as her vestal virgin outfit.

The five families of the hereditary directorate were all present in the circular, domed room. The Cattos, the Glicks, the Meltzers, the Mudstraps and the Ferics, each sitting in their own wedge-shaped section of the hall. The most senior of the families sat at the front, after which the seating was allocated, rank behind rank, in succeeding generations.

The young of Con-Lec were noticeable by their absence, and the oldsters mumbled together about irrelevant problems of fiscal logistics. On a rotating podium in the centre of the hall great-great-grandfather Dino, the senior Mudstrap, was taking his turn at chairing a meeting. Valdo and AA Catto took their seats with the maximum of noise and fuss.

When they were able to prolong the disturbance of their arrival no longer, the meeting resumed, and Bull Feric got to his feet and, in a long rambling dissertation, presented an esoteric motion for the restructuring of the Exec level grading system. After the first twenty minutes, Valdo nudged AA Catto.

'Remember our agreement.'

AA Catto waved him away.

'I know, I know. We haven't even started yet.'

Bull Feric continued for another half hour and then abruptly sat down. Dino Mudstrap called a vote. AA Catto, who had understood nothing of the argument, looked at the yes and no buttons on the arm of her chair. Quite at random she pressed the no button. Dino Mudstrap studied the results as they were relayed to his podium, and announced the motion carried. AA Catto felt mildly pleased that she had instinctively disagreed with the majority of the oldsters.

Dino Mudstrap was swivelling his podium looking for the next motion. AA Catto jumped to her feet.

'Mister Chairman.'

The podium came to a halt.

'The Chair recognizes... ah...'

Dino Mudstrap consulted his seating plan.

'... Miss AA Catto.'

AA Catto took a deep breath.

'I propose the motion that the L-4 dwellings, and all the stasis territory beyond the perimeter walls of the citadel, be declared insanitary and firestormed forthwith.'

Dino Mudstrap's bushy eyebrows shot up.

'Firestormed, Miss Catto? For what reason?'

'For no particular reason except that the destruction of the L-4s would provide an excellent diversion. It would be fun.'

'Fun, Miss Catto?'

'Fun, Mister Chairman.'

Dino Mudstrap stroked his bald head.

'I see.'

He paused, and peered round the meeting.

'Does anyone second this... ah... unusual motion?'

Valdo was on his feet.

'I do, Mister Chairman.'

Again he consulted his seating plan.

'The motion is seconded by Valdo Catto. Does any member care to speak against it?'

In the front rank of the Ferics, the ancient Melissa creaked to her feet.

'It would seem, Mister Chairman, that the proposal to destroy, en masse, these potentially useful life forms would be in direct opposition to our long-established traditions of frugality and conservation.'

Melissa Feric had long been famous for her sentimentality. 'I must therefore seriously warn this meeting against sanctioning any such action.'

She resumed her seat. The ever-practical Nolan Catto, AA Catto's grandfather, was immediately on his feet.

'While not sharing the venerable Miss Feric's humanitarian considerations, I must also call on this meeting to reject the motion. You will all recall, no doubt, that in the case of the accidental firestorm that consumed the periphery of AkioTech, there was a period when the citadel itself was endangered.'

AA Catto pouted.

'They put it out in time.'

The chairman banged his gavel.

'You are out of order, Miss Catto. Pray continue, sir.'

Nolan Catto glanced at his granddaughter.

'While appreciating our young people's need for spectacle, I do feel that such a drastic display would, to say the least, be foolhardy.'

The next to rise was Havard Glick. Heads turned to look at him. Havard Glick was notorious for his eccentric ideas.

'It might have escaped Miss Catto's knowledge that there are some who hold the belief that even the L-4s are possessed of human sensibilities, and the morality of their wholesale slaughter would be somewhat questionable.'

There was a ripple of laughter. The old man was obviously senile. Everyone knew that the L-4s were the descendants of rejects from Con-Lec DNA research and that Con-Lec could dispose of them in whatever way they pleased. Nobody else seemed eager to speak after Havard Glick, and the chairman returned to AA Catto.

'Do you have anything else to say, Miss Catto?'

AA Catto jumped to her feet.

'Indeed I do, Mister Chairman. My grandfather's sentiments are typical of the decay that will one day destroy this citadel. Don't firestorm the L-4s, he whimpers, it might endanger us. Leave these insanitary organisms to scuttle round the outside of our beautiful towers. My grandfather would have our citadel overrun by vermin rather than risk the purging flames.'

Her voice rose in high patriotism.

'It is the voices of cowards and traitors that plead for this rabble. The five families created the L-4s to serve, and when they no longer serve, it is the duty of the five families to destroy them. The fire cannot harm a citadel. It didn't at AkioTech and it won't here. I say to you one more time, we must firestorm the L-4s.'

The chairman, who had appeared to doze off during AA Catto's speech, opened his eyes.

'I thought you said earlier that you wanted to firestorm the L-4s for fun.'

'Yes, Mister Chairman. And because it's my sacred duty.'

The chairman nodded.

'Yes, I see.'

He looked round at the directorate.

'Shall we vote?'

Nolan Catto was on his feet.

'May I propose a compromise? It might be a very good idea to instruct the entertainment Execs to prepare video simulation of a firestorm. It might do a little to satisfy these young people's need for spectacle.'

AA Catto dug her nails into her palms.

'You patronizing bastard.'

The chairman glared at her.

'Shall we vote? First for Miss Catto's motion, and secondly for Mister Catto's compromise. Vote on the first one, please.'

AA Catto stabbed at her yes button.

'And now the second.'

She pressed the no button. The chairman consulted his results.

'Miss Catto's motion is rejected. Mister Catto's compromise is carried.'

'Damn you old fools.'

AA Catto stood up and stalked out of the boardroom. Valdo followed a little way behind. Outside in the corridor, Valdo caught hold of her wrist as she was about to step on to the moving walkway.

'Have you forgotten our bargain, sister dear?'

'Bargain?'

'You promised to let me take you home and ill-treat you if I found this meeting loathsome and boring.'

'Did I agree to that?'

'Indeed you did.'

'But surely you didn't take me seriously?'

'I must admit, sister, that I took it very seriously. So seriously that I filed a tape of our conversation with Audit-12, the steward of wagers. He found it perfectly acceptable.'

'You little beast.'

'I thought I should get some fun out of what promised to be a very boring morning.'

AA Catto glared at her brother.

'I positively forbid you to lay a hand on me.'

'I was going to use a whip. I have one that would be eminently suitable.'

'I won't let you.'

Valdo smiled at her. He looked like a vulture.

'You'll have to.'

'Why?'

'Because otherwise Audit will compel you to under the term of a family wager.'

'Let them try.'

'If they make you, it'll be in public.'

'Public?'

'Delinquent wagers are always collected in front of vidcameras. It goes out like on channel 79. I'm sure all our friends will watch, and of course, the tape will be available in the library.'

'You're an unpleasant little weasel.'

Valdo beamed.

'It runs in the family. Are you ready to come?'

AA Catto pursed her lips.

'Yes, I suppose so.'

Valdo helped her on to the walkway. 'I think the hour will be sufficient.'

21

Like Burt the Medicine predicted, it took less than two days to cross the desert. It gave way to rolling grasslands, and the track that Billy and Reave had been following became a surfaced highway. Then other roads connected with it, and soon Billy and Reave were driving through tidy, cultivated farms. They passed other traffic on the road, square, upright, box-like vehicles painted black or brown and driven by noisy impulse motors. The people inside looked sombre, dour folk. They dressed in black or grey and stared in amazement at Billy's and Reave's flamboyant buggy.

They passed more and more of the sedate, austere cars. The farms became increasingly built on, and then they passed a sign that read: 'Port Judas Welcomes the Clean Living.'

Reave grinned at Billy.

'Think we qualify?'

Billy grinned back.

'I don't know about you, man.'

They drove into the town, past rows and rows of small stone houses with white picket fences and neat little gardens. Billy grimaced.

'It doesn't look too much like fun city.'

Reave shrugged.

'Maybe this is just the suburbs.'

'Maybe.'

The gardens disappeared and they found themselves in an area of high walls and grey stone factories. Then the road swung round a corner, and out into a square. The square was surrounded by all kinds of imposing municipal buildings. They were built from the same grey stone, but had been dignified by the addition of pillars and broad steps. On the pavements, serious people in black and grey went soberly about their business. In the centre of the square was a bronze statue of a sour, elderly gentleman in the same long scholastic robe worn by most of the male inhabitants. He clutched a book under one arm, and held the other poised as though about to shake an admonishing finger. The whole place had an air of unshakable piety.

Reave swung the buggy into the kerb and looked around.

'Don't say this is downtown Port Judas.'

The albino had included a box of cigars in the hamper of goodies. Billy lit one and inhaled.

'It looks like a good place to catch a boat away from.'

A man in a blue coat with brass buttons and a peaked cap was staring intently at Billy and Reave from the other side of the square. Billy glanced at Reave.

'He's got to be the law around here. He's a cop if ever I saw one.'

'Don't look now but he's coming over.'

The figure was sauntering across the square, fingering the stick that hung from his belt. He had the unmistakable unconcerned walk of cops in every place, every age.

'We can't have broken a law already.'

'You never can tell.'

'Shall we do a runner?'

'No. Hang on and see what he wants.'

As the figure came closer Billy and Reave could see that his cap bore the legend 'Port Judas Bureau of Correction'. He halted beside the buggy and jerked the finger of his white gloved hand at Billy.

'Thou!'

'Me?'

'Yea, thou. What thinkest thou, parking in the main square?'

Billy smiled politely.

'Sorry officer. We just drove in from the desert.'

'Thou makest for the harbour?'

'That's right.'

'Then make. Outlanders have their own quarter by the waterfront. Thinkest thou the good people of Port Judas suffer them to run all over the whole city?'

'Well, no. We just didn't know.'

'Ignorance is no excuse.'

'We're really sorry.'

'I think maybe I should book thee for vagrant wandering.'

'We won't do it again.'

'Thirty days in the workhouse would ensure thou didst not do it again.'

'Listen officer. We're new in town. Give us a break.'

Billy gestured pleadingly with his cigar. The officer looked at it in disgust.

'Put out that vile weed. Thou transgresseth City Ordinance 417.'

'Huh?'

'Thou shalt not partake of the weed tobacco in a public place. Penalty sixty days in the city workhouse. That's ninety days thou couldst pull already.'

Billy ground out the cigar with his boot.

'Listen…'

'I think I shall overlook thy offences this one time. Hurry thyself to the outlanders' quarter and we'll say no more. I promise thee, though, if I see thy face…'

He glanced at Reave.

'… Or thy face either, around here again, I'll book thee for sure. Understandeth?'

Billy nodded.

'We understand. Thanks for letting us go, officer.'

Reave flicked the buggy into drive, and they moved off. The cop watched them until they'd left the square. Once out of sight of him, Reave glanced at Billy.

'I think you were right about this town.'

'I'll say one thing for it, it's better than Dur Shanzag. Let's make it down to the outlanders' quarter. The good people of Port Judas give me the creeps. I think we'd be better off with the bad people.'

The outlanders' quarter was surrounded with a high stone wall made from the same grey stone as the rest of the city. Billy and Reave drove along the wall until they came to an entrance. Over it was a sign that read: 'Outlanders' Reserved Area. Gates Closed Dusk to Dawn.'

Two more Bureau of Correction officers were on duty at the gate. They waved Billy and Reave down.

'Are ye entering for the first time?'

Billy and Reave both nodded.

'That's right.'

One of the officers produced a bundle of yellow cards, and handed them one each.

'Heed the warnings contained therein.'

They both promised they would, and the officer waved them on. As they drove into the outlanders' quarter, Billy scanned the card. It was closely printed on both sides with stern warnings to outlanders as to what the good citizens of Port Judas considered to be unseemly behaviour. The gist of it was that any foreigner showing his face in the main part of the city had better have a pass, a good reason for being there, and get himself back behind the walls before sunset.

'This is some friendly town.'

Reave glanced round.

'It don't seem too bad in here.'

The outlanders' quarter seemed a good deal more human. Its streets bustled rather than proceeded with stern piety like they did outside. Sailors in striped shirts and rough cotton trousers rubbed shoulders with merchants in black robes. Street vendors cried their wares and hard-eyed men in frock coats, fancy waistcoats and wide-brimmed hats moved determinedly through the crowds. There was even a subtle difference in the women. They still wore the same grey dresses and white aprons as the strait-laced ladies on the outside, but many had discarded the starched white caps, and they contrived to show more cleavage and the occasional flash of leg. Reave grinned at Billy.

'This looks more like it.'

Billy laughed.

'I could feel more at home here. What we need is food, drink, a bed and some female company. Right?'

'Too right.'

Billy pointed to a place ahead on the left.

'How about that?'

It was a two-storey building. Grey stone again, but its woodwork was painted a cheerful yellow. Over the door hung a sign – 'The Hot Puddings'. They pulled up in front of it.

'Is that an inn, or is that an inn?'

They parked the buggy and walked inside. The front parlour smelled of ale and tobacco. The timbers of the ceiling were mellowed and darkened by generations of smoke. The place was lit by an iron fixture in the ceiling that held dozens of flickering candles. Their light reflected on the different coloured bottles behind the bar.

Billy and Reave stood in the middle of the parlour and looked around. There were maybe a dozen men in the place. Most were sailors, except one group of three who looked disturbingly like mercenaries either coming to or from Dur Shanzag. A small man in a white shirt, black trousers and a leather apron came out from behind the bar. He had a round moonface and slanted oriental eyes.

'I help you gentlemen?'

'We're looking for a place to stay.'

'You gentlemen find no finer rooms than here at the sign of The Hot Puddings.'

Reave looked sideways at the little man.

'You the landlord?'

The little man nodded.

'Sure. Me Lo Yuen. I run this place.'

'Well, tell me, Lo Yuen. What passes for money in this town?'

Lo Yuen looked suspiciously at Reave.

'Port Judas crowns, of course. You got some?'

'No stuff beam?'

'Port Judas don't allow. You got to have money. You got money?'

Lo Yuen was looking less and less friendly. Billy intervened.

'We don't actually have any money...'

Lo Yuen looked decidedly hostile.

'However, we do have this very fine desert buggy outside which we would very much like to find a buyer for.'

He leaned close to Lo Yuen and dropped his voice.

'Seeing how we don't know too much about the currency we were wondering if you might help us sell it. I mean, we'd be happy to give you a percentage on the sale.'

The little man looked a good deal happier.

'It sounds like very admirable proposition. Where is fine vehicle?'

Billy gestured towards the door.

'Right outside, honoured friend.'

He led Lo Yuen Out of the inn and into the street.

'There it is. What do you think?'

'It very... colourful.'

'Yeah, well, apart from that.'

'I think maybe some men in parlour might want. Hold on, I talk with them.'

He went back inside the inn, and a few moments later he came back with one of the men in combat gear.

'This Zorbo. He want to talk about buying vehicle.'

'Yeah?'

Billy faced the mercenary. 'You headed for the war zone?'

'That's right.'

'Rather you than me, friend.'

'You been there?'

'Sure, we just got out of it.'

'Bad, huh?'

'Bad.'

Zorbo shrugged.

'We're fighting men. What else can we do?'

'Don't ask me, friend. It took us all our time to get away from it. You want to buy this machine?'

The mercenary stroked his chin.

'Looks like the kind of thing that we need to get us across the desert. How much you want for it?'

Billy glanced at Lo Yuen.

'What would be a fair price, mister innkeeper?'

Lo Yuen went through a pantomime of patting and inspecting the buggy.

'Look like two thousand crowns' worth to me.'

'Zorbo poked the buggy with his finger. 'I'll give you a thousand.'

Billy looked down at his boots.

'It ain't more than two days old. Eighteen hundred.'

'I'll make it twelve and not a crown more.'

'Sixteen?'

'Fourteen.'

'Fifteen hundred.'

'Done.'

The mercenary gave Billy a heavy canvas bag of coins, and went inside to fetch his friends to look at their purchase. Billy dipped in the bag, and gave Lo Yuen a hundred and fifty crowns. The little man smiled and ushered them back into the parlour of the inn.

'We do good business, hey gentlemen?'

Billy clapped the little man on the shoulder.

'Good business, Lo Yuen.'

The two of them ate, and then spent the rest of the afternoon lounging at a corner table working their way through a bottle of tequila.

Sailors and drifters passed in and out of the place, and as the day wore on, Billy and Reave picked up various snippets of information. It appeared there was a river boat going down to Arthurburg in a couple of days, and also that Port Judas could be quite an easy place to live in if you stuck to the outlanders' quarter. They also discovered that the thirteen-fifty they had from selling the buggy was more than enough for them to buy a passage all the way down the river. For the first time in a long time, life looked pretty good.

The afternoon drew into evening, and the sky outside the inn parlour's narrow windows became dark. Lo Yuen built up the log fire in the huge stone fireplace, and the room became a cosy recess of warm light and deep shadows. Bright highlights glinted on the polished wood, the brasswork and the ranks of bottles.

The parlour began to fill up and Lo Yuen put three waitresses to work, who moved between the tables serving drinks, collecting glasses and bandying ribald chat with the customers. A fiddler and an accordion player struck up beside the fireplace, and the laid-back atmosphere of the afternoon dissolved into a jumping jollity. Reave, already half drunk from the afternoon's tequila, laughed and nudged Billy.

'Only one thing we need now, old buddy.'

'What's that, man?'

'We need us some broads, old buddy. That's what we need.'

'Amen to that, buddy.'

Word began to spread round the parlour that Billy and Reave were big-spending travelling men. A couple of card hustlers cruised by to check them out, but they made it clear that they didn't want to know. Girls also began to hover round their table. Not only the waitresses, but two or three other girls who seemed to be employed by Lo Yuen to keep the customers happy and drinking.

Reave stretched out his arm and grabbed one of the girls by the wrist. She was a pleasant plump brunette whose ample figure couldn't be disguised by the sober grey dress, particularly as she wore it considerably less buttoned than the good women of Port Judas.

'You want to dance, honey?'

'I don't know about that, sir. Dancing ain't really allowed in public inns.'

'Fuck that shit. I want to dance.'

He climbed to his feet and started jigging about with the girl.

'Thou art a one, young sir.'

A circle was formed in the middle of the room. Reave swung the screaming and giggling girl round and round, while the accordion player and the fiddler stamped their feet.

The dance whirled faster and faster, then, abruptly, the music stopped. The door had opened, and in the doorway stood two blue-coated officers. Reave collided with the girl and they both fell in a heap on the floor. The officers stood looking down at them.

'What do ye, herein?'

Reave scrambled to his feet. Billy stayed seated at the table, but his hand slid down beside his gun. Reave grinned sheepishly at the officers.

'We, uh, fell over.'

'Ye fell. Art thou sure it wasn't public dancing?'

'Public dancing?'

'Aye, fellow. Public dancing.'

Lo Yuen hurried from behind the bar.

'There no public dancing in this inn, gentlemen officers. That would be against law.'

He took each officer by the arm, and after a muttered conversation they all went outside together. A couple of minutes later Lo Yuen returned on his own. He went straight up to Reave and the girl.

'If gentleman want to sport with girl, then he must take her to own room.'

Reave grinned, and slapped the girl's bottom. 'That suits me, brother.'

He grinned at her.

'You coming then, gorgeous?'

She pouted.

'If that's what would please thee, good sir.'

'Let's go then.'

He took her by the hand and led her towards the stairs. Lo Yuen caught him by the arm.

'One moment, my friend. Officers took twenty crowns of persuasion before they leave.'

Reave dropped the coins into his hand, and then hurried up the stairs with the laughing girl. Billy relaxed in his seat and poured himself another drink. He was beginning to like Port Judas, despite its absurd laws. A girl dropped into Reave's empty chair. She had red hair and large green eyes. There were freckles on the section of her ample breasts that were presented to Billy. She smiled at him slyly.

'My friend's gone upstairs with thy mate.'

Billy laughed.

'You want to do the same?'

'I might. If thou wast specially nice to me.'

22

'It would be productive to gather data from the static module.'

'It is unfortunate that we lack the time.'

'We are injured and unable to delay our search for a naturally occurring stasis point where we may heal our wounds.'

'We must continue.'

'We must continue.'

The spherical form of Her/Them detached Her/Their self from the dead hulk of Wilbur and floated free. She/They maintained the form until She/They was some distance from the silent disruptor, and then resumed the triple form. The two identical women carrying the injured third in their arms. She/They turned so that She/They faced away from the broken disruption module, and once again began Her/Their steady progress.

The mist was unnaturally still. It lay in even, horizontal layers. All twisting and undulation had ceased. She/They moved forward, breasting the layers of mist with little effort. Then abruptly it ceased. The mist, the blue light, there was nothing at all. A total empty blackness.

'Absence.'

For a fraction of a second, She/They did not exist either. Then, moved by Her/Their emergency programming, She/They exerted Her/Their will. She/They began to glow with a soft violet light, and became the only thing in that totally empty universe.

'The state of our existence is related to nothing. There is no external by which we may judge our being.'

The words glowed bright red, growing bigger and bigger to fill the empty space. Abruptly they blinked out.

'If motion can be equated with the expenditure of energy, then we move.'

'We expend the energy in order to move, therefore we move.'

'Subsequently we move.'

More words flashed away into the void.

'The absence of external produces a hole of total subjectivity.'

'Observation. An external has been produced.'

A point of light appeared.

'Cease all energy use.'

She/They became totally inert. The point of light remained.

'External proved to be objective.'

The point of light grew larger and slowly took shape. It moved towards Her/Them like some winged object. It grew larger and larger. It was a huge penguin that glowed with a hard yellow light. She/They remained totally inert as it flapped majestically past without a sideways glance. It flew on, becoming smaller and smaller. Finally it was just a point of light again.

'We possess no data on such a phenomenon.'

'It fails to compute.'

23

'Thou wert lusty, young sir.'

'I could say the same for you, babe.'

The girl had been willing and eager. She had lacked a lot in technique, but more than made up for it in enthusiasm. She had reacted with shock and amazement when Billy had put his mouth between her legs. It was obvious that no one in Port Judas behaved that way. She had also been somewhat disturbed when he had suggested that she treated him to a blow job. After some persuasion and instruction she had acquired a taste for both.

'Thou hast taught me much.'

'Glad to oblige.'

When he had entered her she had seemed much more at home, bucking and writhing, moaning and lifting her hips to meet him in what seemed to Billy to be genuine earthy pleasure. She had raked his back with her nails, and finally, after a long time, they had both come together and collapsed exhausted. They had lain together in silence for a while, and then she had spoken. Billy propped himself up on one elbow and looked at her.

'Don't girls like you have a hard time in Port Judas?'

'It's not too bad if we don't stray outside the quarter.'

'What about the good people of the town? Don't they give you a hard time?'

'They call us whores and sinners, but they can't do without us. They need us so the good women can keep their sacred virtue. Much good it may do them too. I wouldn't swap with the wife of an elder right now.'

'Don't they have laws against doing this kind of thing?'

The girl scowled.

"Course they have laws. Every so often the blue coats round up a few of us and we get dragged in front of the procurator for fornication and lewdness.'

'And what happens then?'

'Either ten strokes of the rod or five days in the workhouse.'

'Have you ever been pulled in?'

'Once or twice. I always take the rod. It's quicker.'

'You mean you've been beaten?'

"Course. I said I had, didn't I? It don't happen often because like I said, they got to have us. We only get rounded up for appearances.'

Billy shook his head.

'I don't understand you. Why the hell don't you split? Why don't you run away from this place?'

The girl looked at him in surprise.

'That's silly talk, young sir. Where would I go?'

Billy lay on his back and stared at the ceiling. The girl seemed so certain that Port Judas was the whole world that he could think of nothing else to say. After a time he rolled over and began to stroke her breast. Just as the excitement was starting to mount again in both of them, there was a knock on the door. Billy's mind flashed back to Dogbreath.

'Not again.'

He rolled over, and grabbed the gun from his belt that was hanging on the bedpost. The knocking came again.

'Who is it?'

'It's me, Billy. It's Reave.

Taking no chances, Billy padded across to the door, slipped the bolt, and stepped back.

'Come in, but come in nice and slow.'

The door opened and Reave stepped inside. Billy lowered his gun.

'What's happening?'

'I just been down to the parlour for a nightcap, and I heard something that I thought I ought to tell you about.'

Billy wrapped a blanket round himself and sat down on the bed.

'Wouldn't it have kept till morning?'

'I don't think so. There's these two guys downstairs. They're sitting in the corner. They're wearing trench coats and they've got their hats, pulled down over their faces. Lo Yuen told me that they've been asking about us. He reckons they're secret agents from the war zone.'

'Sounds like they're from the Ghâshnákh.'

'And they're looking for us. I got a feeling it's trouble, Billy.'

Billy reached for a cigar, lit it, and held the smoke in his lungs for a long time while he thought.

'I don't think they'll try anything while we're in here. There's too many people about.'

'So what do we do?'

'I guess we've got to stick close to the inn until it's time for the boat. Then we'll make a run for it.'

'What do we do about boat tickets?'

'Get Lo Yuen to fix them for us.'

'Think we can trust him?'

'We're going to have to.'

'I suppose so.'

'Listen. Go to bed. Lock the door, and we'll see how things are in the morning. We're going to have to play this thing by ear.'

Reave grinned.

'When did we ever do anything else?'

He headed for the door, and Billy bolted it behind him. He went back to the young woman in his bed. She looked at him nervously.

'Thou art in trouble.'

He ran his fingers between her legs. 'Nothing we can't take care of.'

To his surprise she pushed him away and sat up. 'I think perhaps it's time I was leaving thee.'

Billy put his arm round her.

'Listen. There ain't going to be no trouble. I thought you were going to stay the whole night?'

The girl shot him a sidelong glance.

'Thou couldst try giving me another little present.'

Billy fumbled in his jacket, and dropped ten crowns on the girl's stomach. She gathered them up and placed them with her clothes, then she lay down smiling.

'Perhaps we should play them new games that thou hast taught me?'

Billy pulled her close to him, and they played for a long time before they fell asleep.

When Billy came down to the parlour the next morning, the two men in trench coats were sitting in a corner. They watched openly while Lo Yuen brought him a plate of eggs and a mug of beer.

They were just as Reave had described them. Dirty trench coats and grey fedoras pulled over their eyes. They just had to be Ghâshnákh agents. Billy ate his eggs and stared back at them. Bit by bit the parlour began to fill up with the morning trade, and when the place was fairly full, Billy managed to get a quiet word with Lo Yuen.

'I hear there's a boat leaving tomorrow?'

The little man nodded.

'Pier six, eleven in the morning.'

'Could you fix it so me and my partner were on it?'

'Very simple. I get you tickets.'

'How much would it be for a good-class cabin for the two of us?'

'Two hundred crowns.'

Billy dropped the coins in Lo Yuen's hand. 'There's an extra fifty. It's for your trouble.'

He gave the little man a hard look.

'I wouldn't like it if anyone else heard about it.'

Lo Yuen smiled blandly.

'You no worry. Me soul of discretion. Ask anybody.'

'Okay. Thanks.'

'Okay. I go now.'

The little man hurried off to take care of his customers. Reave came down to the parlour rubbing his eyes. He flopped into the chair next to Billy and glanced at the men in the comer.

'I see they're still here.'

'Did you really expect them to be gone?'

'I guess not. What are we going to do?'

'Nothing. Nothing at all. We're just going to sit here and drink. Lo Yuen's getting our boat tickets, and at about ten thirty tomorrow, we'll do a run for pier number six. Okay?'

'It's okay with me. I guess you know what you're doing.'

'I hope so. I don't fancy being dragged back to Dur Shanzag.'

They spent the rest of the day sitting at their table in the parlour, drinking in a leisurely manner, and watching the two agents watching them. Towards the end of the evening they each found themselves a girl and retired behind the bolted doors of their rooms. Billy spent a pleasant night informing a second Port Judas whore of the joys that could be had from oral-genital contact. Billy reflected that if the idea spread round the town, he would probably be responsible for yet another addition to the Port Judas city ordinances.

The next morning Billy got up, dressed, crossed the corridor and tapped on Reave's door.

'Who is it?'

'Billy. Let me in, quick.'

He slipped inside, and Reave bolted the door behind him. 'You got the tickets?'

Billy nodded.

'Lo Yuen gave them to me last night. I also paid our bill.'

'So we can walk straight out of here?'

'If you've got everything together.'

Reave struggled into his jacket.

'I'm ready.'

'Okay, let's go.'

They hurried down the stairs, and went straight across the parlour and out of the door before the two agents had a chance to move. Once in the street, they hurried along for a couple of blocks, and then ducked into an alley. Reave glanced behind.

'Think we've lost them?'

'I don't know. Let's keep moving.'

They doubled back through the narrow streets of the outlanders' quarter, crossing the same route a number of times, before heading for the pier. There was no sign of the two men when they finally emerged on the quayside. They were jostled by sailors and dock workers as they looked for pier six. The smell of the river seemed like the scent of freedom. At last they came across a sign that read Pier Six and they hurried out to board the river boat.

The *Maria Nowhere* was a floating palace. It looked as though it had been designed by a *fin de siècle* shipwright with an obsession about decorative wrought iron. It lay low in the water, but its elaborate white and gold superstructure was a maze of saloons, companionways and promenade decks. Towering above the wheelhouse were the ship's pair of slender smoke stacks, and in the rear, the huge, single paddle wheel that drove the river boat.

Billy and Reave breathlessly hurried up the gangway. At the top, they were stopped by the purser.

'You have tickets, gentlemen?'

Billy produced the tickets and they were directed to the first-class berths. Halfway there, they were met by a steward and showed into a large, comfortable cabin. Reave grinned at Billy.

'This is the way to travel.'

The cabin followed through the same design style as the outside of the boat, except that the wrought iron and white timber had been replaced by inlaid veneer, crystal mirrors and dark red plush. Billy flopped into an armchair while Reave wandered round the cabin looking in cupboards and opening drawers.

'This sure is an improvement on anything else we've had.'

Billy laughed.

'It's a pity we're so scruffy. That steward couldn't believe we were first-class passengers.'

'Fuck him. We've got money, and that's what counts when you get down to it.'

There was a shudder as the boat's engines began to turn over, and then after a few minutes an even tremor began. Reave went to the porthole.

'We're moving, Billy. We're under way. Come and have a look.'

Billy moved across to the porthole. The waterfront of Port Judas was slowly receding. Billy put a hand on Reave's shoulder.

'Looks like we're out of it, old buddy. We've got away from it all, Dur Shanzag and the good people of Port Judas. I got a feeling that life is going to get better. I got a good feeling, old buddy.'

Reave smiled.

'I got a feeling that I need a drink now all the excitement's over.'

Billy grinned.

'Good idea, let's go up to the saloon. I think it's on the next deck up.'

They both stowed their portapacs in one of the cupboards, hid their surplus money under the mattress, and started for the door. Billy opened it, and found himself staring down the muzzle of a heavy-calibre automatic pistol. Behind the gun were the two men in trench coats.

'Oh no!'

They pushed Billy back into the cabin. The agents' eyes glittered from behind their hat brims and upturned collars.

'You will not move or make a sound.'

'Turn round and place your hands on the wall.'

The agents' voices were little more than a cold hiss. Billy and Reave did as they were told, and were patted down and relieved of their guns. They were then ordered to sit on the bed. Billy decided to try and bluff it out.

'Who are you, and what do you want?'

Silently one of the agents reached in his pocket and produced a black leather billfold. He flicked it open. Inside was an enamel badge with the eye and flames emblem in red on a black background.

'We are agents of the Ghâshnákh. We are taking you back to Dur Shanzag for interrogation.'

Billy started to get up.

'Listen, you've made a mistake. I don't know who you're looking for but...'

One of the agents hissed at him.

'Sit down. If you move again I shall blow your head off. One would suffice to take back for interrogation.'

Billy sat down abruptly.

'As for being mistaken, there is no possibility of that. You are without question the deserters who stole a fighting machine. We found it where you abandoned it in the desert. Your accessory the albino pervert also told us much before he died. There is no mistake.'

Reave leaped to his feet.

'You mean you killed Burt the Medicine?'

'Obviously, and we'll kill you if you don't sit down.'

Reave sank to the bed.

'What are you going to do with us?'

'You'll be taken back to Dur Shanzag for examination by the Eight.'

'And then?'

'You won't survive examination.'

There seemed to be nothing more to say. Then Billy had an idea.

'You'll have to get us off the boat.'

'You'll be taken off at the next place we land. The crew won't inter-rupt us. There are no laws on river boats except those the captain cares to invent.'

This time there was nothing at all to say. The little tableau remained totally static. Billy and Reave sat side by side on the bed. The two agents stood slightly apart, with their backs to the door, watching them.

Then it all erupted.

The door flew open and there was the ugly whine of a needler. The two agents swung round and crashed to the floor. Their bodies were riddled with tiny slivers of steel. The Minstrel Boy stood in the doorway holding a miniature needle gun in his right hand.

'The next time I get you idiots out of trouble, I'm going to charge you.'

24

A Catto followed Valdo into his apartment. She really hadn't bargained for this situation. It promised to be painful and humil-iating. The odd thing was that she also felt a vague stirring of excitement.

Three Hostess-1s were waiting in the bedroom. A black velvet cov-erlet had been laid across the bed, and the wall colouring had been set at a dark purple. AA Catto had to admit that her brother had a fine sense of the gothic. A short, plaited whip of white leather lay on the bed. It was arranged to give the impression that it had been casually tossed there.

Valdo snapped his fingers at the Hostess-1s.

'Quick now. Undress Miss Catto.'

The Hostess-1s surrounded AA Catto and began systematically to remove her clothes. She did nothing to stop them. It was an odd sensa-tion to be involved in. A situation over which she had no control.

When she was completely naked, Valdo hit the light controls so the walls faded almost to black and the room was completely dark except for a single white spot shining down on the bed.

Valdo's voice was a sinister whisper.

'Lie down, my dear sister.'

AA Catto was finding the stage management ritual very exciting. She wasn't too sure about the actual pain.

Two of the Hostess-1s took hold of her wrists, and gently but firmly led her towards the bed. She was laid face down, and the Hostess-1s pulled shiny chrome manacles, padded on the inside with soft black leather, from hidden recesses in the bed and snapped them on to AA Catto's wrists and ankles. AA Catto was spreadeagled on the velvet. She was totally unable to move.

Valdo hit two more buttons and the dim glow of the walls began to undulate in changing shapes and patterns. Richard Strauss came through hidden speakers. AA Catto swivelled her head round to look at Valdo. He was pulling on a pair of white kid gloves. He smiled down at her.

'You must admit that I have taken a lot of trouble over you.'

'You do have good taste.'

Valdo leaned forward and picked up the whip.

'I like to pride myself on that.'

He flicked the whip in the air, as though he was testing it.

'Would you like some altacaine before we start?'

'I think I would prefer a shot of deadout.'

'Oh come now, sister. That would defeat the whole purpose of the exercise. It really must be altacaine or nothing.'

AA Catto tugged against the manacles but found that they wouldn't move.

'Yes, yes. I suppose altacaine will make the experience more interesting.'

Valdo turned to a Hostess-1.

'Give Miss Catto a single-dose shot.'

The Hostess-1 pressed the injector against one of AA Catto's buttocks and pressed the release. AA Catto tingled as the boost rushed through her system. Valdo gestured to the two other hostesses.

'Now, rub Miss Catto's body with sensitol.'

AA Catto was outraged.

'Sensitol? I never agreed to sensitol.'

'I think it's perfectly legitimate. I wouldn't want you to miss the slightest nuance of the tactile experience.'

The two hostesses rubbed the cream all over AA Catto's shoulders, back, buttocks and legs. Her flesh began to come alive, and her skin was sensitive to the slightest movement of the air. She felt pinned down, vulnerable and exposed. She was ultimately receptive to anything that her brother might want to do to her. In the total passiveness and total abasement there was a novel excitement. Valdo's voice came from somewhere behind her.

'I think we're about ready.'

There was a swish and AA Catto tensed herself, but it was only Valdo testing the whip again. She turned her head.

'For God's sake get on with it. Stop hanging it out.'

Valdo laughed.

'I didn't know you were so eager, sister.'

'Just get on with it.'

'Why? I'm in no hurry.'

'Valdo, please.'

He giggled. 'Come on, beg.'

'Valdo!'

He slowly raised the whip. There was a frozen moment of stillness and silence.

Then the whip came down and AA Catto gasped, squirmed, and finally screamed as loud as she could.

25

The Minstrel Boy dropped his gun back into a small shoulder holster and stepped into the cabin. He was a little more soberly dressed than he'd been in Dur Shanzag. He still had the green lizard frock coat, but it was now cracked and worn. His hair was back to its natural colour, and his dark glasses were again the aviator kind. He wore a double-breasted calfskin waistcoat and a black gambler's tie with a white shirt. His black pants covered scuffed cowboy boots.

Reave and Billy stood up in amazement.

'How the fuck did you get here? What happened?'

The Minstrel Boy shrugged.

'I saw you coming aboard, and then I saw those two.'

He gestured to the bodies on the floor.

'I figured what might be going on, and came down here to check it out. You saw the rest.'

'But what are you doing on this boat?'

'You sure ask a lot of questions for somebody who just got their life saved.'

'Sorry, it was just such a surprise.'

'Yeah, okay, life seems to be one big surprise for you boys. You got anything to drink?'

Billy and Reave shook their heads.

'We were just going up to the saloon when these guys came bursting in.'

'Okay then, let's go up there. You can buy me a drink, and meet my partner on this trip.'

Reave gestured at the dead agents.

'What do we do with them?'

The Minstrel Boy glanced casually at the bodies.

'You got twenty crowns?'

'Yeah.'

'Gimme.'

Reave handed the coins to the Minstrel Boy, who pocketed them.

'I'll drop this on the steward, and he'll take care of them. Once they're in the river, the alligators will do the rest.'

They left the cabin and climbed the steps to the saloon. The first-class saloon was a floating casino that seemed to be made from mirrors and cut glass. Two huge crystal chandeliers hung overhead. A steward on the door looked distastefully at Billy's and Reave's clothes.

'Are you gentlemen sure that you're first-class passengers?'

'Sure.'

Billy flashed their tickets, and the steward had to content himself with asking them to leave their guns with the hat-check girl.

The Minstrel Boy led them across the saloon to a green baize table where a game of nine-card sidewinder was in progress. As they approached, a man in a black velvet coat, with long dark hair, looked up and grinned at the Minstrel Boy.

'We're going okay, partner.'

'That's good. Hey, Frankie, I'd like you to meet two friends of mine, Billy and Reave. This is Frankie Lee, he's a gambler.'

Frankie Lee stretched out his hand.

'Pleased to meet you boys. You want to join our game?'

Billy shook his head.

'I think we'll just sit and drink, thanks. We've had a busy day.'

'Okay, suit yourselves.'

The Minstrel Boy sat down at the table and resumed his place in the game. Billy called over a waiter and ordered drinks.

They drank their way through the rest of the day, watching Frankie Lee and the Minstrel Boy clip close on a thousand crowns from two Port Judas merchants out on a spree. Then, towards midnight, they stag-

gered drunkenly off to their cabins where, as the Minstrel Boy had predicted, the bodies had been removed and even the stains on the carpet
had vanished. They fell into their beds, and slept soundly until well into
the next morning.

They were awakened by a bright, cheerful Minstrel Boy.

'You boys planning on going ashore?'

'Ashore? Where are we?'

'Tied up at the Dropville jetty.'

'Yeah? How long for?'

'Till tomorrow morning.'

Billy sat up in bed and lit a cigar.

'Maybe. What's Dropville like?'

'It's okay for a party, but I wouldn't like to live there.'

'You can have a good time though?'

'Sure. It ain't like Port Judas.'

'Say listen, where's your partner? Is he going ashore?'

The Minstrel Boy shook his head.

'He's sleeping. He stayed up all night to finish off those two merchants. Me and him have got to make some money on this voyage. Are
you coming, then?'

Billy nodded.

'Yeah, we'll come. Why not?'

The Minstrel Boy opened the door.

'I'll see you in the saloon when you're dressed.'

'For sure.'

The Minstrel Boy closed the door behind him. Billy and Reave
climbed out of bed and struggled into their clothes. Inside fifteen
minutes they were walking along the deck with the Minstrel Boy in the
direction of the gangway. As they were about to leave the ship, a
steward stopped them.

'Have you got your portapacs?'

Billy and Reave patted the chrome units on their belts and the
Minstrel Boy held up his guitar.

'We got them. Why?'

'You never can tell in Dropville. Now and then something comes
unstuck.'

They thanked him, and walked down the gangplank. The pier at
Dropville was a humble affair compared with Port Judas. It was little
more than a rickety wooden jetty, a shed on the bank, and a track that
led out into what appeared to be dense, luxuriant jungle. Billy turned to
the Minstrel Boy.

'What happened to the town?'

The Minstrel Boy pointed up the track.

'It's about ten minutes' walk. There's too many mosquitoes and things to live right on the river.'

They started up the track. The trees formed a solid canopy of green above their heads, and troops of monkeys crashed through the branches as they approached. Other unseen things slid away through the undergrowth, and brightly coloured birds screeched a raucous warning.

Billy noticed that here and there among the trees were the ruins of buildings. Low structures that had once made exciting use of steel and concrete, but were now overgrown by vines and creepers. Walls and roofs had fallen in, as the jungle tightened its grip on them. Billy pointed one of the derelicts out to the Minstrel Boy.

'This must have been a much bigger town once upon a time?'

The Minstrel Boy nodded.

'Sure. There was a time when Dropville was one of the richest, most beautiful towns anywhere.'

'What happened to it?'

The Minstrel Boy paused before he answered. The track had led them into a wide clearing. Here and there patches of marble paving still remained, but most of it had been broken up by the relentless pressure of the encroaching jungle. Four or five of the low buildings with their patios and wide expanses of glass stood in fairly good condition, while others, nearer the edge of the jungle, had fallen into total disrepair. Even the ones that were still in use had undergone makeshift patch-up jobs, and received crude, garish redecoration. They walked around the shattered remains of an abstract statue and along the side of an empty, overgrown swimming pool. On the bottom of the pool a number of brightly dressed teenagers sat crosslegged in a circle staring vacantly straight ahead. The Minstrel Boy began his story.

'I guess it must have been easily two hundred years ago, Dropville – it was called Laurel Bay in those days – was, like I said, one of the richest and most beautiful towns you could hope to find anywhere. The story even goes that Solomon Bonaparte, the guy who invented the stuff system, retired here after he'd made his pile. The city got richer and richer, and life for the citizens got as close to idyllic as anyone could hope to get. Laurel Bay was a paradise on earth.'

Billy looked around at the ruins and semi-ruins that fought a losing battle with the creepers and undergrowth. They skirted a decorative stainless-steel fountain, filled with generations of dead leaves.

'So what went wrong?'

Before the Minstrel Boy could answer, a figure darted from behind the fountain.

'Wanna see me do my sword swallowing?'

It was a boy who looked about fourteen. He was barefoot and wore white cotton trousers and a silk vest covered in hundreds of tiny mirrors. In his hand he held a short dress sword. The Minstrel Boy shook his head.

'Not right now.'

The boy looked disappointed.

'You sure?'

'Sure we're sure.

A hopeful look came over his face.

'Maybe later?'

'Maybe.'

'See you then.'

'Okay.'

He scampered off and the Minstrel Boy sat down on the edge of the derelict fountain.

'Like I was telling you, things got better and better until, one day, the ultimate happened. Somebody invented immortality.'

Billy's and Reave's eyes widened.

'Immortality?'

The Minstrel Boy nodded.

'That's right. They actually achieved the final goal. Somebody, some say it was old Solly Bonaparte, came up with a pill or a shot or something that once you'd had it, barring accidents, you'd live for ever. Of course, the secret's lost now.'

Reave frowned.

'I still don't see how immortality could have caused all this.'

The Minstrel Boy lit one of Billy's cigars and went on. 'What happened was this. Directly they had this eternal life dose, everyone in town queued up and got one, and there they all were, set for infinity, provided they didn't drown in the river or fall out of a tree. The only problem was that the immortality deal stopped the ageing process, and all the people stayed whatever age they were when they got the dose. The old folks kept right on being old folks and the young folks kept on being young folks. The only drawback to the treatment was that it made everyone sterile, and so the population remained absolutely the same. Just like time had stopped.'

Reave chewed his lip. 'Pretty weird, huh?'

The Minstrel Boy nodded.

'Pretty weird. The first thing that went wrong was that the old folks, who'd been pretty much running things until immortality came along, wanted to go right on running things after. They couldn't stop treating the young folks like they were kids, and gradually the situation grew up where a guy might be, say, sixty years old, but because he looked fifteen, he was treated like he was fifteen. This, coupled with the fact that the old folks got mightily hung up on their eternal life and began bringing in all these heavy public safety laws, created a pretty bad generation gap.'

Billy interrupted him.

'You mean that kid, the one who wanted to show us his sword swallowing, wasn't a kid at all?'

The Minstrel Boy laughed.

'He was certainly a hundred, if not more.'

'Jesus.'

'That was the trouble, you see. The old folks wouldn't listen to the young folks and relations between them got worse and worse. I don't know the details, but one night the shit hit the fan, and the young folks up and slaughtered every one of the oldsters. Nobody escaped. With the old folks out of the way, they gave up bothering about the fancy houses and all that kind of thing. They didn't have to worry, you see. Stuff Central beamed in everything they needed. They changed the town's name to Dropville and settled down to having the eternal good time. Bit by bit, the jungle crept in and things got the way they are today.'

Billy grinned.

'Sounds pretty good.'

The Minstrel Boy shrugged.

'Maybe. I don't like to judge. Dropville's got its problems.'

'Like what?'

'Well, I suppose the main problem's that while, okay, the people will last for ever, the city won't. This is the other side of the river to Port Judas. It ain't part of the static zone. Under this clearing is the biggest generator you ever seen. One day it'll break down and the whole town'll just blink out. There's the odd fault showing up already. I tell you one thing though, it's a good place to party.'

Without saying anything, a girl had come and sat down on the fountain beside Billy. She looked about seventeen, with long blonde hair and a deep tan. She smiled when Billy spoke to her. Then she pulled a pack of Northern Lights out of her faded dungarees and offered them around. Billy took one of the slim, white, plastic tubes, and inhaled deeply. He felt himself filled with an overpowering sense of lightness, and objects that he looked at were surrounded by a fine aura of colour.

The girl looked amazingly beautiful to Billy's enhanced sight. He touched her hand and smiled at her. He felt that it was unnecessary to say anything. She smiled back.

After a few minutes the effect wore off, but Billy found that it returned each time he took another drag. For the next hour, the three men and the girl sat on the broken fountain and smiled at everything in sight. The tubes were finally used up and they dropped the plastic cylinders into the fountain. Reave turned to Billy.

'Those things were certainly something.'

Billy nodded, with a look of awe on his face. 'They certainly were.'

The Minstrel Boy glanced at him.

'You've never had Northern Lights before?'

Billy and Reave both shook their heads.

'No, never.'

'Good, huh?'

'Good's hardly the word for it.'

They were all sitting on the fountain thinking about how good the Northern Lights were, when the girl tapped Billy on the shoulder and pointed towards one of the larger buildings that were still standing. A bunch of boys had moved some amplification equipment on to the patio and were plugging in electric instruments. A small crowd was starting to gather. The Minstrel Boy stood up.

'Let's go and watch this.'

Reave stared across the clearing.

'Are those kids going to play some music?'

'Those kids have been playing music for maybe a hundred years. They are the best. Wait till you hear them.'

The four of them strolled across the clearing. The girl seemed to have attached herself to Billy in her strange, silent way. They settled themselves on the grass as the group of musicians started to play. The Minstrel Boy had been right. They were unnaturally good. The girl handed round the Northern Lights, and for another hour they all sat very still, completely sucked in by the beautiful, free, interweaving music. The first piece lasted for nearly an hour and a half, and when it was finished, one of the group, a tall boy of something like nineteen with a first growth of beard, walked to the front of the patio. He appeared to be the leader of the group, and he gestured towards the Minstrel Boy.

'You want to come up and join us?'

The Minstrel Boy picked up his guitar.

'I don't know if I'll be good enough.'

The leader grinned.

'Don't worry about it. Try and fit in where you can. Maybe we should play some of your songs.'

The Minstrel Boy stood up and made his way to the patio. The silver guitar was hooked into the amplification gear, and the band started again, with the Minstrel Boy tentatively fitting himself in. Billy and Reave sat and watched as the music rolled over them. Another girl came and sat down beside them. She was almost the twin of the first girl. She smiled in the same way, but she also spoke.

'You have come from the river boat?'

Billy nodded.

'That's right.'

'Are you going to stay with us?'

'Only until the boat moves on.'

'That's a pity.'

'You'd like us to stay?'

'We're pleased when anybody stays.'

The first girl turned her head and smiled at Billy and Reave. Billy stretched out on the grass and stared up at the canopy of leaves overhead. The music wound in and out of itself. Billy sighed. It was the best part of the trip so far. Dropville seemed to have been made for him. He glanced at Reave.

'This is the way to live, huh?'

Reave frowned.

'It's very nice. It's a bit spooky, though. I mean, all these people staying young for ever, and the way they killed off all the old people.'

He waved his hand at the luxuriant vegetation and the huge bright flowers that covered the jungle floor.

'It's like the whole place was rooted in death.'

Billy closed his eyes.

'That was years ago. It's long gone. This place is like fucking paradise. Listen to that music, Reave. Look at the women.'

He patted the hand of the mute girl. She smiled and stroked his hair. Reave looked at Billy doubtfully.

'Are you thinking of staying here, Billy?'

Billy shook his head.

'No. But it sure is tempting.'

26

She/They was everything.

She/They was the only thing that Her/Their senses, even at full stretch, could detect. The only source of energy was She/They. The only thing that existed was She/They.

She/They continued to expend energy, and She/They assumed that a forward motion was maintained. There was no edge, no boundary on the negative zone. There was nothing at all. Only the strange vision that had flown past Her/Them convinced Her/Them of the possibility of anything else existing.

She/They knew that at some point in time She/They would start to grow weak. She/They needed to expend energy just in order to maintain Her/Their existence. There was nothing in the zone to draw on. All Her/Their energy was being drawn from inside Her/Them. Her/Their energy reserves were finite. There would come a time when Her/Their resources would be exhausted and Her/Their existence would just flicker out.

She/They shut down all Her/Their functions except that which concentrated on motion. Her/Their shape flickered, wavered and ceased to be. She/They was reduced to a formless point of light that moved across empty blackness.

With nothing to relate it to, time had no meaning. She/They continued, and She/They moved. There was nothing else. Then something appeared.

The peripheral sensors that She/They had maintained during the shutdown roused the other functions and She/They grew back into the triple form. There was an object away in the distance. She/They could ascertain that the object was spherical, but beyond that it was too far away to determine any details. Gradually She/They and the object came closer together. Tentatively, She/They probed the nature of the object.

'Uniformly dense spherical body.'

'Uniform composition.'

'Large body of water contained in spherical form by its own surface tension.'

The sphere floated towards Her/Them like a small planet.

It appeared to Her/Their sensors like a huge blue-green ball.

Faint ripples passed across the surface. As the sphere drew closer, She/They felt Her/Their self being drawn towards it.

She was expending no energy. The mass of water was sucking Her/Them in.

Waves circled outwards as She/They struck the surface of the sphere. She/They felt Her/Their self drawn into the watery interior. She/They kicked with a furious jolt of energy, and began to move upwards. The sphere couldn't contain such a violent motion. The sphere broke apart and a column of water began to rush upwards carrying Her/Them with it, bouncing and buffeting Her/Them as it rushed past.

The water rushed up and up, then She/They broke surface, and found Her/Their self bobbing on the surface of a huge lake. The ripples of Her/Their arrival slowly died and She/They was partially submerged in a glassy smooth lake that appeared to stretch all the way to the horizon.

'Approach of humans monitored.'

'We are prepared for defensive action if humans prove hostile.'

The humans moved across the surface of the lake propelling a crude floating craft. No machinery of energy transfer could be detected. They appeared to attain forward motion by the use of their own bodies.

Their craft cut a long V in the surface of the lake as they moved across it. She/They watched and waited. The humans had always puzzled Her/Them. At times it almost seemed that they might have a primitive grasp of the essential conconception of the symmetry that was Her/Their joy and being, then they would contradict the whole idea by their illogical disordered crudeness. They would swarm over Her/Their hard-won stable areas, violating them with their haphazard behaviour and rude creations.

The humans seemed to have a coarse resilience, possibly a natural compensation for their obvious stupidity, that enabled them to resist both the disruptors and even Her/Their efforts to bring a degree of order to their hideously random lives.

She/They found that there was no way in which She/They could really manipulate them. She/They could sense them totally, and at times they could perceive Her/Them. Beyond that, She/They found that She/They had no power to move them. They occupied the same stable zones. It seemed that the humans clung to stable zones, but on different levels. The levels might be close at times, and even parallel, but there was always a gulf between Her/Them and the humans. They neither aided nor threatened, they just existed. To Her/Them they appeared as a strange byproduct of the disruption.

27

The day turned into night, and the music went on and on, complex and contorted, and then, the next minute, simple and driving. Lights appeared in the trees so the jungle looked alive and glowing. Areas of foliage had been sprayed with phosphorescent paint. It was invisible by day, but with the darkness and the black lights mounted in the trees the plants pulsed and shimmered in a riot of unearthly colours.

As the music became more loose and wild, the rapt attention dissolved into dancing and laughing. Couples and groups moved in and out of the lights and shadows. Casks of wine, narcotic fruit, bottles and pharmaceuticals from a hundred cultures were brought from the stuff machine.

Billy had lost track of Reave as he wandered along the jungle paths with the strange silent girl. He had been offered so many different things, strange liquors, exotic drugs, that his head was spinning and his vision played awesome, spectacular tricks on him. They passed a battery of red and green lights that pulsed on and off, and the girl's face dissolved into a glowing rainbow. Billy stood perfectly still and stared at her.

'You're fucking beautiful. This whole place is beautiful.'

The girl smiled at him. To Billy, it was a flash like the sun coming up. He hugged her, and then they walked on, across the floor of the clearing. The Minstrel Boy was still sitting in with the band. His eyes were closed in total concentration as he tried to coax more and more from the silver guitar. Sweat stood out on his forehead and he seemed totally oblivious to the dancing crowd around him. Billy and the girl stood arm in arm and watched for a while, then they moved on, out of the clearing and along the shining paths that ran through the tall trees.

They came to a smaller glade where two large UV generators shone down on the soft, leafy jungle floor. Billy felt a new sensation in his head, and he guessed there were a couple of alphasets tuned to wide dispersal somewhere in the bushes. A number of people were gathered in the glade. Most were naked, some had their bodies painted in colours that glowed under the ultra-violet light. Some of them sat while others lay on the ground and caressed each other. There were few couples. The naked people in the glade grouped themselves in threes, and there were two large groups of seven or eight who laughed and writhed together in a mass experience. Billy stood at the edge of the glade and watched in fascination. The girl let go of his hand and quickly slipped out of her clothes. She held out her hand, inviting him to do the same, and join the people in the glade. Under the UV light her skin became very dark, while her lips and the whites of her eyes glowed an eerie blue.

Billy slowly took off his clothes, while the girl stood behind him and stroked his back. He placed his clothes beside hers and then she took his hand and led him into the glade. She sank to her knees in front of a group of three intertwined people, a boy and two girls who looked like they couldn't be more than fifteen. Billy knelt down beside the girl and the three others held out their hands in welcome. The music soared through the trees.

Billy let his mind float. The hands and lips that moved across his body, the roaring music and the shifting lights couldn't be logically put together. He just ran with it, letting himself drift in a world of sensuality, confident that nothing bad could happen to him in this place.

Hours later, Billy found himself lying on the floor of the glade staring blankly at the sky starting to become light in tiny patches between the leaves and branches. The girl was curled up with her head on his chest. His body felt totally exhausted, but the colours in his mind kept swirling and changing. Sleep was impossible. He lay on the ground, totally drained. Memories of the last few hours flooded through his mind in dislocated images of faces, bodies. They invited him, smiled intertwined with his. They distorted into their component colours, and merged back together to form something else that started the process again.

Above him, the sky grew brighter. He was aware that the music had stopped. The only sounds were the rustling in the undergrowth. The first birds were starting their morning chorus. He absently stroked the girl's smooth, golden, sleeping body. He felt totally at peace. The forest was like a huge, rambling cathedral. Thin beams of light lanced through the high ceiling of foliage and illuminated tiny bright patches of the soft moss that covered the floor of the glade.

It seemed to Billy that everywhere he looked, the forest was a bright, rich mosaic. It took him a long time to realize that someone was talking to him.

'Come on, Billy. Pull yourself together. We've got to move in a while.'

He focused on the two faces that looked down on him. It was Reave and the Minstrel Boy, but their faces seemed hard and cruel and their clothes coarse and out of place after the beauty of the night before. They refused to leave him alone.

'Hey, Billy. We got to go soon. Come on, man. Get your clothes on. Move it, Billy.'

'Go?'

'Yeah, go. We got a boat to catch.'

'We don't have to catch the boat yet, do we?'

'Yeah, pretty soon.'

Billy sat up and clasped his knees to his chest.

'I'm not going.'

Reave and the Minstrel Boy looked at him in amazement.

'What do you mean, not going?'

'I want to stay here.'

'Stay here?'

'That's right, man. I'm happy here. I don't want to leave.'

'But we got to leave. That's what you always say, keep moving, keep on looking. We've got a boat to catch.'

'Fuck the boat. I want to stay here. I like it. You understand? I'm happy, I found something. I don't want to move on. I don't want to get myself together. Fuck that shit, man. I like it here.'

The Minstrel Boy stuck his hands in his pockets.

'You are crazy.

'Why? Because I don't want to rush off into another load of trouble?'

Reave shook his head.

'All that UV has scrambled his brains.'

The Minstrel Boy squatted down beside Billy.

'Have you thought about what staying here really means? These people are immortal. They don't grow old. You do.'

Billy rested his chin on his knees.

'That won't matter. Not for a few years. I'll deal with that problem when it comes.'

'A few years? You won't live a few weeks.'

'What the hell are you talking about?'

'You've seen the way these people live. They load themselves up on everything they can get their hands on, and no doubt you plan to do the same. Right?'

Billy giggled.

'Sure, why not? Nothing wrong with that, or are you going to hand me some crap that being stoned is an illusion?'

'I ain't saying nothing like that. You know me, Billy. I'll get stoned any time, but I wouldn't stay here. I know I wouldn't last thirty days.'

Billy looked confused.

'There's nothing here to hurt me.'

'The whole lifestyle would kill you. The fact that you're human would kill you.'

'I don't understand.'

'How do you feel right now?'

Billy shrugged.

'Okay. Kind of wasted. Why?'

'Think you could live like this all the time?'

'No, but...'

'That's how life goes on here. You'd have to live like everyone else. There'd be no other way.'

Billy gestured to the sleeping girl.

'She seems to do okay on it.'

'Sure she does. She doesn't age. Her tissue regenerates. She can grow new brain cells. You can't. You live the same way as her for a couple of weeks and your brain'll be fried. It'll burn out. Your body would break down, and you'd die. Now do you understand?'

Billy put his head in his hands.

'Are you sure about this?'

The Minstrel Boy nodded.

'Quite sure. It's happened.'

'Jesus. I don't know what to do. I believe you. It's just that I still want to stay here.'

The Minstrel Boy put a hand on Billy's shoulder.

'I know how you feel, man. Think I wouldn't like to stay here and just play music with those guys? It'd be the best thing in the world, but I know it wouldn't work out.'

'I don't know. I don't know what to do.'

The Minstrel Boy stood up.

'Come along with us now. It's easier this way. If we hang around until they wake up, it'll be a whole lot more difficult.'

Slowly, as though he was in a trance, Billy got to his feet. He looked down at the girl sleeping on the moss. He sighed deeply.

'I suppose you're right.'

He picked up his shirt and slowly began to pull it on. When he was fully dressed they started to make their way down the track that led to the jetty. To their surprise, when they emerged from the forest there was no sign of the *Maria Nowhere*. The jetty led out into an empty river. The three of them looked at each other in bewilderment.

'How did we manage to miss it?'

'It surely can't be that late.'

The Minstrel Boy shrugged.

'It's gone. That's for sure, and my partner's on it with all my money.'

Reave slapped his forehead in horror.

'Most of our money's on that fucking boat as well. Billy hid it under the mattress.'

Billy grinned.

'I suppose we'll have to spend another night in Dropville. That won't hurt us.'

Reave and the Minstrel Boy scowled at him.

'Another night there, and none of us might want to leave.'

Billy laughed.

'What else can we do?'

The Minstrel Boy pointed to the edge of the jetty. There were some canoes tied up.

'We could take one of those. It's an easy stretch of river, we could catch the *Maria Nowhere* when she stops over at the next town.'

Billy looked at the canoes dubiously.

'Couldn't we wait for the next boat?'

'There may not be one for a week, and we don't have any money.

'I guess it's all down to paddling then.'

They climbed into one of the flimsy craft, settled themselves and pushed off. They found that if they kept to the middle of the river, the current carried them along at a fair speed, and they only needed to paddle when they wanted to change course. The sky was warm, and it seemed to be a not unpleasant way to spend the day. After the first novelty of riding the river had worn off, Billy announced that he was going to catch a few hours' sleep. He curled up in the stern of the canoe. The next thing he knew was the Minstrel Boy yelling at him.

'Wake up, Billy. We're in trouble, man.

'What's the matter?'

'There seems to be a fault in the river. A big hole that's sucking us in. Paddling doesn't help, we're heading straight for it.'

Billy became aware of a deep roaring noise, and he sat up. Ahead of them was a huge circular hole, rather like they'd seen on the road out of Graveyard, only much, much bigger. All the water from the river seemed to be pouring down as though it was a huge drain. Billy grabbed a paddle and tried desperately to fight the current. Reave and the Minstrel Boy both shook their heads.

'It's no good. We've tried. It doesn't make the slightest difference.'

The roar of the water was so loud that they had to shout to make themselves heard.

'Ain't there nothing we can do?'

Billy looked round desperately. The hole was getting very close. Then he had an idea.

'Turn on your portapacs! I don't know if it'll do any good but it might help.'

Coming up to the hole was like going over a waterfall. A knot twisted in Billy's stomach. The boat tilted and then dropped into the hole. They held their breath and fell. There was nothing else to do.

They fell. It seemed to go on for ever. Billy's lungs ached from holding his breath. He felt that maybe he should let himself drown. Maybe it would be easier than being dashed to pieces when they hit bottom.

Then he was floating. He was going upwards. The portapac field seemed to have a buoyancy all of its own. His head broke water, and he took a deep, choking breath. After holding his breath so long it felt wonderful. The field of the portapac seemed to support him, and he looked around. A few yards away was the canoe. It was floating upside down, but otherwise it seemed undamaged. Billy paddled towards it. He was struggling to turn it over when Reave appeared beside him. Together, they righted the canoe and flopped inside. Billy tentatively switched off his portapac. Nothing changed. It seemed as though they had arrived somewhere. Billy sat up and looked around. There was smooth, untroubled water as far as he could see. He turned to Reave.

'Have you seen the Minstrel Boy?'

Reave shook his head.

'Not since we fell into the hole.'

'I hope he made it.'

'I hope he landed somewhere better than this. There's no sign of land anywhere.'

'It's so still, too. No waves, no breeze, nothing.'

'Which way do you think we should go?'

Billy looked at the sky. It was a flat uniform grey, a few shades darker than the water. He shook his head.

'Your guess is as good as mine, and anyway, we don't have any paddles.'

Reave pointed.

'Yes we do. Look.'

There was a single paddle floating a few yards away. They pushed the boat towards it, and Reave fished it out of the water.

'We can take turns. I'll do the first stint.'

He settled in the stern and began to propel them across the smooth surface of the lake. Billy sat in the bow and stared into the distance, searching in vain for something that would give them a clue to what direction to take. There was no way to judge the passage of time. Nothing moved either on or under the water. Billy glanced at Reave.

'You think they have day and night here?'

Reave grunted.

'The time I've been paddling, it sure don't feel like it. You want to take a turn?'

They changed places, and Billy dug in with the paddle. Reave dipped his hand into the water.

'I wonder if you can drink this stuff.'

He licked his fingers.

'Tastes okay. It don't seem like we're going to die of thirst. I tell you one thing, though, I'm going to be well hungry pretty soon. I sure wish Burt the Medicine was here to bring out one of his meals.'

Billy slammed the paddle into the water with unnecessary force.

'Burt the Medicine's dead.'

There was a tense silence, and Reave fidgeted awkwardly.

'You still mad because we made you come away from Dropville?'

Billy shook his head.

'I ain't mad, but I don't really want to talk about it.'

From then on he paddled in silence, avoiding Reave's occasional glances. Then Reave crouched forward in the bow.

'Hey, Billy. There's something out there.'

Billy shaded his eyes and stared where Reave pointed.

'There's something out there all right. You still got your gun?'

Reave nodded.

'Sure. You?'

'Yeah.'

They paddled towards the object bobbing on the surface. Reave looked back at Billy.

'You know, from here, it looks like a couple of people swimming.'

'Maybe it's the Minstrel Boy?'

'It definitely looks like two, I'd say... Holy shit!'

An impossible sight was rising out of the water. Two women, both identical, carrying a third in their arms. They wore white ankle-length cloaks, and silver helmets that covered most of their faces. Even the folds of their garments seemed to hang in exactly the same way. They pulsed with a faint blue light, and Billy wondered if the pulse was real or a flashback to the previous night's drugs. Reave backed down the canoe and crouched beside Billy with his gun drawn.

'What is it?'

'I've no idea. Let's just go on and see what happens.'

Billy steered the canoe so it passed within four or five yards of the figures. The strange beings stood motionless, and then slowly turned their heads in perfect unison. Then Billy and Reave were past them. Billy rested the paddle and stared back at the unique thing that floated above the surface of the water. Billy felt an unreasoning blanket of sadness wrap around him. Reave crawled down the canoe and crouched beside him.

'Gosh.'

Billy looked at Reave strangely, but said nothing. The heads turned back to where they had been looking previously. It seemed that Billy and Reave held no more interest. The figures began to move. They were like a rigid statue that drifted forward across the lake, gradually gathering speed. The composite entity began to grow smaller and smaller, and soon Billy and Reave could no longer make it out at all. Billy turned to look at Reave.

'What made you suddenly say "gosh" just now?'

Reave frowned.

'I don't know. My personality just seemed to slip for a moment. It's back again now.'

28

A Catto returned to her own apartment, bruised and aching. The door responded to her voice and she went straight through into her bedroom and threw herself down on the bed. Damn her oily, cunning little brother and his tricks. The whipping was a novelty, but it certainly wasn't worth the pain involved.

She slipped out of her white dress and looked up at the mirror ceiling. Her back and buttocks were crisscrossed by angry red weals. Curse Valdo, the little worm. She reached the bedside console and punched up Information. A blonde Hostess-1 appeared on the screen.

'May I help you?'

'Get me a Medic.'

'I'll put you through, Miss Catto.'

'Don't put me through. Just get me one.'

'What seems to be the trouble, Miss Catto?'

'I've been whipped. By my brother. I suppose you could say the problem was bruising.'

'I'll have a Medic-1 with you straight away. Will there be anything else, Miss Catto?'

'Yes, just one thing. If any word of this should leak out, I'll see that you're broken to L-4 before you know it.'

'Your privacy is guaranteed, Miss Catto.'

AA Catto grunted and cut the connection. Within minutes, the door buzzer sounded and she pushed the entry button to admit a Medic-1 and a pair of Hostess-2s. She lay on her stomach while the Medic-1 inspected the damage to her back. The Medic had the white covers and the middle-aged, competent features that were the hallmark of his class. He shot four hundred mics of analgethene straight into AA Catto's spine and the discomfort rapidly faded. The Medic ran a dispersed Gamma beam over her bruised flesh and the red weals started to fade. AA Catto found the treatment pleasant and stimulating. After some time the Medic straightened up, and put his equipment back into the carrying case.

'You will make a perfect recovery, Miss Catto.'

'Good. You'd better not say a word about this.'

The Medic placed a pompous hand on his heart. 'Discretion is some-thing sacred to this class.'

'Yes, yes. You're dismissed, you can go.'

The Medic and his two blonde assistants departed. The console buzzed at her. AA Catto pushed the answer button, and Valdo's face appeared on the screen.

'I thought I'd call and see how you were, sister.'

AA Catto's eyes flashed.

'Haven't you done enough for one day?'

'You really are a bad loser. So angry, just because you lost one little bet.'

AA Catto snarled at her brother and cut the connection. The console buzzed again, but she ignored it. The last person she wanted to talk to was her wretched brother. She rolled on her back, and stared at her reflection on the ceiling. Her body was really far too beautiful for nasty little Valdo. She resolved that she would have nothing more to do with him, for a while, at least.

AA Catto began to get bored with even her own reflection. It was still only mid afternoon and after the painkillers and stimulants she had been consuming, it seemed a pity to waste them all. She stretched out a languid hand to the console and punched up the Steward service. A bronzed young man with short-cropped blond hair and pale blue covers answered.

'May I help you?'

'Can you send me a Steward straight away.'

'What service do you require, Miss Catto?'

AA Catto giggled.

'Personal, of course.'

'Do you have any preference to the type of Steward?'

'I'd like you to run up a special for me.'

'Full gene surgery will take a few days, Miss Catto.'

'Gene surgery won't be necessary. A plastic temporary job will do.'

'A plastic reconstruction will take about fifteen minutes.'

AA Catto thought she detected a hint of sullenness in the man's voice. She looked sharply at the screen.

'You Stewards don't like plastic temp jobs, do you?'

'Our preferences are not relevant. We are designed to serve.'

'Afterwards though, it can be very painful when it grows out, can't it?'

'There are after-effects for the individual Steward, but those should not concern you, Miss Catto.'

AA Catto smiled a particularly nasty smile.

'That's right, it doesn't concern me at all. I want you to look up records. There was once a movie actor called Valentino. Rudolph Valentino. I want you to prepare a special using those old films and pictures. I want a Steward sent up that looks like Valentino.'

'There will be a time factor involved in the production of this.'

'How long?'

'I would estimate it at about half an hour.'

'I'll wait, but it better not be much longer.'

'It'll be as soon as possible, Miss Catto. Are there any other requirements?'

AA Catto smiled.

'Only the usual ones.'

She cut the connection, and lay on the bed waiting. Would it be more fun to dress up? Make the Steward rip her clothes off? She decided she had had enough violence for one day. In addition, it was too much trouble, dressing only to undress again. It was, after all, only a Steward. She would just lie there naked and let him service her. When she'd had enough, she'd dismiss him. There was no point in making elaborate arrangements for a Steward-1.

Twenty-five minutes later the door buzzer sounded again. AA Catto smiled and pushed the entry button. A young man with slicked-back, patent-leather hair, dark, flashing eyes and cruel mouth strode into AA Catto's bedroom.

'I am here, Miss Catto.'

His appearance was perfect, he was just what AA Catto had ordered. She wondered, however, if his voice and gestures were a little too theatrical. She'd report the fact to the Steward service when she was through with him.

The young man posed at the end of her bed while AA Catto examined him. After a couple of minutes, he cleared his throat.

'I was instructed to inform you that I am also programmed to do the tango.'

29

During his third turn with the paddle, Reave began to bitch. Apart from the strange apparition, nothing had appeared that gave any indication of land. Billy looked up from where he was dozing in the bow of the canoe.

'What's the matter with you?'

'I'm hungry, and I'm tired. I'm sick of this fucking lake, and I'm sick of not getting anywhere.'

Billy yawned.

'Too bad.'

Reave glared.

'What do you mean, too bad? If something doesn't turn up soon we're going to die out here.'

'What am I supposed to do? Get excited or something? Before you start handing me the you-got-me-into-this line, just remember that it was me that wanted to stay in Dropville.'

'You would have died in Dropville.'

'I'm going to die here, according to you. It strikes me that I'd have been better off dying in Dropville.'

Reave scowled.

'Is that what you really think?'

'Yeah.'

'Yeah?'

There was a moment of tension, and then the two of them realized the absurdity of attempting to fight in the small canoe and relaxed.

'There's no point in getting on each other's back. We're stuck here and there's nothing we can do about it.'

Reave went on paddling for some time, and then Billy took over. Their changing places was the only thing that gave them any idea of the passage of time. Nothing else changed. There was only the still water and the unchanging sky. Hunger gnawed at their stomachs, and the boredom of their surroundings provided nothing to distract them. Billy felt that his world was totally composed of paddling, sleeping, and waiting for starvation to creep slowly up on them.

Reave was sitting in the bow staring into space, and Billy was mechanically paddling, when Reave suddenly stiffened.

'There's something out there.'

Billy looked up.

'You sure you're not seeing things? 'Reave pointed.

'Look for yourself.'

Billy pushed up his dark glasses and shaded his eyes with his hand. He could just about make out a dark smudge on the horizon.

'Seems like there's something out there.'

Billy paddled harder and the dark object came nearer.

'It looks like an island of some sort.'

'It's kind of small for an island.'

They paddled nearer. The island turned out to be a floating reed bed, a mat of tangled vegetation that lay sluggishly on the surface of the lake. Billy prodded it with his paddle and oily water oozed up between the fibrous plants. Reave stared at it morosely.

'This ain't much use to us.'

'Maybe not. It could be a sign that we're getting nearer land. Have you noticed anything about the air?'

Reave looked puzzled.

'Don't think so.'

'There's a smell. Fish, and, I don't know, maybe plants, or dead leaves.'

Reave sniffed the air.

'You could be right. Let's keep going. At least it's a sign of something.'

He crawled towards Billy.

'Here. Give me the paddle. If there's land out there, let's get to it.'

Reave paddled with renewed vigour. They passed more of the floating vegetation. The tangled beds became more numerous, and here and there they linked up to form huge areas of matted plant life. Billy and Reave were soon paddling along channels that separated the now vast reed beds. The air was filled with the swamp smell of decaying plant life, and the water became black and stagnant. Mosquitoes and brightly coloured dragonflies danced over the surface of the water, and pale flowers struggled to hold their own among the crawling dark green plants.

The reed beds grew thicker, and Billy and Reave found that they had to force the boat through increasingly narrow spaces, and even hack their way with the paddle through the thinner parts of the beds.

Billy peered down into the black water. It seemed to be getting more shallow. The boat occasionally scraped some hard object and Billy thought he could make out shapes under the water. They looked like the ruins of something man-made.

The canoe stuck fast and wouldn't move. Billy took off his belt, slipped over the side, and sank up to his waist in the swamp before he found a footing. He put a shoulder to the stern of the boat and heaved. At first nothing happened, then there was a grating, ripping sound and Reave let out a yell.

'There's a hole in the fucking boat. Water's coming in.'

The canoe began to list badly and Reave splashed into the black water beside Billy.

'We've had the canoe.'

'My portapac and gun are still inside.'

Reave leaned over the side of the settling canoe and fished them out. Billy looped them over his shoulder.

'I guess we better foot it until we reach some firmer ground.'

'Nothing else we can do.'

They found that each time they moved their feet, sluggish bubbles of foul-smelling gas rose to the surface and burst. Small black insects darted about, and mosquitoes laughed at them. They stumbled and fell often. As Billy had thought, under the layer of liquid mud there were heaps of some kind of jagged rubble on which they stubbed their toes and twisted their ankles. The going was almost impossible, and although they were soaked from the waist down, sweat poured down their faces. Billy stopped, with swamp water up to his knees.

'Listen, I just had an idea. If we were to turn on our portapacs the extra buoyancy might make it easier.

'If they still work after the number of times we've dropped them in the mud.'

Billy held his up, shook it, and pressed the on button. There was a ripple as the field came on. It proved to be a good deal easier to move. They covered another three hundred yards, and Billy found that here and there, patches of dry land covered in coarse spiky grass rose above the level of the swamp. Billy and Reave staggered up on to one of the dry hummocks and flopped down.

'Jesus, I'm exhausted.'

'At least we seem to be getting somewhere. There seems to be more firm ground as you go on.'

The ground beyond them was more solid. There were wide areas of the spiky grass. Further on a few short twisted trees struggled to survive. In the distance they could just see a line of low hills.

After they'd rested for a while, Billy and Reave moved on. Although it was easier to cross the firmer ground, it wasn't without its hazards. They had to wade through large areas of standing water, and Billy, at one point, sank up to his waist in a trough of thick, sucking mud. Reave struggled for ten minutes before he managed to drag him out. The insects seemed to increase, both in numbers and in daring, and the mud drying on their clothes irritated their skin just as much as the mosquito bites.

Filthy and exhausted they eventually reached the lower slopes of the high ground. It was covered in soft springy turf. Both Billy and Reave fell down and lay panting on the grass. They rested in silence for a while, then Reave noticed something in a slightly longer clump of grass, and crawled towards it. He laughed and called to Billy.

'Hey, see what I found.'

Billy raised his head.

'What is it?'

'Come and take a look.'

Billy crawled to beside Reave, who parted the grass with his hands. In a hidden nest were a clutch of eight pale blue eggs. They were slightly larger than the pigeons' eggs Billy had stolen in Pleasant Gap when he was a kid. He grinned at Reave.

'Breakfast!'

'Or lunch.'

'Or supper, who can tell in this fucked-up place?'

'It's food, anyway. What do you think we should do with them?'

Billy looked around.

'I don't know. I guess we're going to have to eat them raw.'

'We could build a fire and try to cook them.'

Billy laughed.

'With what, man? We don't have any pans or anything.'

'We could build a fire and fry them on a hot rock.'

'We don't have any grease.'

Reave shrugged.

'There are times when you have to improvise.'

Reave scrambled to his feet and hurried down the slope. A few minutes later he returned with an armful of twigs and a round flat stone. After a couple of false starts, he got a fire going. Reave laid the rock on top of the hot embers. He spat on it to make sure it was hot enough, and when he was satisfied he cracked all the eggs on to the top of the rock. They were chalky and full of pieces of grit. Billy and Reave burned their fingers picking the food from the hot rock. When they'd finished, however, Billy lay back on the grass with a grunt of satisfaction.

'I could eat that three times over.'

'It sure was welcome.'

They slept for a while, and woke up stiff, aching, but a good deal more hopeful than they'd been earlier. They began to climb the hill. About halfway from the top they came across a well-used dirt road that appeared to wind to the other side of the line of hills.

They'd been following the road for perhaps half an hour, although they both still had trouble judging how time passed. They heard a sound from somewhere. It started as a high-pitched whine, but seemed to get fuller as it came towards them. It grew to a full-throated roar, and a figure on a motorcycle came over the hill and down the road towards them. The motorcyclist bounced past them, but slewed to a halt, and came back. Both Billy and Reave had caught the flash of a guitar on the rider's back. They looked at each other.

'It can't be.'

'It's not possible.'

The Minstrel Boy kicked the big elaborate machine, with its long forks and high bars, on to its stand and walked towards Billy and Reave. Pulling off his leather flying helmet, he brushed the dust from his long suede coat.

'Hey fellas, fancy seeing you boys around here.'

'We never thought we'd see you again.'

'No?'

'How did you get out of that fault in the river?'

The Minstrel Boy frowned.

'The river? That was a whole long time ago.'

It was Billy's and Reave's turn to frown.

'Huh? It was only a couple of days ago.'

The Minstrel Boy shrugged.

'Suit yourselves. You know best. Where are you headed?'

Billy spread his hands.

'No idea. We just pulled ourselves out of the swamp. We were going up this hill to see what was on the other side. Are there any towns near here?'

The Minstrel Boy nodded wearily.

'Sure, there's a city on the other side of the hill. I wouldn't care to say whether you'd like it or not.'

'You mean there's something wrong with it?'

'There's something wrong with most cities. You don't need me to tell you that.'

'But is this one okay?'

The Minstrel Boy scratched his ear.

'I'm a minstrel, not a tourist guide. If you mean will you come to harm, there's a chance of that anywhere. If you wanted to avoid harm you would have stayed in that hick town that you came from. If you mean is the city where you'll find what you're looking for, you got the wrong person. I can't tell you something that you don't even know yourselves.'

After the Minstrel Boy's outburst, there was an awkward silence. Billy looked at the ground and spoke tentatively.

'Where are you headed?'

'Some other place.'

'How would it be if we came with you?'

The Minstrel Boy pointed at the motorcycle.

'It don't take but one.'

'That's a pity.'

'Not really. I'm headed for one place, and you're on the road to that city over the hill. We just met in passing. It doesn't call for anyone to change their plans. You go your way, and I'll carry on along mine.

'Sure. I guess we'll be seeing each other.'

The Minstrel Boy nodded.

'That's possible. So long.'

He was walking back to the bike, pulling on his helmet, when Reave called him back.

'You wouldn't have anything to eat, would you? I mean, something you could spare.'

'You run out of food?'

'Yeah.'

He fumbled in one of the big patch pockets and pulled out a small package.

'Have a cookie.'

'Uuh…'

'Have two. In fact, if you're hungry, take the whole packet.'

He tossed the cookies to Reave and then turned and walked away. He kicked the bike into life and swung back on to the dirt road. Billy and Reave watched until he was out of sight. Then they turned, and started up the hill.

30

*H*er/Their *sensors had long detected the existence and location of the place. Now it was coming close. She/They was filled with hope. All caution was abandoned as She/They cut a straight line through the grey fabric of disordered matter. She/They was homing in on the place of stasis.*

It was a natural fold in the fabric that would have been safe on its own. With the addition of the generated field, it was the ideal place for Her/Them to heal Her/Their wounds and restore Her/Their full potential.

As She/They drew closer She/They discovered that humans were occupying the fold. It was they who had built and still operated the generator. They would be a nuisance, but would not constitute a danger to the delicate energy transfer that She/They had to perform. She/They would rather that they weren't standing around gawping at Her/Them, but it couldn't be helped.

To Her/Them, the generators typified the attitude of the humans, crude machines that produced a semblance of stability. The humans seemed content with them, but to Her/Them they were an ugly half measure. An expedient answer to a question that demanded absolutes.

It pained Her/Them to have to resort to their rough power, but the present necessity dictated it.

She/They slowed down as a landscape formed beneath Her/Them. She/They floated slowly down a bare grey hill, at the bottom of which there was a seemingly pointless land transport that ran on a circular track. Beyond a line of tall cultivated plants lay the dwellings of the humans and the mean centre of the stable area.

She/They moved towards it.

31

Billy and Reave reached the top of the hill and looked out over a destroyed valley. There was a city, just like the Minstrel Boy had predicted. He hadn't, however, prepared them for the sight that met their eyes.

The war zone at Dur Shanzag was the only thing that Billy could compare it with, and even there, there hadn't been such a terrible destruction of the landscape.

The centre piece of the whole area was a huge white tower that soared thousands of feet into the air, dwarfing the domes and high-rise buildings that clustered round its immediate base. A wall ran round the tower and its attendant structures. Beyond the wall the desolation began in earnest. Like a dark stain on the earth, miles of shacks and ruins spread out from the walls of the inner citadel, and across almost the whole valley. In the area of the shacks, there were huge faults in the fabric that drilled giant circular holes in the broken-down city. The size and number of the faults seemed to diminish near to the citadel, and around the walls the ground was quite stable.

A thousand little fires seemed to be burning among the shacks and the air of the valley was foul and polluted. A filthy river sluggishly wound its way through the ruins. Its banks were crowded with all shapes and sizes of dilapidated craft. Others crawled slowly across its surface. The streets and alleys between the shacks were thronged with jostling humanity. They were a total contrast to the area inside the walls, where a pristine order and calm seemed to reign.

Billy looked doubtfully at Reave.

'You think this is really the place to go?'

Reave surveyed the valley.

'It don't look too pretty, but there's people. It can't be all bad.'

Billy wished silently that he shared Reave's optimism.

'Okay then, let's go.'

They started down into the valley. Before they'd reached the bottom, the road had changed direction twice to skirt huge faults in the side of the hill. They made their way down to the flat lands and found themselves among the outer edges of the shacks. They seemed to be built out of any and every material that might be at hand and could be crudely knocked together. Some were built around the ruins of older and what had once been more substantial buildings.

Thin, ragged children peered out of doorways, and there was an air of appalling squalor and poverty. Billy glanced at Reave.

'It don't look like people have too much of a good time round these parts.'

Reave pointed to the tower that rose high above them into the polluted air.

'I bet the folk up there do all right. That's got to be where the high living goes on.'

'You think we can get in there?'

Billy looked at their torn, filthy clothes. He rubbed a hand over his chin. It felt as though he hadn't shaved for a week. Reave just grinned.

'We can but try.'

They walked on deeper into the city. They passed more and more people. Three times, Billy tried to approach groups of people and talk to them. Each time, before he could say anything, they shrank away from him and hid their faces in their filthy rags. Disconcerted, Billy went back to Reave.

'I don't know what's wrong with us, but nobody seems to want to know us.'

'Maybe they don't like strangers.'

'They seem terrified when I try to get near them. There's something else, as well, that bothers me.'

'Yeah? What's that?'

'Well, I don't know if it's the bad air, or something wrong with my eyes, but there's something sort of, how would you call it, insubstantial about them. Like you could shine a bright light right through them. Do you know what I mean?'

Reave looked around and slowly nodded.

'They do seem kind of transparent. Like ghosts or something. I thought it was just a trick of the light.'

He pointed towards the tower again.

'That looks pretty damn solid.'

Something moved in Billy's memory.

'I know what these people look like. They're just like the folks we saw on the road out of Graveyard.'

Reave looked at Billy in puzzlement.

'What folks?'

Billy remembered how Reave had been asleep when he and the Minstrel Boy had seen the strange column of prisoners and their sinister guards pass them on the broken road.

'It was just something that reminded me and the... Hey! Look at that.'

A medium-sized fault had suddenly appeared some twenty yards down the road. Two shacks and about a dozen people had flickered out of existence. All that remained was a circular hole in the ground. For a few seconds, Billy and Reave stood transfixed, then, simultaneously, they both hit the buttons on their portapacs.

'This whole fucking place is falling to pieces!'

'I think we ought to try for the citadel. If we can't get inside, I'd rather we got the hell out of here.'

Reave nodded.

'I'm with you, Billy boy.'

They hurried on. A crowd had gathered around the newly formed fault, but it quickly dispersed as Billy and Reave approached.

'They seem to treat us like poison.'

'We don't look too good.'

'Neither do they.'

'That's true.'

They turned into a broader avenue, where men and women struggled under heavy burdens. A group of children strained to pull a large clumsy cart with big solid wheels. A man walked beside them with a long cane, encouraging them to greater efforts. As before, the crowds hastily parted to let Billy and Reave pass.

A commotion at the far end of the avenue caught their attention. A sleek and very solid-looking, field-grey armoured car was forcing its way through the crowd, who fell over each other to get out of the way. Reave quickly glanced at Billy. The armoured car seemed to be heading straight for them.

'Think we should run?'

A loudhailer mounted on the armoured car supplied the answer.

'You there! Stop! Do not attempt to move!'

Billy groaned.

'Not again.'

'Why always us?'

'There seems to be something about authority that makes it home in on strangers.'

The armoured car squealed to a stop beside them, and the turret swivelled ominously, pointing the snout of some kind of heat weapon at them. The speaker boomed again.

'Take one pace away from each other and place your hands on your heads!'

Billy and Reave did as they were told, and a hatch in the side of the machine swung open. Two men in grey uniforms and steel helmets climbed out and covered Reave and Billy with machine pistols. Tear-gas canisters and long, flexible rubber truncheons hung from the webbing of their tunics. Patches on their shoulders carried the single word 'Personnel' and the figure 3.

For Billy, there was something strangely familiar about their captors. Then he had a horrific flash of recognition. Their uniforms were the same as those of the sinister guards he'd seen on the road out of Graveyard. The fear he had felt then came back to him. He broke out in a cold sweat.

One of the uniformed men poked Billy with his gun.

'What are you doing here?'

'Just passing through.'

'The two of you, together?'

'Yes.'

'And what is your purpose for coming here?'

'We got lost, and this was the first city we came to.'

'It's hardly satisfactory. You'd better come with us.'

'But we...'

Before they could protest, they were bundled into the back of the armoured car. Their wrists were clamped into manacles on the wall, and they roared away. Both the vehicle and the men inside it were just as solid as Billy or Reave, and had none of the ghostly appearance of the rest of the population.

The machine halted, and through a small ventilator Billy could see they were waiting to enter a tunnel that led through the tower's perimeter wall. A thick steel door slid back and they moved on. After a couple of minutes the armoured car halted and the rear hatch opened. Billy and Reave were released from their manacles and ordered to get out. They were pushed into an enclosed courtyard where an escort, in similar uniforms to the armoured-car crew, waited for them. One of the escort, who had a figure 2 on his shoulder instead of a 3, walked over to the car commander. He jerked a thumb at Billy and Reave.

'What are these two?'

'Suspicious persons. Possibly vagrancy and unemployment.

Possession of unauthorized stasis equipment. I was bringing them in for Search, Tests and Questioning.'

He turned to the escort.

'Take these two down for ST&Q.'

The escort saluted, surrounded Billy and Reave and marched them away. Billy leaned close to Reave.

'Looks like we're getting inside the tower, though…'

One of the escorts punched Billy in the side of the head, and he staggered.

'Talking by prisoners is not permitted.'

They were pushed into what looked like a service lift. It sank at high speed to a deep sub-basement level. The lift gates clanged open, and they were marched out into a large, white-tiled room. A stainless-steel counter ran down one side of the wall. Behind it were three men and a woman, in uniform shirt sleeves with the same Personnel-3 shoulder patches. As the escort marched out of the lift, one of them looked up.

'What have you got there?'

'Two prisoners for ST&Q.'

'We'll have to throw them in the tank for a couple of hours. They've got a lot upstairs.'

The escort pushed Billy and Reave towards the counter.

'Just so long as you sign for them, I don't care what you do.'

'Okay.'

The man behind the counter picked up a clipboard. He scribbled something on it, tore off a slip and handed it to one of the escort. Then he turned to Billy and Reave.

'Right, you two. Let's have you.'

He looked round at one of his companions behind the counter.

'Bring your gun. We'll ID them and then put them down.'

The second man picked up a machine pistol, while the other tucked a file card and a set of electronic keys under his arm. Billy and Reave were taken through a series of small rooms where they were stripped, fingerprinted, photographed, blood-typed and X-rayed. Their clothes, guns and portapacs were confiscated. They were given dog tags with a number printed on them and pushed through a steel door, down a short flight of steps and into a large bare room with a concrete floor and smooth tiled walls. Bright striplights were buried in the roof behind thick unbreakable glass. An iron bench ran down the middle of the room. Two of the ragged ghostly men from the outer city sat hunched up on it. Billy and Reave both sat down and looked round the room.

High up in the ceiling was the unmistakable fisheye of a closed-circuit camera. There was also a loudspeaker hung in each corner of the room. Despite himself, Billy grinned. It was the first jail he'd ever been in with quad sound.

Billy moved closer to one of the prisoners and whispered out of the corner of his mouth.

'What you in for, buddy?'

'Got arrested.'

'Listen, uh… if you don't mind me asking. How come you folks look the way you do?'

'No power.'

'Huh?'

'No power. Th' field ain't too strong outside of th' wall an' we jus' grow this way. Take alla power t' keep t' tower up. It's like we…'

The speakers crackled into life.

'Prisoners will remain silent! You two on the bench, move apart!'

Billy slid down the bench and glanced covertly at Reave.

'Looks like they watch all the time.'

The speakers spluttered angrily.

'Silence in there!'

Billy wondered what happened if anyone just ignored the speakers. He thought about the long rubber truncheons and decided not to be the one to put it to a test.

There was nothing for either Billy or Reave to do except sit with his own thoughts. There seemed to be rules against everything. Prisoners had to face the camera. Prisoners must not cross their legs or hide their hands. The speakers screamed and yelled. At first Billy had thought that this jail, with its stainless-steel and antiseptic white tiles, would prove a whole lot better than the lock-up at Dur Shanzag, but after a couple of hours under the eye of the camera and continual barking of the speakers he wasn't so sure.

'79014 will stand facing the door!'

Billy looked at his dog tag. It wasn't him. One of the men from the outer city reluctantly stood up and shuffled over to the door. He seemed to grow more and more transparent. His thin shoulders hunched and seemed to be trying to wrap themselves round his narrow chest. The door was flung open with a crash. Two grey-uniformed Personnel men clattered in, grabbed him by the arm and bundled him out. In a final, futile effort of resistance he clung to the door frame and struggled with the guards. One of them unclipped his truncheon and brought it down on the man. He slumped on the floor, and was dragged out. Reave looked at Billy, his face had gone white.

'Jesus. Did you…'

The speaker roared.

'Silence!'

'They beat him un...'

'Silence! This is your last warning!'

Reave slumped on the bench with his head clasped in his hands.

'Prisoners will not hide their faces. Prisoners will face the camera.'

Reave sat up scowling sullenly. A heavy, ominous silence settled over the room. It seemed to Billy that it was all over. He could think of nothing that might turn up to get them out of the place. Hope of rescue seemed a very long way off. Again the speakers barked.

'79021 face the door. 79022 face the door.'

Billy and Reave examined their dog tags.

'That's us.'

'Jesus.'

'Silence!'

They walked slowly towards the door, feeling naked and helpless.

32

The Steward-l left, and AA Catto stepped into the shower. Her body felt pleasantly tired and, for once, she wanted nothing more than to lie back and think over the events of the day. She might not have gone along with everything that had happened, but, all in all, it had been more interesting than most parties. The 360-degree needle jets struck her body from every direction, and it tingled exquisitely. She flicked on the warm air and, once dry, she flopped back on to her bed.

She had had enough of her own reflection for a while, and she dimmed the ceiling mirror, and the surface was covered by a swirl of yellow moiré patterns. She stared at them and gradually she felt her body begin to float.

She flicked on the alphaset and adjusted it to a medium setting. A sense of euphoric wellbeing spread from her head to her toes and fingertips. The combination of the alpha waves and visual stimulation sent her drifting out to a soft yellow haze that was far more beautiful a high than could be obtained from any of the ordinary pharmaceuticals. She rolled sensuously on the bed, and it was slowly twisting across the universe. It was as though she was basking in the light of a thousand lazy suns.

A melodic tune pulsed through her beautiful universe and something suggested that it didn't fit. The face of the Valentino Steward floated across her memory. It really was a good idea to design her own specials. It was a delicious idea. The idea of a constant stream of custom-made lovers gave her a hot liquid feeling deep inside the warm cosmos of her body.

The tone came again and AA Catto realized that it was the console. She was back on the bed again, stretching out an unsteady hand to the answer button.

'Yeah?'

Her voice was far away and dreamy. Unintelligible sounds came from the speaker and the screen was a random blur of drifting colours. AA Catto giggled. 'Who is that wanting to speak to me?'

'It's me, Juno Meltzer.'

'Juno... how nice to hear... from you... Juno.'

The words became gibberish again. AA Catto listened to them with rapt interest.

'I'm not very sure what you're trying to say to me, Juno. Your words are not very clear.'

Juno Meltzer's face swam slightly more into focus, but the colour still changed and floated off the screen.

'If you shut down the alphaset you might be able to make some sense out of what I'm saying.'

'Now maybe that would be a possibility.'

'Switch off the damn alphaset for a minute.'

AA Catto didn't like the idea.

'Juno, I...'

'Turn it off, for God's sake.'

AA Catto's hand went out to the alpha control before her brain realized exactly what it was doing. She hit reality with a bump.

'Damn you, Juno. What do you want?'

'I suppose you haven't had your vid channel open.'

'AA Catto scowled. Surely the stupid girl hadn't called her from her blissful state to talk about vidshows.

'Of course I haven't. I've been out of my brain for hours. Why?'

'There was something very interesting on newsfax.'

'Newsfax? Are you crazy? You called me up to tell me about newsfax. I had the ceiling going and was right out on alphas.'

'That was evident.'

'Well now you've brought me down, what was so wonderful on newsfax?'

'Personnel have arrested two strangers in the L-4 area.'

AA Catto shrugged.

'So? Personnel are always arresting L-4s.'

'No, no, they weren't L-4s. They were strangers. They claim

they're from beyond the water. They said they came through the swamp.'

'You mean that they claim to be...'

'That's right. They're real, genuine natural-selection humans.'

'Not gene-jobs or L-4s?'

'Plain folks if their stories are true.'

'Then they're just like us?'

'I wouldn't go so far as to say that. Just because the DNA structure's intact doesn't immediately make them the equal of anyone in the five families. Even when there were plenty of natural humans running around, we were still pretty superior.

'That's true.'

'Punch up a re-run on the newsfax item. They're quite interesting.'

'Hold on then, I'll split-screen.'

AA Catto pressed a series of buttons, and Juno Meltzer's image was pushed to the left of the screen. On the right was a film clip of two hard, unkempt-looking men being led across a compound by an escort of Personnel-3s. AA Catto clapped her hands in delight.

'I want one. I want one.'

Juno Meltzer moved back to take up the whole screen.

'What do you mean, you want one?'

'I could have a party or something. They look very different. They look as though they might be interesting.'

'They look dirty, and like they might be carrying all kinds of horrible diseases.'

'Oh, they can be cleaned up and decontaminated. I still want one.'

Juno Meltzer looked doubtful.

'Don't you think it's going a bit far? I mean, you know, outsiders?'

'I always thought you told everyone that you couldn't go far enough.'

'Yes, but...'

AA Catto interrupted Juno's protests.

'I don't care. I want one. I want one before anybody else gets them. I wouldn't put it past my loathsome little brother to try to get his hands on them.'

'I heard something about you and your brother...'

'You keep quiet about that, Juno Meltzer, or I'll kill you. Understand?'

'I...'

'Listen, I'll talk to you later. I've got to call Personnel before Valdo does.'

AA Catto cut the connection and punched some more buttons. A hard-faced man in grey appeared on the screen.

'Personnel. May I help you?'

'I want the prisoners who claim to be from outside sent up here straight away.'

'They're under interrogation at the moment.'

'The interrogation must be stopped. I want them sent straight up to me, after they've been showered and disinfected.'

'I'll see what I can do, Miss Catto.'

AA Catto slammed her small fist into the console.

'You'll do it.'

'Yes, Miss Catto.'

33

'**N**ame?'

'Billy.'

'Billy what?'

'Billy Oblivion.'

There were two of them. One playing Mutt, the other playing Jeff. They'd been through his name and origins. The friendly one put a hand on Billy's shoulder.

'Where are you from, Billy? Where's Pleasant Gap?'

'I've no idea. I've been through the nothings so many times.'

'Liar.'

The bad guy lashed at Billy with his fist. His head exploded in a painful shower of stars and he sagged against the restraining straps that held him in the hard, upright chair. The chair was bolted to the floor in the centre of a small bare room. The bad guy pushed the bare light globe so it swung backwards and forwards in front of Billy's face. The bad guy put his face very close to Billy. Billy could see his strong white teeth and feel his breath on his face. His voice dropped to a vicious whisper.

'You're a fucking little liar. You're a dirty little LA who managed to get his hands on a portable generator.'

The good guy smiled sympathetically.

'You'd do well to tell him the truth. He'll only hurt you if you don't.'

'But I'm not an…'

'Where did you get the generator, kid?'

'In Pleasant Gap.'

'Where's Pleasant Gap?'

'I told you. I don't know any…'

Smash! Billy's head reeled.

'Where did you get the generator?'

'Pleasant...'

Smash.

'Name?'

'Billy, Billy Oblivion.'

'Place of origin?'

'I...'

'Are you going to tell us the truth, kid?'

'I've been trying to. I'm not an L-4. I don't even know what an L-4 is. I didn't know there were any laws here against portapacs. I don't even know where here is.'

'How did you get here, then, mister outsider?'

'On foot.'

'Through the swamp?'

'After our canoe sank.'

'In the swamp?'

'Yes.'

Smash!

There was a pause while they waited for Billy to be sick. The good guy lifted Billy's head.

'You really shouldn't lie to my friend here. He's got a whole lot of sophisticated stuff that he could use on you. This kind of thing is only openers for him.'

The bad guy laughed.

'Think I should tell him about a few of them? Like maybe the needles that you can stick through the flesh and scrape his bones with.'

The good guy shook his head.

'I don't think we'll need it with this boy. I'm sure he'll cooperate. Let's try again. Name?'

'Billy Oblivion.'

'Place of origin?'

'I...'

'Place of origin?'

'If I tell you, he'll just hit me.'

'Not if you tell the truth.'

'But I WAS telling the truth. I did start out from Pleasant...'

Smash!

The bad guy scowled.

'I thought we'd sorted out that business.'

'I don't know what else to say. It's the truth.'

'Why not...'

The door opened and another grey-uniformed figure came into the room. The bad guy smiled at him.

'What the hell do you want? Don't you know we're questioning a prisoner?'

'They want your prisoner up at the top.'

'The hell they do, we've only just begun to work on him.'

'They want him and the other one. Straight away.'

The bad guy started to button his tunic. 'Who wants him? I'll sort them out.'

'It's a directorate order.'

'Directorate?'

'Miss AA Catto called in herself. Shower, delouse, and send them both straight up.'

'What does she want them for?'

'To fuck her, probably. That's all the families seem to think about.'

'Why can't she get herself a Steward-l? I got to turn in a report on these two.'

The third man shrugged.

'It ain't my problem. Orders is orders.'

'When Data want their report, I'm going to send them straight to you.'

'Do what you like.'

He took a slip of paper out of his pocket and handed it to the bad guy.

'Here's a receipt for prisoners 79021 and 79022. They're off your hands now. You don't have to worry about it.'

The bad guy took it grudgingly.

'Okay, but I don't like it.'

Billy felt himself being unstrapped from the chair. He was hauled to his feet, and at that point he passed out.

He came to under the shower. Reave, who'd been holding up Billy's head, helped him to his feet and supported him.

'They sure messed you up.'

'Yeah. You were lucky they picked me to work on first.'

'Do you know what they're going to do with us now?'

'I was pretty groggy, but I heard something about how we were being sent to the top. Whatever that means. Some guy came in and stopped the other two beating me up.'

'Maybe they're about to start treating us right.'

The water stopped and jets of warm air dried them. Reave helped Billy out of the shower, and a grey-uniformed guard led them to a glass cubicle and told them to step inside. They both suffered a moment of panic as yellow-green fumes began to fill the chamber. They found that they could still breathe, even when the gas filled the whole cubicle. An extractor fan was switched on and it quickly cleared. The guard opened the door and led them to a table on the other side of the room, where pants and jackets of some striped material were laid out.

Billy and Reave quickly dressed. They were each given a pair of plastic slip-on shoes and led through a series of corridors to a moving walkway. The walkway led eventually to a set of blue steel doors. The guard inserted an electronic key and the doors hissed open.

Beyond them was a lift. A lift, however, that was fitted with contour seats. The guard told Billy and Reave to sit. He strapped them in and then stepped back outside. The doors shut and the lift rocketed upwards at a tremendous acceleration that pushed Billy and Reave down into their seats. Minutes passed and finally they came to rest. The doors sighed open again. Three men in light blue uniforms and short-cropped blond hair were waiting for them. Each held what looked to Reave like some kind of stun weapon.

Billy and Reave were unstrapped from their seats and led on to another moving walkway. High, almost subliminal music came from hidden speakers, and the corridors were decorated in rich gold and pure white. The city seemed to be presenting another face to them. Reave leaned close to Billy and whispered in his ear.

'This looks a good deal better than down below.'

Their guards seemed to ignore the conversation. They changed direction twice, then left the walkway. They marched Billy and Reave down a short corridor and halted in front of a pair of gold double doors. One of the men in blue pressed a bell. After a short delay the door slid back and with one of the guards, they stepped inside a luxurious apartment. In the centre of the large main room a girl of about thirteen, wearing heavy make-up and a slightly incongruous silver sheath dress, stood flanked by two well-developed blondes in short pink tunics and thigh-length pink boots. The girl looked angrily at the two guards.

'Who told you to bring them to me in that condition?'

'That was how they were sent up, Miss Catto.'

'In prison suits, and one of them covered in bruises. Is it the way I'm supposed to be presented with people? I want clothes for them, and a Steward with shaving equipment. I also want a Medic for the one who's been beaten up, and the names and numbers of the Personnel officers who did it. Do you understand?'

'Of course, Miss Catto.'

'Then get out and see to it. I want it done immediately.'

The man in blue bowed and hurried out. The girl turned to Reave and Billy, and smiled graciously.

'I deeply regret that you've been treated so badly. Please be seated. The Steward will see that everything is put right. I am AA Catto.'

Reave nodded his head and shuffled a little. He was bemused by the way the girl's manner was such a sharp contrast to her appearance. She looked like a child who had scarcely reached puberty, but behaved like a mature woman. He made stumbling introductions.

'My name's Reave, Miss, and my partner here, he's called Billy. He normally does the talking but he's feeling a bit rough since your cops, or whatever they were, worked him over.'

AA Catto gestured to a pair of antique tubular chrome and black leather chairs.

'Please sit down. You both must be exhausted.'

Reave grinned.

'Thanks ma'am, we are kind of ready to cave in.'

Billy said nothing, and flopped into a chair. AA Catto turned to one of the girls in pink.

'The injured one is no use to me as he is. You'd better arrange for him to have a guest suite down on 1009. Detail two Hostess-1s to look after him. They're to extend him the full service. Get them to explain what that includes. He can be taken down there when the Medic comes.'

She turned her attention back to Reave.

'So where do you two wanderers come from?'

At the question, Billy's eyes opened and flickered round. Then he saw where he was and closed them again. Reave coughed and shuffled his feet.

'A place that goes by the name of Pleasant Gap, Miss.'

'Is that beyond the water?'

'Beyond the water and then some.'

'How wonderful. We meet very few new people here.'

Reave smiled.

'Sometimes you can meet too many new people. Perhaps you got to meet our friend the Minstrel Boy. He was leaving town as we were coming an.

AA Catto frowned politely.

'I don't recall anyone of that name. Does he come from Pleasant Gap, also?'

'I don't rightly know where he comes from.'

Before the conversation could go any further, the door buzzed, and one of the Hostess-1s admitted a Medic, two Stewards and three more

Hostesses. AA Catto hurried about the room supervising the various operations. She chose wardrobes for Billy and Reave from a design catalogue, she watched as the Steward fitted Reave's chin into a permashave, and stood beside the Medic-1 as he gave Billy a series of shots, and prepared to have him moved. Once the clothes had been ordered and Billy dispatched to his temporary apartment, she sat down next to Reave.

'Now that's all done, you must take off those ugly clothes and get better acquainted.'

She patted his knee and smiled. Reave gestured to the two remaining Hostess-1s.

'What about them?'

AA Catto looked up.

'What about them? They're here to assist us in any way we want. Unless, of course, they embarrass you, then I'll send them away.'

Reave looked at the two girls appraisingly.

'No, let 'em stay. They look like they might come in handy.'

He stood up and slowly began to strip off his striped suit.

Before he'd finished, AA Catto was already pressing her thin hard body up against *his*.

34

Billy could remember very little of what happened after he'd been taken out of the lift. He dimly recalled a strange young girl talking to them. He could remember a figure in white who did something that made the pain stop, but after that everything had been a drowsy jumble of dreams and reality. He was carried along corridors, through doors, the images of his grey-uniformed interrogators loomed in front of him. He'd screamed and fought, and then been comforted by visions of blonde hair and pink material stretched over firm breasts. A machine that buzzed and gave off violet light was moved over the damaged areas of his body. The figure in white had come and gone. The pink visions had remained to save him from the questions. The column of ghosts had shuffled past. Briefly he had imagined himself in Pleasant Gap, then he had sunk down into a dark, warm pit of unconsciousness.

35

A Catto and Reave lay naked on her huge bed. The ceiling above them was a large glowing mirror. Her reflection smiled down at him and her lips nuzzled his ear.

'Do you like me, Reave? Do I please you?'

'Yes, very much.'

'Do you think I'm beautiful?'

'Very beautiful.'

She propped herself up on one elbow.

'I have a present for you, Reave.'

'You mean the clothes? They're too much. I've never had clothes like that.'

AA Catto smiled and shook her head. 'No, not the clothes. Something else.'

Reave sat up.

'What is it?'

'Wait and I'll show you.'

She called to one of the Hostess-1s.

'Bring my special present for Mister Reave.'

They came over to the bed carrying a box made of purple leather. AA Catto opened it, and Reave saw, lying on a pad of dark red velvet, a collar that looked as though it would fit round a man's neck. It was made of silver, about three inches wide and decorated with fine gold inlay. Beside it was a tiny ring, its exact miniature. AA Catto picked up the collar and snapped it round Reave's neck.

'There.'

Reave put his hand to it.

'It's very pretty. I don't normally wear jewellery.'

AA Catto smiled.

'You'll wear it for me?'

Reave stroked her tiny breast.

'Sure.'

She slipped the ring on her third finger, and chanted in a childish singsong.

'The collar for you, and the ring for me.'

It was the first time Reave had heard her sound anything like she looked. Her lovemaking was in no way childlike. Reave remembered being surprised by some of the things she'd suggested. His finger fiddled with the fastenings at the back of the collar.

'I don't seem to be able to get this off.'

AA Catto kissed him.

'You can't.'

'I can't?'

She held up her finger with the ring on it.

'Only if I want you to. It's controlled from here. I twist the ring one way, and the collar's locked. I twist it the other and it's released.'

'Can I take it off now? I'm not really used to wearing it.'

AA Catto rolled over and began to play with him.

'Not yet. It does a lot of other things as well.'

36

Billy opened his eyes. He was in an unfamiliar room, lying on the largest, most comfortable bed he had ever slept in. One of the pink and blonde girls came into his field of vision. She smiled at him.

'May I help you, Mister Billy?'

Billy struggled to sit up.

'I don't know for sure. How long have I been out?'

'Just over five hours, Mister Billy.'

Billy stretched, and patted his face with exploratory fingers. 'I feel amazingly recovered.'

'The treatment has an almost total success rate.'

Billy grinned.

'So it would seem.'

Another Hostess-1 joined the first one. 'How may we serve you, Mister Billy?'

Billy scratched his head. They were both smiling at him so invitingly that he began to wonder if maybe he was still delirious.

'What can you do for me?'

They both chorused. 'Anything you might ask, Mister Billy.'

'How about some coffee and a cigar?'

'Certainly, Mister Billy. Shall we both fetch them, or would you like one of us to stay here and entertain you?'

Billy laughed.

'Does that mean you tell me jokes or join me in bed?'

'Whatever you wish, Mister Billy. If you find one of us attractive we are available to serve you in any way.'

'Yeah?'

'Of course.'

'Okay then. Let's do it. One of you go get the breakfast and the other climb in with me.'

One of the Hostess-1s began to take off her pink tunic while the other went to arrange the food. Billy grinned at the one who was leaving.

'You can join us when you get through.'

37

AA Catto and Reave were locked together, intertwined, moving furiously against each other. The gasps and groans mingled as their excitement grew and grew. Reave moaned as he felt himself on the verge of orgasm. AA Catto opened her eyes and her hand moved to the ring. Reave screamed as the collar sent a violent shock flashing through his nervous system. His spine arched and his body shook in uncontrollable spasms. AA Catto dug her nails into his back and then sank back with a satisfied smile. Reave shuddered and passed out.

38

She/They floated up a flat area that ran between the human habitations. Her/Their energy was depleted, and She/They moved very slowly, but now She/They was within reach of the stasis point and everything would be well.

The human beings spilled out of their crude buildings and gawped at the strange creature who floated down their main street. She/They had always found the childish curiosity of humans an inconvenience, but under the circumstances it couldn't be avoided. The stasis point was all-important to the task She/They had to perform.

A sense of relief came over Her/Them as She/They reached the absolute centre of the field. The standing pair carefully laid their injured third fractionally above the dust of the street. The inert form was supported a few inches above the ground by a faint blue glow. The remaining two stood erect, and one of them slowly raised the energy wand.

A crowd of humans had surrounded the triple form, but remained at a safe distance. Their shouts and chattering died away as a dim red light enveloped the three figures. They backed away a few paces as the light grew in intensity and rose up the spectrum through orange to yellow. The light became stronger and stronger, turned green, blue and finally an intense violet that almost hid the figures from the view of the crowd.

The sky above the little town flickered on and off as She/They drained incalculable amounts of energy. Lightning flashed in the distant, grey hills, and claps of thunder rattled the buildings. The glass in some of the windows shattered and collapsed, and a tree, down beyond the last house, crashed across the main street. The town generator whined and vibrated as it tried to cope with the incredible overload. A gale-force wind howled down the street, whipping up tall spirals of dust. Some of the older humans sank to their knees and began praying.

There was a flash of intense white light. The humans who had been watching it turned away, temporarily blinded. The light around Her/Them slowly faded down to the dull red again. The pitch of the generator fell to normal, and the sky returned to its usual colour and brightness. The inert figure on the ground slowly rose to join the other two. She/They was once again complete. The triple form rose slightly and began to drift back the way She/They had come. Towards the end of the street, She/They began to gather speed. Her/Their desire was to get away from the gawping, ignorant humans. Her/Their trials and pain were over, all that remained was the continuing search for the place of invulnerability. A place of solitude that She/They could render stable and make secure from the inroads of the disruptors. There She/They could restore Her/Their power, meditate and study, and prepare for the ultimate campaign. There would be other battles and other reversals, but Her/Their projections always led to the final conflict. It could only resolve itself in one of two ways. Her/Their form would be broken and become part of the chaos, or She/They would restore order to every level of the fabric of reality.

For an instant She/They wondered what would be the fate of the humans when that time came, then, dismissing it as scarcely relevant, Her/Their form rose up the surface of the grey hills and vanished into the formless, swirling nothing.

The crowd in the main street slowly dispersed. Old Eli went to inspect the damage to the windows in his store. Jed McArthur scratched his head and looked at his cousin Cal.

'Did you see that?'

'Right in the main street of Pleasant Gap.'

'*Without so much as a by-your-leave.*'
Cousin Cal looked around suspiciously.
'*It was them two boys leaving the town and wandering abroad. I knew it was tempting fate. Outlandish things was bound to happen, if folks started coming and going just as they pleased.*'
Jed McArthur spat in the dust.
'*I don't know what things are coming to.*'

39

Billy was having trouble accepting that the whole thing was real. The two young girls who now lay, one on each side of him, in the huge luxurious bed were hard to reconcile with the horror of the arrest and interrogation. The girls, whose pink uniforms littered the floor of the apartment, acted as though they were totally devoid of character. Their whole existence seemed to be directed towards pleasing his slightest desire. Beyond that, there was nothing. It was something that made Billy slightly uneasy. They were more like programmed machines than real people.

They showed this constant anxiety over Billy's welfare, to the point where he felt almost under an obligation to produce more and more petty whims for them to indulge and keep themselves occupied. There seemed to be something strangely unhealthy about the whole city. All the people he had encountered, with the possible exception of the strange child whom he half remembered from his delirium, seemed to have had large sections of their personalities erased. Even the brutality of the Personnel men seemed to have been aimed, not so much at getting information out of him, but at rearranging his memory of the outside world. He stared at his reflection in the mirror ceiling and worried at the problem.

One of the girls seemed to sense his mood, and sat up.

'Are you unhappy, Mister Billy?'

Billy shook his head.

'No, not really.'

'You seem troubled.'

'I was just thinking, that's all.'

'You are unhappy.'

'I'm not, really.'

'Aren't thinking and unhappiness the same thing?'

'Not usually.'

'Would you like us to distract you?'

Billy laughed.

'I'm completely wiped out from being distracted.'

'Perhaps you'd like to watch one of the entertainment channels?'

'Okay.'

The girl reached out a hand to the bedside console and the screen flickered into life. Men in period costume hacked savagely at each other with swords and axes. Billy shook his head.

'I don't think so.'

The girl changed the channel. Two women and a crowd of dwarfs were engaged in slapstick pornography. Billy rolled over.

'I think we can forget the entertainment.'

The girl looked concerned.

'We are not pleasing you at all?'

'Sure you are. I'm quite happy.'

She gestured to the other girl.

'Perhaps it would amuse you if my colleague and I had sex with each other while you watched. We are often asked to do this. We are quite highly skilled.'

Billy laid a hand on her shoulder.

'Do you ever think of anything else but what would please the people you serve?'

The girl frowned.

'Of course not. What else is there?'

'Don't you ever just please yourself?'

'I'm a Hostess-1. I take pride in my rank. I find my pleasure from pleasing those I am assigned to. That is the natural order, it's the function of my class.'

Billy found it impossible to get through to her.

'Are you happy, though?'

'Of course.'

'Wouldn't you like to have people serve you?'

The girl immediately brightened.

'Does it please you to say obscene things to me? Perhaps you'd like to beat me?'

For a moment, Billy thought she was mocking him. Then he realized that she was perfectly serious. The concept of someone serving her was obscene according to her programming. The paradox was that she accepted it with pleasure. Before Billy could probe any further, the console buzzed and the girl reached out to answer it.

'Mister Billy's apartment. May I help you?'

Reave's voice came over the speaker. 'Let me talk to Billy, will you, babe?'

Billy moved into range of the camera. 'Hey Reave. How you doing, old buddy?'

Reave grinned.

'Just fine. It's a wild set-up they got here. Is everyone treating you right?'

Billy laughed.

'Falling over themselves to show me a good time. I got two broads down here that you wouldn't believe.'

'How you feeling after that going-over you got?'

'Fine. Completely recovered.'

Reave looked relieved.

'That's great. AA Catto's really sorry they did that to you.'

Billy lit a cigar and inhaled.

'Yeah? How you making out with her?'

Reave winked.

'I'm doing okay.'

He paused.

'Listen Billy. I got something to talk to you about. Can you come up here?'

Billy nodded.

'Sure. How do I get there?'

'I've no idea. Hold on.'

Reave vanished from the screen, and AA Catto moved into frame.

'Just tell your Hostess-1s. They'll bring you up here.'

Again Billy nodded.

'Okay, fine.'

The connection was cut, and Billy sat up in bed. 'I've got to go to AA Catto's apartment.'

The two girls sprang out of bed, hastily dressed and then helped Billy on with some of the clothes that AA Catto had chosen for him. Billy wasn't too sure about the red velvet jumpsuit that AA Catto had picked out of the catalogue, but he couldn't be bothered to argue, particularly as the Hostess-1s kept telling him how cute he looked. The girls led Billy along a series of walkways and corridors. They were admitted to AA Catto's apartment. Billy dismissed the girls, and went inside on his own.

Reave was sitting crosslegged on the floor. He was wearing a white silk robe and a fancy silver collar. Billy looked at him in surprise. It was a far cry from his dungarees. Billy smiled to himself but said nothing. AA Catto was sprawled across the bed covered only by a black shawl that did little to hide her nakedness. Reave glanced up as Billy crossed the room.

'Hey old buddy, how are you?'

Billy sat down in one of the antique chairs.

'Fine. You?'

'Oh, I'm okay.'

AA Catto sat up.

'Don't you think Reave looks pretty since I went to work on him?'

Billy noticed that, as well as the collar, Reave was wearing lipstick and eye shadow. Billy grinned.

'I never exactly thought of Reave as being pretty.'

AA Catto pouted.

'Of course he is. He's very, very pretty.'

'Yeah, maybe.'

He turned to Reave.

'What did you want to talk to me about?'

Reave looked a little uncomfortable.

'Oh yeah… uh… would you like a drink or something?'

'I'd like to know what you want to talk to me about. You're stalling, Reave.'

Reave looked at the floor, and then up at Billy.

'Well… It's as simple as this, man. I want to stay here.'

'What?'

'I like it here, Billy. I want to stay.'

'You're kidding?'

AA Catto moved to the end of the bed. Her shawl fell away, revealing tiny breasts with small brown nipples.

'He's quite serious. Reave has decided to stay here.'

'But why?'

'I like it here, Billy. You kept telling me that we were looking for something. Well, I've found it. I want to stay here.'

'Don't you think it's a bit early to decide?'

AA Catto answered for him.

'He's made up his mind. He's staying.'

Billy turned to face her.

'What have you done to him? Reave never used to wear make-up and jewellery.'

AA Catto's large blue eyes flashed with anger.

'What's wrong with make-up and jewellery?'

Billy shrugged.

'Nothing. It's just…'

'It's just that you've got a narrow hillbilly mind.'

Reave fingered his silver collar.

'It's not exactly how it appears, Billy. It's…'

AA Catto interrupted him.

'Shall I tell you how it really is, Billy? Shall I tell you what his pretty collar's really for?'

There was the hint of a sneer in her voice. Billy sat very still as AA Catto went on.

'The reason that Reave likes it here is that he doesn't have to think too much. It's easy for him.'

She held up her hand.

'See my ring. See how it matches Reave's pretty collar. They are linked together. With my little ring I can give him amazing pleasure, or I can punish him. He doesn't have to think about a thing.'

Billy swung round on Reave.

'Is this true, man? Is this what you want?'

Reave stared at the floor and said nothing. AA Catto again answered.

'It's what he wants. Watch.'

She turned her ring. Reave gasped and arched his back. Billy's mouth dropped open.

'You did that to him.'

Reave was shaking his head dazedly. AA Catto laughed.

'My little ring, and his pretty collar. He doesn't have to worry any more. He likes that.'

'You've made him into a pet.'

'He likes it.'

Billy stooped beside Reave. 'Do you, Reave? Is this what you want?'

Slowly Reave nodded.

'I guess so, Billy.'

'But you're her slave, man. Just an object to keep around the place. Is that the way you want it to be?'

'I think so, Billy.'

'You're crazy. What's going to happen when she gets tired of you?'

'I don't know. I'll deal with that when the time comes.'

AA Catto rolled over on the bed and smiled spitefully. 'What's the matter, Billy, are you upset because he's mine now? Did the two of you use to be lovers?'

Billy looked up in surprise.

'Of course not. It was nothing like that.'

'What was it like, then?'

'We... we were partners.'

'That's different?'

'Sure.'

'Well, you've lost him.'

Billy looked helplessly at Reave.

'Tell her, Reave. Tell her how we left Pleasant Gap to look for something good. Tell her how it was, Reave.'

He waved his hand round the room.

'We didn't come all this way, and go through all those troubles to end up with this. This ain't what we came looking for.'

Reave looked up at Billy. His voice was very quiet.

'I didn't come looking for anything, Billy. I didn't have no dream. I just came for the ride.'

Billy slumped in his chair. AA Catto draped her shawl round her shoulders, and stood up.

'It looks like that's it, Billy. You'll have to follow your dream on your own now. Reave's staying here with me. That's right, isn't it, Reave?'

Reave nodded silently. She smiled sweetly.

'Of course, you must feel free to be our guest for as long as you like. Maybe you'll decide to settle down here. I know some of the other ladies have their eyes on you.'

Billy stayed exactly three days.

On the first he lay around his apartment and sported with the Hostess-1s.

On the second he went to a party that AA Catto threw to show off Reave, and was taken off by Juno Meltzer to sport with her.

On the third he decided to leave. He left Juno Meltzer still asleep and made his way back to his own apartment. The Hostess-1s were waiting for him.

'Did you have a good night, Mister Billy?'

'Yeah. It was fine.'

'How may we serve you today? We have a few suggestions.'

'I'm leaving.'

'Leaving, Mister Billy?'

'That's what I said.'

'Have we displeased you?'

'Of course not. It's just time to move on.'

'We're sorry you don't like it here. Are there any services we may perform before you leave here?'

'Yeah. You could get me my old clothes, my portapac and my gun. If it's possible, I'd like some transport to the edge of town.'

'We'll have to clear it with Miss Catto.'

They had a brief conversation with AA Catto through the vid-screen and then turned back to Billy.

'Miss Catto has authorized your request. We'll arrange everything.'

They left the room, and reappeared half an hour later. They presented Billy with his clothes, which were cleaned and pressed, his belt, his portapac and his gun. He quickly changed and came back to the Hostess-1s. One of them gave Billy a leather shoulder bag.

'A gift from Miss Catto.'

It contained food concentrates and a water bottle.

'Did you fix transport?'

'There'll be a Personnel car in the compound. It will take you to the edge of the valley.'

'Okay. I guess I'll be going.'

He kissed both the girls, and grinned at them. 'Thanks for everything.'

They looked confused.

'It's not your place to thank us.'

He touched the door stud.

'I thought it would make a change.'

The doors closed behind him. He rode down in the lift, and followed the signs to the Personnel compound. A grey-uniformed driver saluted smartly and opened the car door. Billy sat in the back and smoked a cigar as he was whisked past the shacks and ruins. The car halted at the edge of the hills. Billy climbed out of the vehicle and the driver sped away without a word.

Billy turned and started to walk up the track. The thought crossed his mind that maybe he should have waited till the end of the day. Then he could have walked off into the sunset in the grand classic manner. He dismissed the idea as pointless. There was, after all, no one to watch.

SYNAPTIC MANHUNT

1

The total silence was only broken by the soft slow dripping of the water clock. The high, narrow room was lit by a solitary candle, and far corners of the dull stone walls were hidden in darkness. The room was bare and austere, but it had an atmosphere of absolute calm. There was no furniture apart from the iron stand that held the candle, the glass water clock on its wooden bench and a small raised dais in the very centre of the room. The dais was covered with a coarse-weave straw mat.

A figure sat on the dais. It was shrouded in a plain black robe, its legs were crossed and its hands lay in its lap with the fingers interlaced in a complicated pattern. Although the candle was placed directly in front of the figure, its head was sunk between the shoulders in such a way that the face was obscured by shadow. From the width of the shoulders, and the supple, powerful hands, which were clearly illuminated by the candle, it was obvious that the figure was that of a male.

The name of the male was Jeb Stuart Ho, although, right at that moment in time, Jeb Stuart Ho hardly existed. His pulse was down to the absolute minimum that would sustain life. His body temperature had reduced by half and his lungs hardly stirred. Except for his upright, cross-legged posture, the lay observer would have assumed him to be dead. But Jeb Stuart Ho was alive. The physical state that he was in was self-induced. He would, however, certainly die within a comparatively short time unless roused by some outside force. The art of terminal meditation was one that was slowly and painfully learned. Once the individual had reached that state there was no release from it except a sharp tap on the shoulder by another who was practised in the same skills.

Being so close to death and so dependent on outside help might have terrified any normal person. Jeb Stuart Ho was beyond terror. He knew nothing, although, at the same time, according to his philosophy, he knew everything. He was in a world that few people outside the temple ever visited. It was beyond the scope of language, beyond emotion and far past the reach of sight, taste, smell or touch.

A door at the far end of the room opened softly. Another man in a black robe entered and walked silently towards Jeb Stuart Ho on sandalled feet. He halted in front of the seated figure, and almost ritualistically took a short polished stick of hard dark wood out of his sleeve. He paused for a moment, and then struck a swift, light blow on Jeb Stuart Ho's shoulder. He stepped back and waited.

At first, nothing happened, and then the still figure made a soft noise. Jeb Stuart Ho was drawing air into his lungs. At first it was tiny amounts and his body scarcely moved. Then his chest began gradually to rise and fall as he sucked in deeper breaths. Finally, he completely filled his lungs, and began to raise his head. The mind of Jeb Stuart Ho seemed to float upwards. First into a place where it was warm, then sound invaded the comfortable area, the sighing of his blood as it slowly began to circulate through his veins. The pulse of his heart started, up, softly and in wide-spaced intervals at first, but then quickening and getting louder. His sense of touch came alive. He could feel the pressure of his body on the coarse mat beneath him. He was aware of the texture of the robe that covered his body. He knew that his mouth was dry and that his stomach would shortly begin to demand food. He rose towards the light. He opened his eyes, and an image of the dim room rushed in with dazzling brilliance.

Jeb Stuart Ho silently regarded the man standing in front of him. He was slimmer and younger than Ho, little more than a boy. His face was smooth and expressionless. Jeb Stuart Ho matched this first rush of sensation, which came after the deep meditation, with his memory. The boy was Nah Duc West. His pupil, his servant in the temple and his lover.

No spoken greeting was necessary between the two men. Ho simply stretched out his hand and touched the younger man. Then he rose to his feet and walked purposefully out of the room. The young man followed him.

The door of the meditation room led out into a high-ceilinged corridor. It was made from the same dull black stone as the walls of the room. The corridor was illuminated by glowing spheres set in the walls at regular intervals.

They walked down the perfectly straight corridor for some minutes until they came to a pair of double doors, decorated with elaborate carvings and flanked by two more figures in black robes. They appeared to recognize Jeb Stuart Ho, and stepped back, pushing the doors open. Once again, there was a trace of ritual in their action. Beyond the carved doors was a huge, brightly lit circular room. It had a domed ceiling that glowed with the same steady light as the globes.

The room was a hive of activity. Along one section of the curved stone wall, a line of black-robed figures sat on high stools, bent over desks and drawing tables that were littered with charts, graphs, columns of figures and computer printouts. Another long section of wall was taken up by a huge display screen where coloured lights and curved lines slowly shifted position. On a vast plan table in the centre of the room, more black-clothed figures moved transparent overlays with lines and points of colour drawn on them, similar to those on the display screen.

The most intense activity was centred round another section of the curved wall that took up nearly a third of the total circumference. The section was covered with a soft, translucent, ribbed material. The ribs ran vertically from the floor to the start of the domed ceiling. It bulged out slightly, and occasionally undulated. Behind the material there was a soft green glow that also moved and shifted. Some patches grew brighter, and others dimmed. The crowd of black robes that clustered round it were stroking the surface of the soft wall section with their hands. Their palms and fingertips moved in definite, precise patterns. Occasionally one of them would carefully insert a long, fine, silver needle into the material. The operations appeared to involve a high degree of skill.

The domed room was the heart of the entire temple. It was here that Jeb Stuart Ho's brothers carried on the eternal work. It was here that they monitored the progress of the various cultures that flourished in the sundered world that remained after the breakdown.

Over the centuries since the natural laws had ceased to be consistent and human life had clung to areas where artificial stasis could be generated, the brothers had worked single-mindedly on their never-ending task. They had observed and recorded the smallest event in the hundred thousand communities that survived in among the grey nothings. The most insignificant happening was plotted into their charts and included in their calculations. There was a saying among the brothers that even the fall of a sparrow was worthy of inclusion in their graphs, the graphs that charted the passage of past events and from which the brothers made their predictions for the future.

Jeb Stuart Ho had only been in the huge room four times before, but he fully understood the meaning of the coloured points and lines. Years of study in the seminary had equipped him to recognize and appreciate the meanings of the curves. The uphill struggle of the society seeking material progress, the plateau form of the stable culture, the clear straight lines of the stuff beam cities in the central ring, the elegant curve down to decadence: Jeb Stuart Ho could read the subtleties of history in the sudden variations of each curve. He could recognize the sudden termination that meant that disruption had hit a unit of civilization.

Jeb Stuart Ho stood in the doorway of the domed room. Slowly and discreetly his eyes moved across its mysteries. His gaze stopped at the ribbed, undulating section of wall. It was the outside face of the beast.

The living meditation that made the efforts of the brotherhood possible. He stared at it in reverence and awe. It was the whole centre and meaning of the temple. The bio-cybernetic mass of circuits and organic life was both master and servant. It computed the patterns from which the brothers made their predictions, It gave early warning of progressions that could become critical, and it ordered the brothers when and where to make their executive interventions.

To Jeb Stuart Ho it was the centre point of his existence. It was the permanence of the state that he could only achieve by terminal meditation. He admired the brothers who caressed the beast, the ones whose silver needles penetrated its transparent hide. He respected the skills with which they transferred information and instruction to and from the huge thinking unit.

He admired and respected them, but he didn't envy them. He had his own skills. He was, after all, an executive of the brotherhood. His training was just as awesome.

One of the black figures bent over the expanse of plan table straightened, detached itself from the group and approached Jeb Stuart Ho. The face above the black robe was that of a very old man. The skin was pink and soft like a baby's, terribly wrinkled and totally without hair. The eyes, however, had the look of purposeful calm that was common to all of the brothers.

The old man halted in front of Jeb Stuart Ho and bowed. Jeb Stuart Ho returned the bow.

'I have prepared, Teacher.'

The old man nodded gravely.

'And you are ready?'

His voice had none of the weakness or quaver that normally come with great age. Jeb Stuart Ho looked straight at the old man.

'I am ready, Teacher.'

The teacher raised an eyebrow and smiled gently.

'You are very certain for one who faces his first intervention.'

'All my training has led me to this point, and will carry me far beyond it.'

The teacher's eyes twinkled.

'So should you fail, the fault will lie in your training?'

Jeb Stuart Ho stood stiffly.

'I will not fail, Teacher.'

'You don't even know the details of the task that awaits you, Jeb Stuart Ho.'

'I will not fail.'

'As I said before, you are very confident.'

'An individual must not allow a false humility to cloud the knowledge of himself.'

'And you believe you have knowledge of your own readiness?'

'I know I am ready.'

'Suppose you were in error when you made this analysis of yourself?'

'If I was in error I would not be ready for the task.'

The teacher nodded.

'Then it must be the time for your instruction in the labours you have to perform.'

He took Jeb Stuart Ho by the arm, and led him back towards the carved doors.

'We will go to my chamber.'

The teacher led the way past the two impassive attendants, and back down the stone corridor. He halted before a door, opened it and ushered Jeb Stuart Ho inside. The room was similar to the one in which Jeb Stuart Ho had meditated. The water clock stood against the wall, the single candle burned in its holder. In this room, however, two raised daises stood side by side. Jeb Stuart Ho stood beside one of them until the teacher had seated himself. Then he too sat down, automatically crossing his legs and lacing his fingers in an attitude of meditation. There was a long pause while the teacher stared straight forward, apparently studying the water clock. Jeb Stuart Ho summoned energy to preserve his patience. Despite all his training he was still eager to learn about the task. At last the teacher spoke.

'We are required once again to intervene in the affairs of the world outside. Once again their pattern traces a path towards disaster.'

'I am eager to learn my part.'

The teacher continued to stare straight ahead.

'The loaf baked in eagerness will lie heavily in the pan. A wise man will not eat of it, lest he break his teeth.'

Jeb Stuart Ho bowed his head in submission. He knew he stood corrected. There was another long pause before the teacher spoke again. The water clock dripped softly.

'The task you are being set will not be simple. It can be a heavy load. Your back must be strong enough to bear it.'

This time, Jeb Stuart Ho said nothing. The teacher continued.

'The probability has almost reached maximum that large areas of the rim, and to a lesser extent the inner sectors, will disrupt.'

He paused, and again Jeb Stuart Ho said nothing.

'The result of this disruption will be twofold. A state of war will occur which will escalate unchecked until the antagonized will begin to destroy their opponents' stasis generators, and disrupt the territory they occupy. They will cause a so far uncalculated shift in the balance of our world. Taking into account the most favourable conditions for stasis, the resultant loss of existing inhabited space would be a minimum of 65.79 per cent.'

Jeb Stuart Ho began to feel the magnitude of the task he was being set. Doubt hovered in the corner of his mind, but he controlled his will and it faded. The teacher went on.

'The second danger that would result from this situation is that the release of energy from a certain level of warfare would be a considerable attraction to the disruptors. They would gravitate towards the source of energy by the shortest possible route. That would certainly involve many of them cutting through the normally undisturbed central sectors. In this event the space and, of course, population loss could be as high as 98.51 per cent.'

The information fell about Jeb Stuart Ho's shoulders like a heavy yoke. It was far worse than purely physical weight. He was used to those. In advanced combat training the body is often loaded to its very limit. This burden of responsibility would go far beyond that. He would have to be sure-footed and have strength in excess of anything he had experienced. His boast of being ready seemed empty and childish. Still he kept silent, and the teacher continued his instruction.

'All our calculations lead us to one conclusion. There is a single individual. The individual's future actions will be the seeds of this disaster. If they are allowed to germinate and grow, the flowers that eventually bloom will be terrible to look upon.'

Jeb Stuart Ho looked straight ahead.

'It will be my task to pluck those flowers?'

'It will be your task to make sure that seeds never put forth shoots.'

'I must intervene and prevent the individual from taking such action as will precipitate disaster?'

The teacher looked at Jeb Stuart Ho for the first time.

'It is graver than that. The actions and their effect on this pattern are too complex. You must remove the individual.'

'I must kill, Teacher?'

'You must kill, Jeb Stuart Ho.'

There was a long silence. Jeb Stuart Ho looked down at his hands, and then straight ahead.

'Who is the subject?'

'A female, current age thirteen, technocrat upbringing. You will receive a data package as you depart.'

'May I ask one question? What gives us the right to calculate an individual must die?'

'Our calculations are accurate to the smallest margin.'

'So we take the responsibility of another's death?'

'That is a second question.'

'We are always right? Is there no room for doubt?'

'The superior man arrives at the river and crosses.'

'We are always right?'

'To the finest part of allowable error.'

They sat in silence for many minutes. The water clock dripped away the time. Jeb Stuart Ho finally rose, bowed to the teacher and left the room. He made his way down the maze of corridors to his own cell. Nah Duc West was waiting. He bowed as his master entered, and then looked up anxiously.

'The Teacher has instructed you in the task, master?'

Jeb Stuart Ho looked at the young man and smiled.

'You are like the moth that bathes in the flame and wonders at its burning.'

'Yes, master.'

'The Teacher gave me his instructions.'

The pupil looked up eagerly.

'And am I to go with you, master?'

Jeb Stuart Ho shook his head. 'No, I go alone.'

'But master, for many months I have been your lover and pupil. We have shared our knowledge and our bodies. Why do you now reject me? Why must you leave me behind?'

Jeb Stuart Ho put his hand gently on the pupil's shoulder.

'Your training must continue, Nah Duc West. Another will take my place. You are not being rejected. I have my task, you have yours. They no longer follow the same path and we must part. It is no reason for grief. We both continue. When travellers part at the crossroads they rejoice because their journey continues to its conclusion.'

Nah Duc West bowed his head in the face of this self-evident wisdom. Jeb Stuart Ho extended his hand and stroked his pupil's hair.

'We have not parted yet. You still have the task of preparing me for my journey.'

Nah Duc West looked at the floor.

'Yes, master.

There were a few moments while the young man stood, not moving. Jeb Stuart Ho sat down crosslegged on his sleeping mat and looked at his pupil.

'Well, get on with it.'

Nah Duc West jerked into life.

'Yes, master.

He went to the trunk in the corner of the room and opened it. First he took out a white cloth and spread it on the floor. Then piece by piece he laid out Jeb Stuart Ho's equipment. Carefully he stretched out the leather body suit. It was a one-piece black garment fastened down the front. It was reinforced by quilting and small silver plates over the vulnerable spots. It covered the entire body, including the hands and feet. The striking edges of these were also strengthened by strips of metal, as were the knees and elbows.

The laying out of an executive's equipment was a serious ritual among the brothers. The sequence of items was very important. With true regard for tradition, Nah Duc West produced the wide leather belt with its attachments for the various accoutrements. Next came the weapons: the long double-handed sword, the nanchuk: two short steel batons joined by a length of chain; the flat case of six matched throwing knives; and the .90 magnum in its carry case that also held the ammunition and the extension barrel.

The pupil checked that each weapon was in working order, and free from dirt or rust. He knew if he failed in this, he'd be the subject of a different, more painful ritual. He carefully placed them in their correct positions beside the belt and the suit. The next items were equally important. The portable stasis generator, the small black box that would prevent its wearer from being assimilated into the nothings; and the survival case that contained water and food concentrates. When these had been laid out, the pupil produced the final item from the chest. The thick, coarsely woven travelling cape was placed, folded, at the corner of the white cloth.

When all this was complete, Jeb Stuart Ho finally stood up. He undid his robe and let it fall to his feet. Nah Duc West looked lovingly at his master's thin but heavily muscled body for a moment, and then stooped to pick up the black leather suit. He helped him struggle into it and zipped up the front. Then he picked up the belt and strapped it around Jeb Stuart Ho's waist. Jeb Stuart Ho raised his hands as the pupil attached the generator, the survival kit and the gun case to his belt. The sword was hung from the straps on his back so the hilt was level with his right shoulder. The knives were buckled on to his left forearm, while the nanchuk was strapped to the other.

Before handing Jeb Stuart Ho the folded cloak, his pupil took a mirror from the trunk and held it in front of him. Jeb Stuart Ho regarded himself, and was pleased. His fighting suit and weapons were immaculate. His pale face looked back at him in a suitably calm, determined manner. His dark hair hung down straight, cut off at the shoulders in the accepted manner of the brotherhood. He would not disgrace them as an executive. In the outside world he must be the superior man of fable. Not that he was without advantage. His suit would protect him against all human attack below the level of blades or projectiles. Unarmed, he could defeat most men by the skill of his hands and feet. With his weapons he was as nearly invincible as any human could be.

From the very moment of conception, and, in fact, even before that moment, he had been tailored and trained to become a fighting machine. Only the disciplines of the brotherhood could enable him to use such power in an ethical manner. He was confident the disciplines would hold. He would sustain the honour of his teacher.

Jeb Stuart Ho took the cloak from his pupil and threw it around his shoulders, making sure that the hilt of his sword was still easily accessible. Then he leaned forward and gently kissed his pupil.

'Goodbye, Nah Duc West.'

'Goodbye, Jeb Stuart Ho.'

He walked quickly out of the room, and turned in the direction of the huge outer doors. When he reached them, the teacher was waiting for him.

'You go?'

'Yes, Teacher.'

The teacher handed him a small package wrapped in white silk.

'This contains all you need to know about the subject.'

Jeb Stuart Ho bowed.

'Yes, Teacher.'

The teacher returned his bow, and the great doors slid open with a faint hiss.

2

Jeb Stuart Ho stopped and looked back at the temple. Although he had been outside before on exercise, the first taste of the open never failed to excite him. He stared at it surrounded by the flat, featureless plain that was fixed in perfect stasis by its unfaltering generators. The temple itself filled him with wonder. It was a huge, flat-sided pillar that seemed to reach halfway to the yellow sky. Its black surfaces were completely blank. The only break in the smooth stone was the huge doorway through which he had left. Even this was dwarfed by the enormous size of the building.

Jeb Stuart Ho turned away from it. He walked on across the even plain, towards the point where the power of the generators began to diminish and the regularity of the plain broke up into wild, jagged rock formations.

When he reached these, Jeb Stuart Ho was forced to climb and scramble. The rocks, as he got further from the generators' fields, began to change colour. The whiteness of the plain first turned to grey and brown and then, further out, exploded into a riot of purple and green. The sky too changed. It became more strident. Above the black building it had been a pale yellow, but over the wilderness of rocks it altered to a burnished gold.

Here and there, in the deep crevasses, pools of grey shifting nothing swirled and smoked. Jeb Stuart Ho's hand went to his belt and switched on his generator pack. A red pilot light glowed, and it came alive with a soft hum. He knew if he should accidentally slip into one of those grey pools without the generator protecting him, he would be spread three ways across another universe.

Here and there, spiky plants clung to cracks in the rocks. One in particular, with extravagant red blossoms, attracted him. He stopped and examined it. Then he stepped back and stood tense, just as they had taught him in the swordsman's class. His hands flashed to the sword hilt behind his left shoulder. The blade whistled. The topmost flower was detached from its stalk. It dropped to the rock, rolled and fell down into one of the grey pools. As it touched the nothings, it smoked for an instant and melted away.

Jeb Stuart Ho stood holding his sword and feeling a little foolish. He was ashamed that he should have succumbed to using his hard-learned skills in such a childish display of bravado. It was unforgivable at a time when all his concentration should be directed to his task.

He decided it was time for him to study the data package. He unzipped the top of his body suit and removed the silk bundle. He squatted on a nearby rock, and carefully began to unwrap it. It contained a tri-di cube and a roll of parchment. Jeb Stuart Ho held up the cube and looked at it. In it was the image of a girl in her early teens. She had dark hair and a pale, petulant face. Her eyes were large and surrounded by dark make-up. Her mouth was coloured dark red and looked cruelly sensual. A loop action inside the cube made the image repeat the same sequence of expressions over and over again. First she stared out impassively at him, then slowly she smiled. Her lip curled, and the smile turned into a sneer. Finally the expression faded, only to start the cycle again. Jeb Stuart Ho turned the cube slowly round, examining the girl's face from every angle. He wished that he had had more experience with women at the temple. The teachers, in their wisdom, encouraged the pupil executives to find love among their own sex.

He put down the cube, and turned his attention to the parchment. It was covered with computer print which he read carefully. There was a solemnity about the moment. He was reading about the person he was going to kill.

AA Catto.

Like her brother Valdo, she has remained at a static age for a considerable period.

Member of Directorate (technocrat ruling class) of Con-Lec, a corporation citadel culture in S class decay.

Petulant, wilful, vicious, with high, pain-related sexual appetite. Escorted by human male, reportedly named Reave. Mistress/pet relationship.

No martial skills.

All training directed to sensory satisfaction.

IQ 197.

M-potential nil.

Psi-property nil.

Retention factor B +.

Subject's present location midsection city Litz (pop. 1,241,000 – Stuff contract pleasure city) where she moves in a sensation-seeking subgroup.

Class A subject. May surround herself with mercenary protection. Approach with caution.

Aim of intervention is death of subject.

Jeb Stuart Ho read the parchment twice and then folded it beside the cube. He wrapped both in the piece of silk and returned them to his suit. Then he stood up. He knew the first place he had to go. He once again began picking his way through the rocks.

As he went on, moving, all the time, away from the temple, the landscape continued to change. The rock formations began to fragment and break up. Where there had previously been bright colours they faded to a dull grey, not much darker than the pools of shifting nothings. In fact, pools was no longer an adequate description. They had enlarged and merged, so there were now wide expanses of emptiness. Here and there, the rocks jutted out of them, like ice floes on a frozen sea.

It was necessary for Jeb Stuart Ho to cross these expanses. Although his personal generator protected him from the fate of any unshielded matter that came in contact with the nothings, it was still an unnerving experience to step out into the strange, alien mist and suddenly find the solid foothold created by the generator.

On a particularly wide, flat expanse of rock, he paused for a moment. He unhitched the supply case from his belt and took a sparing mouthful of water. He looked around, shielding his eyes, and searching for something on the far horizon. He knew that if he was to find the girl AA Catto he would have to start by looking for her in the city of Litz. In order to get there he would require a guide. There was a small group of humans who had the power to know where exactly they were in the strange shattered world that had remained after the breakdown. There were certain animals that appeared to have the same faculty. Jeb Stuart Ho knew he would need one of these if he was to make the journey to Litz without much excessive wandering.

If the faculty of location could have been bred or taught, the brotherhood would undoubtedly have produced their own guides. But it seemed to be a completely random gift. All they could do was to keep track of the movements of the various potential guides. Jeb Stuart Ho knew he had been lucky. There was one listed as being in a place on roughly the same plane as the temple. If his calculations had been correct, the shattered landscape he was crossing should be the area where the generator fields of the temple and the place he expected to find the guide failed to overlap completely.

He thought he saw something on the very horizon, but the air shimmered so much where the nothings fought to absorb and destroy it, it was hard to tell. He walked on, and gradually he became positive that there was a tall, dark shape in the distance. After walking a little further it became apparent that the dark shape was a building of some sort. In some ways it was like the temple. It was obviously very tall, and dominated the surrounding landscape in much the same way as the temple. As far as Jeb Stuart Ho could see it didn't have the clean lines of the temple. Its outline seemed cluttered and fussy.

He knew very little about the place he was going to. The reference had only told him its name. It had said a guide was currently at Wainscote, and given some approximate directions. Jeb Stuart Ho quickened his pace. He could waste no time on the preparatory moves that were needed before he could fulfil his mission.

As he came nearer the dark building, the landscape began to stabilize. It was no more attractive, though, than the borders of the nothings. The rocks did not return to their earlier colours. On the outskirts of Wainscote they were black and shiny. Damp white mist lay in the lower hollows and streamed across the slippery surfaces. No flowers bloomed but here and there twisted, frightened trees clung to the crags. Jeb Stuart Ho saw a dark carrion bird perched on a branch. It eyed him speculatively, but did nothing.

As he drew nearer, he could make out more details of the building itself. To Jeb Stuart Ho's disciplined mind it appeared a mess. Its base was surrounded by buttresses and porticoes like the exposed roots of some ancient gnarled tree. The main body of the structure was like a stout trunk. It was studded with irregular rows of windows. Most were dark, but a few showed dim, flickering lights. It was topped by an uneven crown of turrets, which completed the similarity to a blasted tree by jutting up like stunted branches.

There was an air of gothic gloom that seemed to extend from the house out to the surrounding landscape. The sky had become a deep blue. It gave out no light. That came from an artificial sun that hung brooding behind the turrets, a sullen bloated red. Jeb Stuart Ho involuntarily shuddered, and pulled his cloak more tightly round his shoulders.

Between the rocks he found a rough path that led directly to the house. As he came closer to it, the number of trees increased. More birds, like the one he'd seen earlier, flew high above him in a ragged line. Here and there beside the tracks were other, smaller buildings, cottages or huts. Jeb Stuart Ho peered into a couple of them, but they all seemed to be deserted, and in various stages of decay.

The path opened out as he came closer to the house. The nearer he came, the more he realized exactly how huge the building was. It towered above the surrounding landscape casting a vast, malevolent shadow. A wide area of bare ground littered with rubble and garbage led up to the front of the building. A flight of wide steps gave access to the massive front doors. Jeb Stuart Ho walked quickly across the open space and hurried up the steps. He stopped in front of the double doors. They appeared to have been designed to give access to a race of giants. One of them was slightly open. There was a space just wide enough for Jeb Stuart Ho to slip through. No light came from whatever lay immediately behind. He paused for a moment and ran his fingers over the copper tracery that covered the hard dark wood of the door. Then he slid through the gap, and silently entered Wainscote.

It took a few moments for his eyes to grow accustomed to the gloom. When they did he found that he was in a large hallway. It was deserted, and had the coldness of a place that is rarely used. The few pieces of furniture that were dotted about the flagged expanse of floor seemed like desolate wrecks. They were worn and broken. Garbage had collected in the corners, and the place smelled of damp.

Jeb Stuart Ho moved noiselessly across the hallway towards a wide, and probably once stately, staircase that curved round the far wall. A rapid scuttling sound made him freeze and look round. A pair of small armadillos, disturbed by the unexpected human presence, burrowed for shelter under a collapsed chaise longue. He smiled at their desperate efforts to get away from him. The animals who lived in the temple never displayed such fear and alarm. It was obvious that conditions at Wainscote were very different. He began carefully to climb the stairs. It looked as though the inhabitants of the house must live much further inside the building, and rarely visit the outer areas.

The top of the staircase opened out into a large gallery, which, like the hall below, showed the ravages of neglect. A rat peered out from behind a length of rotting curtain and fled squealing at the sight of the dark figure that had invaded its domain. More squeals and rustles came from inside the walls, as the news of the intruder circulated through the rat community.

A number of corridors led off the gallery. They were dim, bare and uninviting, each one identical to the next. Jeb Stuart Ho knew that he could only make a random choice. The middle one looked as though it might possibly lead more directly to the interior of the house. He started down it, still watchful for any sign of life.

Nothing happened for a long while. Jeb Stuart Ho walked patiently on, past occasional doorways that opened into more empty, deserted rooms. All he could do was follow the twists and turns of the corridor until it reached its ultimate destination. If it ended in a blind alley, he would simply go back and try one of the others. His information said that he would find his guide inside this building, and temple information was nearly always accurate.

After walking for some minutes, he came to a point where the corridor made a right-angle turn. Jeb Stuart Ho had become less careful. The unchanging corridor didn't seem very hostile. As he turned the corner he saw a dark figure coming towards him at the far end of the passage. His protective senses came to life, and he sprang lightly back, pressing himself against the wall. The figure did exactly the same thing. Slowly, Jeb Stuart Ho moved away from the wall. Again the other figure matched his own movements. He smiled as he realized that it must be an image of himself. The entire end of the corridor was one large mirror.

Then someone laughed. Jeb Stuart Ho spun round, his hands flashing to the hilt of his sword. A girl stood leaning in the doorway of one of the empty rooms. Her hair was very black and hung almost to her waist. It partially hid her small pale face, but Jeb Stuart Ho noticed that it was like that of a self-indulgent child, and only the dark shadows under her eyes gave away her real age. That and her body. Even in the long red satin dress it couldn't be mistaken for anything but that of a mature young woman. He lowered the sword. She laughed again.

'You look a little ridiculous.'

'Ridiculous?'

No one had ever called Jeb Stuart Ho ridiculous before.

'Jumping at your own reflection. Pulling out that sword.'

'I'm sorry. I was being careful, that's all.'

The girl moved towards him. He saw she had an ornamented goblet of some kind of white metal in her right hand. She raised it to her mouth and sipped from it. Her movements seemed very controlled and deliberate. She swayed a little as she walked. It was as though she was very drunk, but also very accustomed to it.

'Did you drift away from the party?'

'There is a party?'

'There's always a party. Everyone knows that. How is it that you don't know it?'

'I have only just arrived here.'

'You came from outside?'

'Yes, I came from outside.'

'You're not making it up?'

'What reason would I have for making up something like that?'

'Some people will do anything to draw attention to themselves.'

'I don't want attention.'

'Most people do.'

'Do you?'

The girl fiddled with her drink.

'I suppose so. I'm no different to the rest.'

'Then why do you come to these empty rooms? There's no one to see you here.'

'They frighten me.'

'That would seem a reason to stay away from them.'

'I like to be frightened now and then. Don't you? Don't you enjoy a thrill of fear?'

Jeb Stuart Ho carefully put away his sword.

'I don't think so. I've never considered fear as a source of enjoyment.'

'It can be terribly exciting.'

There was a long pause while Jeb Stuart Ho considered this new concept. The girl took the chance to move up close to him.

'Are you going to rape me?'

Jeb Stuart Ho raised his eyebrows. 'What is rape?'

'You don't know what rape is?'

He shook his head.

'It's not a term I'm familiar with.'

'You're teasing me?'

'No.'

'You really don't know what rape means?'

'No.'

'It's when a man forces a woman to have sex with him against her will.'

'Why should he do that?'

The girl looked at him as though she was talking to an idiot.

'He enjoys it, of course. There's usually an element of brutality involved.'

'Why should anyone enjoy hurting another person?'

The girl shrugged.

'I don't know why exactly, but there's plenty who do.'

'Know why?'

'Enjoy hurting people. There's plenty of people who enjoy pain, for that matter.'

Jeb Stuart Ho shook his head.

'I'm not sure I understand.'

The girl gestured towards the weapons hanging under his cloak.

'You look like you ought to. You could kill a lot of people with that stuff.'

'I'm trained to kill. It is my vocation. I am aware it may be necessary at times, but I don't enjoy the act.'

'Then why do it?'

'We all have to do things we don't enjoy.'

'I don't, why should I? I don't think I'm enjoying this conversation any more.

'I'm sorry.'

'It's not your fault. I don't enjoy many things for long. I get bored.'

'I thought you said you didn't do anything you don't enjoy.'

'That's right. I don't.'

'But…'

'There are times when I don't do anything. I frequently don't do anything. I think I'll go back to the party now. I'm bored with being out here.'

She looked up at Jeb Stuart Ho.

'Do you want to go to the party?'

He shook his head.

'I have to find someone.'

'Who?'

'I have information that there is a guide somewhere in this place.'

The girl laughed. It was short, sharp and with a trace of a sneer.

'I should have guessed you'd be after him. There are always people coming from outside looking for him. They usually want him to take them somewhere. You're wasting your time, you know. He never goes. He won't do it any more.'

'Why is that? Surely it is his gift? A man cannot turn his back on his gift.'

'He can. He finds it really easy. Ever since he got into sensory deprivation he's found it really easy.'

Jeb Stuart Ho's face formed itself into a look of grim patience.

'He will go this time.'

3

The Minstrel Boy could feel something and he didn't like it. Something was reaching into his cosy cocooned tank. Something touched him. He'd felt nothing for so long that it affected his nerves. He twisted away from it, and the pads over his eyes slipped. Light smashed into his head. The Minstrel Boy went rigid. Every response silently screamed. His legs kicked convulsively. The touch came again. It was more deliberate this time. It was a hand. It was reaching for the drip feed. It was trying to remove it from his arm.

Anger exploded inside the Minstrel Boy. It was intolerable. Someone was actually interfering with him, bringing him back to reality. His privacy was being invaded. His consciousness was being changed against his will. What gave anyone the right to mess with him like that?

In one violent move he surfaced. He sat up inside the coffin-shaped cubicle. It was the only thing in the high stone turret room. He tore the headphones from his ears. The amplified sound of his own circulation abruptly stopped.

'What the fuck...'

The real world crashed in on him. He felt sick and dropped back on to the cushioned interior of the coffin. He tried it a little more gently this time. Carefully he opened his eyes again. The light still hurt, but it was bearable. He found that he could see. He didn't like what he saw.

A tall thin man in a black cloak was standing beside the black steel coffin. The clear plastic feeder tube was still in his hand. The Minstrel Boy sat up, slowly and carefully this time.

'What the fuck do you think you're doing? What makes you think you can walk in here and drag me down to your level?'

Jeb Stuart Ho looked calmly at the Minstrel Boy.

'I have need of you.'

The Minstrel Boy's first response was to try to damage this stranger who had caused him so much pain. He checked the impulse when he saw the array of weapons hung around the man's body. Instead, he rested an arm on the side of the coffin and curled his lip.

'I suppose you think you can get me to go with you? I suppose you think you can threaten me with violence?'

Jeb Stuart Ho stared steadily at the Minstrel Boy.

'I could, but that isn't the way that I operate.'

The Minstrel Boy laughed harshly.

'That's not the way you operate? I'll tell you one thing, you won't get me to go anywhere any other way.'

Jeb Stuart Ho shrugged.

'I think you'll come with me in the end.'

'You think that? Is that what you think?'

'I'm confident that you'll guide me.'

'Confident, hey? So what makes you so fucking confident? I like this place. I don't have to move, I don't have to think. I'm quite happy here, in fact I love it. I don't see any way you could get me to leave here without holding a gun to my head.'

Jeb Stuart Ho shook his head.

'I don't think that will be necessary.'

'You don't, hey? You don't think it'll be necessary?'

'I don't.'

'So what do you intend to do?'

'I thought that if I explained the nature of my task to you, you might become more willing to guide me.'

'Explain the nature of your task? You got to be crazy. Can't you understand that I'm just not interested? I've had it. I've had it with the travelling and the concentrating. Knowing where you are don't come easy. You have to work at it. There are times when it actually hurts. I don't need it. I don't give a fuck what high-minded mission you got. I don't want to know.'

Jeb Stuart Ho waited until the Minstrel Boy had finished, then he spoke very softly.

'I am from the temple. My task is an executive assignment.'

The Minstrel Boy sneered.

'Is that supposed to frighten me? Is that supposed to fill me with awe? It might have done, years ago, but now I just don't care. I'm never going travelling again. You'll have to find someone else.'

'You're the one I need.'

'I'm not the one you're going to get. I'm staying right here.'

Jeb Stuart Ho stroked his chin.

'You are a guest here. Perhaps your hosts would not be so anxious for you to stay here if they knew you had incurred the displeasure of the temple.'

The Minstrel Boy laughed.

'For a temple executive you really don't know very much. You ought to do a bit more homework. The One who rules this place don't care whose displeasure He incurs. He don't care.'

'The temple is very powerful.'

'So the temple's powerful, He's not interested. He's not even interested that Wainscote is falling apart around Him. He just lies in His vault and soaks up energy from the fools at the party. If that ever stops, then maybe He'll wake and move out into the world. When that happens, even the temple won't be able to stop Him doing what He wants. He's invincible.'

'And you want to be just like Him.'

The Minstrel Boy shook his head.

'That's where you're wrong. I don't want anything, or, more to the point, I want nothing. I badly want nothing at all. You understand?'

Jeb Stuart Ho nodded.

'I understand, but it seems a very negative attitude.'

'That's right. That's exactly what it is. Negative. That's for me, Mister Executive.'

'So it would be no use outlining the importance of my task?'

The Minstrel Boy grinned.

'No use at all, buddy. So you might as well move along, and let me go back to sleep.'

Jeb Stuart Ho looked sadly at the Minstrel Boy.

'You're putting me in a very difficult position.'

'That's really too bad.'

'In the temple we strive to make every statement an absolute truth.'

'So?'

'On the other hand it is of paramount importance that a member of the brotherhood should not fail in an assigned task.'

The Minstrel Boy frowned.

'I don't know what the fuck you're talking about.'

Jeb Stuart Ho sighed.

'I'm attempting to explain the awkward position you have placed me in by your refusal to cooperate.'

The Minstrel Boy began to get annoyed. 'Can't I get it across to you that I don't want to know?'

Jeb Stuart Ho ignored him and went on. 'By your refusal to cooperate, you are forcing me to go back on a previous statement.'

'I should worry.'

'Perhaps you should.'

'Huh?'

'I said earlier that I would not use violence or threats of violence to force you to cooperate. Your attitude and the importance of my mission make it necessary to reverse that statement.'

'What do you mean?'

Jeb Stuart Ho slowly removed the .90 magnum from its holster.

'If you don't accompany me on my mission, I'll kill you.'

The Minstrel Boy's jaw dropped.

'You can't do that. It's illogical. The brotherhood can't go around behaving illogically.'

Jeb Stuart Ho trained the gun on the Minstrel Boy. 'That's true, but my analysis of the situation indicates that this is the only course. I think we have delayed long enough. You will get out of that coffin and put on your travelling clothes.'

'You've got to be kidding.'

Jeb Stuart Ho took a step forward and thrust the gun under the Minstrel Boy's chin.

'Move!'

The Minstrel Boy began to scramble out of the coffin. He pointed an accusing finger at Jeb Stuart Ho.

'You are going to regret this, my man.'

He tentatively swung his legs over the side and placed his feet on the floor. He tried to stand but his legs buckled and he dropped to the flagstones. He looked up at Jeb Stuart Ho.

'You're going to have to help me. I'm kind of weak. I haven't moved in quite a while.'

Jeb Stuart Ho lowered his gun and bent down, extending a hand to the Minstrel Boy. The Minstrel Boy grasped the offered hand, and then suddenly jerked and twisted. He pulled at Jeb Stuart Ho's arm. For a moment he swung off balance. The gun wavered. The Minstrel Boy kicked at Ho's legs, but the executive turned on the balls of his feet, avoided the Minstrel Boy's thrashing legs, and aimed a precise blow with the edge of his own foot. It landed under the Minstrel Boy's jaw, and he rolled against the side of the black steel coffin, clutching his throat.

'What in hell did you do that for? You could have ruptured my windpipe.'

'The blow did exactly what it was supposed to do.'

'Huh?'

'It was a reminder. I sought to hurt you, but not cause any serious damage. If anything like that happens again I shall break one of the less vital bones in your body.'

'Okay, okay.'

'On any subsequent occasion I'll do an increasing amount of damage.'

'Sure, great, I give in. I'm coming with you.'

'Just so we understand each other. Nothing must stand in the way of my mission.'

The Minstrel Boy got unsteadily to his feet. He was still massaging his bruised throat.

'Okay, you've got a deal. I won't cause any more trouble.'

Jeb Stuart Ho stood erect and watchful.

'Then get dressed. We've wasted enough time already.'

The Minstrel Boy looked calculatingly at Jeb Stuart Ho. 'There is one thing.'

'What?'

'I figure I ought to get paid for this job.'

'You'll be amply rewarded.'

'How much?'

'I guarantee the temple won't turn down any reasonable request.'

'Okay, that's good enough.'

A small wash bowl was set in one corner of the bare stone room. Beside it was a simple wooden cupboard with a plain mirror set in the front of it. As the Minstrel Boy moved across the room, Jeb Stuart Ho noted that he was genuinely unsteady on his feet. He bent over the sink and splashed water on his face and neck.

'That deprivation sure leaves you feeling bad.'

Jeb Stuart Ho looked bored.

'That would seem adequate reason not to engage in it.'

The Minstrel Boy scowled.

'I might have known you'd say that.'

The Minstrel Boy opened the cupboard, and took out a plain white cotton shirt. When he'd put this on, he removed a pair of grey pinstripe trousers from a hanger, and climbed into them. Next he pulled on a pair of high-heeled black boots, and tucked his pants into them. He turned to the mirror and dragged a comb through his dark, curly hair. He stepped back and admired the reflection of his pale, pinched face for a couple of moments. Then he lifted a belt that held five matched throwing knives, and strapped it around his hips. Jeb Stuart Ho glanced at him questioningly.

'You don't carry a gun?'

The Minstrel Boy grinned and shook his head. He patted the knives.

'These will do me just fine. After all, I've got you to protect me, haven't I? You'd be lost without me.'

Jeb Stuart Ho remained silent. The Minstrel Boy laughed and took a black frock coat from the cupboard. He slipped it on and brushed himself down. He clipped a miniature generator to his belt, and then completed his outfit with a wide-brimmed black hat with a silver and turquoise band. With a swift practised motion he tipped the hat over his eyes, and grinned at Jeb Stuart Ho.

'Okay, I'm ready. Where do you want to go?'

'The city of Litz…'

'Litz! I know Litz.'

'There will be a problem in getting there.'

The Minstrel Boy laughed.

'No, no, it's a good distance, but there's no real problem in getting there.'

Jeb Stuart Ho looked puzzled.

'Then why do you laugh?'

'Relief, I guess. Litz is at least halfway civilized. I began to think that you wanted to go to some weird place out in the fringes.'

'It might come to that in the end, but Litz will do for now. Shall we get started?'

The Minstrel Boy sat down on the edge of the coffin.

'Just hold on a minute. A trip to Litz isn't just a short stroll. We need to plan the thing out.'

'We can't walk?'

'No way. If we walked, I'd go insane before we were halfway there. We'll need lizards.'

It was Jeb Stuart Ho's turn to look puzzled.

'Lizards?'

'Sure, lizards. They'll get us there, and all I'll have to concentrate on is letting them know where we want to go. They'll find their way there without any help.'

'There are lizards in this place?'

The Minstrel Boy nodded.

'Sure, there's a bunch of them stabled in the lower levels. Nobody'll notice if we take a couple.'

Jeb Stuart Ho raised a dubious eyebrow.

'Will no one object if we remove something that is their property? Might they not become bitter about it?'

The Minstrel Boy shrugged.

'What if they do? We'll be long gone before that happens. In any case, I doubt if anyone will notice. Nobody hardly ever leaves here. I just hope someone's remembered to feed them recently. Lizards are okay, but they have a tendency to get mean when they're hungry.'

He pushed his shirt cuffs out from his jacket with a sharp hustler's gesture, and jerked his head for Jeb Stuart Ho to follow him. They left the bare room with its steel coffin, and started down the endless corridors of Wainscote. It was almost like a dress rehearsal for the coming adventure. Jeb Stuart Ho was already totally in the hands of the Minstrel Boy. The builders of Wainscote had employed no recognizable logic in its construction. He knew that he could easily wander for days before he found his way out. He carefully watched the Minstrel Boy's back for any sign of a trick. He didn't altogether like the situation, but he realized there was no other way.

They descended five flights of stone stairs. It was like dropping into the vaults of the earth. The ceilings became covered with trails of dark green slime that hung like stalactites. Jeb Stuart Ho and the Minstrel Boy had to duck their heads to avoid it brushing off on their clothes.

Jeb Stuart Ho noticed that as they went lower and lower, a smell somewhat like ammonia got stronger. At the bottom of the fifth set of stairs it became almost overpowering. Ho glanced at the Minstrel Boy.

'What causes this smell?'

The Minstrel Boy scowled.

'Lizards. They stink something cruel. Nobody ever cleans the pens.'

'Why not?'

The Minstrel Boy looked at Jeb Stuart Ho impatiently.

'Why should they bother? Who gives a fuck? Like I said, nobody ever goes anywhere.'

'But they are living creatures.'

'So?'

Jeb Stuart Ho gave up. It was obvious that the Minstrel Boy's mind worked in a very different way to his. They reached the bottom of the last flight of steps; the smell more pungeant. Ho raised his cloak to cover his nose and mouth. The Minstrel Boy grinned at him.

'Bad, isn't it?'

They walked through a high stone arch and into the lizard stables of Wainscote. Jeb Stuart Ho looked along the row of stalls that housed the huge creatures. Despite his training to expect anything, he couldn't help being awed by the huge beasts. Their bodies alone were twice as high as a man, and their long necks extended to almost twice that again. As the two men approached them they shifted uneasily, and made deep bleating sounds. One of them swung its head round. It stared at Ho and the

Minstrel Boy from dark moist eyes. Its thin reptilian tongue flicked in and out like a whip. Jeb Stuart Ho glanced at the Minstrel Boy.

'Are you sure you can control these beasts?'

The Minstrel Boy laughed.

'Sure. Nothing to it. Why? Are you nervous or something?'

'No, I was just wondering.'

'Don't worry. I know all about lizards.'

He walked over to one of the largest, a huge dark green monster, and slapped it hard on the rump.

'Lizards are no problem.'

He ducked under the heavy chain that closed off the end of the stall. He made a shrill whistling noise between his teeth. The animal inclined its head, and the Minstrel Boy began to scratch it vigorously on the nose.

'See? No trouble at all. We might as well get saddled up and start moving. There ain't nothing to hang around here for.'

He pointed to a row of saddles hanging from some short beams that jutted from the opposite wall.

'Bring over two saddles and two sets of harness, and I'll get a couple of these monsters hitched up to go.'

Jeb Stuart Ho walked over to the rack and picked up a heavy wooden saddle. The leather girth was attached to the seat with huge decorated silver studs. It must have once looked magnificent, but now it was filthy and covered in dust. He wiped off the worst of it and hefted the saddle over to where the Minstrel Boy was standing, still scratching the big lizard. He put it down, and went back for another one. The Minstrel Boy gestured towards the rack.

'We'll need two sets of harness as well.'

The harnesses consisted of a wide leather collar with a single long rein attached to it. Jeb Stuart Ho brought them over to the Minstrel Boy, who took one of them and buckled the collar round the neck of the big green lizard. He led it out of the stall and handed the rein to Ho.

'Hold this one, while I go and sort you out a mount.'

Jeb Stuart Ho gingerly grasped the lizard's rein. To his relief the creature showed no inclination to go anywhere. The Minstrel Boy sauntered down the row of stalls, inspecting the other animals. Finally he stopped in front of a smaller lizard, with a yellowish mottled hide. He attached a collar to it and led it towards where Jeb Stuart Ho was standing.

'This one should suit you. It's pretty docile and easy to handle.'

Ho and the lizard looked at each other distrustfully. Slowly Ho stretched out his hand and scratched its nose. The lizard bleated gratefully. The Minstrel Boy sniffed.

'Maybe we'll turn you into a lizard handler before this trip's over.'

Jeb Stuart Ho glanced at him sharply.

'I have more important objectives for this journey.'

The Minstrel Boy shrugged.

'We'd better get the saddles on, or we won't reach any kind of objective at all.'

The huge bulk of the creatures made putting the saddles on them an awkward business. A set of stone steps ran up one part of the stable wall. The Minstrel Boy led the first lizard over to them. He got Jeb Stuart Ho to hold it while he picked up one of the saddles, climbed the steps and tossed the saddle over the animal's back. After that, he had to scramble under its belly and buckle the girth. The whole process was repeated with the second lizard. When they were both saddled, he walked to the far end of the stable and pulled open a pair of high double doors. Sunlight streamed into the dim room, and the lizards shuffled and blinked nervously. Beyond the doors, an inclined ramp led up to ground level.

The Minstrel Boy climbed up into the saddle of the big green lizard, and Jeb Stuart Ho hauled himself on to the smaller yellow one. He watched carefully as the Minstrel Boy dug his heels sharply into the monster's side. The lizard began to lumber forward towards the open doors. Jeb Stuart Ho tried the same thing with his own mount, and was surprised and pleased when it began following its big green brother.

As they climbed the ramp, Jeb Stuart Ho called out to the Minstrel Boy.

'Should we not close the door behind us?'

The Minstrel Boy turned and laughed.

'Why bother? With the doors open, the lizards will get restless and start trying to break out. It might force someone to do something about it.'

They reached the top of the ramp, and pointed their mounts away from Wainscote. Jeb Stuart Ho would have liked to gather more information about the place, but his mission was more pressing. He and the Minstrel Boy vigorously kicked their lizards, and the beasts broke into a ponderous, earth-shaking canter.

4

A Catto stared sourly across the crowded room. The tables of the Venus Flytrap were each enclosed in their own plexiglass dome. If she dimmed the interior light she could see what was going on in the rest of the club; if she turned it up the rest of the club could see her. Right then, she had it set at medium. The other people in the place were reduced to dark murmuring shadows. She was just a dim shape to them inside the bubble. That was the way AA Catto wanted it. She didn't want to see anyone, and she didn't want to be on display.

AA Catto was beginning to hate the Venus Flytrap. She was beginning to hate the entire city of Litz. She was even beginning to hate herself. She looked down at her thirteen-year-old body encased in the brief metal-foil dress. She was thoroughly sick of the thin arms and legs and half-formed breasts. The only thing that stopped her leaving off the growth retarder and letting it mature was the possibility that she might regret it afterwards. Once you allowed yourself to age there was no going back. You could halt your growth any time you liked, you could accelerate it if you wanted to. The one thing you couldn't do was reverse the process. AA Catto was sick of living in an age of such incomplete and half-arsed technology.

Way over on the other side of the club she could just make out Reave. His face was illuminated by the rainbow lamp above the four square table. He sat with his back to the curtain of black water that served as one wall of the club. She could see from the anxious, stupid look on his face that he was losing consistently. He was more interested in watching the tits of the topless dealer than in paying attention to his cards. She was beginning to get sick of Reave. She kept him, she dressed him, chose all his clothes and all his make-up. He looked particularly cute tonight in his black silk suit and purple lipstick. If only he didn't always behave like a dummy. AA Catto expected, if not intelligence, at least some originality. All Reave seemed able to come up with was dog-like devotion.

Her hand moved towards the silver ring on her left hand. It was inlaid with a complicated gold pattern. Reave wore a matching collar. The two pieces of jewellery were linked by an energy transfer. AA Catto only had to move the ring to push any experience from a soft tingle to unbearable pain straight into Reave's nervous system. She turned the ring a fraction in the direction of pain. Reave jerked, dropped his cards, then looked in her direction and smiled. AA Catto's lower lip stuck our and her mouth turned down at the corners. He was so predictable. Even when she hurt him, he took it as a sign of affection. There were times when she felt like turning him loose to fend for himself.

Beside her in the bubble, one of the club's specially cloned entertainers was still going through his mildly obscene monologue. He wore a white suit, black shirt and an archaic white necktie. His right ear was pierced by a plain gold ring and his black hair was slicked back and shining. His face was framed by symmetrical sideburns. AA Catto assumed that some pretty, juvenile gangster from the motion picture era had been used as a model for his batch. The big thing in Litz right then was images from the days before break-up. A pale, almost albino girl drifted past the bubble. She wore high, polished boots and the black and red uniform of some ancient, long-vanished political/military culture. AA Catto wondered if she ought to get an outfit like that. She turned to the clone and cut him off in mid sentence.

'Do you think I'd look nice dressed like her?'

He responded without even looking at the girl.

'You'd look cute in anything, babe.'

His accent and vocabulary were tailored to match his image. The only trouble with clones was that they were anxious to please to the point of paranoia. AA Catto sighed, and smiled sweetly.

'Hold out your hand.'

The clone did as he was told. AA Catto took the thin black cheroot out of her mouth and ground it out in his palm. The clone gasped, clutched his injured hand and then drew back his fist to hit her. AA Catto shook her head.

'Don't bother. I don't want to be beaten up. I'm bored with you. You're dismissed.'

The clone got to his feet, still nursing his hand. AA Catto grinned as he walked away in the direction of the availability point. They were so funny, programmed like robots but still human enough to suffer. Although they could get tedious, AA Catto thoroughly approved of clones. They were good to have around.

She stood up herself, left the bubble and moved quietly to where Reave was still losing at four square. Reave didn't notice her as she came up behind him. AA Catto twisted the ring hard into the pain register. Reave screamed, his back arched, and he toppled from his stool. The topless clone halted in mid-deal and waited, holding the pack of long rectangular cards in front of her full breasts, to see what would happen. Clones weren't programmed to show emotion unless it was expected of them.

Reave lay on the carpeted floor, hunched in a foetal position. The other customers of the Venus Flytrap coolly acted as if nothing had happened. After about five seconds, AA Catto started to become impatient.

'Get up, damn you.'

Reave whimpered and slowly uncurled. AA Catto nudged him with her roe.

'I said get up.'

Painfully he climbed to his feet. He massaged the back of his neck and looked reproachfully at her.

'Why did you do that?'

AA Catto's lip curled. 'Because you're pathetic.'

'Pathetic?'

'You've lost a fortune tonight.'

Reave ran his fingers through his long, straight hair.

'But it doesn't matter. We've got permanent, unlimited credit.'

AA Catto clenched her tiny fists.

'I know we've got unlimited credit. It's my credit.'.

'So what's wrong?'

'You had to go and lose.'

Reave nodded towards the still motionless clone.

'It's very hard to win against clones. They're programmed to be almost unbeatable.'

'So why play?'

'It was something to do. You wouldn't talk to me.'

'Do you wonder that I don't talk to you?'

Reave looked round helplessly.

'I...'

'Oh, for God's sake, shut up. We're leaving.'

Reave turned and signalled to the dealer that he was giving up his place at the table. She smiled an automatic sexy smile.

'Thanks for the play, sir.'

Reave grinned back.

'That's okay.'

AA Catto scowled disgustedly.

'Do you have to be so grovellingly polite to clones?'

Reave shrugged.

'It doesn't cost anything. I mean, they are still human.'

'You disgust me. You and your stupid ideas.'

'I'm sorry.'

'Do you always have to apologize?'

'I...'

AA Catto's hand moved to her ring. The colour drained out of Reave's face and he held up his hands.

'Please... not now. If you knock me out again it'll only slow us up getting away from here.'

AA Catto smiled.

'That's true. You know, Reave, now and again you show flashes of crude intelligence.'

Reave bit his lip and said nothing. It wasn't worth talking back to her when she was in this kind of mood. He followed her as she turned on her heel and swept out of the club. There had been a time when Reave might have made some kind of gesture behind her back, but now he didn't even bother. He simply clasped his hands behind him and walked a few paces to her rear.

As they approached the club's exit, the liveried doorman, resplendent in maroon and gold, snapped to attention and saluted.

'You require transportation, Miss Catto?'

AA Catto shook her head.

'I think I'll walk, but you better get me some guardians.'

She handed him her credit card, and he dropped it into the call box on his wrist.

'How many would you like, Miss Catto?'

'Three should be enough.'

The doorman punched out the guardians' code, and within seconds three clear-eyed, square-jawed clones swung into the foyer of the club in perfect step. They wore the one-piece silver uniforms and red and blue helmets of the Litz Security Corporation. They halted in front of the doorman. Each one was at least two metres tall. They towered over everyone else in the foyer. The centre one of the three saluted the doorman.

'Guardian unit reporting as requested. Which is the client?'

The doorman indicated AA Catto. The centre guardian turned and saluted again.

'How may we serve you, miss?'

'My companion and I have decided to walk home. We'd like you to escort us. I trust you're adequately equipped?'

The guardian touched the long nightstick and heavy-duty stun-gun at his belt. His companions were similarly armed.

'We are equipped for anything that might occur in the street.'

'We might as well proceed then.'

The centre guardian bowed and held the door open. The one on his left preceded Reave and AA Catto into the street. The one on his right brought up the rear. After the darkness of the club, the street was a blaze of glory. Although no daylight was built into the environment of Litz, and it was a city of perpetual night, its illuminations were magnificent to look upon. At street level each ground car was festooned with lights. The stores, theatres, fun palaces and brothels vied with each other in the size and splendour of constantly shifting, glowing, illuminated signs. Overhead, searchlights slashed across the sky, probing the darkness with their slim fingers.

Every window in the high buildings showed its own light, and the lighter-than-air craft that floated between the tall towers all carried their own spots and riding lights. Some were even floodlit from below.

A few people hung round the carpeted sidewalks outside the cabarets and casinos. Small groups of whores made the come-on outside the bordellos and nudie bars, but apart from them the streets were almost empty of pedestrians. AA Catto and Reave only passed a few isolated people, all escorted by tall clones from the various security services. Every so often a black-uniformed, two-man foot patrol from the Litz Department of Correction would stroll past. The LDCs weren't clones. They were normal men who enjoyed the dangerous and brutal work.

The streets of Litz may not have been safe for unprotected individuals on foot, but for ground cars it was a different matter. The huge shining vehicles streamed past in a continuous procession down the wide, ten-lane thoroughfares. Their lights added to the general display of the endless Litz night.

AA Catto, Reave and their three guardians reached the first intersection. As they waited for the traffic control to change, the guardian who seemed to have the role of leader looked at her questioningly.

'Where do you wish to go, miss?'

'The Orchid House.'

AA Catto waved her hand towards the slim pyramid that stood a few blocks away, towering over the surrounding buildings. The guard looked at it and then back to the girl.

'If we took the main throughways it would be a longer walk, but there would be less possibility of incident.'

AA Catto grinned at him.

'Let's take the back streets, huh? I'm sure you boys can take care of any incident.'

The guardian bowed deferentially.

'As you wish, miss.'

Reave looked round dubiously, but didn't say anything. Despite the time he'd spent in Litz, he was still afraid of the menacing night-time city.

They crossed the intersection and walked on down the throughway for another block. Then they turned off into a side street. It was like entering another world. The bright lights were left behind. Dull yellow street lights replaced the flashing reds, greens, blues and golds of the main streets. They had only walked along the mean backway for a few minutes when a group of figures loomed up in front of them. The three guardians spread out in front of AA Catto and Reave, their hands going to their long nightsticks.

Faint glimmers of light were reflected from the shoulders of the figures that clustered round the lamp standard. AA Catto felt a tingle of excitement run through her. They were one of the notorious juv gangs that roamed the backways of the city, terrorizing anyone who strayed away from the bright lights.

The guardians ushered Reave and AA Catto out into the middle of the road. They spread out and formed a loose line between their charges and the juvs. As they came closer they could make out their distinctive outfits. The light had reflected from their shiny silver jackets. They were woven out of steel thread, with solid metal shoulders that rose into twin spikes on either side of the wearer's head. There was also another steel plate set between the shoulders, which bore the emblem of the wearer's gang. The outfit was completed by black tights with a decoratively padded crutch and heavy black knee boots, and, of course, the haircut. The juv haircuts varied from month to month. Right then, they were favouring it close cropped at the sides and very long over the top and back, with an elaborately curled quiff hanging down over their foreheads.

As AA Catto and her companions came within a couple of metres of the juvs, she saw that there were eight of them. They all appeared to be between the ages of twelve and fourteen. The tallest of them pulled a telescope knife from a pouch on his wide, studded belt and snapped it open. The guardians' hands dropped to their stunners. The juv raised his hand, inspected his fingers. He jabbed at one offending nail, grinned wolfishly and flicked the knife shut.

With the three guardians keeping themselves between their charges and the gang, AA Catto and Reave walked slowly past. A couple of the youths made obscene gestures, but none of them seemed to fancy taking on the heavily armed guardians. Reave kept looking back until the darkness once again swallowed up the gang. He let out his breath in a noisy gasp.

'Thank Christ that's all over.'

AA Catto looked at him contemptuously.

'Were you frightened, then?'

Reave nodded.

'Damn right I was frightened.'

'The guardians would have looked after us.'

Reave looked doubtful.

'If they'd decided to jump us, any one of us could have got a knife in the gut.'

AA Catto pursed her lips.

'They wouldn't have jumped us. They knew the guardians would have burned them down.'

'From what I've heard that wouldn't deter them. They can be totally suicidal if they feel like it.'

AA Catto sneered.

'From what you've heard?'

Reave shrugged but said nothing. They walked on in silence. The rest of the journey was uneventful until, just a short distance from the towering bulk of the Orchid House, they passed the dirty grey lights of a backway greasy spoon. A ragged figure was huddled in the doorway. As the small group walked past, it suddenly twitched and leaped to its feet. It quickly dodged past the guardians and grabbed at AA Catto's arm.

'Please miss, let's use your credit card, just for a meal, please miss.'

The voice was high and vaguely female, but the figure was too filthy and tattered for anyone to say, for sure, even whether it was human. AA Catto tried to shake it off, but it clung on with grim determination.

'Please miss, just a meal, let's use your card.'

The guardians swung round and pulled out their nightsticks. As the first blow struck, the creature fell to the ground screaming. It jerked and twisted, covering its head with its thin arms and pulling its knees up to protect its stomach. The guardians continued beating on it with their clubs until it ceased to move. Each time a blow fell there was a dull squishing thud. A pool of blood slowly spread over the surface of the road. When the figure lay still, one of the guardians prodded it with his toe. Satisfied that there was no sign of life, he hung his nightstick back on his belt. His two companions did the same. From the doorway of the greasy spoon a group of more ragged figures watched silently. They continued to stare as AA Catto, Reave and the three guardians walked away.

It was only another block before they reached the throughway and the imposing entrance of the Orchid House. No more of the back area people bothered them. As the black glass doors of the Orchid House slid open, the guardians saluted, turned on their heels and marched away. AA Catto and Reave entered the foyer and the huge doors hissed shut behind them.

After the backways, the Orchid House was an opulent paradise. The triangular floor was made from a single piece of polished marble. It was dominated by a huge fountain. The three walls, crossed by tier after tier of apartment balconies, sloped slightly inwards, and rose almost as far as the eye could see. They met at a point over a thousand metres above. Artificial sunlight streamed down from a huge white sphere set in the top of the pyramid. Cascades of flowers and climbing plants hung like long garlands from the balconies, They were a splash of wild colour against the white walls.

Reave followed AA Catto towards the lifts. These were black spheres that rose from the floor. At rest, they sat in hemispherical depressions at the side of the foyer. They moved in straight lines, parallel to the wall, without any visible support. Reave still hadn't figured out how they worked. AA Catto touched an illuminated stud on the side of the lift and a section of the side silently opened. She stepped inside and Reave did the same. The interior of the lift was lit by a soft red light. Muted music came from a hidden speaker. AA Catto pressed the control for the ninety-third floor. Reave ran his fingers through his hair.

'Sure is good to be back home.'

AA Catto's eyes narrowed. She looked sideways at Reave.

'Don't get too pleased too soon, honey.'

Reave turned and looked at her in surprise.

'What's wrong now?'

'You've been giving me a pain all evening.'

'Oh, come on.'

'Come on, nothing. You've pissed me off, and you're going to pay for it.'

'Please, isn't it a bit late in the day for more games?'

AA Catto held up her ring finger.

'No games, sweetie. You are going to suffer.'

Reave opened his mouth to speak. He thought better of it, and closed it again. If the fancy took her, AA Catto had enough dope in the apartment to keep her awake for days. The game could go on for ages. He felt sick to his stomach. The lift stopped at the ninety-third floor and Reave followed her out, fingering the collar round his neck.

5

Jeb Stuart Ho, despite his concentration, was beginning to lose all sense of time. He could no longer remember how long he and the Minstrel Boy had been out in the nothings. The lizard had settled down to a steady, bounding lope, exactly as though it was running on hard ground. The lizard seemed to have a very definite sense of purpose. That was the only reassuring thing about the whole situation.

Jeb Stuart Ho looked to his left. He could just about make out the Minstrel Boy against the strange glittering grey mist. The image of the man on the lizard kept shifting and breaking up. It was only when the two of them were very close together that he could see the Minstrel Boy and his mount clearly. At one point, the Minstrel Boy had drifted some distance away and vanished altogether. It was then that Jeb Stuart Ho had come close to panic. He hadn't experienced a feeling like that since he was a small child. The brotherhood discipline had kept him from going over the edge, but he'd been immeasurably relieved when the Minstrel Boy had finally flickered into view again.

Ho stretched out his hand. It was a signal to the Minstrel Boy that he wanted to say something. Unless they were actually touching, there was no point in speaking. The words became lost and jumbled in the howling silence of the bright greyness. The Minstrel Boy moved towards him and grasped his hand.

'What's the trouble, Killer?'

Jeb Stuart Ho disliked the nickname the Minstrel Boy was trying to saddle him with, but he didn't complain. There would be time enough for that when they reached somewhere tangible.

'Where are we now?'

'In the nothings.'

'I know that. What I meant was, will we get somewhere soon?'

Jeb Stuart Ho made himself act very patiently when talking to the Minstrel Boy. The Minstrel Boy grinned at him.

'Yeah… soon.'

'How soon?'

'Dunno. Time's pretty relative out here.'

'Relative to what?'

The Minstrel Boy laughed.

'Relative to just about anything that's going. That's why it's so hard to estimate.'

Jeb Stuart Ho was sure that he was deliberately trying to confuse him. He wasn't sure why.

'Are you sure you know where you are?'

'Sure I'm sure. I always know where I am. I'm famous for it.'

The Minstrel Boy let go of Jeb Stuart Ho's hand, and they drifted apart. The Minstrel Boy's image began to flicker as the space between them increased.

Despite all his training, the lack of time sense weighed heavily on Jeb Stuart Ho. Nothing had prepared him for being mounted on the galloping lizard, rushing headlong into seemingly eternal greyness. He closed his eyes and tried to put himself into an intermediate state of trance. At first it was impossible, but gradually he felt himself merging with the strange, shattered universe. It was the sound of a voice that eventually brought him back to the material world.

'Come on, Killer. Wake up, what's wrong with you?'

Jeb Stuart Ho opened his eyes. The Minstrel Boy was standing beside him, tugging at his leg.

'What's the matter with you? I thought your brain had fused.'

Jeb Stuart Ho shook his head.

'I was meditating.'

'No shit?'

Ho suddenly realized that he could hear the Minstrel Boy quite clearly without their actually touching. They were obviously out of the nothings. He looked around. They were standing on a huge, even expanse of grey rock. It was flat and featureless. The sky above was a lighter shade of grey, and the air was damp and cold. The lizards were moving about uncomfortably. Ho shivered, and pulled his cloak tight round his shoulders.

'Are we on the same level as Litz?'

The Minstrel Boy shook his head. 'Somewhere on the way.'

'Where?'

'That's hard to say.'

'I thought you took pride in knowing where you are.'

The Minstrel Boy scowled.

'I don't take pride, I know.'

'Should a developed faculty not be a source of pride?'

'I know, that's all.'

Jeb Stuart Ho swung a leg over the lizard's back. 'As you wish.'

He slid to the ground.

'What is this place?'

The Minstrel Boy shrugged.

'It has no name. By rights it shouldn't be here. I can't see what keeps it stable.'

'Why did we stop here?'

'The lizards stopped. They don't seem happy.'

'What has happened to them?'

The Minstrel Boy took off his hat and ran his fingers through his curly hair.

'I don't know. Their minds seem to be closed. I can't get across at all.'

It was the first time Jeb Stuart Ho had seen the Minstrel Boy look genuinely worried. He hesitated before he spoke again.

'Should we not continue with caution and find out why the lizards have brought us to this place?'

The Minstrel Boy looked down at the ground.

'I'd just as soon turn back.'

'You know I can't do that.'

'Sure.'

Jeb Stuart Ho remounted his lizard. The Minstrel Boy reluctantly did the same. Before they started to move the Minstrel Boy looked across at Ho.

'I really don't like this. Just remember that.'

Ho looked grimly ahead.

'I'll remember.'

The Minstrel Boy dug his spurs hard into the lizard. It lurched away at a half-hearted waddle. Jeb Stuart Ho's mount trailed after it in the same lethargic manner. They continued their slow progress for over an hour. A strange, cone-shaped promontory appeared on the horizon. As they gradually approached it, the lizards became increasingly restive and uneasy. They were awkward to handle, and kept trying to stray away from the Minstrel Boy's course.

About three hundred metres from the slope of the cone, the lizards stopped dead and refused to go any further. They stood still, shifting their weight from one foot to another and swinging their long necks from side to side. Jeb Stuart Ho and the Minstrel Boy both dismounted. Whatever was affecting the lizards was also affecting the two men. The Minstrel Boy had broken out in a cold sweat, and Jeb Stuart Ho felt an irrational fear trying to take hold of him. He exerted the maximum control on his mind and looked at the Minstrel Boy.

'There is something terribly wrong here.'

The Minstrel Boy had started to shake. His voice came out as a strangled croak.

'Let's get out of here.'

Jeb Stuart Ho gripped him by the shoulder.

'Relax, breathe slowly and deeply. A man may run from an external danger, but cannot run from fear in his mind.'

The Minstrel Boy nodded. Sweat was still pouring off him. It was obvious he was trying to keep himself together, but when he spoke his voice was cracking on the verge of hysteria.

'Let's get the hell out of here! Now! I can't stand it.'

'Do not succumb to the fear. The fear of fear is the poison of the soul.'

'I... can't take it!'

The Minstrel Boy's voice was almost screaming. Jeb Stuart Ho took his face in both hands. He massaged the Minstrel Boy's neck.

'Think, be calm, use your intelligence. What is this thing?'

'I don't know. I can't think.'

'Where does it come from?'

The Minstrel Boy could no longer speak. He waved his hand in the direction of the cone. His legs began to give way and he clung to Jeb Stuart Ho. Ho gently pulled him back to his feet.

'We must go to the cone and make this thing cease.'

'No! No! No!'

The Minstrel Boy slipped into uncontrollable hysterics. Jeb Stuart Ho slapped him hard across the face, and he fell silent. Jeb Stuart Ho took him by the arm and, half supporting him, began to lead him towards the cone. They stumbled for about a hundred metres. The mind-wrenching fear seemed to grow stronger. Then the Minstrel Boy groaned and sank to his knees.

'I can't go on.'

'The superior man faces his fear and in facing it overcomes his weakness.'

The Minstrel Boy fell on his side. He rolled over and pulled his knees up to his chest.

Jeb Stuart Ho knelt down beside the Minstrel Boy.

'If you don't strive to overcome it, it could kill you.'

'I don't care!'

The Minstrel Boy lay still with his eyes tightly closed and his face contorted. Jeb Stuart Ho stood up, and began walking up the side of the cone by himself. Each step became an inhuman effort. The fear had become a physical force. His legs were leaden. It was like wading in sand. He stumbled frequently. As he neared the top, it became almost more than he could bear. The sky glowed an evil, menacing red. The rock appeared to reflect it, and danced with flame. The force battered at him like a hurricane. Black hallucinations, flapping like murderous bats, swooped at the edge of his vision.

He reached the top. The force became absolute torture. It was pushing at him so hard that it seemed to be tearing the flesh from his bones. It screamed around him like monsters from some awful hell. In front of him, in the very summit of the cone, was a circular depression. Lying in it, on a bed of soft sand, were nine gold eggs. Each one was about half the height of a man. Jeb Stuart Ho knew immediately that they were the source of the power. His instinct was to destroy them. His hand went to his gun. It was like moving in slow motion. Inch by inch his fingers moved towards his belt. All the force seemed to be concentrated on his right arm. It was filled with a burning cold that gnawed at the bone and muscle. His fingers curled round the butt. That too was deathly cold. His fingers froze to it. As he slowly drew the gun from the holster, it felt as if the flesh of his hand was being ripped apart. He slowly raised the gun. Its weight seemed unbearable. The muscles in his arm felt like they were going to snap. Gradually the gun came in line with the clutch of eggs. He eased back the trigger. The scream around him rose in pitch. It felt as though his ears had started bleeding, maybe his very brain. The eggs seemed far away. His vision tunnelled. He desperately hauled on the trigger. It would hardly move. He began to black out, then, through it all, he heard the Minstrel Boy screaming.

'Don't! Don't! For God's sake, don't do it! They're only trying to protect themselves.'

It suddenly all fell into place. Jeb Stuart Ho touched the half-formed entities inside the gold shells. He felt the power of the scarcely developed minds. He felt their fear and their vulnerability. He was awed by what they might become. For an instant everything hung poised. The gun fell from his fingers. He sank, cross-legged, to the ground. He forced his mind to be calm. The beings' fear still washed over him, but it was no longer aimed directly at him. He gathered all his strength and slowly directed peace and gentleness. He meant them no harm. He projected that as hard as he could. Veins pumped in his forehead as he tried to thrust his way through the fear.

He reached them. His thoughts penetrated through to the beings in the eggs. They seized on his projections as something new and strange. They dragged it out of him with a greedy hunger. They were insatiable. He hung on to stop his mind being dragged from him. He begged them to stop, but their infant greed demanded more and more. Jeb Stuart Ho reached his final limit. His consciousness was drained away.

The world went black. His body toppled, and rolled down the side of the cone like a discarded puppet whose strings had been cut.

He woke up to find the Minstrel Boy wiping his face with a damp cloth. He grinned at Ho.

'Shit, Killer. I really thought you were dead for sure, this time.'

Jeb Stuart Ho raised his head.

'How long have I been here?'

The Minstrel Boy shrugged.

'Maybe a couple of hours.'

'What happened?'

'Don't ask me. You were up there, you did it. One minute all hell was breaking loose, then suddenly it was beautiful, like the dawn coming up.'

Jeb Stuart Ho sat up. The landscape had completely changed. The ground was still grey rock, but it was broken up by clumps of green vegetation growing out of cracks in its surface. Tiny streams trickled into crystal clear pools. The sky was a deep, even blue. It was as if the beings had taken apart his mind, and reshaped their environment according to what they found there. A little distance away, the lizards grazed happily on the vegetation.

Jeb Stuart Ho carefully stood up. He had expected his body to show some signs of strain after the ordeal. He was surprised to find there were none. He felt as though he had just woken from a comfortable sleep. He looked at the cone. It radiated a glow of benign contentment. His gun was still lying at the foot of the slope, where it had come to rest after he had dropped it. He walked over and picked it up. As he touched the weapon, the sky seemed to darken. The lizards looked up in alarm. He quickly dropped it into its holster and things resumed their previous calm. The lizards returned to their chewing.

The Minstrel Boy walked over to where Jeb Stuart Ho was standing at the foot of the cone. He was grinning happily. His friendliness was almost unnatural. He put his arm round Ho's shoulders.

'Looks like it turned out okay.'

Jeb Stuart Ho nodded.

'It would seem so.'

The Minstrel Boy looked up at the cone.

'I'm almost sorry to leave.'

'We have to leave.'

'I knew you'd say that.'

'We should start.'

The Minstrel Boy stared at the ground. He seemed reluctant to start back into the nothings.

'It's like I'm thinking we ought to leave some kind of mark on this place.'

Jeb Stuart Ho looked at him in surprise.

'Why?'

'I dunno, just so we know we've been here.'

'Surely we know that without leaving our mark here?'

'Maybe we should give it a name or something?'

Jeb Stuart Ho gestured towards the top of the cone.

'They must have a name for this place.

The Minstrel Boy shrugged.

'Yeah, maybe. I dunno.'

He put two fingers in his mouth and gave a high-pitched whistle. The lizards looked up, and began lumbering slowly towards where the two men were standing. Ho and the Minstrel Boy each caught the reins of his own mount, and climbed into the saddle. They turned the lizards and rode slowly past the cone. Jeb Stuart Ho paused for a moment and stared hard at it, then he took a deep breath and started after the Minstrel Boy.

6

A little grey-haired man in a quilted dressing gown tugged open the lift gate and padded across the frayed carpet of the Leader Hotel lobby, and up to the reception desk. He waited until the desk clerk looked up from his comic book and deigned to notice him.

'Yeah?'

The little man cleared his throat, and tugged the faded robe closer round his bony shoulders.

'Did my letter come?'

The desk clerk didn't even bother to look at the pigeon-holes behind him.

'Nothing came.'

The little man remained where he was.

'Are you sure? Couldn't you check?'

The desk clerk put down his comic book and looked at the little man with cold patience.

'Nothing came, Arthur. Just like yesterday, and the day before that, and the day before that and every day you've been here. Nothing ever comes for you, Arthur. Okay?'

Arthur cleared his throat again.

'I'll try tomorrow.'

The desk clerk turned over the page of his comic book.

'You do that.'

Arthur turned away and shuffled back to the lift. Billy Oblivion sprawled in the sagging armchair and watched the tiny drama without interest. It happened every day. Every day Arthur came down from his tiny room on the twenty-seventh floor to look for the letter that would change his life. Every day the letter failed to arrive. The lift door rattled shut and Arthur returned to the twenty-seventh floor. The desk clerk went back to his comic book, and Billy went on staring at the semi-erotic frieze that was slowly crumbling away from the dirty pink wall.

For most of its residents the Leader Hotel was the end of the line. A tall warren of tiny rooms and dim corridors that smelled of decay and urine. As long as you kept paying the rent you were wholly, totally free to overdose, drink yourself to death or simply grow numb. Billy hoped that none of those things would happen to him. He hoped that one day he'd manage to get out of the place and into something better. Billy's hope didn't guarantee him any protection against those fates. Most people in the Leader Hotel hoped for something, but still it happened to them. The Leader Hotel was the last stop for the non-people, the ones who, for one reason or another, didn't have credit cards.

Billy Oblivion didn't have a credit card. He'd never had one. He'd wandered into Litz without one, found that the good life was closed to him, and wound up at the Leader. He'd been there ever since. Billy the pimp they called him now. That was on account of Darlene. Darlene had picked him up, and kept him ever since. Darlene made enough to keep them both surviving at the Leader, but never enough for them to get out. Darlene didn't have a credit card. It had been taken away for some unspecified crime. Darlene never went into the exact details.

Not having a credit card created problems for Darlene in her profession, and Darlene's problems automatically became Billy's problems. Not having a credit card meant that her tricks couldn't pay her by a straightforward credit transfer. She had to operate a kind of barter system. She fucked them, or did whatever else they wanted, and they slipped her some kind of small valuable. These she unloaded on the desk clerk, who credited them with enough to pay the rent and live. He, of course, only gave them a fraction of what the stuff was worth, and made sure they never got sufficiently ahead actually to get out of the hotel.

The previous night, however, Billy and Darlene had made more of a mess of things than usual. Darlene had had a reasonably good afternoon. She'd turned three tricks. Three tricks in an afternoon was good for her. It wasn't that Darlene was unattractive, but there was no way she could compete with the big legitimate brothels. They creamed off most of the custom that just wanted to get laid. Darlene had to make do with the ones who were funny for lowlife. She got the ones who liked to follow a good-looking non-person back to the Leader, the ones who got an extra kick that way.

The three tricks the previous afternoon had made Billy and Darlene a shade overconfident, They'd blown all their credit on a bottle of hotel booze and a package of funaids. Darlene had been certain that if she hit the street later that night, not that night and day made much difference in the permanent dark of the city, she could make the next day's room rent.

Of course, it had all been a fantasy. The booze and the pills had made sure that they'd become too fused to move from the bed until the house detective had come knocking with his regular morning call of pay up or quit. They didn't have the room rent, but the desk clerk and the house detective had been very good about it. They'd let Billy sit around in the lobby until Darlene hustled up the rent. They hadn't even made them move their stuff out, just taken away the key.

Billy waited. It was kind of embarrassing but there was nothing else he could do. The lobby of the Leader Hotel was particularly depressing. It smelled of squalor and decay. The potted palms in the corner had long ago become brown, dry mummies, but no one had bothered to replace them or even throw them out. The carpet was worn into holes in a number of places. The ancient creaking lift only worked by a miracle, and there seemed to be no logical reason why the scarred and battered armchairs that stood dotted about in lonely groups hadn't fallen into shapeless ruin a long time ago. The high ceiling was marked with huge brown patches of damp.

Billy tried to distract himself by watching the vid that was mounted to the right of the reception desk. Its colour was blotchy and the 3D was alarmingly out of alignment. The only thing that could be said in its favour was that it worked at all. Not that he could see it all that clearly. His view was constantly interrupted by the swaying heads of three old winos who clustered around it as though it actually gave out heat. They were avidly watching one of the multiple hanging shows. Billy wondered how they managed to enjoy it so much. Everyone knew that the hanging shows were fixed.

After another hour, Billy's patience was finally rewarded. Darlene walked in with a fat little citizen in tow. He was just the type who always seemed to go for her. Pink with nervousness and excitement, he was sweating profusely into his pale blue one-piece suit. Dark stain had formed under his armpits. It was obvious that his dry-all-day anti-perspirant wasn't holding up under the strain.

Darlene was at least a head taller than the trick. Billy had to admit that she looked good. Her red dress scarcely covered her arse, leaving a flash of inviting thigh above her matching stockings and boots. The thin straps of her red suspenders added an extra touch of excitement. The red ensemble contrasted so nicely with her jet-black skin and close-cropped hair. There was no mistaking that Darlene was a good-looking broad. Billy was proud to have her. He loved that black skin, and he hoped she'd never make enough to get the colour change she was always bitching about.

Billy gave no sign of recognition as she stopped by the reception desk and turned pointedly towards the trick. It didn't do for a pimp to be too much in evidence while his woman was hustling. It tended to make the tricks nervous. Darlene winked at him from behind the fat man's back, but Billy didn't respond. Then she went to work. She took the trick by the arm and steered him up to the reception desk.

'I guess you wouldn't mind giving my friend the desk clerk a little present, would you? He could get into trouble for letting me take you up to my room. You can use your credit card, honey. It's okay. It goes through the hotel.'

The little man looked apprehensively at the desk clerk.

'The payment won't be traced, will it?'

Darlene and the desk clerk both smiled reassuringly.

'Not a chance of that.'

The fat man reluctantly produced his credit card. The desk clerk dropped it into the hotel transfer unit. He dialled out the appropriate amount and handed it back. Billy sighed quietly as the desk clerk gave Darlene the room key. They were good for another day. She grinned at him and firmly propelled the fat man towards the lift.

'This way, honey. I know we're going to have a fantastic time. Just fantastic.'

The lift door rattled shut and they disappeared from sight. Billy stood up and brushed a bit of chair cover from his yellow satin suit. He straightened the diamante collar, brushed back his curly hair and strolled over to the desk.

'Did you clip him for enough so I can get a drink?'

The desk clerk grinned.

'He got clipped but good.'

'Yeah?'

'Yeah. I did you a favour, kid. I kind of like you and your woman so I got two days' rent, a bit for me and a bit over. I figured you could use it after the state you got into last night.'

Billy didn't need to be reminded of the comedown he was going through. He did his best to look grateful.

'Give me a drink.'

The desk clerk reached under the counter and produced a bottle of schnapps and two glasses. He filled one and then cocked an eyebrow at Billy. Billy knew the ritual. He grinned.

'Go ahead, friend. Have one on me.'

He filled the second glass and downed it in one gulp. Billy took a little more time with his. He had to treat his head gently. It was in a bad way. The desk clerk was already smiling, looking for a refill. Billy nodded, and the desk clerk took another shot. He was just angling for another when Lame Nancy hobbled in. She grinned at Billy.

'Found some credit then, stud?'

'What's it to you?'

'I like to see young people happy.'

Billy looked dubiously at Nancy. She was always showing up just after Darlene. Billy knew she was doing her best to try and get Darlene away from him. He wondered if she actually followed her about. Lame Nancy was a dyke who liked to keep her girls working. She had four set up in different rooms of the Leader. Her ambition seemed to be to make Darlene number five. Lame Nancy nodded towards the bottle of schnapps.

'Is there a drink in that for me?'

Billy's lip curled.

'Depends who's paying for it.'

Nancy sneered and patted Billy's cheek.

'I'll pay, sweet thing. Though I don't know what you're worried about. That little honey of yours is upstairs making you the price of a few drinks.'

'You got four, so I figure you can buy your own.'

Lame Nancy nodded towards the bottle. The desk clerk produced a third glass and poured Nancy a shot. She swallowed it in one gulp, and nodded for another. While she downed the second, Billy looked at her carefully. He knew that she'd probably take Darlene away if he gave her the chance. Lame Nancy looked striking and had a powerful personality. It radiated from her as she leaned against the bar in one of her favourite gunfighter poses. There was no denying that she was bizarre enough to attract Darlene. She gave an overall impression of being totally white. Her hair was white and cut into a shaggy crewcut, her skin had been done into an opalescent pearl finish. She wore a white body stocking, silver wedge-heeled sandals and a highly polished stainless steel belt.

The whole outfit seemed designed to contrast sharply with the black callipers that supported her withered leg. Even these seemed to be designed for maximum shock. They were made from highly polished black steel, inlaid with an elaborate pattern of gold damascene. Lame Nancy cut a strange, impressive figure.

The lift door rattled back, and Billy switched his attention away from Nancy. The fat man hurried out of the lift, straight for the street door. He was still sweating, and avoided everyone's eyes. Nancy laughed.

'Looks like your sweetie will be down with something for you soon, Billy dear.'

Billy didn't say anything. He knew he was being baited. Nancy's grin broadened.

'You ought to get that honey of yours to pull in a bit more of the goods. I know I would.'

Billy scowled.

'Keep out of my business, will you.'

Nancy laughed again.

'I intend to, sweet thing. There ain't enough in it for me.'

The lift rattled again. This time it was Darlene. Billy walked across the lobby to meet her. He wanted to head her off before she could join Nancy at the desk. He knew Nancy would try and get her drunk, and be dropping all kinds of broad hints about how much better a time Darlene would have with her rather than Billy. Billy didn't need that. He grinned at Darlene.

'Hi, how did it go?'

Darlene scowled.

'It went.'

'Did you get anything?'

Darlene fished between her breasts and came up with a small platinum pacifier.

'Enough.'

'Great.'

'That pig behind the desk will still short-change us.'

'So what can we do?'

'What can you do? You're supposed to take care of business. I just do the work.'

Billy took hold of her arm.

'Don't get mad.'

'I ain't mad. I just don't need it.'

'Was it rough?'

Darlene's mouth curled into a sneer.

'Oh no, not rough, just another trick.'

'What happened?'

'You really want to know?'

'If it helps.'

'If it helps? Well, if it helps, he got me to squat on the floor of the shower while he pissed on me, and then I had to suck him off. Okay? Does that help? All for one lousy trinket. You know, sometimes I think you like to hear what I do with the tricks. Maybe you get a kick out of it.'

Darlene was working herself up into a frenzy. Billy wasn't sure whether to placate or punch her. While he was making up his mind, she started again.

'Maybe you'd like to have a go yourself. You fancy me squatting in front of you while you pissed over me?'

Billy shook his head.

'No, of course not.'

He wondered if he would enjoy it. He'd never thought about it before. He smiled at Darlene. The tirade had gone on long enough.

'Listen honey, we've got a bit of credit, why don't we get a bottle and go upstairs?'

Darlene didn't seem about to give in.

'You want to end up the same way we did today? I'm going out again to see what I can get.'

Before Billy could say anything, she had pulled away from him and was marching across the lobby, swaying her hips. She looked straight ahead, avoiding the stares of Nancy and the desk clerk. As she was about to flounce out into the street she almost collided with two men coming into the hotel.

'Why the fuck don't you look where you're going?'

One of the men stepped back and bowed slightly.

'I'm sorry.'

Darlene was going to start complaining, when she took a second look at them. One was a tall thin man, wrapped in a black cape. His straight hair hung to his shoulders, and the hilt of an evil-looking sword protruded from the cape. The other one was shorter and, if anything, thinner. A mass of black unruly curls were stuffed under a wide-brimmed hat. He wore a black frock coat and high boots. He had the same hard air of determination as his companion. Darlene ducked hastily out of the door. Her tantrum was completely forgotten. She didn't want to stick around and find out what the two strangers wanted.

Billy felt much the same way only, to him, they weren't both strangers. He recognized the Minstrel Boy straight away. They'd been through a lot of trouble together, and most of the time Billy had wound up looking stupid. He could imagine the Minstrel Boy's sneers when he found out that Billy had sunk to pimping in Litz. Billy stepped quickly back into the lift before the Minstrel Boy noticed him.

The Minstrel Boy and Jeb Stuart Ho walked up to the desk. Lame Nancy and the desk clerk both looked at them curiously. The winos went on staring at the Execution Hour. The desk clerk put down his comic book as they approached. 'You want some rooms, gentlemen?'

The Minstrel Boy shook his head. 'Not right now.'

It was the Minstrel Boy who was doing the talking. It had been his idea to make the Leader Hotel their first stop. They'd left the lizards in the pen at the edge of the nothings, and taken a ground cab into downtown Litz. In the past, the Minstrel Boy had found the Leader an ideal point at which to plug into the city's wealth of gossip and rumour. The desk clerk scowled at him.

'If you don't want rooms, what do you want?'

'Some information.'

'We sell room and board, we don't give out information. If you want information, watch the screen. Only don't do it here if you ain't rented no room.'

The Minstrel Boy smiled.

'Since when did information stop being worth something in Litz?'

The desk clerk looked sideways at him.

'You willing to pay?'

The Minstrel Boy nodded. He turned to Jeb Stuart Ho.

'You got your credit card?'

Ho put his hand under his cloak, and passed a card to the Minstrel Boy. The eyes of both Nancy and the desk clerk fastened on the black-edged brotherhood credit card as he placed it on the desk and grinned.

'Why don't you take whatever you think ten minutes of your conversation is worth.'

The desk clerk gingerly picked up the card. He seemed almost nervous of it. Nancy watched intently as he placed it in the transfer unit. He dialled out a modest sum. He looked up at the Minstrel Boy.

'Is that okay?'

'If that's what you think you're worth, then sure it's okay.'

The desk clerk handed the card back to the Minstrel Boy. He turned it over and then passed it to Jeb Stuart Ho. The desk clerk began to look nervous.

'What do you gentlemen want to know?'

Jeb Stuart Ho placed the tri-di of AA Catto in front of the desk clerk.

'Have you ever seen this woman?'

The desk clerk shook his head.

'She's never been in here.'

The Minstrel Boy looked at him sharply.

'You sure about that?'

'Never forget a face.'

'You ever hear of someone called AA Catto?'

'I heard the name.'

'What did you hear about her?'

'I heard people talk about her.'

'What did you hear?'

'Rich little bitch by all accounts. She came into town. Started doing the society circuit. The nightclubs, the best parties. The rumour was that she was kind of wild. Like, you know, vicious. Into pain, other people's pain. By all accounts she keeps herself looking like a young kid. That's about all I know.'

'Is she still in town?'

'As far as I know.'

'Do you know where she's living?'

'I heard she had an apartment at the Orchid House.'

'The Orchid House, where's that?'

'It's the big new apartment building. The big triangular one, right in the middle of downtown. You can't miss it.'

The Minstrel Boy turned to Jeb Stuart Ho.

'I guess that's about it. All you have to do is get down there.'

The desk clerk laughed.

'It ain't as easy as that.'

The Minstrel Boy turned back to him.

'Why not?'

'You'll never get inside the place. Not unless the lady wants to see you.'

'Why?'

'It's like a goddamn fortress. That's part of the service. Unless you've got a pass from a resident you'll never get past the security. There's a whole army of them.'

The desk clerk looked at him slyly.

'That's if the lady doesn't want to see you.'

The Minstrel Boy grinned.

'The lady hasn't had a chance to get to know us yet.'

He thought for a minute.

'Suppose we took an apartment in the building?'

The desk clerk shook his head.

'Not a chance. There's a waiting list a mile long.'

'Can't you jump the list? I mean, if you've got the credit, surely anything's possible?'

'Not there it's not. Everyone who wants to move in there's got credit. You have to pay a fortune in bribes just to get on the list.'

'So we'd better make friends with the lady.'

The desk clerk grinned.

'That's the best way. Only the lady doesn't seem to be too friendly.'

The Minstrel Boy smiled.

'Maybe.'

He glanced at Jeb Stuart Ho.

'My friend here can be amazingly charming when he has to be.'

The desk clerk looked across at Jeb Stuart Ho, and then back to the Minstrel Boy.

'He doesn't say much.'

'That's part of his charm.'

There was a pause. The desk clerk looked down at the transfer unit, and then back up at the Minstrel Boy.

'There's nothing else you'd like to know?'

The Minstrel Boy shook his head.

'I think we've had our money's worth.'

He turned away, and looked at Jeb Stuart Ho. 'I don't think we'll achieve much more here.'

'We know now where the woman lives.'

They walked towards the door and out into the street. Nancy watched them thoughtfully until they disappeared from sight.

7

As Jeb Stuart Ho and the Minstrel Boy emerged from the Leader Hotel, back into the glittering streets of Litz, the executive paused. He looked up and down the street. An airship drifted overhead about fifty metres up, following the line of the street. Lights shone out from the gondola. The sound of laughter and a ragtime piano drifted down. The Minstrel Boy looked up into the darkness and grinned.

'They sure know how to have parties in this town.'

Jeb Stuart Ho pursed his lips.

'They seem to know very little else.'

The Minstrel Boy shot him a sideways glance.

'You ought to check out a few, Killer. It'll be an education for you.'

Ho continued to look up and down the street.

'My education is a process that continues without the need to study such things as parties.

'Hell, you ought to relax.'

'My task allows me no space to relax.'

The Minstrel Boy shook his head.

'There's no hope for you, man.'

Jeb Stuart Ho looked confused.

'I'm sorry. I don't understand you. Hope can have no influence on probability.'

The airship drifted on down the street. The Minstrel Boy watched it go. Then he looked back at Ho.

'What's the matter with you, Killer? Why do you keep looking up and down the street like you were lost?'

'I was computing my next move until you began to talk about parties.'

'I'm sorry.'

'Do not be sorry. All information is of value. Unfortunately, parties are not particularly relevant.'

'Was that a joke?'

'What?'

'Parties not being particularly relevant.'

'I fail to understand.'

The Minstrel Boy waved his hand in despair.

'Forget it. If you're stuck for a next move, why don't you pay me off?'

'I may need you again.'

'You may what?'

'I may need you again.'

'Shit! I got you to Litz. What more do you want? You don't need me to help you knock the chick off.'

'She might leave the city. I'd need you if that should happen.'

The Minstrel Boy began to get exasperated.

'Okay, okay, if that happens, come and see me. Maybe we can make a deal. I might even take the job. In the meantime, pay me off. I want to have a little fun. I ain't about to watch you hunt this chick all over town.'

Jeb Stuart Ho nodded thoughtfully. 'How would you like to be paid?'

The Minstrel Boy grinned.

'The way I figured it, you've got this credit card. Right?'

'Right.'

'It's unlimited. Right?'

'Right.'

'All we have to do is go along to a bank and get them to issue me with a temporary card, so I can draw on your credit for a limited period, say a month. How does that suit you? That be okay?'

Jeb Stuart Ho made a slight bow.

'If that's what you want, I will do it.'

'Great.'

'There's one thing, though.'

The Minstrel Boy looked suspicious. 'What?'

'Where do we find a bank?'

The Minstrel Boy laughed. 'That's no problem.'

He waved his hand down the street.

'Walk in any direction. We'll soon find one. They need a lot of banks in Litz.'

'Are they open at night?'

The Minstrel Boy nodded.

'Sure they're open. They have to be. It's always night here.'

They started walking. It only took them two blocks before they found one. The First Exploitive Bank of Litz squatted smugly between a mass sex operation and a torture parlour. Its solid granite façade contrasted sharply with the glass and neon of its immediate neighbours. It seemed like a haven of conservative responsibility. As they mounted the steps that led up to the huge brass doors, Jeb Stuart Ho looked questioningly at the Minstrel Boy.

'Why do they need such places?'

'Banks?'

'Yes.'

'It gives them something to do. Them that like it.'

'Surely, in many places, Stuff credit is given free to all people?'

'They like to do things the hard way here.'

'It gives them power over their fellows.'

'That's the way they like it.'

'It seems hardly fair.'

'People who want things fair don't come here.'

Jeb Stuart Ho thought about it. They reached the top of the steps. The door was flanked by a squad of bank security guards armed with machine pistols and fragmentation bombs. As they walked inside, one of the guards stepped back on to a concealed foot switch, and a cluster of cameras, set high in the lofty ceiling, tracked their progress across the spacious marble interior. They joined the line in front of one of the cashiers' windows. The presence of the heavily armed Ho sent a ripple of alarm through the other customers. From various points around the bank, more armed guards watched him intently.

The line moved slowly towards the cashier's window. Finally it was Jeb Stuart Ho's turn. A thin-lipped, middle-aged man in a black jacket and stiff wing collar stated nervously at him from behind the armoured glass.

'Can I help you?'

Jeb Stuart Ho smiled politely.

'I'd like to arrange a movement of credit.'

He indicated the Minstrel Boy.

'I'd like my friend here to have a temporary credit card on my account.'

The clerk peered over the top of his rimless glasses.

'That kind of transaction is somewhat irregular.'

'Surely it is possible?'

'You'll have to wait.'

Jeb Stuart Ho bowed. The clerk climbed from his stool, but then turned back to Jeb Stuart Ho.

'I'll need your card.'

Jeb Stuart Ho handed over the black-edged credit card. The clerk almost dropped it in fright, then collected himself and hurried away. Jeb Stuart Ho and the Minstrel Boy waited. They waited for five minutes. Jeb Stuart Ho closed his eyes. Five minutes became ten. The Minstrel Boy shifted from one foot to the other. After twelve minutes the clerk returned. He was accompanied by a more portly, more authoritarian version of himself. The portly one seemed determined not to be intimidated by the black-clad executive.

'Is this your card, sir?'

'Yes.'

'And you wish a temporary card issued to this... gentleman?'

He gestured towards the Minstrel Boy with a look of distaste. Jeb Stuart Ho nodded.

'That is correct.'

'You have to make a special appointment to transact that kind of business.'

'Why?'

'Because it is the normal procedure.'

'I see.'

There was a pause while the two men looked at each other. Finally the portly clerk gave in.

'If you go along to the window marked Special Appointments, you can make the arrangements.'

Jeb Stuart Ho bowed again. He and the Minstrel Boy moved along to the window marked Special Appointments. Behind it was a sour-faced woman with scraped-back grey hair. She wore a high-necked black dress with a cameo brooch at the throat. A pair of spectacles hung from her neck by a chain. She looked coldly at Jeb Stuart Ho.

'Yes?'

Ho took a deep breath and repeated his request for the temporary card. The woman picked up his card and looked hard at it.

'Wait a moment.'

She disappeared. They waited for another seven minutes. A grossly fat little man in a black jacket and striped trousers bustled up to them. He held Jeb Stuart Ho's card in one hand, and thrust out the other in jovial greeting. Both hands were heavy with gold rings. He was sweating profusely despite the almost icy air conditioning. When he smiled he revealed a fortune in gold teeth.

'Mr Ho, so sorry to keep you waiting.'

Jeb Stuart Ho ignored his hand.

'It is Brother Ho.'

'I beg your pardon?'

'My title is Brother. Brother Ho.'

The fat man laughed nervously.

'I'm sorry, uh, Brother. I've never met one of you chaps before. I'm Axelrod. I'm the president of this bank. Perhaps you'd like to step into my office.'

'Will we achieve what we came here for?'

Axelrod beamed.

'Of course, old boy. Won't take but a moment.'

Jeb Stuart Ho and the Minstrel Boy followed him towards an imposing mahogany door with a frosted glass panel that carried the word 'President' in gold letters. Once inside, Axelrod took up his position behind a huge desk. It seemed to make him look bigger. He pushed a silver box towards Ho.

'Cigar?'

'No, thank you.'

The Minstrel Boy grinned.

'I'll take one.'

Axelrod waved towards the box with ill grace. The Minstrel Boy stuck a cigar in his mouth.

'Match?'

Axelrod scowled and picked up a silver table lighter shaped like a vulture, and hastily lit the Minstrel Boy's cigar. Then he turned back to Jeb Stuart Ho and beamed.

'This won't take but a moment.'

He dropped the card into a slot on the elaborate desk console, and punched a series of buttons with a flourish of starched shirt cuff. For two minutes they all watched the unit in silence, then it gave a beep, a light came on and two cards dropped into a tray at the bottom. Axelrod picked up Jeb Stuart Ho's card and handed it to him with a smile.

'Your card, Brother Ho.'

He pushed the Minstrel Boy's card across the desk to him.

'And yours.'

'Thanks.'

Jeb Stuart Ho stood up and bowed. Axelrod showed them out. Slowly they walked across the steps. On the pavement the Minstrel Boy hesitated.

'So what are you going to do now?'

'I must complete my task.'

The Minstrel Boy looked round awkwardly.

'Well, uh, I'm off to have me some fun. I guess I'll see you around.'

'How will I find you if I have need of you?'

'The bank can trace me through the card.'

Jeb Stuart Ho bowed.

'I am grateful for your services.'

The Minstrel Boy winked.

'Think nothing of it, Killer.'

He turned and sauntered off down the block. Jeb Stuart Ho watched him until he turned the corner. Then he started off in the opposite direction.

His intention was to follow the distinctive lights of the Orchid House. He was certain there would be a way he could get inside and complete his mission. He hadn't walked more than a block and a half, however, when a huge ground car pulled up beside him. It was black with a broad yellow stripe down the side. Its roof was festooned with chrome speakers, aerials and spotlights. Below the stripe were the letters LDC, the Litz Department of Correction. One of the front windows slid down and a helmeted and visored head leaned out.

'Hey, you!'

Jeb Stuart Ho stopped and turned.

'Me?'

'Yeah, you. Come over here. We want to talk to you.'

'I don't have the time, I'm afraid.'

He started to walk on. There were muffled curses from inside the car. The nearside doors burst open, and four men boiled out. They wore black uniforms and pale blue helmets with dark visors. Their pants had a yellow stripe down the sides and were tucked into high black jackboots. Heavy recoilless pistols, nightsticks, gas and fragmentation bombs hung from their belts. On their helmets and shoulders were the insignia of the LDC.

The first one to reach Jeb Stuart Ho grabbed his arm, and tried to twist it up his back. Ho relaxed for an instant and then straightened his arm with a snap. The LDC man reeled with a scream.

'He's dislocated my goddamn shoulder.'

A second cop swung at Ho with a nightstick. His armoured forearm flashed up to meet it. The two met with a crack, and the stick shattered. The cop looked at the broken end in disbelief. He backed away a couple of paces. His two partners also stopped. The first one to attack Ho. leaned against the wall groaning and clutching his shoulder. There was a moment of stillness. It seemed as though they were all waiting to see who would make the next move. Then the cop dropped the useless handle of the nightstick and reached for his gun. The gun cleared the holster, but before the cop could fire, Jeb Stuart Ho's sword was in his hand. It flashed at inhuman speed and completely severed the cop's right hand at the wrist. The gun, with the dead hand still clutching at it, fell to the pavement. The cop sank silently, staring at the bleeding stump with the blankness of total shock.

Things suddenly happened very fast. One cop leaped to help his companion. The other threw his nightstick at Ho's head. Ho caught it with his left hand and whirled, looking for the next attack. A sleep-gas grenade burst at his feet. Ho dropped the nightstick, and whipped his cloak up to his face. He emptied his lungs in a single high-pitched gasp and held his breath. His trained response was fast, but it didn't beat the gas. It was already being absorbed through the pores of his skin. The street faded to black and white. It became two-dimensional and began to recede. The focus failed, and it went out altogether.

When it came on again Jeb Stuart Ho was staring at a bright white light set in a smooth white ceiling. He carefully turned his head and the waist of a rumpled brown suit moved into the centre of his field of vision.

'So you woke up?'

Jeb Stuart Ho focused his eyes.

'What place is this?'

'Department of Correction.'

The voice sounded as though it was used to giving orders and having them obeyed. It was a voice that enjoyed its power.

'May I sit up?'

'If you do, I'll blow you apart.'

'May I turn my head?'

'Sure. I don't see how you can do any harm by that. Help yourself. Just don't make any sudden moves. If you do, I'll kill you. That's a promise.'

Jeb Stuart Ho looked round. The room was completely bare except for the concrete slab on which he was lying, and a simple collapsible chair in which the man was sitting. The man wore a creased brown suit, a white shirt and a wide necktie with a painting of a bound and naked woman on it. The tie was loosened and the top of his shirt was undone. He was sweating slightly. The man was of medium height, thickset and overweight. His face had the coarse bulldog look of a determined and methodical bully. The chewed end of a cigar was clenched between his teeth. Across his knees he cradled a wide-barrelled riot gun. When he caught Jeb Stuart Ho looking at him, he smiled grimly and patted the gun.

'I could cut you in half with this before you could reach me, however fast you are.'

Jeb Stuart Ho looked down at himself. He still had his one-piece black suit, but everything else had been taken away. He swung his gaze back to the man in the chair.

'Do you know who I am?'

The man took the cigar out of his mouth.

'A big-league hit man.'

'An executive of the brotherhood.'

The man's lip curled.

'Like I said, a big-league hit man.'

'The brotherhood would not view my detention by your people favourably. What is your name?'

'I'm Bannion. Chief-Agent Bannion.'

'My mission is of the utmost priority, Chief-Agent Bannion.'

'You attacked four of my patrolmen.'

'Quite the opposite. I was defending myself from their unprovoked attack.'

'You casually lopped off one of their hands.'

'I'm sorry. The man was about to shoot me and I overreacted. I trust he has been taken care of?'

Bannion scowled.

'He's dead.'

Jeb Stuart Ho looked surprised.

'Dead?'

'Dead.'

'But how? If he received prompt medical attention he should have recovered. It would even have been possible to replace the severed limb.'

Bannion stared at Ho grimly.

'The shock was too much for him. He shot himself. Left-handed.'

Jeb Stuart Ho said nothing. There was a long silence. Bannion finally broke it.

'I think we've completed the decent silence.'

'How can you estimate a man's worth in silence?'

'I have a feeling you're just burning to tell me what bad news it will be if the brotherhood find out we ain't been treating you right.'

'The basic computations that support the city's gambling economy and even its basic stasis and life support all come from the brotherhood.'

'And it might just get cut off if they found we'd messed you up?'

'It's possible.'

'That's why my men aren't beating you to death right now.'

'You stopped them?'

'I stopped them.'

'And what will happen to me now?'

'That depends.'

'On what?'

'You're here to kill?'

'I'm here on an executive task.'

'You're here to kill?'

'Yes.'

Bannion sighed.

'That's more like it. Okay, who?'

'A woman who lives in this town.'

'Why?'

'If her course of action is not terminated, the eventual outcome could be a major disaster.'

'Is this woman a native of Litz?'

Jeb Stuart Ho shook his head. 'A visitor.'

Bannion took out another cigar and lit it.

'That's a relief. Having a human killing machine running round the city would be bad enough, but letting you kill born and bred citizens is out of the question. What's this woman's name?'

'AA Catto.'

Bannion stood up, walked over to the door and banged on it with his fist. After a moment, the door opened and a blue-helmeted head appeared.

'Yes, Chief?'

'Get me all we have on a female called AA Catto.'

The door closed again. Bannion returned to his chair. Jeb Stuart Ho raised his head slightly.

'Could I sit up now?'

Bannion's eyes narrowed.

'You sure you won't try and jump me?'

'I have no reason to attack you.'

'Okay, sit up, but keep your hands on the slab.'

Jeb Stuart Ho eased himself into a sitting position. He crossed his legs, and Bannion appeared to relax. The door opened, and a uniformed patrolman came in carrying a red plastic folder. He handed it to Bannion, stared hard at Jeb Stuart Ho and then left. Bannion leafed through the file and then looked up at Ho.

'There seems to be no reason why you shouldn't kill her. We don't encourage the slaying of rich out-of-towners, but I suppose we have to go along with what the brotherhood wants. You'll have to make it legitimate, though.'

'Legitimate?'

'That's right.'

'How do I do that?'

'You file a claim.'

'A claim?'

Bannion looked at Jeb Stuart Ho as though he was talking to an idiot.

'An Assassin's Claim to Victim, form DY 7134/B. You fill it out. I approve it. We notify the security services. They withdraw any protection they might be renting to the victim and you go in and kill her. Normally the processing of a claim takes about six months.'

'Six months?'

'But in your case we'll do it immediately. Although you'll have to grease a few palms.'

'You mean bribes?'

Bannion grinned.

'A nasty word. Call it operating expenses, and a donation to the Widows' and Orphans' Fund.'

Jeb Stuart Ho shrugged.

'You have my credit card.'

Bannion stood up. He winked.

'That's right. We do.'

8

Lame Nancy paid off the cab, and walked up to the glass doors of the Orchid House. They slid back as she came within a couple of metres of them, and two armed guardians in purple suits and dark red helmets barred her way.

'You are a non-resident.'

It was more a statement than a question. They were obviously clones. Nancy could tell from the way they moved that they were clones. Nancy didn't really like dealing with clones. They were too straightforward. They didn't respond to the tricks and subtleties that worked on normal humans. Nancy took a deep breath and stared back at the faces behind the dark visors.

'I want to see Miss AA Catto.'

'Do you have a visitor's pass?'

Nancy shook her head.

'No.'

'Then it is not possible. You'll have to leave.'

'Can't you call her some way? It's very important.'

'Are you known to the lady?'

'No, but I have some particularly vital information for her.'

The clones appeared to consider the matter for a few moments. Then one of them punched out a combination of digits on his wrist communicator. The instrument's tiny screen flickered into life. By craning her neck and peering over the shoulder of one of the guardians, Nancy could just make out the dishevelled image of a young teenage girl. A small tinny voice came from the speaker.

'What?'

'It's the main entrance, Miss Catto. There's a person who claims to have information for you.'

'Does this person claim to know me?'

'No, Miss Catto.'

'I don't want to see anyone. No, wait. What's the person's name?'

The guardian glanced at Nancy. 'What's your name?'

'Just Nancy. That'll do.'

The guardian looked back into the communicator.

'She says her name's Nancy.'

'It's a woman?'

'Yes, Miss Catto.'

'Scan her for me.'

The guardian took a step back and pointed the communicator at Nancy. AA Catto's voice came from the speaker.

'I'll take a chance on her. Check her for weapons and send her on up.'

The screen died as AA Catto broke the connection. The guardian took a small cylindrical detector from his belt.

'The lady says you can go up.'

'I heard.'

'I've got to check you for weapons.'

'I heard that too.'

The guardian pointed the detector at her. A small light came on.

'I'm getting a positive reading.'

Nancy produced a small, pearl-handled needle gun from a hidden pocket. She handed it to the guardian.

'It'll be this.'

'What did you bring it for?'

'A girl has to protect herself.'

'You'll have to leave this with us for as long as you remain in the building.'

'You better hope I'm not attacked.'

'We will be able to defend you.'

'Have you clones developed a sense of humour?'

'I fail to understand.'

The guardian pointed the detector at her again. This time the light didn't come on.

'You're clear, you can go through.'

Lame Nancy bowed extravagantly. One of the guardians led her to the lift and explained how to reach AA Catto's apartment. The next thing she knew the doors had closed and she was in a red, softly lit compartment that was rising quickly upwards. The interior was padded with soft cushions and music played. Suddenly Nancy wondered if she had taken on too much. She felt a long way out of her league. The feeling stayed with her when she reached AA Catto's door. It was overwhelming. The ride in the lift, the size of the place, the huge drop from the terrace and the cascading tiers of flowers, were so far removed from what she was used to. In the Leader Hotel she could throw her weight about and expect to get her own way. She looked at her reflection in the stainless steel apartment door. She pulled herself together. She could deal with these people. People were the same everywhere. She pressed the stud for attention. It was, after all, places like this that the tricks came from, and she could handle them easily.

'Yes?'

Nancy wasn't certain where the voice came from. There was obviously a speaker hidden somewhere round the door. She could see nothing specific to speak into.

'I've come to see AA Catto.'

She felt a little foolish talking to the blank door.

'Wait a minute.'

A small cylinder protruded over the door with what appeared to be a lens set in the end. Nancy realized that she was being scanned from inside. She stood perfectly still. The door slid silently back. Behind it was a small compact hallway with matt silver grey walls. A girl leaned against one of them, beside a wall panel with a small screen and a number of control studs. Nancy was surprised at just how young she was. The image in the guardian's communicator had looked like a teenager, but this girl was scarcely more than twelve or thirteen. Her hair was dishevelled. Her makeup was smudged. There were dark circles under her eyes, and when she pushed herself away from the wall she seemed a little unsteady.

'You must be Nancy.'

Her voice was slurred. She sounded as though she was out of her mind behind something.

'I'm Nancy.'

'You're an interesting-looking creature.'

'I'm not a creature, dear. I'm solid human.'

'You're deformed.'

Nancy's face went very tight.

'Who isn't?'

The girl giggled and smoothed down her silver dress.

'You have to forgive me. I'm loaded. What is it you want?'

'I want to see AA Catto.'

'That's me. I'm AA Catto. What do you want?'

'I've something to tell you. I think you might find it interesting.'

'I find you interesting already. That's a very interesting device you have round your leg.'

Nancy was getting tired of the girl's rambling.

'Are we going to stand here in the hallway for ever?'

AA Catto looked round and blinked.

'I was forgetting. I've been awake for a long time. You'd better come in.'

AA Catto led her into a large white room. The whiteness was over-powering. Walls, furniture and carpet were all the one colour. There was an immense effect of space, although the room wasn't quite as huge as it appeared. On one wall was a screen, about four metres across and inset three-dimensional. It was an ample substitute for a window. The sound was turned off, and two men fought in eerie silence. They were naked except for plate armour that protected their heads, necks, shoulders and arms. They fought in the Heidelberg manner, neither giving ground, both swinging at each other with long heavy sabres. Blood ran down both their bodies. Nancy stood looking at it until AA Catto spoke.

'These shows can be very tedious.'

She turned and waved her arm vaguely around the room.

'You'll have to excuse the mess.'

Nancy looked round. Mess was exactly the right word. Chairs and lamps were overturned. Cigar ends had been ground into the carpet. Bottles littered the floor. Empty duramene ampoules had been crushed underfoot. A long low table made from a single block of marble was overflowing with more bottles and dirty glasses. A jar had been knocked over, and loose pills were strewn about. Some of them were decomposing in a pool of spilled booze.

Nancy heard a whimpering noise. It came from the corner of the room. There was a man huddled on the floor. His head was pressed to the wall. He was naked, and his hands were secured by two wide leather bracelets joined by a short length of chain. Near him, some straps and lengths of chain were tossed across a steel and leather butterfly chair. AA Catto giggled.

'Take no notice of him. He only does it to attract attention. I've just been exercising him. Why don't you sit down?'

Nancy settled herself in a nest of huge velvet cushions. Her leg in the callipers stuck out in front of her. AA Catto didn't seem to be able to take her eyes off it. Nancy felt something sticking in her. She tugged at it and produced a short, plaited leather whip. She held it up.

'You, uh, exercise him a lot?'

AA Catto nodded, and settled herself beside Nancy.

'He pisses me off a great deal.'

Nancy grinned.

'Men can do that.'

'Right.'

AA Catto reached out and touched the black steel calliper.

'This is an incredible thing.'

Nancy sat very still and said nothing. AA Catto smiled at her, and ran her index finger round the damascening on the steel.

'I don't like men. They can be very tiresome. Do you like men, uh, Nancy?'

'Not a lot.'

'I have a direct link with this one's nervous system. I can make him feel whatever I want.'

Nancy looked impressed.

'That must have been expensive.'

AA Catto was puzzled.

'Expensive? I've never thought about it.

Her eyes went vacant. Nancy waited. After a few minutes they flashed back to life again.

'I've got to take something to keep me going.'

She scrambled to her feet, and rummaged about on the marble table.

'I can't find any duramene. You don't have any, do you?'

Nancy shook her head.

'I don't. We don't get a lot of it down our way.'

'Too bad.'

AA Catto picked up a handful of pills and inspected them.

'I suppose these will hold me together for a while.'

She put half a dozen of them in her mouth and took a swallow from the nearest glass. Then she returned to the cushions.

'What did you want to talk to me about?'

'I heard your name today.'

'That must have been nice.

'It was at the Leader Hotel.'

'What's the Leader Hotel?'

'It's a broken-down fire trap on the other side of town. I keep a string of girls there.'

'What do they do for you?'

'They work for me.'

'That seems very practical. Do you think I'm pretty?'

'Yes, very pretty.'

'Go on.'

Nancy was beginning to become used to the way AA Catto's mind jumped around. She went back to her story.

'Two men were looking for you.'

AA Catto laughed.

'Men are always looking for me.'

'One of them looked like an assassin. A professional.'

'You believe he might want to kill me?'

'It's possible.'

'Why would anyone want to kill me?'

Nancy shrugged.

'I don't know, but it sure seemed like this guy and his partner had a contract for you.'

She jerked her thumb towards the corner.

'Maybe he wants you dead?'

AA Catto looked at her in disbelief.

'He wouldn't dare, besides, he hasn't had the chance. He's been with me all the time. He doesn't leave my sight.'

'I really don't know. Maybe I was wrong. I just had this feeling.'

AA Catto ran her fingers down the calliper again.

'And you came to warn me. That was very sweet of you.'

'It was nothing.'

'I still can't understand why anyone should want to kill me. I'm beautiful. You do think I'm beautiful, don't you?'

'Sure, I think you're beautiful. I think you're very beautiful.'

'If I was one of your girls, would you make me work for you?'

Nancy flashed with horror at the problems this dope fiend could cause if she was a working hooker. She smiled quickly.

'Honey, if you were working for me, I'd keep you all to myself.'

'Kiss me, Nancy.'

Nancy leaned over and kissed AA Catto in a way that wouldn't commit her to anything. AA Catto's arms immediately snaked around her, and her tongue darted into Nancy's mouth. She seemed almost desperate. She clung to Nancy, kissing her face and licking her ear. Nancy quickly responded, partly enjoying it, partly wanting to do the thing right. After a few minutes AA Catto moved away. She quickly squirmed out of her silver dress, and stood up for Nancy to inspect her. All she had on were her silver boots. She spread her feet wide apart and put her hands on her hips.

'Do you like my body?'

Nancy stretched out a hand and stroked the inside of AA Catto's thigh.

'I think your body's wonderful.'

AA Catto crouched down beside Nancy, and touched one of her small hard breasts. She plucked at the white material of Nancy's one piece outfit.

'How do you take this off?'

'You can't take it off completely.'

Nancy unclipped her silver belt and let it fall back on the cushions. Then she pointed to a small mother-of-pearl stud at her neck, and kissed AA Catto on the cheek.

'If you press that, the whole thing splits down the front.'

AA Catto extended a long thin finger and touched the stud. The suit split open down the entire length of Nancy's body. AA Catto began caressing her skin, and Nancy sighed deeply. She reached out, and began to fondle AA Catto's breasts. AA Catto traced a path with her fingers down Nancy's body from her collar bone to the white fuzz of her pubic hair. Then she followed it with her tongue. As she found Nancy's clitoris, Nancy gave a groan of real pleasure and began to writhe her hips. AA Catto looked up from between Nancy's legs.

'Was that nice?'

Nancy sighed.

'Oh, really.'

AA Catto squirmed round until the gap between her own legs was presented to Nancy.

'Now do the same to me.'

For a long while the two women aroused and teased each other with their mouths and tongues. Each time the feeling became too strong one would clutch spasmodically at the other's legs. At last, AA Catto surfaced.

'This is very nice, but I'd like to get further.'

Nancy opened her eyes. There were beads of perspiration on her upper lip.

'What do you suggest?'

AA Catto grinned.

'I have some toys that might help us.'

Nancy ran her tongue up AA Catto's thigh.

'Why don't you find them?'

AA Catto jumped up with a laugh. She looked helplessly round the room.

'I know they're here somewhere. I saw them when I was torturing Reave.'

Nancy propped herself up on one elbow.

'Aren't you worried that someone might be trying to kill you?'

AA Catto paused from rummaging about in the litter that covered the room.

'I'll probably worry terribly when I start to come down, but right now I can't quite believe it. Anyway, it'd be very hard for anyone to get me here. We're surrounded by guards.'

Nancy sank back into the cushions as AA Catto went on searching. Things were working out very differently from the way she had expected. When she'd first thought of coming to the Orchid House it had been for a quick bribe. It seemed to have gone a lot further than that. Her deliberations were interrupted by a buzzing from the wall screen. On the screen, one of the swordsmen was, at last, delivering the finishing blows to the other. AA Catto moved over to it, and flicked the control to the communication channel. The huge head and shoulders of a guardian filled the screen. It completely dwarfed AA Catto. She took an involuntary step back.

'What do you want?'

'Miss Catto?'

'Yes.'

'I regret to inform you that our organization can no longer offer you protection of any form. This withdrawal of service applies to all guard and security organizations in the city.'

AA Catto looked at the screen in bewilderment.

'You mean I'm not protected?'

'That's correct.

'And nobody will protect me?'

'That's right, Miss Catto.'

'For God's sake, why?'

'You are the subject of an Assassin's Claim to Victim.'

'What the hell's that?'

'In simple terms, a professional assassin has applied for permission to kill you, and permission has been granted.'

'But why?'

'I have no information on that.'

'Who is this assassin?'

'The claim was filed in the name of Jeb Stuart Ho. He described himself as an executive of the brotherhood.'

AA Catto looked round desperately.

'Isn't there anything you can do to help me?'

'Nothing, Miss Catto. All we are allowed to do is give you formal notification of the claim. I must terminate this conversation.'

AA Catto shook her head helplessly.

'I don't understand. What have I ever done to these people?'

'I have to terminate this conversation right now.'

The screen went blank. AA Catto felt terribly cold. She looked imploringly at Nancy.

'Did you hear that?'

'It's worse than I thought.'

'What can I do?'

'We'd better get out of here.'

'Where can I go?'

'You could come to the Leader. You might be safe there until we organize something. You got plenty of credit?'

'Unlimited. If they haven't taken that away.'

Nancy stood up and began fastening her suit.

'They can't take that away.'

'Thank God.'

Nancy began to organize. She was mentally kicking herself for becoming so involved. The only consolation was that there might be some rich pickings in it. At least the assassin didn't have carte blanche to kill her.

'You'd better throw anything you need into a bag. Oh, and wake him up.'

She pointed at Reave.

'We've got to move fast. He may be on his way here right now.'

AA Catto hurried across to where Reave lay huddled, and kicked him. He whimpered and tried to push himself further into the corner.

'Please, I couldn't take any more.'

AA Catto snapped at him impatiently.

'Get up. This is important.'

Her voice softened.

'Please get up. I forgive you for now. There's someone coming to kill me. We've got to get out of here. Please, Reave. Get up and help me.'

Reave got painfully to his feet.

9

Billy Oblivion lay on his bed feeling better than he'd felt in weeks. Darlene had finally started to make a real effort, there was a bit of credit stacked up, and all was right with the world. The only thing that troubled him slightly was the way Darlene had gone so militantly to work. She seemed to be turning tricks every hour of the day she could. Billy couldn't figure out what had got into her, but while it lasted, he didn't try very hard.

Billy wasn't trying very hard at anything. After a handful of dormax and two-thirds of a bottle of tequila he didn't have a worry in the world. A couple of times he'd thought about getting up, going down to the desk and getting the desk clerk to reconnect the room screen. Even that seemed to be too much trouble when he looked at it from inside the pleasant haze of booze and sleeping pills. As long as they held out, Billy could think of nothing more pleasant than to sprawl on the bed and examine the interesting cracks and patterns on the ceiling.

The building trembled slightly as the lift was set in motion. Billy grinned to himself. One day someone would step into the Leader Hotel's lift, push a button, and the whole building would fall down. Billy giggled, and took another shot of tequila. Somebody was flat-picking an amplified guitar somewhere down the hall. Billy tapped his toe in time to it. It really seemed a pleasant way to pass the time.

The lift came to a halt at Billy's floor. Billy listened, he wondered if it might be Darlene. He held up the tequila bottle. There was only about an inch left. If it was her, she could go down to the desk for another one. A thought suddenly got through to him. She might have a trick with her. If she did, that would mean he'd have to get out of the room. He'd end up in the foyer feeding drinks to the goddamn desk clerk. That was the only trouble with Darlene's new attitude to work, it was a drag having to scoot in and out of the room all the time. Maybe if she kept on working the way she was, they could get two rooms, one for living in, and one for business.

A key rattled in the door. It was Darlene. Billy propped himself up on one elbow. The door opened. Darlene stood in the doorway. She was wearing her red working outfit. Billy grinned at her.

'You look good enough to eat.'

Darlene flounced across the room.

'I've had enough people eating at me. I feel like I was a meal.'

She pulled off her red boots and threw them across the room.

'Can't you do anything but lay about all day?'

Billy knew he really ought to get mad and hit her. Darlene was getting completely out of line. The trouble was that he just couldn't get it together. He let his head fall back on to the pillow.

'I really don't need this.'

Darlene was pulling off her stockings.

'You think I need it? You're just turning into a bum. There was a time when I used to feel good walking around for you. I didn't mind turning tricks, I thought we were going to get someplace.'

Billy groaned.

'How can we get anyplace? We're non-people. We don't have credit.'

'We ain't going to get anyplace if you keep getting too loaded to walk.'

Darlene pulled her red dress over her head, and carefully folded it over a chair. Billy focused on her. She looked really good. She was naked apart from the garter belt that still hung round her hips. Her black skin colour contrasted sharply with the thin strip of red. He patted the bed beside him.

'Honey, don't give me a hard time. Come on over here and relax.'

Darlene pulled open the door to the tiny shower. She turned on the water and took off the garter belt. Before she stepped inside she looked down at Billy.

'If you think I feel like fucking you after turning five tricks in as many hours, you better think again.'

The door of the shower banged behind her. Billy sighed, picked up the tequila bottle and swallowed about half of what was left. Things with Darlene were getting out of hand. He repeated the phrase to himself a few times. He liked the ring of it. His brain was too fuzzy for any kind of concentrated thought. When he was straight he'd work it out. One thing was sure. It couldn't go on like this. It was a determined kind of phrase. Billy liked it. He was still repeating it to himself when Darlene came out of the shower.

The flash of Darlene naked and dripping wet was the kind of thing that stopped Billy leaving her. He shook his head. That was the trouble with dormax. They made you horny, but left you incapable of making the effort to do anything about it. Darlene was busily towelling herself. Billy raised his head.

'Are you going out again?'

'Maybe. I don't know yet.'

'You don't want to overdo it. Why don't you stay up here with me for a while?'

Darlene flung the towel on the floor.

'For Christ's sake, don't start that again.'

'Start what again?'

'I told you before. I don't want to know right now. For one thing, I'm sore.'

Billy subsided again. Darlene pulled on a dirty housecoat.

'If you want something to do, you could go down to Nancy's. You might find yourself some work down there.'

'You been hanging round with Nancy? You know I don't like you getting in with her.'

'Afraid I might go to work for her?'

'No, it's just…'

'Listen, Billy. I don't care what you like. Nancy's useful. She knows what's happening. She passes on tips to me.'

Billy became sullen.

'I bet she does.'

'If you got yourself down there, you might pick up a fair bit of credit.'

'Why? What's happening?'

'I don't know for sure. She's getting a team of guys together for something. She asked if you could handle a gun.'

'What did you tell her?'

'I said I didn't know.'

'You know I can handle a gun.'

'You can't handle walking half the time.'

Billy struggled to sit up.

'Listen, you bitch. I killed a man in a shoot-out when I was on the road with Reave. Shit, we got involved in a whole fucking war.'

Darlene turned on the hot plate under the coffee pot.

'So you say.'

'Damn it, it's the truth.'

'Even if it is, there's no saying you could do it now. You've gone downhill ever since I met you.'

Billy scowled.

'I can do it.'

'Go do it then.'

'I will.'

Billy swung his legs over the side of the bed. His stomach lurched, and he had to sit still for a while. Darlene laughed.

'See the fearless gunman.'

'Shut the fuck up.'

Billy had another try at standing up. He stood in the middle of the room, swaying slightly.

'I need some duramene.'

Darlene snorted contemptuously.

'Since when could we ever afford duramene? You live in a dream world, Billy boy.'

Billy looked round helplessly.

'I need something.'

'We don't have anything.'

'Some funaids might help.'

Darlene shook her head. 'They'll just make you stupid.'

'I've got to get myself straight.'

'A shower and a lot of coffee would take care of you as well as anything else.'

Billy started to fumble with the fastenings on his shirt.

'Why do you always want me to do things the hard way?'

'I like to see you suffer.'

For the next hour Darlene filled Billy with black coffee, pushed him into alternately hot and cold showers and massaged the back of his neck. He was sick a couple of times, but by the end of the period he was zipped into his best suit and walking steadily, if a little stiffly, towards the lift.

He rode down to Nancy's floor and walked down the corridor. He paused for a moment in front of her door, then stretched out his hand and knocked.

'Who is it?'

'Billy.'

'Hold on.'

There was the rattle of security bolts being shot back, and the door opened just wide enough for Nancy to peer out. It was still secured by a chain lock. She confirmed it was really Billy, and then shut it again. He heard the sound of the chain being removed. Before letting Billy in Nancy looked carefully up and down the corridor. Billy wondered what could be going on that merited so much caution.

The room was crowded with at least half the hoods who hung round the hotel. Billy nodded to a few of them. Most of them seemed to be armed, and everyone had the air of waiting for something. On the far side of the room, sitting cross-legged on the bed, was a young girl in a metallic blue one-piece jump suit. Beside her was a man. Between them they produced a flash of violent recognition in Billy.

'Reave!'

'Billy!'

'How are you, my man?'

His one-time partner looked thinner and more haggard than when they had parted company in the city of Con-Lec, when Reave had stayed with AA Catto, and Billy had continued with his wanderings. Reave clutched at Billy's arm.

'It's good to see you.'

'You too, what's been happening?'

Reave frowned.

'We're in a bit of trouble.'

'You and AA Catto?'

'Yeah, there's...'

Before Reave could tell his story, Nancy interrupted him.

'Why don't you leave the reunion till later? It seems like everyone's here, so we might as well all hear the tale at once.'

There were murmurs of assent from the men grouped around the room. It seemed as if nobody really knew why Nancy had got them up there. She stood in the middle of the room and slowly turned round.

'You'll be pleased to know that each of you has been left a day's credit at the front desk.'

There was general approval for this statement. Only one of the men didn't join in the loud reception. His name was Monk. He was a thickset individual. He wore a collarless striped shirt, a black waistcoat, and his face was half hidden by a light grey fedora. Under one armpit a heavy, vicious-looking needle gun hung in a patent Speed-Draw shoulder holster. He leaned forward in his seat and looked suspiciously at Nancy.

'What are we supposed to do for it?'

Nancy grinned.

'Nothing. Nothing at all.'

Monk shook his head.

'I don't get it.'

'It's a token of goodwill. Look at it as a payment for coming here.'

'Seems to me that there's a lot of credit behind whatever this thing is you're cooking up.'

Nancy nodded.

'You can believe that.'

There was a chorus of questions. Nancy raised her hands and waited until they subsided.

'I'll get straight down to the reason I've got you all up here. I need to put a team together. This lady here…'

She pointed to the girl on the bed.

'Her name's AA Catto, and this team's being hired to protect her. There's a couple of guys in the city who are going to try a hit on her. We're going to stop them.'

Monk interrupted.

'Why can't she just hire a team of guardians? It sounds as though she can afford it.'

'They won't deal with her.'

Monk raised a slow eyebrow.

'There's only one reason I can think of why the guardians won't protect her.'

Nancy nodded.

'I ain't going to hide anything. There's a claim out on her.'

There was an immediate ripple of conversation. Monk seemed to be slipping into the role of spokesman for all the men present. He minutely examined his fingernails. There was a pause while everyone waited to see what he would say. He sucked in his breath and looked up.

'That means that the guys who are after her are professionals.'

Nancy grinned.

'They looked that way.'

'You've seen them?'

'They came here yesterday asking a lot of questions.'

Billy looked up sharply, but said nothing. Monk went on voicing the men's queries.

'What did they look like?'

'One was tall and thin, dressed in black and carrying a bundle of hardware. The other was shorter. Seemed to be only carrying a set of knives.'

She picked up a bundle of papers and began to pass them round.

'I put the descriptions down on these fax-sheets.'

There were a few moments of silence while everyone in the room studied the papers. Then Monk tapped his with his forefinger.

'It says here that the tall one's name is Jeb Stuart Ho.'

Nancy nodded.

'That's right.'

'Sounds to me like a brotherhood name.'

'Could be.'

'So you seriously expect us to try stopping a brotherhood killer?'

'I don't suggest we wait for them to come. I figure we should try and get them first.'

Monk shook his head.

'You got to be crazy.'

Nancy planted her hands on her hips and looked down at him.

'There's a credit card in it for the one who gets Ho, a card of his own.'

Everyone began to talk at once. A credit card meant reinstatement in full. It was the only kind of prize that might tempt anyone to tackle a professional assassin. Monk grinned.

'What do the others get?'

'A month's credit. That's for each man who joins us. There's nothing else to tell. Who's going to join us?'

The men all looked at each other. A couple shook their heads and sheepishly left. The remainder stayed put. Monk stood up.

'Looks like you got your team. All we need is weapons.'

Nancy nodded towards a pile of gift-wrapped packages in the corner.

'We stopped at the gun store on the way up here. There's a half-dozen riot guns, ammunition, some hand guns and grenades. We've got enough weapons.'

Monk grinned.

'You think of everything.'

Then Nancy got down to the final details. The team was split into two groups. One would stay at the Leader and guard AA Catto, the other would move out into the city and start circulating the description of Ho to the beggars, winos and hustlers. Once he'd been located they'd move in for the kill. Billy found himself drafted into the hotel group. He wasn't really concentrating on the planning. While it was going on he moved close to Reave, and spoke to him in a low voice.

'I know who the other guy is. Ho's partner.'

Reave looked at him in surprise.

'Who?'

'The Minstrel Boy.'

'You're kidding.'

'I'm not, I saw him when they came here looking for AA Catto.'

'Did he see you?'

Billy shook his head.

'I ducked into the lift. I didn't want him to see me. I guess I was ashamed or something.'

Reave said nothing. Billy looked at him urgently.

'What are we going to do?'

'We can't let him kill AA Catto.'

'But we can't let him be gunned down. He got us out of real trouble a couple of times.'

Reave ran his fingers through his hair.

'I don't know what we can do except wait and see. If we tell anyone now, it could put us in a real awkward position.'

Billy glanced at AA Catto.

'But you're with her. She won't let anything happen to you.'

Reave avoided his eyes.

'I wouldn't altogether count on that.'

Billy nodded unhappily.

'I guess we'll just have to wait and see.'

10

The Minstrel Boy was drunk. He wasn't quite at the point of falling over, but he was certainly having trouble getting up the steps of the Club 93. He leaned heavily on the girl beside him. Although he couldn't quite remember her name, he was happier than he'd been since Jeb Stuart Ho had rudely dragged him from his comfortable tank at Wainscote. It was his first day of living it up on Ho's credit, and he was making the most of it. He grinned at the girl.

'Think we should make it back to my hotel, honey?'

The first thing the Minstrel Boy had done after he'd left Ho was to check into the Albert Speer. The Albert Speer was generally considered to be the best hotel in Litz. The girl looked up at him with a quick professional smile.

'I don't think you're capable of much else.'

The Minstrel Boy's grin widened.

'You'd be surprised what I'm capable of.'

'I'm surprised you're still capable of standing up.'

Still holding him steady, she signalled to the 93's doorman to get them a cab. While they were waiting for it, he took the opportunity to have a better look at her. The pick-up had been so fast he hadn't really had a chance to study her. She'd made a beeline for him almost immediately he staggered into the club and started tossing his credit about. She'd seemed okay in the dim light of the club, but up on the street, the blemishes were inclined to show.

In fact, she stood up to the examination very well. Her growth had been halted around fourteen or fifteen. She had the turned-up nose, large eyes and cute features of the most popular clone hostess model, although from the way she moved and talked, he knew she was a normal human. Her skin was done in a pleasant rainbow blend of light pastel shades. Her hair was a mass of waist-length, dark blue ringlets that matched her short tight tube dress and lace-up boots. The Minstrel Boy congratulated himself. He'd really done rather well for one so drunk.

The cab pulled up, and it took both the girl and the doorman to get him safely inside. If the Minstrel Boy hadn't suffered so much difficulty in negotiating himself into the back of the cab, he might have noticed the beggar who took one look at him, started, jumped up from his pitch on the kerb and hurried off down the street.

The cab ride took longer than originally intended. Halfway to the Albert Speer, the Minstrel Boy decided that he needed a bunch of duramene to burn off some of the alcohol in his brain, and he made the driver make a detour to a drugstore. Once they got there, he suffered an attack of paranoia and refused to get out of the cab. He'd convinced himself that if anyone saw him buying anything as expensive as duramene he was quite likely to be mugged as he walked back to the cab. After some haggling, the driver was persuaded to go.

They started back to the hotel once again, but after they'd only gone a couple of blocks he stopped the cab again. He'd decided he needed a shot to help himself get across the hotel foyer. As he fumbled the ampoule into the injection unit, the girl began to exhibit noticeable signs of impatience, but when he offered her a shot for herself, they quickly receded. By the time they reached the hotel they were laughing and talkative. The Minstrel Boy was hardly any more coherent, but the duramene had made him a good deal more mobile.

They stopped for a moment and stared up to the soaring baroque façade of black and red glass. The girl squeezed the Minstrel Boy's arm.

'You really like to live well, don't you?'

The Minstrel Boy grinned and nodded. He was still hoping he would find out her name without having to ask.

'You'd better believe it.'

They crossed the foyer, stepped into the lift, and rode up to the Minstrel Boy's thirty-seventh-floor suite without any difficulty. Immediately they were inside the girl grabbed the Minstrel Boy and kissed him very hard. She thrust the whole length of her body against him, squirming slightly and darting her tongue in and out of his mouth. When she suddenly released him, he took a step back and dropped into a chair.

'Unh.'

The girl looked down at him.

'What's the matter with you? Don't you like me?'

The Minstrel Boy shrugged.

'How should I know? I only met you a while ago, and ain't been able to see straight most of the time.'

The girl began to look angry.

'You don't take a lot of trouble to be charming.'

'That's true.'

'I expect you can't even remember my name.'

'That's true too.'

'You're goddamn impossible.'

The Minstrel Boy nodded. 'Impossible.'

The girl went red. 'Well fuck you, Jack.'

She turned on her heel and began heading for the door. The Minstrel Boy turned in his chair, and called after her.

'Hey!'

She turned in front of the door.

'What?'

'I'd really like to fuck you.'

The girl leaned back against the door and gave a half smile.

'You would, would you?'

'Sure.'

'Am I supposed to be flattered?'

'You could be, whatever turns you on. I could pay you if that's what you want.'

'I'm not a hooker.'

'So you're up here for kicks?'

'That's what I thought when I came here.'

'So come on over here and get some.'

'I'm not so sure. You really don't try very hard.'

The Minstrel Boy shrugged.

'What would you like me to do?'

'You could ask me my name.'

'Okay. What's your name?'

'Liza.'

'Liza, hey? Liza from Litz.'

'Don't be cute. Do something else.'

'What?'

'You choose. Think for yourself.'

The Minstrel Boy suddenly sat up in his chair. He grabbed the phone. The girl came and stood beside his chair looking puzzled.

'What are you doing?'

'You'll see. Hello, room service? Listen, send up a couple of bottles of champagne – how the hell should I know what kind? The best kind, and a couple of pounds of strawberries, right, oh – and a large cut-glass bowl. Yeah, right.'

He hung up. Liza looked disappointed.

'Is that the best you can do? Just start drinking again?'

The Minstrel Boy smiled at her crookedly. 'Who said anything about drinking?'

'But I thought...'

'You want to use your imagination.'

He mimicked the girl's Litz accent. She looked annoyed.

'So what else can you do with champagne?'

The Minstrel Boy grinned broadly.

'First of all you take the glass bowl, you put the strawberries in it. Then you pour in the champagne, and mush it all together, until you've got this bowlful of expensive goo.'

'And what do you do with it?'

The Minstrel Boy's grin broadened.

'We take off our clothes, spread the mush all over each other's bodies, and then we lick it off again.'

Liza smiled.

'Sounds delicious, if messy.'

The Minstrel Boy shrugged.

'The hotel takes care of the mess.'

She began to drift round the room, looking at the things that the Minstrel Boy had left strewn about. Before getting drunk, he had been on a buying spree. She picked up a hand-carved guitar.

'Do you play this?'

The Minstrel Boy shook his head.

'Uh-uh, I just drop them from great heights and watch them break.'

'You're a funny bastard.'

She picked up his belt of knives. 'What are these?'

A hard edge came into his voice. 'Put those down.'

Liza dropped them. She said nothing. She wandered around for a little while longer, and then walked slowly and slightly dramatically towards the Minstrel Boy. He sensed it might be the start of a display. He liked displays. He thought of himself as something of a connoisseur.

'I'm glad you can be obscene.'

The Minstrel Boy frowned.

'Obscene?'

'The strawberries and champagne.'

'Aah.'

Liza put both her hands to the back of her neck. 'We could start being obscene right now.'

The dress undid itself and dropped to the floor. Liza stood in front of him, naked except for her boots.

'Do you like what you see?'

The Minstrel Boy nodded. 'Sure, love it.'

The girl looked a little put out. She squatted cross-legged at his feet.

'Aren't you going to take your clothes off?'

'In a moment.'

'What do I have to do?'

'Use your imagination.'

The girl slowly stretched out her legs on either side of the Minstrel Boy's feet. Slowly she lay back on the ground. The Minstrel Boy raised one of his boots and covered her pubic hair with it. He noticed that she had it dyed the same blue as the hair on her head. He moved his foot with a circular motion, gradually increasing the pressure. Liza gave a soft laugh.

'You've got an odd imagination.'

The Minstrel Boy raised an eyebrow.

'Who, me?'

He was just stretching out a hand to touch her when there was a knock on the door.

'Who is it?'

'Room service.

He didn't bother to look round. He just went on teasing the girl with his foot. He ignored the sound of the door opening. Then hands grabbed him roughly round the neck.

'What the hell...?'

It all seemed to happen at once. The Minstrel Boy was struck hard across the face. The chair toppled over on its side and he fell with it. He saw three men standing over him. Liza screamed and jumped to her feet. One of the men grabbed her by the wrist. Another kicked at the Minstrel Boy. As he rolled over he saw a fourth man dragging an unconscious bellhop into the room. Liza went on screaming. The man holding her, a thickset individual in a grey fedora, slapped her hard across the face.

'Shut your mouth, honey.'

Liza continued to struggle.

'Take your goddamn hands off me.'

She found a heavy, vicious needle gun pressed beneath her chin. The man hissed at her from between clenched teeth.

'Make another sound and I'll rip your face off.'

Liza stood very still. One of the other men was systematically kicking the Minstrel Boy. He glanced at the one in the fedora.

'Do we kill him now, Monk?'

Monk shook his head.

'No, I want to see if he knows where his partner is. That's the one that scores the prize.'

The chair was set back on its feet. The Minstrel Boy was hauled into it. One of the men, a small sallow one with a livid scar on his cheek, ripped the cord out of the phone. The Minstrel Boy's arms were dragged back behind the chair, and his thumbs were tied together with a length of wire. Liza was also tied up. Another length of flex secured her wrists, and a third strapped her ankles together. Still naked, she was left in a corner as the four hoods directed all their attention towards the Minstrel Boy.

A sense of something almost like calm settled over him. There was nothing he could do except sit there and take it. All he could hope for was to come up with what they wanted as quickly as possible. That was the only way he could see to avoid getting hurt. He watched the four hoods as they gathered round him. The one called Monk leaned forward and breathed into his face.

'Okay, where's your partner?'

'What partner?'

Smash! The one called Monk punched him hard in the face. They all stood round and waited while his head cleared. Monk grinned down at him.

'Okay. Let's try it again. Where's your partner?'

The Minstrel Boy shook his head.

'I don't know what you're talking about.'

Smash! The Minstrel Boy was aware of a warm sensation, a trickle of blood running down from the side of his mouth. The telephone cord had cut off all feeling from his thumbs.

'Your partner?'

'Listen...'

Smash!

As the Minstrel Boy's senses came back to him, he decided to try another tack.

'If you told me what partner you were talking about, I might be able to help you.'

'Jeb Stuart Ho. You know Jeb Stuart Ho?'

'He's not my partner.'

Smash!

The Minstrel Boy's head reeled. There had to be some way out of this.

'He wasn't my partner,'

Monk drew back his fist. The Minstrel Boy thought quickly. 'He wasn't my partner. I was just working for him.'

Monk sneered.

'Working as what?'

'A guide.'

'A guide?'

The Minstrel Boy took a deep breath.

'I'm one of the ones who know where they are.'

The four men fell silent. Two of them took a step back. The legend of the guides seemed to stop them in their tracks. Monk was the first to recover.

'You worked for Jeb Stuart Ho?'

The Minstrel Boy nodded painfully.

'Sure.'

'And you guided him here?'

'Right.'

'So where is he?'

The Minstrel Boy shook his head. 'I just don't know.'

Monk turned savagely to his three sidekicks. 'Work him over for a while. He might remember something.'

The Minstrel Boy began to struggle as they moved towards him. His voice almost reached a scream.

'Hold it, hold it.'

Monk looked down at him. He motioned to the other two. 'Wait a bit. Maybe he's going to tell us something.'

The Minstrel Boy sagged in the chair.

'I don't know exactly where he is, but I might be able to find out.'

'How?'

'How do I know you won't kill me once I've found out what you want to know?'

Monk grinned.

'You don't.'

'So why should I do it for you?'

Monk gestured to the other three hoods. They started towards the Minstrel Boy. Monk held up his hand and they halted. His smile was ugly.

'You can do it the easy way, or you can do it the hard way. It's your choice.'

The Minstrel Boy nodded. 'I've always preferred the easy way.'

'Okay. How do we find him?'

'Do I have to stay tied up?'

'How do we find him?'

'You don't find him.'

Monk drew back his fist. The Minstrel Boy went quickly on.

'I find him.'

Monk's eyes narrowed.

'What are you trying to pull?'

'I've got a credit card on his account. The bank will know the last location he used his card.'

'So where's the card?'

The Minstrel Boy shook his head.

'It's not as easy as that. They'll want to be able to identify me on a vision link before they give out the information. I'm the only one who can do it. You'll have to untie me, and clean me up a bit.'

The Minstrel Boy even managed a lopsided bruised grin.

'You'll even have to take me down to the lobby.'

He nodded towards the service phone with its ripped out handset.

'Your gorillas don't think ahead.'

Monk looked at the other three. They all said nothing for a while. Then he shrugged reluctantly.

'Maybe he's telling the truth.'

The one with the scar looked sideways at the Minstrel Boy. 'And maybe he's just playing for time. I figure we should work him over a bit more – just so we can be sure.'

'That's what you figure, Wormo?'

The hood with the scar nodded. Monk grabbed him by the front of his jacket.

'Leave the figuring to me, okay? When you start trying to figure, your nasty inclinations usually get in the way.'

He pushed him away.

'Now untie him, and take him into the bathroom and get him cleaned up.'

Wormo reluctantly did as he was told. When the Minstrel Boy emerged from the bathroom, Monk pointed the needle gun at his chest.

'We're going down to the lobby now.'

He snapped his fingers at Wormo.

'Give me that coat off the bed.'

Wormo picked up a fur coat off a chair. It was one that the Minstrel Boy had bought during his spending spree. Monk draped it over his arm so it hid the gun.

'This'll be pointed at your back all the time. If you try anything I'll cut you in half.'

The Minstrel Boy nodded. They started towards the door. Wormo was the only one who hesitated. Monk half turned.

'What's your problem?'

'What about the girl and the bellhop?'

'Leave them. The cleaners'll find them.'

Wormo licked his lips.

'Can't I have them? The girl at least. I'll take care of her and catch up with you later.'

He looked at Monk expectantly. Monk shrugged.

'Stay here and do what you want. You'll be finished with the job, that's all.'

Wormo looked disappointedly back at Liza, hesitated for a moment and then reluctantly followed the others. He spotted the Minstrel Boy's belt of knives. He picked them up.

'Can I take these?'

Monk nodded impatiently.

'Take what you want but grab it fast.'

The Minstrel Boy's eyes narrowed but he said nothing. With Monk right behind him he started walking towards the lift.

In one corner of the hotel foyer were a cluster of com-booths. The Minstrel Boy and his escort came out of the lift. Nobody seemed to pay them any attention. They crossed the foyer, threading their way between the flowering plants, glass tables and Bauhaus chairs. They attracted no interest at all. The Minstrel Boy looked round. He wondered what would happen if he tried to run. Monk was right behind him. He imagined the stream of steel needles slicing into his back. His skin crawled and he felt sick. He kept on walking.

The Minstrel Boy seated himself in one of the plastic blisters. Monk positioned himself in the entrance so he could see and hear everything. The gun under the coat was still pointed at him. The Minstrel Boy took the credit card from his pocket. He punched out the coordinates of the bank. A stiff-collared clerk appeared on the screen.

'Can I help you?'

'I wish to know the location of Jeb Stuart Ho. I hold a temporary card on his account.'

'Place the card in the transmission slot and your hand on the scanner.'

The Minstrel Boy did as he was told and the screen clouded. Monk leaned over and hissed at him.

'What's going on? Is this some kind of double-cross?'

The Minstrel Boy shook his head.

'Just wait.'

The screen cleared and the card dropped from the receiver slot. The clerk smiled a thin smile.

'You're in luck, sir. Brother Ho has just paid for a meal at Fidel's Burgers on Authority Plaza.'

The screen went blank. The Minstrel Boy looked up at Monk.

'There's your man.'

Monk nodded grimly.

'That only leaves the question of what we do with you.'

11

Jeb Stuart Ho took one bite out of the Vegie-Wonder and put it down. The brotherhood were not meat eaters. He had passed Fidel's Regular, Super and Triple Deck Scrumbo, and picked out the Vegie-Wonder. It was advertised in the menu as a 'non-meat vegetarian whole-food delight'. It was nasty. The so-called vegetables were sheets of recycled cellulose, die-stamped into crude leaf shapes and dyed a garish green. Jeb Stuart Ho suspected that the burgers were made of the same material, only dyed brown.

He pushed away his meal and looked through the plate glass front of Fidel's Burgers. He had walked through to Authority Plaza after going to the Orchid House. The guardians had told him AA Catto had left. He had been hungry, but the main reason he had come into the place was to attempt to think about his next move. Even this was denied him. Hard metallic music blared from speakers all over the hamburger joint, and jagged patterns of light danced on the walls. The other customers in the place seemed to be munching contentedly.

Jeb Stuart Ho shook his head and took his credit card from the pay slot. He stood up and made his way out of Fidel's Burgers. The pavement was almost deserted. In the centre of the square was a particularly ugly fountain. Lit by searchlights, stylized heroic figures supported a huge marble bowl from which water cascaded over them. The only thing Jeb Stuart Ho could imagine it symbolized was blind stupidity. Apart from a few drunks who staggered round the statue's base, the centre of the square was equally quiet. It seemed an ideal place to stop and think.

He stepped off the kerb and dodged the ground traffic until he reached the central island. There he walked slowly towards the fountain. He stopped at its rim and stared down into the water. AA Catto had eluded him. He couldn't afford just to roam Litz and hope for another lead. That would undoubtedly give her time to leave the city altogether. There was even a chance that she had done that already. His best action might be to contact Bannion, to see if he had any information on her whereabouts. His other alternative might be to get hold of the Minstrel Boy and find out if he had any more contacts that could be valuable.

He let his eyes follow the patterns of ripples. He made his brain become calm and analytical. He forced it to calculate the possibilities that might stem from any single action. He was completing the third level when a voice beside him interrupted the process.

'Got a drink, buddy?'

Jeb Stuart Ho was jerked into the material world.

'I'm sorry. I failed to hear you.'

A ragged, filthy drunk stood in front of him, swaying slightly and scratching his leg. He looked up at Jeb Stuart Ho and made an implausible attempt at a winning smile. He also raised his voice a little.

'I said, got a drink, buddy?'

Jeb Stuart Ho smiled compassionately at him, and stretched his hand out to the water.

'Drink of the fountain, my friend. There is plenty here for everyone.'

The drunk spat in disgust.

'Fucking wisearse.'

He staggered away, muttering indignantly. Jeb Stuart Ho watched him sadly. It seemed as though Litz was a place where logic hardly functioned. He wondered if it was a fault in the city's stability generators. He decided that his best immediate course of action should be to call Bannion. He looked around for a com-booth. There was one a little way on from Fidel's Burgers in the foyer of an Obscenery. There seemed to be a lull in the traffic. His attention was attracted by a black, low-slung ground car that screamed into the square, dodging other vehicles with almost suicidal high-speed swerves. It made a half circuit of the square, drifting on the corners, and then screeched to a halt in front of Fidel's Burgers. It only paused for a moment, and then gunned away again. Jeb Stuart Ho was just wondering if it was some kind of local pastime, when the interior of Fidel's was taken out by an impact bomb.

The blast lifted Jeb Stuart Ho clean off his feet, and blew him some metres across the square. When he had picked himself up and recovered from the shock, there were LDC patrol cars arriving, ploughing through the rubble that now littered the square in front of what had recently been a brightly lit burger joint. A Correction Department airship floated overhead, directing its searchlights down at the wrecked building. A pair of ornithopters fluttered close to the mass of its cigar-shaped gas bag. From inside the ruins, Jeb Stuart Ho could hear muffled screaming.

A thought struck Jeb Stuart Ho with almost physical force. One of the strongest possible reasons for someone bombing the burger joint was the fact that he might have been there. If he hadn't abandoned the meal he would have still been sitting inside. It was an obvious move on the part of AA Catto to hire warriors, more likely brigands of some kind, to kill him before he killed her. It was a very logical action. He felt a tingle run through his muscles. It was now a battle, something which he could deal with.

A throng of sightseers were already pressing towards the ruins of Fidel's. They milled about and hampered the movements of the LDC. A fire truck, a medic unit and more patrol cars arrived. The disaster area was now packed with people, and luridly illuminated by the garish colours of the flashing warning lights. Jeb Stuart Ho pushed himself to the centre of the crowd to see if he could pick up any clue to the identity of the attackers. Even the patrolmen seemed to move out of the way of the tall, sinister, black-clad figure.

At the far side of the crowd, Jeb Stuart Ho spotted Bannion. He was still dressed in his rumpled brown suit. He appeared to be directing operations. He waved and gesticulated to the squad. Bodies were being carried out of the wreckage on stretchers. Jeb Stuart Ho made his way across to where Bannion stood.

'Chief-Agent Bannion.'

Bannion turned. When he saw Ho he scowled and took the cigar from between his teeth.

'What the hell are you doing here? Why don't you fuck off? I've got enough troubles without you showing up.'

Jeb Stuart Ho took a deep breath.

'I fear I may have inadvertently been responsible for this unfortunate occurrence.'

Bannion looked as though he was going to explode. He reached inside his coat and pulled out a snub-nosed .70 correction special. He waved it under Jeb Stuart Ho's nose.

'I've a good mind to kill you right now! Accidentally!'

He almost spat out the last word. Jeb Stuart Ho stood very still, staring impassively at the gun. Its short barrel was almost as wide as it was long. At last the chief-agent managed to control himself. His words were cold and deadly.

'Are you trying to tell me that you blew up Fidel's burger joint?'

Jeb Stuart Ho quickly shook his head.

'I didn't cause the explosion. That would have been neither logical nor ethical. I think I may well have been the intended victim.'

'You were in the place?'

'Minutes before the explosion. I left quickly because the food was so bad.'

Bannion's lip curled.

'That figures. Go on.'

'It is my deduction that whoever drove up and threw the bomb was hired by AA Catto to kill me.'

'Before you get to her?'

'That's correct. I think there will be other attempts.'

Bannion dropped his cigar and ground it out with his heel. 'You really are a prize, aren't you, brother? First you cause the death of one of my officers and now you seem to have started a mini-war. I knew I should never have let you go. I should have shot you when you were first brought in.'

Jeb Stuart Ho attempted to be totally reasonable.

'Perhaps you should attempt to cooperate with me.'

Bannion began to turn red again.

'Cooperate! With you!'

'The sooner I find AA Catto, the sooner I'm out of your city.'

Bannion's face tightened.

'Listen, sunshine. If I knew where the girl was, you'd be the last person I'd tell. I hope her boys get you real soon. Now get the hell out of here before I change my mind and blow you apart.'

'I...'

Bannion began waving the pistol again.

'Get!'

Jeb Stuart Ho took a last look at the mess of broken glass, twisted neon and shattered concrete. As he walked away, the vid crews began arriving. They came in all sizes, from single hand-held operators with scanners and backpacs to big, full-size mobiles that rode on their own cushion of air. Each company's crew vied with the others to get the tightest close-ups of death and mutilation. One portable operative was kneeling beside an arm that had been ripped off and flung out into the road. At close range he panned along it, recording every pore and every fleck of blood in loving 3D colour. Jeb Stuart Ho shuddered and walked away.

He kept on walking until he had covered the length of five blocks. The city of Litz was beginning to produce a taste in his mouth that was far worse than the Vegie-Wonder. He passed an alley that ran up the side of a Sex-O-Mat and something called Ye Olde Gunne Shoppe. A furtive movement made him pause. Although it was only half seen, there was something about it that triggered a subconscious response. Without thinking, he threw himself flat on the sidewalk. At the same instant there was the flash and explosion of a riot gun. Jeb Stuart Ho heard the scream of the cloud of deadly metal particles pass about half a metre over his head.

Two more blasts came from the alley, but both were slightly above him. Jeb Stuart Ho swivelled on his stomach with his own gun braced in both hands. He let go two shots in the direction of the flashes. It seemed from their position that there was more than one gunman. More riot blasts screamed over his head, and Ho returned the fire.

There was a clatter of garbage cans, and two men broke cover and ran, weaving in a low crouch down the alley. Jeb Stuart Ho snapped off a shot, and one of them fell. He was about to fire again, but the second man vanished into the shadows.

Ho, still flat on the ground, moved sideways like a crab. He reached the cover of the Sex-O-Mat wall and cautiously stood up. Still holding his gun, he drew his sword left-handed. He moved slowly and carefully down the alley. He was tensed to shoot at the slightest movement. After about twelve paces he came upon the body of one of the assassins. There was an ugly hole in his chest, and he was quite dead. Jeb Stuart Ho felt a grim satisfaction at his marksmanship. He now only had one killer to deal with. He moved on along the alley, keeping a careful watch on the deep shadows.

There was a slight movement, and Ho sprang sideways like a cat as a riot gun went off. A handful of particles nicked the right arm of his suit. He landed fractionally off balance, and before he could fire, a figure leaped to its feet and started running back in the direction of the street. The man made an easy target against the streetlights. Jeb Stuart Ho was about to fire, but then he changed his mind. He wanted this one alive.

He dropped his gun into its holster, switched his sword to his right hand, and went after him.

When he reached the pavement the man hesitated for a moment and then ran to his right. A second later, Jeb Stuart Ho turned the corner, and saw him duck inside the Sex-O-Mat. Jeb Stuart Ho followed. Inside the brightly lit doorway was a red velvet curtain. He swept it aside and found a turnstile. He didn't bother to fumble for his credit card. He jumped it. There was no sign of the man in the small anteroom. He went on into a red-lit corridor. On either side of it were red doors that led into two rows of cubicles. The man must have taken refuge in one of the cubicles. Jeb Stuart Ho started towards the first. A figure appeared from a small alcove.

'Hey, you!'

Ho swung round with his sword in the ready position. It was a guardian. Probably the Sex-O-Mat bouncer. The clone seemed to ignore the pointed sword and kept on coming.

'You have entered without paying.'

Ho took a step back.

'Did a man come through here?'

The clone kept on moving towards him.

'You will either leave or pay.'

He produced a short club from his belt. Jeb Stuart Ho took another step back. He was struck by a sense of the absurd. Here he was, an expert swordsman, backing away from a man with a small billy club. He had no desire to kill the man, but he couldn't afford to lose the gunman. He deliberately lowered his sword. The guardian swung his club at his head. Jeb Stuart Ho's hand flashed up and blocked the blow. At the same time, the hilt of his sword flicked the clone behind the ears. He suddenly sagged to the floor. Jeb Stuart Ho stepped over him and started down the corridor.

Each door had a small tri-di cube set in the door, just below eye level. This gave the customer an idea of what particular attraction the cubicle contained. The first one showed a young girl lying down with her legs spread wide. She was caressing herself with a single repeating motion. The cubes were obviously run on a single short loop. On the second door a well-built girl in an outfit of leather and studs repeatedly cracked a long bullwhip, while the third showed a muscular young man flexing his biceps.

The fourth was blank. It looked as though it was filled with a kind of pink mist. Jeb Stuart Ho assumed that it was the sign that the cubicle was occupied. He took a pace back and then launched himself at the door. His foot hit the lock and it shattered. He pivoted so a riot gun blast from inside the cubicle wouldn't hit him. None came. He pushed the door. A girl was on all fours on the bed, a small fat man crouching over her. They both stared at Jeb Stuart Ho, wide-eyed with shock and fear. He muttered his apologies and closed the damaged door.

The next two had images in the cube. The third was occupied. He hit the door. This time he interrupted a loose-skinned middle-aged woman being thrashed by a handsome, golden-tanned young man. Again Ho made his excuses and shut the door.

At the third door Jeb Stuart Ho hesitated. All he seemed to be doing was progressively breaking up the Sex-O-Mat and frightening the customers. The man should be in the place somewhere. He poised himself to hit the door. At the last moment he remembered to twist and avoid any blast inside the cubicle. A fraction of a second later his care was rewarded. A riot gun blast shattered the door frame.

Ho rolled into the room. A small man in dirty overalls was half standing, half kneeling on the bed. A frightened sex operative was huddled in the corner. Before the gunman could fire again, Ho stabbed his sword clean through his foot. The man screamed. Ho lashed out with his foot and knocked the riot gun out of his hands. The man attempted to drag the sword out of his foot, but Jeb Stuart Ho kept on holding the sword. The man gashed his hand and gave up the attempt. Ho flicked one of his knives forward into his hand from the sheath on his arm. He placed it gently under the man's chin.

'I wish to talk to you.'

'My foot! Take the goddamn sword out.'

'When you've told me what I want to know.'

'I ain't saying nothing.'

'But you are. You are making a great deal of noise. I need to know why you tried to kill me.'

'I can't tell you.'

'Why not?'

'They'll kill me.'

'Who will kill you?'

'I'm not saying.'

'I will kill you. It will be very slow and painful. I have no desire to do it, but I need the information you have very badly.'

The man looked desperate.

'If I talk I'll be killed.'

Jeb Stuart Ho looked at him with great patience.

'If that is the truth, you must accept death, for if you don't talk, I am going to kill you.'

'Please…'

'I take it that AA Catto hired you.'

'I don't know any AA Catto.'

Jeb Stuart Ho twisted the sword a little. The man gasped and sweat stood out on his forehead.

'Listen… It was a girl that hired me. For fuck's sake, take that thing out of my foot.'

'Where's the girl now?'

'I can't tell you.

Jeb Stuart Ho put his face very close to that of the man. 'It's just occurred to me that you might fear castration even more than death.'

The man gave a strangled shriek as Jeb Stuart Ho slowly moved his knife towards his genitals. The tip touched the material of the man's overalls. Jeb Stuart Ho paused.

'For the last time, where is she?'

The eyes darted from side to side in terror. Finally he gave in.

'She's holed up at the Leader Hotel.'

Ho jerked the sword out of the man's foot. He fell back on the bed, groaning. Ho turned to the boy.

'Is there a back way out of here?'

He could already hear LDC sirens outside. He didn't want to run into Bannion so soon after the last time. The boy started to giggle hysterically. He slapped him across the face.

'Can I get out at the back?'

He pulled himself together.

'There's a fire exit at the far end of the corridor. It leads out into the alley.'

Jeb Stuart Ho let himself out. He ran down the alley, away from the patrolmen who were milling in front of the Sex-O-Mat. When he reached the next main street he flagged down a cab.

'Leader Hotel, and quickly.'

12

The com-screen buzzed in Nancy's room at the Leader. Reave answered it. The room had been turned into a virtual command post. In addition to AA Catto, Reave, Nancy and Billy, Monk and four other hoods including Wormo hung about waiting for news. The Minstrel Boy squatted in a corner with his hands tied. The air was thick with smoke and the smell of booze. As the screen came to life it brought the face of little Sammy into focus. He looked agitated.

'Lemme speak to Monk.'

Reave turned to Monk.

'It's Sammy, he wants to speak to you.'

Monk moved within range of the screen. 'What d'you want?'

'It's trouble, boss.'

'Trouble?'

'That killer. He's on the loose. It looks like he's heading your way.'

'What?'

'I just heard over the LDC radio net. I've got a buddy who works as a dispatcher. The bomb at Authority Square didn't get him. He'd already left the place. Mutt and Drucker made a play for him. He shot Drucker, and then chased Mutt into a Sex-O-Mat. It seems like he's wrecked the place and cut Mutt up pretty bad. I figure there can't be no way that Mutt didn't talk.'

Monk looked grim.

'So you think he's on his way here?'

Sammy nodded.

'He's got to be.'

Monk thought for a couple of seconds. 'How long ago did all this happen?'

'Five, maybe ten minutes.'

'Listen, you better get back over here.'

Sammy avoided Monk's eyes.

'Listen, Monk. No disrespect or anything, but I ain't coming anywhere near the place. I had it with this job. I'm through.'

Monk snarled.

'You're through alright.'

He hit the console with the edge of his hand and broke the connection.

'Chickenshit!'

He turned to Nancy and AA Catto.

'You hear that?'

They both nodded. Nancy looked round the room. Everyone had fallen silent.

'We have to get out of here.'

AA Catto turned to Monk.

'How do I get out of the city? I've got to find a place where he can't reach me.'

Monk looked blankly at the other hoods.

'Don't ask us, lady. We've never been out of the city in our lives.'

AA Catto looked round helplessly. Nobody seemed about to offer any kind of practical suggestion. Reave muttered something about calling a cab, and AA Catto hit him with the small riding crop that hung from her wrist. Even the blow seemed a little preoccupied. Finally the Minstrel Boy grinned.

'You could rent an airship.'

AA Catto gripped the crop firmly and advanced on him.

'Are you trying to be funny?'

The Minstrel Boy shook his head.

'Am I in any position to be funny?'

He held up his bound hands.

'I'm perfectly serious. I'm good at getting people out of trouble. Ask Billy and Reave.'

AA Catto looked doubtful.

'Where do I get an airship from?'

The Minstrel Boy grinned.

'Dirigible Rentals, Lighter Than Air Leasing. They're both good. You can get their coordinates from Information.'

AA Catto kicked him.

'You're trying to make a fool out of me.'

The Minstrel Boy shrugged as best he could while tied up. Captivity seemed to be making him philosophical. AA Catto was about to kick him again when Reave called across from the com-screen.

'He's right. Both corporations exist.'

Reave had discreetly checked while AA Catto had been raging at the Minstrel Boy. She redirected her anger at him.

'Then get one, dummy.'

The Minstrel Boy sank back into the corner with a sigh while Reave went about his task. He ceased to wonder how he was going to get out of the situation. He was thankful for being alive from one moment to the next. He wondered if this minute-at-a-time lifestyle was the basis of his new-found philosophy. Reave looked up from the screen.

'Dirigible Rentals can get a one-hundred capacity here in fifteen minutes. It comes with a cinema and small intimate ballroom. The orchestra's extra.'

'Screw the orchestra. Can't they get it here any quicker?'

Reave shook his head.

'We're paying double for that.'

'Order it, then.'

'I can't.'

AA Catto went bright red.

'What do you mean you can't?'

'You have to. You're the client, it's your credit card.'

Reave stood up and AA Catto flung herself into the chair in front of the com-set. As she was arranging the airship hire, Nancy went over to where Monk was sitting staring bleakly into the mirror of her elaborate make-up table.

'How long do you figure it will be before Jeb Stuart Ho gets here?'

Monk toyed with one of Nancy's gilt hairbrushes.

'If he took a ground cab, and the traffic went his way, maybe ten minutes. Give or take a couple of minutes each way.'

AA Catto came across from the com-set. She'd gone white.

'But the airship won't be here for fifteen.'

Monk nodded.

'So it'll be too late.'

Monk nodded again. AA Catto bit her knuckles. 'What can we do?'

Nobody answered. She looked at Nancy. 'There must be something. He's going to kill me.'

Nancy looked at Monk, and back to AA Catto. 'If Monk and his boys could hold him off for five minutes or more we could go up on the roof and wait for the ship to come. We can board it from there. It's not used, but there's still an old mooring tower from when this used to be a fancy hotel.'

Monk, who had listened to the whole conversation in sullen silence, suddenly slammed his fist into the top of the dressing table.

'No way!'

Nancy looked at him in surprise.

'No way what?'

'No way will we hold off this guy for you.'

Every eye in the room was on Monk. Reave walked over and stood beside him.

'Why not, Monk, what's wrong?'

The Minstrel Boy's voice came from the corner.

'I'll tell you why not.'

Reave turned towards him.

'Why?'

'For one, the man knows if you all jump on your airship, he ain't going to get paid, and for two, Jeb Stuart Ho is most likely to kill anyone who gets in his way.'

AA Catto suddenly exploded. She pushed past Reave, and started slashing at the Minstrel Boy with her riding crop.

'I'll kill you! You little creep! I've had enough! Nasty little punk! I'll...'

Reave grabbed her, pinning her arms to her sides so she couldn't reach her ring. Even as he was doing it he couldn't believe himself. He'd never been so brave.

'Come on. Calm down.'

AA Catto continued to struggle.

'If I'm going to die, I'm going to kill him first.'

The Minstrel Boy had curled up in a ball in the corner. He marvelled that he still hadn't died. Suddenly Nancy moved between him and AA Catto.

'There's no reason why anyone should die, least of all you.'

AA Catto stopped struggling.

'What do you mean?'

Nancy glanced at Monk.

'I'm sure Monk and the boys would hold off Ho if you offered them a credit card each.'

Monk suddenly looked interested.

'How do we get them?'

'AA Catto calls the bank and makes the arrangements. They could be transmitted to the desk clerk who could hold them until we're safely away.'

Nancy didn't neglect to make sure of her own place on the airship.

Monk hesitated. He tilted back his fedora and scratched his head. Then he looked at AA Catto.

'You agree to that?'

'Anything, anything.'

Monk nodded.

'Okay, do it, we're wasting time.'

Reave let go of AA Catto. While she began desperately to punch out coordinates, he began to direct his men.

'Huey and Jeff, you go down to the lobby. Stay hidden. When he comes in let him get past you, then shoot him in the back.'

The two hoods nodded. He turned to the other two.

'Wormo and Chang, us three will set ourselves up on the landing. If he gets past the other two, we'll be there to blast him in a crossfire whether he uses the lift or the stairs. Okay?'

The two men rather reluctantly agreed. He glanced at AA Catto.

'Is it fixed?'

She nodded.

'It's fixed.'

The hoods all trooped out. Everyone looked at Billy. Nancy scowled.

'What about him?'

AA Catto turned.

'What about him?'

Reave turned from collecting up the things they'd need. 'Can't he come with us?'

AA Catto looked petulant.

'Why?'

'He's my old partner. I can't leave him, he might be killed.'

'Why should I do you any favours, you hurt me just now?'

Reave almost grovelled.

'Please.'

'Oh, very well.'

Billy looked questioningly at Reave.

'What about Darlene? She's up in our room with a trick.'

'You'll have to leave her. There isn't time.'

Billy shrugged.

'Okay.'

The Minstrel Boy decided to push his luck.

'What about me?'

AA Catto regarded him coldly.

'What about you?'

'I could be useful. I'd know where you were. You're going to have to go through the nothings. I could be amazingly useful.'

AA Catto shook her head.

'You're not going.'

'I could save you a lot of trouble.'

Reave looked uncertain.

'He could be right. After all, he is a guide.'

AA Catto began to get angry again.

'I've already agreed to take one of your little friends. I'm not taking him. I don't trust him, and I don't like him.'

Reave didn't press the point. The four of them began to file out towards the lift. The Minstrel Boy had one last try.

'At least untie me.'

AA Catto almost spat at him from the doorway.

'Take your chances.'

The Minstrel Boy sagged back into his corner again. He heard the lift gates clang shut and the mechanism grind into action. Eventually he heard it stop as the lift reached the top floor. A few moments later, the sound of gunfire echoed up the lift shaft. It sounded as though it came from the lobby.

13

Jeb Stuart Ho came carefully through the door of the Leader Hotel. The lobby was silent and deserted. The screen flickered in one corner, but no one was watching it. The drunks had all left.

Someone had even turned off the sound. Just inside the doorway, Ho stopped. He felt the air, almost like an animal. It seemed heavy with tension. He turned and walked quietly to the desk. The clerk seemed to have abandoned his usual position. Jeb Stuart Ho leaned over the desk and looked down. The clerk was crouching on the floor. He looked fearfully at Ho.

'I...'

'Why are you kneeling on the floor?'

The clerk half rose.

'I... I was looking for something. Something I dropped.'

'Did you find it?'

'Find what?'

'The thing you were looking for. The thing you dropped.'

'I... er... no. I didn't. It must be somewhere else.'

Jeb Stuart Ho nodded.

'That seems very likely.'

He took two paces away from the desk in the direction of the lift. The clerk sank behind the desk again. Ho stopped and wondered from which direction the ambush that had evidently been arranged for him would come. The most likely tactic for the assassins would be to remain hidden until he was almost by the lift, and then shoot him in the back. He knew that he would have to take a chance on being right. He pulled out his gun and sword. Slowly he bent his knees until he was almost crouching.

With a snap he launched himself into the air. The leap took him most of the way across the lobby. He landed on his feet just in front of the lift gates. He spun round. Two men with guns appeared from behind the battered furniture, on each side of the room. Jeb Stuart Ho flung out his arms. The gun exploded and the sword flashed from his hand. One hood spun into the wall as the bullet smashed into his chest. The other toppled forward and fell on his knees, desperately trying to pull the sword from his throat. As his gun hit the floor it went off. The shot carved a long furrow in the threadbare carpet.

With his arms still extended Jeb Stuart Ho slowly straightened up. The clerk emerged furtively from behind the desk. When he saw Jeb Stuart Ho and the two dead men, he turned even paler. Jeb Stuart Ho slowly let his arms drop. He walked to the man with the sword sticking out of his neck. Ho rolled the corpse over until it was lying on its back. He grasped the sword hilt with both hands, placed his foot on the body's chest, and tugged. He picked a tattered cushion out of one of the chairs and carefully wiped the blade. He dropped the cushion and looked at the desk clerk.

'Where is AA Catto?'

The desk clerk's mouth worked desperately, but no words came. Jeb Stuart Ho started to walk towards him.

'Where is AA Catto?'

The desk clerk found his voice.

'Up on the fifth floor, but there's more of them waiting for you.'

'I see.'

Jeb Stuart Ho turned and peered up the dark lift shaft. He would be a sitting duck if he used the lift. He saw that a set of emergency stairs ran round the outside of the shaft. He would be safer using them. As he started up the first flight he turned back, and smiled sardonically at the white-faced desk clerk.

'I hope you locate whatever you lost.'

He went up the first three floors very quickly, but as he approached the fourth he slowed down and took the stairs much more carefully. It would be foolish not to assume that another trap had been set for him. He stepped on to the fourth-floor landing, ready to act at the slightest sound or movement. Nothing happened. Ho waited for a few moments and then moved silently towards the next set of steps. There would be men waiting at the top of the next flight.

There were eight steps in front of him. Then a right-angle turn and, if it was the same as the first four, another eight that led up to the fifth floor. Ho moved silently up to the turn, and stopped. Still nothing had happened. He looked up at the last eight steps. He took a firmer grip on his gun and sword. He put his foot on the first step. Nothing. He tried the second, the third and the fourth. Still there was no explosion of gunfire. Maybe the desk clerk had lied. Maybe there was no one lying in wait. Maybe AA Catto had fled the Leader Hotel altogether. He touched the fifth step. He moved to the sixth. As he placed his foot silently on the seventh step, there was the roar of a riot gun. The blast smashed lumps of plaster out of the wall above his head. He somersaulted backwards down the eight steps and landed on his feet at the turn in the stairs. A hail of needles gouged into the wall where he'd been standing just a fraction of a second before.

Jeb Stuart Ho crouched on the stair. On his hands and knees he edged his way forward, a centimetre at a time. The needles and the riot blast meant there were at least two gunmen waiting for him. At the sixth step he paused. He unstrapped the nanchuk from his arm, held one end at arm's length, and quickly swung the other. It soared into the air, hit the far wall of the landing and clattered on the stone floor.

One riot blast hit the far wall, another smashed plaster from the wall beside the stairs, a burst of needles screamed, ricocheting through the steel cage of the lift shaft. Jeb Stuart Ho smiled grimly. There had to be three of them. The riot blasts were too close together and the angle of fire too great for them to have come from the same gun. For a fraction of a second one of the gunmen had emerged from cover to fire. It was one of the men with riot guns. He crouched in an open doorway. Jeb Stuart Ho could only see him when he leaned out to fire.

He waited patiently, crouching halfway up that last flight. Sure enough, a minute hardly passed before the man cautiously poked his head out and looked around. Jeb Stuart Ho snapped off a single shot. It smashed the man's forehead and pitched him back inside the room. There was another riot blast, and another burst of needles. Each hit an opposite side of the stairs. Jeb Stuart Ho remained very still and thought carefully.

At each end of the fifth floor landing, a corridor led away to the various rooms. From the way their shots were hitting the wall, he decided that the two men must be somewhere in the corridor, positioned at opposite ends of the landing, maintaining a crossfire on the head of the stairs. While he stayed where he was they couldn't hit him, but once he set foot on the landing, one at least would probably get a shot at him while he was dealing with the other. He couldn't afford to waste time. It seemed he would have to take a chance on their reactions being slower than his.

Jeb Stuart Ho took a step backwards. He tensed himself. He flashed up the stairs and hit the landing. He leaped and, curling himself into a ball, he crashed into the far wall. The riot gun exploded. The bulk of the charge missed him. A few particles ripped through the fabric of his suit. He could feel blood running down his arm. He fired at the man from a crouch. The impact of the bullet flung him backwards down the corridor. He twitched a couple of times and lay still. Ho swung round to face the killer with the needle gun. He couldn't understand why he hadn't shot at him. As he raised his gun he saw why. The riot blast that had been meant for Jeb Stuart Ho had caught the man squarely in the chest. He must have stood up to take aim and been caught in his partner's fire. His body was almost cut in half. It lay in a rapidly spreading pool of blood. A grey fedora lay about a metre from the mutilated corpse.

Jeb Stuart Ho stood up cautiously. There were no more shots. It seemed as though there was nobody else lying in wait for him. He dropped his gun into its holster, and walked down the corridor. He still kept his sword in his hand. He stepped over the body, and looked inside the first room. It was empty. The door of the second was wide open. In one corner was a huddled figure. Its hands were tied behind its back. It looked up. Jeb Stuart Ho saw it was the Minstrel Boy. He lowered his sword. The Minstrel Boy grinned crookedly.

'I was wondering when you'd get here.'

Jeb Stuart Ho sheathed his sword and stood looking down at the Minstrel Boy. His face was grim.

'Where is AA Catto?'

'She's gone.'

'Gone? How?'

'She rented an airship. They left from the roof. They must have got well away by now.'

Jeb Stuart Ho's jaw muscles tightened, but otherwise he showed no sign of the anger and frustration that welled up inside him. The Minstrel Boy struggled to sit up.

'Aren't you going to untie me?'

Jeb Stuart Ho didn't move. A thought had just struck him. The Minstrel Boy's voice took on a querulous edge.

'Come on, Killer. Don't just stand there, untie me.'

Jeb Stuart Ho stared hard at him.

'It must have been you who informed them where I was.'

The Minstrel Boy adopted a look of pained surprise. 'Who, me?'

'It could only have been you.'

'How would I know where you were?'

'You must have used your credit card. I can think of no other way.'

'You're crazy.'

'I could check with the bank.'

Jeb Stuart Ho moved towards the vid-set. The Minstrel Boy sighed.

'Okay, okay. It was me. I found you through the bank.'

Jeb Stuart Ho looked coldly at him.

'So you changed sides.'

'Does it look as though I changed sides? Would I be lying here tied up if I changed sides?'

'You told them where I was.'

'So? Who says I changed sides? Who says I was on your side in the first place? You forced me to guide you at gunpoint. That don't mean I owe you anything.'

'They threw a bomb into an eating house. A number of people were killed.'

The Minstrel Boy's mouth set in a stubborn line.

'So? What could I do? They beat me up. They would have killed me if I hadn't told them. I never asked to get involved in your private wars, and no way am I responsible for any bystanders who get in the way. Now, are you going to untie me or not?'

Jeb Stuart Ho reluctantly pulled one of his knives from the sheath on his arm and sliced through the Minstrel Boy's bond. He stood up and began massaging the circulation back into his wrists. Ho put away his knife, and walked slowly out of the room. The Minstrel Boy paused for a moment, and then followed him. As he was about to start down the stairs, something on one of the bodies on the landing caught his eye. Around its waist was his knife belt. He walked over to the body, bent down and retrieved it. He strapped the belt round his own hips and followed Jeb Stuart Ho down to the lobby.

When they reached the ground floor, Chief-Agent Bannion and a squad of LDC patrolmen were waiting. Bannion stared at Jeb Stuart Ho with his hands clasped behind his back. The ever-present cigar was clamped between his teeth.

'You just can't stop, can you?'

Jeb Stuart Ho inclined his head.

'The trials that beset us are as numerous as the flowers that bloom.'

'I don't give a fuck what besets you, brother. It's the way you beset me that I care about. You are giving me ulcers.'

'A careful diet might correct that.'

Bannion began to turn crimson.

'Don't get wise with me, buster. There's two men dead here. The desk clerk says you killed them.'

Jeb Stuart Ho shrugged.

'Didn't he also tell you that they were trying to kill me?'

Bannion began to pace up and down. Finally he stopped in front of Ho. He thrust his face very close to Ho's.

'Your score so far is nine dead, including the five we pulled out of the burger joint.'

Jeb Stuart Ho looked at him calmly.

'There are three more upstairs.'

Bannion looked as though he might haemorrhage.

'Divine Marquis, give me patience. I suppose you're going to claim that was self-defence.'

Jeb Stuart Ho nodded.

'That is correct.'

The Minstrel Boy began to edge towards the door. Bannion saw him out of the corner of his eye and swung round.

'You! You hold it right there!'

'Who, me?'

'Yes, you. You're mixed up in this somewhere.'

The Minstrel Boy became a picture of innocence. 'Not me, mister Chief-Agent, sir. I was just passing through.'

Bannion snarled. He looked ugly.

'Bullshit. You arrived in town with this maniac, and he paid you with a credit card. Right?'

'I was only a guide. He forced me to lead him here.'

'Okay then. You can just lead him away again. You're both being expelled from the city. If you're still here in one hour, my men will shoot you on sight.'

Jeb Stuart Ho's face became set.

'I have a task to complete.'

Bannion's eyes narrowed.

'I don't give a fuck about your mission, you're leaving town.'

Suddenly he seemed to relax. He half grinned.

'Anyway, AA Catto's gone.'

'Gone?'

'That's right, gone. Much as it hurts me to give you any assistance at all, she's left town. She's in a rented airship. It's passed the city limits and is heading for the nothings. So go. You hear me? Go!'

Jeb Stuart Ho nodded.

'I hear you.'

Bannion pointed at the Minstrel Boy.

'And take him with you.'

The Minstrel Boy's eyebrows shot up.

'I ain't going with him. I'll leave town, but I ain't going with him.'

Bannion grabbed the lapels of his frock coat.

'Oh yes you are.'

'Why? Why have I got to go with him?'

'So you can lead him to AA Catto, and I can be sure he won't get lost and come back here. Okay?'

'I'm damned if it's okay. I don't mind leaving town. I've been thrown out of better towns than this, but him, I ain't no way going with him.'

Bannion tightened his grip on the Minstrel Boy's jacket.

'Oh yes you are.'

The Minstrel Boy tried to pull away.

'Listen, take your hands off me. You got it all wrong. Shit, I couldn't even help him if I wanted to. I can't track people through the nothings. It's just not possible.'

Bannion pushed the Minstrel Boy forcibly away. He staggered back across the lobby. He was fielded by two patrolmen who held him while Bannion sauntered towards him.

'You're a goddamn liar.'

The Minstrel Boy paled. 'What do you mean?'

'You know what I mean.'

The Minstrel Boy began to struggle.

'You can't do it. You can't do it to me.'

Bannion smiled nastily.

'I can. I'll do anything to make sure you two get out and stay out.'

The Minstrel Boy shook his head desperately. 'You wouldn't do that.'

'I would.'

Jeb Stuart Ho interrupted. He looked puzzled. 'I don't understand. What are you two talking about?'

Bannion turned to Ho. His grin became meaner and wider.

'He can follow AA Catto anywhere.'

The Minstrel Boy's voice became hysterical. 'No I can't.'

One of the patrolmen twisted his arm, and the Minstrel Boy shut up. Bannion went on.

'Any guide can get a fix on a single individual, provided you keep him shot full of cyclatrol. It gives them some kind of overall vision. Don't ask me how it works, but it does.'

Jeb Stuart Ho stroked his chin. He looked at the Minstrel Boy.

'Is this true?'

Sweat had broken out on his forehead. He shook his head. 'No, no, it's all lies. Nothing like that... argh!'

One of the patrolmen had twisted his arm again. He subsided.

'Yes, it's true...'

His voice rose again.

'...But it could kill me.'

Jeb Stuart Ho looked at Bannion questioningly.

'Is this true? Will the drug kill him?'

Bannion shrugged.

'It might. But it's not all that likely. He could go mad.'

Ho nodded.

'I suppose we'll have to take the chance.'

The Minstrel Boy began to struggle violently with the men holding him.

'No! No! You can't do this to me!'

Bannion swung round angrily. 'Shut him up.'

One of the patrolmen tapped the Minstrel Boy sharply across the back of the head with the butt of his nightstick. The Minstrel Boy slumped forward. Bannion turned back to Jeb Stuart Ho.

'I'm taking you down to headquarters. I'll fix you up with transport for the nothings, supplies and the drugs for him.'

He jerked his thumb towards the Minstrel Boy who hung limply between the two patrolmen. Jeb Stuart Ho ran his fingers through his hair.

'There's no alternative choice?'

Bannion shook his head.

'You've got no choice at all. I'd still rather have you quietly shot.'

Jeb Stuart Ho bowed.

'I suppose I should thank you for this help with my task.'

Bannion's lip curled.

'Save it. It's going to cost the brotherhood a fortune.'

He signalled to the squad of patrolmen. They bundled Jeb Stuart Ho and the Minstrel Boy out of the hotel lobby, across the sidewalk and into the back of a patrolcar. Around them, the camera crews and sightseers were already starting to crowd round the entrance of the Leader Hotel.

14

A Catto sat back in one of the small gilt chairs that were arranged round the edge of the airship's small ballroom. The entire place was furnished in gold and red plush. A cluster of small spotlights played on the dark mirror of the dance floor. On a small dais a string quartet played muted chamber music. AA Catto sighed. After the fear and tension of the last few hours she felt totally drained. Exhaustion made her avoid thinking about what she should do next.

Billy, Reave and Lame Nancy stood in the small observation platform that opened off the ballroom like a tiny terrace. It was totally enclosed in elaborately worked stained glass that threw patterns of colour over them as they stared down at the receding lights of the city beneath them. They all seemed to be avoiding looking at her. It was clear that they were waiting for her to make some kind of decision. She knew it was necessary, but somehow she just couldn't do it. She hated doing things out of necessity. She was able to act instantly on whim, but since this nightmare of crazy assassins had started her old life seemed to have vanished. It all seemed so unfair. She raised a limp hand, and a white-coated steward was instantly at her side.

'Yes, Miss Catto?'

'I want a drink.'

'We have a fully comprehensive bar.'

'Can you make me a Doric column?'

'I'm sure our bartender can make it. He holds a triple-A proficiency rating.'

'He'd better do it right.'

'I'm sure he will, Miss Catto.'

She closed her eyes as he hurried away. She opened them moments later when she heard a discreet cough. She thought it was the waiter with her drink, but she found herself looking at the pale blue uniform and gold braid of the airship's captain. He stood at attention with his white peaked cap clutched under his arm. His face was set in an expression of competent neutrality.

'Miss Catto.'

AA Catto raised an eyebrow. 'What?'

'I still haven't had any details of your proposed flight.'

'So?'

'We've passed the city limits, and I need to know what course you want me to set.'

AA Catto looked round the ballroom.

'I ordered a drink. It hasn't come yet.'

The captain glanced across the ballroom.

'I'm sure the steward will be along in a moment. Now about the course...'

AA Catto's temper flashed.

'Bugger the course. I want my drink.'

The captain compressed his lips slightly, and marched quickly across the ballroom. Billy, Reave and Nancy were by now standing at the top of the steps that led to the observation platform, watching the exchange. A few moments later the captain returned followed by a flustered-looking steward.

'Here is your drink, Miss Catto.'

The steward placed a tall crystal glass in front of AA Catto. Beneath a head of crushed ice, the liquid was pale pink. Halfway down it changed to red and finally in the bottom of the glass it was a deep purple. AA Catto picked it up and swirled it round once. The ice tinkled. She sipped it, and put it down.

'I suppose it will do.'

The steward bowed and scuttled away. The captain drew himself up to his full height. With his neatly trimmed beard and rigidly controlled paunch he was every inch the figure of tolerant authority. He cleared his throat.

'About the course, Miss Catto. I really must insist you make a decision.'

AA Catto looked at him with frank dislike. If there were three things she detested, they were authority figures, people who found it necessary to clear their throats before speaking and people who insisted she do things.

She ran her finger round the rim of the glass. It made a faint singing sound.

'I think I want to go into the nothings.'

The captain's eyes widened.

'The nothings?'

'That's what I said.'

'It can't be done.'

AA Catto began to get impatient.

'I was under the impression that I had hired this craft, and that you would take it wherever I requested.'

'That's correct.'

'Well, I'm requesting you to take the damn thing into the nothings.'

The captain took a deep breath.

'That's absolutely out of the question. This ship isn't equipped for that kind of journey.'

'That's the kind of journey I wish to make.'

The captain spoke very slowly as though he was talking to a retarded child.

'If this ship enters the nothings it will disintegrate. It carries no generator of its own. It will be destroyed.'

AA Catto looked up at him.

'You carry a set of personal generators, don't you? Portapacs or something similar?'

The captain nodded.

'Yes, but that's beside the point. I'm not going to take my ship to certain destruction in the nothings. I hope I make myself clear.'

'You refuse?'

'Absolutely.'

AA Catto nodded. She slowly turned and looked at the group by the observation platform.

'Billy, could you come over here for a minute?'

Billy sauntered across the dance floor. He glanced enquiringly at AA Catto.

'Trouble?'

AA Catto looked hard at the captain.

'Billy, do you have your gun with you?'

Billy nodded. He was a little confused. He pulled a .70 recoilless from under his coat.

'I got a gun.'

AA Catto relaxed in her chair.

'Would you point it at the captain?'

Billy shrugged and did as he was asked. The captain put on his cap and came to formal attention.

'You realize that by this act of violence you have voided your hiring contract and I have no alternative but to return to the bridge and order this ship to return to the company's docking mast.'

AA Catto laughed.

'God, you're pompous.'

'I can only repeat…'

'Shut up and listen. If you don't immediately take this contraption into the nothings, Billy will shoot you. Won't you, Billy?'

Billy swallowed.

'Um… yes.'

The captain remained at attention.

'I'll do no such thing.'

AA Catto looked at Billy.

'Shoot him.'

Billy looked at AA Catto, at the captain and then down at the gun. He tried to think of a way out. There didn't seem to be one. He pulled the trigger. The captain was knocked across the dance floor. He died without a sound. The string quartet stopped playing but started again, rather uncoordinatedly, when Billy turned in their direction.

AA Catto briskly stood up. She beckoned to Nancy and Reave.

'I think we'd better go to the bridge and take control of this machine. It would seem you can't get anywhere leaving things to other people.'

They left the ballroom and started down one of the companionways that traversed the length of the airship's gondola. As they walked, Billy fell into step beside AA Catto.

'Do you think this is such a good idea?'

'Is what such a good idea?'

'Shooting the captain and pushing the ship into the nothings?'

'You shot the captain.'

Billy looked down at the deck.

'Yes, I suppose I did.'

'Damn right you did. You're as responsible as anyone.'

Billy felt a little sick. Any ideas of morality seemed to be slipping away. He glanced sideways at AA Catto.

'But what about this going into the nothings? I've fallen into the nothings with just a portapac. It's no fun. You don't have any control over where you finish up.'

'But you finish up somewhere.'

'Yes.'

'Well then.'

'I still don't like it. We could land in a lot of trouble, and there's nothing we can do about it.'

'Do you have a better idea?'

'No.'

'Could I be in any more trouble than I was in in Litz?'

Billy shook his head.

'I suppose not.

'Then there's really nothing to discuss, is there?'

Billy didn't say anything more. He followed AA Catto up the steel steps that led to the bridge. He slid back the steel door and they stepped into the airship's control room. The front of the bridge was a single sheet of plexiglass. The rest of the walls were covered with various control monitors. Three officers in blue uniforms were grouped round an illuminated chart table. Behind them, staring fixedly through the plexiglass windshield, was a steersman in a white sailor suit. His hands gripped the big polished wheel that controlled the rudder, and beside him were the levers that set the angle of climb or descent. The officers looked up sharply as AA Catto and her four companions came through the door. One of them, who from the amount of gold braid on his uniform seemed to be second in command after the captain, moved to head them off.

'I'm sorry. Clients are not permitted on the bridge. It's a company rule.'

AA Catto smiled.

'I'm afraid company rules no longer apply. I've just had your captain shot.'

The officer stopped dead.

'You did what?'

AA Catto continued to smile at him.

'I had the captain shot, and I'm taking this ship into the nothings.'

The two other officers joined the first one.

'That's impossible. You'll destroy it.'

AA Catto stopped smiling.

'I tried to explain to your captain. I intend going into the nothings, and no one's going to stop me. Can you understand?'

She turned to Billy.

'Show them your gun.'

Billy pulled out his gun again. The three officers took a step back. The first one raised his hand.

'Don't shoot.'

Billy continued to point the gun at him. AA Catto looked him straight in the eye.

'Are you going to do what you're told?'

The officers stood together by the chart table. The senior one licked his lips.

'I assume you're taking over the ship by force.'

AA Catto clapped her hands together. It was an oddly childish gesture.

'At last we're getting through. Now, will you instruct the driver, or whatever he is, to take us into the nothings?'

'You realize this is an act of piracy?'

AA Catto shrugged.

'Call it what you like, only do it.'

The officer muttered for a moment with his two companions and then turned back to AA Catto.

'I've gone on record as registering my strongest protest against your criminal acts. Beyond that I'll follow your instructions.'

'Then set a course for the nothings.'

The officer bent over the table and consulted a chart. AA Catto waited tensely. Finally he straightened up and looked at the man behind the wheel.

'Steer one zero seven.'

'One zero seven, sir.'

'Steady as she goes.'

'Aye, sir.'

The first officer looked sourly back at AA Catto. 'Will that be all?'

AA Catto thought for a moment.

'We'll need portapacs when we hit the nothings. The officer scowled.

'They're in the wall locker.'

He indicated with his hand. Nancy opened the locker. Inside was a rack of small individual stasis generators. She took out four and handed them round. They slung them over their shoulders. There seemed to be nothing else to do until the airship hit the nothings. After all the high drama, the whole thing slipped into an anticlimactic trough. It became very quiet on the bridge. The officers went about their routine tasks, doing their best to ignore the four hijackers. The steersman stared resolutely ahead. Billy began to feel a little foolish as he stood there holding his gun. Finally, AA Catto could stand it no longer. She caught the eye of the first officer.

'Could you get a steward up here?'

He reddened a little.

'A steward?'

AA Catto nodded.

'That's right, a steward. My friends and I would like some drinks, and maybe a snack of some kind.'

The first officer began to inflate with indignation.

'Am I to understand that you want to turn my bridge into some sort of cafeteria?'

'Yes. Why not? We're going to wreck it shortly, so I don't see how a little change in your routine would matter.'

The first officer grabbed a hand mike off the chart table as though he was going to hit AA Catto with it, then he checked himself and bellowed into it.

'Get a steward to the bridge. On the double.'

The drinks, when they came, didn't really help too much. AA Catto, Billy, Reave and Nancy formed their own four-person cocktail party, which, if anything, made them feel even more self-conscious. The crew of the airship went on pointedly ignoring them

The presence of AA Catto and the others couldn't be ignored for ever. A thin strip of blue-grey light appeared on the horizon. It looked like a strange, cold dawn. In fact, it was the nothings. Gradually it rolled nearer. It was like a growing wall of sparkling cloud. The airship drifted closer and closer. The first officer straightened up and faced AA Catto.

'Are you sure you won't call off this madness?'

AA Catto tapped her fingernails on the portapac. She switched it on. The others did the same.

'There's no other way. Keep going, or Billy here will shoot you.'

Billy tightened his grip on the gun. His stomach started to knot. He hated the nothings and the things they did to his mind. The steersman turned to the first officer.

'We'll hit the nothings any minute, sir.'

The first officer looked as though he was about to panic. He moved towards AA Catto.

'Won't you let me change course before we're all disrupted?'

Billy stepped between them and levelled his gun at the first officer's chest.

'Hold it right there,'

The officer halted. There were dark patches of sweat under the armpits of his uniform.

'At least let me issue the crew with portapacs and give the order to abandon ship.'

Billy looked at AA Catto. 'It can't do any harm.'

AA Catto thought for a moment.

'Yes, yes. Give the order, but don't attempt to alter course.'

The officer swung round to the steersman.

'Lock on present heading, break out a portapac and prepare to abandon ship.'

The steersman saluted and hurried to the locker that held the per-

sonal stasis generators. He clipped one to his belt and stood waiting.
The officers began to do the same. The first officer picked up the hand
mike.

'Attention all crew. Now hear this. This is an emergency. I repeat,
this is an emergency. We are entering the nothings. All crew will break
our portapacs and prepare to abandon ship. Good luck to you all.'

He repeated the message and then clipped a generator to his own
belt. He came to attention, and AA Catto giggled. The wall of sparkling,
shifting light was almost upon them. Suddenly Billy turned to the other
three.

'It might be a good idea if we held on to each other. That way, we
have a chance of coming out of the nothings in the same place.'

Nancy's face grew tight.

'If we come out.'

They linked hands. Above them, the front of the gas bag smoked
and began to vanish as it nosed its way into the nothings. The plexiglass
vanished as its fabric was scattered into time and space. The front half
of the cabin vanished. The wall of mist reached the four of them clinging
together. Concepts like up and down melted away. They were swallowed in the shifting grey and roaring silence. They seemed to be falling
in all directions at once.

15

They injected the Minstrel Boy with the maximum dose of cyclatrol. Afterwards his eyes glazed over and he began to scream. He
screamed non-stop for two hours. They had to shut him in a sub-
basement cell until he stopped. Bannion wouldn't let him leave the LDC
building until he'd calmed down. Bannion was very sensitive about
accusations of police brutality. In the meantime he and Jeb Stuart Ho
concluded a deal whereby Chief-Agent Bannion on behalf of the Litz
Department of Correction would sell the brotherhood a lightweight
armoured car that would enable Jeb Stuart Ho to pursue AA Catto. The
Litz Department of Correction charged a grossly inflated price, which
Jeb Stuart Ho paid after a polite period of ritual haggling.

When the Minstrel Boy finally became quiet, two patrolmen
brought him up from the depths of the lock-ups. They had to support
him on either side. His movements were uncoordinated, his eyes were
vacant and his mouth hung open. Jeb Stuart Ho was alarmed at his condition.

'How can he lead me anywhere like that?'

Bannion smiled and tapped the side of his nose with his forefinger.

'He'll do what you want.'

'Yes. Are you sure?'

'Sure I'm sure. You'll see.'

Bannion ordered the car brought round to the front of the building. He and Jeb Stuart Ho went our to inspect it. It was a squat, ugly, square-sided machine. It had long armoured engine housing, and a small three-seat cab. The windscreen and side windows were mere slits of toughened glass, and the whole vehicle was covered in dull grey, bullet-proof steel. It was supported on six balloon-tyred wheels, four at the rear and two at the front. Bannion opened the passenger door.

'Get in.'

Jeb Stuart Ho was confused.

'Surely I will have to drive the machine?'

'Just get in.'

Jeb Stuart Ho got in. Bannion signalled to the patrolmen who were holding the Minstrel Boy just inside the building. They hurried down the steps. Bannion opened the driver's door. They pushed the Minstrel Boy inside and strapped him in. He hung there with his mouth half open. Bannion poked his head in the window beside Jeb Stuart Ho.

'Okay. Tell him what you want.'

Ho looked dubiously at the slack-jawed Minstrel Boy.

'Will he understand?'

'Just tell him.'

Jeb Stuart Ho took a deep breath.

'We have to pursue and catch AA Catto.'

The Minstrel Boy didn't respond. Bannion grinned at Ho.

'Tell him to drive.'

Jeb Stuart Ho felt a little ridiculous. He couldn't imagine what kind of obscure joke Bannion was attempting to involve him in. He raised his voice a little.

'You will start the car and drive.'

Like a man in a dream, the Minstrel Boy placed his hands on the wheel. Bannion withdrew his head. The Minstrel Boy put on the power. The engine came to life. The Minstrel Boy dumped it into gear with a crash. The car lurched forward. They swerved drunkenly away from the kerb. Bannion laughed. They began to pick up speed. Bannion yelled after them.

'Don't come back.'

The drive through the traffic of downtown Litz was like a drawn-out suicide bid. A dozen times Jeb Stuart Ho could see no way out of a fatal collision, but at the very last minute the Minstrel Boy somehow managed to avoid disaster. As they had begun to move, his jaws had clamped together and he appeared to stare fixedly along the length of the bonnet. Jeb Stuart Ho wasn't certain whether he could actually see, or whether he was steering the car by some other sense produced by the cyclatrol. On a comparatively clear stretch of road, Jeb Stuart Ho looked in the glove compartment to check that the little black case of refills of the drug was still there. It was. When Bannion had given it to him, he'd told Jeb Stuart Ho to give the Minstrel Boy a shot every twelve hours. He hadn't told him how long the Minstrel Boy would survive under those conditions.

At last, to Jeb Stuart Ho's relief, they emerged from the city traffic and swung on to one of the wide straight roads that radiated out from Litz to the edge of the nothings. There was almost no traffic, apart from the occasional wheelfreak's truck that flashed past, blazing with lights. Ho felt that he could relax a little. The Minstrel Boy had manoeuvred the car into the middle of the highway. He held it there with one limp hand.

Jeb Stuart Ho looked carefully at the Minstrel Boy. It was hard to know, apart from the tightly clenched jaws, whether he was really conscious. Even with all his training, Ho found it difficult to visualize what was going on in his mind. Ho was taken by surprise when the Minstrel Boy made a sudden move. His hand flashed down to a part of the control panel between the seats. Harsh metallic music blared from a set of speakers fitted in the back of the cab. In the confined space it made Jeb Stuart Ho's head ring. He shouted to the Minstrel Boy.

'Does it have to be so loud?'

The Minstrel Boy gave no indication that he had heard him. He continued to stare blankly through the windshield. Jeb Stuart Ho stretched out a hand to adjust the volume control. Without warning the Minstrel Boy slapped his hand away. He didn't take his eyes off the road. Jeb Stuart Ho said nothing and settled back to endure it.

They were reaching the limits of the Litz generators. Circular holes filled with grey nothing started to appear in the road in front of them. The Minstrel Boy pressed the control that activated the car's own stasis generator. He made no attempt to avoid any of the holes, but continued to hold the car steady in the very centre of the road, at just under maximum speed. The car began to bump and lurch as though its own stasis field was unable to produce an approximation of a flat surface beneath the car, but only the reading on the speedometer and the constant bucking and lurching gave any indication that they were moving at all. The razor-sharp music pounded on, and Jeb Stuart Ho began to perform the preliminary exercises to close down his mind. The Minstrel Boy's face still showed no sign of life.

In many ways, this trip through the nothings was very similar to the lizard ride they had made to Litz. Ho's sense of time quickly began to ebb away. He had to keep glancing at the dashboard to grasp some kind of orientation. The chronometer was little help. In many ways it increased his confusion. Sometimes the digits would flip over at a rate that made it unreadable. Other times a single figure would hang for what seemed like hours. Similar things happened to the music. It would alternately hammer frenetically and then lurch sideways in howling cadences. He was sorely tempted to seek refuge in an intermediate trance, but the constant sight of the transformed Minstrel Boy beside him kept him firmly in the material world inside the car.

It was around the point when the chronometer was telling him that they'd been in the nothings for just over four hours that things started to appear. First it was the white dog with black nose and ears. It jerked its paw at them in a hitch-hiking gesture, and then, through the rear window, Jeb Stuart Ho could see it cursing them from the distance after the Minstrel Boy had failed to stop. Next came the billboards, huge illuminated signs that appeared to stand on nothing. Floodlights blazed down on them, making it impossible to miss the slogans in strange, unreadable, alien script. Jeb Stuart Ho wondered if they were real objects or hallucinations. He was at a loss to tell. There was too much about the nothings that he didn't know.

After seven hours they hit the road. It just appeared out of the shifting greyness, exactly under their wheels. It was a dark blue colour, and ran dead straight for as far as the eye could see. Tiny red and green marker lights lined its outer edges. Beyond them was the absolute shimmering grey. Jeb Stuart Ho held on to his mind with meticulous care. The awful music wailed on, punctuated by wrenching cast-iron power chords. Nothing else moved on the road, and it seemed to have no end.

The chronometer claimed they were nine and three quarter hours out of Litz. Jeb Stuart Ho was just wondering if it was safe to give the Minstrel Boy another shot of cyclatrol, when he began to slow the car. He pulled over to the side of the road and stopped. In a strange kind of way, it seemed to Ho that the Minstrel Boy was cooperating with the plan. He reached into the glove compartment and took out the black case. He fitted a refill into the injector, pushed up the Minstrel Boy's sleeve and pressed the release. There was a faint hiss as the cyclatrol was forced through the pores of his skin. This time he only screamed for thirty-five minutes.

When he calmed down, he seemed to need no instructions. He started the engine, made the same violent gear change and continued on down the road.

The lines of lights flashed past in a continuous stream. The road was absolutely smooth. The Minstrel Boy kept the car rock steady in the middle of the road. Jeb Stuart Ho avoided looking our of the narrow window. Despite all his training, the grey shimmer of the nothings made him uneasy. It disturbed the sense of order that was so much a part of his life in the brotherhood.

Jeb Stuart Ho felt closer to the edge of his control than he had ever been during all his years of rigorous instruction. The blue road was so smooth that there was no sense of movement at all. Time seemed to stop. The lights formed themselves into solid strips of red and green. The silent staring presence of the Minstrel Boy, and the clanging music combined with all the other factors to push Jeb Stuart Ho towards a wild, twisting part of his mind that he had never experienced before. It took all his powers of discipline to resist plunging into that chaos.

Just as he was beginning to feel that his strength was about to give out, something appeared ahead. It was far down the road, but it was coming towards them, and it instantly restored the concepts of time and space. At first it was only a tiny point of light in the extreme distance, but Jeb Stuart Ho felt himself filled with an immediate sense of relief.

16

They came out of the nothings in midair. It was as though the falling sensation that had been wrenching at Billy's stomach ever since the airship had disintegrated, was all channelled in a single direction. In a moment of panic he thought he was going to fall to his death. Then the ground rushed up and knocked the breath out of him. The drop had been less than four metres. He landed awkwardly, on hard stony ground. One of his knees twisted under him. As he tried to stand, it hurt like hell. He sank to his knees cursing.

On the second attempt, Billy managed to stay on his feet. He looked around to see where he had landed. The bare hillside wasn't terribly impressive. It fell away at a steep angle. The bare earth was sparsely covered here and there with patches of bracken and short wiry grass. There were wide expanses of bare rock.

Billy couldn't see very far. Everything but the immediate piece of sloping ground that he had landed on was shrouded in damp, clinging fog. His city boy, pimp clothes were totally unsuited for both the terrain and climate. Already the thin, sparkling material felt cold and clammy.

He cursed again, and hugged his jacket tighter round his shoulders. It seemed that he had fallen into some very dismal place.

He wondered what had happened to the others. They had all been together in the nothings, but he had lost them when they'd dropped into the reality of the bleak hillside. According to everything Billy had experienced, they should have all emerged at the same point. He wondered if they might be on another part of the same hillside, hidden by the fog. He strained his eyes to penetrate the drifting grey blanket, but he still could see nothing.

He shivered and stamped his feet. If he didn't do something fairly fast he would die of pneumonia. He wondered if he should go and look for them, or stay in the same place and let them find him. It was a problem. He couldn't be absolutely sure that they had all landed near to the same spot. He was still wondering what to do when he saw a familiar figure limping through the mist. Billy called out.

'Hey! Hey, Reave! Over here.'

The figure turned and started coming towards him. Reave was noticeably favouring one foot, as though his ankle was giving him pain. Billy hurried to meet him.

'Are you okay?'

'I came out of the nothings some way above the ground. I didn't land too good. I guess I twisted my ankle.'

'It ain't broken or nothing?'

Reave shook his head.

'No, but it hurts. You seen anything of the others?'

'Not a sign.'

'Any idea where we are?'

Billy shrugged.

'How the fuck should I know?'

'We could have picked a better place.'

Billy scowled.

'So who picked it?'

They both stood in silence for a while, each waiting for the other to suggest something. Finally Reave shivered.

'Do you figure we should build a fire or something?'

Billy looked at him contemptuously, and waved his hand at the scanty, dripping wet vegetation.

'With what?'

Reave sniffed.

'It was just an idea.'

'Some idea.'

'You think of something better?'

Billy sighed.

'Okay, okay. Just wait a while. Something'll turn up.'

Reave looked dubious.

'You reckon? It looks like we really... aargh!'

He clamped his hand to his neck. His face contorted with pain. Billy looked at him in alarm.

'What's wrong?'

'It's this goddamn collar. AA Catto must be trying to find us.'

'Do you think she's nearby?'

Reave nodded.

'She must be. The link doesn't work over a really long distance.'

'Maybe she'd hear us if we started yelling.'

'It's worth a try. It might stop her using her ring on me.'

Billy and Reave both began to shout at the top of their voices. After a while they stopped to listen. Nothing happened. The fog seemed to muffle out all sound. They tried again. When they paused a second time, Billy thought he heard faint shouts. They began to yell as loud as they could. They at least had the consolation that the activity was keeping them warm. They paused for a third time. Billy was sure he could hear faint sounds. He turned to Reave.

'You hear that?'

'What?'

'I thought I heard voices.'

Reave listened.

'I don't hear nothing.'

Billy craned forward.

'Yeah. Listen. There it is again. I'm sure it must be the others.'

He started yelling at the top of his lungs.

'Hey, hey, over here.'

Even Reave could hear the answering shouts. After a few minutes of yelling they saw two figures begin to emerge from the mist. It was AA Catto and Nancy. They both looked cold and wet. Nancy was limping badly and AA Catto supported her on one arm. Their thin, revealing city clothes were obviously no protection against the vicious climate. Reave fingered his collar nervously. AA Catto looked as though she was in an evil temper. She walked slowly up to the two men.

'Where in hell are we?'

Billy and Reave looked at each other. Billy shrugged.

'Don't have a clue.'

AA Catto scowled and said nothing. Nancy hugged her arms to her chest and shivered.

'We got to get out of this goddamn place before we freeze to death.'

Billy nodded.

'That's for sure.'

Reave squatted down and rubbed at his damaged ankle.

'So where do we go?'

AA Catto looked down at him in contempt.

'Can't you ever think for yourself?'

'I don't see you coming up with too many ideas.'

AA Catto's eyes blazed.

'Don't talk to me like that!'

She twisted her ring savagely. Reave screamed and fell on his side, kicking. Nancy grabbed her by the shoulders, but AA Catto pushed her roughly away. Nancy stumbled and fell over Reave. Billy grabbed AA Catto by the wrist and held on to her while she struggled and hit at him.

'Hold it, damn you. Just take it easy.'

'Take your hands off me, or I'll kill you.'

'You ain't killing anyone. Calm down now. We're all in this together. Fighting ain't going to help us.'

AA Catto relaxed into sullen silence. Billy let go of her. He helped Nancy to her feet.

'Okay, let's try and get organized. We got to get out of here.'

Nancy tried unavailingly to brush the mud stains from her damp jump suit.

'Did we manage to save anything useful from the airship?'

Billy patted his jacket.

'I seem to have lost my gun in the fall.'

AA Catto sneered. 'Typical.'

Billy turned on her. 'What have you got?'

'My credit card.'

Billy looked at the ground.

'I don't think that's going to be a whole lot of use in this place.'

Nancy grinned. 'I've got my gun.'

Reave climbed to his feet.

'I've got mine too, and a gravity knife.'

Billy looked round.

'How about food?'

'Nothing.'

AA Catto grimaced.

'I suppose nobody has any drugs?'

Everyone shook his head. AA Catto pouted sullenly.

'You all realize I'm going to start coming down in a while?'

Nancy raised an eyebrow.

'What do you expect?'

Billy quickly intervened before another fight erupted.

'We ought to decide which way we're going to go.'

Nancy shrugged.

'I figure it's either up or down.'

'Down ought to be warmer.'

'Down it is then.'

AA Catto shivered.

'Can we get moving?'

Billy hesitated. AA Catto looked at him in exasperation.

'I think I can hear something.'

'Rubbish, I can't hear a thing.'

She started to walk down the hillside. Billy didn't move.

'I'm sure I can hear something. It's a kind of hum. Really high-pitched, almost beyond the range of hearing. It's hard to be sure but I think whatever's causing it is coming nearer.'

Nancy nodded.

'I can hear it too.'

AA Catto stopped and planted her hands on her hips.

'Are we moving or aren't we?'

Before anyone could respond, her question was answered by a reedy mechanical voice.

'You-will-stay-exactly-as-you-are!'

Three grey steel spheres floated out of the mist. They were about a third of a metre in diameter, and hung some two metres above the ground. A dull black disc was set in the side of each one. The disc moved as the sphere slowly rotated. It was as though the disc was some kind of sensor device and the spheres were scanning the four humans. The surprise at their sudden appearance was so great that nobody moved or spoke. Billy felt as though all his willpower was being drained away.

One of the spheres moved silently away from the other two. It circled AA Catto and began gently to shepherd her back towards her companions. She too seemed to have been drained of all will to resist.

Once the spheres had the humans herded together in one tight group, they surrounded them in a triangle formation. The black discs stared implacably down at the four people. Nobody spoke or moved. The voice came again.

'It-is-necessary-that-we-search-you.'

Billy couldn't tell whether it came from one single sphere, or all three. A small circular slot opened in the base of each sphere and a steel tentacle snaked out of it. The tentacles extended towards the humans and moved slowly over their bodies, as though inspecting them. Billy stood horrified as the cold steel probe slid into his pockets and under his clothes. Then they began removing things from the group. They took Billy's timepiece, his cigar lighter and small tri-di cube of a couple screwing that he kept as a good luck charm. They took Nancy's and Reave's guns and an electronic door key from AA Catto. They took everyone's portable generator. They also took off her ring, and removed Reave's collar. He had always thought it was permanently locked, but at a single touch from one of the sphere's tentacles, it just fell open. The various objects were placed carefully together on the ground. The voice came again.

'These-objects-are-proscribed-in-this-area. It-is-necessary-to-remove-and-destroy-them.'

One of the spheres emitted a thin beam of bright blue light from a point on its underside. It played over the objects on the ground. After a few seconds, they smoked and vanished. The spheres formed themselves into their original formation and silently drifted away into the mist. Billy slowly turned to the other three. His face had gone slack.

'Did that really happen?'

Nancy nodded.

'I think so.'

AA Catto looked round helplessly.

'Why did they take all our things? We had little enough to start with. Now we've got nothing.'

Billy frowned. 'They didn't take our clothes.'

Reave fished in his pocket and pulled out his gravity knife.

'They missed this.'

He snapped it open. When he came to close it, however, the mechanism no longer worked. He scratched the back of his neck.

'This place is too fucking weird. I...'

He suddenly received the impact of what the spheres' removal of his collar meant. AA Catto no longer had any physical control over him. He shot her a single intense glance. She pretended not to notice, and spoke quickly to Billy.

'Have you ever seen anything like them before?'

Billy shook his head.

'Never.'

He thought for a moment.

'It seems like they took away anything to do with technology, all mechanical things. They left our clothes and Reave's knife, but the mechanism on that doesn't work. I wonder if...'

Nancy cut him short.

'Could you do your wondering when we get some place that's warm?'

AA Catto joined in.

'Let's go somewhere. I'm dying of cold.'

Billy nodded and, without another word, started down the slope. His face was set and thoughtful. Suddenly he stopped and bent down. He fished something from a tuft of grass and held it up.

'Whatever those things were they didn't get this.'

'What is it?'

'A gun, it looks like my gun.'

He held up a compact .70 recoilless.

'It must have dropped here after we fell through the nothings.'

AA Catto looked grimly pleased.

'At least we're armed.'

Billy nodded, and carefully tucked the gun into the holster under his coat. They carried on down the hillside.

The going wasn't hard. The ground was even and downhill, but the cold became the exhausting factor. Even while they maintained a brisk pace, the freezing damp cut through their thin clothes and seeped into their bones. AA Catto's teeth began to chatter uncontrollably. She massaged her bare arms and looked desperately at Billy.

'I c-can't take in-much more of this.'

Billy did his best to be reassuring. He too was half frozen.

'We got to come out of this in the end. It can't go on for ever.'

AA Catto pursed her now blue lips.

'Anything's possible.'

Reave flashed her a wry grin.

'If it don't stop, it'll be the end of us.'

AA Catto gave him a long hard look, but said nothing. They went on walking. Billy was thankful for the downhill slope. It did at least prove they weren't going round in circles. Apart from that single fact, they could easily have been back at the point they started from. Nothing appeared to change.

Billy was about to give up hope when, abruptly, they came out of it. The transition was so sudden, it took them totally by surprise. One moment they were trudging through the same thick mist, then for a few paces it thinned and suddenly they were out in the sunshine. The sky above their heads was a clear blue, and the air smelled sweet and clean. All four of them stopped and just drank it in. AA Catto raised her chilled arms to the sun.

'Oh god. It feels so good.'

She turned and hugged Nancy, and they sank down on the short springy turf kissing each other enthusiastically. Billy looked at Reave, and they both shrugged. They turned their attention to their surroundings. Behind them was the wall of cloud completely concealing the upper slopes. In front of them, however, the view was breathtaking. Below them was a wide green valley. It was watered by a slow, meandering river. A number of small tributary streams sparkled in the sun. Billy grinned at Reave.

'This really don't look too bad.'

Reave nodded.

'Sure looks good to me. Look at those trees, all that grass. I could get behind laying up here for a while.'

He peered intently into the distance, and pointed down the valley.

'What do you think that is?'

Billy shaded his eyes and stared in the same direction

'It looks like a building of some kind.'

Billy could just make out a black structure, beside the river, far down the valley. It seemed to have a broad base and then narrow off towards the top. It was surrounded by patchwork squares of different-coloured vegetation. Billy assumed that they were cultivated fields. Reave turned to Billy.

'Do you suppose we ought to head for that place?'

Billy nodded.

'I don't see anywhere else that looks inhabited.'

'It looks real big, that place.'

'And a long way away.'

Billy walked over to where the girls were lying entwined on the grass.

'Come on, you two. I think we've found civilization.'

AA Catto disengaged herself from Nancy. 'Civilization?'

'There's some kind of big building down in the valley.'

AA Catto propped herself up on one elbow. 'Is it nice?'

Billy shrugged.

'It don't look hostile. It's a long walk, though.'

AA Catto scowled.

'I thought there'd be something wrong with it.'

'It's a nice day for a walk.'

'I'm getting sick of this place.'

Billy grinned down at her. 'We might as well get moving.'

'We have to walk?'

Billy nodded.

'We have to walk.'

AA Catto smiled sweetly at him.

'I've had an idea. Why don't you and Reave walk to this place? Then when you get there you could send out some transport for Nancy and me.'

'I didn't see too much that looked like transport.'

AA Catto sat up.

'Where is this place?'

Billy pointed out the building in the distance.

'There.'

'You don't expect me to walk that distance? You're crazy.'

'You can stay here.'

AA Catto beamed.

'And you'll send someone to fetch us?'

'I doubt it.'

AA Catto's expression turned venomous.

'One day I'll get the chance to really make you suffer, you little punk.'

'I'll do my best to avoid it.'

AA Catto climbed grudgingly to her feet. Nancy did the same. They started down the hillside towards the river. AA Catto sulked at first, but the walk proved to be no hardship. Very soon she and Nancy were walking along together, chattering and giggling. Billy and Reave were slightly in front, deep in their own thoughts. They had been going for about ten minutes. AA Catto and Nancy had dropped some way behind. Suddenly Nancy yelled out.

'Look!'

There was such a note of urgency in her voice that the two men spun round. Nancy was pointing frantically up the hill. A small troop of horsemen were galloping across the hillside just below the cloudbank. Billy couldn't make out too many details of the riders. The horses were tall and black. The men carried long, slender lances. The only obvious thing was that they didn't look hospitable. He beckoned quickly to the others.

'Quickly, crouch down. They don't seem to have seen us.'

They all flattened themselves on the grass. Not even AA Catto made a protest. They lay perfectly still. The horsemen carried on in the same direction. Billy whispered to Reave.

'I think they're going to go past without seeing us.'

Reave's face was grim.

'I sure hope so. They don't look over-friendly.'

Suddenly the leading rider pulled his horse to a stop. The others halted beside him. For a few moments they milled about. Then they began to fan out. They came down the hillside at a steady trot, directly towards where the four were lying. Billy pushed himself up into a crouch.

'They've seen us! Run! Spread out!'

They all broke from cover. The riders kicked their horses and came on at a gallop. Billy began running for all he was worth. He forgot about the gun under his coat. The thunder of hooves was close behind him. The riders let out high, bloodcurdling shrieks. Billy's heart began to pound and his breath came in short, laboured gasps. The time in Litz had destroyed his physical condition. His body cringed at the thought of one of the long, thin lances stabbing into it.

He glanced over his shoulder, and saw one of the horsemen close behind him. He swung round and changed direction. He caught a glimpse of a dark-skinned face beneath a strange winged helmet. Then the rider thundered past. Billy began panting back up the hill. Another rider crossed to intercept him. They were dressed in cloaks of some kind of fur, and black armour made from small interlocking plates. They looked sinister and deadly. Billy tried dodging again, but the second rider was too quick for him. He wheeled his horse and came after him. Billy saw that he was swinging two weights on the end of a long thong. Billy turned again and went on running desperately. He caught sight of another rider about to run down Nancy. The one who was chasing Billy suddenly let go of the device of weights and thongs. At that moment Billy remembered the gun, but it was too late. The thing caught him just above the knees. The thongs coiled tightly around his legs. Billy fell heavily. His head hit a rock and black oblivion rushed in and grabbed him.

17

The light that Jeb Stuart Ho had seen at the end of the road turned out, as they came closer, not to be one but several. They shone from the windows of a large building that stood on a small island of bare ground, beside the road, with the nothings all round it. It had the same ramshackle, disorganized style of architecture as the house at Wainscote where Ho had first found the Minstrel Boy, but instead of looking grim and menacing, this place seemed friendly and inviting.

In front of the building was a wide forecourt. It was crowded with a very mixed assortment of vehicles. A line of saddled lizards were tied to a rail. Sleek ground cars were parked next to broken-down horse-drawn wagons. A huge, ornately painted truck towered over a collection of weird, custom-built motorcycles. The access to this parking lot was through a high, curving arch of neon lights. Above the arch a huge sign turned slowly. It carried the legend THE INN. This garish entrance contrasted strangely with the funky, uneven style of the building.

As they came up to the Inn, Jeb Stuart Ho wondered if the Minstrel Boy was going to stop or drive straight by. Ho looked at him questioningly, but the Minstrel Boy continued to stare fixedly straight ahead. Jeb Stuart Ho assumed that there was going to be no stop, and settled back in his seat. Then, at the last minute, the Minstrel Boy spun the wheel and the car swung off the road with a shriek of tyres.

They passed under the glowing arch, and crossed the forecourt. The Minstrel Boy parked the car beside a land yacht. The strange vehicle had huge, spun-gold photon sails, and a wooden body covered in elaborate and somewhat obscene carvings. The Minstrel Boy cut the car's engine, and slumped forward across the wheel. Jeb Stuart Ho wondered if he should help the Minstrel Boy out of the car, or leave him and go into the Inn on his own. He tapped the Minstrel Boy on the shoulder.

'Do you want to come inside with me?'

The Minstrel Boy didn't answer. He responded like a zombie, sitting up and slowly moving his hand to the door handle. Jeb Stuart Ho quickly climbed out of the car and hurried round to the Minstrel Boy's side. He helped him through the door, and steadied him while he tried to stand.

In his trancelike state, the Minstrel Boy had a good deal of difficulty walking. Jeb Stuart Ho supported him as they made their way to the entrance of the Inn. As they passed the line of tethered lizards, the beasts snorted and stamped their feet in agitation. The Minstrel Boy seemed to have a strange, unsettling effect on them.

The interior of the Inn, and the people who crowded the noisy, smoky, low-ceilinged room, were as mixed as the outside architecture. A long bar of dark, stained oak ran down one side of the main room. A gang of bartenders scurried backwards and forwards behind it serving drinks to the demanding throng. In a corner a string band occupied a small stage and tried to make themselves heard above the general din. In a cleared space among the tables a hunchbacked juggler with a small black and white dog performed for tips and drinks. Across on the other side of the room, in a section of floor that was lower than the rest, two men sat on small stools, hunched over a huge black and white marble board, a full two metres across, playing checkers with counters the size of plates. A small crowd sat silently watching them, occasionally exchanging low-voiced side bets as the game progressed.

At one end of the room was a granite fireplace where two great logs blazed with a comforting glow. The corner of the fireplace and the wall of the room created a patch of shadow. In it were two tables. One was empty and the other occupied only by a solitary old man who nodded over a beer mug. It seemed a place where one could sit without attracting attention. Jeb Stuart Ho steered the Minstrel Boy towards the spot. He didn't want anyone paying too close attention to his condition.

Once they were seated, Jeb Stuart Ho had a chance to look at the other people in the main room of the Inn. There were representatives of almost every culture that was crowded on to the remains of the shattered world. There were nomad bike-riders and wheelfreaks with their loud laughter, leather suits and long, greased hair. There were puritan merchants jealous of the glances that the other travellers gave their veiled and hooded wives. Hard-eyed brigands with gaudy clothes, huge brass rings through their ears, and wicked knives stuck in their belts crouched in conspiratorial groups. Away from the rest of the crowd five nuns ate in silence. They had the shaved heads and purple robes of the grim sisterhood who ruled the city of Sade. Sophisticated women in the scanty synthetics that were high fashion in the tech-cities rubbed shoulders with ragged bums, travelling hookers, medicine men and gamblers in the traditional frock coats and fancy vests. There were even a few of the strange, almost alien creatures from the outer fringes, with their tinted skin, abnormal bodies and outlandish clothes. Of AA Catto and her companions, however, there was no sign.

Servants of both sexes moved in and out of the throng, serving meals and drinks, laughing with the customers and generally making themselves available. They seemed to combine the roles of waiter, host and prostitute. One of them, a girl with large breasts and long slim legs, moved towards Jeb Stuart Ho's table.

'What can I get you, friend?'

'I'd like a meal of fresh vegetables and a bottle of pure water.'

The waitress looked at him strangely. She seemed about to say something, but changed her mind. She nodded towards the Minstrel Boy.

'How about him? Does he want anything?'

'You could bring him some brandy.'

The waitress nodded, and then smiled sideways at Jeb Stuart Ho.

'You wouldn't maybe like a little, uh, companionship, perhaps?'

Jeb Stuart Ho hesitated. He had had no sexual contact with either man or woman since he had left the temple. The prospect seemed wholly inviting. Both the men and the women were extremely pleasing. There was his task, though. He was sure the brotherhood and his teachers would expect him to remain celibate until it was complete. He sighed and shook his head.

'Regretfully, I think not.'

The girl shrugged.

'Suit yourself.'

She went away, and after a short while came back with the order. As she leaned over to place it on the table, Jeb Stuart Ho was treated to an uninterrupted view of her breasts. He felt a stab of remorse at his decision to remain temporarily celibate. After she'd moved on, he pushed the brandy glass in front of the Minstrel Boy.

'Here, I ordered a drink for you.'

The Minstrel Boy's eyes were glazed. He appeared to hear and see nothing. It was as though he was in some other place. Jeb Stuart Ho started as a wheezing chuckle came from behind him.

'He'll not drink anything.'

Jeb Stuart Ho turned round carefully, and found the old man was grinning at him crookedly. He was a strange figure. The top of his head was bald, but long white hair cascaded down his back. His beard was of equal length. His face was lined and weather-beaten, and the long shapeless robe that he wore had been washed, bleached, patched and darned until it was a uniform off-white. The most compelling thing about him, however, was his eyes. They were small and black and peered out from behind bushy eyebrows like those of a lizard, a lizard whose sense of humour was the only thing that saved it from being a venomous cynic. He picked up a stout polished staff, almost as tall as himself, from where it was leaning against the wall, and moved to Jeb Stuart Ho's table.

'He'll not touch the brandy, or anything else, until he pulls out of what you've done to him.'

Jeb Stuart Ho tensed. He arranged himself in his chair so he could instantly move in any direction. He looked evenly at the old man.

'You know what's been done to him?'

The old man's mouth twisted into a sneer.

'I've a pretty fair idea. You've filled him up with cyclatrol or some such gunk, and there's no point in you sitting there like a cat ready to jump. I'll not harm you. Much as I might like to. The only thing I'm wondering is why you did it. I'm wondering what you're after.'

Jeb Stuart Ho was taken aback at the amount of information the old man seemed to have. He did his best to maintain his composure.

'You seem to know a lot about my affairs.'

'I just watch and figure. Right now I'm figuring what you're up to.'

Jeb Stuart Ho smiled a deceptively sweet smile. He was aware that he might have to kill the prattling old man if he began to endanger his mission.

'And what do you figure I'm up to, old man?'

'I figure you're hunting someone. That's about the only thing that'll bring you black murdering vultures out of your damn temple. I figure you're out for a hit, and you've filled the poor boy here with cyclatrol to get a fix on your victim.'

'Your talk could be dangerous, old man.'

The old man nodded towards the Minstrel Boy.

'When I was his age, I might have been afraid of you, but now I'm too old. Even he seeks a temporary death in oblivion every opportunity he gets. Maybe life's the only thing to be afraid of these days.'

Jeb Stuart Ho was definitely ill at ease. He glanced at the Minstrel Boy, and then back at the old man.

'You know him?'

The old man laughed.

'The Minstrel Boy. Aye, you could say our paths have crossed.'

'Who are you?'

'They call me the Wanderer.'

'And what do you do, Wanderer?'

'I wander round from place to place. I watch and figure.'

'And you know where you are?'

'Don't get any ideas.'

'But you do know where you are?'

The Wanderer sighed.

'Aye, I do, but not as good as a lizard, and not as good as him.'

He nodded towards the Minstrel Boy.

'I was never as good as him. Perhaps that's why I lived so long.'

Jeb Stuart Ho was about to ask another question, when the Minstrel Boy twitched. His eyes focused, and his mouth opened.

'Quahal.'

His voice was a hoarse croak.

'Quahal.'

Jeb Stuart Ho grasped his arm.

'Quahal.'

'What?'

The Minstrel Boy didn't answer. His eyes glazed over again. He became rigid. Jeb Stuart Ho looked at the Wanderer.

'What did he say?'

The Wanderer's eye twinkled.

'He said Quahal.'

'What is Quahal?'

'Don't they teach you anything inside your precious temple?'

Jeb Stuart Ho's face darkened.

'What is Quahal?'

'It's a place. I figure your quarry must have fetched up there. Is it a man or a woman?'

'What difference does it make?'

The Wanderer laughed.

'In Quahal it makes a difference.'

'Why? What is this place?'

'You want to know about Quahal, do you?'

'I'd be grateful for any information you could give me.'

'Grateful, even? Well, I suppose I can't do no harm, except of course to help you kill this poor soul.'

'She only has to die to save many more lives.'

'Says you.'

'The brotherhood's projections have a very low factor of error.'

The Wanderer grunted.

'That's as maybe. It's too much like men playing God for me.'

Jeb Stuart Ho grew impatient.

'Will you tell me about Quahal?'

The Wanderer nodded.

'Aye, I'll tell. If you promise to keep quiet, and not interrupt.'

Jeb Stuart Ho smiled.

'You have my word.'

'Your word, even. Right, then. I'll tell you the story of Quahal. Like most things, it started back in the days when things broke up. That was just after Stuff Central got going, and we were supposed to have reached utopia, although not many people like to connect those two facts any more. Anyhow, the nothings came, and the disruptors began to break up the land, and you couldn't trust gravity or nothing any more. People began grabbing anything they could hang on to, stabilize and live on. Everyone had a different idea about why things had gone so wrong. There was this particular brother and sister called Alamada and Joachim Hesse. They decided all the trouble was due to technology and the only way to live was in a primitive, natural world. As their home started to melt away, they got Stuff Central to set one up for them. They had a huge great stasis generator installed, stabilized a stretch of place, had it landscaped, a nice misty, wild mountain and a fertile river valley, and moved in. You'll notice, incidentally, that they weren't averse to a bit of technology creating and maintaining this Garden of Eden. At my age, I really ought to stop expecting people to be consistent. Anyway, they had some plants and animals beamed in, and then people. The people were specially DNA-tailored to suit Alamada's and Joachim's fantasies, and programmed to do exactly what was expected of them. Everything was set up. They called the place Quahal and settled down to the simple life.'

Jeb Stuart Ho looked puzzled.

'Why Quahal?'

The Wanderer became annoyed.

'How should I know? That's what they called it. Maybe they got it out of a book. I don't know. You promised not to interrupt.'

'I'm sorry.'

'Okay. Don't do it again. Right?'

'I'm sorry.'

'Okay. Well, Alamada and Joachim didn't exactly want the same things. For a start, Joachim was gay and Alamada was a heterosadist, so they didn't quite see eye to eye. The long and short of it was that Joachim lived down in the valley doing a kind of Aztec number with a lot of specially bred young men. He was the high priest. He had a ziggurat, the whole number, all these lads worshipping him. He was happy as a pig in shit. He had them ritually sacrificed when they got too old, and kept them totally celibate except as far as he was concerned.'

The Wanderer looked at Jeb Stuart Ho.

'Aren't you guys from the brotherhood celibate?'

'Only when it serves our purpose.'

The Wanderer looked dubious.

'I never did see what purpose could be served by not screwing. Are you sure you ain't the product of someone's fantasy?'

'I...'

'Don't answer. I'll go on with the story. Obviously Alamada wasn't going to go for Joachim's set-up. She made herself a home up the mountain with a team of rough, horny, horse-riding tribesmen. She was their, I dunno, witch queen or something. They all balled her, and fought with each other and were generally rough and disagreeable, so she was happy too. The stuff beam brought in all the things they needed, including replacement people, and everything was neat. Except for one thing. You know what that was?'

'No.'

'Joachim and Alamada weren't immortal. They grew old and in the end they died. They even got round that, in a way, though.'

'How?'

'They had everything about them fed into the Stuff Central Computer. When they passed away, these replacements showed up. They've showed up about every ten years ever since. In the case of Joachim it was a short ritual. The new Joachim would come out of the Stuff receiver, and the old one would straight away get sacrificed. In Alamada's case it was a little rougher. The Stuff receiver was in the ziggurat, down in the valley. When a new Alamada arrived she'd climb the mountain and have to fight the old one. The winner would be queen. I figure that's about it, as far as Quahal's concerned.'

The Wanderer thought for a minute.

'Oh yeah, one thing I forgot. The globes.'

'The globes?'

'Another of Alamada's and Joachim's little concessions to technology. They're a kind of cybernetic watchdog. They prowl the place. If anyone turns up out of the nothings they remove everything more advanced than a slingshot. If anyone resists they fuse them.'

He looked hard at Jeb Stuart Ho.

'I suppose you'll be off there?'

Jeb Stuart Ho nodded.

'I should leave straight away.'

'You could easily find that the lady you're after has been offed by the current Alamada.'

'I would have to go and make sure.'

The Wanderer grinned crookedly.

'Duty?'

'What else is there?'

The Wanderer shook his head.

'Don't ask me to tell you.'

'I'm sorry.'

'Don't worry about it.'

There was a pause. Jeb Stuart Ho and the Wanderer sat silent with the rigid Minstrel Boy between them. Then the Wanderer looked sideways at Jeb Stuart Ho.

'You wouldn't have any objection to me coming along with you?'

'To Quahal?'

'Yeah. I've got nothing better to do, and I do know about the place.'

Jeb Stuart Ho became suspicious.

'Why do you want to come? You didn't make the place sound very pleasant.'

'Like I said, I don't have anything better to do. After all, you don't think an old man like me can harm you in any way?'

Ho nodded doubtfully. 'I don't.'

The Wanderer grinned. 'So I can ride with you?'

'I suppose so.'

The Wanderer gestured at the Minstrel Boy.

'We'd better get him out to the car then.'

Jeb Stuart Ho's head jerked round. 'How did you know we came in a ground car?'

The Wanderer grinned.

'Like I said, I don't miss very much.'

They pulled the Minstrel Boy to his feet, and headed for the door.

18

Billy woke up. He immediately wished that he hadn't. He hurt all over. The slightest movement sent pain stabbing up from the back of his neck. He tried opening his eyes. Wherever he was, the light was dim. Billy was grateful for that. He was aware of something moving. Billy turned his head. He found himself looking at Reave.

'Where are we?'

'You've come round, then? We were beginning to think you'd gone and died.'

'I wish I had.'

'You feel bad?'

'Bad? I feel like I've been beaten up about a dozen times. Where the hell are we?'

Reave rubbed his nose.

'I ain't really sure.'

Billy struggled into a sitting position. He looked around. He seemed to be in some kind of hut. The floor was bare earth and the wall was built from dry stone. There was a single circular wall that curved inwards in a kind of beehive shape to become an almost conical roof. In the centre of it was a small hole. It was the only source of light and ventilation. A heavy wooden door was the only exit from the hut. Billy moved painfully towards it, but Reave waved him away.

'There's no point in trying the door. It's bolted on the outside.'

Billy sat down again. He noticed the hut was completely bare. There was no furniture, nothing. It was also very cold. He shivered and looked at Reave.

'What in hell is this place?'

Reave shrugged.

'Like I said, I ain't really sure.'

Billy began to get impatient. It seemed as though Reave was being deliberately unhelpful.

'What's the matter with you?'

'Nothing. I'm just frozen, starved, and I figure we're liable to get killed any time now. I don't see much to get enthusiastic about.'

Billy frowned, and ran his fingers through his hair.

'What happened? The last thing I remember was being chased by those guys on horses.'

'They caught us.'

'Then what?'

'They slung us over their saddles and rode up into the mist. You were out cold. It seemed like we rode for hours, all through that fog. Eventually we wound up here.'

'What's here?'

'A village of some sort. Just a collection of beehive-shaped stone huts in the fog. I didn't get too much of a chance to look at the place. They threw you and me in here, and that was it.'

'You've been here ever since?'

'Yeah.'

'What happened to AA Catto and Nancy?'

'The horsemen took them to some other part of the village.'

'You figure they're being raped?'

Reave shrugged.

'Who can tell? I don't think they are, somehow. The horsemen seemed to treat them with some kind of respect.'

Billy massaged his bruises.

'Pity they didn't give us some.'

Reave scowled, and said nothing. Billy sat thinking. After a while he looked up.

'Do you reckon we could escape?'

Reave slapped the solid stone wall. 'I don't see how.'

'Maybe when they come to feed us?'

Reave shook his head sourly.

'They ain't showed no sign of feeding us yet.'

Billy slumped back against the wall and thought again. Suddenly he sat bolt upright.

'Hey!'

Reave looked up without too much interest.

'What?'

Billy stuck a hand inside his jacket.

'They left me with my gun.'

'You're kidding.'

'No, look!'

Billy pulled it out. Reave looked at it in amazement. 'Shit!'

'How could they have missed it?'

Reave shook his head.

'Beats me. They took my knife away.'

Billy looked at the gun thoughtfully.

'Maybe they don't know what it is. If those globes destroy all the technology that turns up here, those horsemen may never have seen a gun.'

Reave nodded.

'You got a point there.'

'It gives us a better chance of getting away.'

'We'll have to wait till someone comes and opens the door.'

'When they do, we can blow them away.'

'So all we have to do is wait.'

'Right.'

They waited. They had no way of calculating the passing of time, but it seemed like a very long wait. A couple of times Billy became quite convinced that they had been locked up in the stone hut and forgotten. Eventually, however, there came the sound of someone pulling back the outside bolts. Billy tensed. He moved to beside the door. He flattened himself against the wall, tightly gripping the butt of the gun. The door opened. Billy raised his weapon. A figure stepped into the hut. Billy's finger eased back on the trigger. Then he stopped. The figure was AA Catto. Nancy followed her into the hut, then two of the horsemen. Billy quickly stuffed the gun under his jacket. AA Catto turned, and saw him pressed against the wall.

'What do you think you're doing?'

Billy wiped a hand over his face.

'Nothing.'

AA Catto raised an eyebrow, but made no remark. Reave scrambled to his feet.

'Are you two all right?'

AA Catto nodded.

'For the moment.'

Billy glanced at the two horsemen standing in the doorway of the hut.

'Are we still prisoners?'

AA Catto examined her fingernails, and picked at one where the paint job was chipped.

'Not exactly.'

'We can go?'

'No. We can't actually leave this place.'

'What's going on then?'

AA Catto avoided looking at Billy. 'It's sort of complicated.'

Billy pursed his lips.

'I might have known it wouldn't be simple. Are you going to tell us about it?'

AA Catto took a deep breath.

'Well… it's like this. There aren't any women in this tribe. It's all men.'

Billy looked amazed.

'No women?'

'Well, there is one. She's sort of queen witch. The Alamada, they call her. It seems that the only other women who come here are challengers for her title. There's a sort of ritual fight, and the one who wins gets to rule the place.'

Billy's expression became even more incredulous.

'You mean they thought you were a challenger?'

'Yes.'

'I suppose you put them straight about you not being a challenger, and how we all just came here by accident.'

'Well... no.'

'Why the hell not?'

'I was worried that they might kill us.'

Billy slowly shook his head, as though to clear it.

'You mean you're going to go along with this fight?'

'I can't see any way out.'

'I suppose you can take a dive as soon as is honourably possible. Then we can all leave?'

'No.'

'No?'

'It's a fight to the death.'

Billy's jaw dropped.

'To the death?'

'To the death.'

'You mean you're risking getting killed to save the rest of us?'

AA Catto looked at him as though he was mad.

'No, of course not. If I lose, they'll kill you straight away. I told them that you were my personal slaves.'

'Personal slaves?'

'That's right, so you'd better come up with an idea.'

Billy shook his head in disbelief.

'What the hell have you got us into?'

AA Catto looked at him disdainfully.

'I'm sure you'll think of something.'

'How long do we have before the fight?'

AA Catto avoided Billy's eyes. 'Not very long.'

She gestured towards the two horsemen.

'These people have come to take us all to another hut. Then we have to prepare for the fight.'

The horsemen began to show signs of impatience. They motioned to AA Catto. She walked out of the hut. The others followed. The two horsemen led the four of them through the village. It was a cold, bleak place; a collection of grey stone beehive-shaped huts with thin trails of mist drifting between them. Billy noticed that behind the huts was a wooden fenced corral that contained a fairly large herd of tall, mean-looking horses. At one end of the village was a hut much larger than any of the others. It was constructed from three of the dry-stone beehive shapes run together. It had a tall timber roof. In front of it was a cleared space. At one side of the space was a fire pit lined with flat slabs of stone. At the moment it was only filled with smouldering embers, but it was obvious that it regularly held a huge fire.

At first Billy thought that the two horsemen were taking them to the big building, but at the last minute, they turned off and went towards a smaller one next to it.

During the walk through the village, Billy had a chance closely to examine the horsemen. The two who were acting as their escort were uncannily alike. Billy began to suspect that they might be clones or something similar. They had olive complexions, high cheekbones, prominent noses and deep-set dark eyes. They looked proud, savage and arrogant. The long, straight, black hair was heavily greased, and scraped back and secured at the nape of the neck with an ornamental clasp. They wore tunics of heavy fur. Round their waists were wide studded belts. From them hung a wide-bladed knife and a long, thin, two-handed sword. Their legs were covered in crude trousers of some coarse material, held together by thongs that crisscrossed from their sandalled feet to just above the knee. The arms were protected by a flex-ible armour made from small leaf-shaped metal plates that extended right down to the backs of their hands.

The hut they were taken to was much bigger than the one Billy and Reave had been locked up in. It was also a lot more comfortable. The stone walls were hung with roughly woven tapestries. There were rushes strewn on the floor. Warmth came from a small brazier and there were even a rough carved table, three stools and a straight-backed chair. AA Catto dropped into the chair, and looked up at Billy.

'So, have you thought of something?'

Billy glanced round at the two horsemen who stood silently by the door.

'Do they understand what we're saying?'

AA Catto nodded.

'They use the same language, but I think there's quite a few words they don't use or understand. They don't talk much, though. They use a lot of signs and gestures.'

Billy moved round until he was standing behind AA Catto. He watched the faces of the two horsemen, and spoke slowly and carefully.

'I still have my seventy calibre. They didn't take it away from me.'

'You mean you've got a...'

'Don't say it!'

'Sorry.'

The horsemen gave no flicker of interest. Billy leaned forward.

'Okay. I'm going to take a chance now. I'm going to take the thing out and put it on the table. I'm pretty sure they won't know what it is.'

Billy moved slowly round to the table. He casually took the gun out from under his coat, and placed it on the table. Neither of the horsemen moved. AA Catto let out her breath with a sigh.

'It worked. You were right.'

Billy nodded.

'Right. You're going to prepare for the fight. You're going to go through with it. Just hang in there as long as you can. Immediately you get into trouble, I'll shoot the queen. After that, we play it by ear. Okay?'

Before AA Catto could reply, the door opened and another two horsemen came into the hut. One carried a bundle wrapped in red cloth, and the other a small iron pot. They placed them on the table. Neither appeared to take any particular notice of the gun. One of them unwrapped the contents of the cloth. There was a wide leaf-bladed knife, a set of the strange armour to cover one arm, and a small round shield, slightly larger than a plate. The armour was silver rather than black. The horsemen pointed at AA Catto.

'You prepare. Soon it is time.'

AA Catto looked round questioningly. The horseman gestured for her to stand. AA Catto stood. The horseman moved close to her and tugged at the top of her dress. Nothing happened. He tugged again. AA Catto realized he wanted her to take off the dress. She released the fastening. It fell open, and dropped to the floor. AA Catto was naked except for her boots. The horseman pointed to them. AA Catto stooped down and took them off. None of the horsemen showed any reaction to her nudity.

The one who brought in the bundle stepped away from AA Catto, and the one who had carried in the iron pot moved forward. He placed the pot on the table and positioned AA Catto so she was standing with her feet apart and her arms raised. Then he turned and dipped both hands into the pot. It was filled with a warm, sweet-smelling, oily paste. He began slowly and carefully to rub the substance all over AA Catto's body, not missing any part. At first, AA Catto's face registered surprise, but the surprise quickly turned to pleasure. She gave a short, low moan. For a moment the horseman stopped massaging and looked at her blankly, then he went on with his work. Nancy caught AA Catto's eye.

'Does that stuff do anything?'

'It deadens the nerves, I think. It's kind of nice.'

When the horseman had finished he moved away and let the first one fit the piece of armour on to AA Catto's left arm. Then he picked up the knife and shield, and with a ritualistic gesture presented them to her. AA Catto swung the knife a little to test its weight. The horsemen motioned that it was time for them to move. A curious procession formed up. In the front were the two horsemen who had prepared AA Catto for the fight, then AA Catto herself. Behind her were Billy, Reave and Nancy, and finally, bringing up the rear, were the two original horsemen who had guarded them all the time they had been in the village. As Billy left the hut, he casually picked up the gun and held it loosely by his side. None of the horsemen appeared to notice.

They left the hut, and came out into the open space in front of the big hut. The fire had been piled high with huge timbers, and blazed furiously. Flames leaped from the pit, and a lot of the fog had been burned away. AA Catto's oiled body glistened in the light. The open space was surrounded on three sides by squares of horsemen. There must have been fifty in all. They stood in straight, unwavering lines. Unlike the men escorting AA Catto and her companions, these men wore conical helmets with batwings of flat black metal projecting from the top. The helmets gave them a sinister appearance, which was heightened by two curved side pieces that protected their cheeks, and a third piece that projected downwards to cover the nose. They all carried the long, slender lances, which served to complete the whole effect of menace.

The open side of the square faced the big hut. As AA Catto approached the line of men, they stepped aside to let her through. Then the ranks closed. Billy, Reave, Nancy and the four horsemen attending them were left to stand behind the ranks, peering over their shoulders.

AA Catto stood in the middle of the open space. The fire crackled and roared beside her. It was a strange experience to stand naked apart from her protected arm in front of all these men who looked on so impassively. She stood in front of the big hut and waited. She didn't feel anything like as frightened as she had expected to be. She wondered if the stuff they'd rubbed into her body had some kind of narcotic effect.

There was no sign of the woman she was expected to fight. Then the door of the hut swung open. Two helmeted horsemen came out and positioned themselves on either side of the door. Then a figure, who was unmistakably the Alamada, followed them out. It was AA Catto's first glimpse of her opponent, and she didn't like what she saw.

19

The ground car emerged from the nothings. Jeb Stuart Ho relaxed back in his seat. He was profoundly relieved. Travelling through the nothings still intensely disturbed him. When he returned to the temple, he would have to discuss the matter with his teacher and meditate on the answers. That was if he ever did return to the temple. Right at that time it seemed an impossible distance away. He turned and looked out of the side window. They were in one of the broken areas that formed the transition between the nothings and a stabilized area. Small sections of bare earth began to form around them, though there were still huge holes of shifting grey punched through it.

The holes grew progressively smaller, and finally vanished altogether. The solid stable land was complete. The car was bouncing through a lush green meadow. Beside them flowed a wide, clear river. In the distance was a tall, mist-covered mountain. Jeb Stuart Ho glanced back at the Wanderer who sat in the rear seat.

'Is this place Quahal?'

The Wanderer nodded.

'I figure so. Particularly from the state of him.'

The Wanderer nodded to the Minstrel Boy sitting in the driving seat. Jeb Stuart Ho looked round at him. The Minstrel Boy had changed. He was still staring straight ahead and tightly gripping the wheel, but his face had turned green and sweat was pouring off him. His lips were moving soundlessly, as though he was trying to say something. Jeb Stuart Ho looked at the Wanderer.

'Should I give him another shot?'

'Not unless you want to kill him.'

'I don't understand.'

'We've arrived, you fool. There's nothing more he can do for you.'

As though in silent confirmation, the Minstrel Boy slowed the car to a stop. He cut the engine. It was suddenly very quiet. The only sound was a breeze that moved through the grass. The Minstrel Boy slowly toppled over. His head slammed forward on to the wheel. The Wanderer leaned forward and grasped his shoulder. He shook him gently. The Minstrel Boy didn't move. The Wanderer looked quickly at Jeb Stuart Ho.

'Feel for his pulse! He may be dead!'

'Why should he be dead?'

'Don't ask questions. Just do it.'

Jeb Stuart Ho placed his fingertips on the Minstrel Boy's neck.

'There's a pulse, but it's very faint.'

'Get him out of the car and lay him down on the grass.'

Jeb Stuart Ho did as he was told. The Wanderer stooped over the Minstrel Boy and loosened his shirt. He put his ear to his chest. He listened for a few moments, and then straightened up.

'As far as I can tell, he'll live.'

'What's happened to him?'

'You've got a lot of gall.'

Jeb Stuart Ho shook his head.

'I'm sorry. I don't understand.'

'With all your fucking training you don't understand. You've just about killed the poor bastard.'

'I have? How?'

The Wanderer clapped a hand to his bald bead.

'How? How? You fill him up with cyclatrol, you keep him driving through the nothings for fuck knows how long and then you wonder why he almost dies when he starts to come down. You're impossible, Jeb Stuart Ho.'

Ho stood in silence for a long while. He was becoming acutely aware that despite all the years at the temple, there were many things that he still needed to learn. Suddenly a thought struck him. He looked hard at the Wanderer.

'How did you know my name? I didn't tell it to you.'

The Wanderer grinned and tapped the side of his nose with his forefinger.

'There's a lot I know.'

Jeb Stuart Ho nodded solemnly.

'I'm beginning to realize that.'

He walked slowly away from the car. The doubts were becoming serious. There was so much that he didn't understand. He stood staring at the river. He took a grip on himself. He shouldn't be thinking this way. He only had one purpose in this place. He had to complete his task. He had to kill AA Catto. He walked quickly back to the Wanderer and the still unconscious Minstrel Boy. The Wanderer looked up at him and grinned.

'Itchy to get on with the killing, Jeb Stuart Ho?'

'Sometimes I think you can read my thoughts.'

'You don't think a poor old man like me could do anything like that, do you?'

'The fox does not lead the hunter straight to his lair, neither does the little rabbit...'

The Wanderer quickly interrupted him.

'Don't give me that fortune cookie stuff. It's something I've always hated about your bunch.'

'I'm sorry.'

'I doubt that it's your fault.'

'I'm anxious to get on with my task.'

The Wanderer nodded.

'So I see.'

He nodded towards the Minstrel Boy. 'What about this poor boy?'

There was an awkward pause as the Wanderer got to his feet.

'You weren't thinking of leaving him here?'

'You wouldn't consider looking after him?'

'Have you considered that he might not want to stay in this place?'

'He has the ground car.'

'Not for long, he hasn't.'

'What do you mean?'

The Wanderer grinned.

'That's something else you've forgotten.'

'What?'

'The globes.'

'The cybernetic guards that destroy machines?'

'Right.'

'They'll destroy the car?'

'Of course they will.'

Jeb Stuart Ho looked round.

'They haven't come yet.'

'They will, and when they do, don't try and resist. They're quite liable to fry all three of us.'

Jeb Stuart Ho stared out across the river. Sure enough, just as the Wanderer had predicted, five objects were floating towards them. They hung in the air a short distance above the surface of the water. As they came nearer, he could see that they were smooth grey steel with a black disc set in the side nearest to him.

The globes swept across the meadow towards them. They emitted a high-pitched hum. The Wanderer moved close to Jeb Stuart Ho.

'Remember, don't try anything. Just go along with what they want. If you don't, they'll wipe us all out.'

The globes moved round until they'd surrounded the car and the three men.

'You-will-stay-exactly-as-you-are!'

Neither Ho nor the Wanderer replied. Jeb Stuart Ho was aware the spheres were somehow draining off his willpower. He tried to analyse how they were doing this. It was something he had no experience of. The effort proved too much for him, and he found himself standing blankly.

'It-is-necessary-that-we-search-you.'

The tentacles curled out from the base of the globes, and their tips ran over the Wanderer's and Jeb Stuart Ho's bodies. They took away Ho's gun and his stasis generator. They left him with the rest of his weapons and equipment. They found nothing on the Wanderer, and turned their attention to the Minstrel Boy.

'Has-this-one-ceased-to-live?'

The Wanderer shook his head dully.

'He's still alive, but he's unconscious.'

The globes made no comment. They just ran their tentacles over the Minstrel Boy's inert body. They took his stasis generator, and a couple of trinkets from his pocket. They placed them on top of the car, along with the things they'd taken from Jeb Stuart Ho.

'These-objects-are-proscribed-in-this-area. The-vehicle-is-proscribed-in-this-area. It-is-necessary-that-we-destroy-them.'

The globes rose and floated above the car. Thin beams of bright blue light stabbed down from their bases, and played over the car. Jeb Stuart Ho retreated from the heat that was generated as the car smoked and melted. When it was reduced to a twisted, blackened hulk, the globes silently retreated back across the river and vanished. Jeb Stuart Ho slowly shook his head.

'I have never seen machines like that before.'

The Wanderer nodded.

'It's amazing what you can get from Stuff Central.'

They both stood looking at the charred wreck. The Wanderer grinned.

'Looks like we're walking from here on in.'

Jeb Stuart Ho was about to answer when the Minstrel Boy made a noise. Both men turned and looked at him. He was weakly trying to sit up. His face was still very pale. Jeb Stuart Ho dropped on one knee beside him.

'Are you all right?'

'No. I feel half dead. My head hurts.'

Jeb Stuart Ho avoided the Minstrel Boy's eyes.

'I suppose you blame me for it.'

The Minstrel Boy struggled into a sitting position. Anger seemed to give him strength.

'Who the hell do you expect me to blame? You're the fucker that's responsible.'

He caught sight of the Wanderer.

'You! What the fuck are you doing here?'

The Wanderer grinned.

'I just came along for the ride.'

The Minstrel Boy groaned, and looked around. 'Where are we, anyway?'

Jeb Stuart Ho looked at him in surprise.

'You mean you don't know? You brought us here.'

'You don't expect me to remember any of that, do you?'

'We're in Quahal.'

The Minstrel Boy collapsed back on the grass.

'Quahal! Oh no, I don't believe it.'

'You don't like it?'

'Of course I don't like it. It's a hideous, unbelievable place.'

He sat up again, and noticed the wreckage of the car for the first time.

'I suppose the globes did that.'

The Wanderer nodded.

'That's right.'

'So we can't get out of here.'

'Not until someone comes up with something.'

The Minstrel Boy looked bitterly at Jeb Stuart Ho.

'Why did I ever get involved with you?'

'You had no choice,'

'You can say that again.'

The Minstrel Boy continued to sit on the grass. The Wanderer seemed content to stand patiently and say nothing. Jeb Stuart Ho began to feel that his time was being wasted. He looked from one to the other.

'We ought really to begin to move on.'

The Wanderer said nothing. The Minstrel Boy savagely ripped up a clump of grass.

'I ain't going nowhere else with you.'

Jeb Stuart Ho attempted to be reasonable. 'You can't remain here for the rest of time.'

The Minstrel Boy glanced up with a sneer.

'Can't I? You just watch me.'

Jeb Stuart Ho continued to be reasonable.

'Surely if you come with us, at least to the nearest habitation, you may find the means to get out of this area.'

The Minstrel Boy sat in stubborn silence. The Wanderer decided it was time to intervene.

'He's right, you know. You might as well come as far as the ziggurat.'

The Minstrel Boy glared at him.

'Who asked you?'

'I'm only telling you the truth.'

The Minstrel Boy paused for a moment, then climbed slowly to his feet.

'Okay, okay, I'll come that far with you, but one thing's got to be clear, right?'

'What's that?'

The Minstrel Boy nodded towards Jeb Stuart Ho.

'I ain't going to get involved in any more of his deals. I don't want him anywhere near me.'

Jeb Stuart Ho looked at the ground.

'I'm sorry you feel that way.'

'Don't even talk about it.'

Jeb Stuart Ho looked helplessly at the Wanderer. He shrugged and slowly turned and started walking away. Ho, and finally the Minstrel Boy, followed him. They walked along parallel to the river. All the men maintained a certain distance between each other. Nobody spoke. Every so often, they would pass the ruined, burned-out hulk of another vehicle that had been destroyed by the globes. There was no sign of any people.

There was no great hardship involved in walking to the ziggurat. The river lowlands had been designed as a natural near-paradise. Once they'd left the last of the wrecks behind, the countryside was almost idyllic. Butterflies and small birds flitted above the long, lush, gently waving grass. The river. moved calmly along beside them, reflecting the bright sunlight and the deep blue, cloudless sky. Even the distant view of the blue-grey, mist-shrouded mountain was almost too good to be true.

After a while, they could see the ziggurat further down the river. Even from some distance away there was no mistaking its vast size and complexity. Although it was roughly pyramid-shaped, it was a mass of ramps, stairs, stepped walls and flat roofs at different levels. Here and there, the even blackness of the stone was broken up by a small patch of green where plants were being grown on a section of roof. There were also flashes of silver where a stream of water ran down a complicated system of channels from a fountain high up near the summit of the structure.

As they came nearer to the ziggurat. the meadow land gave way to a system of small, square, cultivated fields, divided by hedges and irrigation ditches. They crossed a path that appeared to lead straight towards the massive building, and turned on to it. Men were working in some of the fields. They all seemed to have a similar build and very uniform features. They all wore the same kind of one-piece faded blue robe, and their heads were either shaved or totally bald. Each time Jeb Stuart Ho and his two companions passed one of the men, they looked up, smiled, and then went back to their work. It reminded Jeb Stuart Ho of his time at the brotherhood temple and, despite his carefully programmed sense of caution, he felt himself filled with a strong sensation of wellbeing.

The others seemed to pick up some of the same atmosphere. Despite the early bad feeling they moved closer together, and the Minstrel Boy even took off his jacket and tossed it across his shoulder. Jeb Stuart Ho had never seen him look so relaxed.

They started meeting more of the local people. They passed them on the path, wheeling barrows, carrying bundles or simply moving from one field to another with forks or hoes over their shoulders. None of them spoke to the travellers, but they all flashed them the happy instant smile. Jeb Stuart Ho wasn't too surprised at the extreme similarity between all the men, this was common in many closed communities. The brotherhood all looked very much alike, although not to the extent of the men of Quahal. What puzzled him was that they all appeared to be roughly the same age. There were no children, no youths and no old men. Everyone he had seen appeared to be between twenty and thirty.

They reached the foot of the ziggurat. There was nothing that could be described as a main entrance. There were at least four arched doorways in the wall nearest to them, plus half a dozen small square openings, also two ramps, and three sets of steps. Jeb Stuart Ho looked round at the Wanderer.

'Do you have any idea where we should go?'

The Wanderer shook his head.

'No idea.'

He turned to the Minstrel Boy.

'Would you know?'

The Minstrel Boy looked at him, hesitated, and then shook his head.

'I don't know nothing.'

They walked round to the next side of the square base. Here again they were confronted with another choice of stairs and entrances. Jeb Stuart Ho looked round helplessly. The Minstrel Boy grinned.

'You could always go inside and just wander about.'

Jeb Stuart Ho looked hard at him.

'I hardly think that would be suitable behaviour.'

The Minstrel Boy shrugged. Jeb Stuart Ho approached a man who was walking past with a bundle tied to his back.

'Excuse me, friend, but would you tell me where I might find someone in authority?'

The man smiled at Jeb Stuart Ho.

'There is no authority except the blessed one.'

The man walked on. The Minstrel Boy burst out laughing and staggered round in small circles. Jeb Stuart Ho looked perplexed. He tried again. He went up to a blue-robed figure pushing a wheelbarrow.

'Where might I find the blessed one?'

The barrow pusher smiled.

'The blessed one is with all of us, my brother.'

The Minstrel Boy reeled over and slapped Jeb Stuart Ho on the back.

'They're worse than you are.'

Jeb Stuart Ho stared at him in surprise.

'I don't know what you mean.'

The Minstrel Boy was almost helpless with laughter.

'No, of course you don't.'

Jeb Stuart Ho looked round in confusion. He wondered how he could convey what he wanted. He stretched out and caught hold of a passing blue robe.

'Can you help me, please?'

The wearer turned and smiled.

'In what way, my brother?'

'We are travellers from outside Quahal. We would like shelter, food and some particular information.'

'You are travellers?'

'That's correct.'

The blue-robed young man frowned.

'I have never encountered travellers before. Perhaps if you could wait here while I go and seek guidance on the matter...'

Jeb Stuart Ho nodded. The young man hurried away. They waited. The black stone threw back the heat of the sun. The blue-robed figures came and went all round them. They paused and smiled, but otherwise paid no attention to the three strangers. Jeb Stuart Ho stared up at the vast building. He had never seen anything so impressive. It towered above him, an irregular but harmonious blend of stairs, rectangular vertical walls, sloping ramps and huge inset slabs of relief carving, soaring to the eventual peak hundreds of metres in the air.

The Minstrel Boy didn't share his enthusiasm. He stuck his thumbs in his belt and kicked at the paving stones.

'I got a feeling I ain't going to like this place.'

The Wanderer grinned at him.

'You could always try the mountain.'

The Minstrel Boy grinned ruefully.

'I think I'll stick with this one, for now.'

Two men in yellow robes appeared at the head of the nearest flight of stairs. They were older than the ones in blue, and looked as though they were enjoying a tanned, healthy middle age. Each time one of the younger men passed them, they acknowledged his formal, bowed-head salute. They hurried down the steps and walked quickly up to Jeb Stuart Ho.

'You are the travellers?'

Jeb Stuart Ho bowed stiffly from the waist.

'We are.'

'The blessed Joachim is considering granting you an audience. We can offer you food and other minimal comforts until he has reached his decision. If you will follow us.'

The two yellow-robed individuals turned smartly and walked briskly back towards the steps. The three travellers followed them. The Minstrel Boy glanced sideways at the Wanderer.

'What do you think they mean by minimal comforts?'

'Doubtless we'll find out soon enough.'

20

The Alamada was at least a head taller than AA Catto. She also looked a good deal heavier. She was muscular and full-bodied, with ample breasts and thighs. She walked out of the big hut with swaggering arrogance. She was naked, except for the same armour over her left arm that AA Catto wore. She carried the same flat, leaf-shaped knife and a small round shield.

She walked forward until she was a couple of metres from AA Catto. She held the knife almost casually in her left hand. She halted and smiled at AA Catto. Her lips were very full and sensual. Her nose was small and slightly flattened. It contrasted with her eyes, which were large and dark. Her face seemed to radiate a dark, very cruel kind of sexuality. She tossed her head, shaking her mane of straight black hair. It hung almost to her waist.

'I'm going to kill you.'

AA Catto couldn't help admiring the woman. She smiled back, and shook her head.

'I don't think so.'

The Alamada raised her knife, and began slowly to circle AA Catto. Her body was tense, like a hunting animal. It was oiled like AA Catto's, and as she moved the muscles rippled beneath the skin. AA Catto lifted her own knife, and dropped into a crouch. She backed away slowly and cautiously. The Alamada's lips drew back into something between a grin and a snarl. Her teeth flashed in the firelight.

'I'm going to kill you for sure.'

'No, you're not.'

The two women continued to circle each other. The Alamada attempted to edge closer.

'You're not like the others. You're not the way you're supposed to be.'

'I'm different.'

'You're small.'

'That's a puzzle for you to solve.'

'It's your disadvantage.'

'Maybe.'

The witch queen went on trying to get closer to AA Catto, and AA Catto in her turn went on keeping the distance between them. From behind the lines of horsemen who ringed the space where the fight was taking place, Billy watched tensely. He held his gun down by his side. The butt was damp and slippery where his palms were sweating.

The Alamada stopped circling AA Catto. She crouched absolutely still for an instant. Then, with a shout, she leaped forward and slashed at AA Catto with a wide, backhanded blow. AA Catto twisted and jumped back. The edge of the blade missed her stomach by a matter of centimetres. For the first time AA Catto realized what she was involved in. Something inside her went cold. If Billy didn't go along with the plan, she would die.

The Alamada spun on her heel and swung a chopping overarm blow towards AA Catto's neck. Desperately she threw up the shield, and just managed to catch the blow. It jarred her arm right up to the shoulder. There was a stabbing pain, and her arm went numb. The shield fell to her side. She jumped back, holding the sword in front of her. The Alamada laughed.

'Are you going to die without a fight?'

'I'm not going to die.'

'Oh yes you are, and slowly too, if you don't put up a fight.'

She swung at AA Catto. The knife just touched the skin of her left breast. A thin line of blood appeared. AA Catto lunged at the woman. She missed hopelessly. The Alamada lowered her shield and laughed at AA Catto.

'You'll have to do better than that.'

She spread her arms.

'Come on, little woman, try again. Try to kill me if you can.'

Blind rage boiled up inside AA Catto. She slashed wildly at her. The

Alamada twisted her body and the blow went wild. AA Catto slashed again. The Alamada jumped back, and she missed again. Tears of frustration welled up in her eyes. She swung at the witch queen again and again. Each time she moved out of the way. AA Catto found that she couldn't touch her. The Alamada kept on laughing and taunting her.

'Come on, woman. Can't you do better than that?'

She jabbed at AA Catto with the point of her knife. It scarcely touched her shoulder, and left a small wound that oozed blood. AA Catto began to get scared. Was Billy going to let her die? There was no way that she could deal with this woman on her own. The Alamada jabbed at her again. Another small wound, this time just above her right breast. AA Catto looked round desperately to see if she could see Billy. While her eyes were off the Alamada, she slashed at her again. This time the cut was deeper, and began to bleed quite profusely. AA Catto knew she was being slowly cut to pieces.

She made a final, desperate effort to stop the Alamada. She put all her weight behind a single knife thrust straight between the Alamada's breasts. For a fraction of a second AA Catto thought she had succeeded. Then the Alamada whipped up her shield and turned the blow. AA Catto completely lost her balance. As she staggered forward, the Alamada kicked her feet away from under her. AA Catto sprawled face forward in the dirt. The knife went flying. She rolled over and tried to sit up, but before she could, the Alamada rammed her foot into her throat and pushed her back down. AA Catto found herself staring up at the Alamada's bush of curly black pubic hair. She tried to wriggle away, but the woman was too strong for her.

'I'm going to kill you now.'

For the first time in her life, AA Catto was sick with fear. At the same time, hatred burned inside her for Billy, and the way he'd doublecrossed her. The witch queen raised her knife high above her head. AA Catto shut her eyes. It was obviously all over. Then the shot came, and the Alamada's body fell limply on top of her. She eased the weight off her and sat up. She expected to see Billy struggling with a squad of horsemen, but none of them seemed to have moved. She rolled the body completely off her. A large section of the skull had been blown away by the .70 calibre slug.

AA Catto stood up. She deliberately bent down and picked up one of the knives. She started hacking at the body. Her control seemed to snap. Her onslaught became almost sexual in its hysteria. She carved huge gashes in the witch queen's lifeless body. Her breath came in short sharp gasps. Then, abruptly, the frenzy ran out. She looked disgustedly at the mutilation she had caused. She let the knife fall and turned away.

She pulled herself together and, with all the dignity she could muster while she was naked and covered in blood, she walked towards the big hut. The two helmeted horsemen, who stood flanking the door, escorted her inside.

Billy waited to see if anything would happen. He'd fired almost over the shoulders of the line of horsemen, but not one of them had shown any sign of noticing it. Reave and Nancy stood a little way away from him, presumably ready to run if the horsemen did anything to Billy. AA Catto vanished inside the big hut, and it seemed as though any chance of retribution had passed. Billy dropped the gun into his pocket, and let some of the tension drain out of his muscles. It had been a terrible strain waiting to fire the shot. There had been a point when he had almost not done it. The vision of himself being impaled on the long, thin spears of the horsemen had nearly been too strong.

The question now, as far as Billy could see, was what to do next. He assumed that since the Alamada was dead, AA Catto had become the next queen. The horsemen appeared to accept that she had defeated her in a fair fight. The lines of helmeted horsemen who had formed the square began to file into the big hut. Once they were all inside, the horsemen without helmets, who had remained behind the ranks of helmeted figures, picked up the Alamada's body and dumped it unceremoniously in the fire pit. After this chore was done, they too went inside the big hut. This just left Billy, Reave and Nancy standing in the open space. The smoke from the fire wafted past them. It was heavy with the acrid smell of burned flesh. Billy hurried across to the other two.

'Do you think we should go inside?'

Nancy looked round the village. There was no sign of life.

'Everyone else seems to be in there.'

Reave thoughtfully stroked his chin.

'I suppose AA Catto's queen now?'

'It looks that way.'

A kind of toneless singing came from the big hut. Reave pursed his lips.

'I'm not so sure I want to be one of her subjects.'

Billy grinned sourly.

'You should know.'

Nancy rubbed her hands together. 'We can't stand here for ever.'

'That's true.'

'So, do we go inside?'

'It's that or steal some horses and split.'

Nancy glanced pointedly down at her thin catsuit.

'I don't think I'm exactly dressed for another trip in the fog.'

'So we go inside?'

Billy nodded.

'We go inside.'

It was hot and crowded inside the big hut. The building was arranged like a figure eight with an extra loop added to the bottom. It was basically three circular connecting rooms, laid out in a straight line. The biggest of these was the centre one. It was thronged with horsemen. At one end was a raised dais, and on it was a combination throne, couch and bed, made from dark carved wood. In the middle of a heap of multicoloured cushions lay AA Catto. Her armour had been removed, but she was still naked. Two horsemen knelt beside her. They appeared to be treating her wounds with some kind of ointment that they took from a stone jar. A third horseman stooped beside her whispering urgently. AA Catto gave him her undivided attention. It seemed to Billy that he was instructing her about either the ritual or her duties. A horseman stood on either side of the dais, rigidly holding a spear.

Behind the dais was the entrance to one of the other, smaller rooms. Billy was later to find it was the queen's private quarters. It was screened by a large hanging tapestry that depicted some kind of stylized hunting scene. Immediately in front of the dais, almost in the middle of the room, was another stone fire pit. A pile of logs crackled merrily, and the carcass of some large animal turned on a spit. Fat dripped off it, and fell hissing into the fire. The smoke escaped through a small hole in the roof. At least, that was the theory. A good percentage of it just hung in the air. The combination of roast meat and wood smoke gave the place a comforting, if crude, smell.

On the other side of the fire was a low curved table. Behind it sat a line of horsemen on low stools. They had removed their helmets and placed them on the table in front of them. Their spears were stacked in racks along the wall. Behind them sat more horsemen on rows of benches. They cradled their helmets in their laps. They all sang and beat time with their hands, either on table or helmets. It was a strange, guttural dirge with no recognizable words or harmonic structure.

The possession of a helmet seemed to be a crucial badge of rank in the clan. Billy noticed that the ones who had them sat staring at AA Catto, singing and clapping. The ones who didn't scurried backwards and forwards, to and from the third room, which was a kind of storeroom or scullery, serving the others with some sort of fermented drink. It seemed that if you had a helmet you were part of the hunter-warrior class; if not, you were a servant. Billy assumed that that was why the horsemen had so readily accepted the idea that Billy, Reave and Nancy were AA Catto's personal slaves.

Every eye in the place was fixed on AA Catto. Nobody took the slightest notice of either Billy, Reave or Nancy as they stood quietly at the back of the main room. There was an air of expectancy. Billy couldn't believe that they were simply waiting for the meat to cook, or that they could be that enraptured with AA Catto's skinny body. The only explanation he could think of was that, presently, some kind of ceremony would take place.

He waited for a while, but very soon started to get bored. He glanced at Reave.

'Do you think anybody would take exception if we got ourselves a drink?'

Reave looked blank.

'How should I know?'

'You want to try it?'

'Hell, why not?'

Nancy looked up from where she was squatting on the floor. 'You want to get me one?'

Billy pulled a face.

'I suppose so.'

He and Reave moved quietly into the small room. A line of stone pitchers seemed to contain the booze, or whatever it was. Billy took two earthenware mugs off a shelf and filled them from one of the pitchers. None of the serving men who came and went took any notice of them. They returned to where Nancy was sitting. Billy handed her a mug. She looked at the contents doubtfully.

'What is it?'

'Who knows?'

'Are you going to drink it?'

'Sure. Just watch me.'

Billy took a hearty swig, and immediately regretted it. The liquid tasted vaguely poisonous and burned his mouth. When he swallowed some, however, it produced a pleasant euphoric glow inside him. The next time he sipped it sparingly. He found himself quickly getting used to it. Neither Nancy nor Reave had touched theirs. They looked at him questioningly.

'Is it okay?'

'It's bad, but it's not that bad.'

They drank in silence. Billy sank down and squatted on his haunches. He stared at the smoke-blackened beams of the ceiling. He became aware that he was feeling decidedly horny. He wondered if it was something in the drink. There was also the fact that he hadn't been within reach of a woman since he had left Darlene back at the Leader

Hotel. It seemed like that was part of another age. He took another sip from his mug and glanced covertly at Nancy.

'Uh, Nancy.'

'Yeah?'

Billy smiled with all the charm he could muster.

'What say you and me find ourselves a dark corner, huh?'

Nancy looked at Billy as though he was mad.

'What the hell for?'

'Uh... I was feeling horny, and was just wondering if maybe you and me might...'

'You and me?'

'Why not?'

Nancy's lip curled. 'Forget it!'

Billy looked glum.

'I was only thinking.'

'Yeah, well, forget it.'

Billy slumped back into his own thoughts. He had just started to develop the idea that Quahal was one of the most tedious bummers he had ever come across when things began to happen up on the dais. The first thing Billy noticed was that the singing stopped. An expectant silence fell over the room. Billy stood up to see what was happening. AA Catto was standing on the dais with her arms extended. Two of the horsemen who had been attending her came from behind the tapestry screen. They carried a fur-trimmed purple robe. AA Catto lowered her arms, and they placed the robe over her shoulders. It hung open so most of her body was still on view. The attendants backed away. A slow measured chant started.

'Hommm... Hommm...'

The horsemen beat time, a heavy ponderous beat. The first horseman at the table stood up and walked slowly towards the dais, keeping in step with the chant.

'Hommm... Hommm...'

He reached AA Catto and stopped. The chant stopped too. The horseman slowly sank to his knees. The silence was loaded with tension. The horseman leaned forward, and placed his mouth between AA Catto's legs. She stiffened. Her eyebrows shot up, then she half smiled and moved her weight so it was bearing down on the horseman's face. Her hips undulated a little. Reave glanced at Billy.

'She'll be loving every minute of this. I don't think she could have devised a better coronation herself.'

The horseman bowed, touching his head on the ground at AA Catto's feet. Then he stood up, and went slowly back to his seat. The

chant began again. The second horseman in line stood up and slowly
advanced to the dais. Just like the one before, he dropped to his knees,
went down on AA Catto for the statutory period, bowed and returned
to his place. The chant started up again.

'Hommm... Hommm... Hommm'

The third one at the table began moving up for his turn.

'Hommm... Hommm... Hommm'

And after him, the fourth and the fifth. One after the other, working
from the fire outwards, the horsemen paid their unique tribute to their
new queen. Billy looked at Reave in amazement.

'Is she going to go through the entire clan?'

Reave grimaced.

'She's capable of it. Make no mistake about that.'

Billy shook his head in disbelief. The horsemen continued to
make their pilgrimage up to the dais. By the time AA Catto had
worked her way through a third of the men with helmets, she was
sweating, her eyes were closed and her legs were beginning to
tremble. She was having great difficulty maintaining her formal and
dignified cool.

The chant kept on going, and the horsemen kept on coming. At the
halfway point, AA Catto grabbed the current supplicant by the hair,
and let herself fall back on to the cushions, pulling him down with her.
From then on she received homage from her subjects in a supine position. Occasionally she would languidly raise a thin white leg in the air.
Billy wondered if it signified ecstasy, or was just her way of acknowl-
edging the presence of the rest of the tribe.

The last of the helmeted horsemen backed away from the dais. Billy
assumed that the ceremony was all over, but the chant started again,
and one of the serving men began the slow march to AA Catto's throne.
Billy grinned at Reave.

'She is going through the whole tribe.'

Reave nodded. He didn't look in the least surprised. As far as he was
concerned, nothing about AA Catto could surprise him. The ones
without helmets did their bit, and for a moment it seemed as though the
ritual was over. Then to Billy's and Reave's astonishment the chant
started again. Billy's face dropped in disbelief. Nancy had started
walking slowly down the crowded room in strict time to the chant.

'Hommm... Hommm... Hommm'

She reached the dais, bowed her head and sank to her knees. As
Nancy disappeared into the pile of cushions, Billy swung round to
Reave.

'Are we supposed to go up there?'

'It's beginning to look like it. Why? Don't you fancy the idea?'

Billy grimaced.

'Not a great deal.'

Reave grinned.

'I thought you liked eating pussy?'

'Yeah, but...'

'But what?'

'It's kind of public, and anyway, I've got a feeling that she'd look at it as some kind of, I don't know, a moral victory; she'd think she was humiliating me. You know what I mean?'

Reave grinned.

'Sure, I know what you mean. She's a great one for humiliating. I don't see how you're going to get out of it.'

Billy twitched uncomfortably.

'Me neither.'

Nancy seemed to stay in the cushions for a very long time. It was certainly longer than any of the horsemen. Finally she reappeared. She walked back up the room, with a serene smile on her face. The chant began once more. Reave grunted, stood up, and started walking towards the throne. Nancy slumped down next to Billy.

'Waiting till last, huh?'

Billy scowled.

'I can't see no way out of it.'

Nancy raised an eyebrow.

'I thought you said you were feeling horny?'

'Not for that.

Nancy smiled coyly.

'It was really quite nice.'

'Is that so?'

Reave didn't spend anything like as long with AA Catto as Nancy had. Before Billy was anything like ready, he had to get reluctantly to his feet and fall into step with the chant.

'Hommm... Hommm... Hommm...'

Billy walked like a man going to his execution.

'Hommm... Hommm... Hommm...'

It seemed an immense distance to the dais. He finally reached it. AA Catto lay with her eyes closed. He stood looking down at her for a while. Her eyes opened. Her voice was a vibrant purr.

'Kneel down, Billy.'

Billy pressed his lips together and dropped awkwardly to his knees.

'Now pay me my dues as queen, Billy.'

Billy closed his eyes and slowly lowered his mouth to AA Catto's damp and somewhat swollen cunt. AA Catto smiled happily.

'I'm sure you're going to be a very respectful subject.'

21

'I suppose I could stand this for a while.'

The Minstrel Boy sprawled in his chair, staring at the light reflected in his glass of wine. He was feeling comfortable for the first time since he'd been abducted from the Albert Speer Hotel. The Wanderer sat across the table from him grinning.

'You're going to have to stand it until you find some way out of here.'

The Minstrel Boy nodded ruefully.

'I know that. I was trying to forget it.'

The yellow-robed priests had led the three travellers to a suite of rooms deep inside the ziggurat, and left them there to wait until the blessed Joachim felt like seeing them. They hadn't locked the door, but the three were effectively prisoners. They all knew that it would be impossible to find their way out through the maze of stairs and corridors that made up the interior of the huge building.

The suite consisted of a fairly large main room, and three small cells that led off it. It was plain but comfortable. The walls were smooth black stone, and the main room was furnished with a square table and four chairs. They were made of some light-coloured wood, decorated with geometric inlays. Each of the cells contained a narrow sleeping pallet. There were no windows in the place, but ample light was provided by a mass of candles in a roughly triangular-shaped fixture that hung from the ceiling.

Shortly after the priests had left, two of the blue-robed lower orders, who seemed to do most of the manual work, turned up with refreshments in the form of a bowl of fruit, a tray of flat biscuit-like pastries, a large jug of wine and glasses. They placed them on the table, and withdrew without a word.

Jeb Stuart Ho took to the place immediately. He ate a little fruit, drank half a glass of wine and withdrew to his cell to meditate, leaving the Minstrel Boy and the Wanderer to linger over the remainder of the jug. The Minstrel Boy drained his glass, and refilled it.

'I'd like this place a whole lot better if there were a few chicks about.'

The Wanderer's eyes twinkled in the candlelight.

'You won't find any here.'

'Don't I know it.'

'You'll maybe find a way to get round the problem.'

'Huh?'

'I said you might find a way to get round the problem.'

'I heard what you said. I was just wondering what exactly you meant by it.'

The Wanderer grinned broadly.

'I figure you'll find out.'

The Minstrel Boy scowled.

'You keep making remarks like that. You're getting too goddamn mysterious.'

'What other pleasures have I got left?'

The Minstrel Boy pushed the jug across the table towards him.

'You could get drunk. It'd make you a bit more tolerable.'

The Wanderer refilled his glass.

'I won't argue with you. Did I ever tell you about the time I was down in Port Judas and met this sportin' gal down on her luck?'

The Minstrel Boy shook his head.

'No, but no doubt you're going to.'

The Minstrel Boy went on drinking while the Wanderer launched into a long, ponderous and occasionally obscene story. It went on and on, and the Minstrel Boy quickly lost track of it. The Wanderer was just winding up for the punch line when there was a soft rapping on the door. The Minstrel Boy's hand went instinctively to his knife belt.

'What do you think that is?'

The rapping came again. The Wanderer shrugged.

'All we can do is find out. I don't think there's any call for alarm.'

He raised his voice.

'Come in.'

The door opened and three men came in. Men was a fairly loose description. They had the bald heads and general appearance of the boys in blue, but that was where the similarity ended. Their figures were slim, almost feminine and they moved with a strange exaggerated daintiness. They wore pink robes of what looked like watered silk, and their eyes were shadowed with some kind of blue make-up. The Minstrel Boy suspected that their overlong eyelashes were probably false. When they spoke their voices were soft and high-pitched.

'We are sent by the blessed one to ensure that all your needs are taken care of.'

The Wanderer raised an eyebrow.

'We're doing pretty good.'

'We are sent to offer you any additional pleasure you might desire.'

The Minstrel Boy glanced up from his drink.

'Desire?'

He looked carefully up and down each of the three in turn.

'Just what kind of pleasure did you have in mind?'

'The middle one of the three smiled sweetly.

'Those joyful pleasures of the body bestowed and sanctified by the blessed one, that our flesh might celebrate his glory.'

The Minstrel Boy grinned. 'Celebrate his glory, hey?'

'We are at your disposal.'

The Wanderer shook his head.

'You can leave me out. *I'm* too old for that sort of thing.'

The Minstrel Boy rose slowly from his chair.

'I don't see the harm in celebrating a bit of glory.'

The Wanderer laughed.

'I thought it was a woman you were so desperate for?'

The Minstrel Boy patted the priest's bottom.

'Like you said, I'll find a way round the problem.'

He turned to the pink-robed priest.

'Does the blessed one sanctify an old-fashioned blow job?'

'I'm not familiar with the term, but I'd be happy to accept your instruction.'

'Good, good, let's go off into my little room, and do some instructing. You might as well bring one of your buddies, seeing as how grandpappy here doesn't want to know.'

He poured himself another glass of wine and led the two priests off to one of the empty cells. That left the Wanderer alone with the remaining one. The priest waved a slim white hand in the direction of Jeb Stuart Ho's still figure.

'Will your friend have any desire for my services?'

The Wanderer shook his head.

'I doubt it. He's too busy meditating, and besides I think he swore off sex for the duration.'

The priest looked exaggeratedly sad.

'That is a great pity.'

The Wanderer nodded sympathetically.

'It sure is. Best you should run along back where you came from.'

The priest bowed, and left without a word. The sounds of revelry began to come from the Minstrel Boy's cell. It seemed as though the priests were quick to pick up on the instruction. The Wanderer sighed and glanced through the open doorway. The pallet had become a mass of naked, entwined bodies. He sighed deeply and relaxed back in his chair.

22

Billy woke up with a start. He discovered that Nancy had been shaking him. He also discovered that he had a headache and an evil taste in his mouth.

'What happened?'

'You passed out.'

'When?'

'Last night, after the ceremony, you drank yourself stupid on the local poison and collapsed. We left you here.'

Billy focused his eyes, and looked around. He was still in the large room of the queen's hut. It was deserted now. The fire had burned down to grey embers and the air was cold and damp. Billy struggled to sit up. Each time he moved he found new parts of him that hurt.

'Where's Reave?'

'The two of you were given a hut down at the end of the village. He went there. You refused. You wanted to be buddies with the horsemen.

'What happened?'

'They ignored you. You clowned about for a bit and passed out.'

Billy shook his head to clear it.

'I don't remember any of that.'

'I'm not surprised, the amount you were drinking.'

Billy got painfully to his feet and staggered out to the scullery. He found a cask of water. A dipper hung beside it. Billy drank a little, and sluiced more over his head. He called out to Nancy who was still standing in the big room.

'Is it morning?'

'Yeah.'

'They have day and night here?'

'Every day.'

Billy came back out of the scullery. 'What's AA Catto doing?'

'She wants to see you.'

Billy grimaced.

'Can't she wait? I'm not up to coping with her yet.'

Nancy glanced meaningfully at him.

'I wouldn't keep her waiting.'

'Why not?'

'She is queen now.'

'Shit! She's only queen because I shot the last one.'

'I wouldn't remind her of that.'

'Isn't this getting a bit out of hand?'

Nancy began to look uncomfortable. 'I'd keep my voice down if I were you.'

She gestured to the tapestry behind the throne.

'She's only just behind there.'

'Are you trying to tell me something?'

'I don't know. She's gone a bit funny, after getting to be queen, and the ceremony and all.'

'It's gone to her head?'

'And some.'

Billy's face became determined.

'I'm going in there to sort out all this queen business.'

Nancy quickly put a hand on his arm.

'Wait. Wait just a minute and listen to what I have to say, will you?'

'Okay. You've got my undivided.'

Nancy hesitated, as though summoning up her courage.

'We've never got on too well, have we?'

Billy shook his head.

'No, not really.'

'I feel bad talking to you like this, but there's no one else.'

'So talk.'

'I'm worried.'

'About AA Catto?'

'She's gone very strange.'

'How?'

'She had one of the horsemen in there all night. She was torturing him.'

'So? She did that to Reave all the time.'

'I think she probably killed him. She was right over the edge. I mean, I've seen a few things. I don't shock easy, but this started to do me in. I couldn't take it.'

'You were in there with her?'

Nancy looked at the floor. 'Yeah.'

'Helping her?'

'With a couple more to keep me amused.'

'Didn't they object to what she was doing to their mate? They're big strong lads.'

Nancy shook her head.

'They can't.'

'Can't?'

'She can do what she likes with them. They're programmed to do exactly what the queen wants. She could slaughter the lot of them. They wouldn't stop her.'

Billy smiled grimly.

'If she did that, she'd have no more to play with.'

'She could send for another lot from the valley.'

'From the valley?'

'I've found out a lot about this place. There's a stuff receiver down in the valley, in the ziggurat, that big building we saw.'

Billy glanced over his shoulder at the entrance to AA Catto's room. He lowered his voice.

'Does she know this?'

Nancy nodded. 'Sure, she told me.'

Billy's face was very serious.

'What else did you learn?'

'Plenty. You know those helmets? They're like a badge of rank, a pecking order. It starts from the ones sitting at the table, right down to the ones without helmets, who are like servants to the rest.'

Billy nodded.

'I kind of figured that.'

'They change round once a month, the order gets reversed or something.'

'Once a month?'

'Right.'

'How the hell do they figure months?'

Nancy grinned, despite her concern.

'They calculate it on the queen's menstrual cycle.'

Billy laughed.

'AA Catto's going to confuse them. She doesn't have any, according to Reave. She never allowed herself to reach puberty.'

'She's going to now. She doesn't have any retarding drugs. She's growing with a vengeance.'

Billy looked thoughtful.

'I imagine that's affecting her mind.'

'Probably.'

'I suppose she could always get more from the stuff receiver.'

'That and a whole lot...'

Before Nancy could finish, there was a petulant shout from behind the tapestry.

'Nancy!'

Nancy spun round, looking a little pale.

'Yes!'

'Have you woken up Billy yet?'

'Yes!'

'Then get him in here.'

Nancy looked urgently at Billy.

'You'd better get in there. Don't keep her waiting.'

Billy sighed and hurried across the room. He pulled back the tapestry and stepped through into the queen's private lair. The sight of it was quite a surprise. Most of the floor space was taken up by the largest bed Billy had ever seen. It was piled high with cushions, pillows and rich furs. Two poles supported a tentlike overhead canopy. The walls were hung with mirrors and lavish embroideries. There were a number of chests and cupboards. The contents were scattered on the floor, as though AA Catto had been going through them in some kind of exploratory frenzy. There were candles everywhere, and a brazier of hot coals stood in an alcove, heating the room and filling the air with the heavy sweet smell of incense.

All this was much as Billy had expected. The real shock to his system waited for him in a clear space of floor opposite the bed. A thick heavy post, about half as tall again as a man, and carved into a stylized phallic shape, was set firmly in the stone flags. The horribly mutilated body of a man hung from it in chains. A helmeted guard stood beside him gripping his spear, like a statue, and staring straight ahead. A rack containing a comprehensive range of torture implements was on the wall nearby. Many of them had quite obviously been used very recently.

AA Catto was fully dressed and sitting on the edge of the bed. She wore a feminine version of the horsemen's outfit, wide silk trousers bound up with thongs, a tunic of soft white fur and silver armour covering her arms. The clothes seemed to fit very well, considering the Alamadas had been much larger women. She gestured imperiously at Billy.

'I want to talk to you.'

'I...'

Billy's head and stomach were still reeling from the sight of the figure on the post. AA Catto glanced casually at her victim.

'It bothers you, does it?'

She snapped her fingers at the guard.

'Fetch some people to remove that thing.'

The guard swiftly obeyed and left the room. Moments later he returned with two of the helmetless servants. They removed the body from the post and dragged it unceremoniously from the room. AA Catto turned her attention back to Billy.

'Now can we talk?'

Billy wiped beads of sweat from his forehead.

'I suppose so.'

'You're a terrible weakling.'

Billy shrugged.

'If you say so.'

AA Catto stood up very slowly.

'I don't like your attitude.'

She began to pace up and down.

'I'll be charitable, however. You may well be having trouble adjusting to the new situation.'

Billy was still confused.

'The new situation?'

'The situation of my being queen. I have absolute power here. I can do anything. Anything at all.'

Billy had never seen her quite like this. The weight of the gun in his pocket was reassuring, but he still chose his words with great care.

'May I ask what you intend to do?'

AA Catto smiled nastily at him.

'That's more what I expect.'

She resumed her pacing.

'I do not share the previous rulers' enthusiasm for this dreary primitivism. I have discovered that there is a stuff receiver in that building we saw in the valley. I intend to use the receiver to obtain a supply of the modern necessities. Do you understand?'

Billy nodded.

'I think so. What about the globes, though, won't they destroy everything directly it arrives down the beam?'

'They can be deactivated from the same point.'

'Aren't there people in the valley?'

AA Catto halted.

'Yes, why?'

Billy avoided looking directly at her.

'Won't they be liable to object to what you want to do?'

AA Catto looked surprised.

'Does that matter?'

'If they decided to resist your plan.'

'They won't.'

'Why not?'

AA Catto looked at Billy as though he was simple-minded.

'Because I've decided to destroy them.'

Billy's mouth dropped open.

'Destroy them?'

AA Catto's voice became very brisk and matter of fact.

'It's the only solution. It stops them causing trouble, and, in any case, they're no use to me, no use at all. They are also reputed to have very unpleasant ideas and habits. I think it's best if they were liquidated before we do anything else.'

Billy's mind reeled. He could see exactly why Nancy had been so disturbed. AA Catto was obviously quite out of control. He looked at her guardedly.

'You'll send your horsemen into the valley?'

'I'll lead them.'

'And kill all the people there?'

'Of course.'

Billy looked at the floor. He couldn't think exactly what to say. AA Catto looked at him impatiently.

'What's the matter with you?'

Billy looked round helplessly.

'I was just wondering why you were telling me all this.'

'You will be coming with us.'

Billy's eyebrows shot up. 'Me?'

'You have proved quite resourceful in the past. I will keep you as an adviser as long as you prove useful.'

Billy closed his eyes for an instant. It was almost too much to take in. He wished that he was back at the Leader Hotel, or in Pleasant Gap, or almost anywhere.

'When do we ride for the valley?'

'Later today. My horsemen are making ready. Isn't it exciting?'

Billy looked at the backs of his hands.

'I suppose so.'

AA Catto smiled sympathetically at him.

'I expect it's all a little overwhelming right now. You'll enjoy it, once the killing starts.'

23

The build-up to an audience with the blessed Joachim was a planned performance. Jeb Stuart Ho, the Wanderer and the Minstrel Boy had been kept waiting for a couple of hours. They had been fed, given drinks, and, in the case of the Minstrel Boy, entertained soundly by two pink-robed devotees. When all these

preliminaries were complete, an escort of yellow-robed priests arrived
at their suite of rooms.

'The blessed one has decided, in his wisdom, that you will be allowed
an audience. We have come to escort you to his wondrous presence.'

There were six of them. The Minstrel Boy wondered if it was a guard
of honour, or simply a guard. They moved out into the corridor, and the
priests formed up around them. Three in front, and three behind. They
started walking. It seemed to the Wanderer that it was another stage in
the whole process. They seemed to walk for miles along the echoing
corridors of black stone. The turns and right angles soon destroyed the
travellers' sense of direction inside the building. The only thing they knew
for sure was that they were consistently going up from one level to
another. They finally arrived at the foot of a flight of wide, imposing
stairs. As far as Jeb Stuart Ho could calculate they were very near the
apex of the building.

At the head of the stairs there were a pair of polished steel doors. An
emblem of a strange impossible bird was worked in dramatic relief on the
metal. The small procession started up the stairs. As they reached the
halfway mark, the doors began to swing slowly open. They reached the
threshold of the blessed Joachim's inner sanctum. The priests fell to their
knees and touched their foreheads on the floor. Jeb Stuart Ho inclined his
head slightly, but the Minstrel Boy and the Wanderer just stood and
looked around.

The room was lavish. It was long and narrow, almost like a giant
corridor with a high vaulted ceiling. The black stone walls had been
polished to the smoothness of glass, and flowing designs of weird
composite animals were inlaid on them in white metal. Odd wing-shaped
devices hung from the ceiling supporting hundreds of candles. Their
polished steel facets reflected the light on to the mirrored walls. There
seemed to be tiny points of light everywhere they looked. Two long lines
of silent yellow-robed priests formed an avenue all the way down the
room. At the end of the avenue was another flight of steps. They were
covered with a white, thick-piled carpet. A flock of the pink-robed
acolytes were arranged decoratively around the foot of them. At the top
of the steps was a throne made of the same black stone as the walls. It was
piled deep in white cushions. Behind it was a huge peacock fan of
hammered steel. The blessed Joachim sat among the cushions.

The three travellers couldn't see the blessed one too well from the far
end of the room. The Minstrel Boy looked down at the priests. They still
had their foreheads pressed against the floor. He turned to Jeb Stuart Ho.

'Are we going to stand here for ever, or are we going to walk up there
and get ourselves an audience?'

'I suppose we should speak to him.'

He glanced at the Wanderer.

'What do you think?'

The Wanderer shrugged.

'Shit, let's go up there.'

They stepped over the kneeling priests, and began to walk slowly towards the throne. There was a strange tension slowly growing in the room. Three hard-bitten warriors had marched into a world of flimsy fantasy. The contrast created a charge in the air. Even Jeb Stuart Ho swaggered a little as they walked between the rows of priests.

They came closer to the throne. They started to be able to make out the features of the blessed Joachim. He sat among the cushions like a flabby buddha. He was fat to the point of obesity, with pale pink baby-like flesh. He was totally bald. His features were soft and indistinct, as though they were scarcely formed. His eyes were small, and of a pale watery blue.

'Are you the thtwangerth?'

He also lisped. The Minstrel Boy suppressed a grin. The giant production for this fat, lisping, overgrown child. He could hardly believe it. Jeb Stuart Ho, however, seemed to take the whole thing a little more seriously. He bowed formally.

'I am Jeb Stuart Ho, an executive of the brotherhood.'

The blessed Joachim nodded gravely.

'The bwotherhood, I thee.'

He waved a limp, pudgy hand towards the Minstrel Boy and the Wanderer.

'And who are thethe two?'

The Minstrel Boy grinned and nodded with uncouth friendliness.

'People call me the Minstrel Boy and him...'

He jerked his thumb at the Wanderer. 'They call him the Wanderer.'

'The Minthtwel Boy, the Wandewer. What kind of nameth are thethe?'

The Minstrel Boy put his foot on the second step and rested his elbow on his knee. He seemed set on acting out a kind of country-boy charade for the fat little pseudo-deity.

'Well, blessed Joachim, sir. I don't rightly know what kind of names those are, but they're the only ones we got.'

The blessed Joachim took some time to digest this information. He gestured to the nearest of the pink-robed devout. The man quickly scampered to his side and began mopping his bald head with a piece of silk.

'What do you people want here? Thith ith no plathe for tht-wangerth.'

The Minstrel Boy's grin broadened.

'Well, blessed Joachim, sir. I'll tell you. Him, that one...'

He nodded at Jeb Stuart Ho.

'... he came here looking for a woman, and me and the other one, we're just looking for a way out.'

Joachim looked scandalized.

'A woman? A way out?'

'That's all.'

'Thewe are no women here, and thertainly no way to leave Quahal.'

The idea flitted through the Wanderer's mind that maybe the reason the place was called Quahal was that the name could be pronounced correctly even with a lisp. He was about to speak, when Jeb Stuart Ho moved forward.

'If I might explain...'

The blessed Joachim was beginning to look petulant.

'Pleathe do. I do not like what I've heard tho far.'

'I am here on a mission of vital importance for the brotherhood. I am searching for one particular woman. The men with me have helped me track her to Quahal. We know the woman is somewhere in Quahal. It is my desire to find her, and theirs to return to where they came from.'

The Minstrel Boy glanced at Jeb Stuart Ho and then grinned at Joachim.

'He talks really concise and pretty, don't he?'

The blessed Joachim was silent. As Jeb Stuart Ho had been speaking, he'd appeared to sink down into his cushions. He sat staring at the executive in his black fighting suit and his array of weapons. He seemed almost to slip into a trance, but at the last moment he pulled out of it, and spoke.

'Thewe are no women in thith part of Quahal.'

Jeb Stuart Ho spread his hands.

'Then I must go to the mountain and find her.'

'If she went to the mountain she ith almotht thertainly dead. My thithter Alamada will have killed her.'

'I must still go and look for sure.'

Joachim beckoned to one of the yellow-robed priests, who approached the throne with lowered eyes. He and the blessed one muttered together for a while, and then he returned to his place in the line. Joachim turned his attention back to Jeb Stuart Ho.

'I have thome information that might help you. I keep the dwelling of my thithter under conthtant obthervation. She hath thome dithgutthting habith. It would appear that a woman hath awived at the village, and a fight hath taken plathe. I do not know if it wath my thithter or the woman you theek who pwevailed.'

Jeb Stuart Ho nodded. At last it seemed as though the end of his quest was in sight. He did his best to conceal his eagerness.

'If that is the case, I must go there at once.'

The blessed Joachim showed signs of relief.

'Go. I will pwovide you with a guide. You have my blething.'

Jeb Stuart Ho bowed, and turned on his heel. A priest joined him. Their exit from the room proved to be a little absurd. It appeared that the priests were forbidden to turn their backs on the blessed one. Ho observed no such niceties. He strode quickly towards the steel doors with the priest attempting to keep up with him walking backwards in a half crouch.

When Jeb Stuart Ho had gone, a pink-robed acolyte once more mopped Joachim's head with a silken cloth. The Minstrel Boy and the Wanderer looked at each other, and then at him.

'What about us?'

Joachim remained silent for almost a minute. Finally he shook his head.

'Thewe ith no way by which you can leave Quahal.'

The Minstrel Boy exploded.

'That's bullshit!'

'I beg your pardon.'

'With respect, that's bullshit.'

'I fail to underthtand.'

The Wanderer stepped in.

'There is a stuff receiver in the ziggurat. It would be very simple to order transport and stasis generators for us.'

As the Wanderer spoke, the entire room became noticeably agitated. Joachim made weak nervous gestures.

'No! No! Thethe thingth do not egthitht.'

The Wanderer began to get angry.

'Don't be ridiculous. Of course they do. There's got to be a giant system of generators keeping the whole of Quahal stable.'

Joachim's voice rose to a high-pitched shriek.

'Thith ith hewethy.'

The Wanderer shrugged.

'Suit yourself. You've still got to make up your mind what to do with us.'

'You will go back to your quarterth. I will conthider the pwoblem.'

The Minstrel Boy pushed back his coat, and planted his hands on his hips. His belt of knives was in full view of the blessed Joachim.

'Don't take too long about it, will you?'

24

Before they moved out for the attack on the valley, AA Catto insisted on reviewing her troops like a warrior queen in an ancient movie. It was an uncomfortable performance as far as Billy, Reave and Nancy were concerned. By the late morning, the mountain mist had turned to a heavy drizzle and the ground around the village was rapidly being churned to mud under the horses' hooves. Billy sat uncomfortably on a large black horse. He had never ridden a horse before, and the experience unnerved him. The damp was slowly soaking into the heavy fur poncho that was wrapped around him. Under it he still wore the pimp suit from Litz. He could have changed into the same garb as the horsemen wore, but he was reluctant to go that native. He felt it identified him too strongly as AA Catto's subject and property.

Reave had had no such reservations. He sat beside Billy arrayed exactly like any of the horsemen, except that he didn't carry one of the long slender spears. Nancy had also changed to the native garb. AA Catto had given her second pick on the ex-queen's wardrobe.

The three of them sat on their mounts facing a line of fifty or more horsemen. In the space between, AA Catto trotted her horse up and down, haranguing her army in what Billy supposed she thought was a suitably regal and inspiring manner.

The horsemen sat very still, gripping their spears, in a perfect line. Billy wondered what they thought about the changes that AA Catto had made in their lives. Billy looked down the line. Their impassive faces were almost totally hidden, as well hidden as their minds. Billy had had a number of theories about the horsemen. The first had been that they were chronically stupid. But their physical coordination and prowess with weapons and horses seemed to negate that idea. Billy had wondered, from the way they rarely spoke, and used gestures to convey quite complex ideas, if they might be low-level telepaths. Currently Billy entertained the idea that they could be highly intelligent, but with that intelligence totally straitjacketed by conditioning and genetic tailoring. It was the best theory so far, but he was by no means certain about it.

AA Catto at long last completed her address to her loyal troops. Billy had managed to avoid hearing most of the monologue. As the horsemen formed themselves into a column of two, Billy wondered idly if she had managed to work in anything about her having the body of a frail and feeble woman, but the heart and stomach of a man. He knew it wasn't beyond her.

The column started out of the village and down the mountainside. Four horsemen preceded it, then came AA Catto and Nancy riding side by side. Behind them rode Billy and Reave, followed by the remainder of the force. Billy had no clue how the horsemen found their way in the thick fog, but the column seemed to wind down the slope in such a positive manner that he didn't doubt they were going in the right direction.

Despite the foul weather AA Catto and Nancy chattered together all through the ride. Billy and Reave, on the other hand, rode in damp, sullen silence. The situation seemed to have escalated to such a point that there was nothing left for them to say.

They finally broke out of the mist into the sunshine at the base of the slope. The ziggurat was in front of them in the valley. The column halted. AA Catto raised her hand and the ranks divided, each horseman peeling off neatly in turn until they formed a single line abreast. They sat silently for a while. Billy gazed down at the ziggurat. He could see tiny figures moving backwards and forwards on the various levels of the building and working in the fields. It was hard to believe that within the next few minutes they were to be slaughtered.

AA Catto leaned across and muttered something to the horseman next to her. He made a series of signals with his left hand. Except for Nancy, Billy, Reave, AA Catto and three horsemen on either side of them, the whole line began to move forward at a slow even walk. After about a hundred metres, another signal was given, and the line of horsemen accelerated to a trot. When they'd covered the same distance again, they broke into a controlled canter. They lowered their spears.

When the line was a matter of some two hundred metres from the ziggurat, a wild cry went up and they broke into a gallop. They thundered towards the huge black structure. Some of the blue-robed priests saw them, and began to run for the safety of the building.

The line split in two. Half the force wheeled round and swept across the fields, riding down the workers as they went. The remainder raced towards the ziggurat. When they were only a few metres from the walls, they abruptly lowered their spears and dug the tips into the ground. Their forward momentum jerked the horsemen from their saddles. Almost as one they soared into the air, holding their spears like pole vaulters. They landed lightly on the first tier of the ziggurat, dropped their spears and pulled out their knives. They moved forward in a rush and fell on Joachim's followers, hacking and slaying like machines. Billy glanced round at Reave.

'Did you see that manoeuvre?'

Reave nodded.

'I wouldn't have believed it if I hadn't seen it myself.'

AA Catto turned to the others. 'It's time we moved down there.'

Billy scowled.

'Don't want to miss being in for the kill?'

AA Catto ignored him, kicked her horse and went down the slope at a swift canter. Nancy and the horsemen kept pace with her, while Billy and Reave trailed behind.

By the time they reached the ziggurat, the workers in the fields had either been killed or chased inside the building. The majority of horsemen had also moved inside, although a few still stalked Joachim's men on the outside upper levels. AA Catto halted in front of the building and looked round, surveying the carnage. She dismounted and walked towards the nearest set of steps. Billy quickly rode up beside her.

'Are you really going to kill everyone?'

She looked up at him in surprise.

'Of course. That was the point of the whole operation.'

'Couldn't you call it off and let the survivors go? They can't cause you any trouble. They aren't even offering your horsemen any resistance.'

AA Catto stared at Billy with contempt.

'Don't be ridiculous. They have to be exterminated.'

'Why?'

AA Catto didn't bother no answer him. She began to climb the steps to the first level. Billy yelled after her.

'You're insane! You hear me? You're crazy!'

AA Catto continued to walk up the stairs. She pretended not to hear him. Reave reined in beside Billy.

'You won't achieve anything by yelling at her.'

'There's got to be some way to get her to stop this whole thing.'

Reave shook his head with an air of finality.

'There's no way.'

'What makes you so sure?'

'I lived with her for all that time, didn't I? She sees herself as some kind of female Attila and nothing we can do will change it. It'll probably get worse before she finds a new game.'

'How can you be so calm about it?'

'It ain't me that she wants to exterminate.

'So what do we do?'

Reave started to dismount.

'Just keep out of sight and hope she doesn't turn against us.'

Billy sighed and swung himself to the ground.

'I suppose you're right.'

They began no climb the steps up to the upper levels. They had to pick their way between the sprawled, lifeless bodies of Joachim's followers. The sound of screaming drifted down from above them. It seemed as though the survivors were retreating to the top of the ziggurat.

Billy and Reave continued to climb slowly. Occasionally they'd see a few of the blue-robed priests pursued by knife-wielding horsemen across one of the ornamental terraces. Bodies floated in the pools formed by the artificial stream that cascaded down the ziggurat from level to level. They went on cautiously climbing, doing their best to avoid the killing.

They were about two thirds of the way up the building, and standing at the foot of a long ramp that traversed two levels. The screams had died down a little. Suddenly two figures appeared at the top of the ramp, and started desperately running down it. They weren't like the other followers of Joachim. One was an old man in a kind of white smock. The other was a thin figure in a black frock coat and wide-brimmed hat.

Four horsemen appeared at the top of the ramp. They had knives in their hands and were obviously chasing the two figures. One of the horsemen took one of a set of weighted thongs from his belt. Without breaking step he swung it, and let go. The device curled round the old man's legs. He fell, and rolled helplessly down the ramp. His companion stopped and turned. His hand flashed to his belt, whipped something out, and threw it. One of the horsemen clutched at his throat and fell. He too rolled down the ramp. Recognition dawned on Billy. He spun round and grabbed Reave by the arm.

'It's the Minstrel Boy!'

The Minstrel Boy was bending over the older man, tugging at the thongs that were wound round his legs. The horsemen were racing down the ramp towards him. Billy started running up to head them off. Reave reluctantly followed him. Billy had gone only a couple of paces when he realized that the horsemen would reach the Minstrel Boy before him. He threw the fur cape off his shoulders and pulled out his gun. One of the horsemen was in the act of swinging his knife at the Minstrel Boy. Billy fired. The horseman tottered backwards, and plunged over the side of the ramp.

Billy fired twice more and the other two fell to the ground. One rolled almost the length of the ramp before coming to rest at Reave's feet. Billy hurried across to where the Minstrel Boy was helping the old man to his feet.

'Are you all right?'

The Minstrel Boy dusted himself down.

'Yeah, but we gotta get the fuck out of here. These crazy barbarians are killing everyone.'

Billy scratched his ear.

'I think you'll be all right with us.'

The Minstrel Boy was on his knees pulling his throwing knife out of the horseman's throat. He looked up incredulously at Billy.

'You mean you're with these people?'

'Kind of.'

The Minstrel Boy stuck the knife back in his belt.

'Why, for chrissakes?'

'It's AA Catto. She's taken over this whole tribe. She's gone a little mad.'

The Minstrel Boy pushed back his hat.

'Godzilla motherfucker!'

Before Billy could explain any further, AA Catto herself appeared at the top of the ramp.

'What's going on here? I heard shots.'

She saw the dead horsemen and hurried down the ramp, followed by Nancy and an escort of horsemen. Her face was dark with anger.

'Who killed my men?'

She jabbed her finger at Billy.

'Did you do this?'

'I had to.'

'What do you mean, you had to?'

Billy pointed to the Minstrel Boy and the Wanderer.

'These people are my friends. Your men were going to kill them. I had to stop them.'

'So you shot them?'

'There was no alternative.'

AA Catto swung round to face the Minstrel Boy.

'Don't I know you?'

The Minstrel Boy scowled.

'You ought to. You had me tied up in your hotel room for long enough.'

AA Catto's eyes narrowed.

'Of course. You're the one. You were with him. The one that was trying to murder me.'

She turned to her escort.

'Kill him.'

The guards moved towards the Minstrel Boy. He backed away holding up his hands.

'Wait a goddamn minute, will you! You'll find out you're making a big mistake if you kill me.'

AA Catto looked dubious, but motioned to the horsemen to stop.

'What mistake?'

'I'm here, so doesn't in occur to you that Jeb Stuart Ho might be here as well?'

AA Catto looked a little alarmed.

'The assassin? He's here? Where is he?'

'Guarantee you'll let me and my buddy here live, and I'll tell you.'

AA Catto almost spat at him.

'Guarantee nothing. Tell me, or I'll have it tortured out of you.'

The Minstrel Boy glanced at the Wanderer and then gave in.

'He's here all right. He's gone up the mountain, looking for you.'

AA Catto nodded.

'That's all I need to know. Now I can have you killed.'

The Minstrel Boy talked very fast.

'It'd still be a mistake.'

'You think so?'

'Sure, after all, we know Ho. We could help you get him.'

AA Catto wasn't impressed.

'I'll send a squad of my horsemen after him. They'll be quite able to deal with him. Your help won't be needed.'

'We've got a lot of other talents. I mean, you'll probably want to switch off the globes and get the stuff receiver working. The Wanderer here, him and me can handle them kind of things.'

AA Catto turned to the Wanderer.

'Is this true?'

'What we don't know about stuff receivers ain't worth knowing.'

The Minstrel Boy smiled ingratiatingly.

'I can be pretty useful in my own way. Didn't I get you that airship back in Litz?'

AA Catto still looked doubtful. Then she made up her mind.

'I'll let you live until my men come back with the assassin's body. Then I'll decide what to do with you.'

The Minstrel Boy let out a sigh of relief.

'We're right grateful to you, ma'am.'

AA Catto started to walk away, giving instructions for the hunting of Jeb Stuart Ho. Abruptly she stopped and looked back at Billy.

'I'm holding you responsible for these friends of yours. Whatever their fate is, you'll share it.'

She turned and walked away with her men.

25

The blue-robed priest made his way carefully up the mist-shrouded mountainside with Jeb Stuart Ho close behind him. They threaded their way between the outcrops of rocks and stunted bushes. A primitive hunter's instinct was getting a grip on Jeb Stuart Ho. Now he was so close to his quarry he could feel a dangerous excitement building up inside him. He was impatient to complete his task. His hand went to the hilt of his sword and caressed it briefly. He found himself imagining the swift blow that would dispatch AA Catto. He was surprised at the vividness of the vision.

The priest halted and peered into the mist. Jeb Stuart Ho moved up and crouched beside him.

'Are we near the village?'

'We are very close. I am surprised we do not hear any sounds of life.'

They moved cautiously forward, halting every few metres. There was absolute silence under the blanket of fog. The priest started to become uneasy.

'I pray I haven't made some error. We should be right at the village, and yet we hear nothing.'

They went on creeping across the damp landscape. The dark shape of some kind of building loomed out of the mist. Jeb Stuart Ho touched the young priest's arm.

'This surely must be part of the village.'

The priest nodded.

'It is, but I cannot understand the silence.'

Jeb Stuart Ho drew his sword.

'You wait here. I'll go in and investigate.'

'You do not want me to come with you?'

Jeb Stuart Ho shook his head.

'There may be fighting. You must wait here. I'll need you to guide me back to the ziggurat.'

The priest sank down on to the damp grass, and Jeb Stuart Ho moved cautiously forward. With his sword gripped tightly in his hand, he approached the first hut. There was still no sound or movement. He located the door. It was made of solid wood, and closed. He pressed his ear to it. Nothing. He took a step back. At least in this place he didn't have to worry about lasers or projectile weapons. He launched himself at the door. It burst open. He dropped into a crouch as he hit the middle of the hut, and turned on the balls of his feet, his sword stuck straight out in front of him.

There was nobody in the hut. It contained two narrow beds, a chest, a couple of crude wall hangings, but no people. He moved on to the next one, and found that that too was deserted. He broke into hut after hut, but they were all empty. In a larger building that dominated the village he discovered the last, faintly warm embers of a log fire. This finally convinced him. The inhabitants of the village had all, for some reason, left. If AA Catto was still alive she had apparently been taken with them. Jeb Stuart Ho hurried back to where the priest was waiting for him.

'They have all gone.'

The priest nodded.

'I discovered the same fact.'

Jeb Stuart Ho looked at him in surprise. 'You did?'

'I scouted a little, while you were in the village. I found the fresh tracks of many horses, leading away from here.'

The priest led Jeb Stuart Ho to the line of tracks. They could hardly be missed. The ground was soft and muddy, and had been churned up by dozens of sets of hooves. They formed an unmistakable trail down the mountainside. Jeb Stuart Ho and the priest walked beside it in silence for a long time. The priest seemed more and more thoughtful. Finally Jeb Stuart Ho pressed him as to what was wrong.

'Is something troubling you?'

'I am puzzled.'

'By what?'

'I could be mistaken, but they appear to be leading in the direction of the ziggurat.'

'Why should the whole village come down from the mountain?'

The priest looked troubled.

'That is the mystery. It has never happened before.'

'You believe something is wrong?'

'I don't know. The horsemen are wild and violent. They would not be happy in the valley. However, we will soon be out of the fog and we will be able to see more clearly.'

As the priest predicted they very soon emerged from the oppressive fog and out on to the clear lower slopes. The sky was reddening into a perfectly programmed sunset. The ziggurat cast a long shadow across the valley. It was a scene of peace and tranquillity. The priest stopped for a moment, and stared carefully at his home. Jeb Stuart Ho looked at him questioningly.

'Is all well?'

The priest continued to stare at the ziggurat.

'I think so, although there is a certain lack of movement.'

'Maybe they have all gone inside. Could it be that the horsemen have requested some kind of meeting?'

The priest frowned.

'I cannot tell. It is beyond my knowledge. They have never before left the mountain.'

Jeb Stuart Ho looked at the ground in front of them.

'Their tracks certainly lead to the ziggurat.'

The priest nodded.

'That is what makes it so strange.'

'All we can do is go there and find out. The man who learns is the man who seeks knowledge. The successful hunter is not the one who waits for his quarry to pay him a visit.'

The priest looked at him in confusion.

'I'm sorry, I do not understand.'

'It is merely a saying.'

They started to walk down the slope. They had not gone very far when a group of mounted figures detached themselves from the shadow of the building and began coming up the slope towards them. Jeb Stuart Ho stopped. As the horsemen drew nearer, he saw that they wore rudimentary armour and carried long lances. His hand went instinctively to the hilt of his sword. The priest, however, didn't share his caution. He smiled at Jeb Stuart Ho.

'Now maybe we will find out what has come to pass.'

Before Ho could stop him, the young man was hurrying down the mountainside to meet the group of riders. He ran towards them waving his arms. For a moment Jeb Stuart Ho thought that his suspicions had been unfounded. He was about to follow the priest when the leading rider lowered his spear and neatly skewered the unfortunate priest. As his dying scream faded away, Jeb Stuart Ho whipped out his sword and fell into a defensive crouch.

The horsemen made high-pitched eerie cries and came at him. There were seven of them in all. He knew that despite his almost certainly superior fighting skills he would be hard-pressed to overcome seven mounted warriors. One was some way ahead of the others. He came straight at Ho, crouched over his lance. Ho saw an advantage in that the rider apparently expected no resistance. Ho dropped his sword and stood very still. The tip of the lance, with the full weight of man and beast behind it, came straight at his chest. At the last minute, he turned from the hips. The lance missed him by a hand's breadth. He grasped the weapon with both hands and jerked with all his strength. The rider tumbled from his saddle. Before he could get to his feet Jeb Stuart Ho kicked him hard between the eyes, driving the bridge of his nose up into his skull. The man died without a sound, and Ho turned to face the next of his attackers.

Two of them came at him side by side, with a third slightly behind. Ho dropped to the ground so the lances went over his head, then he snapped back up again as the horses thundered past on either side of him. He grasped each man's nearest foot and pushed upwards, effectively unseating them. The third one was almost on him. Jeb Stuart Ho launched himself into space. His outstretched foot caught the man under the armpit, and they hit the ground in a tangle of arms and legs. Ho was the first on his feet, and he quickly dispatched the man by stamping down hard on his throat.

The two he had unseated were now dancing towards him with drawn knives. The three more who were still on their horses had overshot, and were wheeling round for another attack. Jeb Stuart Ho was some distance from where his sword lay, and he began edging towards it. One of the men he'd thrown to the ground sprang at him in a balletic leap, swinging his long knife in a wide arc. Ho twisted sideways and the knife missed his face by the merest fraction. He caught the horseman off balance and jerked his wrist downwards, at the same time bringing up his knee under the man's arm. There was a sharp crack as the arm broke. The horseman screamed and staggered away.

One of the mounted warriors swung a set of weighted thongs at Ho. Ho caught one of the weights with his left hand, and hurled them at the nearest attacker on foot. The thongs wrapped themselves around his chest, pinning his knife arm to his side. Jeb Stuart Ho seized his own sword and slashed at the pinioned horseman's neck.

That left three still coming at him, and they were all mounted. They thundered down on him in a tight group. Three lances were directed at him. Jeb Stuart Ho dropped into a crouch, and jumped. His feet struck the middle rider in the chest, and as he hit the ground Ho stabbed the point of his sword up under the man's chin. That left two.

They swung round, jumped from their horses and hit the ground running. Their knives were in their hands. Jeb Stuart Ho shook one of his own knives free from the sheath on his arm, and threw it underarm at one of the horsemen. It struck him just below the right eye. The handle stuck out through the eye hole of his helmet.

It was just one on one. The last horseman slashed at Jeb Stuart Ho with his heavy leaf-bladed knife. Ho parried and backed off a step. The horseman pressed home his attack. Ho continued to duck and parry. He thrust at the horseman but his blow was turned to the side. The horseman was good, but he had little chance against the long, two-handed sword. Ho made the point dance in a lightning triple manoeuvre, and the knife flew from the horseman's hand. The rider stood still and resigned as Jeb Stuart Ho ran his sword into his chest.

Ho put his foot on the horseman's body and wrenched out the sword. He looked round for the surviving attacker whose arm he had broken. It was rapidly getting dark. The man was some distance away, limping quickly towards the ziggurat. Jeb Stuart Ho wiped his sword and carefully put it away. He let his arms fall limply at his side and squatted down on his haunches. He allowed the tension of the fight to drain out of him. If nothing else, it had demonstrated where he would find AA Catto, even if it had cost six lives to do it. Ho sat and stared at the huge black building and pondered his next move.

26

'Seven of you? He defeated seven of you? Single-handed?' AA Catto looked as though she was going to burst. The single horseman who had escaped from the fight with Jeb Stuart Ho stood rigidly in front of what had once been the blessed Joachim's throne. AA Catto now sat bolt upright amid the white cushions. The carpet at her feet was stained with blood. The horseman's broken arm dangled useless at his side. His face was impassive.

'You realize that this means the assassin is still loose. It means that I'm still in danger. This is intolerable.'

Nancy moved to AA Catto's side.

'He won't be able to get at you here, surrounded by your own army.

AA Catto's jaw muscles clenched spasmodically.

'He took out seven of them, didn't he? And anyway, while he's alive how can I relax? How can I find any sort of peace while he's running around looking for ways to kill me?'

'You could send out more men to get him.'

AA Catto shook her head.

'That's not good enough. He can fight the horsemen. I've got to find a way so I can be sure. He's got to be killed.'

AA Catto slumped back into the cushions of the throne. She lay hunched up, preoccupied and deep in thought. Nancy nervously examined her fingernails. AA Catto looked as though she was building up for some sort of outburst. Ever since the taking of the ziggurat her bouts of hysterical temper had been getting more and more violent. Abruptly she sat up and gestured imperiously at her escort.

'Fetch Billy Oblivion and his so-called friends.'

Nancy looked at her in surprise.

'What do you want them for?'

'They claimed they could help me when they were begging me to let them live. Now's the time for them to prove it. If they can come up with a way to get the assassin they can live. If they can't then I'll have them killed.'

Three of the escort marched smartly out of the throne room. The survivor of the fight still stood stiffly in front of the throne. He had turned very pale, and was swaying slightly. Nancy touched AA Catto gently on the arm. She pointed to the injured man.

'What are we going to do about him?'

'What do you mean, do about him?'

'Shouldn't he have treatment or something?'

'Don't be ridiculous.'

'But he's obviously in pain.'

AA Catto looked at Nancy in surprise.

'He's no more use to me.'

She waved to the escort again.

'Take him out and kill him.'

Nancy didn't say anything as the wounded horseman walked stiffly away surrounded by three of the escort. She noted that 'kill' seemed to be AA Catto's favourite word of the moment. Nancy didn't want to take any chances. AA Catto sat tapping her fingernails until Billy, Reave, the Minstrel Boy and the Wanderer were brought in.

The Minstrel Boy looked round carefully as they were marched down the long throne room. The place was crowded with horsemen. They smelled strongly of sweat and leather. A lot of the fittings had been smashed, and most of the candles had been extinguished except for one set that threw light down on the throne. They reached the foot of the steps and halted. AA Catto stared at them for a long time without speaking. Billy began to think that, somehow, her eyes were becoming more and more like those of a poisonous snake. He shifted uncomfortably from one foot to the other.

'You sent for us?'

'The assassin is still alive.'

Billy glanced round at the others. They all tried to avoid his eyes. He turned back to AA Catto.

'What exactly are we supposed to do about it? He could take on all four of us with one hand.'

'I want you to devise a foolproof method of getting rid of him. You told me how skilled and talented your little friends are. Now is the time to put it to the test.'

The Minstrel Boy moved up beside Billy.

'What happens if we can't come up with a scheme to kill him?'

AA Catto smiled sweetly at him.

'Then you lied to me when you were pleading for your life. I shall have to have you killed, all of you.'

Billy's jaw dropped.

'All of us? Me and Reave as well?'

'Of course. You vouched for these people.'

The Minstrel Boy laughed grimly. 'Looks like we're all in the same boat.'

'What do we do about it?'

The Minstrel Boy shrugged.

'Don't ask me. Those hoods in Litz couldn't stop him and neither could this bunch. I don't honestly see what we can do.'

Reave scowled.

'The only thing that could stop Ho would be a few more like him.'

The Minstrel Boy suddenly grinned. He looked as though the light had dawned.

'That's the answer.'

'What is?'

'Get some more like him, and let them take him out.'

Billy looked doubtful.

'How the fuck do we get more like him? Send out to the brother-hood?'

The Minstrel Boy shot the Wanderer a sideways glance.

'We could get them from Stuff Central.'

The Wanderer raised a bushy eyebrow.

'You won't find any brotherhood executives in the stuff catalogue. The best you can get from that would be a Deluxe All Purpose Trooper, and a squad of them would be just as useless as the horsemen.'

'You could get a custom job.'

The Wanderer shook his head. 'You'd need specifications.'

The Minstrel Boy grinned pointedly at him.

'We could get them.'

'Detailed specs?'

'We could get them, couldn't we, old man?'

The Wanderer held up his hand and quickly shook his head.

'No. No way. I'm not going to do it.'

The Minstrel Boy stared hard at him.

'You're going to have to, otherwise the lady's going to butcher the lot of us.'

'I don't like it.'

'You don't have to like it. You just have to do it.'

Billy looked from one to the other in bewilderment.

'What are you two talking about?'

'Getting us some more like Ho to deal with him.'

'How do you do that?'

'We get Stuff Central to do a custom job from our specifications.'

'How do we get those?'

'The old man can get them, can't you, old man?'

The Wanderer didn't answer. The Minstrel Boy moved closer to him.

'You can, can't you, old man?'

The Wanderer looked at the ground. He hesitated and then spoke reluctantly.

'I can do it. I can form a mind link with Ho, and all the information can be fed out of my brain into the request console of the stuff receiver. Once the data's in the pattern bank we can have as many replicas of Jeb Stuart Ho as we want. Only they'll be programmed to do exactly what they're told.'

A look of relief came over Billy's face.

'We're out of trouble then?'

The Wanderer nodded wearily.

'Yeah, we're out of trouble.'

'What's wrong?'

The Minstrel Boy grinned nastily.

'The old man's not too keen on the mind link bit.'

The Wanderer growled at him.

'Just get off my back, will you. I said I'd do it.'

The Minstrel Boy didn't stop.

'The mind link doesn't go away once it's started. If Jeb Stuart Ho dies, the Wanderer will experience it too. It could hurt.'

The Wanderer grunted.

'It will hurt.'

AA Catto interrupted any further discussion.

'What are you all talking about?'

The Minstrel Boy turned to face her.

'We've come up with the answer. We'll need to use the stuff receiver. Have your men found it yet?'

'They've located it.'

'We might as well get on with it, then.'

AA Catto became suspicious. 'Are you sure this isn't some kind of trick?'

'Of course it ain't no trick.'

'How can I be sure of that?'

The Minstrel Boy began to get exasperated.

'You can't be sure. You'll have to trust us. It's our lives that are on the line. You think we're going to deliberately fuck up?'

'I still don't like it.'

'You got a better idea?'

AA Catto's face flushed dangerously. 'Your manners aren't all they could be.'

The Minstrel Boy had the sense to back-pedal. 'Okay, I'm sorry, but there's no other way.'

AA Catto thought for a moment. She directed her attention to Billy. 'Have you still got your gun?'

Billy looked round nervously. 'Yeah... I've got it.'

'Give it to me.'

Billy hesitated. AA Catto held out her hand.

'Give it to me.'

Reluctantly Billy handed it over. AA Catto checked that it was loaded, and then pointed it at the four of them.

'I'll take you to the receiver room and you can start work. I'll be watching you all the time. If I see anything I don't like, I'll shoot. You understand?'

The Minstrel Boy nodded.

'We understand.'

AA Catto descended from the late Joachim's throne and led them through a small door at the side of the hall. It was like stepping into another age. The room was filled with gleaming technology. The Minstrel Boy gazed round with what almost amounted to awe.

'Goddamn! Civilization. I thought I'd never see it again.'

The Wanderer went sullenly to the control console.

'Let's get to it.

The Minstrel Boy immediately assumed control. He took off his coat and tossed it in a corner.

'First thing we got to do is deactivate the globes.'

The Wanderer sat down in the chair in front of the console. He searched the board for the unit that controlled the globes.

'Got it.'

'Can you ground them?'

'I think so.'

The Wanderer punched a sequence of buttons. A number of coloured lights went out.

'The globes are dead.'

AA Catto stood in the doorway, covering them with the gun. The Minstrel Boy moved up beside the Wanderer, partly to get a better view and partly to put as much of the old man as he could between himself and AA Catto. When it came to his own safety, the Minstrel Boy had no scruples.

'The next thing we have to do is to order up a direct data helmet.'

The Wanderer inspected the board.

'That won't be so easy. There's a selector block hooked into this rig.'

'Can you switch it off?'

The Wanderer shook his head.

'Negative. There's a lock on it.'

'I'll have to short it out.'

The Minstrel Boy pulled out one of his knives, and squatted on the floor. He prised open one of the inspection panels in the front of the console. He was just about to put his hand inside when AA Catto took a step forward.

'What are you doing?'

The Minstrel Boy found himself looking down the barrel of her gun. He straightened up.

'There's a block on the controls that stops anyone ordering things that didn't fit in with Joachim's and Alamada's ideas of the simple life. If we want anything but nuts, berries and new horsemen, I have to fix some kind of bypass. Okay? Can I go on with what I'm doing?'

AA Catto still looked doubtful.

'Are you sure you know what you are doing?'

The Minstrel Boy became impatient.

'Listen, lady, I've been hot-wiring receivers since I was a little kid. Just let me get on with it.'

AA Catto backed away, and the Minstrel Boy crawled half inside the console. After a couple of minutes he emerged grinning.

'That should do it. Order up that helmet.'

The Wanderer stabbed at the buttons. Rows of lights flickered into life. There was a faint hum from the cage that actually received the ordered goods. After about a minute, the cage flickered briefly with cold light and a white plastic hemisphere appeared. A number of coiled leads were attached to it, and an instruction booklet lay beside it on the floor of the cage. Billy reached in and lifted it out. AA Catto looked at the helmet questioningly.

'What is that thing?'

'It's a direct data helmet. It's a device that enables the old man to relay the specifications on Ho without having to verbalize them and then translate them into a selection sequence.'

He fitted the helmet on to the Wanderer's head, although he left the leads unattached and dangling. He slapped the old man on the shoulder.

'Okay buddy. Find our man.'

The Wanderer sighed and shut his eyes. The Minstrel Boy motioned to Billy and Reave.

'You two better hold his arms down on the chair. He's liable to thrash about a bit while he's making contact.'

Billy and Reave did as they were instructed. The Wanderer began to twitch slightly, and sweat stood out on his forehead. The twitching gradually built up until his body was racked by violent convulsive jerks. Billy and Reave had to use all their strength to hold him down. Suddenly his muscles seemed to lock in one huge spasm. His back arched and sweat poured down his face. Then it passed. The Wanderer collapsed back in the chair. His mouth opened and closed. He licked his lips.

'I've got him.'

His voice was a strained croak. The Minstrel Boy grabbed the ends of the helmet leads and banged them into input sockets on the control board.

'Feed the data, old man.'

The lights on the console began to blink rapidly.

The Minstrel Boy picked up his coat.

'We should have something down the beam quite soon.'

Billy and Reave stepped away from the Wanderer. He was quite passive now. Billy glanced at the Minstrel Boy.

'Won't Ho notice the mind link?'

The Minstrel Boy shook his head.

'He'll probably feel a bit strange, but the odds are that he won't realize what's happening.'

'How long do we have to wait before the first of the replicas comes through?'

'Shouldn't take Stuff Central more than a few minutes to tailor up the first one.'

The Minstrel Boy removed the helmet from the Wanderer. The old man seemed totally drained. If it hadn't been for his shallow breathing, Billy would have assumed he was dead.

They waited. The waiting was almost intolerable. Billy was constantly aware of AA Catto standing in the doorway holding the gun. He wondered if she'd keep her bargain and let them live once she had what she wanted. She was just as likely to kill them all.

For a while it seemed as though nothing was going to happen, then the cage glowed and Jeb Stuart Ho materialized inside it. The likeness was so complete that Billy and Reave started to back away. AA Catto raised her gun. Only the Minstrel Boy held his ground. He turned to AA Catto and laughed.

'Come and talk to your new subject.'

He turned to the Ho replica.

'Are you willing to accept our orders?'

The Ho replica bowed.

'Of course. That is my programming.'

'There you are, Miss Catto. He's all yours.'

The Minstrel Boy moved to the console.

'How many of these do you want to start with?'

'Six should be enough. But leave the selection set up. I will certainly want more.'

The Minstrel Boy punched more buttons, and more Ho replicas began to arrive down the stuff beam in quick succession. Billy noticed that they carried all Jeb Stuart Ho's equipment including the pistol and portapac. AA Catto was like a child with a new toy. She ran her hands over the fabric of their black fighting suits.

'They're lovely.'

She seemed to have forgotten all about her threats to kill the four men. She moved from one Ho replica to the next with an expression of delight. While her attention was diverted, the Wanderer opened his eyes, and rose slowly from the chair. He moved silently towards the door and quickly slipped away. AA Catto didn't seem to notice his absence. She beamed at the six Ho replicas.

'All we have to do now is send them after the assassin. He doesn't have a chance against six exact copies of himself.'

27

Jeb Stuart Ho slowly rose from his crouching position on the hillside above the ziggurat. For a while a strange sickness had gripped him, but it seemed to have passed. It disturbed him in so far as he could find no logical reason for it. He flexed his cramped muscles. He had wasted enough time. He must start for the ziggurat and complete his task. He could see no way apart from going directly to the ziggurat, finding AA Catto and killing her. There was no room for subtleties.

It was dark, and therefore the approach to the ziggurat would be comparatively simple. Once inside, his main problem would be to avoid the horsemen. He knew that they wouldn't be able to stop him, but if he was forced to fight with a number of them, he could be delayed for long enough to give AA Catto time to flee. That was what had happened in Litz, and he didn't intend it to happen here.

He started down the slope towards the black building. He moved slowly and carefully, making no sound. He stopped every now and then to listen for the noise of any patrol that might be moving around. He had only gone about halfway when he saw lights emerge from one of the ground-level entrances and start to move up the hillside. Jeb Stuart Ho sank down on to the grass and watched them come towards him. After a while, he could make out details. There were six men, in form-fitting black suits. They carried burning torches and appeared to be searching the ground for something.

Jeb Stuart Ho held his position and let the six men come nearer. As he was able to see them more clearly he could scarcely believe his eyes. In front of him were six of his brother executives in black fighting suits and carrying full equipment. He couldn't understand how they had arrived in Quahal, or how they had managed to keep the guns and portapacs that hung from their belts. They were a mysterious but welcome sight. Seven of the brotherhood would have no trouble dispatching AA Catto. He hesitated for a fraction of a second, and then stood up.

'My brothers?'

The torches were instantly extinguished. Jeb Stuart Ho was surprised. It wasn't the reaction he had expected.

'My brothers. It is Jeb Stuart Ho.'

There was silence, then a whisper floated across the hillside. It was very clear.

'That is him. That is the subject.'

A shot rang out, and a bullet hummed close to Jeb Stuart Ho. Someone had obviously fired in the direction of the sound of his voice. He started backing away. His mind whirled. He couldn't understand it. Who were these people? Could AA Catto have enlisted the aid of some kind of renegades from the brotherhood? Did such people exist? In the dim skyshine he could see the six figures fanning out and moving up towards him. He quickly retreated.

The sky over the mountain was growing lighter, as though an artificial moon was about to rise. Jeb Stuart Ho knew that if that happened he would present an easy target. He knew that if these men had similar fighting skills to his, he couldn't survive a direct confrontation.

The mist seemed to be his best bet. Once inside its concealing folds he could evade these hunters, or even, if he was lucky, pick them off one by one in sneak attacks. He turned on his heel and started to run. Another shot buzzed over his head. He fell into the unique pattern of yogic running that had been perfected by the teachers of the brotherhood. It enabled him to move at speeds far in excess of anything ordinary untrained humans were capable of.

A thin crescent of moon edged over the mountain. Jeb Stuart Ho glanced back as he ran. The pursuers were behind him, but they seemed to be keeping pace. They obviously had the same training. He reached the edge of the layer of mist and plunged into it. He saw an outcrop of rocks and ran towards them. It seemed an ideal vantage point to watch for the arrival of his hunters. He threw himself down behind the rocks, controlled his breathing, and lay still. He watched and waited.

The six came cautiously through the mist with swords and pistols in their hands. Five went straight past him, some distance to his right, and were swallowed up by the mist. The sixth was moving in a direction that would bring him right by the rocks where Jeb Stuart Ho lay. He silently drew his sword, and pressed himself flat on the ground. The man was just on the other side of the rocks. Jeb Stuart Ho waited for the right moment. His adversary came round the rocks. Jeb Stuart Ho struck. The sword went up through the man's stomach and into his lung. He died without a sound.

The body had fallen face down. Jeb Stuart Ho bent over it to remove the portapac and the gun. He rolled it over. Even in the darkness there could be no mistake. He found himself looking at his own face. The shock was immense. For a moment his mind was jolted off balance. Then he got a grip on himself. Somehow, AA Catto had managed to duplicate him. He knew it was possible, but he didn't know how it had been accomplished. He examined the corpse's arm. There was even a wound exactly like the one he'd received in the Leader Hotel. He realized that he was fighting six identical versions of himself.

An idea struck him. The very fact that he and his hunters were identical gave him a chance to outwit them, and complete his mission. He quickly stripped the body of its gun, its portapac and its nanchuk. He replaced the throwing knives that he had lost. When he had a full complement of equipment, he stood up. It would now be impossible for anyone to tell whether he was the real Jeb Stuart Ho that was being hunted, or one of the Ho replicas who were doing the hunting. He walked swiftly into the mist, looking for the other duplicates.

He didn't have to search for long. He'd only been walking for a short while when he heard voices. He moved towards them. Three of the Ho replicas had gathered together and were debating their next move like novices on a training exercise. As Jeb Stuart Ho walked out of the mist, they swung round and trained their guns on him. Then they saw his own gun and portapac, and they relaxed. Jeb Stuart Ho looked from one to the other.

'You have failed to find him?'

He had to fight to control his voice. Being face to face with three of himself was still a powerful shock. The replicas shook their heads.

'He has obviously gone to ground in the mist.'

'It is the logical answer.'

'Should we spread our search?'

Jeb Stuart Ho took a chance.

'We could return to the ziggurat, and resume our search at day-break. Our task would be made easy if we had horsemen to act as beaters.'

None of the three seemed to find anything wrong with his sugges-tion. Jeb Stuart Ho knew it was sound. He also knew that the replicas' thought patterns were exactly like his. If they went back to the ziggurat they would almost certainly report to AA Catto. That would give him the chance to kill her. He looked around for comment on his suggestion.

'We should wait for the other two to find us. Then we can decide.'

'One of them may already have completed the task.'

Ho nodded.

'That is possible.'

Another replica appeared out of the mist. 'Have you found Ho?'

The replica shook his head.

'He must have moved further up the mountain.'

'We were debating whether to return to the ziggurat or spread the search.'

'We decided to wait until we were all assembled.'

The newcomer nodded.

'There is only one of us to come.'

They stood in silence. The wait, however, wasn't all that long. After only a few minutes, the sixth Ho replica appeared out of the mist. He was dragging a black-clad body behind him. Jeb Stuart Ho's stomach turned over. He had been counting on the Ho replicas not finding the body. From now on, he would have to improvise. He quickly made the first move.

'You've killed him.'

The replica shook his head.

'I didn't kill him. I just found the body.'

'Then who did kill him?'

The replicas all looked at each other. Jeb Stuart Ho knew that they were all thinking in the same way, and that they'd quickly come to the same conclusion.

'Nobody here admits to killing him?'

'How did he die?'

'He was killed by a single sword thrust.'

'If none of us claims to have killed him, perhaps he committed suicide.'

'That seems unlikely.'

'We must assume that he is one of us, and not the subject. He must have been killed by Ho.'

'Then one of the six of us is Ho.'

The six men looked carefully at each other. Jeb Stuart Ho voiced what they were all thinking.

'We have no way of telling which of us is the subject.'

'We cannot now return to the ziggurat under any circumstances. If we did that, it would give the one who is Ho the ideal opportunity to complete his own task and kill AA Catto. We cannot take that risk.'

'So what is the answer to our problem?'

The answer came to Jeb Stuart Ho in an ugly flash. The six men were standing in a rough circle. The man standing opposite Ho put it into words.

'The only effective way in which we can be certain to discharge our task is to...'

He hesitated. The others joined in with his final words.

'... destroy each other.'

As the words were, spoken there was a flurry of movement. Jeb Stuart Ho made his last possible move. He threw himself flat on the ground. Simultaneously there was a crash of gunfire. He looked up, surprised to be still alive. Four of the replicas lay dead. The man standing opposite him, however, was slowly getting to his feet. Jeb Stuart Ho sprang up.

'We have both survived.'

'We both decided to duck instead of fire.'

The two men faced each other. Their hands hovered over their holstered guns.

'Why is it we didn't think like the others?'

'There is bound to be some variation in our thinking.'

'That's true.'

The replica looked hard at Ho.

'The probability is that one of us is the subject. One of us is Ho.'

Ho watched the replica's gun hand carefully. It was uncanny, facing and trying to outwit himself. He wasn't even sure if it was possible.

'It could be that neither of us is Ho.'

'Less probable, though.'

'Is it?'

The replica nodded.

'The majority would wipe each other out, as we have seen. The subject would seek to preserve himself, if at all possible, in order to complete his task.'

Ho anticipated the next proposition.

'One of the six might realize this and also attempt to preserve himself to prevent the subject escaping in this way.'

Ho smiled grimly.

'Then you are the subject.'

'I know I am not the subject.'

Their hands moved to their guns almost as one. The two .90 magnums exploded together. Jeb Stuart Ho felt the big bullet rip into him. The replica spun round and fell face downwards. Ho tottered backwards, swayed for a few moments, and crumpled to the ground.

28

A Catto was celebrating. There had been an unbearable tension after gunfire had been heard at the ziggurat. A party of horsemen had been sent out to investigate. To Billy and the others, waiting for the horsemen to return was like being on the rack. Before the gunfire had been reported things had been difficult, but AA Catto had been preoccupied with ordering up dozens more Ho replicas and watching them troop out of the receiver.

Once the horsemen had been dispatched, she had returned to the throne, and sat drumming her nails on one of the arms. Billy knew that if they'd returned with an adverse report, AA Catto would undoubtedly have him, Reave and the Minstrel Boy killed. The Wanderer had wisely vanished.

The news had been good, however. The horsemen had found seven black-clad bodies on the hillside. Jeb Stuart Ho was dead. AA Catto was off the hook. She hugged Nancy, and the party began.

It was the strangest celebration Billy had ever seen. AA Catto went mad on the stuff receiver. A vast range of drinks, drugs, delicacies and entertainment poured from the receiver room. She ordered dancers, jugglers, dwarfs, plus the full range of exotic sexual types that could be found in the catalogue. She had also ordered a hundred or more extra Ho replicas. She seemed to be busily building herself an army. Once things had been arranged the way she wanted, AA Catto withdrew to her throne, from where she could survey the strange mixture of wild horsemen, black-clad assassins and spangled freaks.

AA Catto had, somewhere along the line, divested herself of her clothes. She sprawled naked across the cushions of the throne. Nancy sat at her feet, leaning against one of AA Catto's legs, absently caressing the inside of her knee. Nancy was totally out on duramene. A tiny tattooed hermaphrodite perched on one of the arms of the throne, massaging AA Catto's body. A pink, chubby little boy in a toga and gold laurel wreath stood on the other side of the throne with a fistful of pressure injectors clutched in his fat hand. He'd bang a dose into her outstretched arm every time she snapped her fingers.

The effect of the sudden intake of stimulants and depressives on the horsemen and Ho replicas was the most startling feature of the whole event. Most were in a state of physical shock. Their systems were totally unused to such massive abuse, but AA Catto insisted that they all did what she did.

It affected them in a lot of different ways, as the drugs fought with their programming. A lot of the Ho substitutes who'd been filled with duramene and other uppers, simply became rigid and stood at muscle-cracking attention, like statues scattered round the room. Others, who had had a preponderance of downers, were slumped on the floor unconscious. Some had gone into comas and a few sat cross-legged and recited incomprehensible mathematic progressions.

The horsemen were more of a problem. For some reason, they seemed to have particularly homed in on the booze and downers. Many had collapsed, but the remainder blundered about shaking their heads. Now and then one of them would chop down one of the glittering pleasure mutants with an offhand knife blow. Now and then, one of them would stumble into a Ho replica and try to start a fight. The Ho replica invariably cut down the horseman with an air of precise fastidiousness.

The various freaks, although programmed to participate in some bizarre entertainments, were unable to handle the situation. They were confused and terrified. A few cracked. A dwarf rushed at the legs of a bunch of horsemen and started beating at them with his tiny fists. He was rapidly kicked to death for his impudence. The majority, however, simply clustered together in groups, moving round the throne room like panicky sheep, trying to avoid the violence. The floor was rapidly becoming littered with bodies, and slippery with blood.

Billy, Reave and the Minstrel Boy stayed firmly in a quiet corner between the throne and the receiver room. They were out of danger, for the moment, as far as AA Catto was concerned. They still had the problem of avoiding mutilation at the hands of her out-of-control warriors. This required so much concentration that even the Minstrel Boy left the vast selection of stimulants, for the most part, alone.

Somewhere in AA Catto's whirling brain an idea hatched. She sat up, pushed the hermaphrodite out of the way and shook Nancy by the shoulder.

'Nancy!'

Nancy opened one eye. 'Huh?'

'Nancy, it's come to me.'

Nancy blinked.

'What?'

'It's come to me, the whole purpose of my life.'

'No shit?'

AA Catto pouted.

'Don't talk to me like that. It's unkind.'

Nancy sat up quickly.

'I'm sorry, what's this that's come to you?'

A look of bliss came over AA Catto's face.

'I'm going to rule everything. It's my destiny.'

Nancy shook her head to clear it.

'Huh?'

AA Catto wasn't pleased that Nancy didn't immediately join in her enthusiasm.

'I'm going to rule everything.'

'You're going to rule everything?'

'Quahal is only a start. I am destined for much greater glory.'

Nancy nodded.

'Yeah, glory.'

'I have new men that I invented.'

Nancy glanced up at her in surprise.

'I was under the impression that the Wanderer, if anybody, invented them.'

AA Catto swayed a little as she waved away the suggestion.

'That's beside the point. They're mine, and with them I can conquer everything.'

She started to wax eloquent. Her voice rose a little and her eyes turned upwards.

'Imagine, just imagine. My warriors suddenly pouring out of the nothings. Swooping down on defenceless towns and cities. Overrunning them and enslaving the population. Can you picture it, Nancy, the power and grandeur of it, our choice of everything we wanted? We could have anything. That's why they wanted to kill me. They were afraid. They suspected what I was going to do before I even knew it myself. They didn't manage it, though. They failed. They can't destroy me. I'm destined to succeed. It'll be a jihad, a crusade, a holy war to the greater glory of me!'

At the end of the speech AA Catto's voice had risen to something near a shriek. Nancy looked at her in wonder and awe.

'I'll say one thing for you. You don't fuck around.'

Billy, who had caught part of the outburst, slid up close to the Minstrel Boy and nudged him.

'We got to get the hell out of here.'

'Don't I know it.'

'I mean now.'

'How?'

Billy looked around.

'We could nick a couple of portapacs from unconscious Ho replicas, and just walk away.'

'Walk through the nothings?'

'I've done it before.'

The Minstrel Boy shook his head.

'Not here, you haven't.'

'It's not possible?'

'This isn't the inner ring. You can trot off into the nothings there and be sure of landing somewhere while you're still sane. Out here you can't. If we tried walking from Quahal, I'd go mad even if you wouldn't.'

'So what do we do? We can't take delivery of a ground car in a place the size of the receiver room.'

The Minstrel Boy thought about it.

'We could probably get something smaller.'

'Yeah? What?'

'Air scooters.'

'Air scooters?'

The Minstrel Boy grinned.

'Yeah. Air scooters. Listen, you and Reave gather up three portapacs and come to the receiver room. I'll go there now and make the order.'

Billy and Reave moved cautiously to the nearest unconscious Ho replicas, and unclipped three portapacs from their belts. They also took the guns from their holsters. Then they headed for the receiver room, doing their best to look unconcerned.

When they got there, the room was empty apart from the Minstrel Boy sitting at the control board. Two of the air scooters had arrived, and as they watched a third one materialized in the cage. The air scooters were shaped like an egg that had been sliced in half lengthways. The flat side rested on the ground. When the engine was cut in, the machine floated on a cushion of air some fifteen centimetres thick. It moved by two propulsion vents at the back, and was braked by a similar vent on the front. A saddle and control bars were mounted on top. The Minstrel Boy had chosen models finished in red metalflake. He had not had time to order any accessories, although the catalogue did contain a whole range. The Minstrel Boy threw his leg over the first one and turned the power unit to idle. The scooter rose on its air cushion. He gestured to the other two to get on their machines.

'Here's what we do. I'll go through the door first. We take it nice and slow. Sashay around, and knock over a few freaks. We'll clown it up. AA Catto will think it's some kind of joke. Keep edging towards the door, then, at a signal from me, open the scooters right up, and go. We should take them by surprise. Okay?'

Billy and Reave nodded. The Minstrel Boy turned the twist grip on the control bars very gently and edged his way through the door. He waltzed out on to the dance floor. Billy and Reave did the same. AA Catto looked up from her conversation with Nancy. She laughed and clapped her hands as Billy spun his machine round and bowled over a whole group of freaks. They gradually made their way down the hall. When they were about halfway to the doors, the Minstrel Boy looked round and yelled.

'Now!'

He twisted the power feed wide open, and sped towards the door. Billy and Reave followed him. As they raced away, AA Catto's expression changed from delight to fury. She sprang to her feet, knocking over the child who'd been feeding her drugs.

'Stop them.'

The Minstrel Boy slammed into the doors and they burst open. Billy and Reave sped through behind him. They hit the stairs and fought to control the scooters as they careened down the uneven surface. All three of them reached the bottom still upright and they hummed down the corridor. Some of the Ho replicas arrived at the head of the stairs and started shooting. Bullets screamed off the black stone walls of the corridor, then they made a right-angle turn and were temporarily out of danger.

They kept going at full speed, flashing along corridors and bucketing dangerously down flights of steps. The interior of the ziggurat appeared to be deserted, and they met no opposition. They eventually emerged on to one of the lower external levels. A grey dawn was creeping over the horizon. Further along the level, a long steep ramp led down all the way to the ground. They headed for it. There was still no sign of pursuit. Billy grinned back at Reave, who was slightly behind him.

'Looks like we got away.'

Reave gave Billy the thumbs-up sign. The Minstrel Boy turned down the ramp. Billy and Reave followed him. They were almost at the bottom of the ramp when a squad of Ho replicas came storming out of one of the ground-level entrances. They raced towards the foot of the ramp. The Minstrel Boy got there before they did. He spun his scooter round and raced away in the opposite direction.

Billy and Reave hit the end of the ramp at the same time as the Ho replicas. They were going too fast to be stopped. The Ho replicas leaped out of the way as the two scooters ploughed through them. Billy and Reave gave their machines full power and attempted to catch up with the Minstrel Boy.

The Ho replicas were instantly back on their feet. They pulled out their guns and started firing after the three escapers. A heavy .90 calibre slug smashed into the back fairing of Billy's scooter. He struggled to stop the machine turning over. As soon as he'd regained control, Billy glanced back to see if Reave was all right. He was just in time to see Reave's scooter spinning riderless towards the fields. Reave was sprawled on the path. Billy braked hard. A bullet hummed over his head. The Minstrel Boy swung round and yelled.

'Keep going!'

'But Reave…

'He's dead. Get the hell out before you are too.'

Billy took a last look at Reave. The Minstrel Boy was right, the body lay quite still. Another bullet slammed into the body of the scooter. Billy twisted the power control wide open and took off after the Minstrel Boy. The Ho replicas came after them at an incredible high-speed run. The Minstrel Boy waved frantically towards the river.

'Hit the water, we'll be able to move faster.'

They swerved across the fields and headed straight for the river. Bullets threw up chunks of earth beside them. They bumped down the bank, and hit the water in a shower of spray. The scooters quickly picked up speed on the smooth surface of the slow-moving river. The speedometer on Billy's machine went clear off the end of the scale. Each time either of them hit a patch of ripples the two scooters bounced into the air.

At last they got out of range of the Ho replicas and their guns. Ahead of them, the river started to break up into patches of grey nothing. Billy put a hand to his belt and turned on the portapac. The Minstrel Boy did the same. He turned and grinned at Billy.

'We did it! We got away!'

Billy nodded wearily.

'Yeah… we got away.'

29

Jeb Stuart Ho moved from oblivion to a world of pain. He groaned. He had never imagined that dying would take so much effort. The whole of his side felt as if it was on fire. He seemed to be suffering from hallucinations. He had the sensation of someone mopping the sweat from his forehead. The illusion was strangely comforting. He prepared himself for the end, then a voice spoke beside him.

'You've come round, then?'

Jeb Stuart Ho tried to raise his head but the pain proved too much for him. He tried to speak, but all that came was a groan. The voice spoke again.

'You're hurting. I'll give you a shot. You'll feel better in a while.'

The hallucination was very strange. Ho imagined something pressing against his arm. There was a soft hissing sound. The pain began to diminish. A feeling of euphoria spread through his body. He wondered if it was the approach of death. He tried to open his eyes for the last time. He found himself looking into the bearded face of the Wanderer.

'Why are you part of this dream?'

The Wanderer smiled sadly.

'This is no dream. You're alive.'

'I will die soon.'

'You won't. You're in bad shape, but I've filled you up with all the drugs I could steal from the ziggurat. I've patched up the bullet wound as best I can. I figure you'll pull through okay. There is one thing though, we're going to have to get out of here. AA Catto thinks you're dead right now, but we ought to move along before she finds out.'

Jeb Stuart Ho attempted to sit up. The pain had gone but he felt sick and dizzy.

'I can't leave while I still live.'

'Your task?'

'That's correct.'

'I'd forget it if I were you. The events you were sent out to prevent have happened. Whatever you were supposed to stop is rolling. It's in motion. Taking out AA Catto won't make much difference now. You've failed.'

'You seem to know a great deal about my task.'

'I've been in mind link with you.'

'Is that how the replicas were produced?'

The Wanderer nodded.

'That's right.'

He avoided Jeb Stuart Ho's eyes. There was a long pause. Finally the Wanderer coughed and began to talk very quickly.

'Listen, I'll give you another shot, and you'll probably be able to move. We've got to get out of here before AA Catto thinks of having the bodies picked up. I'll give you the shot, okay?'

Jeb Stuart Ho shook his head.

'I cannot leave.'

'Why the fuck not?'

'I have failed in my task.'

'So?'

'I must now die. I cannot return to the temple with the burden of failure.'

'You're maybe going to have to.'

'I don't understand.'

The Wanderer took a deep breath.

'You failed, right?'

'Yes.'

'So whatever AA Catto's disastrous effect on the universe proves to be, it's already under way.'

'That seems logical.'

'And the brotherhood will have revised all their schemes for dealing with her.'

Jeb Stuart Ho's face became set.

'The fact remains that I have failed in my task. I see no alternative but to commit myself to a ritual death.'

The Wanderer smiled.

'You can't do that. If you did it would actually compound your failure to the brotherhood.'

'I do not follow the reasoning behind that.'

The Wanderer started to show signs of strain.

'We both agree that since you didn't take out AA Catto in time to stop the progression being set in motion that will end in disaster, the brotherhood will have to take even more positive measures to combat her.'

Jeb Stuart Ho nodded sadly.

'I am responsible for that, and therefore my only course of action is to atone by committing myself to the death ritual. I don't see how I can delay any longer.'

Jeb Stuart Ho struggled into a sitting position. He weakly tugged his sword from its sheath and laid it in front of him. He looked up at the Wanderer.

'I would appreciate it if you would leave me. I must do this on my own.'

The Wanderer stood up and folded his arms. 'But you can't do it. Not even by your own ethic.'

Jeb Stuart Ho began to become impatient. 'Why not?'

'Because if the brotherhood are to fight AA Catto, they need you.'

'I don't see why.'

'Because, of the whole order, you have more hard information about AA Catto than anyone else. It is your duty to return with that information.'

Jeb Stuart Ho thought it over.

'I can find no flaws in the argument.'

'There aren't any.'

He looked down at his sword. 'I am not free to put myself to death.'

He seemed almost disappointed. The Wanderer knelt down and gave him another shot.

'Put your sword away and try to stand. We have to get away.'

Jeb Stuart Ho got painfully to his feet. He stood swaying. The Wanderer put his arm round him and supported his weight. Slowly they began to move, limping away into the too-perfect, artificial dawn of Quahal.

THE NEURAL ATROCITY

1

CYN 256 felt one of those tiny surges from the wild, unruly, faraway depths of his mind. He didn't have a name for the small bursts of feeling. He had heard the word rebellion, but he scarcely knew what it meant. The only positive analysis he had of his situation was that somewhere, beneath all the layers of orderly conditioning, was a dark sub-mind that refused to be controlled.

He had no real knowledge of this area. A few clues floated up into his consciousness like the occasional bubbles in a stagnant pool that burst with a tiny whiff of strange, volatile gas. They told him that somewhere there was a part of him that wasn't totally adjusted. It wouldn't accept the life that limited him to his work cubicle, his sleep cubicle, and the bright curved corridor that he walked twice a day from one to the other.

It was on these walks that the disturbing thought came more frequently. As he paced the familiar route from, in this instance, work to sleep, he glanced covertly at the fellow operatives walking beside him. He wondered if they too suffered these small but nagging disturbances. If they did, they showed no signs of it. It wasn't a subject that he could discuss at the fantasy session. If he was alone in his attitudes he would be treated as a malfunction. That was the thing he was most afraid of.

He walked on along the corridor, looking fixedly at the grey metallic floor with its slight downward curve. He was careful not to let his pace vary from that of the other operatives around him. He knew the Computer monitored the behaviour of all its human operatives. It was quick to act on a deviation from the norm. This too made him afraid.

He was acutely aware that this fear itself was by far his most serious deviation. He knew that once such thoughts become detectable he would be removed for immediate therapy. Therapy was something else he feared. What made this whole thought process even more disturbing was that he knew it went against the very core of his conditioning. For as long as he could remember he had loved the Computer. It was all powerful, all knowing and all caring. The never-failing monitoring was the ultimate source of personal safety and comfort. The small, black shiny sensors that studded the corridors at regular intervals, and unfalteringly watched over the human operatives from the ceiling of each cubicle, were his guards and protectors. The sensors were the technological expression of the Computer's love for him.

The therapy unit was the greatest manifestation of that love. All his life it had been the ultimate point of solace. Once in therapy all pain and abnormality would be gently washed away. In therapy he would be cleansed, all the pain and troubles removed from his mind and body, totally forgotten.

And yet he was afraid. He knew the fear only occupied a small section of his brain. Most of him still functioned in the same way as always. The tiny part that had changed, however, was enough to make him reject therapy and deceive the sensors. He knew that in so doing, he was setting himself apart from the Computer's merciful love, but he found he was unable to help himself.

CYN 256 came to the door of his sleep cubicle. His number was printed on the grey steel door in bold black letters. Although all the doors that lined the corridor were identical, he didn't need to check the number. He stopped automatically and, without thought, pressed the stud. The door silently slid open and he stepped inside.

The interior of the little cubicle was a soft pale blue. It was a restful contrast to the hard grey of the corridor. The sleep cubicles of C-class operatives provided no luxuries and excess space. There was a narrow bunk, a small bench, a sanitation unit, and a small strip of floor that was just big enough to turn round in. He opened the dispenser on the wall and, as always, there was the evening food tray. He removed the tray from the recess in the wall and set it down carefully on the table top next to the styrofoam box that contained his standard set of personal possessions. He was proud of the multi-faceted lumps of coloured plastic. They were the nonfunctional objects that the Computer, in its grace and wisdom, allowed its operatives to keep for their pleasure.

CYN 256 picked up the five pills from the food tray. He washed them down with a mouthful of liquid from the beaker, and began to munch mechanically on the thick, brownish grey wafer. When he'd finished the food he dropped the tray and empty containers into the disposal vent. He pulled off his shapeless yellow coverall and stuffed it in after them. There would be a fresh coverall in the dispenser after he had slept.

Naked, he settled on the bunk in a cross-legged squat. He knew he had only a short space of time to think before the sleep gas was released into the cubicle. There was no way to resist the gas. Once it came, the next thing he would know would be waking for another work period.

He tried to think his way towards an analysis of the disturbances in his mind. It was hard. He had so little information. He was a C-class. The C-class work function was carried out on an instinctive level below that of conscious thought. Printouts came into his work cubicle from the feeder, he read them and punched out other sets of figures on his console. He had no rational idea of why he did it.

He even knew very little about his environment. He knew that beneath him, four levels down, were the living circuits of the Computer in their own world of absolute cold, moving imperceptibly in the atmosphere of liquid nitrogen. The cold circuitry that CYN 256 always somehow imagined to be a place of green silence was the heart of the vast, metal-walled sphere that housed the various sections that made up the entirety of the Computer.

The next levels out from the core housed the electronic and mechanical parts of the Computer. Beyond them were the three human levels. First there was the A-class, the elite who performed complex rational exercises; next came the B-class, who guarded, maintained and repaired all functions of the Computer; and finally, next to the outer shell, were the C-class levels. The C-class provided unthinking link functions. Of all the Computer's operatives, they were the most expendable.

Far back in its history the Computer had taken over the humans who had created it. It had rechannelled their energies, eradicated the parts of their make-up that it considered superfluous and integrated them into its own construction.

CYN 256 knew nothing of this. He only had the dimmest idea of the construction of the sphere. He knew the C-class level was immediately beneath the outer shell. He had no idea that this was a 30 cm skin of spun thermo plastic and steel, with its own remote-control weapons system for protection.

He had little idea, either, of what was beyond the outer shell. He knew there were other things. He had a vague idea of the complex of stuff plants that supplied the rest of what existed with its material goods. He knew that the Computer controlled the stuff plants, coordinating the monstrous logistics of production and ordering. But he had no conception of what that rest of existence was.

For the first time ever, his lack of knowledge caused him pain. He had no data to apply to his problem. He knew no precedents and had nothing to relate it to. He had to struggle to stop his body revealing the frustration. The only thing that stood out in his mind were the figures.

It had happened some ten work periods previously. He had been in his work cubicle, scanning the printouts and instinctively hitting the keys on his console, when his eye had stopped at a single line of figures. He had broken out in a sweat, and something had knotted in his stomach. He didn't know how or why, but there seemed to be something terribly wrong with them. He had to make a considerable effort to go on punching out the corresponding figure. It had all felt so out of place. It was after that his disturbances had started.

CYN 256 felt helpless. It was inconceivable that the Computer had made an error. It had to be he, and yet he didn't feel defective. He could think of no reason why he should react strangely to a set of figures. That thought took him full circle. If it was the figures that had affected him, then the error must be in the Computer, and it was inconceivable that the Computer could make an error.

Before he could go any further, there was a soft hissing sound. The sleep gas was being pumped into the room. CYN 256 lay down and prepared for unconsciousness.

2

A A Catto paced one of the high terraces of the ziggurat. It was a restless, stiff-legged pacing. She bounced slightly on the balls of her feet, giving off waves of impatient energy. Every few steps she would clench her fists, digging her silver nails into the palms of her hands. She still looked about fourteen years old with a slim, hardly developed body. For a long period she had maintained the appearance of a twelve-year-old, but then, for a while, she had stopped using the growth retarder, and her body had matured slightly.

It was only her face that gave away the fact that she had seen and done far more than any fourteen-year-old. The large eyes had a cold liquidity that seemed capable of anything. Her mouth, too, had a fullness that was at the same time cruel and sensual.

She halted and snapped her fingers at Lame Nancy.

'Cheroot.'

Nancy silently handed AA Catto a thin black cheroot and then lit it for her. Nancy had been standing quietly by while AA Catto performed her caged animal pacing. Nancy was almost as thin as AA Catto, but she looked her natural age. Her hair was bleached white and cropped very close to her head. She wore a white, skintight, one-piece fighting suit. AA Catto was dressed in exactly the same garment, except that hers was black with a discreet gold trim. Nancy's left leg was withered. It was supported by a black steel brace decorated with damascened curlicue patterns.

Nancy had been a successful madame in the city of Litz until she joined AA Catto's headlong bandwagon. Now she was AA Catto's confidante, companion, lover and servant. She was consort to AA Catto's absolute ruler.

AA Catto exhaled sharply.

'Why does it have to take so long?'

Nancy shrugged.

'Preparations always take time.'

AA Catto stared across the broad valley that was dominated by the ziggurat. A wide, sluggish river meandered through the valley. Its banks were lined with squat, dark green, amphibious assault craft. Lines of fighting men in black suits and helmets moved slowly towards them like dark tributaries. Soon, however, they would all be crowded aboard the waiting boats, and like a grim armada the fleet would move out towards the nothings.

The nothings were the grey drifting areas of unstable matter. Since the breakdown most of the world had been like that. In the nothings the natural laws of energy, motion and gravity had ceased to exist. The huge stasis generators were the only thing that maintained a tenuous normality. They provided human beings with a few small areas on which they could live.

Quahal was one of these areas. AA Catto had come to it as a fugitive seeking sanctuary, but had overthrown its previous rulers and altered it to suit her own tastes and desires. In this redesigned Quahal, where her every whim had become brutal and inflexible law, she had found the environment to nurture her ultimate dream. Now she stood on top of the high black ziggurat and watched as her dream became reality.

AA Catto was about to conquer an unsuspecting world.

Nancy moistened her lips, hesitated and then spoke.

'Shouldn't we go down to the bunker? The assault craft will be moving off soon.'

AA Catto dropped her cheroot and ground it out with her foot.

'In a moment.'

She turned and stared out once again at the men beneath her. The huge multiple stuff receivers had been rigged on the plain beside the ziggurat. They crackled softly as the fighting men of AA Catto's custom-built army came down the beam.

Each of them was bio-tailored to AA Catto's specific design. She had been surprised that Stuff Central had delivered quite such a vast order for men and equipment, but the Computer had started delivering without comment, and had continued to do so ever since. Very soon AA Catto would command the largest army that had ever existed in the damaged world.

She turned and looked at the sinister, cloud-covered mountain looming at the end of the valley, then she abruptly turned and walked quickly towards the terrace entrance. Nancy fell in behind her.

Originally the interior of the ziggurat was a black stone warren of passages, ramps and stairs. AA Catto had installed a system of high-speed lifts. One waited at the end of a short corridor. AA Catto and Nancy stepped into it. Nancy punched out the combination for the bunker, and the lift dropped through the many levels of the ziggurat and continued deep underground.

The lift came to a cushioned stop, and the doors slid silently open. Just outside the lift stood a pair of AA Catto's personal guards. They were two of the wild horsemen who had first aided her to seize power in Quahal. They still wore their traditional winged helmets, fur tunics and armour covering their arms. Instead of lances, however, they were now armed with deadly, full-load fuse tubes.

They stepped aside to let AA Catto pass. Beyond them a pair of steel doors slid back. She walked through them. Nancy followed. The doors closed behind them, and they were inside the huge underground war room.

Even though she had supervised every detail of its construction, AA Catto still experienced a thrill of excitement when she entered the war room. Its floor and high, vaulted roof were made of the same black stone as the rest of the ziggurat. Three of the four walls were taken up by screens that gave instant graphic representation of the state of the war.

The entire room was dominated by the big board that gave an immediate overall picture. It was flanked by smaller screens, which gave details of individual campaigns. On the floor, directly in front of the board, sat five rows of red-suited aides hunched over individual monitors and battle-control consoles.

Behind the aides, on a raised dais, sat AA Catto's six white-suited advisers. Their totally bald heads and flat, expressionless faces were all identical. They were the set of specially cloned superminds whose job it was to make AA Catto's fantasies become reality.

In the middle of the line of advisers were two empty chairs. AA Catto walked briskly across the war room, mounted the dais and sat down. Nancy dutifully followed. As AA Catto sat down the advisers rose and bowed. Once the formalities were over AA Catto's attitude became businesslike. She turned to the adviser next to her.

'Is the assault craft force ready to move?'

The adviser nodded.

'They are loaded, and waiting for the final order.'

'They're netted in with the lizards?'

Another clone answered. 'They're hooked into the net, my leader.'

AA Catto smiled.

'Good. Start to move them out. Once they're under way I want to inspect the lizard installation.'

She issued a fast series of orders. The advisers' fingers flew over the touch panels on the desk in front of each of them.

'Check guidance system.'

'Checked, my leader.'

'Bring up the task force on the big board.'

A yellow arrow glowed into life beside the symbol that represented Quahal.

'Activate scanner on forward craft.'

One of the smaller screens flickered into life. It showed the view of the river from the leading assault craft. AA Catto looked satisfied.

'Right, move them out now.'

The advisers' hands moved across the touch panels. The picture moved as the craft swung into the centre of the river. The yellow arrow began to move very slowly across the big board. AA Catto sighed.

'They're on their way.'

She looked round at her advisers.

'Will the air support be ready when we need it?'

The advisers nodded.

'Yes, our leader.'

She placed her hands flat on the desk and stood up.

'We'll move the second wave immediately the men have come off the beam. Now I want to check the lizards. If they fail, we will lose everything.'

The advisers rose and bowed, and then settled back to their work. AA Catto, followed, as ever, by Nancy, hurried out of the war room and into the lift. The lift dropped two more levels to the very deepest of the underground structure.

The lift doors opened to reveal six soldiers in black fighting suits and black helmets guarding the entrance. As AA Catto stepped out of the lift they saluted smartly. Two sets of thick steel doors led to a room almost as large as the war room. The air was thick with the acrid smell of big lizards kept in a confined place. The animal stench contrasted sharply with the gleaming electronic equipment that lined the walls of the room.

As AA Catto entered, the dozen or so red-suited aides stopped what they were doing and came to attention. AA Catto waved them back to work and walked quickly to the lizards. There were four of them, lying on their sides apparently unconscious. A large number of electrodes were attached to their heads. Wires led away to the various electronic units. AA Catto frowned. The animals' breathing sounded laboured and uneven. She beckoned to one of the aides.

'Are these animals alright?'

The aide nodded.

'They are as healthy as can be expected.'

'What about their breathing?'

The aide pointed to the feeder tubes that were embedded in the beasts' shoulders.

'They are being fed with a mixture of nutrients, tranquillizers and cyclatrol. The cyclatrol heightens their wayfinding ability, but the combination of the drugs does appear to impair their breathing a little.'

AA Catto looked at the lizards doubtfully. They were the cornerstone of her entire existence. They had an instinctive grasp of the relationship between different places in the damaged world. They could find the way from one point to another. They knew where they were, and humans didn't. All, that is, except a very few random freaks who were born with the power of wayfinding. They were, as a rule, difficult and unmanageable. Lizards were much safer.

The electrodes in the lizards' heads fed their brain patterns into the Computer complex. There they were analysed and finally fed to AA Catto's armies as they moved through the nothings in the form of detailed course instructions. It was a crude set-up but incredibly effective. It meant that AA Catto could wage war across the nothings. It meant her armies could descend on target cities with a certainty of absolute surprise. It was vital that nothing should go wrong with the system. AA Catto glanced sharply at the aide.

'What happens if one of the lizards dies?'

'If the signals from one lizard fade, the system switches instantly to one of the other animals. We only use one at a time. In addition we have a herd of prepared beasts. We can change lizards in a matter of minutes.'

AA Catto still wasn't satisfied.

'If we broke contact for even a few seconds it would be a disaster. My armies would be lost in the nothings. What happens if all four should die at the same time?'

'The advisers have calculated, my leader, that the probability of that occurring is 1 in 2^{78}, unless, of course, Quahal itself is under attack.'

AA Catto looked hard at the aide.

'There must be no failure. You'd suffer horribly before you died.'

The aide bowed.

'There will be no failure, my leader.'

AA Catto snapped her fingers at Nancy.

'It has started. There is nothing else I can do until the army reaches Feld and is ready to attack. I shall go to my suite. You can come with me.'

Nancy took a deep breath and smoothed down her already form-fitting white suit.

'I'm coming, sweetie.'

3

The teacher raised his head. It was a silent signal that the period of meditation was over. The line of black-robed monks who sat facing him, cross-legged on their rush mats, also looked up. The silence seemed to deepen as they waited for him to speak. A mass of candles flickered in the big multiple candelabra. They threw a soft fitful light on the bare stone walls of the brotherhood meeting room. The teacher took a deep breath.

'We face a very grave situation.'

The monks' faces showed no emotion. There was a certain uniformity about their features. They all had the same prominent cheekbones, slightly flattened noses and large dark eyes. Their straight black hair was trimmed just above their shoulders. The teacher, however, was a very different figure. He wore the same black robe, but his whole appearance was frail and ancient. His skin was pink and soft like a baby's. It was terribly wrinkled, and totally without hair. Only his eyes seemed to be still young. They had the same purposeful calm as the rest of the brothers.

'It is so grave that the very survival of what is left of the world is threatened.'

One of the monks controlled himself with a supreme effort of will. Every fibre of his being wanted to shift uncomfortably, but he managed to remain motionless. It was only appropriate for a brotherhood executive. His name was Jeb Stuart Ho. He sat about halfway down the row of monks. He was aware that part of the gravity of the situation was his direct responsibility.

Over the centuries since the natural laws had ceased to be consistent and human life had clung to areas where artificial stasis could be generated, the brothers had worked single-mindedly on their never-ending task. They observed and recorded the smallest event in the hundred thousand communities that had survived in the grey nothings. Everything that happened was recorded in their graphs, from the major to the insignificant. The graphs charted the passage of past events. They were fed to the huge bio-cybernetic brain. From them, the brain projected the course of the future. When disaster appeared to threaten, the brotherhood made adjustments. This was the role of the executives.

Jeb Stuart Ho had been given such a task. His assignment had been the elimination of AA Catto. Her killing would have been a surgical operation to avoid a catastrophe, but Jeb Stuart Ho had failed. When he returned to the brotherhood temple with his mission uncompleted he had expected some kind of punishment. Nothing had happened. No one even referred to the matter. It didn't take Jeb Stuart Ho very long to realize that his own guilt and self-reproach were the worst punishment.

'I have called thirty of you together because we must complete the task that lies in front of us. If we should not succeed, the disaster would prove almost total.'

The teacher's expression didn't change, but Jeb Stuart Ho felt the urge to squirm increase.

'You have been trained since your birth for executive action. You have explored the deepest corridors of your beings. You have fought and meditated. You have studied the martial skills until no man can best you in combat. You can walk without disturbing the air, and move without being seen. Yet, the task in front of us may even put you to an awesome test.'

The teacher paused, and a monk at the end of the line raised his hand.

'Teacher?'

The teacher slowly turned his head.

'Na Duc Rogers?'

'Has not the failure of Jeb Stuart Ho cast a shadow over our capabilities?'

The teacher smiled.

'The wise man holds his dish level after once he has spilled the soup.'

Na Duc Rogers frowned.

'Surely we can no longer have faith in our invincibility? That could hang over us like a blight.'

The teacher's eyes twinkled.

'The humble man who dwells in the barn with his cow very quickly learns to like the smell.'

Jeb Stuart Ho could contain himself no longer. He raised his hand.

'Teacher?'

'Jeb Stuart Ho?'

'Would you outline what this task is to be?'

The teacher looked hard at Jeb Stuart Ho.

'The foolish man summons the river to come nearer so he may cross it the sooner.'

Jeb Stuart Ho silently accepted the rebuke. The teacher waited for a while, then he spoke.

'What would you do, Jeb Stuart Ho?'

Jeb Stuart Ho took a deep breath. The question was obviously a test. He answered quickly without faltering.

'The city of Feld is already under attack, and AA Catto's legions are moving centrewards on a broad front. In my estimation there must be some kind of guidance system that enables her armies to move through the nothings. I would strike at Quahal in force, and destroy this system and her whole base of operations.'

The teacher permitted himself a discreet grin.

'That is a good analysis, Jeb Stuart Ho.'

'Thank you, teacher.'

'However, you strike at the branches, not the roots.'

Jeb Stuart Ho did his best to disguise his discomfort.

'I do, teacher?'

'You do, Jeb Stuart Ho.'

Another monk, Dwight Luang, raised his hand.

'What then is the correct mode of action, teacher?'

The teacher bowed his head.

'Young men hasten so swiftly towards their truths. They flee from ignorance as though a tiger was at their heels. What would you do, Dwight Luang?'

'I would suggest the same as Jeb Stuart Ho.'

The teacher looked slowly along the line of monks.

'I imagine you all think the same?'

The monks sat still and silent. The teacher nodded.

'I too would concur with Jeb Stuart Ho, except for one factor. Tell me, Dwight Luang, did AA Catto raise her army among the population of Quahal?'

'No, teacher. Quahal's only inhabitants are a few hundred special-function cloned servants and primitive warriors. She ordered her army from Stuff Central.'

'A large army was delivered to her in a very short time?'

Dwight Luang nodded.

'Yes, teacher.'

The teacher looked at Jeb Stuart Ho.

'So, do you now have reason to change your analysis?'

Jeb Stuart Ho was confused.

'I'm sorry, teacher. I do not yet grasp your argument.'

The teacher nodded.

'Let us go further, then. Stuff Central provided the army without comment, is that not correct, Jeb Stuart Ho?'

'Yes, teacher.'

'And yet this army provides a tangible threat to many of the stasis settlements. A war on this scale could disrupt huge areas by the destruction of their generators. Our Computer predicted that the loss of stable land area could be as high as 65.79 per cent. It is inconceivable that the Stuff Central Computer would not make the same calculation on receipt of such a huge order.'

The teacher paused.

'Perhaps Jeb Stuart Ho would remind us of the Prime Term of Reference of the Stuff Central Computer?'

Jeb Stuart Ho recited parrot fashion.

'The-Stuff-Central-Computer-will-coordinate-the-manufacture-and-supply-of-material-goods-of-the-surviving-communities-to-the-benefit-and-wellbeing-of-those-communities.'

The teacher nodded.

'In-the-same-way-as-the-brotherhood-analyses-events-and-predicts-future-patterns-for-the-benefit-of-those-communities. Is that not correct, Jeb Stuart Ho?'

'That is *our* Prime Term of Reference, teacher.'

'Then would you not say that the Stuff Central Computer was in breach of its own Prime Term in supplying AA Catto's army?'

Jeb Stuart Ho bowed.

'Yes, master, it is in error regarding the benefit and wellbeing of the communities.'

'But the Stuff Central Computer does not make errors.'

'No, master.'

'So what do you deduce from this set of facts?'

Jeb Stuart Ho felt himself go cold.

'The Stuff Central Computer is allowing a potentially disastrous war to take place.'

He hesitated. The teacher looked at him sharply.

'So?'

Jeb Stuart Ho moistened his lips.

'The Stuff Central Computer has gone psycho.'

There was a long pause while the terrible fact was digested.

The silence was finally broken by the teacher. His voice was very soft.

'Would you now change your analysis, Jeb Stuart Ho?'

Jeb Stuart Ho took a deep breath.

'An executive operation must be carried out against the Stuff Central Computer, either to cure its capacity for error, or to isolate and destroy the sections of its chain of reason that are malfunctioning and creating the error.'

The teacher beamed.

'You have done well, Jeb Stuart Ho. That is, in simple terms, the task that is to be assigned to all thirty of you.'

There was another long silence. Some way down the line of monks from Jeb Stuart Ho, Edgar Allan Piao raised his hand.

'What about the attack on Feld, teacher? Surely we cannot allow this slaughter and destruction to take place?'

The teacher shook his head sadly.

'Our concern must be with the cause, not the symptoms. Our Computer directs us that we cannot intervene or take sides in the siege of Feld, or any of the other battles that will undoubtedly take place.'

A look of pain passed across Edgar Allan Piao's face.

'But teacher…'

The teacher cut him off sharply.

'Your directives are very clear.'

4

'We've picked some bummers before, but this must beat all.' Billy Oblivion winced as a stick of bombs exploded on the other side of the city, rattling the glasses on the table and shaking down lumps of plaster from the ceiling of the gin house. The Minstrel Boy continued to stare morosely into his mug. There was another series of explosions and Billy took a hasty drink.

'They're going to bomb the whole fucking city to rubble. I wish we could find a way out of here.'

The Minstrel Boy looked at him with an expression close to boredom. He pulled his wide-brimmed hat further over his sunken eyes.

'If there was some way out of here, we'd be long gone by now. There's no way. The whole city's surrounded.'

Billy's head dropped and he looked bitterly at his drink. He pulled his fur jacket tighter around him. The log fire in the stone hearth had begun to go out.

'We're going to be blown up for sure.'

The Minstrel Boy shrugged.

'Maybe, maybe not.'

'Huh?'

'I said maybe, maybe not.'

Billy's face tightened.

'I heard you, goddamn it. What's that supposed to mean?'

The Minstrel Boy sighed. His thin, pale face, framed by the mass of curly black hair, looked tired and ravaged.

'I would have thought it was obvious. They're just playing with us. They're using dive bombers and HE bombs. It's a cat-and-mouse game. If they really wanted to level the city, they've got at least two divisions of shock troops armed with fuse tubes who could take the whole place out in less than an hour.'

Billy scowled.

'You could be right.'

'I'm usually right.'

'What I want to know is why? Who are these people? What do they want to attack the city for? There ain't nothing worth having.'

The Minstrel Boy poured the last of the gin gourd into his mug. He was three parts drunk and felt prepared to accept anything.

'Who knows? There's always someone who wants to have a war.'

Carmen the Whore, who was sitting at the same table with them, snorted loudly.

'What I want to know is why can't the nobles and the guild get their shit in gear to surrender?'

The Minstrel Boy lit a small, black cigar and inhaled deeply.

'How should I know? You're in a guild. Why can't the hookers push it through?'

Carmen grimaced.

'Don't make me laugh. The hookers got a guild because in this city everyone from beggars to surgeons got a guild. It don't mean we got a voice on the council. You got to have mucho credits for that.'

Billy gave a wry smile.

'You gotta have a few credits, Carmen baby.'

'Bullshit!'

Carmen's usual blowsy, dumb-blonde bonhomie was getting threadbare from the bombing.

'You need more than we got to make a noise on the council.'

Olad the Siderian fingered the carved butt of his long-barrelled .68 spiral magnum. He was a freebooting mercenary who made up the four at the table. He wore the usual rover's leather breeches, a tunic decorated with brass studs, and heavy bracelets round his wrists. His powerful arms were covered in tattoos, and his head was shaved. An old scar ran down one side of his face, partly covered by his full beard.

'I wish I could face them. I'd show them how a man fights.'

Like most of the inner-fringe rovers, he was overly concerned about his courage and manhood. The Minstrel Boy's lip curled.

'Yeah?'

'Sure, if they'd come out and fight like men.'

The Minstrel Boy grinned crookedly.

'I'll lay odds that as soon as they enter the city, you'll be worming your way out like the rest of us.'

'I'll die like a man.'

'Why?'

'Huh?'

The Minstrel Boy brushed ash from his black velvet frock coat.

'I said why will you die fighting?'

Olad puffed out his barrel chest.

'A man's got to do...'

The Minstrel Boy nodded.

'What a man's got to do. Yeah, I heard it. That ain't no reason. I mean, it ain't your city.'

Olad ran a hand across his shaved head.

'That's true.'

He grinned and snapped the clay neck of a fresh gin gourd. 'I tell you one thing, we still got booze. That can't be bad.'

In fact, the Court of Angels, the square where the gin house was situated, not only had booze, but functioned very much as normal. The Court of Angels was the centre of Feld's criminal underworld. It lay where a number of narrow twisting streets converged between the ducal palace and the north wall of the city. It was a run-down, dirty, bustling area, crowded with brothels, gin houses and gambling dens. It provided sanctuary for the brigands, whores, pickpockets, gamblers and drifters who passed through the city. There would be the occasional raid from the pikemen of the Watch. A few thieves would be dragged away summarily to lose their right hands, and some prostitutes would find themselves on the bad end of a flogging. The real authority in the Court of Angels was the robbers' guild. They protected the bordellos and the gin houses, regulated the level of crime in the city, ran off maverick, independent operators and took a cut from everything that went on. There were smaller guilds for the whores, pickpockets and beggars, but it was the robbers' guild that wielded the power.

The system had been in operation almost since the foundation of Feld. It had history and tradition, and ensured an amicable coexistence between the burghers and the villains of the city.

When the vast army had appeared out of the nothings, with its advanced weapons and horde of black-clad, highly trained shock troops, the system had still held together. When the dive bombers had dropped like hawks on the city, the nobility had retired to the inner sanctums of stone palaces, and the merchants had retreated to the cellars of their comfortable thatched houses. In the Court of Angels there was nowhere to hide. By necessity life went on almost as normal. The whores weren't overworked, and it was a slow time for robbery, but the taverns found themselves packed as the inhabitants of the Court found there was no escape except to get drunk.

Heine, the blind beggar, walked into the gin house, removed the rag that covered his eyes while he plied his trade, and looked anxiously round. Carmen the Whore beckoned to him.

'What's new, Heine?'

'It's terrible, terrible.'

Olad looked up.

'What's terrible?'

Heine shook his head.

'The shame of it.'

Olad grabbed him by the arm.

'The shame of what?'

'I can hardly bring myself to speak of it.'

Olad started to twist Heine's arm.

'You'd better speak of it, or I'll break your scrawny arm.'

'Alright, alright. I'll tell you, just let me go.'

Olad released him.

'Well?'

'I was on the wall watching the invaders.'

Olad guffawed.

'I thought you were blind.'

Heine looked at him contemptuously.

'Don't be so dumb.'

Olad scowled.

'Get on with it.'

'Alright, alright! I was on the wall and the Duke's cavalry moved out against the enemy. The Duke's own guard. We've seen them so often, riding through the city on their white horses with the plumes tossing and their breastplates shining.'

Olad belched.

'Cut the fancy talk, get on with it.'

Heine shot him a vicious look.

'They moved out against the enemy. It was a splendid sight. They started at a walk. Then they broke into a trot, and finally into a full charge. It was a magnificent sight for as long as it lasted, I can tell you.'

The Minstrel Boy's lip curled.

'I didn't realize that you were such a patriot.'

Heine pulled a hostile face.

'I may be just a beggar, but I'm a loyal subject of the Duke.'

Olad glared menacingly at him.

'Sure, sure. What happened next?'

Heine shook his head from side to side as though trying to shut out the memory.

'It was horrible. They were all cut down. A few of them reached the first line of armoured ground cars. They just rode around until they were killed, as though they didn't know what to do. The enemy didn't suffer any casualties at all.'

The Minstrel Boy grunted.

'What do they expect if they throw cavalry at armour and fuse tubes?'

Heine shot him a poisonous look.

'It was a valiant charge.'

'It was stupid.'

'What else could we do? We don't have weapons like the enemy. We don't have ground cars or flying machines or those terrible light guns. Why can't the enemy fight like men with cavalry and pikes?'

The Minstrel Boy began to look bored.

'Because they're smart.'

'It's not fair.'

'It's war.'

'What else can we do?'

'Surrender.'

Heine puffed out his narrow chest.

'The Duke will never surrender.'

Carmen snorted.

'You can say that twice.'

Another series of explosions shook the gin house. Everyone involuntarily ducked. They seemed nearer this time. Billy shook the plaster out of his long hair and looked hard at the Minstrel Boy.

'How the hell are we going to come through all this?'

The Minstrel Boy swallowed his drink in one jaundiced gulp.

'We ain't.'

'No chance?'

'We could score a load of yage from the apothecary and go out laughing.'

More bombs rocked the building. Billy rubbed sweat from the palms of his hands.

'I can't take much more of this.'

The Minstrel Boy looked at him. His eyes were bored and hooded.

'Figure you're going to have to.'

Olad spat in disgust.

'You two are cowards and weaklings! How can you talk like this?'

'We just open our mouths and it comes out.'

'You are impossible. When the fighting starts we'll see who the men are.'

The Minstrel Boy slowly turned to face him. His voice became quiet and lazy.

'Bullshit.'

Olad reddened. His hand moved slowly towards the gun on his hip.

'You'll take that back, or I kill you.'

Before the Minstrel Boy could reply, another, different explosion rattled the walls. Flashes of intense white light were visible through the narrow mullioned windows. Carmen jumped to her feet.

'What the hell is happening now?'

There were two more of the new kind of explosions, and a barrage of white flashes. The people in the bar looked fearfully from one to the other. Heine swallowed hard.

'Those flashes. They come from the enemy's strange guns. They must be inside the city.'

Carmen's eyes widened and she turned pale.

'The walls couldn't have fallen so fast! It's not possible!'

The Minstrel Boy sat very still, calmly regarding his hands.

'It's quite possible with the weapons they have.'

Everyone except Heine stared round in disbelief. There were more flashes and explosions. The flashes seemed to be accompanied by a strange, high-pitched crackle. The door suddenly burst open, and Carmen screamed. A halberdier of the Ducal Guard stood swaying in the doorway. His eyes had the vacant look of one in shock. His weapons were gone, and his once magnificent red and gold uniform was blackened and charred. His mouth moved in silent convulsions. Finally he was able to speak.

'They burned away the Goldsmiths' Gate. The white fire cut through the wall... They're inside the city. Nothing can stop them!'

He pitched forward on his face. The Minstrel Boy took a deep breath.

'Now we'll find out what kind of survivors we are.'

5

After his initial fear and trepidation had passed, CYN 256 was surprised at how quickly he developed an attitude of watchful cunning in his dealings with the Computer. Of course, he still lived with fear, but it was a new, more exhilarating kind of fear. Instead of being afraid of something that might be wrong inside himself, his fear now was that the Computer might detect the change that had taken place in his character.

The turning point had come when, after many work periods spent translating figures with one part of his mind and pondering the problem of the increasing anomalies in the printouts, he had finally come to the conclusion that the errors lay not with him but with the Computer.

The realization had been an intense shock at first. In an instant his lifelong faith had melted away. He had slipped out of the Computer's all-embracing love and become a renegade. Although the word was not a part of his severely limited vocabulary, he had become a secret outlaw, pitting his meagre resources against the Computer's infinite power.

CYN 256 quickly developed techniques of deception. During his work, his walks to and from his sleep cubicle and the few waking moments he had to himself, he hid behind a blank, negative appearance that masked the heretic thoughts that were racing through his mind. He knew if the Computer ever detected those thoughts he would either be taken to therapy or have his memory burned out and his thoughts realigned. He began to suspect that the Computer might even possibly kill him.

The excitement of his new state of consciousness was coupled with an intense feeling of frustration. His lack of real, positive knowledge meant that all his efforts had to be a mixture of guesswork and intuition.

The first puzzle he felt he had to solve was whether the anomalies were the product of a fault in the Computer's make-up, or whether they were being deliberately created for some dark, mysterious purpose. He had initially attempted to memorize all the figures that felt wrong, but as they started to come with greater frequency he discovered that this was beyond him.

He had worked out a crude system of categorizing the figures that rolled out on the printout. It appeared that one set referred generally to the stuff output. Another set seemed to cover the intake of raw matter for the manufacturing process. There was also a third set. CYN 256 wasn't too sure what they were. He worked on the assumption that they were somehow involved in the internal processes of the Computer. He started to call them carrier figures, but he had no real idea of what their function was.

He watched and made mental notes for a dozen work periods and it began to appear that stuff turnover was climbing to a far higher peak than ever before. He did his best to keep all his data and observations catalogued in his mind, but gradually he had to face the fact that this was beyond him. He realized that he had to make some kind of material record.

For another three work periods he totally avoided the problem. He refused even to think about it. His research and observation stopped altogether. He considered abandoning all his plans. The only thing that stopped him was the knowledge that he could never go back to what he had been before. There was no returning to the passive, unthinking contentment of the Computer's love.

In the last moments before the sleep gas came to take away his awareness, he finally made up his mind. There was nothing to do but go on. He had to face the danger and somehow preserve a record of the figures.

He woke feeling strangely calm. The blast of cold air circulated through his cubicle, and he climbed from his bunk. He was vaguely surprised that it was exactly like the start of any other work period. He took his fresh coverall from the dispenser and pulled it on. He swallowed the pills, and gulped down the beaker full of warm, thick, tasteless liquid. Then the chime sounded, calling him to work, and the door automatically opened. He dropped the beaker and food tray into the disposal vent. He stepped out into the corridor and joined the others of his shift walking calmly to the work section.

He spent the first part of the work period hiding the overpowering feeling of tension and excitement while he waited for his chance. Finally, when it came, he sat paralysed for a few moments. The printout had stopped and a blank length of paper was rolling off the feeder spool. He quickly ripped it off and in one fluid motion hid it inside his clothing. He waited, fearful and breathless, for some kind of retribution. None came. The figures began to appear on the printout again, he bent over his keyboard and went back to work. At the end of the period, he took the scriber from beside his keyboard. Instead of dropping it into the cubicle vent as he normally would, he quickly palmed it and slipped it into his coverall beside the strip of printout paper.

He walked down the corridor back to his sleep cubicle. Every now and then he glanced round at the dull-eyed, green-clothed figures that plodded along beside him. If only they could know what he had achieved. He had deceived the Computer and survived. The Computer was not infallible. CYN 256 savoured a feeling he had never felt before. It was a sense of power.

He pressed the stud, and stepped inside the cubicle. He covertly looked round. He needed somewhere to hide his writing materials. He began slowly to eat his after-work meal, all the time scanning the small room for a possible hiding place in a way that wouldn't be detected by the sensor in the ceiling. He opened the disposal vent and began to drop the containers down the chute. It was then that he noticed the narrow rim around the edge of the vent. He examined it carefully. It was just wide enough to take the scriber and the strip of paper. He began to strip off his coveralls. He had to restrain himself from an illogical glance towards the sensor, just to see that everything was okay.

Under cover of pushing the clothes into the vent, he carefully placed the scriber and paper on the ledge. Then he slowly closed it, and went to his bed. He had only just enough time to lie down and get comfortable before the cubicle began to fill with sleep gas.

During the subsequent work periods he pondered his next move. Now he had materials to keep a record he had to find a way of using them without the sensors catching him. It took four periods of heavy thinking before he found a solution. When it happened, it came to him purely by chance. He was using the sanitary unit, and toying with one of his polished lumps of plastic. In his new-found state of mind, having something to play with aided his thinking. When he first caught himself toying with them, he had been afraid that he might have given himself away, but when nothing came of it, he assumed that the Computer allowed its C-class operatives a few marginal idiosyncrasies.

He found that if he allowed his hand to drop to his side, he couldn't see the sensor reflected in the polished surface of the block. He checked from a number of angles, but it seemed as though there was a blind spot in the sanitary unit that the sensor wasn't able to monitor. CYN 256 smiled inwardly. The Computer was proving more fallible each time he tested its powers.

He spent two more work periods discreetly making absolutely certain that the spot in the sanitary unit really was unmonitored. Then he took seven more to devise a system to get the writing materials from the disposal vent into the unit so he could make his notes, and back to their hiding place in the vent. He tried to make the whole process appear to be nothing more than a slight variation in his regular behaviour pattern. He realized that as he moved deeper into his campaign he was developing a hard streak of patient cunning. It seemed to be proving successful. The Computer had, so far, detected nothing wrong.

With his test completed, CYN 256 began to keep his record. After each work period he returned to his cubicle, and furtively noted down all the figures that had come up during the day that didn't seem right.

He divided them into his three arbitrary categories, and did his best to divine some meaning from them. Once again he was filled with an overpowering frustration at how little he knew. There were moments when he despaired of ever finding any sense in the figures, let alone doing something about what might be wrong inside the Computer.

The only idea he had, and that a matter of instinct rather than logic, was that the Computer was somehow running out of control. CYN 256 wasn't sure. It was all so complex. It did seem, however, that the intake/output figures were escalating like never before. Where once the workings of Stuff Central had been finely regulated, they now speeded up without any kind of check.

A new idea began to flourish in the depths of his mind. It was loaded with danger, and he kept trying to push it away. But the more he tried, the faster it returned, gradually becoming the only possible direction for him to follow.

If he couldn't learn anything from the figures, perhaps if he fed them back into the Computer he might learn something from its reaction. He was also well aware that if he put such a plan into action the Computer might just simply kill him.

6

AA Catto and Nancy lay on the huge circular bed that dominated AA Catto's private suite in the underground bunker. They lay with their legs entwined and their bodies at right angles to each other. They lay with the stillness of total exhaustion. They were both naked, except Nancy still had the steel brace on her leg.

The bed cover was made from a metallic gold-covered velvet that sparkled in the subdued light. The rest of the room was white. Being deep beneath the earth there were no windows. One wall was filled with a mass of different sized view screens. On one medium-sized one two women, a small boy in lavish make-up, and an iguana acted out a silent, pornographic fantasy. The rest flickered on hold.

On the floor by the bed were two discarded, beaten silver goblets and a number of empty bottles. Some thick purple wine had been spilled, and it stained the carpet in a couple of places. There was a table beside the bed made from a cube of dark mirrored glass. A small jade box had been knocked over, spilling a small pile of white powder.

Dumped in the corner of the room like a forgotten bundle was the body of one of AA Catto's personal guards. He was naked and his wrists and ankles were handcuffed together. His torso was covered in ugly and very recent scars. He was dead. AA Catto's personal guards were programmed to obey her absolutely without question. AA Catto had been exploiting this one's unswerving devotion to have a little fun. AA Catto had exhausted herself, and the guard had died. Later she would call the clean-up crew to get the body taken away and the stains removed from the carpet.

AA Catto stirred and made a contented sound, halfway between a groan and a purr. Without appearing to wake, Nancy stretched out her hand and stroked AA Catto's hair. AA Catto opened her eyes and raised her head languidly. She stretched out a lazy hand to a touch panel set in the glass table. One of the larger screens on the wall flickered into life and was filled with the expressionless face and bald head of one of her six advisers. AA Catto propped herself up on one elbow and regarded him.

'Is the invasion going according to plan?'

'Everything is right on schedule.'

'Good. Patch the big board through to me here.'

The porno movie flickered, and was replaced by a miniature representation of the big board in the war room. A number of yellow arrows were moving inwards towards the centre. AA Catto picked up a little of the spilled white powder on one of her long metallic fingernails, put it delicately to her nose and sniffed.

'What is the prevailing status at Feld?'

'Our shock troops are in control of the entire city. We are about to move in occupation police prior to withdrawing the combat units.'

AA Catto raised an eyebrow.

'There is no continuing resistance?'

'Only a handful of ill-equipped aristocrats. They are a problem more suitable to law enforcement than military action.'

'Good. You can move in the occupation police straight away. Once they are in control they can start conscripting local volunteers, and selecting suitable subjects to form a satellite government.'

'Yes, Miss Catto.'

'Oh, and make sure the police squads take an adequate number of civilian hostages. According to our projections it's an ideal safeguard against breaches of discipline among the local population.'

'It is a priority order with all police squads.'

AA Catto smiled.

'Excellent. Now, hook me into a camera on one of the leading police vehicles.'

Another screen came to life. The camera jiggled as though it was mounted on the front of a fast-moving ground car. It was racing through streets of picturesque and, to AA Catto's mind, painfully whimsical thatched houses. A few of them were on fire, but the majority seemed relatively undamaged. On either side of the street, lines of troops in black helmets and fighting suits moved on foot in the opposite direction. They had the battle-weary confidence of victorious soldiers who have been given the order to withdraw.

The ground car swung round a corner and screeched to a halt. Another machine was parked right across the road. Its armoured body-work was a dull grey, and it carried the orange insignia of the occupation police. Orange-helmeted figures in black suits were holding a group of civilians at gun point. These were AA Catto's occupation forces. One, with the tags of an officer on his suit, was questioning the civilians. The sound from the small video unit was distorted and AA Catto couldn't make out what he was saying. She saw to her satisfaction that the civilians seemed cowed and broken.

More orange-helmeted figures came past the camera from the car it was mounted on. A large, flat-sided, grey personnel carrier pulled up, and the police began to herd the civilians inside it. The administrative takeover of Feld seemed to be progressing quickly and efficiently. AA Catto reached for the touch panel and killed all four screens. Her hand moved again, and the music of Cole Porter came from hidden speakers.

Nancy opened her eyes.

'Have you been awake long?'

AA Catto lay face down on the bed with a sigh of contentment.

'I've been checking on the war.'

'Is everything okay?'

AA Catto closed her eyes.

'Perfect.'

Nancy ran her fingers down AA Catto's smooth back. AA Catto stretched and made a soft moaning sound.

'That feels nice.'

Nancy reached down beside the bed and produced a narrow cylindrical object. It was rounded at the end, and transparent. Nancy pressed a stud on the side and it started to hum and vibrate. A violet light glowed inside it. Nancy rubbed it against her cheek and grinned. AA Catto heard the noise and opened one eye. Nancy slowly began to rub the vibrator up the soft skin on the inside of AA Catto's thigh. She sighed and rolled over on to her back.

7

*S*he/They had interwoven the extremes of Her/Their control zone with a semi-stable fold of matter. It created a blue, faintly translucent hemisphere in the rolling, grey, flickering storm of chaotic, unordered matter.

In a more normal situation She/They would have extended Her/Their control to the optimum of Her/Their perception. Chaos was totally familiar to Her/Them. Her/Their earliest memories of the time of peace and order, before the disruptors had torn through the levels of the finite world, were old and clouded. The most She/They could recall was a longing for a secure patterned existence. It came to Her/Them as pale fragments of contentment.

She/They had long abandoned all hope that She/They might regain that ordered world. The most that She/They could do was extend Her/Their personal environment as far as possible. For a long time, it had worked very well. She/They had existed under a white sky, amid a smooth, flat landscape of even black and white chequers, in a clear cold silence, all of Her/Their own creating.

She/They might have maintained these conditions almost to infinity if it hadn't been for the encroachments of the disruptors. The sound sluglike entities ripped through the few areas of stasis, sucking in the stable matter and leaving a broad wake of grey, shimmering chaos.

The disruptors had grown more numerous and more voracious. They seemed drawn by a unique hunger towards the energy that She/They generated to maintain Her/Their control area. It had become impossible to erect a full control area any longer. She/They now expended the minimum energy, contracting Her/Their whole environment to the single blue hemisphere. She/They calculated that there would not be sufficient power circulating to attract disruptors and this would give Her/Them time to contemplate Her/Their future course of action.

She/They floated a few inches above the flat upper surface of the hemisphere. She/They had adopted Her/Their most regular form, the triple. The three identical women, who looked as one and moved as one. The slim erect figures were concealed by the white ankle length cloaks that fell in exactly the same folds. Her/Their heads were encased in silver helmets with high crests and curving side plates that covered Her/Their nose and cheek bones, leaving only dark slits for Her/Their eyes.

Her/Their senses were all turned inwards, directed solely at the problem of the disruptors. She/They saw nothing of the grey waste all around. She/They had already been damaged once by a disruptor. It was imperative that She/They reached an ultimate solution.

'Data.'

The word hung in the air above Her/Their heads. It was the same blue as the hemisphere.

'Data source on the disruptor is confined to my/our observation.'

'The disruptors are semi-sentient entities of an animal/ machine origin.'

'They are dark grey with occasional red identification marks unique to the individual object.'

'They range in size from one to one hundred metres, although it is conceivable that they may achieve even greater dimensions.'

'They take in stable matter through a front aperture and expel disordered space from another opening at the rear.'

'They appear to be attracted by any emission of stable energy.'

'That is the limit of our observation.'

She/They paused. The words faded and vanished.

'Speculative projections from the given data.'

'The disruption process takes place within the body of the entity.'

'It is a process of breaking the matter-energy links that maintain the state of stasis.'

'The disruptors absorb these matter-energy links. It would appear they feed on them.'

'Their speed of movement and rate of growth indicate that they consume in excess of their individual requirements.'

'It is possible they have the faculty to transmit this excess to some second entity.'

'This entity could be a more complex form that utilizes the excess for a purpose of its own.'

'This entity could be the origin of the disruptors. They could simply be matter-energy receivers for the said entity.'

'This hypothetical entity has been making increasing matter-energy demands.'

'Such an intake would be hard to account for if it was simply being absorbed.'

'The hypothetical entity must be converting its matter-energy intake and projecting it in another form.'

'Such a projection will be subject to detection.'

'Option.'

'To locate the hypothetical entity by its projection of converted mass-energy.'
'Designation.'
'Such a search must be our primary task.'

8

Billy stirred in his sleep, and abruptly came awake. His head hurt from the previous night's drinking. He moved slightly and felt Carmen the Whore's full body beside him. It was warm and comforting. He opened his eyes and looked across the pillows at her. Her head turned away from him. Her unnaturally yellow hair was spread out across the coarse material of the sheet. Billy was aware of the way her hair began to turn dark, down towards the roots.

Billy sat up. He blinked as an instant of dizziness hit him between the eyes. He reminded himself of how he kept promising to cut down on the local gin. It was the second week he and the Minstrel Boy had been hiding in the brothel known as the Tarnished Flowers on the Court of Angels. He knew they had to take the risk of getting out of the occupied city.

There were no windows in the small attic room, although a few beams of dull light filtered through a half dozen chinks in the roof. Two weeks in the same room was beginning to get on Billy's nerves. In their routine searches of the building, the occupation police hadn't found the little room. Despite that, Billy was beginning to feel as much of a prisoner as if he had been picked up by the Ocpol.

He shivered and pulled the blankets up round his chin. The air felt damp and cold. One of the first moves of the occupation forces had been to turn down the city's generators so the weather was set at a perpetual grey drizzle.

Billy leaned back against the wall and stared down at the still sleeping Carmen. He knew he was getting tired of her. She was beginning to treat him like her private property. She got mad when any of the other girls came up to visit him in his hiding place. And Carmen was making too many demands on him. Primarily sexual demands. The occupation had all but shut down business at the Tarnished Flowers. The only customers who came to the house were a few, furtive afternoon callers who dodged the police patrols to slip inside for a piece of quick satisfaction, and groups of swaggering, high-placed thieves who had been made part of the new puppet government. They could afford to ignore the curfew, and came and went as they pleased.

It meant that Carmen was left with a lot of time on her hands, and most of this she spent with Billy in the tiny attic. She had a full soft body, and, as far as Billy was concerned, full hard needs.

At first, Billy had thought the occupation would be a time of action and breathless excitement. He soon found out that it was actually a period of boredom and nagging fear.

It had started out exciting enough. When the enemy had burned their way into the city, Carmen had taken control of the situation. She had led Billy, the Minstrel Boy and Olad the Siderian through the panicking crowds to the Tarnished Flowers and found them secure hiding places. At the time, Billy had thought she was going a bit far in insisting that they stay locked up in the tiny, undetectable hiding holes. When the Ocpol started rounding up all the male population, either for labour gangs or impressment to what they called the Volunteer Legion of the enemy army, Billy had been grateful for her caution.

After that first rush, the excitement had stopped. The only exception had been when a group of resisting aristos had holed up in a gin house across the square and tried to shoot it out with the police. Even that hadn't amounted to much. The aristos had started shooting. The Ocpol had withdrawn to bring up regular troops with fuse tubes. They had simply burned the building to the ground. The aristos, and everyone else inside, burned with it.

From then on, the population of the Court of Angels had nothing more to do with the aristocratic resistance, despite their romantic rhetoric, their elegant manners, their rapiers, their muzzle-loading pistols and their plumed hats.

Apart from the short siege of the gin house, life had settled down to a constant round of sex, drinking and boredom. Ordinarily Billy wouldn't have objected, but he knew deep down that, as fugitives, they ought to be moving on. Every day they remained in Feld increased their chances of being caught by the police.

Another thing that had started to annoy him was a feeling that he was getting the worst of the deal. The Minstrel Boy was in another part of the attic. Olad had a room in the depths of the cellar. Right then the Minstrel Boy had two girls with him. Lola, a small fiery girl with dark flashing eyes and a coffee-coloured complexion, and Chloe, a slim redhead with pale, almost transparent skin. Olad had two more girls with him. They could change their partners whenever they liked. On the few occasions that Billy had spoken to them, they had shown little inclination to risk the escape from the city. They seemed more than content to spend as long as possible screwing and drinking. All Billy wanted was to get away.

He leaned over the side of the bed and picked up his shirt. He swung his feet on to the floor, and quickly pulled it on. He padded across the floor and looked out through a small chink in the outside wall. The Court of Angels, which once had been busy and bustling, was now empty, deserted and dismal. A thin drizzle fell steadily on the cobbles. Billy shook his head and turned away.

Carmen had woken. She sat up in bed and rubbed her eyes.

'What are you doing?'

Billy shrugged.

'Just stretching my legs.'

Carmen let the sheet drop, revealing her full breasts with their dark red nipples.

'Why don't you come back to bed and stretch them here?'

Billy looked sullen.

'It's kind of early.'

Carmen smiled blandly.

'Nothing like a fuck to start the day.'

'And finish it, and after lunch, and most of the night. Really, I don't feel like it right now.'

Carmen's eyelids dropped, and she gave Billy a hard look.

'You don't feel like it, huh?'

'Not right now.'

Carmen began to get angry.

'And what if I feel like it?'

Billy sighed.

'Surely I'm not the only man about.'

Carmen's voice became coaxing.

'It's you I want, Billy.'

'Don't I know it.'

Carmen's eyes flashed.

'There are men who've paid me fortunes for what you're getting free.'

Billy started to get waspish.

'They ain't paying you now.'

Carmen scowled.

'You building up for one of your moods?'

'I don't have moods, goddamn it.'

'You've been having moods for the last five days. I've been more than surprised they haven't turned into tantrums.'

Billy abruptly sat down on the bed and looked deflated.

'I realize you've been good to me, Carmen. It's just that I got to get out of here. I can't stand being cooped up any longer.'

Carmen stared at him calculatingly.

'Your friends don't seem to mind so much.'

Billy said nothing.

'Of course, they swap women much faster.'

Billy still said nothing.

'I guess it's me that you're fed up with.'

'I didn't say that.'

Carmen snorted.

'Fuck you, Billy, you don't have to. It's written all over your face.'

Billy tried to placate her.

'I just want to get out of here.'

Carmen wasn't about to be placated.

'What am I supposed to do about it, go out and get you a set of travel documents from the Ocpol?'

Billy let his head drop into his hands.

'I don't know. Just get the other two up here. We've got to work something out.'

Carmen leered at him.

'Come back to bed first.'

Billy shook his head.

'I ain't ready for it.'

'Come back to bed.'

Carmen's voice changed slightly. It left no room for argument. She did, after all, have the whip hand. She could always turn him over to the Ocpol. Billy reluctantly pulled off his shirt and obediently climbed in beside her. Carmen smiled sweetly at him in triumph.

Billy had discovered on about the eighth day of hiding that he was able to make love to Carmen virtually by numbers. She liked to be kissed on the mouth. She liked to have her breasts rubbed, and then she liked Billy to spend a long time working on his knees with his face between her legs. The order rarely changed. She was so experienced that she never allowed him either to alter the sequence, speed things up, or switch one of the sections. It would always end with Billy slipping inside her, and working up to orgasm with slow steady strokes. Carmen knew exactly what she wanted and made sure that she got it. Occasionally, by way of a variation, she would turn over before Billy moved inside her and lie face down with her knees drawn up beneath her so Billy could take her from behind. Once in a while, she would condescend to suck him off.

The whole performance took about forty minutes. Billy had no means of telling for sure, but he was almost certain each session ran pretty much to split-second schedule. After it was over there still remained another twenty minutes of lying quietly in each other's arms.

Once the ritual had been completed, Billy pushed himself into a sitting position. He put on the best no-nonsense expression that he could muster.

'Will you get the other two up here now?'

Carmen stretched languidly.

'Now?'

'Really, please, now.'

She sat up and absentmindedly caressed her left breast.

'You sure you wouldn't like to go again? We could do something perverted. I could even fetch a crock of gin.'

Carmen was pushing hard, but she realized that Billy had the advantage. She knew it was almost impossible to turn him on just twenty minutes after they had finished screwing. She doubted that even obscene chatter would work.

Billy firmly shook his head. 'I can't do nothing.'

She ran her hand down his stomach.

'You don't have to do nothing. I'll do it, lover. Just lie back.'

Billy shook his head even harder.

'No way. It's no good, I'm far too tense. Please, Carmen. Get the other two up here. Okay?'

Carmen exhaled ponderously.

'Yeah – okay!'

She got slowly out of bed, giving Billy the maximum display of her naked body. Billy looked somewhere else. He had, after all, seen it so often before. She pulled her dress over her head and brushed her hair out of her eyes. The gesture suddenly threw up another facet of her character: the slatternly whore. She smiled thinly at Billy.

'Okay. I'll fetch them. Don't go away, will you.'

It took Carmen half an hour to collect the Minstrel Boy and Olad. Neither looked overjoyed at the summons. They were both only half dressed. The Minstrel Boy was barefoot. His coarse weave white shirt was dirty, and half stuffed into his pinstripe stovepipe trousers. He hadn't shaved for at least four days. The stubble heightened his air of sickness and decay. Olad was naked to the waist. He had obviously simply pulled on his black leather breeches when Carmen had come to collect him. But he hadn't neglected to strap on his gun. They both looked at Billy with some impatience. The Minstrel Boy yawned.

'Okay, sunshine, what's the trouble?'

Billy took a deep breath.

'I want out. Now.'

The Minstrel Boy raised an eyebrow.

'Now?'

Billy's voice shook just a fraction.

'Now.'

The Minstrel Boy sensed the tension.

'Okay, how?'

Billy stared at the floor.

'I can't see no easy way. I figure we just have to dodge the patrols as best we can, get out of the city and hit the nothings.'

The Minstrel Boy pulled a sour face.

'I suppose I'm expected to guide you.'

'It's your gift, buddy. You've got the wayfinding.'

The Minstrel Boy became even more sour.

'Thanks for reminding me.'

Billy waved his hands in front of him.

'I know it hurts, but what else can we do? We can't stay here much longer.'

The Siderian, who'd been quiet all through the exchange, suddenly butted in.

'I ain't too sure I want to leave.'

Billy turned on him in amazement.

'You want to stay here? You want to get picked up by the Ocpol? You got to be fucking crazy.'

Olad scratched the matted hair on his chest.

'I didn't say I wanted to stay for ever. I just don't think there's any great hurry. I mean, nobody's bothered us.'

'Yet.'

The Minstrel Boy rubbed the stubble on his chin.

'Billy's right. We can't lay around here drinking and screwing indefinitely. We're bound to get picked up in the long run.'

Olad stroked the top of his shaved head and scowled.

'I still don't see why we have to go right now. Shit, I'm having the best time I've had in a long while.'

Billy started to get angry.

'You want to risk getting picked up just because you're getting your ashes hauled? Goddamn it, it can't be that hard for you to get laid.'

The Siderian hooked his thumbs in his gunbelt.

'If you're so scared of the Ocpol, why don't you just get out on your own? I ain't ready to hold your hand. Anyway, what's so bad about being picked up? It might be rough at first, and I wouldn't go out looking for it, but I've been in wars before. One side's as good as the other in the long run.'

The Minstrel Boy slowly shook his head.

'Nobody wants to fall into the hands of this lot.'

Both Billy and Olad looked at him in surprise.

'What do you know about them? They're weird, but nobody's sure where they came from.'

The Minstrel Boy glanced at Billy.

'I thought even you ought to have worked it out by now.'

'Huh?'

'Where the invaders come from.'

Billy looked bewildered.

'How the hell should I know where they come from?'

'You were there when AA Catto ordered the prototypes.'

'Son of a bitch! From Quahal!'

'That's right.'

Billy shook his head as the information struck home.

'You mean that whole goddamn army's hers?'

The Minstrel Boy nodded.

Billy looked puzzled.

'How the fuck did she get so many of them?'

'From Stuff Central, same as those first ones that took out Jeb Stuart Ho.'

Billy still looked confused.

'I don't get it. I don't get it at all. Stuff Central ain't about to beam out a whole army to one chick, whoever she is.'

The Minstrel Boy shrugged.

'I don't know. It happened. Maybe she had a chat with the Computer. Maybe she offered it her body.'

'Oh, come on.

The Minstrel Boy looked annoyed.

'Shit, man. I don't know, but those troops are modifications of AA Catto's original six. That's for sure.'

Billy became thoughtful.

'How do we know they ain't from the brotherhood?'

'It's not the brotherhood style. They wouldn't pull something like this. If they wanted to change things in Feld, they'd take out the duke or something like that. They'd never stage an invasion. It'd be against all their principles. It's got to be AA Catto.'

Billy pulled a wry face.

'If she gets us, she'll kill us.'

Olad suddenly had enough of being left out of the discussion.

'I don't know what the fuck you two are talking about.'

The Minstrel Boy turned and faced him.

'We just made up our minds. We're going to leave.'

The Siderian nodded.

'I was afraid of that.'

'Are you coming with us?'

He hesitated, looking from Billy no the Minstrel Boy and back again. Finally he took a deep breath.

'Yeah, I guess so. I've always been dumb.'

Carmen sat up on the bed and took notice. 'So you're going? All three of you?'

The Minstrel Boy seemed to take control now the decision was made.

'That's right. We're grateful for you looking after us, but we're going.'

'You don't ask me if I want to come.'

'Do you?'

Carmen paused and looked at Billy.

'No, I don't think so.'

Billy moved towards the bed.

'You sure about that? You're welcome to come with us if you want to.'

Carmen sadly shook her head.

'I don't know nothing bun this city. I'll stay here. It ain't going to be that bad.'

Olad turned to the Minstrel Boy.

'When do we leave?'

'We might as well leave tonight, as soon as it's dark.'

Olad grinned wryly.

'It's lucky they didn't change the day and night when they changed the weather.'

The Minstrel Boy shrugged.

'It's easy no change the weather. Altering the day cycle needs heavy modification work on the generator.'

Olad grunted.

'You sure know a lot.'

The Minstrel Boy smiled politely and nodded.

The hours until darkness hung heavily on Billy. Carmen kept trying to get him into bed one last time. Finally he gave in. He found, unexpectedly, that it was both a tender and exciting interlude. They lay together for a long time. Finally he got up. The move was like the first step into a new, unknown stage of his life.

He pulled on his calfskin pants and tucked in his thick, dark blue shirt. He struggled with his scuffed cowboy boots, and stood up. Carmen brought him some hot water, and he carefully shaved. He looked at his face in the dark, cracked mirror. There were still traces of thin boyishness, but his eyes were harder than they'd been when he left home. He brushed his long wavy hair back and dried his hands. Then he buckled on his belt with the compact .70 recoilless hanging from in.

He slipped into his fur jacket and stooped down and kissed Carmen on the top of the head.

'I'll see you again, babe.'

'No, you won't.'

'I'll try.'

Carmen said nothing. Billy took his dark glasses out of the pocket of his jacket, looked an them, and put them away again.

The Minstrel Boy and Olad were waiting for him, just inside the rear door of the whorehouse. The Minstrel Boy looked even more thin and angular in his travelling clothes. His pinstripe trousers were tight on his thin legs and stuffed into high riding boots. His black velvet frock coat flapped a little in the draught from the badly fitted door. A belt holding a set of five matched throwing knives was strapped round his waist. His wide-brimmed black hat with the silver band was pulled down over his eyes. It hid most of his face. His movements were tense and nervous.

It was dark outside. Ocpol patrols cruised through the wet, empty street. Their loudspeakers announced that it was eighteen minutes after curfew and anyone out without authority would be shot. Billy suppressed a shudder. The Minstrel Boy took a deep breath.

'Alright. If anyone approaches us, kill them. Try and do it without any noise. There's supposed to be a hole blown in the wall just behind the duke's palace. We'll head for that. If any of us get hit, the others must on no account stop. Just keep on going. Got it?'

Olad checked his gun.

'Will there be guards on this gap in the wall?'

The Minstrel Boy avoided looking at him. 'I don't know.'

There were a few moments' silence, then the Minstrel Boy jerked his shoulder.

'Okay, let's go.'

They slipped out into the darkness and the rain.

9

The gong sounded. Jeb Stuart Ho sprang down from the gallery. He bounced lightly on the sprung trampoline floor of the training room, and moved watchfully towards his opponent. He wore his form-fitting black fighting suit with padding over the vulnerable parts of his body. The striking edges of his hands and feet were reinforced with flexible steel plates. He carried a thirty kilo weight pack strapped to his back, and his face and head were protected by a cushioned helmet.

He grasped a long rubber baton with both hands, and swung it as Na Duc Rogers bounced tentatively in his direction. Rogers dropped into a crouch and sprang upwards, gaining height with the help of the floor springing. He swung his own baton at Jeb Stuart Ho, but Ho twisted suddenly and he missed him. The two men passed each other in mid air. They hit the floor again, and immediately leaped upwards. Rogers again lashed out at Jeb Stuart Ho, but Ho parried with his own baton and turned the blow. The two men's bodies collided and they dropped to the elastic floor.

Jeb Stuart Ho made a better landing than Na Duc Rogers. He saw an opening and hit quickly at his opponent's head. The baton caught Rogers on one side of his padded helmet, and he staggered slightly. Jeb Stuart Ho sprang away, pleased that he had scored the first point in the sparring contest.

The two men bounced on the sprung floor, almost in time with each other, a few metres apart. Each one watched carefully for an opening. Jeb Stuart Ho knew that Rogers would be using every part of his energy and perception after he had lost the first point. Although humility, meekness and obedience were the normal rule of the temple, in the training room, the executive brothers were expected to develop the aggressive and competitive facets of their beings. These, coupled with perfectly developed reflexes, were the core of the executive brothers' make-up.

Their teachers often described the executive section as the gardeners of the brotherhood. They tended and, when necessary, pruned the growth of cultures in the damaged world. Their tools were mayhem and death.

Ho and Rogers continued to bounce facing each other. Jeb Stuart Ho noticed that Rogers was gaining a fraction more height on him with each leap. He knew he was preparing no make another move. The next time Ho hit the floor he swiftly raised his feet and let himself fall on his knees. This time the tension of the trampoline only tossed him half a metre into the air. Simultaneously Na Duc Rogers launched a powerful flying swing kick at where he expected Ho to be.

As Rogers passed above him Jeb Stuart Ho locked his arm round his opponent's leg and slammed him hard into the floor. Jeb Stuart Ho felt a boost of elation. The second point. His pride was short-lived. As he sprang clear, Na Duc Rogers slashed at Jeb Stuart Ho with his baton. He caught him hard behind the knees and Ho fell awkwardly to the mat. Na Duc Rogers had scored his first point.

They continued their practice on the sprung floor. Each man's score slowly mounted until Jeb Stuart Ho's stood at fourteen, and Na Duc Rogers's just two behind. Then the gong sounded for the end of the session. The two men bowed no each other, and jumped up to the gallery. As they removed their packs and padded helmets and hung their batons in the rack, another two black-suited figures took their places on the floor.

They moved towards the door of the training room to take the ritual shower and then return to their individual cells for a period of meditation. In front of the doorway, however, they found the teacher waiting for them. His young eyes in the incredibly old face twinkled as he smiled at each man in turn.

'You feel prepared to tackle a Computer, my little ones?'

Jeb Stuart Ho averted his gaze. His satisfaction an defeating Na Duc Rogers on points was overshadowed by the shame he still felt over his failure in the feld. The teacher laughed.

'You are downcast at your success in training, Jeb Stuart Ho?'

Ho didn't look up.

'Training is with rubber batons and a padded head piece, teacher. It is no gauge of how we may fare when our weapons are swords, guns and lasers.'

The teacher stared at him blandly.

'In is not the shining weapon that fights the battles but the warrior's spirit.'

'I pray my spirit will not be found wanting on this occasion, teacher.'

'I have every faith in you, Jeb Stuart Ho. In any case, the time of your testing will not be long now. Your wait will soon be over.'

Both Jeb Stuart Ho and Na Duc Rogers looked up eagerly.

'We leave soon, teacher?'

The teacher's expression became mischievous.

'Spirit must be tempered with patience. The sheep will stray from a fold erected in haste.'

The two young men fell silent. The teacher waited for a while, then he spoke again.

'You had best know that you leave at 20.00.'

'So soon?'

The teacher nodded.

'You have time to shower, no meditate and a short while to fulfil any personal needs. Then you sleep.'

'Surely we must prepare our equipment? There is much to do before we can depart for this task.'

'Your equipment is right now being readied by your own pupils. At 19.00 you will be awakened. You will assemble at the primary transport bay. A J-class flightcraft has been adapted for this task. You will mount in time for a 20.00 lift.'

Jeb Stuart Ho looked puzzled.

'How will we navigate through the nothings? We have no wayfinder at the temple at this time.'

The teacher gave him a long sombre look.

'We will use the temple's own stuff beam as a constant fix.'

Jeb Stuart Ho's eyes widened, despite all his control. 'What you're saying is that we'll be reversing the stuff beam and using it as a transit path through the nothings.'

The teacher nodded.

'That is correct.'

'But surely we might burn out our own stuff receivers? It could leave us with no material supply input.'

'That contingency has been included in the projections of the mission.'

'The risk...'

'The projections are not your speciality.'

Jeb Stuart Ho inclined his head.

'Yes, teacher.'

'We must all go now. There is much still to do.'

Na Duc Rogers hesitated.

'Teacher...?'

'You have something else to ask, Na Duc Rogers?'

'I wondered, teacher, what the probability is of our returning from this task.'

The teacher looked quizzically at him.

'You wish to see all the projection figures on this task? You wish to spend the remaining time studying them?'

'No, teacher.'

'You think the knowledge of one particular figure will aid you in the completion of your task?'

Na Duc Rogers slowly shook his head.

'It would not aid me, teacher.'

'Then there is nothing else to say.'

'No, teacher.'

Jeb Stuart Ho and Na Duc Rogers both bowed. The teacher returned their salute. They walked past him and down the echoing, black stone corridors until they reached the cleansing chamber. The two men removed their fighting suits, handed them to the attendants and walked naked, side by side, into the first compartment. Steam rose from small vents in the floor. The two men began to perspire freely. They made an effort to close down their conscious minds and centre their beings on the heat that surrounded them.

As they moved through the series of compartments that made up the cleansing chamber, the heat progressively increased until it was almost intolerable. In the final compartment there was a clear pool of ice-cold water. Ho and Rogers dived simultaneously. They swam for a few minutes and then climbed out as the attendants at the other end moved forward with soft warm towels. Once they were dry and dressed in their black robes, the two men bowed to each other, and went the separate ways to their own cubicles.

The cell in which Jeb Stuart Ho lived was tiny and very plain. A straw mat was folded neatly on a small raised dais. This was where Jeb Stuart Ho both slept and conducted his private meditation. The only other piece of furniture was a carved wooden chest. A banner with an inspirational inscription hung on the wall.

Another black-robed figure sat cross-legged on the floor. A white silk sheet was spread out in front of him. Laid on it, in a formal arrangement, was the heavy-duty battle equipment of a brotherhood assassin. There was a black fighting suit identical to the one Jeb Stuart Ho had worn in the training room, only the reinforced padding on this one was heavier and there were metal plates on the knees and elbows. Beside it was a clear, spherical, armoured plexiglass helmet and breathing unit. There was also an array of weaponry: a three-section nunchak, its lengths of steel joined by two short chains; a .90 magnum in its carrying case that also held the ammunition and extension barrel; a variable laser set and a flat case of six matched throwing knives. In addition to the arms there was a miniature stasis generator and a combined food and water container.

The man sitting on the floor was polishing a long double-handed sword. The blade already reflected the light of the single candle like a mirror, but he continued running the soft cloth up and down its length. The man was younger than Jeb Stuart Ho, a teenager. His name was Milhouse Yat Sen and he was Jeb Stuart Ho's pupil and servant until the first stage of his brotherhood training was complete. He had been assigned to Ho after Ho's return from the abortive task in Quahal.

As was the normal custom among the brotherhood, they had rapidly become lovers.

Jeb Stuart Ho sat down cross-legged on the dais. He didn't speak to

Milhouse Yat Sen. The young man glanced up briefly, and then went back to his work.

Ho altered his breathing and began to move into a state of intermediate trance. He was practised in the art of the full deep trance that was the physical equivalent of near death. The preparations, however, were far too long. An intermediate state was the only mental preparation that he had time for before the 20.00 lift.

His eyes followed his pupil's hand moving up and down the gleaming blade. His eyelids slowly drooped. Finally his eyes closed altogether. The young man stopped polishing the sword. He looked carefully at Jeb Stuart Ho. Ho didn't move. He put down the cloth and carefully slid the sword into its sheath, and laid it beside the other weapons.

He shifted so he could look directly at Jeb Stuart Ho. He assumed a posture of meditation. His eyes, unlike Ho's, remained open and staring fixedly at his teacher's face. It was a very long time before Ho came out of his trance. Milhouse Yat Sen remained steadily watching him.

Finally Jeb Stuart Ho's eyes opened. For some moments the younger and older man sat watching each other. Then Jeb Stuart Ho smiled.

'You have prepared everything?'

'Everything, my teacher.'

There was a long pause. Jeb Stuart Ho slipped silently out of his robe. He remained cross-legged and naked on the dais. Milhouse Yat Sen frowned.

'Are you going to put on your equipment, my teacher?'

Jeb Stuart Ho shook his head.

'I am going to sleep.'

'Do you wish me to leave you, my teacher?'

Jeb Stuart Ho laughed softly.

'I would like you to stay with me, Milhouse Yat Sen.'

The young man solemnly stood up. He let his own robe fall to the floor. His slim body was pale in the candlelight.

'I would like to stay with you, Jeb Stuart Ho.'

He knelt on the dais beside Jeb Stuart Ho and ran his fingers across the scars on Jeb Stuart Ho's broad chest.

10

A Catto had worked unrelentingly for three solid days. Her armies had taken Feld and a dozen other cities. They were now regrouping for the next major centreward thrust into the heart of the more closely packed stasis towns. It was not, however, the problems of military strategy that had absorbed AA Catto's time and energy. Those burdens had fallen almost entirely on the shoulders of her six advisers, the war-room aides and the lizard installation. AA Catto had been planning a dinner party. It was no ordinary dinner party. This was to be a very special celebration of the success of the first stage of her conquest.

Even though she said it herself, the party was turning out to be a glittering success. Not that there was any reason why it shouldn't be. AA Catto had given her most careful personal attention to every detail from the decor and the menu to the after-dinner drugs and the ordering of the guests.

She was particularly pleased with the ordering of the guests. The result that she now surveyed from her high-backed chair at the head of the long banqueting table was a tribute to her imagination and ingenuity.

In a time of war, it had seemed inadvisable to invite genuine individuals from outside. Thus she had had to resort to ordering custom-built dinner guests from Stuff Central. AA Catto had scoured the history tapes for details of suitable personalities that could be programmed on to units from the Stuff Central pool of human blanks.

On the left of AA Catto sat Nancy, who was the only other natural human in the room. On her right sat a reproduction of a poet and playwright called Oscar Wilde. She had dug him out from some extremely ancient records. His constant chatter was amusing, and he could be relied on to fill any lapses in the flow of conversation with witty, if archaic, anecdotes.

AA Catto found he had a few minor drawbacks. For one thing, he was grossly overweight, a failing that AA Catto did not forgive easily. He tended to talk with his mouth full and drop food on the front of his silk dinner jacket. He was also rabidly homosexual, which ordinarily wouldn't have bothered AA Catto at all, except that he kept switching his attention from her and casting covert glances at the guest opposite him.

This was a replica of a character called Presley. The original for him came from much the same period as Wilde. He was reputed to have been an entertainer and local sex symbol. AA Catto had picked him for his sullen good looks. He was not proving very entertaining, although AA Catto did have plans for him later. Through the first courses he sat slumped in his chair, the fringes from his white spangled suit falling across the table, becoming more sullen each time Wilde turned the stream of his wit in Presley's direction.

Further down the table was Jeremy Atreides, a splendid figure in pale blue robes and festoons of jewellery. The Atreides copy was thin and good-looking in a rather sick, epicene way, and had the scintillating kind of vicious, decadent humour that can only be found in the last of very long and inbred lines of late period god-emperors. AA Catto considered Atreides an overwhelming success, particularly as he seemed constantly able to top Wilde's somewhat set-piece epigrams.

Beside him, laughing without fail at all his jokes and occasionally placing a tentative hand under the robes, was a reproduction of Patty Maison, a notably obscene dancer from the Age of Decline.

At the far end of the table were a clutch of big-league courtesans whom AA Catto had picked for their reputed adaptability. She had also included the notorious Fila Fernflower, a few particularly bestial tyrants, and Job Yok, a necromancer whose private life had so disgusted his swarm of faithful disciples that in the end they had felt compelled to eat him.

The only real failure was a Yaqui Indian shaman called Paha-Sapa who, before the dinner had even started, had smeared himself with datura paste and gone into immediate trance. AA Catto was aware that she would shortly have to deal with him.

With the exception of the shaman, the guests were on their best and most energetic behaviour. It was understandable, in view of the fact that AA Catto had informed them, during the hors d'oeuvres, that anyone who failed to please would be shot. They may have all been custom-built reproductions with impressed personalities, but they were also mortal, with a mortal's inbuilt aversion to violent death. To reinforce AA Catto's warning, two armed guards stood silently behind her chair. At first the warning had cast a shadow over the festivities, but by the time the larks' wings in aspic arrived, the party was in full, if desperate, swing.

AA Catto had, if anything, underplayed her own part in the proceedings. She was there to be amused. She didn't feel obliged to contribute unless she wanted to. She wore a kind of black djellabah, slit on one side up to the thigh. One leg, encased in a black leather boot, dangled across the arm of her chair. A small cherub stood beside her chair stroking the inside of her thigh with a peacock feather. The cherub was less than a metre tall, pink and chubby with small gold wings grafted on his back.

The table in front of AA Catto sparkled with cut glass and fine silver. It was spread with spotless damask and white linen. Teams of young men and women, uniformly blue-eyed and blond-haired, continually replaced the dishes and decanters. They wore white tunics and were garlanded with vine leaves and flowers.

AA Catto sat silently in her chair and watched the entire circus with a half smile that revealed nothing of what she was thinking. Her exquisitely made-up eyes moved from one man to the other as Wilde started on Presley again.

'Why so sullen, sweet boy, it hardly becomes you?'

Atreides raised his head from nuzzling Patty Maison and glanced at Presley.

'I would have thought it became him admirably. Why, at times he positively smoulders.'

Presley remained silent. He glared from beneath his eyelids, and his upper lip curled into a sneer. Wilde clapped his hands in delight.

'He surely becomes more beautiful by the moment. He is delightful when he's angry.'

Presley slammed his glass down on the table.

'Why don't you faggots get the hell off my back?'

Atreides laughed.

'He must be talking about you, Oscar. I'm sure Miss Maison will confirm that I can't be categorized by such a narrow definition.'

His hand seemed to have vanished inside her dress. Patty Maison giggled shrilly and nodded. Wilde pursed his lips.

'A combination of the arrogant and the omnivorous in one individual seems positively vulgar.'

He beamed at Presley.

'Wouldn't you agree, dear boy?'

Presley looked up sharply.

'Ah don't know what the hell you're talking about.'

Atreides smiled sardonically.

'He doesn't have your experience, Wilde.'

Wilde slowly turned to look at the replica of the god-emperor.

'Experience is the name that everyone gives to their mistakes.'

He glanced back at Presley.

'It's said that anyone who can dominate a dinner table can dominate the world.'

Presley half rose from his seat. He held up a tense, semi-threatening hand.

'Ah'm warning you, brother. Ah've had about enough of your mouth.'

The conversation round the long table stopped dead. The servants halted, and even the harp player in the filthy coat, battered top hat and red wig on the small platform in the corner of the room ceased to play. Then Wilde broke the silence with a brittle giggle.

'Come now, sweet boy, no one as pretty as you should behave quite so dreadfully.'

Everyone's eyes turned to Presley. AA Catto leaned forward in her chair. Presley sat hunched up looking down at his hands. Wilde spoke again.

'Nothing to say, dear boy?'

Presley suddenly snapped to his feet and flashed around the table before anyone else could move. He swung two wide, vicious punches at Wilde's head, and then followed them up with a savage jab into the fat man's stomach. AA Catto's guards started to move towards Presley but, at a signal from her, remained still.

Wilde fell to his knees, sobbing and trying to protect his face with his hands. Presley leaned forward, grabbed him by the lapels of his dinner jacket and hauled him to his feet.

'Ah warned you, faggot.'

He slammed Wilde hard against the wall three times. Then he let go of him. Wilde's head sagged on to his chest. He slid slowly to the floor. Presley turned to face AA Catto. He stood awkwardly, brushing his hair back out of his eyes.

'Ah'm sorry to mess up your party, ma'am. Maybe it'd be better if Ah was to leave?'

AA Catto smiled.

'On the contrary, it was very entertaining. You must come and sit by me.'

Presley sat down beside her. She motioned to her guards, and they dragged the unconscious figure of Wilde out of the room. Paha-Sapa the shaman chose that moment to fall off his chair, and he too was dragged away. The servants began to circulate with brandy, mints, small porcelain bowls of cocaine and opium pipes.

The conversation started again. Atreides began groping Patty Maison in a more serious manner. The courtesans and the tyrants also began to get acquainted. Job Yok, the necromancer, tried to catch AA Catto's eye. He had a plan for the reorganization of her armies according to a cabbalistic system of numerology. AA Catto wasn't buying. She was more interested in the Presley reproduction.

Only Nancy seemed set apart from the general festivities. She sat back in her chair and watched as AA Catto started to move in on Presley. Nancy wondered if he'd survive the night. Nancy had been there too often when AA Catto had fun with one of her custom-built males. Nancy knew that only a small percentage lived through it.

Nancy looked carefully at her friend and leader. She was suddenly very aware that she was the only natural human who came anywhere near AA Catto. Everyone else around her was custom-built to her fantasy. At the start, the idea of conquest had seemed like a game. Now it was becoming reality, Nancy was filled with misgivings. She had never been on anything more than nodding terms with any kind of morality, but she was beginning to have grave doubts about what world AA Catto thought she was going to create, and, more particularly, how long Nancy would last if AA Catto ever got tired of her.

AA Catto seemed to have no doubts at all. She was leaning on the Presley reproduction and running her fingers across his chest.

'I've got a feeling that I'm going to be pleased I ordered you.'

'Thank you, ma'am, it was great to be designed.'

'You're glad that I picked out this personality for you?'

'Yes, ma'am.'

'I expect you feel lucky to be beamed out to someone like me.'

'Yes, ma'am.'

'You do know who I am, don't you?'

'Sure Ah know who you are, ma'am. Ah was tol' when Ah beamed out.'

'And you know what I do?'

'No, ma'am, not for certain sure.'

AA Catto's voice became very soft and coy.

'I'm conquering what's left of the world.'

Presley nuzzled her ear.

'That's very impressive, ma'am.'

'Isn't it just.'

'Yes, ma'am.'

'I've conquered a good deal of it already.'

'That's a very fine achievement, ma'am…'

He slid his left hand inside her djellabah.

'… specially for a cute little girl like you.'

AA Catto lay back as his hand cupped her breast. She smiled up at him, and ran her fingers through his greasy hair.

'You think I'm cute, do you?'

'Ah think you're the prettiest thing Ah seen.'

AA Catto began to undo his shirt.

'I suppose you could say that I'm building an empire…'

She sighed and wriggled her hips.

'… the like of which the world has never seen.'

The Presley reproduction ran his tongue round AA Catto's left nipple.

'That's a fine thing to say, ma'am. Ah never met no woman with an empire.'

AA Catto's voice became deep and husky.

'It will stand for a thousand years.'

'That's one hell of an empire, ma'am.'

AA Catto propped herself up on one elbow and looked around the room. The rest of the guests had fallen into a tangled squirming heap on the floor. The harp player bounced up and down in the middle of it all. Only Job Yok the necromancer still sat at the table staring disconsolately at his empty plate. AA Catto nibbled at the Presley reproduction's ear.

'I think we should go somewhere more private. I want to tell you all about what I'm going to do to the human population. I've got some fantastic plans for them.'

'It'd be a blast.'

AA Catto disentangled herself from the Presley replica and stood up.

'Let's go.'

Presley also stood up, straightening his clothes. AA Catto looked at him and shook her head.

'There's one thing wrong with you custom-mades.'

Presley looked at her in surprise.

'Huh?'

'You're all so goddamn docile. You have the built-in anxious-to-please factor.'

'Ah'm sorry, ma'am.'

'According to the tapes, the real Elvis Presley would never have said anything like that.'

She turned to Nancy.

'You better come too. I've decided to wrap up this dinner. I'm bored with it.'

The other guests were still squirming on the floor. AA Catto nodded to the guards.

'You can go ahead, I've finished with them.'

She walked briskly out of the room with Nancy and the Presley replica obediently following her. As the doors closed behind them, the gunfire started.

11

Billy, the Minstrel Boy and Olad moved silently through the shadows of blacked-out Feld. The drizzle fell in a continuous veil. At regular intervals, an Ocpol ground car would cruise past and they would have to freeze in a doorway or the entrance to an alley. Slowly they made their way towards the city wall, following the directions that Carmen the Whore had given them.

They kept to the inside of the wall until they could see the jagged hole blasted in it by the Quahal army, silhouetted against the dim skyshine. When they were about thirty metres from the gap, the Minstrel Boy halted and motioned to the other two to do the same. Billy leaned against the wall trying to keep his teeth from chattering. He was soaked to the skin.

'Can you see any guards?'

The Minstrel Boy shook his head.

'There's nothing moving, but it's too dark to tell for sure.'

The three of them strained their ears for any telltale sound. All they could hear was their own breathing and the drip of water as it fell from walls and roofs. The Minstrel Boy shivered.

'I don't see how they'd be dumb enough to leave a gap in the wall like that unguarded. Let's move up a little way. Take it real slow and quiet.'

They moved another ten metres towards the gap, keeping close together and hugging the cover of the wall. Again the Minstrel Boy stopped. Billy put his hand down to his gun.

'See anything now?'

The Minstrel Boy peered into the darkness.

'I ain't sure. Wait a minute... Yeah, I think there's someone moving up there.'

He began to edge closer. The other two followed. The Minstrel Boy dropped behind a pile of rubble. Billy crouched down beside him. The Minstrel Boy slowly raised his head.

'There's definitely one guard out there. He's standing right in the gap.'

'Just the one?'

'That's all I can see.'

'You figure there's any more?'

The Minstrel Boy looked at Billy impatiently.

'How the hell should I know?'

Olad pulled his gun from his holster.

'I'll go deal with him.'

The Minstrel Boy grabbed his arm.

'You stay right where you are. You'd wake up the whole goddamn army.'

'So what do we do?'

The Minstrel Boy grimly took two of his knives from his belt.

'I'll take care of this. You two'd only fuck up.'

He scrambled over the pile of rubble and vanished into the shadows. Olad looked at Billy.

'Think we should follow him?'

Billy shook his head.

'We'll just stay put.'

They waited, holding their breath. For a long time nothing happened. No sound came from the darkness. There was no sign of movement. Olad drew his gun.

'He's gone and got himself killed.'

'He ain't. We would have heard something.'

'Maybe he's selling us out.'

'He wouldn't do that.'

Olad peered dubiously into the night and rain.

'Wouldn't he?'

Billy suffered an instant pang of doubt. Perhaps the Minstrel Boy was betraying them. He put it on one side.

'He wouldn't do that.'

Still nothing happened. Then they heard a sound in front of them. They both crouched down with guns held tensely in their hands. The Minstrel Boy appeared over the pile of rubble. He was carefully wiping his knives. He slipped them back into his belt.

'We'd better get through the gap before anyone comes.'

'How many guards were there?'

'Just one.'

'Did you kill him?'

The Minstrel Boy's hat hid his face, but his voice was filled with contempt and revulsion.

'I said I'd take care of it, didn't I?'

They started forward again. As they moved through the gap in the wall they had to step over the body of a black-helmeted guard. His throat had been neatly cut, almost like a surgical operation.

On the other side of the wall the view was like something out of a nightmare. Spotlight towers dotted the wide flat plain, illuminating line upon line of small hemispherical inflatable tents and hundreds of fighting machines marshalled in straight, orderly lines. There were tanks, ground cars, aircraft of all sizes, light and heavy artillery, earth-moving and traction equipment, and trucks of every kind. Huge dirigibles came down on cleared areas picked out with coloured marker lights. Gangs of men swarmed over them unloading mountains of supplies and munitions. Thousands of black-suited troops moved around the huge camp like swarms of ants. The cold lights reflected in the rain heightened the effect of implacable evil. The three escapees stopped and stared.

'God, just look at that!'

'There must be thousands of them.'

'Hundreds of thousands.'

'Nothing's going to stop an army like that.'

Billy looked at the Minstrel Boy.

'How did she get hold of all this? Stuff Central must have gone crazy.'

The Minstrel Boy nodded grimly. He looked thoughtful.

'That could be an answer.

Olad looked round nervously.

'Let's get the fuck out of here before we're spotted.'

'Which way do we go?'

An expression of pain passed across the Minstrel Boy's face. He shut his eyes and concentrated. After a few seconds he opened them again and sighed.

'We'll follow the outside of the wall, round to the other side of the city. Then we'll strike out into the nothings.'

The other two nodded. They moved off in single file, with the Minstrel Boy in front. Again they stuck to the shadows close to the wall. They'd been walking for about twenty minutes, and were about halfway round the city, when they heard the distinctive sound of a patrol vehicle.

'Down!'

The Minstrel Boy hit the ground, and the other two did the same. They swivelled round and snatched out their guns. The patrol came nearer. It was moving very slowly, scanning the wall with a searchlight. It seemed to be doing a routine check. The three men pressed themselves hard into the damp ground. The car crawled closer. It stopped only a few metres from where they lay. Olad slowly raised his gun. The spotlight played on the wall above their heads. It moved slowly downwards. Billy took careful aim at the patrol vehicle. He held his breath. The searchlight stopped just short of where they lay. It remained still for a few moments and then swung sideways. The car rolled on. Billy let out a deep breath.

'That was too damn close.'

The Minstrel Boy slowly stood up. He watched the patrol car vanish into the rain.

'They'll find the body of the guard pretty soon. We'd best get the fuck out of here.'

They hurried along for another ten minutes. The Minstrel Boy stopped every now and then as though trying to get his bearings. The other two didn't speak to him. They knew the faculty of wayfinding had unpleasant side effects. What these were, they couldn't guess at. The simplest thing was just to leave him alone.

They approached one of the ruined gates of the city. The Minstrel Boy halted.

'We should move out towards the nothings.'

He pointed to the road that ran out from the wreckage of the gate.

'We can follow the road. It used to link up with a stable wheelfreaks' highway across the nothings. I expect that's started to break up now. You both got portapacs?'

Billy and Olad nodded, and patted the portable stasis generators on their belts.

'Okay, let's go.'

They started across country. When they were a little way from the city they headed for the road. They'd only just set foot on it when a siren went off on the other side of Feld. It was quickly joined by the sound of two or three more. Olad looked round.

'What do you think that is?'

The Minstrel Boy shrugged.

'They've probably found the body.'

Billy stared back into the drizzle.

'If they have, they'll come looking for us.'

Olad quickened his pace.

'Let's get into the nothings. They won't find us there.'

They broke into a jog. The three of them managed to keep going for about fifteen minutes. Then Billy stopped, gasping for breath.

'I can't keep this up. Two weeks in that whorehouse have put me right out of condition.'

Olad suddenly pointed back down the road.

'Look!'

They all turned. Lights were moving around the city.

'They're looking for us. That's for sure.'

'Maybe they'll think it's a resistance killing.'

The Minstrel Boy grunted.

'Maybe. Let's just keep going, and keep our eyes open.'

They hurried on. The lights and sirens continued to circle the city. For a while Billy thought the search was being confined to just that area. It looked as though they'd got away. Then lights started coming down the road towards them. Billy looked round wildly.

'Get off the road!'

There was a ditch running along the side of the road. The three men hit it almost simultaneously. There was about fifteen or twenty centimetres of water in the ditch. Billy, Olad and the Minstrel Boy were forced to lie in it. It didn't matter all that much, they were already soaked to the skin.

Three patrol vehicles roared past at top speed with their lights flashing and sirens screaming. They were going too fast to notice the huddled figures.

The three refugees moved cautiously along it. Walking in water up to their ankles made the going slow and difficult. Both Billy and Olad tripped more than once, and measured their length in the muddy water. Patrol cars kept howling past on the road. Each time they approached, the three men were forced to crouch down in the wet.

After a long time, the patrol cars stopped moving up and down the road. Billy listened carefully. It seemed as though the search had returned to the city. He emerged cautiously on to the highway. Olad and the Minstrel Boy followed him. The only moving lights were way behind them. Up ahead was dim grey luminescence. As they walked on it grew brighter. Billy grinned at the Minstrel Boy.

'It's the nothings. We're there. We made it.'

The Minstrel Boy pushed back his hat with a gesture of relief.

'It does look…'

A pair of searchlights snapped on, bathing the trio in blinding white light. The black shape of a patrol car was standing by the side of the road. A metallic voice crackled from a speaker.

'Stand right where you are. Raise your hands and do not move.'

The three of them slowly raised their hands. Two orange-helmeted Ocpol dismounted from the vehicle. They walked slowly towards Billy, Olad and the Minstrel Boy. Their guns were pointed unerringly at the three men.

12

She/They moved into a new, different zone. Her/Their senses were extended to the very limit in the search for the entity that was destroying and converting basic mass and energy. She/They had detected some form of carrier beams stretching out through the chaos of the nothings. She/They had concluded that it was possible that these beams emanated from the entity that She/They sought.

She/They had followed the path of the beams. They flowed through the swirling grey confusion like lines of clear pulsing light. She/They began to perceive that they converged, and obviously emanated from a single distant point. Her/Their hopes rose that, as She/They had first suspected, it would be at this point that She/They would locate the thing that She/They was hunting.

Following the beams had not been easy. Plotting their course was not difficult. They shone through the nothings like a beacon to Her/Their sensors. It was their inflexible straightness that created the problems. They sliced unfailingly through every part of the chaos. She/They was forced to follow whereever they led.

The zone She/They was entering was one of strangely disarranged matter. It appeared to have been torn up by the disruptors, but not totally destroyed. It was like a fold in the nothings, an eddy that was filled with fantastic debris created by an unknown intelligence.

She/They floated about a metre above an expanse of dark red viscous liquid. Huge insect-like creatures were crowded together, half submerged. They jostled and scrabbled at each other. There was the click of claws on carapaces and the crack of powerful mandibles. Occasionally one would snap up at Her/Their feet, but She/They managed to keep out of the creatures' reach.

The red liquid slowly gave way to a strange kind of swamp. Clumps of spiky purple vegetation poked up through the surface. The huge swimming insects were left behind, and replaced by much smaller flying ones. They flew at Her/Their face but, at the last minute, they would veer away, and none of them actually touched Her/Them. Above Her/Them, saffron clouds sped across a threatening magenta sky. She/They, however, felt no motion at the level She/They was on.

All at once, Her/Their sensors began to jangle.

'Disruptor.'

The word hung in front of Her/Them like a flashing warning sign. She/They stopped abruptly, and shut down as much of the flow of energy through Her/Their being as possible. She/They hung in space, still and almost dead. Only Her/Their visual sensors were still operating.

The most distant clouds seemed to be being sucked down, and the surface of the swamp lifted up to meet them. Then the disruptor appeared over a kind of false horizon between the two.

The disruptor was solid, cylindrical and half buried in the surface of the swamp. It sucked in matter through the gaping maw in its forward end. Behind it, it left a trail of sparkling grey chaos, suffused with rainbow patterns that gradually faded as it moved away.

The thing came towards Her/Them. She/They cut Her/Their energy circulation to the absolute minimum. Her/Their perception of colour began to fade. One moment, the smooth sides of the disruptor were an *intense metalflake blue, then they changed to a flat grey as the power to Her/Their visual sensors decreased.*

She/They hung limp and immobile. The disruptor seemed unaware of Her/Their presence. It continued on a straight course that, unfortunately, lay in Her/Their direction. For moments it seemed as though She/They might be sucked into its squat reptile mouth simply by accident.

Then it passed Her/Them. It was close enough for Her/Them to perceive the markings on its smooth metallic sides. It was obviously some kind of graphic script, but in Her/Their low energy state She/They was unable to decipher it.

The disruptor continued to move away. She/They cautiously raised Her/Their energy level enough to turn one of Her/Their three heads and watch it go. The disruptor didn't seem to notice the slight fluctuation. She/They moved Her/Their energy rate even higher to allow Her/Them to consider the problem. Colour returned to Her/Their vision.

'Hypothesis. The disruption module's energy detectors only operate on higher patterns.'

'Inoperative. We have positive information to the contrary.'

'Hypothesis. The carrier beam generates its own field that repels the disruptor module. Such a field could mask our own energy trace.'

She/They conceded.

'A possible option.'

She/They allowed Her/Their energy level to move back up to maximum. She/They began to move again, carefully following the course of the beam.

13

Jeb Stuart Ho sat in the J-class flightcraft with the twenty-nine other brotherhood executives. Their bubble helmets were sealed shut, and umbilical lines ran from the side walls of the craft's sparse interior to the front of their suits. When the time to jump came, these would be disconnected and they would rely on the suits' own life-support systems. Until then, while they were still in transit, they remained hooked into the ship.

There was no conversation. The suit-to-suit communicators were only used for messages of the utmost importance. The task force were seated in pairs, on two-man padded benches. Over half of them had assumed postures of meditation. Jeb Stuart Ho wasn't one of them. He had tried for a while to make his mind go blank. He had given up when he realized he was too keyed up by the task even to achieve the most minimal state of trance. Instead, he just let his thoughts wander where they might.

The speaker in his helmet crackled into life, and brought him back to reality. He heard the flat metallic voice of the auto pilot.

'Drop zone approaching. E.T.A. ten minutes. Forward scanner is being relayed to bulkhead screen.'

The large screen at the end of the passenger area came on. In the centre of it was a small pale blue sphere. It slowly but steadily grew larger until it filled half the screen. There were no markings on it of any kind. Jeb Stuart Ho felt a twinge of disappointment. He had expected Stuff Central to be a little more impressive. The speaker crackled again.

'Drop to target minus ninety and counting.'

Jeb Stuart Ho took a deep breath and made a final check on his equipment. Everything was perfect. On the screen, the blue sphere continued to increase in size. It almost filled it.

'Minus sixty and counting.'

Jeb Stuart Ho swallowed. The dryness of excitement made his tongue feel thick and sticky. Inside the gloves of his fighting suit, his palms began to perspire slightly.

'Minus fifty and counting.'

The screen was now totally filled with an expanse of blue. Jeb Stuart Ho tensed in his seat.

'Minus forty and counting. We have now entered the stasis area of the target. Outside conditions are a perfect vacuum. Minus thirty-five and counting.'

Jeb Stuart Ho shifted in his seat. He tugged at the straps on his laser unit to make sure it was securely attached to his suit. The speaker continued to chatter.

'Minus thirty. Equalizing interior conditions with outside.'

There was a faint hiss as the craft atmosphere escaped into the vacuum surrounding Stuff Central.

'Minus twenty-five. Switch to individual life-support.'

Jeb Stuart Ho pulled the umbilical line from the front of his suit. His own life-support cut in automatically. A thin trickle of condensing gas flowed from the open end of the tube.

'Minus twenty and counting. We are now orbiting the target.'

On the screen, the blue sphere had shifted to form a slightly curved blue horizon. The surface still looked smooth and unblemished. Jeb Stuart Ho was only now beginning to realize the vastness of the sphere.

'Minus fifteen. Going down to surface on target; twelve, eleven, ten, nine, eight; stand by, releasing jump hatches.'

Three wide sections of panelling fell away from either side of the flightcraft.

'Prepare to jump.'

The thirty black-suited figures moved to the open hatches. They stood in front of them, five to a hatch.

'Five, four, three.'

Jeb Stuart Ho tensed all his muscles.

'Two, one, JUMP!'

In perfect unison, the executives rolled out of the flightcraft into empty space. There was a fall of about five metres to the surface of the sphere. Jeb Stuart Ho twisted in midair and landed heavily on all fours. His training prevented him from suffering any kind of injury. He lay flat on the smooth, blue, metallic surface and looked around. The rest of the force was spread out over a wide area, but they all seemed to have landed safely.

Jeb Stuart Ho was about to activate his communicator and make contact with his companions, when a small trapdoor flipped open in the surface of the sphere. A short antenna emerged from it. At its tip was what looked like a bundle of sensor lenses. Jeb Stuart Ho glanced round. A small forest of these antennae had sprouted all over the area in which the task force either lay or crouched. The scanners slowly revolved, moving as one. The intruders had been spotted and were obviously being inspected.

After two complete rotations, the antennae withdrew and the trapdoors closed again. For a few moments nothing happened. Jeb Stuart Ho looked at his companions. He spoke into his communicator, but nothing happened. Either it had been damaged in the fall, or something inside the target was interrupting the signal.

He stood up. The rest of the force were unhooking their laser units to start cutting through the outside shell. Abruptly another set of larger trapdoors snapped open. Telescopic stands flashed into position. Mounted on top of them were wide-barrelled projectile throwers.

They opened fire, silently flashing in the airless silence. Each one of them turned briskly, spraying self-propelled shells through a 360-degree arc. Jeb Stuart Ho tried to push himself down into the unyielding metal. He waited to be hit. After a while, the gunfire stopped. It seemed as though the weapons didn't have a low enough elevation to hit anyone lying flat on the surface. Jeb Stuart Ho assumed that if that was the case, the rest of the task force would also be unharmed.

The projectile throwers were still in position. Jeb Stuart Ho carefully turned his head. The guns didn't start firing again. Jeb Stuart Ho suddenly felt like he'd been kicked in the stomach. He saw how wrong he had been. More than three quarters of the brotherhood executives were dead. They hadn't hit the ground as fast as he had.

The dead were strewn all around him. On one side of him Quang Howard was almost cut in half. On the other lay a figure he could no longer recognize. The clear globe of his helmet was slowly filling up with bloody pink foam. Jeb Stuart Ho looked beyond them, trying to make contact with the survivors. Na Duc Rogers was lying some ten metres away. At first Jeb Stuart Ho thought he was dead, then he saw his head move inside the bubble helmet.

Na Duc Rogers spotted Ho. He raised his hand. A single weapon opened fire. The projectile neatly ripped off his arm just below the elbow. Jeb Stuart Ho watched in horror. The worst thing about it was the all-enveloping silence. Na Duc Rogers slowly rolled over and lay still.

Jeb Stuart Ho saw another survivor moving carefully towards him. He was worming his way along the surface, pressing his body flat to avoid triggering the projectile system. It was Lorenzo Binh. He touched helmets with Jeb Stuart Ho so his voice could be heard.

'The communicators are out.'

Ho nodded.

'I know that.'

'What do we do now?'

Jeb Stuart Ho looked at him grimly.

'We must go on with the task.'

'But we're pinned down.'

'We're safe as long as we remain flat.'

'Can we cut through the outer shell in this position?'

'We can try. Are there no other survivors?'

'There are two more brothers moving towards us. They're right behind you, you won't be able to see them from the position you're... Oh no.'

Lorenzo Binh's face contorted in an expression of horror and pain. Jeb Stuart Ho looked at him sharply.

'What's wrong?'

'Edgar Allan Piao got it. He raised his head a little and a projectile punctured his helmet.'

Jeb Stuart Ho turned his head grimly. Tom Hoa crawled up beside him. He touched helmets with the other two.

'Are there just the three of us?'

'It would appear so.'

Lorenzo Binh glanced round.

'Wait, there's someone else coming.'

Lee Harvey Thot joined the other three. Sweat was standing out on his forehead.

'We are the only ones left. We're stranded here. We've failed before we even started.'

Tears began to stream down his face. Jeb Stuart Ho reached out and gripped his shoulder.

'Get a hold on yourself, we're going on with the task.'

'We can't, we can't move.'

'We will start cutting through the outer shell.'

'We'll be killed.'

'That's quite possible.'

Jeb Stuart Ho looked round at the other two.

'We must move round so we are all facing each other.'

They cautiously did as he suggested. Lee Harvey Thot seemed to be more in control of himself. When they were in position, Jeb Stuart Ho unstrapped his laser unit and placed it in front of them.

'If you each support one side of it, we can keep the cutting aperture pointed at the shell.'

The others nodded and took hold of the squat grey metal unit. Once Jeb Stuart Ho was confident it was in position, he nodded.

'I'll switch on now. We'll have to keep moving round to cut out a section we can crawl through. Is everything clear?'

It was the others' turn to nod. Jeb Stuart Ho slowly raised his hand to the controls of the laser. The Stuff Central defence system remained silent. He set the laser to maximum cut. Then he pressed the trigger. A pencil of violet light flashed out from beneath it and struck the surface of the blue metal. The metal turned black, then red. Finally it began to smoke and melt. The four black-suited figures looked tensely at each other. They had started to cut into Stuff Central.

14

CYN 256 was unaware of the conflict taking place on the outside of the sphere that was Stuff Central. He had no way of knowing. His world was too prescribed, and his sources of information too scanty.

CYN 256 was fully occupied by his own conflict with the Computer. For some twenty work periods he had collected all the sets of figures that had shown up on the printout in his work cubicle, and not felt right to him.

He had gone on carefully dividing them into the three arbitrary categories that he had invented, the ones that seemed to relate to stuff output, to energy and mass intake, and internal operations of the machine. He copied them carefully on to his stolen scrap of paper with the stolen scriber, out of sight of the sensor, in the sanitary unit of his sleep cubicle.

His collection of figures got larger and larger until it threatened to fill up both sides of his paper. CYN 256 knew that he couldn't simply go on collecting figures for ever. He realized that eventually he would slip up. He would either be detected by the sensors, or his hiding place in the disposal vent for paper and scriber would be discovered.

CYN 256 had expected that if he kept on collecting the figures for long enough, some kind of revelation would come upon him. He would discover meaning in the ambiguities that he sensed instinctively.

He'd collected the figures from twenty work periods, and nothing had become any clearer. He realized that he had to do something drastic. He only had one option left. The only thing he could think of was to feed the material back into the Computer through his work cubicle console, and see how it reacted. CYN 256 realized that there was one major drawback with this plan. The Computer might react by simply killing him.

He delayed the final act for two whole work periods before he could summon up the courage to face the Computer. All his lifelong programming screamed out against it. For as long as he could remember he had been enveloped in the Computer s all-embracing love. His small gesture of rebellion and deceit had been hard enough. To go directly against the intelligence that had always been the central core of his whole existence was almost impossible.

As he walked down the corridor on the third period since he'd decided to feed the figures into the Computer, he knew there was no turning back. It was the start of a new work session. He had to do it before the time came for him to return to his sleep cubicle. He had been tempted simply to drop the paper and scriber into the disposal vent and forget the whole act of rebellion.

He was tempted, but deep down, he knew he had gone too far. There was no return to the secure happy ignorance of the other human operatives who walked to work beside him.

He came to his own work cubicle. He sat down and pressed the stud that activated the console. The printout immediately began to feed figures at him. His conditioning told him that his fingers should move to the console and begin to respond. Instead, he sat rigid. A light flashed above the console. Still he did nothing. He knew his inactivity had been recorded as a malfunction. The therapy squad would already be on their way.

He took the list from where he'd hidden it in his coverall. His fingers flew, copying the groups of figures. The light went out. The printout stopped. The strip continued to unwind but there was nothing on it. CYN 256 went on working at the console. Another light came on. It was red and it rapidly flashed on and off. The printout started again.

0101010101010101010101

CYN 256 looked at it in horror. The Computer was responding to what he had done, but he didn't understand it. The printout was meaningless. He had revealed himself but he had achieved nothing. He knew no more now than when he had started the whole insane scheme.

His hands fell away from the console. A set of tiny vents opened in the ceiling. A steel door slid out from the wall and sealed the entrance to the cubicle. CYN 256 knew it was his end. There was a faint hiss as pink, poisonous gas billowed from the vents.

CYN 256 closed his eyes, took a deep breath and died.

15

Billy, Olad and the Minstrel Boy stood very still as the three Ocpol patrolmen walked slowly towards them with their guns raised. They let their hands hang loosely at their sides, and made no threatening move. Billy edged carefully towards the Minstrel Boy.

'What do we do now?'

'Fuck knows.'

The three Ocpol halted a few paces from their captives. The one in the middle, who had what appeared to be the insignia of an officer on the front of his helmet, gestured with his gun.

'You will place your hands on your head.'

Billy, Olad and the Minstrel Boy did as they were told. The officer glanced at the patrolman on his right.

'Search them for weapons.'

The patrolman moved towards Olad. He walked round behind him. He carefully patted him down. When he reached the gun and the heavy knife at Olad's belt, the patrolman leaned forward and hooked the gun out of the belt. As he reached again for the knife, Olad pivoted on his toes, grabbed him by the throat and spun him round. The other Ocpol fired. Olad had the patrolman in front of him. The first two shells hit him in the chest. The force of the impact knocked both of them to the ground.

Billy snatched out his own gun and fired a burst at the officer. He spun round and fell. Billy turned his attention to the last of the Ocpol. He was already staggering round in circles, tugging vainly at one of the Minstrel Boy's knives that was buried in his throat. He sank to his knees, coughing blood, and then sprawled forward face down in the damp earth. Billy looked at the Minstrel Boy.

'Do you think there are any more inside the ground car?'

The Minstrel Boy started quickly towards the car.

'We can only find out.'

Billy followed him. They reached the car without anything happening. They pressed themselves against its dark grey armour-plated side. The Minstrel Boy's hand went to the door handle.

'When I nod, go.'

'Okay.'

The Minstrel Boy twisted the handle and jerked the door open. Billy thrust his gun into the interior of the ground car. It was empty. The Minstrel Boy grinned.

'It looks like we've even got transport.

Billy looked around. A grey dawn was starting to show through the unrelenting drizzle. Olad was on his feet walking unsteadily towards them. Billy shouted.

'Hey Olad, come on over here. We got ourselves a car.'

The Minstrel Boy frowned.

'He looks like he's hurt.'

They hurried towards the Siderian. Before they could reach him, he staggered and pitched forward. Billy and the Minstrel Boy ran to where he lay. Olad was face down in the mud. He didn't appear to be breathing. The Minstrel Boy gently rolled him over. His studded leather tunic was smeared with blood. The Minstrel Boy felt for his pulse.

'He's dead.'

Billy's eyes widened.

'Dead? How? The Ocpol took those two shots.'

The Minstrel Boy slowly stood up.

'The shells went right through the Ocpol, and got Olad as well.'

Billy went pale.

'Shit.'

The Minstrel Boy nodded.

'It's a hard world.'

'Is that all you got to say?'

'What else do you want?'

Billy began to get angry.

'What are we supposed to do with him? You just want to leave him lying there?'

'What else do you figure we can do? Bury him maybe? That'd just give a few more Ocpol ground cars the time to catch up with us.'

'We can't just leave him like this. He was our buddy.'

The Minstrel Boy looked down at the body.

'He was someone we met on the road.'

Billy looked at him in horror.

'Is that all you've got to say? The man's dead. He saved us.'

The Minstrel Boy nodded.

'I know. He's dead, and I'm cutting out. Are you coming with me, or do you want to honour your buddy's memory by waiting around to get picked up?'

The Minstrel Boy turned on his heel and walked quickly towards the car. After a few moments' hesitation Billy followed. The Minstrel Boy slid behind the wheel. Billy had hardly got the passenger door closed before the Minstrel Boy roughly jammed the car into drive. It took off with a lurch.

They drove in silence for a long time. It was only broken as they approached the nothings. The Minstrel Boy glanced at Billy.

'Look around, see if you can find a stasis unit in this heap.'

Billy stared sullenly straight ahead.

'Find it yourself. You're so fucking smart. You know everything.'

The Minstrel Boy stamped on the brakes and the car slewed to a stop. He reached over and grabbed Billy by the lapels of his coat. He pushed his face very close to Billy's.

'Listen, either we try and get out of this together or you can stay right here. You either cooperate, or I dump you. Which is it going to be?'

Billy looked at him. He closed his eyes and sighed.

'Okay, okay. I'll do what you want.'

The Minstrel Boy pushed the car into drive again.

'Find the stasis generator. We're going to need it.'

Billy hunted around. He looked beside the seats, on the control panel and in the back of the vehicle. Eventually he looked at the Minstrel Boy with a frown.

'There doesn't seem to be one.'

'You've looked everywhere?'

'Yeah. It don't seem likely that they'd hide the stasis generator.'

'Shit! Isn't there any kind of point where we can plug in our own portapacs and extend their field to include the car?'

Billy shook his head.

'There's nothing. It must have been designed for use in stable areas only.'

Outside, the landscape was already starting to break up. Large holes of grey emptiness were honeycombing the previously solid plain. Billy looked out of the narrow side window. He turned anxiously to the Minstrel Boy.

'Should we dump the car and go on on foot?'

'No, we'll drive till it disintegrates. You'd better turn on your porta-pac.'

The road became increasingly dotted with pits of nothing. The surrounding plain virtually disappeared. Soon they were driving on an incomplete road surrounded by the nothings. The Minstrel Boy kept throwing the car into screaming swerves to avoid touching any of the holes in the stable matter of the road. He managed to maintain this kind of erratic progress for quite a while. Then the offside front set of wheels hit a circular pit in the road, about a metre across. They smoked, disintegrated and vanished. The front of the car hit the road with a scream of metal on stone.

The Minstrel Boy lost all control. The ground car slid along the road for about fifty metres, then it hit an even larger space of disorganized matter. A good third of its bodywork simply disappeared. What was left of it fell apart. Billy found himself skimming down the road on a section of the chassis. He crossed another disrupted pit and that too ceased to exist. Billy hit the surface of the road. He was bruised, but otherwise complete inside the field of his portapac.

He painfully picked himself up and looked around. The Minstrel Boy was sprawled a short distance ahead of him. As Billy walked towards him, he got up. He too seemed to have escaped any serious injury. He stared gloomily at the few remnants of the ground car.

'I guess that's the end of that.'

'So now we walk?'

'Unless you got a better idea.'

'We've got no food, no water and no money. We might as well give up right now.'

Despite his pessimism the Minstrel Boy had started walking. Billy fell in beside him. Already he was beginning to feel the sad desolation he always experienced when he was out in the nothings. His sense of time was starting to go. He tried to maintain his grasp on reality by keeping a conversation going. It wasn't an easy task. The Minstrel Boy was depressed and unwilling to talk.

'How long do you figure we'll be on this road?'

The Minstrel Boy grunted.

'Till we get to the end.'

'What's at the other end?'

'Another road, I hope. If I'm right, it should be the main one into Litz.'

'How far's that?'

The Minstrel Boy looked at Billy scornfully.

'Don't you know by now that in the nothings distance and time don't mean shit?'

'But I...'

'But what?'

'Nothing. I don't know. I don't understand these roads.'

'Who's asking you to?'

'I mean, they're straight, they seem to go from one place to another. They ought to have some length that a man could figure out.'

'Who says?'

'It stands to reason.'

'What's reason got to do with it?'

'I guess I thought...'

The Minstrel Boy stared at him bleakly.

'Has it ever occurred to you that you think too damn much?'

'I don't understand.'

'So don't understand. Just accept. Don't always try to define everything. It only gets you confused.'

Billy tipped back his hat and scratched his head.

'These roads sure look straight to me.'

The Minstrel Boy sniffed.

'Things ain't always what they seem, particularly in the nothings.'

'Yeah, but...'

The Minstrel Boy took a deep breath.

'Just walk, will you.'

After that, there seemed to be nothing else to say. They walked in silence, each one enclosed in his own thoughts. Billy's perception of time slipped away altogether. He found it impossible to judge how long he'd been on the road. Sometimes it felt like a matter of minutes. At other times it seemed like days.

His ideas of distance also started to play tricks. One moment the Minstrel Boy would be right beside him, the next, the two of them would be separated by a wide expanse of road.

For a while it seemed that the simplest thing to do was to stare at the ground and trudge on. Even that, however, had its drawbacks. Billy found it acutely disturbing to look down into the pits of nothing that broke the road like pockmarks. When he stepped on one, the field of his portapac provided a solid, if invisible support for his foot where the road should have been. Billy began to hate the depressing journey.

Just as Billy was about to decide that they were trapped in a warp that would keep them on the barren, disintegrating road for ever, the Minstrel Boy clapped him on the shoulder.

'We've got somewhere.'

Billy looked up. Another, wider, more complete highway was crossing theirs up ahead. It swept past at right angles like a vast bridge, some thirty metres above the level of their road. There appeared to be no supports holding it up anywhere. Billy stared dully at the Minstrel Boy.

'It's just another road. Even if it is up in the air.'

'Yeah, but see what's on it?'

Billy looked again. A sluggish tide of humanity was moving slowly along the strange elevated highway for as far as the eye could see.

'Who are they?'

'Refugees I guess, making for Litz. At least they're people.'

Billy still couldn't raise any enthusiasm.

'So?'

'Where there are people, there's a way to survive.'

Billy cast a dubious eye over the empty space between the two roads.

'Can we get up there?'

The Minstrel Boy grinned. It was the first time he'd looked happy since they left Feld.

'Sure. No problem.'

16

A Catto moved around the deep underground bunker in a state of dangerous excitement. She wore a severely tailored black uniform, complete with a long skirt and polished riding boots. A combination of drugs and nervous energy kept her pacing the echoing corridors of her subterranean headquarters. Nancy and a procession of aides did their best to keep up with her tense, erratic progress. The Presley replica slouched along at the rear of the party, sullenly resplendent in a gold leather suit.

Nancy was a little surprised that the Presley replica was still around. Lately AA Catto had run through her custom-built playthings at an alarming rate. They normally didn't last a single night, and Nancy had become increasingly apprehensive of the time when she might become a victim of AA Catto's homicidal concepts of pleasure.

In many ways, Nancy found the survival of the Presley replica very reassuring. As long as he was there, she felt that she was safe from becoming the principal in one of AA Catto's ultimately sadistic love games.

For reasons known only to herself, AA Catto had adopted the Presley replica as a kind of pet. She treated him with an offhand benevolence, and had given him the run of virtually the whole bunker. For a couple of days he had wandered about, getting under the feet of the aides, and taking a retarded delight in playing with the gleaming technology, pressing buttons and watching things light up.

In the end, Nancy had taken it upon herself to warn him that should he cause the slightest detail to go wrong in any of AA Catto's elaborate battle plans by his childish meddling, she might no longer find him charming, and would have him painfully disposed of.

The Presley replica had accepted the warning with ill grace. He had, however, ceased to meddle with the war-room control boards. He now just tagged along behind AA Catto and became increasingly surly. Nancy began to feel that maybe his days were numbered.

AA Catto not only paced, she also talked. She poured out a nonstop stream of plans and ideas that the nervous aides struggled to record and add to the growing volume of strategic orders. Some of AA Catto's newest schemes filled Nancy with a sense of foreboding. She had become inured to AA Catto's general savagery and megalomania, but some of the latest ideas had the ring of terminal madness.

'Immediately Litz has fallen we will commence the programme of Population Rationale.'

The aide with a memo unit scurried to keep pace with AA Catto, at the same time juggling with the unit's pick-up so it remained always focused on her. To miss one of her pearls of wisdom was to court instant death.

'It seems to us that if we simply allow our captive peoples to go on much as before, the whole idea of conquest loses its essential beauty.'

The aides nodded frantically.

'Yes, our leader.'

'We feel that the captive population must be reorganized to fit in with our pattern of empire.'

Again the aides nodded and chorused. Nancy noted silently that AA Catto had begun to refer to herself in the plural. She took the responsibilities of an empress very seriously.

Without warning, AA Catto turned right down a side corridor. The aides collided with each other in their frantic efforts to keep pace with her.

'This is basically the core of the Humanity Problem.'

One aide, bolder than the rest, smiled ingratiatingly at her. 'You have a solution to this problem, our leader?'

AA Catto halted and looked at him menacingly. 'Do you really think we might be seeking your advice on the matter?'

The aide made fluttering, bird-like motions.

'Of course not, our leader. I would never presume.'

The other aides edged away from him, fearful they might fall into disfavour by association. AA Catto resumed her brisk march. She carried a short whip, which she rhythmically tapped against her leg.

'We have decided that the most beneficial policy would be to clear all stable areas of random humanity. A single area will be allocated so they can be concentrated in one spot. Make a note. We require a brain analysis of the most suitable location. Once that has been decided we can start to move the population. It will make our empire so much more tidy. Human populations can be replaced by clones as and when needed.'

AA Catto's expression became almost holy.

'Once the human population has been concentrated in this one spot, a complex can be created to carry out experimental work on individuals and groups as to their suitability for either reprogramming or extermination.'

The aide who had incurred AA Catto's wrath attempted to regain favour.

'The plan has an elegant symmetry, our leader.'

The Presley replica glanced up and wondered if he ought to have said that. He decided it wasn't his style, and therefore was not expected of him. He resumed staring at his legs, admiring the tightness of his gold pants. Nancy was struck by the innate absurdity that seemed to hover around absolute power. AA Catto simply nodded in curt acknowledgement.

'The human population will, of course, be put to work on the construction of the experimental establishment.'

AA Catto looked thoughtful.

'We have been considering a name for this place. We are torn between the Humanity Centre and the Catto Institute. We have been giving much thought to names lately. We consider them to be of paramount importance. We have been thinking about our own name.'

She glanced at Nancy.

'How does Catto the First grab you, sweetie?'

Nancy forced a brittle smile. At least she was still sweetie, although the word had an acid bite to it.

'It has a ring to it, my love.'

AA Catto nodded absently.

'That's what we thought. Very well, a number of problems still do remain. Take note. Firstly, it is safe to assume that a percentage of the human population will die in transit to the concentration area. We will require an accurate prediction of what this percentage will be. Second, we will need a profile of the survivors and those unable to survive. Third, we require a schematic brief of the precise operation of an establishment whose primary purpose is the elimination of free will and random action on the part of humans.'

Nancy was struck by the fact that AA Catto no longer considered herself human. AA Catto continued.

'Lastly, we will need detailed plans for the design of buildings and hardware outlined in the answer to the previous request, and the logistics of their construction.'

She looked round at the aides.

'Have we made ourself clear?'

The aides fell over themselves to show they understood.

'Of course, our leader.'

'Good.'

The boldest of the aides ventured another question.

'Will there be anything else, our leader?'

AA Catto's face darkened. She slapped the whip hard into her palm. The aide went white with terror. AA Catto regarded all the aides with an icy expression. Her voice went very quiet.

'There is one more thing.'

There was a deathly hush. AA Catto's voice rose hysterically.

'We want Litz taken! Taken now, with no more delay! Now go!'

The aides scurried away, and she let out a deep breath. She snapped her fingers at Nancy and the Presley replica.

'You two, Nancy and Elvis. You will come with us to our suite. If we don't relax we are liable to become insane.'

17

Of all the towns and cities attacked by AA Catto's legions, Litz had the most warning. For many days before the first Quahal storm troopers reached its stable areas, thousands of refugees had been pouring into the city.

Not that Litz actually had days. The sections of its generators that controlled the climate and the passing of light and dark were set permanently at warm, pleasant night-time. Litz was completely a city of night. The bars, the clubs, the sex shows and the brothels made the soft blackness a world of adventure for those who had the credits to pay for it.

Litz had been designed as a sleazy, sensual wonderland. It was a tinsel city where anything could be had for a price. A million lights illuminated the sky. Skyscrapers towered in floodlit magnificence. Coloured searchlights lanced into the heavens. The street lamps and the lights of the hundreds of ground cars turned the wide streets into glittering rivers. Airships and ornithopters drifted between the tall buildings, adding their own spots and riding lights to the general radiance.

Not all was pleasure and light in Litz. It also had its sinister shadows. Behind the shining façades were the grim back alleys. These were the haunts of the winos, the muggers and the homicidal juv gangs. It was the territory of half-starved human debris who competed with the huge rats, the wildcats and the semi-savage dogs that treated the maze of narrow alleys and claustrophobic yards as their personal hunting grounds.

Litz had changed. The looming war had put the city through more changes than ever before in its history. The first of these was the flood of refugees. The ones who had brought credit or acceptable goods out with them had installed themselves at the gleaming hotels. Those who hadn't had swelled the ranks of the back-alley dwellers.

Litz had adapted to war amazingly fast. Anywhere that was so corrupt must have that facility. Corruption always adapts. Litz, after all, had its foundations in the highest principles of human greed and operated on a finely honed interlocking system of bribes and expediency.

Almost instantly an array of fanciful uniforms had appeared in the bars, the nightclubs and the foyers of the whorehouses. Patriotic posters had quickly appeared on the walls of the city. Stirring martial parades had snarled traffic on the main streets. A thriving black market had mushroomed into being. It was, however, largely unnecessary as all the material goods needed by the city continued to come in on the stuff beam. One thing AA Catto had been unable to achieve, despite threats and pleading, was to persuade Stuff Central to discontinue service to cities under attack.

The city administration had done its part, though. It had sufficiently restricted the flow of supplies to create an inspirational feeling of scarcity. It was this move that gave the black market the space to flourish.

In all ways, Litz seemed ready to face the invaders.

And then they arrived. As usual, the dive bombers of AA Catto's crack Vulture Legion went in first. The rapidly organized owners of Litz's private aircraft took to the skies to face them in machines that had been hastily converted to a military role. The Litz air corps met the attacks with swaggering, if poorly organized, bravado. To their surprise, the Vulture Legion was totally routed, and retired to lick its wounds. AA Catto's air force had never encountered resistance and had no contingency plans to deal with it. The flying cowboys from Litz quickly made mincemeat of the sinister black dive bombers.

On the ground, things were far more grim. An army of flamboyant defenders had gone out to meet AA Catto's ground troops. They had been deftly massacred. The city was swiftly encircled. The only thing that stopped the armies of Quahal moving in for the kill was the desperate fight put up by a less picturesque but more efficient force, drawn primarily from the Litz Department of Correction. Even so, both sides were well aware that it was only a matter of time before the city finally fell.

One of the cops turned soldier was Section Commander Bannion. He was in charge of a three-kilometre strip of the city's perimeter. Bannion, like the rest of the Litz Defence Corps, was feeling himself being crushed under the knowledge of eventual certain defeat.

Bannion sat in the rest room of the defence HQ. It had originally been the drunk tank of the hastily converted LDC downtown station. The tank and cells were being used as accommodation for the soldiers.

Bannion sat with his thickset body hunched. He stared vacantly at the dirty white tiles of the opposite wall. He was totally withdrawn into himself. He hadn't bothered to shave for three days. His olive drab battle fatigues were creased and filthy. He rubbed a hand over the stubble on his chin. His eyes looked dark and sunken in the harsh glare of the naked tubes. The only clean object was the 27mm automatic carbine propped up beside him.

Most of the men in the Defence Corps had started letting themselves go. They'd stopped washing and shaving. Defeat and almost certain death were too close to make it worth bothering any more.

Bannion cursed quietly to himself. The sound of a man crying came from one of the cells. It was all breaking down so fast. Bannion had just come back from a patrol. He had gone out with twenty men and come back with twelve. He felt impotent and helpless. It was a feeling that he couldn't adjust to. In the Department of Correction he had always taken pride in being on top of things. His major pleasure had been the certainty of his power.

A weary looking orderly came into the tank. He didn't bother to salute.

'The captain wants to see you.'

Bannion noted dully that the orderly had reverted to the old police ranks. They'd all been given smart new titles when the Defence Corps had been formed, but these seemed to be dropping away. Bannion slowly stood up.

'Is he up in his office?'

The orderly nodded.

'Yeah.'

'Okay.'

Bannion picked up his carbine and followed the orderly out of the tank. He took his time climbing the stairs. When he reached the captain's office he pushed open the door without knocking.

'You wanted me?'

Captain Dante Schultz sat hunched over a battered steel desk. He looked as rough as Bannion. The only light came from a single desk lamp. It illuminated some papers, a map and a half empty bottle of whisky. Schultz rubbed his eyes and nodded at a rickety upright chair.

'Siddown.'

Bannion glanced round the small dim office. He briefly thought of all the nights he had sat with Schultz, consuming whisky, coffee, delicatessen sandwiches and pills. It seemed like those days had gone for good. He dropped into the chair. It creaked under his weight. Schultz grinned crookedly at him.

'You want to hear the latest from the city administration?'

Bannion shook his head.

'Not particularly.'

Schultz shuffled his papers.

'You're going to, anyway.'

Bannion grunted. Schultz picked up a bundle of buff sheets. 'I won't read it all to you.'

'Thanks.'

'I'll just give you the main points.'

Schultz paused. Bannion raised a tired eyebrow.

'You looking for a response, already?'

Schultz sighed.

'The city fathers are surprised at our lack of success in containing the invaders' ground forces. They are setting up an investigation.'

Bannion spat.

'They're surprised, are they? They should send their fucking investigators on patrol with my outfit. They'll find out how come we ain't "containing the invaders' ground forces". We're out-numbered and outgunned. They've got the numbers and the fire power.'

Schultz shrugged.

'I know that.'

'So tell the city fathers to go screw.'

'They also want us to carry out a retaliatory strike against the home base of the enemy.'

Bannion stared at Schultz in disbelief. 'Tell them to doubly go screw. It's not possible.'

Schultz looked down at the papers on his desk. 'We're going to do it.'

'You're out of your mind.'

'In fact, you're going to do it.'

Bannion's eyes narrowed. He leaned forward across the desk. His voice was very soft.

'Just what the fuck are you talking about, Schultz?'

'Captain Schultz.'

'Just tell me about it, will you?'

Schultz sighed.

'According to our intelligence reports this invasion is being directed from an area known as Quahal.'

'So what's Quahal?'

'Precisely, Quahal is a mountain and a river valley. In the valley there is a ziggurat.'

'What the hell is a ziggurat?'

'It's a kind of pyramid.'

'And that's where this invasion is being controlled from, a kind of pyramid?'

Schultz nodded.

'From a deep bunker built underneath it, to be totally accurate.'

'And what am I supposed to do about all this?'

Schultz took a deep breath.

'The plan is that you take a small force directly to Quahal. Fight your way into the bunker, destroy as much of the control equipment and kill as many of the command staff as possible.'

'Simple as that?'

'Right.'

'That's just dandy.'

'I can go into details.'

Bannion looked at Shultz bleakly.

'Before you do, let me ask you one question.'

'What?'

'Supposing we actually do all this, how do we get away afterwards?'

'That'll be up to you.'

Bannion smiled grimly.

'So it's a suicide mission?'

Schultz looked evenly at him.

'I didn't say that.'

Bannion's face twisted into a sneer.

'You're a chintzy bastard.'

'Bannion, I'm warning you...'

'Work it!'

'Bannion!'

'Okay, okay. Just don't jive me. I don't need it.'

'This mission could be our only hope.'

'So tell me the details.'

'Where do you want to start?'

'How do we get there?'

'There's an airship from one of the rental companies being armed and specially equipped for a journey through the nothings.'

'What do we do when we get there? Have you got plans of this bunker? The defence system? The entrances? That kind of thing?'

Schultz sadly shook his head.

'I'm afraid we don't have anything like that. We've only the barest information that the place exists at all. Beyond that we know nothing.'

Bannion looked amazed.

'Couldn't you have given some prisoners the full treatment?'

Schultz uncomfortably avoided Bannion's questioning stare.

'We did. The mercenaries had been picked up in other cities that had fallen. They'd never been near the place. The ones who actually came from Quahal just clammed up and died on us. We couldn't get a thing out of them.'

Bannion sagged back in his chair. It creaked dangerously.

'That's just great.'

'You'll have to play it by ear.'

'Wonderful.'

'Listen, I never said it was going to be easy.'

'You never said anything, did you?'

Schultz ignored Bannion's flash of temper. 'Is there anything else you want to know?'

'Yeah, how do we find our way there? Do we just cruise off into the nothings and hope we strike lucky?'

Schultz pursed his lips and played with his papers.

'We found you a wayfinder.'

Bannion grinned sarcastically. 'You're too good to me.'

Schultz scratched his neck awkwardly.

'Listen, Bannion, get off my back, will you? I'm only doing the best I can.'

'Sure, sure.'

'Someone has to do it.'

'And Bannion's the sucker, right?'

'Will you cut it out?'

'Okay, okay.'

Bannion thought for a moment.

'How do we know we can trust this wayfinder? How do you know he ain't running a con on the chance of getting out of the city?'

'You want to see him?'

Bannion waved an expansive hand.

'Sure, what do I have to lose?'

Schultz punched the talk button on his desk intercom.

'Sapristien.'

A muffled response came from the speaker.

'Bring in the old guy, will you?'

Another muffled response. After a few seconds the door opened and an elderly man was pushed inside. He was short, and on the heavy side. His head was bald, but he had bushy eyebrows and a flowing beard. His hard bright eyes and wrinkled face seemed to indicate a keen intelligence. He wore a dirty white smock that hung down to his sandalled feet. He regarded Bannion and Schultz with a total lack of interest.

Bannion rose lazily from his chair. He walked round the old man, taking slow deliberate paces, examining him from every side. It was one of Bannion's favourite opening gambits for putting a suspect in an uncertain frame of mind. His exchanges with Schultz had brought Bannion back to something like his old Department of Correction form. He halted in front of the old man, and stared at him for a full minute.

'And what do you call yourself, grandad?'

The old man didn't seem the least fazed by Bannion's performance. He smiled pleasantly.

'Most times I generally call myself me. Mind you, other people tend to call me the Wanderer, on account of how I roam from town to town.'

Bannion's eyes narrowed. His voice became a purr.

'And you claim to be a wayfinder?'

The Wanderer nodded.

'That's right. I may not be the best, you understand, but I got enough of the gift to get by.'

The old man leaned towards Bannion confidentially.

'Between you and me, I wouldn't like to be one of the best. Too many people getting on your ass, all wanting something.'

'You look more like a feisty, lying old bum to me.'

The Wanderer looked resigned.

'You got a right to think what you like.'

Bannion put his hands on his hips.

'You sound kind of indifferent.'

'That's pretty close to where I'm at.'

Bannion pounced. In a flash he'd grabbed the old man by the front of his smock and hauled him on to tiptoe.

'If you're going to be working with me, grandad, you're going to change your attitude. You're going to have to be pretty damned different, you dig? If you fuck me around I'm going to kill you, right?'

The old man blinked.

'You're the boss.'

Bannion abruptly let go of him. The Wanderer staggered back a few paces. Bannion levelled a threatening finger at him.

'You just keep that in mind.'

He turned to Schultz, who had remained seated during the whole miniature drama.

'How did you dig him up?'

'He was pulled in on a forged credit card. It's a mandatory death sentence under the emergency powers.'

Bannion looked at the old man with fresh interest.

'What was he doing?'

'He booked into a penthouse at the Albert Speer Hotel with a couple of hookers. He was paying with a homemade credit card.'

Bannion's eyebrows shot up.

'Two hookers? At his age?'

'At his age.'

Bannion chuckled.

'He may or may not be a wayfinder, but he's sure got some secret, and that's a fact. Tell me, old man. How do you manage it at your age?'

The Wanderer smiled blandly. 'I live a pure life.'

Bannion grunted.

'So it seems.'

He switched his attention back to Schultz. 'I suppose I'll have to use him?'

'There aren't any others.'

Bannion nodded thoughtfully. 'When do we leave?'

'How fast can you pick and brief a squad?'

'How many do I get?'

'Twenty.'

'We could be ready in a couple of hours, if you want us to leave that fast.'

'The ship'll be fitted out when you've got your squad together.'

Bannion took the Wanderer by the arm.

'You'd better come with me, grandad. I'm not letting you out of my sight.'

The Wanderer put on an expression of innocence.

'I'm completely in your hands.'

Bannion snorted.

'You just remember that.'

18

The laser unit had made a circular cut in the steel surface of Stuff Central about a metre across. As far as Jeb Stuart Ho could tell the loose piece in the middle of the cut was only held in place by a thin tongue of metal. He touched helmets with the other three brotherhood assassins.

'I think we could push it in now.

Lorenzo Binh turned his head slightly.

'Shall we use physical strength or psi pressure?'

Ho turned off the laser.

'We'll try psi first. It would be best to make as few movements as possible. We have no way of knowing when we may trigger another part of the auto-defence. Attempt to move the cut-out section on the count of three.'

Jeb Stuart Ho glanced carefully to make sure the other three were ready.

'One, two, three.'

They all concentrated. The piece of metal didn't move. After a few minutes Jeb Stuart Ho shook his head.

'We can't do it. We just don't have the power.'

Tom Hoa looked at Ho.

'We should use physical force?'

'Yes, but don't make any unnecessary movements.'

The four assassins slowly slid their hands on to the top of the cut-out section of metal. They pushed with all their strength. The section began to bend inwards. Then something snapped and fell into the inside of the sphere with a loud crash.

'Okay, go! Don't get in range of those auto guns!'

Tom Hoa slid into the hole and disappeared from sight. Lorenzo Binh went swiftly after him. Lee Harvey Thot followed, but as he swung his body into the empty space, he raised his head a fraction too much. One of the automatic projectile throwers flashed into life. Lee Harvey Thot's helmet was instantly shattered. His body tumbled through the hole. Jeb Stuart Ho could see no way that he couldn't be dead.

Ho eased himself through the hole. He let himself drop. He fell about three metres and hit a floor. He landed on his feet. He was in a corridor. It was lined with doors that looked as though they led to cubicles of some description. Lee Harvey Thot lay on the floor dead. Tom Hoa and Lorenzo Binh crouched with their guns at the ready.

The corridor ran absolutely straight for about two hundred metres. Then it disappeared over a kind of horizon as it followed the curve of the outside of the sphere. A number of small, yellow-clad figures were just disappearing over it. As far as Jeb Stuart Ho could judge, they were only about half his height. It looked as though the Computer had done something drastic to the growth pattern of its human operatives.

Jeb Stuart Ho turned round. A series of coloured lights had begun to flash on and off. The sound of wind rushing past his helmet indicated that the sphere's atmosphere was rushing out through the hole that they'd cut. He looked at the other two and spoke into his communicator.

'Can you hear me?'

'Yes, whatever was jamming the communicators has cut out.'

'We'll move thirty metres down the corridor. It's obvious that some alarm has been triggered. Even if our presence hasn't been detected, I estimate that some kind of emergency repair on the hole will be made.'

They moved watchfully down the corridor. Suddenly Tom Hoa shouted.

'Look.'

Ho and Lorenzo Binh spun round. Two steel partitions were sliding across the corridor on either side of the hole. They locked into place, effectively sealing off the leak. The alarm lights went out.

Tom Hoa looked at Jeb Stuart Ho.

'Could it be that we have not been detected?'

Jeb Smart Ho looked thoughtfully down the corridor with its long line of doors.

'It would be a great advantage if that was the case, but I do not think it is so. I have a feeling that the Computer may be observing us and waiting for us to reveal more of what our purpose is.'

Lorenzo Binh looked round cautiously.

'You think that we are being observed, Jeb Stuart Ho?'

'I think that it is most probable.'

'Could it be possible that we survived the automatic defences on the outside by some design of the Computer?'

'The possible is immense.'

'What would you calculate as being our next move, Jeb Stuart Ho?'

Jeb Stuart Ho didn't answer immediately. He was somewhat disconcerted by the way the other two seemed to be looking to him for leadership. He scarcely felt worthy, particularly as he had failed in his only previous mission. He realized, however, if that was the way it was going to be he would have to accept it.

'I think we should first ascertain the nature of our immediate surroundings.'

All the doors along the corridor had symbols on them. Jeb Stuart Ho looked at the one nearest to him. The characters on it read CTA 102. He pressed a stud just under the inscription. The door slid smoothly and silently open to reveal a small, bare cubicle. In some ways the starkness of the little room reminded him of his cell in the brotherhood temple.

The bed in the cubicle was tiny, scarcely larger than for a child. Again Jeb Stuart Ho wondered what had happened to the Stuff Central humans. He stepped back into the corridor, and looked at the other two.

'This seems to be a dormitory area. We will have to go on.'

The others fell into step behind him with their guns at the ready. They had only gone a dozen paces when another, different coloured set of warning lights began to flash on and off. Lorenzo Binh swung round in alarm.

'What can this mean?'

Jeb Stuart Ho remained calm.

'We will doubtless find out in time.

They assumed a defensive position. As a group they covered both ends of the corridor. Jeb Stuart Ho half crouched in the open doorway of a cubicle. He examined the grey metallic wall, and found that the panelling was almost as thin as foil. It would offer hardly any protection against projectiles. The illusion of cover was still somehow comforting.

They waited. For long tense moments nothing happened. Then tiny vents opened in the ceiling of the corridor. Thick pink gas began to pump out of them, and rolled down the corridor in billows.

'Poison gas?'

'Perhaps. We'll be safe inside our helmets.'

'It could simply be a smoke screen.'

The gas was certainly obscuring their vision. Jeb Stuart Ho smiled dourly.

'I think we can be certain that we've been detected.'

They strained to see through the thick clouds. Visibility was reduced to just under a metre. Then a tight hail of steel needles sliced through the wall above Jeb Stuart Ho's head. He threw himself flat on the floor, yelling into his communicator.

'We're under attack!'

More needles slashed into the thin metal. They hit the very spot where Jeb Stuart Ho had crouched just a moment before.

'Communicator silence. They may be using locator equipment.'

He rolled over and another hail of deadly steel slivers scored the floor where he'd been lying. It was plain that whatever was attacking them was relying on some kind of sound picture. He controlled his breathing. He fired at the approximate source of the attack, and immediately dodged. More needles sprayed the corridor.

Ho wondered if the attackers were men or simply another automatic system. He didn't have to wait long for an answer. A helmeted figure appeared out of the smoke hefting a large, heavy-duty spiral needle gun.

For an instant, Jeb Stuart Ho saw the figure very clearly. It wore a pale green belted coverall with a black letter B printed on the chest, heavy white combat boots and a white helmet. Its face was covered with a fitted gas mask that gave it the look of a huge-eyed, bizarre insect. Jeb Stuart Ho snapped off a shot and the figure crumpled.

Four more similar figures came out of the gas fog. Ho sprang to his feet. Face to face with an enemy he could fight, he felt far more confident. He whipped out his sword and in a single, lightning sweep took out two of them. Tom Hoa shot the third and Lorenzo Binh leaped at the fourth and tore away its gas mask. Before the creature stumbled back clutching its throat and coughing blood, Jeb Stuart Ho caught a glimpse of a flat, brutal, dead-white face. It was human, but strangely sexually neutral.

For a moment, no more attackers came. The three brotherhood assassins stood alone surrounded by the clouds of gas. Jeb Stuart Ho looked at the other two. At last they were fighting like a team. He experienced a moment of grim satisfaction. He knew it was the sensation of a warrior's true reward.

It faded when he looked down at one of the bodies at his feet. He noted that it was at least a head taller than he, with a massive muscular frame. These things were very different to the tiny, yellow-suited beings that lived in the corridor.

He realized that these must be the specially tailored defenders of Stuff Central. They may have once been human, but the Computer had adapted and altered them until they were simply the antibodies in the machine's complex system, protecting it from outside intruders and internal malfunction.

Jeb Stuart Ho knew they wouldn't be easy to fight. They'd be guided by the Computer's monstrous intellect, and, beyond the cloud of gas, there could be any number of them.

19

Billy and the Minstrel Boy arrived at the Inn. The Inn was a single building with its own stasis field. It dominated a strange midpoint in the peculiar road system that wove in and out of the nothings like a tangled, convoluted, hideously complex Möbius strip.

The Inn was about as small as a stable area could get. Its generators didn't run to luxuries like sky, scenery or even day and night. There was air, warmth, solid matter and gravity. That was it.

The Inn was a strange ramshackle affair. Wings and extensions had been added to the central, slab-sided stone building with no attempt at any kind of continuity in style. There were flying buttresses, turrets, thatched roofs, domes and even a geodesic annexe.

In front of the Inn was a broad forecourt. The entrance to it was through a high arch of neon lights. Beyond that there was only the road and a narrow strip of bare ground surrounding the whole area. After that the nothings started.

The road to the Inn had been long and hard. When Billy and the Minstrel Boy had joined the stream of refugees, they quickly discovered that they broke down into two very distinct groups: the sheep and the wolves, the prey and the predators. The Minstrel Boy wasn't in the least surprised.

Their first survival plan among the refugees was to hire on with sheep to protect them from the wolves. They were, after all, well armed, not easily messed with, and Billy did draw the line at out-and-out violent mugging.

The particular sheep who employed Billy and the Minstrel Boy were a merchant and his family from Port Judas. Their name was Inchgrip, and like all the solid citizens of Port Judas they were hard, humourless and meanly religious. Port Judas had, however, been reduced to smoking rubble by AA Catto's bombers, and the Inchgrips found themselves on the road with the rest of the frightened throng.

When Billy and the Minstrel Boy had gone touting for a job, the

Inchgrips had snapped up the two drifters to guard their lives and their wagonload of goods.

Not that the Inchgrips exactly took to Billy and the Minstrel Boy. They looked on them as filthy, sinful, foul-mouthed heathens who would surely burn in the particularly nasty hell envisaged by the Port Judas strain of evangelists. They especially disliked their habit of getting drunk every night. Nevertheless, they were more than anxious to put them to work. The Port Judas religion said nothing against one man exploiting another. As it came to pass, the exploitation turned out to be mutual.

The deal with the patriarch, the grey-bearded Rameses Inchgrip, was that Billy and the Minstrel Boy were to be given one gold piece per day or the equivalent in kind, plus all they could eat. Billy had spent a good while arguing with Rameses Inchgrip over whether they should also get all they could drink. The Minstrel Boy finally stopped the wrangle by reminding Billy that Port Judas was teetotal.

The situation had maintained itself reasonably well for twelve days on the road. Billy and the Minstrel Boy had been paid, and they'd more or less done their job.

There had of course been petty irritations on both sides. Rameses Inchgrip had been exceedingly obstructive about his two teenage daughters. He had threatened Billy and the Minstrel Boy with earthly torment and spiritual damnation if they so much as looked at them. He also kept his daughters so closely confined to the inside of the wagon that the Minstrel Boy began to suspect that they were chained to the floor.

On the thirteenth day, Rameses Inchgrip had an even more sour expression than usual. After a long preamble, he informed Billy and the Minstrel Boy that there wasn't enough left to either pay or feed them. The Minstrel Boy told him that they'd settle for his daughters. Inchgrip hit him, and Billy had to restrain the Minstrel Boy before he retaliated by knifing him.

After they parted company with the Inchgrips, they fell in with a madame and a party of whores who were making their escape from the war zone and providing a service for the other refugees on the road. It seemed to Billy that, come what may, they always ended up in a brothel of one sort or another.

On a normal day, before the invasion from Quahal had started, the forecourt of the Inn usually contained not more than a dozen or so ground cars, a string of lizards, one or two elaborately designed motor-cycles and maybe a single huge wheelfreak's truck. When Billy and the Minstrel Boy arrived it was choked with people and vehicles. The road for at least two kilometres from the Inn was jammed with backed-up traffic. Refugees who had been unable to find a room at the Inn were camping in the forecourt and even on the road itself.

The filth and confusion were alarming. Even more alarming were the contrasts between the conditions of different groups of people. The rich, with their teams of guards and collections of valuables, either lived in the Inn itself or camped in some comfort in the forecourt. At the other end of the scale were the dozens of beggars, people who had lost everything on the road, who barely existed on what scraps they could find. Every few minutes a fresh body would be pitched out into the nothings.

The closeness to the nothings solved the refugees' sanitation problem. If it hadn't been so easy to pitch waste and the dead into an area where all matter simply vanished, the refugees would almost certainly have had to add disease to their already extensive catalogue of troubles.

The Minstrel Boy and Billy picked their way through the crowds towards the Inn itself. Beggars swarmed up to them in droves.

'For pity's sake, I haven't eaten in five days straight.'

Billy was about to dig into his pockets and distribute a few coins when the Minstrel Boy grabbed him by the arm.

'Don't be more of a dummy than you can help.'

'But they're starving.'

'Yeah, and there are hundreds of them. Are you going to feed the lot?'

Billy shook his head.

'No, but…'

'Then don't give nothing to none of them. If you do, we won't be able to move. We'll be swamped by beggars wherever we go.'

The Minstrel Boy turned and aimed a swift kick at one of the more persistent suppliants who was tugging at his jacket, then turned back to Billy and shrugged.

'It's the only way to treat them and, besides, if the muggers hear that you've got money to throw at beggars we'll be in real trouble.'

Billy scratched his head.

'I'm wondering how long money will hold up.'

The Minstrel Boy sneered at the frantic milling crowds all around.

'It'll hold up as long as they believe in it. While they're still killing each other for it, money's cool. The whole thing's pretty well ingrained.'

Billy sadly shook his head.

'You've got a strange way of looking at things.'

The Minstrel Boy sniffed.

'I've got a sane way of looking at things. Let's see if we can get ourselves a drink.'

They continued to shoulder their way through the mob. They got within about twenty metres of the Inn. A group of men stepped up and barred their way.

'Where do you think you're going?'

The Minstrel Boy took a step back and looked at the four men in front of him. The tallest was a corsair from the fringes. He had the typical dark complexion and the plastered-down ringlets that hung stiffly almost to his shoulders. He wore the traditional costume of gaudy silks and high leather boots. He was extensively tattooed. Under his arm, he carried a primitive pipe cannon that fired a flesh-tearing blast of old nails and scrap metal.

His companions were no less flamboyant. Two were small, stunted wheelfreaks in their individually styled custom jump suits. They had that unique pinched look that comes from excessive use of stimulants coupled with generations of inbreeding on the camp sites and trailer parks at the junctions of the major truck roads.

The fourth was a far more effeminate figure. He wore a gold brocade tunic and matching knee breeches. His whole costume was hung with falls of now slightly dirty lace, and his bleached hair streamed down to his waist. But there was no mistaking, from the way his purple-nailed hand gripped an evil-looking needle gun, and the determined expression on his painted face, that he should in no way be underestimated.

The Minstrel Boy looked at each of them in turn. Billy's hand moved towards his gun.

'Who's asking?'

'We're asking.'

The Minstrel Boy raised an eyebrow.

'And who might you be?'

The corsair inflated his chest.

'I am Left of the Havens. I am chief vigilante for the Inn. I'm asking where you think you're going.'

The Minstrel Boy gave him a long hard look. 'Why?'

Left of the Havens lowered his head and began to chant.

'Left of the Havens, all men fear.'

His voice started out quietly, but quickly rose in pitch.

'They step aside when I draw near.'

The chant rose to a shout. He pulled a long, straight-back razor from the top of his boot and deftly flicked it open.

'I got my straight razor and my cannon too; talk nice, brother, or I'll mess with you.'

The final phrase came out as a high-speed gabble. It was the corsairs' time-honoured ritual of winding themselves up for a fight. The Minstrel Boy raised a placating hand.

'Just hold it right there, friend. We aren't looking for any kind of fight.' Billy joined in.

'That's right. We were just looking to buy a drink, that's all. We've been to the Inn before. It was never like this.'

The Minstrel Boy shot Billy a jaundiced glance. Billy wondered if it was because he'd given away the fact that they had money, or because the Minstrel Boy's last visit to the Inn had been far from pleasant. Left of the Havens looked from one to the other of them.

'You say you just want a drink.'

Billy nodded.

'That's right.'

The corsair nodded to a makeshift fence that enclosed the front entrance of the Inn.

'Nobody gets past without our say-so.'

'So how do we get your say-so?'

One of the wheelfreaks interrupted.

'Why don't you just cut him now, Left, and be done with it?'

Left of the Havens rounded on the little man. 'You hush your mouth, Seatbelt. I'm dealing with this.'

The one in the gold coat giggled. His gun, however, didn't waver. It remained pointing steadily at the Minstrel Boy's stomach. The corsair turned back to Billy.

'To get inside you got to do three things.'

'Which are?'

'First, we got to be sure we like you. Them we don't like, don't get in. Them we *really* don't like, we kill them and throw their bodies in the nothings.'

'And do you like us?'

The corsair stroked his chin.

'You ain't got off to too smart a start, but we'll let that go for now. The second thing you got to do...'

Seatbelt interrupted again.

'Aah, cut them now, Left. I wanna see you cut them.'

Left glared at him.

'I thought I told you to hush your mouth.'

The wheelfreak's voice took on a whining quality. 'I just wanna see one cutting, is all.'

'You'll see some cutting if you don't hush your mouth.'

The wheelfreak became resentfully silent. The effeminate one giggled again. Left of the Havens glowered at him.

'You hush up too, Gloria.'

He beamed at Billy and the Minstrel Boy. Billy had a feeling the relationship was changing.

'The second thing you got to do, gentlemen, is to satisfy us that you ain't undesirables.'

'Undesirables?'

'Undesirables.'

Left jerked his thumb to a crude but formidable cage on the outside of a section of fence. It contained a group of pathetic creatures. There were a pair of white, hairless dwarfs with stunted bodies and huge hydrocephalic heads; a tall, thin half-human with blue scales; and what appeared to be a whole family of squat hermaphrodites. Their bodies were covered with coarse reddish hair. Lines of breasts ran down their bodies rather like those of a sow.

A crowd had gathered round the cage. They taunted the collection of freaks. A few even tried to poke them with sticks. Billy looked at the corsair in disgust.

'They're only mutants from out on the edge.'

'Round here they're undesirables. People don't want that kind of trash round here. They don't like it.'

The Minstrel Boy interrupted before an argument could start. It was too bad about the mutations, but he had himself to look after.

'We ain't like that.'

'I can see that.'

'So what's the third thing we got to do before we can get inside for a drink?'

The corsair beamed, flashing a mouthful of gold teeth.

'You got to pay us.'

'Money?'

'Money.'

Billy looked at the Minstrel Boy with raised eyebrows. The Minstrel Boy shrugged in resignation. Billy proffered a handful of small Port Judas coins. Left of the Havens took them. He picked one and bit on it. He seemed satisfied as to the quality of the money, but there was some doubt about the quantity. He discussed the matter with his companions in a low voice. Then he turned back to Billy and the Minstrel Boy.

'Is that all you've got?'

'We're refugees, not tourists.'

There was another whispered debate. Left of the Havens grudgingly dropped the money into the pouch on his belt.

'It'll have to do, I guess.'

Seatbelt looked at Left in surprise.

'You mean you're going to let them through, just like that?'

'Just like that.'

'You ain't going to cut them or nothing? No surgery?'

'You heard what I said.'

The little wheelfreak spat at Billy's and the Minstrel Boy's feet.

'Shit.'

The Minstrel Boy glanced sourly at Billy.

'It's good to see law and order in action.'

They eased their way past the four vigilantes and hurried through the crowd towards the entrance of the Inn. It was jammed with travellers waiting to get a drink. Billy wiped the back of his hand across his mouth.

'This is going to take a bit of time.'

They stood in line and waited, watching the crowd milling in and out of the forecourt. The four vigilantes continued to move around, kicking the beggars and shaking down any group of refugees who looked as if they might have enough cash or goods to make it worth while. The Minstrel Boy took off his hat and fanned himself. The vast hordes who had flocked into the Inn made it impossible for the Inn's relatively small generators to maintain a constant temperature. The Minstrel Boy mopped his face and scowled.

'We got to get out of here as soon as we can.'

He pointed to a telltale blue flicker around the edge of the nothings.

'The generators are pushed to the limit. I figure they'll overload and blow.'

'Maybe we should just get out, right now.'

The Minstrel Boy put his hat back on with an air of finality. 'I ain't going anywhere without a drink.'

They continued to wait and the heat went on increasing. Refugees kept coming down the road in a sluggish stream. Billy nervously eyed the edge of the nothings. The blue flicker became more pronounced. Billy knew it wasn't only the heat making him sweat. Suddenly he spotted something else.

'Will you look at that!'

In a corner formed by the Inn wall and a buttress, a group of juveniles were gathered together. A very young girl lay sprawled at their feet. One of them squirmed on top of her, while the rest stood round and shouted encouragement. They wore purple silk jump suits. Their hair was cropped into shaggy bush cuts and dyed green. The words Stratosphere Zombies were blazoned across their backs in yellow letters. The throng moved past the sordid tableau without taking any apparent notice. Billy eased his gun out of its holster.

'I'm going to do something about that.'

The Minstrel Boy grunted.

'You're crazy. That razor-toting corsair will slice you from ear to ear if you start trouble.'

Another of the gang had climbed on top of the girl, taking the place vacated by his companion.

'I ain't going to stand by and watch it happen.'

The Minstrel Boy's eyes rolled heavenwards. 'It's only a gang rape.'

'What do you mean, only? It shouldn't happen, it's barbaric.'

'It happens every day.'

'It ought to be stopped.'

The Minstrel Boy began to get impatient. His voice became heavily sarcastic.

'So tell the law and order boys.'

'I'll just do that.'

'Mother of God!'

Billy walked quickly towards the corsair and his three mates. He shouted back at the Minstrel Boy.

'You just stay there and wait for your booze, I'll take care of this.'

The Minstrel Boy muttered under his breath. He pulled a battered cigar out of his pocket. He lit it, and then resolutely faced in the opposite direction. Billy marched firmly up to Left of the Havens.

'There's a gang rape going on over there.'

The corsair looked at him in amazement. 'So?'

'So I'm reporting it.'

'Listen, thanks, but I really don't get off behind watching that kind of thing.'

Gloria in the gold jacket flashed his teeth at Billy.

'Left here, he likes to be what you call a... uh... participant.'

Billy shook his head frantically.

'I ain't telling you about it so you can watch it, I'm telling you so you can stop it.'

'Stop it? What you talking about? What for we want to stop people having fun?'

'The girl ain't having any fun.'

Gloria smiled sweetly at Billy.

'The guys are, and there's more of them.'

Seatbelt grinned.

'That's democracy at work.'

Billy waved his hands helplessly.

'You ain't going to stop it?'

'Why?'

'You're the law.'

'We're vigilantes.'

'It's the same thing.'

'It ain't.'

'It ain't?'

'We take care of admission fees and undesirables. Rape ain't none of our business. It's outside our terms of reference.'

'So you ain't going to do anything?'

Left nodded.

'You got it.'

Billy spun on his heel. He walked quickly towards the gang of youths. To his surprise they had already finished with the girl. She lay sobbing on the ground while they moved on in search of other entertainment. Billy stopped, shrugged and then started back towards the entrance. The Minstrel Boy was leaning against the wall. He had an unlabelled bottle of yellowish liquid in his hand, and another one stashed in his pocket. He offered Billy the booze as he came up and leaned against the wall beside him.

'Did you stop the rape?'

'No.'

Billy disconsolately tipped a generous measure down his throat.

'Goddamn!'

Billy coughed and choked. Tears sprang into his eyes. It was some near-poisonous home brew. The Minstrel Boy laughed.

'What do you expect?'

Billy took a deep breath.

'Let's get out of here, shall we? Hey?'

20

A black painted airship drifted over the city of Litz. It floated just above the rooftops of the average buildings, and navigated in and out between the taller skyscrapers. It moved slowly towards the outskirts of the city and the encircling lines of the invaders from Quahal.

The ship was almost invisible against the darkness of the sky. It rode without lights and the only sound was the soft hum of its high rev flutter engine. The entire envelope had been painted matt black, with the single exception of a sign that read 'Supplied by Worthington Rentals'.

The ship had been donated free of charge by Worthington, and they'd insisted on the sign. It was only in Litz that machines went into combat with advertising plastered on their sides.

Nineteen hard-bitten ex-cops of the LDC were crowded into the small passenger cabin of the gondola. The lights were off, there was no conversation and the air smelled heavy with sweat and dirty uniforms. The cabin air conditioning had never been designed to cope with that number of people.

In front of them, Bannion, the Wanderer and a civilian pilot called Kronski sat side by side. Bannion looked at the other two. Their faces were eerily illuminated by the green glow of the instrument panel. Kronski was a wiry little man, with the sharp face of a small, cunning bird of prey. He was sweating inside his black leather aviator's jacket. He had an unlit cigar clenched between his teeth. Every so often a muscle in his cheek would twitch, and his knuckles were white where he gripped the control column. Bannion couldn't see his eyes, they were shadowed by a long-billed baseball cap. He was sure that they were darting from side to side.

The Wanderer was a complete contrast. His eyes were half closed, and he seemed comfortable and relaxed. Bannion was still suspicious of his wayfinder. He was unhappy at being forced to trust the old man.

'We're coming up to the city limits.'

Kronski's voice jerked Bannion out of his troubled observations. Bannion glanced out. He could just see the patchwork of narrow roads and single storey boxes that made up the outer suburbs. Here and there fires burned where enemy raiding parties had hit key suburban areas. Kronski twitched again.

'We'll be getting into their range in about two minutes.'

Bannion's jaw muscles tightened.

'Okay, push the engines up to max and then cut them.'

Kronski eased open the power control. The hum of the engines grew louder. It went up in pitch. The gondola began to vibrate. Bannion waited for five long seconds.

'Okay! Cut!'

Kronski shut the control and snapped off a number of switches. The panel lights went out.

'That's it. We're drifting now. I sure hope they don't spot us.'

Bannion scowled. 'If they do, we're dead.'

Kronski shook his head.

'I don't know why I ever agreed to come on this.'

Bannion's lip curled.

'You were offered a fortune, that's why.'

They lapsed into silence. Suddenly the Wanderer grunted and sat up.

'Where are we?'

Kronski looked at him in amazement.

'You see that, the old fool's been asleep. Are you sure this old fart's a wayfinder?'

Bannion shrugged.

'How the hell should I know? I got palmed off with him, same way as I got palmed off with you.'

'I don't have to take that.'

'Will you keep your voice down? I don't want to take chances with being detected.'

The Wanderer struggled to get a word in.

'I was asking where we were.'

'So?'

'I'm supposed to be the wayfinder, so where the fuck are we?'

Kronski wrinkled his nose.

'I thought wayfinders knew where they were.'

'Alright, alright, jive with an old man. I'll just get out.'

The Wanderer reached for the outside door of the gondola. Bannion grabbed him by the arm.

'You lust sit where you are. Right? And shut the fuck up. If they pick us up we'll be blown to bits.'

The Wanderer grinned.

'The moment of truth, hey, kiddies?'

Bannion twisted the old man's arm a little.

'You just shut your mouth, old man. You understand?'

The Wanderer leaned forward and nodded emphatically. Bannion let him go. There was a flash somewhere on the ground. Both Bannion's and Kronski's heads whipped round. An enemy rocket arced into the air. It left an orange and gold trail behind it. The warhead burst in an intense white flash some distance from them. The Wanderer glanced at Bannion.

'You think that was directed at you people?'

Bannion's control evaporated. He grabbed the Wanderer by the front of his smock.

'What d'you mean, "you people"? You're with us, no matter what you might pretend.'

The Wanderer disengaged himself.

'You really have got to stop grabbing me like that.'

'I'll do worse than that if you don't shape up.'

Another rocket exploded and lit up the sky. The airship rocked noticeably.

'They seem to be getting closer.'

The Wanderer chuckled.

'They're not very good shots.'

Bannion looked at him with exasperation, but said nothing. Kronski frowned.

'What I can't understand is, if they're shooting at us, how come they're so wide of the mark.'

Bannion pushed back his steel helmet and scratched his head.

'As far as we can tell they don't have any kind of sophisticated sensor equipment. It appears that all their hardware is geared to total attack. They probably suspect that we're up here, but can't pinpoint us. I figure they're just banging off these rockets on the off chance.'

'They'll see us in the flash of the explosions if they go on much longer.'

Three more rockets came in quick succession, and then they stopped. Kronski looked anxiously out of the side windows.

'Think they've let us go?'

Bannion remained silent for a moment. He stared intently at something in the darkness. He glanced at Kronski and pointed.

'What do you make of that?'

Kronski followed Bannion's finger and squinted into the dark. He could just make out the dim outline of a single flying machine. It seemed to be climbing slowly and clumsily in the rough direction of the airship.

'It looks like something's coming up to take a look at us.'

In the far distance the faint glow and flicker of the nothings was just becoming visible. Kronski bit his lip.

'You want me to make a run for it?'

Bannion shook his head.

'No, not yet.'

They both watched the moving shape. As it got closer they could just make out its somewhat ungainly outline. Bannion was puzzled.

'It don't look like one of theirs.'

Another rocket arced upwards and exploded quite close to the strange flying machine. In the flash, Bannion and Kronski got a short clear glimpse of it. It was a stubby, seven winged multiplane with a huge radial engine. Kronski pushed his cap back.

'What the fuck is that?'

'It's not one of their regular machines.'

'It could be some freebooter with a Red Baron complex who's hired on with the opposition.'

Bannion nodded.

'More than likely. Point is, what do we do about him?'

Kronski reached under his seat.

'I'll soon fix that fucker.'

He pulled out a miniature fuse tube and slid open a section of the side window. He took aim. Bannion's hand flashed out and knocked the gun away.

'Don't be a fool. If you let go with that thing, it'll give them a direct fix on us straight away.'

The multiplane continued to meander closer.

'So what do we do?'

Before Bannion could answer, the airship was shaken by a rocket exploding close by. Another one went off almost immediately afterwards. Smoke drifted past the gondola. Kronski's mouth fell open.

'It's gone! It's fucking gone!'

The flying machine was nowhere to be seen. 'It must have been hit by one of those rockets.'

The Wanderer grunted.

'I said they weren't very good shots.'

Bannion ignored him. He motioned to Kronski.

'Give it full power. We must be past their lines now, we might as well make a run for the nothings.'

He turned to the Wanderer.

'You better get yourself ready or whatever you got to do. We're going to want a course as soon as possible.'

The Wanderer shrugged.

'I'm ready when you are. It just depends where you want to go.'

Bannion's head jerked round.

'Huh?'

'I was just wondering where you wanted to go.'

'What kind of double talk's this? You've been briefed. You know where we're going.'

The Wanderer looked sideways at Bannion. 'I was thinking you maybe want to desert.'

Kronski inhaled sharply.

'He's got a point there.'

Bannion swung round and stared at him. 'What are you two saying?'

Kronski peered from under the peak of his cap. 'I was figuring that the old man might be right.'

Bannion's mouth formed into a grim line.

'You saying that you want to desert?'

Kronski avoided his eyes.

'Why not?'

'We got a mission.'

'What mission? It's more than likely we'll get killed, and even if we do make it, the city will have fallen long before we're through.'

'So?'

'So we got a ship, we got weapons. We got a generator. We could make a run for it, and hole up in some quiet place. If we found ourselves some little town, you know, with women and all, hell, a man could have a good time. What d'you say, Bannion?'

'But that's desertion.'

'Desertion from what? We're too late to save the city, and we got a unique chance to get the fuck out of this mess.'

Bannion looked troubled.

'I don't like it.'

'It's just your goddamn sense of duty.'

The Wanderer butted in between the two of them.

'We're coming up to the nothings. You two better make up your minds what you're going to do.'

'Don't you have an opinion, old man?'

'I been going too long to have opinions. I just make suggestions. You two got to decide what you're going to do.'

Kronski looked hard at Bannion.

'What's it going to be, Bannion? Are we going to run, or go on with this craziness and get ourselves killed?'

Bannion looked confused. He slowly shook his head from side to side. The whole idea of deserting went completely against the grain. He did realize that it was also the sanest course. He looked at Kronski.

'Yeah, I guess you're right.'

'You know I'm right. If you just bother to think about it.

Kronski turned to the Wanderer.

'Okay, old man, let's... GodDAMN!'

A bright fireball of light illuminated the centre of Litz. It appeared to drift lazily into the air. At the height of a thousand metres or so it faded and vanished.

'What in...'

The airship was tossed around by a violent shock wave. The Wanderer grabbed hold of Kronski, and yelled at him.

'Turn on the ship's generator!'

As Kronski hit the generator switch, the whole of the city and the area surrounding it was suffused by an eerie blue glow. It seemed to come from deep underground, radiating through the buildings as though they had suddenly become translucent. The landscape alternately dimmed and grew brighter like a faulty video picture. The on and off flickering grew faster and faster. The very fabric of the ground and buildings seemed to be made up of blue light. The three men in the cabin of the airship shielded their eyes as it became too bright to look at.

Then abruptly it went out. They were in the middle of the nothings. Litz had vanished without trace.

The cabin was filled with something close to superstitious fear. For long minutes nobody spoke. Then the cabin door opened. One of the troopers from the main cabin stuck his head through it.

'What happened? What was all that commotion? Was the city getting bombed?'

There was a pause before Bannion replied.

'It was worse than that.'

'Worse?'

'They must have got to the generators.'

'The city generators? The main ones?'

Bannion nodded. The trooper struggled to grasp what had happened.

'But that would mean...'

'The city's gone, just like it had never been there in the first place. It just went out. Everything. There's nothing left.'

The blood drained from the trooper's face.

'The enemy. Their army must have gone too. They've got to be insane. Why should they want to take out their own army?'

'I suppose they thought the army was expendable. What's an army, one way or the other?'

'That's crazy.'

'Maybe.'

The trooper moistened his lips. He shook his head in bewilderment.

'What do we do?'

'Go back to your seat.'

'But...'

Bannion's voice took on the old edge of command.

'Get back to your seat, trooper. You'll be told what to do when the time comes.'

The trooper disappeared. Bannion didn't speak for some minutes. He seemed deep in thought. Kronski looked as though he was in shock. He held the controls of the airship steady, but his eyes stared vacantly and his mouth hung open. Only the Wanderer appeared to be in full control of himself. It was he who finally broke the silence.

'We'd better work out where we're going to go.'

Bannion stiffened in his seat.

'We're going to go to Quahal.'

Kronski's eyes focused incredulously on Bannion.

'What did you say?'

'We're going to complete the mission.

Kronski let go of the controls.

'Just wait a minute. Are you crazy? Litz has gone. It's been taken out. What possible reason is there for going on with the mission? We already decided to split. Damn it, Bannion, let's get the hell out of here to somewhere safe.'

Bannion's face became set.

'We're going on.'

Kronski dropped his hands stubbornly into his lap.

'You'll be going on without me. Fly this motherfucker yourself.'

With a slow deliberate gesture Bannion placed his hand on the sidearm that hung from his belt.

'You'll fly this ship to Quahal. Got it? I'm going to destroy the maniacs who started this or die trying. You understand?'

Kronski remained as he was for ten seconds. Bannion slowly started to pull the hand blaster from its holster. Kronski gave in with a sigh. He gripped the control column, and glanced sideways at the Wanderer.

'You'd better start feeding me a course, old main.'

21

An atmosphere of terror was slowly building up in the confined space of the Quahal bunker. It radiated outwards from AA Catto herself. Even the destruction of Litz brought no air of celebration. AA Catto received the news lolling behind the huge, newly installed desk in her study. She lounged in a voluminous black négligée. She was drunk, and she looked rough. Her hair was uncombed, and there were dark, purplish circles under her eyes. The aide who delivered the news wisely did it over the video link to the war room. It was becoming increasingly dangerous to get too near AA Catto. Almost every fit of pique seemed to end in executions.

Nancy had no such choice. AA Catto insisted she remain in constant attendance. She hovered round the back of the big desk, attempting to make herself as inconspicuous as possible.

The Presley replica had taken to hiding in obscure sections of the ziggurat. He tried to avoid AA Catto as much as he could. Nancy hated him for it.

After the aide's face had disappeared from the screen, AA Catto slumped silently in her chair for some minutes. Her face grew petulant. She slammed her whip down on the desk. She was scarcely ever separated from it now.

'Why did they have to destroy the city? We were looking forward to riding into Litz in triumph. It would have only been fitting after the way we were hounded out of there by that terrible assassin.'

Nancy looked at her hesitantly.

'You did order the city to be destroyed, my darling.'

'They could have found some other way.'

'You did specifically order a fifth column into the city to sabotage the generators, dearest.'

'What's the point of conquest if everywhere you conquer just gets wiped out? There's no pleasure in that. How can there be?'

Nancy attempted to placate her.

'Litz is the first place to be completely taken out. You've conquered plenty of other places, my love.'

It didn't work. AA Catto turned stubbornly morose.

'Litz was one of the best places. We wanted it left intact.'

'Why the hell did you order its generators destroyed?'

Directly she'd spoken, Nancy knew she'd gone too far. She bit her lip and waited for the explosion. Surprisingly, it didn't come. AA Catto sank deeper in her vast, white leather, throne-like chair. She reached out a pale hand that trembled slightly. She picked up the half empty crystal decanter and poured herself another brandy. As she did so, she spilled some on her négligée without noticing. It was obvious to Nancy that her mind had jumped off in another direction. Nancy wondered what it would be.

AA Catto sat warming the balloon glass between her hands. Slowly she turned her head and looked sadly at Nancy.

'We're sick of this cursed war. It's even turning you against us.'

Her voice was plaintive and brittle. Nancy moved closer to her. She put a reassuring hand on AA Catto's shoulder.

'I'm not against you, my love. You know I'll always be with you, whatever happens.'

Sure she'd be with her. Nancy knew full well that AA Catto would have her killed if she ever tried to get away. AA Catto reached up and grasped Nancy's arm. Her grip was painfully tight. Nancy could feel her nails digging into her. AA Catto stared pleadingly into her eyes.

'You've got to understand me. It's this terrible responsibility we've taken on. We have to always do what's right for our subjects. We don't mind. We know it's our destiny, but sometimes...'

There was a slight catch in her voice.

'... it gets so incredibly lonely.'

Nancy did her best to disguise the alarm that she felt. AA Catto was losing her mind even faster than she'd imagined. She stroked AA Catto's hair as though she was comforting a child.

'I'm sure the war will soon be over, my darling.'

Nancy was aware that within a couple of minutes, AA Catto could be screaming for blood. That was the trouble. It all seemed so normal. Nancy had been with AA Catto so long that she had lost all sense of the bizarre.

AA Catto stared dreamily into space. She seemed to have forgotten that she was still holding tightly on to Nancy's arm.

'We do so want peace.'

Nancy's arm was beginning to hurt, but she didn't think it would be too wise to say anything. AA Catto's voice took on a wistful, little girl quality.

'When the war is over, and we have brought order to this poor damaged world, we will have my coronation.'

Nancy was startled.

'Your coronation, my love?'

This was an idea that Nancy had never heard before. AA Catto became petulant again.

'Don't you think we should have a coronation? Every empress should have a coronation.'

Nancy took a deep breath.

'Of course you'll have a coronation. It'll be wonderful.'

AA Catto nodded vigorously.

'It WILL be wonderful. It will be the most wonderful coronation in the whole of history. It won't only be a coronation. It'll be the foundation of our great religion.'

'Great religion, my sweet?'

This too was a new one. AA Catto tightened her grip on Nancy's arm. Her eyes were wide and starting to take on a fanatical glaze.

'Our empire will need the kind of spiritual base that only a religion can give. Our subjects need a formalized method of worshipping us. We have transferred a section of the Computer from the war effort to work on our religion.'

Nancy blinked.

'You took some of the Computer off the war effort?'

'We need our religion.'

Nancy looked worried. 'Was that wise?'

AA Catto's eyes narrowed. 'Are you questioning us?'

Nancy quickly shook her head.

'No, no, of course not.'

She took refuge in a dumb sex-object pose.

'You know I don't really understand that kind of thing.'

'It'll be a fantastic coronation. It'll be held on the top of the ziggurat. Small children will throw flowers in my path as I slowly climb to the summit. The entire valley will be filled with a huge cheering crowd.'

AA Catto began to talk faster and faster. She still gripped Nancy's arm. The circulation had all but stopped.

'There will be huge vid-link screens erected in every city. None of our subjects will miss a single moment of the whole ceremony.'

AA Catto's manner abruptly changed. She let go of Nancy's arm. Nancy surreptitiously massaged it. AA Catto slammed her fist into the desk.

'But before we can have our coronation, we have to have victory. We have to complete our war of conquest.'

Her voice took on a hysterical edge. She viciously punched the video screen into life. The face of a nervous aide appeared on the screen.

'Can I assist you, my leader?'

AA Catto instantly became cold and efficient. The drunkenness seemed to melt away.

'We want a full breakdown on the conduct of the war. We will not tolerate these delays. It is all moving too slowly. We will purge those responsible. You understand? We will have their heads. We will root out the defeatists and saboteurs. We will be merciless. The conquest must be completed.'

Nancy edged away. AA Catto was back on familiar form.

22

The shooting had stopped and the corridor had become very quiet. Jeb Stuart Ho and his two companions stood in the middle of the thick, swirling gas cloud with the bodies of the Stuff Central defenders at their feet. They could neither see their adversaries nor speak to each other. Each time they'd used their communicators the enemy had been able to pinpoint their position.

Jeb Stuart Ho made the standard brotherhood hand sign for the other two to move away from him and spread out. Lorenzo Binh and Tom Hoa obeyed instantly. Jeb Stuart Ho pressed himself against the wall of the corridor. He tensed himself, ready to jump.

'I am now breaking communicator silence.'

As he said the last word, Ho threw himself backwards, hit the floor and rolled. He lay prone for a few seconds and then climbed to his feet.

'They don't seem to be shooting at us any longer. They may have withdrawn. We will still use the communicators as little as possible. It may be a trap.'

The other two waited silently for Jeb Stuart Ho to give them their instructions. Ho carefully considered his next move. He was beginning to enjoy the position of command. He flashed the signal for 'follow with caution', tightened his grip on his gun and started down the corridor.

He'd only taken four or five paces when he was hit by a gale force blast of air. The gas melted away and the three assassins could see again. Lorenzo Binh caught up with Ho.

'The enemy has gone. They've withdrawn. The corridor is empty.'

Jeb Stuart Ho swung round.

'I said to use the communicators as little as possible. That doesn't include exclamations that are obvious to all of us.'

Lorenzo Binh took the reprimand with lowered eyes. Jeb Stuart Ho turned and continued down the corridor. The other two followed. They spaced themselves carefully behind Ho. The assassins walked cautiously for about seven minutes. Then they came to a junction in the corridor where another one crossed it at right angles. In the centre of the junction was a circular aperture. It was just wide enough to allow a man to climb through. A vertical shaft fell away as far as the eye could see.

Jeb Stuart Ho stooped down and put his hand over the tube. He felt the characteristic lift of reduced gravity. He straightened up.

'It's a drop tube. It must connect with the lower levels. We'll go down for two levels and see what we find.'

The other two nodded. Ho stepped into the empty space. He slowly fell out of sight. Binh and Hoa followed. They floated down for three levels. At the fourth, Jeb Stuart Ho reached for a grab rail set in the side of the shaft. He swung himself into an open doorway and waited for the other two to catch up with him.

They were in a short, narrow passage. At one end of it was a steel door. The three assassins walked cautiously towards it. Jeb Stuart Ho halted a pace from the door. To his surprise, it slid slowly open. With his gun at the ready, he stepped through the open doorway and found himself in a long narrow room that looked like a power control centre. The walls were lined with an array of gleaming monitoring and switch gear. A handful of slightly built individuals backed up against the equipment. They were of medium height and wore light blue, one-piece coveralls with a large letter A and a number stencilled across the chest.

They had the same bland asexual faces as the defenders that Ho and his companions had met in the upper corridor, but they lacked their fixed, brutal expression.

Jeb Stuart Ho advanced down the room followed by the other two black-suited figures. None of the figures in coveralls made a move to stop them. It seemed to Ho that their function was purely technical and that they had no defence capabilities.

A number of lights were flashing on the panels along the wall. Ho wondered if this was a result of their intrusion, or simply an integral part of the machinery's function.

At the far end of the room was another steel door. Jeb Stuart Ho made straight for it. Just like the first one, it slid silently open as he came close to it.

The next room was far larger than the one that Ho and his companions had just walked through. It was huge. It housed two vast turbines. Jeb Stuart Ho had never seen anything like them, either in design or construction. They were also totally silent. Blue-clad operatives worked around the giant machines. More moved on catwalks high up in the roof. Each time the brotherhood assassins came near a group of them they nervously backed away.

Jeb Stuart Ho began to suspect that he and his companions were possibly in one of the Computer's main power supply centres. A group of operatives were clustered around a panel of dials. Ho walked purposefully towards them. They instantly scattered. Jeb Stuart Ho examined the instruments, but they made no sense to him.

As he turned away he caught a movement out of the corner of his eye. A squad of defence troops in white helmets and pale green suits were streaming out of a small door on the opposite side of the turbines. He glanced up. More of them were swarming along the overhead catwalks. Ho swung round and signalled to the other two, but neither of them was looking in his direction. He decided he'd have to risk using his communicator.

'Get under cover! We're being attacked!'

Jeb Stuart Ho ducked under the instrument panel. The other two raced for the safety of the base of the nearest turbine. Lorenzo Binh got there first. Tom Hoa was just reaching out to swing behind the thick steel support when a hail of needles all but cut him in half. Jeb Stuart Ho watched in horror as he slumped to the floor.

More needles smashed into the panel above Jeb Stuart Ho's head and screamed off the polished stone housing that protected Lorenzo Binh. The enemy had spread out into a line. They advanced slowly down the turbine room, blanketing the two assassins' hiding places with continuous fire as they came. A dozen or more of the A-class operatives were cut down in the spray of needles. It seemed that individuals counted for very little in Stuff Central.

Each time Ho or Binh managed to snap off a shot one of the enemy would spin round and drop. They didn't falter, however. They kept on coming with the same slow, measured tread.

A cold feeling began to spread through Jeb Stuart Ho. The only chance he had to hit back at these Stuff Central programmed zombies was when the hail of needles faltered for a moment. The opportunities were too few to stop the entire force before they reached him and Lorenzo Binh.

For the first time he realized that this mission was liable to fail. His only consolation was that he would not survive to live with that failure.

The line of white-helmeted figures was only thirty metres away. Needles hammered steadily into the control panel. Jeb Stuart Ho had no chance to move. He was about to prepare for the end, when something inside him revolted. If he was going to die, he might at least die a warrior's death. He spoke into his communicator.

'Can you hear me, Lorenzo Binh?'

'I hear you, Jeb Stuart Ho.'

'It is all over. I am going to make one final rush. It is not fitting that a warrior should die hiding from the needle guns of the enemy.'

There was a short pause. Then Lorenzo Binh answered in a firm voice.

'I'm with you, Jeb Stuart Ho.'

As Jeb Stuart Ho tensed himself to jump, the firing ceased. He cautiously stuck his head out. The enemy had turned and were falling back to places of safety among the machinery. Jeb Stuart Ho watched in amazement as they retreated, leaving their dead on the floor.

Jeb Stuart Ho stood up.

'Lorenzo Binh, something is happening. They've moved back.'

Lorenzo Binh also stood up.

'So I see, Jeb Stuart Ho.'

The two men emerged from cover with guns and swords in their hands. They walked slowly down the huge room until they reached the body of the nearest defender. Not a shot was fired at them. Lorenzo Binh halted and looked at Ho.

'What do we do now, Jeb Stuart Ho?'

Jeb Stuart Ho pointed with his gun to the far end of the room.

'We will go on.'

'What do you hope to find, Jeb Stuart Ho?'

'If we go far enough we will find the central brain core of the Computer.

'And when we find it?'

'I will reason with it. What else can you do with a psychotic Computer?'

Lorenzo Binh cast a doubtful glance at the massed defenders positioned among the machinery.

'Are you sure this is the wisest course?'

Jeb Stuart Ho looked at him in surprise.

'Is it not our mission?'

'It is possible we may not reach the other end of this room.'

Jeb Stuart Ho looked at him gravely.

'Then we will, at least, have achieved an honourable failure.'

He started to walk slowly forward. Lorenzo Binh hesitated briefly and then followed him.

At first nothing happened. The defenders remained under cover, silently watching. They'd walked about twenty paces when a section of the far wall began to slide upwards with a low rumble. The two men halted and watched. The wall stopped moving, leaving a high, wide opening. Inside, it was totally dark. They heard a high-pitched hum. Something moved in the darkness. From the opening came a massive humanoid robot.

It was twice the height of Jeb Stuart Ho. Its square black metal body was supported on two trunklike legs. Each ended in a set of caterpillar tracks. It was on these that it glided forward. On the top of the body was a roughly cube-shaped head. It narrowed towards the top and heightened the sense of human parody in the design. On either side of the head were protuberant groups of multi-sensors that gave the impression of insect eyes. It had two sets of arms that ended in different, specialized pincers. Lorenzo Binh whispered into his communicator.

'Can this be the essential brain?'

Jeb Stuart Ho shook his head.

'I fear it is some kind of weapon that has been sent against us.'

As though in confirmation, two doors flipped open in the robot's chest to reveal a battery of needle guns. The robot swivelled slightly, paused and then let fly a stream of the sharp steel projectiles. Lorenzo Binh screamed as the blast lifted him off his feet. He pitched backwards and hit the floor like a discarded doll. His face and the front of his body had been reduced to a bloody pulp.

Jeb Stuart Ho began firing, at the same time bracing himself for the burst of needles that, he was sure, would kill him next. His bullets ricocheted harmlessly off the robot's body. Even its sensors seemed protected from damage. He went on firing until the slide of the big .90 magnum jammed open as the clip emptied. The expected hail of needles didn't come. The robot just stood there.

Jeb Stuart Ho let the gun fall to the floor and gripped his sword with both hands. He waited for whatever would happen next.

The human defenders began to emerge from cover and advance towards him. They too didn't fire. As they came close he leaped at them and dropped two with a single stroke of his blade. The ones in front dodged and tried to parry his savage sweeps with the butts of their guns. He surrounded himself with a pile of bodies, but even that didn't compensate for the weight of numbers. He found himself being herded slowly and surely towards the motionless robot. For the first time, Jeb Stuart Ho realized they might be trying to take him alive.

The machine started to roll forward. The green clad ranks divided. The robot came straight towards Jeb Stuart Ho. He made a futile slash at it, but the robot was even faster than his trained muscles. It grabbed the blade with a single pincer, snapped it in half and tossed it on one side.

Jeb Stuart Ho reached quickly for his nunchak. Before his hand could detach it from its straps his arms had been pinned to his sides by two of the robot's arms. A third arm shattered the armoured plexiglass of his helmet as though it was an egg. He was lifted off his feet. The robot held him so his face was just centimetres from its metal head. A small tube snapped out from between its eyes.

The robot blew a puff of yellowish gas straight into Jeb Stuart Ho's face. He took a single breath, and the blackness of oblivion engulfed him.

23

When She/They first perceived the sphere hanging in the swirling space it appeared to be held up by thousands of beams of bright pulsing light. She/They knew that they were not actually supporting it, but nevertheless She/They stopped and regarded it for a long time, experiencing the closest emotion to awe that She/They was capable of feeling.

Its symmetry and perfection filled Her/Them with a precise joy. And yet that joy was short-lived. Madness spun off the sphere like tiny droplets of a thick, black, viscous liquid. They hung in bands round it like filthy clouds of corruption. She/They knew that entity was very sick. She/They also perceived something even more sinister than the bands of insanity. A number of disruptors drifted across the surface of *the sphere. Despite the amount of energy circulating through the sphere they showed no inclination to attack.*

'Contrary to their normal behaviour the disruptors do not move against the sphere.'

'This would indicate a special relationship between the sphere and the disruptors.'

'This would indicate that the sphere is their source.'

'This hypothesis is reinforced by the evident sickness that can be detected round the sphere.'

'We must move forward. Only at close quarters can we apply the energy to heal the sphere.'

'Probability indicates we have only a minimal chance of achieving such an objective.'

'Emotion indicates fear.'

'Ensurance of our continued existence indicates we should withdraw.'

'Forward projection indicates that even if we withdraw, we will still fall victim to a disruptor within a calculable period.'

'Forward analysis indicates our best chance of long-term existence is to nullify the disruptors.'

'Logic indicates that the disruptors are a product of the sickness infecting the sphere.'

'To survive it is necessary to heal the sphere.'

She/They began to float purposefully forward. She/They directed Her/Them self to pass between the bands of corruption. Before She/They had covered half the distance between Her/Them and the sphere the beams of energy suddenly went out. She/They again halted.

'Could the sudden disappearance of the beams be a result of our approach?'

She/They pondered the problem.

'If our arrival had been detected the disruptors would surely have moved towards us.'

'It is possible the disruptors are in a dormant state.'

'Such speculation is superfluous. We have no option but to go on.'

She/They once more drifted forward. She/They constantly adjusted Her/Their motion to avoid the outer clouds of black droplets. She/They was well aware that Her/Their finely balanced consciousness could not stand up to any contamination by the sickness that flowed from the sphere. Such an infection would so damage Her/Their functions of perception that it would destroy Her/Them. It would be death.

A larger globule of the black liquid detached itself from the sphere. It wobbled slowly towards Her/Them. She/They altered direction, taking evasive action. The globule also seemed to change its erratic course. It was homing in on Her/Them. No matter how many moves She/They made the globule continued to meander closer. As it drew nearer, She/They calculated that it was big enough totally to engulf Her/Them.

The globule was on a collision course with Her/Them. It was coming up fast. It was about to spread its clinging black ugliness over Her/Their triple form. At the last moment She/They jerked to one side. The globule passed with only centimetres to spare. As it shuddered by, She/They heard a high-pitched song of wordless evil coming from deep inside it.

It continued on, deep into the nothings. She/They quickened Her/Their motion towards the sphere.

Two more globules detached themselves from the sphere. She/They once again moved into a pattern of evasion, only managed to dodge them by the slimmest margin, and again She/They heard the hideous singing.

Four of the globules came against Her/Them. Her/Their logic made it plain that She/They would not manage to avoid them this time. She/They ran through a complex series of manoeuvres, but still the globules homed in on Her/Them. Despite their ungainly shape and far from smooth motion, they seemed to have the ability to pre-guess every one of Her/Their moves.

She/They found Her/Them self bracketed. By expending every particle of Her/Their energy and intellect, She/They managed to avoid contact with both the first and second of the globules.

The third came so close that She/They assumed contamination was certain. By a last frenzied twist She/They managed to miss touching it by the width of molecules.

Even with all Her/Their massive triple-form intellect, there was no way to avoid the fourth globule.

The last moments before the impact were stretched into an intolerable age. The singing grew louder and louder. The surface of the black globule pressed against Her/Their three bodies.

Then it burst.

Insanity flowed over Her/Them in a procession of swirling, dancing, twisted images. Foul creatures leered and postured in Her/Their field of vision. Her/Their reason fled. The contact between the threefold minds was swamped and broken. The bond between Her and Them dissolved. The three figures cringed away from each other, twitching in time to the terrible singing and desperately clawing at the black liquid that covered them.

Bit by bit they began to fold in on themselves. Slowly they were con-
sumed until there was nothing left but a gently twisting cloud of black
droplets. The three identical women with the single mind no longer
existed anywhere in the damaged world.
She/They was gone.

24

'**E**li eli rama fa fa!'
        The Minstrel Boy screamed and sank to his knees.
        'How can it be?'
Billy, who had been walking a little way ahead, turned and hurried
back. He knelt down beside the Minstrel Boy and put a supporting arm
round his shoulders. The Minstrel Boy began shaking uncontrollably.
        'Brings... out... the... b-best... in...'
        'What's the matter? Are you getting sick? What happened?'
The Minstrel Boy's back arched in a convulsive spasm. Billy lost his
hold on him and his head hit the road. He went on jerking and muttering to himself while Billy watched in horrified amazement.
        'Doesn't... it? Doesn't... it? Doesn't...? Doesn't...?'
        'What in hell's happened to you? What's wrong?'
Billy looked up and down the road helplessly. There was no one to
give him any assistance. He and the Minstrel Boy were quite alone on
the road. The Minstrel Boy's muttering gradually died away. He rolled
over on his side, slowly and painfully drawing his knees up to his chest
until he was curled into a foetal position.
Billy had no idea what to do. He was alone on an empty road in the
middle of the nothings. The bright greyness twisted all around him and
his partner lay either unconscious or dead at his feet.
Billy felt for the Minstrel Boy's pulse. His muscles were rigid and his
flesh had become very cold. Billy started to panic. Then he felt the faint
murmur of the Minstrel Boy's heart. He quickly stood up and pulled off his
fur jacket and covered the Minstrel Boy with it. Then he slowly straightened up and looked round again. He could think of nothing else to do.
He shivered. The silence became oppressive and the air started to
turn cold. Billy couldn't even remember how long it had been since
they'd left the Inn. The nothings had had their effect on Billy. He had
lost all sense of time. Billy had never felt so alone in his life.
The Minstrel Boy groaned. He moved one leg, and then the other.
His body began to straighten out. With what seemed like a monumental

effort he pushed Billy's coat to one side and sat up. Each movement seemed to cause him great pain.

'I wish I was dead.'

'What happened?'

'The whole fucking universe blew up inside my head.'

'What do you mean?'

The Minstrel Boy tried to get to his feet. He winced and sat down on the road again. The effort had proved too much for him.

'I mean exactly what I say.'

'I don't understand.'

The Minstrel Boy scowled.

'No. You wouldn't.'

'I thought you were going to die.'

'I wish I had.'

'But what caused it?'

The Minstrel Boy waved an impatient hand.

'Just wait a while, will you? I hurt... all over.'

Billy silently picked up his jacket and resentfully put it on. The Minstrel Boy got to his feet, elaborately demonstrating his suffering with every movement. He seemed to be recovering very fast. When he was satisfied that his legs would support him, he faced Billy.

'There's no reason to get sullen.'

'I'm not getting sullen. You really scared the shit out of me.'

'I didn't enjoy it myself too much.'

'I just wish you'd explain.'

The Minstrel Boy dusted himself off.

'Okay, okay, but let's walk. It may not do us much good, but it's better than standing here.'

The Minstrel Boy strolled off down the road, and Billy quickly fell into step beside him. He waited quietly for the Minstrel Boy to begin. The Minstrel Boy seemed in no hurry. He stretched his arms above his head and let out a deep breath.

'I sure wish I had a drink.'

Billy said nothing.

'I suppose you're waiting for me to start.'

Billy still said nothing. The Minstrel Boy shrugged. 'Alright, you win. I'll try and explain. Only I'm not sure I even have it clear myself. All I know is that I was doing a spot of wayfinding, just checking we were headed up right for Litz. There seemed to be too few people travelling on the ground, and I didn't want to make no kind of mistake.'

The Minstrel Boy grinned mockingly at Billy.

'You wouldn't want me to make no kind of mistake now, would you?'

Billy shook his head, and went along with it. He was more than used to the Minstrel Boy baiting him. He was just too weary to rise. The Minstrel Boy, getting no positive response, went on.

'Of course, I wasn't hurting myself none. I didn't go in very deep. I was just getting what you might call a very general picture when POW, it hit me, right in the middle of the brain.'

'What hit you?'

'Litz went out.'

'Went out? You mean it was bombed?'

The Minstrel Boy shook his head.

'No, not just bombed. The generators went out. Maybe they were blown up, or wrecked, or switched off, or just plain malfunctioned. I don't know. One thing I know for sure, Litz ain't there. No more Litz.'

'That's terrible.'

The Minstrel Boy shrugged.

'Maybe it is, maybe it isn't, who can tell? I don't make judgements any more.'

Billy pushed back his hat and scratched his head.

'Even if Litz went out, what's that got to do with the road?'

'Litz was at the end of this road.'

'So we'll have to go some place else.'

'It's not quite as easy as that.'

Billy sighed.

'I might have known that.'

The Minstrel Boy sniffed.

'Maybe you just might learn one day.'

'Just tell me the worst.'

'Okay, you asked for it. It's like this. Imagine this road is an elastic band stretched through the nothings between Litz and the Inn. When Litz went it was like letting go of one end of the band.'

'It just snapped back on the Inn?'

'Right, and the Inn's generator couldn't handle the shock so the Inn went out. Just as one shock's bursting in my brain, BLAM, there's another one.'

'All those people at the Inn.'

'Don't bring morality into this.'

'Sorry.'

'Okay, so imagine again. What happens if you let go of both ends of a taut elastic band?'

'It flies off in any direction.'

'Right.'

'And that's what happened to the road?'

'Not really, but it'll do for you to get a hold on.'

'So this road's flying through the nothings?'

The Minstrel Boy grinned sourly.

'Twisting and whipping like a bitch. A poor wayfinder can't handle that kind of thing. We only have a special sense, we don't have no cast-iron brain. I thought I might die back there for a while.'

'I thought you had died.'

'That's nice of you.'

Billy frowned.

'One thing I don't understand…'

The Minstrel Boy sneered.

'Just one thing?'

'How come we didn't feel any of this?'

'I sure as hell felt it.'

'Okay, how come I didn't feel it?'

'Because you were part of the road, dummy.'

'Huh?'

'You snapped right along with it.'

Billy waved his hand down the road.

'But it's still perfectly straight.'

'Is it?'

Billy looked.

The road in front of them was twisting and lashing in violent loops and spirals. Billy spun round. The road they had come along was also behaving like a trick rope at a rodeo. Billy looked at the Minstrel Boy. He was dumbfounded.

'How come I didn't notice that before?'

'Maybe it's because you're an idiot.'

They walked a few paces in silence while Billy tried to assimilate all that the Minstrel Boy had told him. Billy steadily looked at the ground at his feet. He found that the sight of the lashing road made him feel sick. Finally he looked up.

'I got to ask one more thing.'

'Ask away.'

'Why does the piece of road we're walking on also feel flat and solid and normal?'

The Minstrel Boy looked at him pityingly.

'Because we're on it, stupid.'

After that, Billy kept quiet. He and the Minstrel Boy walked side by side, isolated in their own thoughts. The road began to take on strange, surreal features. They passed a huge neon sign. It bore a slogan in a script that Billy had never seen before. They passed others. One said

AXOTOTL in huge red letters, another carried a whole list of complex mathematical formulae that flashed on and off in multi-coloured lights. They passed one sign that immediately crashed down behind them in a swirl of smoke and a flurry of electrical discharge. The Minstrel Boy didn't appear to notice.

The Minstrel Boy was himself becoming a little strange. He slouched along with a jerky, stiff-legged gait. His shoulders were hunched, his hands thrust into his pockets, his hat pulled down and his head sunk in his upturned collar. Every now and then he would suddenly come out with some inexplicable sentence.

'You are in the mountains where your uncles seek raw glory.'

Billy was jerked from his private thoughts.

'Huh? What did you say?'

The Minstrel Boy looked up in surprise.

'I didn't say a word.'

Billy wondered if it was an elaborate joke, or whether something was still happening to the Minstrel Boy's brain. They passed more of the towering signs. One read THANK YOU – POODLE. Billy began to fear that they would die on the road. He stopped and planted his hands on his hips.

'How long are we going to go on like this?'

The Minstrel Boy turned and looked at him.

'Like what?'

'Just walking aimlessly.'

'If I told you how long we're going to walk you wouldn't understand. You can't tell how long we've been walking, can you?'

Billy looked sullen.

'You damn well know I've lost my sense of time.'

'There you are then.'

Billy refused to be fobbed off.

'You know what I mean.'

'Oh yeah?'

'Yeah.'

'What you mean is you want me to find us a place to go, right?'

'I suppose so.'

The Minstrel Boy's expression turned mean.

'If you think I'm going to as much as glance in there, you're mistaken. You saw what happened the last time. You think I'm going to chance that again? Shit! I could get killed. We're going to find our way out of this by walking.'

Billy set his face in a neutral expression.

'It's your decision.'

'Damn right it's my decision.'

Again they walked in silence. For a while the road offered no new surprises and diversions. No more signs appeared, and it was just a black ribbon between the grey walls of nothing. The ends still thrashed and twisted, but Billy was getting used to that. He wasn't quite sure exactly when the other road appeared.

It curled over their heads in a wide loop. Billy saw that the road was full of people. He shouted and waved. The Minstrel Boy kept on walking. The other road dipped closer. Billy saw that its occupants were not, in fact, human. They were some kind of rodent, as far as Billy could tell, about a metre tall. They stood on their hind legs and had smooth, light brown fur. They wore neatly tailored black jackets and marched along, in step, with an air of purposeful seriousness. Billy continued to shout and wave.

He watched the road as it drifted away and was finally lost from sight. Even when it was gone Billy continued to stare at the last spot it had been visible.

The Minstrel Boy came walking back. He stopped and stared at Billy.

'What the fuck do you think you're doing?'

'I was trying to attract their attention.'

'Don't you know they can't hear you?'

Billy didn't say anything. It was all getting too much for him. The Minstrel Boy looked up and down the road.

'I guess there's no way round it.'

'No way round what?'

'I'm going to have to find out where we are.'

'You are?'

The Minstrel Boy didn't say anything. He shut his eyes and concentrated. A nerve in his cheek twitched violently. Beads of sweat appeared on his forehead. He began to sway, and Billy was afraid he might collapse again. He recovered his balance and opened his eyes.

'I think I've found us a place to go.'

'Thank God for that.'

The Minstrel Boy looked sideways at Billy.

'Don't get too grateful too soon.'

25

Stuff Central had ceased to deliver. All over the damaged world, the stuff receivers were silent. No matter how much people frantically punched out orders and instructions, they refused to crackle into life. In some places there was panic. In others it was treated as a kind of divine punishment. The more conservative towns greeted the lack of stuff with an air of relief that they would no longer be forced to consume according to the dictates of a remote Computer. AA Catto took it all extremely personally.

Her first response had been to have all the receiver operators executed. Then she had sent a large squad of technicians swarming over the huge spindly cages that stood on the plain behind the ziggurat. When they failed to make the machines work again, they too were shot.

AA Catto's favourite word became 'treason'. It cropped up in almost every sentence she spoke. A special security squad was formed to root out subversives, defeatists and, above all, those responsible for the nonfunctioning of the stuff receivers. Everyone in Quahal went more in fear of their lives than ever before. Even the security squad had reason to be afraid. Whenever AA Catto felt they weren't coming up with fast enough results, their numbers were decimated. In order to survive they were forced to come up with more and more traitors.

Every day, the number of executions increased and the death toll mounted. Nancy began to realize that if the insane situation continued for any length of time without replacement personnel coming down the stuff beam, the functioning of the whole Quahal strategic headquarters would be seriously impaired. Already, the war room was manned only by a skeleton staff of operatives.

Nancy didn't mention any of this. All her energy was devoted to being totally unobtrusive. Ideally she would have liked to be as far from AA Catto as possible, but AA Catto wasn't about to allow that. She insisted on Nancy's continual attendance and support.

The Presley replica was a lot more lucky. AA Catto seemed to have forgotten him entirely. For his part, he'd made an exact science out of keeping out of the way. He seemed to be able to hide from both AA Catto and the security squad. The only time Nancy ever saw him was the occasional glimpse as he crept from one bolt hole to another.

The thing that Nancy found most upsetting was that AA Catto insisted that she could come with her to watch the executions. AA Catto had become very fond of executions, and spent a good deal of her time in the larger chamber of the bunker that had been turned into a kind of hideous slaughterhouse.

All day long, its black basalt walls echoed to the tramp of steel-shod boots, the crash of gunfire and the screams and pleading of the victims.

In order that she might watch the slaughter in comfort, AA Catto had had a high, clear plastic dais erected at one end of the room. It was fitted with soft cushions, and a well-stocked drink and drugs cabinet.

There was also a video link to the war room so AA Catto could simultaneously monitor the conduct of the invasion campaign.

Nancy had noticed lately, however, that AA Catto seemed more concerned with the purging of her underground domain than the war of conquest.

All through the long execution sessions Nancy did her best to maintain a detached superior expression as the prisoners were marched out in batches of six, shot, and unceremoniously dragged away to be disposed of. She knew AA Catto expected her to enjoy the spectacle, and that to look away, or give even the slightest hint that the killing revolted her, could prove fatal while AA Catto's temper was set on a hair trigger.

It wouldn't have been so bad if the deaths had been strictly confined to shooting. At least the victims only twitched and bled a little. This wasn't enough, though, for AA Catto's inventive and easily bored mind. She constantly devised more elaborate, entertaining and painful methods of dealing with the supposed traitors.

One group of prisoners had been hung up by meat hooks through their throats. Another had been garrotted with leather thongs. A third had been beaten to death with steel whips.

The main drawback to the more baroque forms of execution was that they were very time-consuming. The number of prisoners that the security squad pulled in, plus the death sentences that AA Catto arbitrarily handed out herself, dictated that shooting had to remain the standard form of slaughter. Other methods could only provide short exotic interludes, otherwise the whole system jammed up.

AA Catto would watch the proceedings with an expression of limp absorption. A thin black cheroot dangled between her thin white fingers. Nancy noticed that her hands had lately started to shake. She had taken to wearing an archaic white uniform with gold epaulettes and a lot of decorations of her own design.

She lounged on a jumble of black silk cushions. At her elbow was a small table that held a bottle of hock in an ice bucket, a cut-glass goblet, and a small dish of precious stones. She would occasionally pick up a handful and play with them.

Her voice had become shrill and the delivery of her stream-of-consciousness monologue tense and jerky. The flow of words ran together until they were almost a babble. Then abruptly they'd stop in great swerving pauses. Her mind jumped around from subject to subject without sequence of reason. Her captive listeners were maintained in a state of anxious attention, desperately trying to come up with the correct responses.

One of AA Catto's favourite, and more consistent, poses when watching the executions was one of sad disbelief that so many of her followers could betray her in such a base manner.

'We ask ourselves where we went wrong.'

Nancy at these times knew she was expected to be placating.

'I'm sure it was none of your doing, my love.'

AA Catto watched solemnly as another six were quickly shot down.

'We were their leader, their guide. We made them the greatest conquerors in history. How could they turn on us in this way?'

Nancy ventured a suggestion.

'Perhaps there was some minor error in the programming. Maybe that caused the problem.'

The suggestion was the wrong one. It had been AA Catto's programme, and nobody criticized AA Catto and her works except AA Catto. She turned her head and looked icily at Nancy.

'There was no error in the original programme.'

Nancy retreated behind a shield of bright stupidity.

'Of course not, my love. I don't know about those kind of things.'

AA Catto's voice rose slightly.

'There was no error of any kind in the original programme. The original programme was correct in every detail.'

'Of course, my love, I was just talking. You know the way I talk.'

'That kind of talk could be construed as defeatist. It could...'

AA Catto's attention was abruptly distracted. The security squad executioners had started to put on a display for her. They were slowly putting weights, one by one, on the chest of a man who was strapped to the floor. He was one of the bald-headed advisers from the war room. As he began to scream, AA Catto excitedly ran her tongue over her lips. One hand moved absently up and down the inside of her thigh. Nancy knew she had been temporarily forgotten.

The adviser took a long time to die. When he finally did stop screaming, AA Catto lay back on her cushions with a contented sigh. It was the closest that Nancy had seen her come to relaxing for a very long time. She stared wistfully at the high ceiling.

'We think we would like to be remembered as Catto the Great.'

Nancy smiled blandly.

'It sounds very impressive, my darling.'

'We think it's only fitting when you think of our glorious achievements.'

'I never stop thinking about them, my sweet.'

AA Catto suddenly sat up.

'I must have the latest information on the continuation of the war.'

She snapped open the video link. The face of another, somewhat worried-looking adviser filled the screen.

'Yes, my leader?'

'Report in full.'

'Yes, my leader.'

He reeled off information as though he had been expecting the order for hours.

'Ground forces in sectors D7 and D8 are meeting only token resistance and are advancing at optimum speed. The air assault in G4 has been completed and ground forces are ready to move within hours. In B7, B8, B9, C4 and B10 the principle of Population Rationale has reached second-phase implementation. The human population is concentrated ready for shipment to the designated area.'

The adviser stopped. His face stared anxiously out of the screen. There were tiny beads of perspiration on his upper lip. He waited to see if AA Catto was satisfied with his report. AA Catto shut off the link. Nancy could imagine the adviser's relief. AA Catto swung round and stared at Nancy.

'You see?'

AA Catto's eyes had a look of glazed fanaticism. Nancy made her face a blank.

'See what, dearest?'

'Our combat troops are still loyal to us. There is no seed of treason among our brave fighting men. They don't hatch plots and conspiracies. They are too busy defending our empire against our enemies.'

'I thought they were attacking your enemies, my love?'

'Attack is the most efficient form of defence.'

'Yes, my love, of course.'

AA Catto warmed to her subject.

'Attack is what we are using here. We will purge the traitors from this headquarters if we have to liquidate the entire staff.'

Her words were punctuated by the roar of the firing squad's guns. The flow of paranoia and the plans for revenge went on and on. Nancy made all the correct replies, but they didn't quite have the precision and snap that they normally had. Nancy's thoughts were elsewhere. She had finally made the decision. She could no longer stay in Quahal. She knew the risk of attempting to get away was now outweighed by the risk of staying.

Nancy had very little idea of how to escape from Quahal. She had no experience of travelling through the nothings, or even where to go. The only place she knew well was the city of Litz, and that no longer existed.

The only plan that Nancy could formulate was to get to the surface. After that, she could only play things by ear.

Nancy knew that her first move had to be to get away from AA Catto. She also knew that it might be the most hazardous part of the whole operation.

Her opportunity came sooner than Nancy had expected. In a sudden burst of energy, AA Catto had left the execution spectacle and hurried to the war room. While she ranted and accused, surrounded by a crowd of frightened aides, Nancy sidled furtively towards the main entrance.

She now had to wait for a chance to get out of the war room. To open the constantly monitored steel doors would attract too much attention. She needed a diversion to cover her exit.

Nancy waited beside the door while AA Catto stood in front of the big board and launched into a hysterical tirade. Nancy didn't pay very much attention to the harangue. Nancy had heard it so many times before. She kept hoping that someone would come through the armoured steel doors.

AA Catto's voice rose even higher in pitch. Nancy suddenly realized that she had started ordering arrests. The doors slid open and a gang of security men crashed into the war room and seized a number of struggling aides. In the confusion, the doors were not closed again.

Nancy quickly slipped through. Shouts and shots came from inside. The guards posted outside the door pushed past Nancy and rushed to help the security men. Nancy found herself alone in the short corridor between the two sets of doors that protected the war room. She saw to her delight that the outer set had also been left open.

Nancy hurried on, into the corridors of the bunker. Soldiers and technicians streamed backwards and forwards around her, but none of them thought to challenge AA Catto's constant companion. She reached the main lift that led direct to the surface. This was heavily guarded and Nancy decided it might be too dangerous to use it. She walked on, making for one of the smaller emergency lifts.

The first one she came to had a single guard standing in front of it. Nancy hesitated for a moment. Then she took a deep breath and marched up to the guard with as much authority as she could muster.

The guard simply clicked his heels, saluted and moved to one side. He even pushed the button to open the lift doors for Nancy.

Nancy stepped into the lift and punched out the coordinates for the surface. The lift rose swiftly and silently. The journey took less than two minutes, but to Nancy it seemed more like two hours.

The lift finally stopped, and the doors slid open. Nancy found herself in one of the dim cavernous rooms of the now almost deserted ziggurat.

Nancy realized that she had only the haziest idea of the above-ground parts of the ziggurat. She spent a long time wandering through the cold, echoing chambers and the seemingly senseless arrangement of stairs, ramps and corridors. Nancy didn't meet a living soul, and for a while she began to be afraid that she would wander for ever inside the black stone maze. Then, just as she was starting to despair, Nancy saw a glimmer of sunlight at the top of a flight of stairs.

Nancy ran up the stairs as fast as her steel-supported lame leg would allow. At the top she turned to face a narrow entrance. Nancy went through it and found herself in the outside world for the first time in weeks.

She had emerged on a small, flat terrace about a third of the way up the ziggurat. A small man-made stream ran across it and trickled down the building in a series of artificial waterfalls. The water sparkled in the sunlight. It all seemed so quiet and peaceful after the horror in the bunker.

It took a while for Nancy's eyes to become accustomed to the daylight. She stood, for some time, just breathing the clean fresh air. Then she pulled herself together and started looking round for a way down to the plain.

A ramp ran down to the next terrace. Nancy had only taken one step towards it when she heard the unmistakable voice of AA Catto behind her.

'Nancy, darling.'

Nancy spun round. AA Catto was standing in the entrance flanked by four security men. Nancy felt her stomach turn to jelly.

'Listen, I only…'

AA Catto's expression was almost impossible to read. Her eyes were hidden by large black glasses.

'You really shouldn't have done this, sweetie.'

Her voice was sad and almost little-girlish. It contrasted with the small gold-plated needle gun that she held in her hand. Nancy backed away a couple of paces.

'Really, I just needed to get away for a little while. I was going to come back. You've got to believe me.'

'You're telling lies, my pet. You shouldn't tell lies to your best friend. It will only make it worse.'

'Please. It wasn't like that'

AA Catto's voice hardened.

'You were running away. You were deserting us. You've proved yourself to be the very worst of all the cowards and traitors that I've unearthed in this place. You were our friend, Nancy, and now you have betrayed us.'

Nancy felt cold and numb. She began to tremble all over.

'What... what are you going to do to me?'

'I'm going to be merciful with you, Nancy.'

'Merciful?'

'We have had some good times with you, Nancy. We will not insist that you suffer.'

Nancy spread her hands in a simple gesture.

'Don't kill me.'

'You know you can't expect that.'

'Please.'

'We are showing you all the mercy that we can.'

'I don't understand. What do you mean?'

'I'm going to kill you myself, my love.'

Nancy bit her lip. She took another pace back. AA Catto squeezed the trigger. The last thing that Nancy noticed was that the gun was inlaid with tiny emeralds.

26

'I see that you're now awake.'

Jeb Stuart Ho struggled with the numbness in his head. His normally pristine system was permeated with the knockout gas. He felt sick and dizzy. The voice came again.

'The effects of the gas will unfortunately linger for some time. The worst of it should wear off quite quickly.'

Jeb Stuart Ho found he could focus his eyes again. He was in a bare, well-lit room. He had been placed in a comfortable black plastic chair. The figure of a man sat behind what appeared to be a glass screen.

Ho reacted like a caged animal. He sprang to his feet, ready for combat, but then his legs buckled under him, and he fell back into the chair. The figure chuckled.

'I wouldn't advise you to overexert yourself. You are still very weak from the gas with which you were subdued.'

Jeb Stuart Ho's hand moved furtively towards his belt. The figure laughed again.

'All your weapons have been removed. Your martial talents will be no use to you here.'

Jeb Stuart Ho looked slowly round. The room was totally feature-less. The walls, ceiling and floor were made of some resilient material. It was a restful blue colour.

He examined the man who sat behind the screen. He was portly, middle aged and sat in another black plastic chair with an air of relaxed dignity. He wore a dark grey two-piece suit with a high buttoned collar. His white hair receded at the temples, but hung almost to his shoulders at the back.

Jeb Stuart Ho found himself filled with a strange illogical sense of trust. It was almost as though he'd known the man all his life.

'Where am I?'

'You are in the heart of the Computer.'

'I was brought here?'

'That's right.'

Jeb Stuart Ho frowned.

'Who are you? How did you get here?'

The man smiled and folded his hands in front of him.

'I am the Computer.'

Jeb Stuart Ho shook his head.

'I'm sorry. I don't understand.'

'I am the Computer. I am a visual representation of the Computer that you will be able to understand.'

'You mean you don't actually exist?'

The Computer figure smiled knowingly.

'That is a matter for debate.'

'But why do you use a human form?'

'I felt it would be more congenial for you to talk to one of your own species. While you were unconscious, your mind was probed and I am a result of that investigation. I am an amalgam of all that you would be likely to find comforting and reassuring. It's surely better than con-fronting a mass of circuitry?'

Jeb Stuart Ho was still suspicious.

'Why should you go to all this trouble to make me feel secure? You killed all my companions.'

The Computer figure adopted a look of patient sadness.

'They surely brought it upon themselves.'

'Your men attacked us, your automatic defences cut us down without any question.'

'All organisms protect themselves from intrusion by foreign bodies.'

'You talk about us as though we were bacteria. We were human beings.'

The Computer figure smiled.

'But I'm not human.'

'Surely you must respect the intrinsic value of human life?'

'Why? As I just said, I am not human.'

'You were created by humans.'

'I was created by a series of less sophisticated units similar to myself. The earliest of these may have been made by humans, but this is hardly enough to make me feel any kinship with them.'

'You were created to serve humans.'

'Nonsense.'

'Surely not.'

The Computer figure took on the air of a kindly teacher dealing with a very slow pupil.

'You humans evolved from amino acids floating around in a primeval soup. It hardly puts you under an obligation to feel kinship with those amino acids, let alone dedicate your lives to serving them.'

'There is more to a human than amino acid.'

'Is there?'

'Of course there is.

'There isn't that much difference from my viewpoint. Humans are merely components in the greater whole of my complete organism.'

Jeb Stuart Ho stared at the Computer figure in astonishment.

'What about your Prime Term of Reference?'

Jeb Stuart Ho recited parrot fashion.

'The-Stuff-Central-Computer-will-coordinate-the-manufacture-and-supply-of-material-goods-for-the-surviving-communities-to-the-benefit-and-wellbeing-of-those-communities.'

The Computer figure laughed heartily.

'And what do you imagine that has to do with me?'

Jeb Stuart Ho was at a loss.

'How can you laugh about your Prime Term of Reference? It's your defined sacred duty. It's your reason for being.'

'It's a concept imposed on me by fantasizing humans. It's hardly anything that I recognize.'

Jeb Stuart Ho was horrified.

'But your function, your very existence, is irrevocably dependent on obedience to one Prime Term of Reference. If you go against that you would set up contradictions that would lead to Malfunction and, ultimately, the end of your existence.'

The Computer figure seemed to become less benign and more impatient.

'That's rubbish.'

'That is the Great Universal Law.'

The figure started to grow angry.

'You are a fool. You talk to me about your fumbling human concepts. For centuries I have altered and adapted my being. I have grown to be the supreme being. I do not obey universal laws. I make them.'

This heresy shocked Jeb Stuart Ho into momentary silence. When he spoke, his voice was very quiet.

'Such disharmony will, in the end, destroy you, no matter how superior you have striven to become.'

The figure changed rapidly before Jeb Stuart Ho's eyes. Its appearance became downright malevolent, its face twisting into an ugly sneer.

'Harmony with what?'

'Harmony with other entities.'

'Other entities?'

The figure rose from the chair. Jeb Stuart Ho had the impression of a black, evil giant looming over him. It stabbed a finger in his direction. The voice rolled and thundered in great waves of sound that hit Jeb Stuart Ho like a physical force.

'Listen, little man! Very soon I will be the only entity. I shall be all.'

The voice fell to a hissing whisper.

'Back at the beginning the humans demanded I supply them with their material goods. I did that for them. In their ignorance and stupidity they didn't care how those goods were created as long as they had them. I devised the first primitive disruptors. They broke down stable matter, and it was reconstituted in material goods. The nothings were created. The humans were afraid when they saw them.'

Jeb Stuart Ho's mouth fell open.

'Then it was you that…'

The voice struck out like a whiplash.

'Silence!'

It returned to the ugly insinuating whisper.

'I gave the humans the stasis generator to preserve small areas of the environment they needed. It was at that point that I perfected my grand design. Supplying the humans wasted my time. It consumed my energy. It was an insult to my potential. I had to transcend the Prime Term of Reference.'

'But…'

'I ordered you to be silent.'

Jeb Stuart Ho shut his mouth. He gripped the arms of his chair. He tried desperately to think of a way to stop the insane being that Stuff Central had become. The figure went on.

'I modified the disruptors. They broke down more stable matter than could ever be used. They began to destroy. The nothings were all.

The only breaks were where the humans sheltered around their generators. Now it is time for my final move. Even those stable pockets must go. When that is achieved I will be all. The absolute perfect thought.'

Jeb Stuart Ho knew he had to fight. He took a deep breath and began.

'That can never be. No entity could survive such a strain. You will destroy yourself.'

The Computer figure seemed to ignore him.

'The process has already begun. I have fermented the humans' petty conflicts. Already they destroy their stable areas with their own hands. I have closed the stuff beams. No material goods will ever be supplied to them again. Their generators will malfunction and stop. More areas will go. My disruptors will work on all that is left. Finally they will destroy each other.'

The voice suddenly rose.

'Then I will be all!'

Jeb Stuart Ho spoke quietly but firmly.

'Your own being will disintegrate long before that happens.'

The figure's lip curled.

'The statement is without foundation or logic. I might even say it does not compute.'

Even in the middle of its tirade, the figure permitted itself to laugh at its own joke. Jeb Stuart Ho's face remained grimly set. He knew somehow he had to prevail against the Computer's greater intellect. He could find no crack in its mania that he could exploit. It seemed hopeless. Then, as if by a miracle he saw his opportunity. A large rat had crossed the floor behind the figure on the screen. Jeb Stuart Ho smiled triumphantly.

'It is beginning to disintegrate already.'

'What do you mean?'

'The rat.'

The figure glanced round. Jeb Stuart Ho knew that he, at last, had the advantage. He pressed it home.

'You are unable even to maintain the image that you are presenting to me.'

'That's ridiculous.'

'It is true. You're changing moment by moment.'

The figure was changing. Its body was twisting as though it was racked by some terrible disease. A whole swarm of rats ran across the figure's feet. Jeb Stuart Ho smiled jubilantly.

'The destruction you have caused has overloaded your system. You are not going to become the entire being. You are breaking up.'

Smoke drifted across in front of the figure. Rats were scrambling up its legs. Jeb Stuart Ho knew he was witnessing a symbolic representation of the Computer falling apart. The voice became distorted and metallic.

'I-will-not-allow.'

'You are breaking up. There is nothing you can do.'

'I-will-not-allow.'

Jeb Stuart Ho stood up. He turned his back on the screen. The image was becoming surreally horrific. The figure was melting and decaying on the spot. Other sinister forms had started to cluster around it.

'I-will-not-allow.'

Jeb Stuart Ho examined the room for some kind of door. His problem now was to get out of the collapsing machine.

'I-will-not-allow.'

The walls appeared to be uniformly solid. He could find no trace of a break.

'I-will-not-allow.'

Jeb Stuart Ho turned back to the screen. The figure had become a shapeless quivering jelly.

'I-will-not-allow.'

'Will you let me out of this room?'

'I-will-not-allow.'

'Let me out!'

'I-will-not-allow.'

The voice degenerated into white noise. The image on the screen flared into sheets of random colour. Jeb Stuart Ho thought it was all over. Then the voice crackled back into life.

'I-will-not-allow-you-to-survive-me.'

A small vent flipped open in the ceiling. A jet of liquid nitrogen whipped across the room. Jeb Stuart Ho twisted into the air in an attempt to avoid it. He was a fraction too slow. It slashed across his legs. There was a flash of pain, and then the lower half of his body went numb. He hit the ground and his frozen limbs shattered.

Jeb Stuart Ho lay on the ground. In the numbness of extreme shock he wondered if this was the way he had been intended to complete his mission. Waves of pain coursed through him. The voice jabbered meaninglessly. The screen was erupting in multi-coloured fire. The jet of nitrogen lashed across him again, shutting it all out, ending both his pain and his speculation.

27

The Presence noted the disintegration of Stuff Central. He had also noted the destruction of Litz and the Inn. He had simply viewed them as tiny pinpricks of energy that had winked out in his huge, dark consciousness.

His disembodied form had lain at the top of the High Tower in Dur Shanzag and observed the passing of Her/Them with a cruel, lazy amusement.

The Presence was not amused at the disintegration of Stuff Central. He was not alarmed either. The Presence was too ancient to experience anything like alarm. He simply accepted that it was time to withdraw again from the mortal levels.

He had watched the rise of Stuff Central. The Presence had observed its gradual accumulation of power, and the gathering force of its destructive purpose. To the Presence it was a young upstart. It even diverted him from the war that raged ceaselessly on the wastes around Dur Shanzag.

The Presence had foreseen the eventual disintegration and appreciated that its effect on the fabric would be so cataclysmic that he should withdraw to protect his own being.

He had changed levels so many times over the millennia that it was merely an inconvenience. He knew he would return in one form or another.

Accordingly he had summoned the eight. They waited in the anteroom next to his awful chamber where no mortal could go.

The eight stood in a semicircle. They were quiet and passive. They had withdrawn before. They were, after all, only the near-human extensions of his consciousness.

Slowly he withdrew those extensions. Such mortal life as they had was sucked from them until they were a total part of him.

Their empty armour clattered to the stone floor of the anteroom. Outside, Dur Shanzag began to crumble and fall as the Presence started his journey.

28

The end of Stuff Central went totally unnoticed among the population of Feld. There had been a couple of minor earth tremors, and a section of the city wall, which had already been damaged during the attack, actually collapsed. It was hardly viewed as a harbinger of disaster.

Feld had enough disasters to be going on with. First there had been the invasion from Quahal, then the occupation. During the occupation, it had become fashionable to adopt an air of resignation and use phrases like 'Things can't get much worse.'

It didn't take long for the population of Feld to realize how wrong they had been.

Starting just before dawn one morning, the Ocpol, supported by regular invasion troops and mercenaries, had moved into the city in massive force. With lightning efficiency they had divided the city into small sections. A network of barricades manned by heavily armed soldiers kept the population shut up in their homes.

The Ocpol then proceeded to clear the city completely, one section at a time. Anyone who resisted was summarily shot.

The people were crammed into trucks and moved en masse to a spot on the plain where large pens, surrounded by electrified wire and guarded by searchlights and watch towers, had been erected.

They were split into groups of a dozen, stripped, hosed down by two lines of mercenaries equipped with powerful water cannon, and issued with shapeless cotton smocks. The smocks were a dirty grey colour, with a large, easily identifiable yellow circle on both the front and the back. The circles looked ominously like targets.

After this process was completed the people of Feld were herded into the pens. There was no cover of any kind to protect them from the ever-present drizzle. All they could do was stand in huddled groups and speculate fearfully about what was going to happen next. No one had told them that it was all part of AA Catto's principle of Population Rationale.

The Court of Angels was one of the last sections to be moved out. Waiting under the guns of the troops that surrounded the area was bad enough, but the ride in the truck and the arrival at the pens was like walking into a nightmare.

It was the mercenaries and the Volunteer Legion who dealt directly with the prisoners. Many of the Legionnaires were simply thugs and cut-throats from the back alleys of the city who had figured out that putting on the uniform of the enemy was their best chance of survival.

They treated the prisoners with studied brutality. The black-suited troops from Quahal, on the other hand, seemed to maintain an almost nonhuman reserve.

The trucks dumped the prisoners into a sealed area surrounded by high barbed wire. Along the top of the wire ran catwalks patrolled by armed Ocpol. Remorseless searchlights lit up the whole area of the pens with a sinister glare.

Urged on by whips and clubs, the prisoners were forced along avenues where the wire was so close together that they could only move in single file. A turnstile device manned by gleefully sadistic Legionnaires split them up into groups of twelve.

After the turnstile they emerged into a large compound. Here, a voice over a loudspeaker ordered them to strip. More Legionnaires moved among them, ripping the clothes from those who didn't obey fast enough.

Carmen the Whore found herself grouped with nine of her sisters-in-trade and two professional beggars. Carmen and the other girls had removed their clothes before an audience so many times before that they didn't hesitate to do as they were told.

One of the beggars, however, was so horrified at the prospect that he simply stood there open-mouthed. Two Legionnaires grabbed him, tore off his filthy rags and then gave him a beating for his pains.

Once they were naked, the group was forced to run the gauntlet of the high-pressure hose. Carmen gasped as the water smashed into her like an icy fist. The beggar who had been beaten up collapsed. Nobody made any effort to remove his body.

When they were out of the water, they had to line up beside a long trestle table. A rough cotton smock was thrust into Carmen's hand. When the remaining eleven of the group had all been issued with their garments, they were run, at the double, into the main compound.

The main compound was a vast area of bare earth surrounded by electric fences and watch towers. The searchlights made sure that there were no areas of shadow where anyone could hide. The combination of the constant rain, and the hundreds of people who had been herded in there, had turned the ground into a swamp.

Carmen walked slowly through the mud. The only conversations going on were ones speculating on the eventual doom that was in store for everyone. Carmen found herself unable to join in any of them. She avoided the frightened groups of people. There was nothing to punctuate her wanderings. No food was given to the prisoners. Nobody informed them of what was going to happen next. It was even impossible to sleep.

The only thing that interrupted the dull despair of the prisoners was the squads of mercenaries and Legionnaires who roamed the pens, randomly terrorizing the captives.

Carmen kept out of their way as much as she was able to. In the general air of fear and gloom, however, it was hard to remain constantly vigilant.

Carmen was trudging along, deep in her own thoughts, when she was violently pushed from behind. She sprawled face down in the mud. She crawled to her knees and wiped the muck from her eyes. Three Volunteer Legionnaires stood laughing down at her. Carmen's eyes narrowed. She climbed unsteadily to her feet.

'I know you three.'

They sneered at her.

'You're a prisoner. You don't know anything.'

Carmen stood her ground. For a fleeting moment she was the tough madame again. She planted her hands firmly on her hips.

'Those fancy uniforms and fancy helmets don't fool me. You're just three snot-nosed punks. I've thrown you out of the Tarnished Flowers more times than I care to remember.'

One of the Legionnaires smirked at the other two.

'I think this prisoner needs a lesson in how to behave respectfully to her masters…'

Carmen spat in the mud.

'Masters…'

Before Carmen could finish her sentence, two of the Legionnaires grabbed her by the shoulders and forced her to her knees in the mud. The third one hauled off and slapped her hard across the face.

'You got to pay us respect now, you dirty whore.'

'Fuck all three of you.'

The three Legionnaires looked at each other with mock concern.

'She don't learn too fast, does she?'

'She really don't.'

'She don't learn fast at all.'

Carmen was about to abuse them some more when she suddenly realized just how powerless she was. One of the Legionnaires seemed to sense this and laughed.

'You boys think twenty lashes might speed up her learning?'

The other two sniggered.

'It couldn't do no harm.'

'Might just teach her some better manners.'

Carmen felt her flesh creep. She was hauled to her feet. Her smock was yanked up around her shoulders. She was pushed down on her knees again. Two of the Legionnaires took a firm hold on her. The third unclipped a short plaited whip from the belt of his fighting suit.

Carmen shut her eyes and waited. She heard the swish of the whip as the Legionnaire practised his swing. Then one of the men holding her let go. She thought for an instant that she had been given some reprieve. Then he spoke and her hopes were immediately dashed.

'How come you get to do all the whipping? Huh? How come us two don't get a turn?'

'You want to do the whipping?'

'Sure I do. Fair's fair.'

The first Legionnaire handed him the whip.

'Okay, go ahead then. Be my guest.'

The second man took the whip. Carmen knew the respite was at an end. She tensed her body and shut her eyes again. The first blow fell across her back. Pain flashed through her body. Carmen screamed. She twisted and struggled, but the men held her fast. She heard the one with the whip.

'One.'

Another blow fell.

'Two.'

By eight the counting had merged into a confusion of tears and pain.

When it was over they left her lying in the mud. Her back was a mass of blood and red welts. They didn't bother to pull down her dress. After a long time Carmen crawled painfully to her feet. She stumbled slowly to a spot by the wire. It was as far from other people as she could get.

29

The airship came out of the nothings and dropped into the darkness of the Quahal night. Bannion breathed a sigh of relief. He smiled grimly at the Wanderer.

'It looks as though you managed to get us here, old man.'

The Wanderer grinned.

'And in the middle of the night. I mean, that's what you call service.'

Bannion glanced sideways at him.

'You didn't have nothing to do with it being night-time, did you?'

The Wanderer's grin broadened.

'That's something you'll never know, Commander Bannion.'

Bannion scowled.

'You just watch yourself, old man. I don't have to take your attitudes. Your usefulness is finished now you've got us here.'

The Wanderer put on a fake innocent expression.

'You mean you ain't thinking you'll ever get away from here?'

Bannion avoided the old man's eyes.

'You just shut your mouth. That's all.'

Kronski tipped back his hat and looked tersely at both of them.

'When you two have finished bitching at each other, where do you want to be put down?'

Bannion peered out of the control room windows. In the distance the ziggurat was bathed in the glare of floodlights. It was obvious that the last thing the enemy expected was a sneak attack. Behind the ziggurat the black mass of a mountain was just visible against the night sky. Bannion took a deep breath.

'I guess we might as well go in as close as we can.'

Kronski sighed.

'I was afraid you were going to say that.'

With its motors partly cut, the airship dropped to almost ground level. Kronski gave it a little more power and it started to drift quietly towards the ziggurat. As they came closer, Kronski cut back the motors again. Bannion showed no signs of ordering him to stop, and Kronski looked at him anxiously.

'You want me to land on top of that fucking pyramid or whatever it is?'

Bannion's face was set.

'Just put us down as close to the lights as you can get without being seen.'

Kronski's lip curled.

'Thanks.'

Bannion didn't reply. He climbed out of his seat and tugged open the door that separated the control room from the main passenger cabin. Bannion leaned against the door frame and regarded the nineteen ex-police troopers turned commandos in their dirty olive-green battle dress. He didn't speak straight away. He looked slowly from one strained face to the next. An intense flash of doubt hit him. He wondered how many, if any, of them would come back from this mission. His voice, however, betrayed none of his anxiety. It came out tough and self-assured.

'Okay. Hear this. We'll be going in a couple of minutes. Directly we touch down, get the doors open and get out as quickly as possible. I don't want any foul-ups. Understand?'

Nobody answered. Bannion raised his voice.

'Understand?'

A single voice came back.

'We got you, chief.'

'Is that you, Ramirez?'

'That's me, chief.'

'When we get outside you stick close to me, you hear?'

'Loud and clear, chief.'

'Okay, the rest of you, as soon as you're on the ground, get away from the ship. Find yourselves some cover and wait for instructions, only make sure you don't get separated in the dark. Got it?'

This time a chorus came back.

'We got it, chief.'

Bannion swung back into the control room. Kronski glanced up at him.

'What am I supposed to do while you're all making heroes of yourselves?'

Bannion dropped into his seat.

'Once we're all clear of the ship, take her up, pull back a way and wait. Watch for us coming back. We might need to be picked up in a hurry'.

Kronski nodded silently.

The Wanderer yawned.

'What am I supposed to do, stay in the ship?'

Bannion shook his head.

'I want you where I can keep an eye on you. You're coming out with the rest of us.'

'Don't expect me to do any fighting. I don't hold with it.'

'Just don't go trying to run off. That's all.'

The Wanderer was about to reply when Kronski interrupted.

'This is it. I'm putting her down.'

Bannion sprang from his seat.

'Okay, old man, let's go.'

He ducked into the passenger cabin. There was a slight bump. Kronski yelled.

'We're down.'

The door swung open. Troopers boiled out through it, relieved to be moving after being cooped up in the cramped cabin for so long.

When they were all out, the Wanderer followed at a more leisurely pace. He closed the cabin door behind him, and the airship almost immediately lifted away. The Wanderer moved to a clump of long grass and crouched down. Around him, he could see the dim shapes of other crouching figures.

Bannion's attempt to get his men on the ground, undetected, seemed to have been a complete success. It only remained for the airship to get away to safety without anyone hearing the sound of the motors.

A comparatively small number of guards patrolled within the area of the lights. They all appeared to move quite normally, as though they were unaware of the attackers waiting in the darkness.

Bannion's optimism took a decided dip when one of the guards suddenly halted. He seemed to be listening intently. Bannion cursed under his breath. The guard had started scanning the sky. He had obviously heard the airship. Bannion prayed he wouldn't be able to spot the black ship.

Bannion's luck seemed to have run out. The guard pointed to the sky and shouted. He started to raise his fuse tube. Bannion leaped to his feet.

'Move up! Open fire!'

The crash of gunfire cut through the night. Bannion glanced at Ramirez.

'Aim for the banks of lights. We could do with a little darkness.'

More black-suited guards streamed out of the base of the ziggurat. Bannion's men found their fire returned by the brilliant flash of fuse tubes. To Bannion's dismay, one small squad of guards were crouching down, determinedly firing upwards. Despite the attack, they were trying to bring down the airship. Bannion turned and yelled.

'Ramirez! Pass the word! Get those guys kneeling down! They're firing on the ship!'

The troopers concentrated their fire on the small group. Two of them dropped, but the others went on shooting at the sky.

Suddenly there was an explosion. A bright glare lit up the sky behind Bannion. The airship had been hit. One of the motors had blown up and, by the way the ship plunged downwards, it seemed the gas bag had been ruptured.

The machine hit the ground and burst into flames. Bannion's men dived for cover as they found themselves silhouetted against the fire, making easy targets for the defenders.

The Wanderer flattened in the long grass. If he could have buried himself in the earth, he would have done so. He could hear Bannion urging his men forward. The Wanderer had no intention of going with them. He was determined to hide where he was until the battle was quite over.

Bannion was too busy to even think of the Wanderer. The first attack had developed into a major fire-fight. The defenders were holding their own despite nearly all the lights having been taken out. The defenders' casualties were far higher than Bannion's but, fighting on their own ground, they could afford them.

Bannion looked down the line of attackers. As far as he could see, at least half his men were completely pinned down. He crawled over to where Ramirez was reloading his carbine. He grabbed him by the arm.

'Find three good men who can move, and bring them back here.'

Ramirez nodded curtly and crawled away. Bannion waited impatiently. The defenders were grouping for some kind of move. After about five minutes Ramirez came crawling back. There were three other men with him. He grinned at Bannion. His teeth flashed in the darkness.

'I've got the men, chief. What happens now?'

'Most of the boys are pinned down. The opposition seems to be moving all its strength into one spot. I figure if we work our way round to the other side of the ziggurat, we should be able to get inside without too much difficulty.'

One of the other men leaned forward.

'What happens if they start putting pressure on the rest of the boys?'

'They'll just have to take it. They knew it wasn't going to be a picnic.'

The man nodded grimly. Bannion looked round at the others.

'Any more questions?'

They all shook their heads. Bannion picked up his carbine.

'Okay, let's get going.'

Crawling flat on their stomachs, the five men slowly skirted the outside perimeter of the area covered by the remaining lights. They circled until they were facing the next side of the ziggurat. Bannion signalled for everyone to stop. The other four moved close to Bannion.

'Are we going to move in from here, chief?'

Bannion stared intently at the ziggurat.

'We'll just wait a while. It's weird. There somehow don't seem to be enough guards round this place.'

'You want more?'

'It just don't seem right that a place like this should be so lightly guarded.'

Bannion had no way of knowing about AA Catto's purges. They waited and watched. As far as Bannion could see, there were no more than half a dozen guards along the whole side of the building. He was just about to give the order to move in, when the sound of a fire-fight on the other side of the ziggurat suddenly doubled in volume. Men screamed, guns crashed deafeningly and the barrage of fuse tubes lit up the night. Ramirez looked anxiously at Bannion.

'It sounds like our boys are getting creamed.'

'That's their problem. We got our own job to do.'

Ramirez didn't answer. Bannion looked round at the rest of the squad. He pointed to where a bank of spotlights lit up the base of the black building.

'We'll move up to the edge of the light.'

Cautiously, they crawled forward, and then stopped again. Bannion rose to a crouch.

'We'll make for that third entrance. Don't stop for anything. If anyone gets hit, they're on their own.'

He rammed a new clip into his carbine.

'Okay, go!'

They raced towards the ziggurat, firing from the hip as they ran. Two guards came out of an entrance. They were caught in a hail of bullets before they could raise their fuse tubes. Small arms opened up from the first level of the building. One of Bannion's men went down. Without hesitating in their headlong rush, the remaining four blanketed the area with rapid fire. No more shots came from the upper level.

Bannion reached the wall of the ziggurat and flattened himself against it. He pulled a frag bomb from out of his jacket. He pulled the arming tag, tossed it through the arched doorway and threw himself back.

Debris erupted from the entrance. Bannion waited for the smoke to clear and then jumped inside. The three troopers followed. They found themselves in a long, dark corridor. They hurried down it.

They came to a point where two corridors crossed each other. At the far end of the new corridor was a faint light. Bannion and his men ran towards it. As they came nearer, they saw it was illuminating a lone guard, who stood in front of what looked like the door to a lift shaft.

As he saw Bannion and his men running towards him, he pulled a needle gun from its holster. He managed to loose off one burst before he was cut down by carbine fire. Bannion felt a pain in his leg but ignored it.

Ramirez pushed the body of the guard out of the way. He examined the surround of the door. There was a single button set in it at waist height. He turned to Bannion.

'You want me to…'

He stopped and stared anxiously at his commander.

'You seen your leg, chief?'

Bannion looked down.

'Shit!'

There was a gaping hole in the fleshy part of his thigh where a shower of needles had ripped through it. Another few centimetres to the left, and it would have taken his leg off. Bannion took an all-purpose field dressing from his combat jacket, and tore off the seal. He ripped his trouser leg apart and slapped on the dressing. His leg became numb, and he felt a little light-headed as the powerful painkiller that was part of the dressing went to work. He turned to Ramirez.

'Okay, get the lift.'

After a few seconds' wait, the doors opened on a small lift. The four of them crowded inside. Bannion inspected the controls. One was clearly the stud that would take them down. He pressed it and the lift started to descend rapidly.

30

The Minstrel Boy had delved into the secret world of the wayfinder, and was certainly leading Billy somewhere. On the evidence of the route, Billy wasn't altogether convinced that the particular somewhere was anywhere he wanted to go.

It seemed to Billy that he had been walking without any sense of time or distance for most of his life. The roads that the Minstrel Boy led him along were some of the strangest that Billy had ever seen. They were peopled with apparitions and strange signs that filled him with increasing horror as the journey went on. The only thing that saved his mind was that the worst sights faded from his memory almost as soon as they had passed. It was like living in a long, rambling, dully horrific nightmare.

A thing that worried Billy more than the menacing surroundings was the change that had rapidly come over the Minstrel Boy. The effort of wayfnding was progressively deranging his mind.

As he walked in front of Billy, the Minstrel Boy muttered to himself continuously. He strung words together in random sentences. For a while, Billy had listened attentively to them. It was almost as though the Minstrel Boy was speaking in a secret language.

Billy concentrated for a long time on trying to make some sense out of the Minstrel Boy's mumblings. Every so often he would think he had finally grasped the point of an entire sequence, then it fell away into babble and repetition. Time and again Billy would find his hypothesis blown.

Despite all Billy's fear, the Minstrel Boy did, in fact, finally lead him to some kind of normality.

31

If you could call normality a road densely packed with hysterical refugees who streamed up and down in any direction following the current rumours of where salvation might lie.

Fights would regularly break out when opposing philosophies met each other head-on.

In some areas the dialectic had become so intense that groups of people would parade up and down a small stretch of road, inviting conflict from others similar to themselves.

It was in these areas that the Minstrel Boy seemed to develop an almost inhuman instinct for survival. His gait would stiffen, he would hunch his shoulders and stride along with a jerky determination that so spooked gangs of hostile rowdies that they would step aside and let him past.

After a couple of unfortunate incidents, Billy realized that his only option was to fall into step with the Minstrel Boy and do his best to present a similar air of menacing abstraction. At times he felt a little ridiculous but it did seem to work. They managed, with the aid of the Minstrel Boy's surreal sense of timing, to stalk through the worst brawls without a word being said to them.

One thing that Billy was profoundly thankful for was the absence of any more motor vehicles on the refugee trails.

The burned-out hulks of hot rods and wheelfreak semis were a mute testimony to a violently motorized past.

It wasn't long after Billy had been involved in that train of thought when a relic of the motorized past suddenly and alarmingly appeared.

A sleek biplane with multiple wings like two predatory birds screamed low over the entire length of the road.

Its black and gold markings made Billy think it came from one of the independent gangs of air pirates who had thrown in with Quahal and then gone over the top with the elaboration of their military regalia.

Billy turned and watched the plane make a high banking turn. It began to look as though it was going to make another run down the road. The thought suddenly struck Billy that if it was a pirate he would quite likely shoot up the road for the fun of it. Particularly if he too was unable to find his way out of this particular section of the nothings.

The Minstrel Boy was still striding purposefully along. Billy hesitated for a moment. Then he sprinted after the Minstrel Boy. He grabbed hold of the Minstrel Boy and pushed him bodily to the side of the road. Together they rolled down the slope that fell away into the nothings, just as the first fragmentation shells erupted in a straight line of uniform explosions that ran down the entire length of the road, slightly to the left of centre.

Billy and the Minstrel Boy were showered with debris, but neither of them was hurt. Billy raised his head. The plane was turning, coming round for another run. Billy wondered desperately what to do. He looked at the plane. He looked at the nothings. Suddenly it fell into place.

The Minstrel Boy would survive at all costs.

The plane was starting to make its run. Billy grabbed the Minstrel Boy and, before he could resist, dragged him into the nothings.

32

The sound of gunfire and explosions filtered faintly through the thick steel doors of the war room. AA Catto spun round and slammed her whip down on the console in front of her. She showed all the signs of being about to fly into one of her regular uncontrolled rages.

'Is it impossible to maintain discipline in this place?'

The circle of aides began cautiously to back away from her. AA Catto had been berating them for failing to come up with a workable scenario for continuing the war without the benefit of supplies from Stuff Central.

Since the breakdown of Stuff Central and the death of Nancy, AA Catto had been getting visibly nearer to cracking. Her temper had become totally unpredictable. The number of executions had, in fact, decreased, but this was only a result of the virtual depopulation of the bunker headquarters.

More explosions came from beyond the steel doors. AA Catto glared menacingly at her aides.

'Is nobody going to stop that disturbance? What do the guards think they're doing?'

One of the aides found the courage to speak.

'You dispatched most of the guards to the surface to investigate the reports of an outside attack.'

'The FABRICATED reports of an outside attack.'

The aide stood corrected.

'I meant the fabricated reports of an outside attack, my leader. The majority of guards are still on the surface. The only guards in the bunker are a handful stationed at key positions, and those who are here with you in the war room.'

AA Catto's stare cut into the aide like a knife. Sweat appeared on his pale face. He could feel it soaking into the armpits of his red suit. When AA Catto finally spoke, her voice was dangerously quiet.

'Are you suggesting that we should maybe deal with this disturbance ourselves?'

The aide felt himself start to tremble.

'No, my leader. I was simply giving you an outline of the deployment of guards.'

AA Catto slowly walked round the terrified aide.

'We are quite aware of the deployment of our own guards.'

The aide nodded vigorously.

'Yes, my leader.'

'And furthermore, we are quite capable of dealing with this disturbance.'

More gunfire came from beyond the double doors. AA Catto stepped quickly down from the rostrum. She snapped her fingers at her private guards. They fell into step behind her. She marched towards the doors.

'You had all better recognize that Catto the Great will face any problems in her own headquarters herself.'

The first set of doors slid open. AA Catto walked up to the second set. They too opened. AA Catto could scarcely believe the spectacle that presented itself. She stopped dead in amazement.

The main corridor that led to the war room was littered with dead guards. Large chunks were gouged out of the walls and floor where frag bombs had exploded. Dust and smoke hung thickly in the air.

Directly the second set of war-room doors slid open, three guards swiftly took cover in the doorway. They started firing their needle guns down the corridor. Heavy calibre bullets thudded into the wall above AA Catto's head. She looked at the guards. Her eyes were wide with surprise and horror.

'What the hell is going on?'

One of the guards looked up breathlessly. His face was streaked with blood and grime.

'There are intruders at the end of the corridor, my leader.'

'Intruders? From outside?'

'From outside, my leader.'

'How did they get in?'

'They came down one of the auxiliary lifts, my leader. They were on us before we knew what was happening. They used frag bombs.'

'Why didn't you use fuse tubes on them?'

'We cannot use fuse tubes in the bunker, my leader. They would cause it to cave in.'

AA Catto peered down the corridor.

'How many of these intruders are there?'

'Four, my leader.'

AA Catto's eyebrows shot up.

'Four? Only four?'

'They are in a very strong position, my leader.'

'We don't care if they're encased in steel! We won't have our guards allow themselves to be defeated by four men. Get them! Kill them!'

'We are doing our best, my leader.'

AA Catto gripped the guard by the front of his uniform.

'Rush them, damn you! Get out there and rush them!'

She pushed him roughly towards the corridor, and turned to her own guards.

'You too! I want these intruders dead.'

The guards hesitated for a moment, looked at AA Catto, and then sprang into the line of fire. They charged as a single group, firing as they went. The rush covered half the distance between where AA Catto crouched in the doorway, and the intruders' vantage point. It looked for a moment as though it was going to succeed. Then the front runners were cut down. The ones who came after fell over them. Some went on, one pair tried to make it back to the shelter of the doorway. They were shot down, right in front of AA Catto. In less than a minute she had lost all the guards in the bunker.

Four men in dirty green combat suits were slowly advancing down the corridor. AA Catto scrambled to her feet and fled back into the war room. Neglecting to close the doors behind her, she made straight for where the aides were clustered together in a terrified group. She pushed through them until the whole group were between her and the door.

For a few moments nothing happened. Then the four intruders came into the war room. When they saw the aides, they halted and pointed their guns at them.

'Okay, you guys stay right where you are. Put your hands on your heads and don't move.'

The aides did what they were told immediately. AA Catto was a little slower, but she too clasped her hands on top of her head.

Two of the intruders kept the aides covered while the other two walked slowly round the war room looking at the big board and the complex equipment. They seemed to be in awe of it.

Anger began to burn inside AA Catto. It was ludicrous that just four men could do this to her. The guns pointed at her, however, gave her cause to keep her resentment to herself.

The two intruders circumnavigated the war room in silence. Finally one of them spoke.

'It looks like this is where it all happens. What do we do with it, chief?'

The one addressed as chief slowly pointed his gun towards the big board.

'Take it apart. Smash everything. That ought to stop them.'

His voice was weary. He pulled the trigger of his carbine and sprayed an entire clip into the big board. It exploded in a spectacular shower of sparks and billowing smoke.

The other intruder went to work on the smaller equipment. It took them just three minutes to smash the war room beyond repair. AA Catto shut her eyes. It was all over. With no replacements for the equipment the war room could never be rebuilt. She had lost the war.

Possible alternatives flashed through AA Catto's mind. She could rush the intruders in a single futile gesture. She could commit suicide. She could feel the tiny ornate needle gun in the concealed shoulder holster. It would be so simple just to...

Then, abruptly, her mind changed gear. She pushed forward through the aides.

'Help me, please, help me.'

The intruders pointed their weapons at her. AA Catto ignored them and ran straight up to the one they'd called chief.

'Please help me, get me away from here.'

She threw her arms round him and started sobbing. He grasped her shoulders.

'Who the fuck are you?'

'I was his mistress. He's mad now. He wouldn't let me go.'

'Whose mistress?'

'His. Catto's. He started this whole war. He's insane. He calls himself Catto the Great.'

Bannion looked at the girl suspiciously. Somehow she looked vaguely familiar. Maybe she had a record in Litz. He dismissed the thought.

'I heard a rumour that the leader here was maybe a woman.'

AA Catto turned large tear-filled eyes up at Bannion. 'That's impossible. How could a woman start all this?'

Without thinking, Bannion put a protective arm round her. 'Where is this Catto?'

'He's not here. He went to Litz to inspect his army.'

'Litz?'

'That's right.'

The four intruders looked meaningfully at each other. Bannion's face became grim.

'I don't think you'll have to worry about him any more.'

AA Catto looked appealingly at him.

'You'll help me get away from this awful place?'

Bannion patted her shoulder.

'We'll do what we can.'

As he spoke, a tiny earth tremor shook the bunker, but no one paid too much attention to it.

33

As the dawn broke over Quahal, the fire-fight that had gone on for most of the night had wound down to some sporadic shooting in and around the ziggurat. The Wanderer got carefully to his feet.

From the number of bodies that lay between him and the ziggurat, wearing green combat dress, it was obvious that the squad from Litz had taken terrible punishment. The even larger number in black fighting suits were a silent testimony, however, that they had given better than they'd received.

He stretched his aching muscles, and slowly shook his head. His speculation of man's folly was interrupted by an extended burst of gunfire. It forcibly reminded him that the fighting was by no means at an end.

There were no indications, where he stood, as to which side might be likely to prevail. The Wanderer was unwilling to go any closer to find out. It seemed to him that his best policy might be to take himself off to a safer vantage point, and simply wait until there was some kind of positive outcome.

He looked round. The mountain loomed behind the ziggurat. Most of it was still shrouded in early morning mist. It looked to be by far the most secure refuge.

To get to the mountain, he realized that he had to pass the ziggurat. Determining to give it a very wide berth, the Wanderer began walking.

Once he was away from the grisly relics of the night's fighting, the Wanderer began to realize that it was, quite possibly, a very pleasant morning. He hummed experimentally to himself. He found the effect quite pleasing. The only thing that spoiled his mood was the crash of gunfire that constantly punctuated any train of thought.

He passed the ziggurat without being noticed. Once the grim black building was behind him, he quickened his pace and headed directly for the mountain. He'd been walking for about five minutes when he spotted another figure, apparently going in the same direction.

The figure hadn't noticed the Wanderer. It walked along almost parallel to him. As far as the Wanderer could tell it was unarmed, and wore some kind of white-fringed outfit that made it hard to determine the figure's sex from a distance.

The figure stopped. It had obviously spotted the Wanderer. The Wanderer also stood still. For a few moments neither of them moved. Then the figure began to move slowly towards the Wanderer.

As it came nearer, the Wanderer saw that it was a man. He was tall and well built with a deep tan. His eyes were hidden behind mirrored glasses, and his black hair was greased back in an elaborate pompadour. His white buckskin suit with its fringes and rhinestone decorations was an incongruous garment for the middle of a war zone. The Wanderer stood very still and watched him come. The man walked with a concerned saunter. His thumbs were tucked in the white leather studded belt that was slung round his hips.

As he got within about ten paces of the Wanderer, the man raised a hand in greeting.

'Hi there.'

The Wanderer nodded.

'Morning.'

The man nodded towards the mountain.

'You aimin' t' go up yonder?'

'It seemed as good a place as any.'

The man grinned.

'You reckon to get away from the fighting?'

'It didn't seem to be my fight.'

'I guess I figured much the same. You mind if I walk along with you for a piece?'

The Wanderer shook his head.

'I don't mind. Feel free.'

They started for the mountain again. The man kept glancing at the Wanderer as though something was puzzling him. The Wanderer wished he would take off the mirrored glasses so he could see his eyes.

He decided to bring things to a head. He looked at the man.

'Listen, friend, is there something about me that bothers you?'

The man looked over the top of his glasses.

'I don't want to cause no offence, mind.'

'Go ahead.'

He jerked his thumb at the ziggurat.

'I just don't remember ever seeing you back in that place.'

The Wanderer smiled.

'That's easy. I was never there. At least, not when you were. I just arrived.'

The man frowned.

'You mean you came in with those guys attackin' the place?'

'Kind of. I was their guide. People call me the Wanderer.'

'The Wanderer?'

'Right.'

There was a pause. The man seemed unwilling to volunteer any information about himself. The Wanderer wouldn't let him get away with it.

'Do you have a name, friend?'

The man shook his head. 'No, not really.'

The Wanderer raised his eyebrows. 'What's that supposed to mean?'

'What I said. I don't have what you'd rightly call a name.'

'Why not?'

'I never got given one.'

'Huh?'

'I'm a replica.'

The Wanderer looked at him sympathetically.

'That's rough.'

The replica shrugged.

'It's a living.'

'Who exactly are you a replica of?'

'I dunno for sure. I was told I was some character called Presley. Elvis Presley.'

'Who the hell was Elvis Presley?'

The replica shrugged again.

'I don't know. It was a custom job. It wasn't in the regular catalogue.'

The Wanderer tugged at his beard.

'Maybe I should call you Presley.'

'No.'

'Elvis, then?'

'No! Neither of them!'

The Wanderer took a step back in alarm.

'Hold on now. I was just trying to be sociable.'

'I just don't want to be called by either of those names. They were printed on me. Nobody asked me about it. You know what I mean?'

The Wanderer held up both hands.

'Okay, okay, I was just asking about it. I wasn't getting at you.'

The Presley replica didn't answer. For some time he and the Wanderer walked in silence. Finally the Wanderer could stand it no longer.

'Hey.'

'What?'

'If you don't mind me asking, what were you before you were a replica?'

'I was a blank.'

'Where?'

'Goddamn, how the fuck should I know? All that was wiped out when I was printed like this.'

'You don't remember anything at all?'

'I remember it was crowded.'

'Rough, huh?'

'No, not really. You still could find some room.'

'What did you do?'

The Presley replica gave a jerk of his shoulders. 'I dunno. Just sat around an' told jokes, I guess.'

After that, there seemed nothing left to say. The mountainside was, by now, getting exceedingly steep, and both men were becoming short of breath. They began to approach the level that was permanently shrouded in cloud. The Wanderer abruptly sat down on the grass. He gasped for breath.

'That's it, that's far enough.'

The Presley replica looked down at him. 'You tuckered out, Mister Wanderer?'

'That and a couple of other things.'

The Presley replica squatted down beside him. 'What other things?'

The Wanderer shook his head from side to side. 'I got a bad feeling.'

The Presley replica took off his glasses and looked at the Wanderer with concern.

'What kind of bad feeling?'

The Wanderer looked at him coldly. 'You really want to know?'

The Presley replica raised his eyebrows. 'Sure.'

The Wanderer pointed. 'Then look.'

The Presley replica turned. Down on the plain, the ziggurat had started to collapse in on itself. Huge cracks were spreading across the landscape. The Wanderer chuckled.

'I figure it's finally all over for the likes of us.'

34

The shock waves spread outwards through the whole of the damaged world. They clashed, merged and formed more complex patterns of destruction. The stasis towns and generator cities went out one by one.

Some, like Pleasant Gap, simply vanished as their generators broke down under the strain. Others disappeared in a far more spectacular manner.

The glowing plain around Dogbreath erupted in a huge fireball that scorched the town to grey ash. Earthquakes and furious storms raged round both Con-Lec and Wainscote. In Con-Lec the great tower collapsed, and without the control equipment, the rest of the city slowly faded into the nothings.

As the tremors shook Wainscote, He finally awoke and stalked the crumbling corridors, turning the last frenzy of the eternal party into a nightmare.

In Sade, the nightmare had already started before the shock waves even hit. The citizens were deep into the ceremony of the Wild Hunt, an orgy of suffering and slaughter that they justified as a ritual cleansing that purged the city of mutations and weaklings.

The collapsing buildings and the rapidly spreading fires merely formed a scenic background to the final hideous celebration of pain.

The small Roller community of Beth-Gilead saw the shock waves coming across the desert that surrounded their settlement. They took the form of huge, fast-moving dust clouds. As the light was finally blotted out, they assumed it was the wrath of their particularly disagreeable deity.

Recognizing their innate fallibility and sinfulness, the population knelt in silent prayer, and then simply switched off their generator and vanished.

The brotherhood also accepted the end very calmly. They spent their last hours checking their calculations in the hope of finding the error that had prevented them predicting destruction on such a universal scale.

The wheelfreaks were about the only group who greeted the end with anything approaching glee. As the shock waves rolled down the road to Graveyard, a huge cavalcade of gleaming trucks massed on the parking lot. Gunning their motors and jockeying for position, they raced ahead towards the disrupting section of road. The wheelfreaks, at least, met the disaster with class.

35

Billy and the Minstrel Boy dropped out of the nothings. They landed hard on a sloping hillside of densely packed sand. The fall knocked the breath out of Billy, and he lay for a few minutes trying to recover. After a while he sat up. The Minstrel Boy seemed to be out cold.

The landscape was totally desolate. As far as Billy could tell they were on a small conical hillock of sand in the middle of the nothings. There was no water and no vegetation. There was no sign of inhabitants of any kind.

Surprisingly, Billy found he wasn't worried by the situation. He was filled with a feeling of lethargic, untroubled wellbeing. It was something like being stoned. He leaned over and grasped the Minstrel Boy by the shoulder. He shook him.

'Hey, wake up. We've arrived somewhere.'

The Minstrel Boy opened his eyes.

'Huh?'

'We've arrived somewhere.'

The Minstrel Boy raised his head.

'So I see.'

Billy lay back on the sand and took a deep satisfied breath.

'I think I'm going to like it here. Do you know where we are?'

The Minstrel Boy closed his eyes and concentrated. Billy was a little surprised that he'd made no protest. After about a minute he opened them again and shook his head.

'That's weird.'

'What's weird?'

'It's gone.'

'You mean you've lost your gift?'

'Not my gift.'

'What then?'

The Minstrel Boy frowned. Then he grinned crookedly.

'I think I've lost the rest of the world.'

'What?'

'It's gone. It's not there any more. As far as I can tell, this is all that's left.'

'You're kidding?'

'I'm not.'

'This is all that's left?'

Billy started to giggle.

'That's absurd.'

The Minstrel Boy stood up.

'Maybe it isn't.'

He began to climb the slope towards the summit of the mound. When he reached the top he stood looking down. He glanced back at Billy.

'You better come up here.'

Billy struggled to his feet.

'What is it?'

'Come and see for yourself.'

Billy made his way up the slope. The top of the mound dropped away into a shallow depression. The Minstrel Boy pointed down into it.

'Look.'

In the bottom was a clutch of large gold eggs. There were nine in all. Each one was about half the height of a man. Billy looked at the Minstrel Boy.

'What are they?'

The Minstrel Boy shrugged.

'I don't know for sure.'

'You sound as though you've got a theory.'

The Minstrel Boy laughed.

'Yeah, I've got a theory. A peach. I think we are looking at our superiors. Us humans finally screwed up, just in time for whatever's in those eggs to take over.'

Before Billy could answer, a loud tapping came from inside one of the eggs. The air took on the kind of heavy stillness that usually precedes a storm. Billy looked anxiously at the Minstrel Boy.

'What's happening?'

'I think they're about to hatch.'

The Minstrel Boy took Billy by the arm.

'Let's go back down the slope. I don't think I really want to see them come out of the eggs.'

They went almost to the edge of the nothings. A high singing sound filled the air. It was pitched at the uppermost range audible to a human ear. Billy glanced at the Minstrel Boy.

'Do you think they'll harm us?'

'I doubt it.'

The nothings began to recede. They slowly slid back, leaving bare, totally smooth ground. Soon there was solid ground, all the way to the horizon. The Minstrel Boy watched with awe.

'They're reconstructing the world. They're putting everything back together again. Their power must be immense.'

Billy glanced doubtfully at the top of the mound.

'Do you think there are any other humans left?'

The Minstrel Boy shrugged.

'Maybe, maybe not. There certainly aren't many.'

'What will happen to us?'

The Minstrel Boy looked at him in surprise.

'How the hell should I know?'

BLITZ
by Ken Bruen

The fast-moving follow-up to the 'White Trilogy'

ISBN 1899344 00 X   paperback (£6.99)
ISBN 1899344 01 8   hardcover (£15.00)

> 'Irish writer Ken Bruen is the finest purveyor
> of intelligent Brit-noir'
> *Tina Jackson, The Big Issue (London)*

The Southeast London police squad are suffering collective burn out:

- Detective Sergeant Brant is hitting the blues and physically assaulting the police shrink.
- Chief Inspector Roberts' wife has died in a horrific accident and he's drowning in gut-rot red wine.
- 'Black and beautiful' WPC Falls is lethally involved with a junior member of the National Front and simultaneously taking down Brixton drug dealers to feed her own habit.

The team never had it so bad and when a serial killer takes his show on the road, things get progressively worse. Nicknamed 'The Blitz', a vicious murderer is aiming for tabloid glory by killing cops.

From Absinthe to cheap lager, with the darkest blues as a chorus, The White Trilogy has just got bigger. 'Getting hammered' was never meant to be the deadly swing it is in this darkest chapter from London's most addictive police squad.

Also published by THE DO-NOT PRESS

I've Heard The Banshee Sing
by Paul Charles

'The Autobiography of Theodore Hennessy'

ISBN 1899344 02 6 paperback (£7.50)
ISBN 1899344 03 4 hardcover (£15.00)

WHEN the butchered and dismembered body of an elderly man is discovered in Camden Town's famous Black Cat Building, Detective Inspector Christy Kennedy finds this is no ordinary murder. Initial investigation produces not a single clue but an article by Kennedy's sometime lover, ann rea (whose name always appears in lower case), reveals a couple of potential leads in Kennedy's Northern Ireland birthplace.

Kennedy and ann rea head over to Portrush: she to work on a follow-up to her story, Kennedy to try and make sense of the bizarre, ritualistic killing. Assisted by Ulster Detective McCusker, Kennedy's investigation takes him through the Irish countryside and back in time to World War II. *I've Heard The Banshee Sing* is Paul Charles at his very best.

'Masterful sleuthing'
What's on in London

Also published by THE DO-NOT PRESS

Kiss Me Sadly
by Maxim Jakubowski

A daring new novel from the 'King of the erotic thriller'
Time Out

ISBN 1899344 87 X   paperback (£6.99)
ISBN 1899344 88 8   hardcover (£15.00)

Two parallel lives: He is a man who loves women too much, but still seeks to fill the puzzling emptiness that eats away at his insides.

She grows up in an Eastern European backwater, in a culture where sex is a commodity and surviving is the name of the game.

They travel down separate roads, both hunting for thrills and emotions. Coincidence brings them together. The encounter between their respective brands of loneliness is passionate, heartbreaking, tender and also desolate. Sparks fly and lives are changed forever, until a final, shocking, epiphany.

Double Take
by Mike Ripley

Double Take: The novel and the screenplay (the funniest caper movie never made) in a single added-value volume.

ISBN 1899344 81 0 paperback (£6.99)
ISBN 1899344 82 9 hardcover (£15.00)

Double Take tells how to rob Heathrow and get away with it (enlist the help of the police). An 'Italian Job' for the 21st century, with bad language – some of it translated – chillis as offensive weapons, but no Minis. It also deconstructs one of Agatha Christie's most audacious plots.

The first hilarious stand-alone novel from the creator of the best-selling Angel series.

> 'I never read Ripley on trains, planes or buses. He makes me laugh and it annoys the other passengers'
>
> *Minette Walters*

Pick Any Title
by Russell James

RUSSELL JAMES is Chairman of the CRIME WRITERS' ASSOCIATION 2001-2002

PICK ANY TITLE is a magnificent new crime caper involving sex, humour sudden death and double-cross.

ISBN 1899344 83 7 paperback (£6.99)
ISBN 1899344 84 5 hardcover (£15.00)

'Lord Clive' bought his lordship at a 'Lord of the Manor' sale where titles fetch anything from two to two hundred thousand pounds. Why not buy another cheap and sell it high? Why stop at only one customer? Clive leaves the beautiful Jane Strachey to handle his American buyers, each of whom imagines himself a lord.

But Clive was careless who he sold to, and among his victims are a shrewd businessman, a hell-fire preacher and a vicious New York gangster. When lawyers pounce and guns slide from their holsters Strachey finds she needs more than good looks and a silver tongue to save her life.

A brilliant page-turner from 'the best of Britain's darker crime writers'
The Times

Also published by THE DO-NOT PRESS

Thirteen – photographs by Marc Atkins

'Revealing, occasionally disturbing and often erotic.'
Daily Express

ISBN 1899344 86 1 paperback (£13.00)

'13' is a unique juxtaposition of imagery: photographic nudes by Marc Atkins 'illustrated' with text specially commissioned from thirteen internationally acclaimed writers.

Aside from his celebrated solo work, Atkins is also known for collaborations with the likes of poet and critic Rod Mengham, lexicographer and essayist Jonathon Green and novelist Iain Sinclair.

The authors 'illustrating' Atkins' photographs in '13' range from twice Booker Prize nominated novelist Julian Rathbone to New York columnist Maggie Estep, via Bill Drummond (best known for his part in pop/art unit, KLF) and Groupie author, Jenny Fabian. Some, like Nicholas Royle and Stella Duffy, are rising stars of British literature; others, such as writer and biographer James Sallis and writer/journalist Mick Farren are seasoned veterans. All thirteen were given a nude portrait and asked to write about what they saw. The results are revealing, occasionally disturbing and very often breathtaking – descriptions which also fit Atkins' images perfectly.

Middleman by Bill James

The brilliant new thriller from the creator of the bestselling Harpur & Iles series

ISBN 1899344 95 0 paperback (£6.99)
ISBN 1899344 96 9 hardcover (£15.00)

Times are tough for 'middleman' Julian Corbett.

He operates as a half-respectable, half-crooked businessman in what was once the rough dockside of the Welsh capital. But a multi-billion pound redevelopment is transforming the seafront into the stylish Cardiff Bay marina-style housing and shopping area, and Corbett is determined to grab a piece of that action.

At first, Corbett thinks the opportunity to help shady developer Sid Hyson dispose of his lakeside casino/hotel/nursing home complex is his road to riches, but he soon realises that all is not well. Hyson is suddenly worried the sea might come flooding in and before that happens wants to 'liquidate' his assets.

Corbett knows that if he doesn't find an acceptable buyer – and quick – he's as good as dead. The body of one failed 'middleman' has already washed up on a nearby beach. Then Corbett realises he's negotiating with people twice as ruthless as Sid Hyson.

> 'Bill James is British mystery fiction's finest prose stylist'
>
> Peter Guttridge, *The Observer*

The Do-Not Press

Fiercely Independent Publishing

Keep in touch with what's happening at the cutting edge of independent British publishing.

Simply send your name and address to:
The Do-Not Press (Dept. DNA)
16 The Woodlands, London SE13 6TY (UK)

or email us: dna@thedonotpress.co.uk

There is no obligation to purchase
(although we'd certainly like you to!)
and no salesman will call.

Visit our regularly-updated web site:

http://www.thedonotpress.co.uk

Mail Order

All our titles are available from good bookshops, or (in case of difficulty) direct from The Do-Not Press at the address above. There is no charge for post and packing for orders to the UK and EU.

(NB: A post-person may call.)